FAMILY FEELING

'Ella, are you awake? It's me, Megan.'

Ella nodded. 'I'm awake. I wish I wasn't.'

'Ella, what has happened is the most terrible and sad thing, and I wish I could help you in some way. I'll stay with you for as long as you want, and . . .' her voice shook a little with the strength of her desire '. . . and, if it would h-help, when I leave I'll take one of the twins with me.'

'Take one of them?' Ella's eyes opened properly and Megan saw that, though they were still drowsy and drugged with pain, there was sanity in them, and understanding. 'Oh Meg, if you took one of them I'd be able to manage so much better . . .'

'I'll take the little one,' Megan confirmed, holding her sister's hand firmly between her own warm and capable ones. 'I'll bring him up right, just the way that you and Ben would want, I promise. And if you ever want him back . . .'

'No. Once he's gone from here he's no son of mine,' Ella said. A tear rolled down her cheek. 'No child of Ben's either, Megan. Do you understand that? If you take him, it's for good . . .'

FAMILY FEELING

Judith Saxton

ARROW BOOKS

Arrow Books Limited
62–65 Chandos Place, London WC2N 4NW

An imprint of Century Hutchinson Limited

London Melbourne Sydney Auckland
Johannesburg and agencies throughout
the world

First published by Century 1986

Arrow edition 1986

© Judith Saxton 1986

Printed and bound in Great Britain by
Anchor Brendon Limited, Tiptree, Essex

ISBN 0 09 937940 6

For Brenda Ferris
who lent me her house
in Valentine Street!

Acknowledgements

I should like to thank Robert Wynn, who lent me invaluable material on mining in Denbighshire, and Ken Howarth, the author of *Dark Days: The Story of Lancashire Mining*, easily the best of all the reference works I consulted.

As always, I should like to thank the staff of the Wrexham Branch Library, and last but not least the people of Wrexham who were always eager to set me on the right track.

PART ONE

One: 1902

Ella lay in the bed and felt the pillows soft beneath her head and shoulders and the goosefeather mattress yielding to her back; she felt, too, the quiet beginnings of pain, a purring warning which would presently intensify until it became next to unbearable. Don't tense, she told herself, don't fight it; go with it, let the pain take you, wash over you, until it gradually ebbs, and then the child will be born before you know it.

This would be her fourth child — and perhaps, this time, it would be the girl she longed for. After all, things were different this time. This baby was coming in winter and not in spring or summer, and it would be born with the evening dusk and not with the rise of the sun. It would be wonderful to have a daughter, a little girl to dress in frills and hair-ribbons, someone to watch you when you were baking or cleaning, someone to whom you could teach all your own hard-won housewifely skills.

Not that she would mind another boy. Ben was one of three sons and he took it for granted that she would bear boys. Since she enjoyed nothing more than pleasing Ben, all she need do was give birth to a healthy child.

Downstairs she heard the clatter as the boys came in with Annie Todd, who was giving a hand. Annie would soon be moving round the kitchen where Ella herself had worked yesterday at this time, getting the tea ready. The poor girl was simple, or so they said, but she was good with the boys. A shout and a cuff perhaps, if they plagued her, but otherwise she would manage them well enough until Ben got home.

Ella went over her preparations for tea, to take her mind off the pain. Yesterday she'd had a batch of homemade bread from the oven, so it would still be quite fresh. With a big family

3

and only one wage coming in you baked once a week, not every day. There was plenty of raspberry jam left, too; it was a bit pippy, because she'd gathered the wild raspberries which grew so abundantly up in the mountains, but the boys loved the sharp, delicate flavour. Then there was pork; belly slices for the boys and Annie and a hefty chop for Ben, with potatoes and winter cabbage if Annie remembered to clean it. When Luke was born Annie had popped a nice drumhead into the pan without noticing the family of fat caterpillars which lived just inside the outer leaves.

Ben had been more amused by Annie's astonishment that children should mind a few boiled caterpillars, Ella remembered now, than the incident seemed to warrant. He had come up to her room later and, sitting on the bed, had re-told the story for her entertainment, his blue eyes straying occasionally to the cradle where the tiny, red-faced Luke lay slumbering.

The pain, steadfastly ignored, built up and then faded. Ella sat up on her elbow and looked out of the window through the increasing dusk. Ben was late, but his shift was over and he would be coming home any moment now, humming to himself as he climbed the hill to a good fire, a good meal, and his family. He did not even know she was in labour, since the pains had not begun until nearly noon. In what was left of the light she could see a shine on the tiles of the cottages on the opposite side of the road, but it did not look much; Ben should get home without a wetting.

Thinking about Ben made her glance at the little table by the bed where his gunmetal hunter had lain during her other confinements. It had been a friend, comforting her with its deep, steady tick; assuring her that time was not standing still, that her pain was not for nothing, that very soon the birth would be upon her. This time, of course, Ben had taken his watch to work as usual, not knowing that she would be needing it.

More sounds from downstairs; the tin bath was being dragged across from the wash-house, where it hung on the wall all day, to the spot before the fire where Ben would have his bath. In summer, he cleaned up in the back yard, but she would not have dreamed of allowing such a thing in winter.

Then, he came indoors, and if there were women visiting they were shooed into the parlour to freeze for half an hour or so on the slippery little satin-striped sofa, beneath the framed print of Justice with a bandage round her eyes, until Ben was decent once more.

Listening hard, she caught the sound of sloshing water and knew that Annie had heard the men approaching from the pit. They usually came back to the village in groups, clogs clattering on the cobbles, talking and laughing, eager for a good wash and some decent food that didn't smell of the coal. She hoped that the water was hot, and that Annie had got the big bar of coarse red soap handy and warmed one of the good towels.

But even as she, too, heard the clogs, the pains began to get closer and she knew that it was time for Annie to get herself up the stairs, and to send one of the boys for Nurse. Nurse had popped in an hour earlier, patted Ella's shoulder, asked a few questions, and popped off again. Old Mrs Macpherson whose big son Donald was the blacksmith a mile or so away needed a visit, and Nurse would guarantee that the young Fletcher about to put in an appearance would not be doing so for the next hour or two.

Ella called and Annie came upstairs, listened and pattered off down again. Stan, the eldest boy, was despatched, but had got no further than the gate before Ella heard Nurse's quick, clipped footsteps as she approached the house. It was odd, Ella thought as sweat poured off her, how your ears became eyes when you were tied to your bed and could not run to the window to look for yourself. She heard the tap of Nurse's heels on the path, the swish of her skirts as her bag brushed against them, even the tiny click of the latch as Nurse, ever careful, closed the gate behind her. And then the pains suddenly changed in a way she knew well but could never remember until it happened. The baby was coming! A present for Ben, a child which would arrive only moments after he did himself, if she was any judge.

Ella was pushing steadily as Nurse came into the room, rolling up her sleeves, smiling, taking off her coat.

'Good girl! The men are on their way, so let's get this over before they're here to bother us.'

*

5

At the very moment when his wife was looking on the bedside table for his hunter, Ben was taking it out of his pocket and glancing at the face. It was not easy to see in the chancy light from the lantern, but he was used to the dimness. Besides, instincts were almost as reliable as timepieces down here in the eternal dark. His body was telling him that it was time to start walking back towards the pit bottom and his watchface had only to be glimpsed to confirm the feeling. Just time to get Charlie, his tub-filler, to shovel the rest of the coal into the last tub so that the boy could take it up to the haulage point. From there the ponies would drag it until they reached the endless rope which would take it to the surface.

'I'm off now, Tab; you coming?'

The other collier, a man in his early forties, grunted, but shook his head.

'Late I was this morning, Ben, mun; can't afford to clear off until I've got another load down. Can you stay to fill for me, Charlie?'

Charlie sighed and agreed. Ben, mindful of Ella, set about clearing all the loose coal so that Charlie could get to work on it at once. He was holing out, which meant, in this particular Place, lying on his side and swinging the pick from his elbow to strike the coal right. The seam was a deep one and still dropping, and because of the incline at which he was working he had folded his shirt round his jacket to make a pad, rested the clothing on his overturned shovel and lowered himself on to the resultant hump to make the work easier. Even so, it was a scramble to get right side up, and to back away from the face so that he could prepare to leave the seam.

'You all right, Charlie? Send it up, then.'

Ben gathered up his tools – props, wedges, a couple of picks and of course his heavy hammer – and secured them, and then he and the boy began to make their way out of the seam. It meant going upwards, of course, but it also meant getting out of bad air and into better, so though it was a tough scramble it was still a pleasanter journey, to his mind, than that which they took each morning to get to work. Charlie usually pushed the tub in front of him but now, because they were both leaving the seam, the boy went ahead, dragging with one hand, his light bobbing erratically as they struggled upwards. Ben, pushing, could feel the sharp stones of the tunnel floor through his leather knee-pads, but even so he continued to crouch as low as he could. He did not want to crack his scalp on the low rock ceiling and he had never fancied pushing the tub with his head, as a good many of the fillers did when they were working on a steep gradient. It made them go bald, Ben thought disapprovingly, proud of his own thick crop of fair curly hair. Not that it would look fair now, of course. Darkened by sweat and coal dust, he could be black for all you could tell at a glance. No, this way might be hard on the knees, since you had to use your hands to shove the tub, and you certainly couldn't see much as you didn't have a spare hand to hold your lamp so it had to hang round your neck, but it was still preferable to premature baldness.

He felt the roof grate along his spine and hastily ducked again. In these very narrow, low seams you filled a half-tub because the full-sized ones would not go through, and if you forgot that the tub before you was smaller than usual it sometimes made you careless. Ben felt blood trickle down his back and thought longingly of the bath he would have as soon as he got home. Ella made a lovely bath! He was hot now, but by that time the sweat would have cooled on him and he would be quite cold, eager for the silky touch of warm water and the sweet smell of the soap. And Ella, clucking and murmuring, would clean his back, wincing at the ugly scabs on his spine, awkward now because of the baby she carried but still glad and proud to help her man with his bath.

Ben pushed harder and heard Charlie, in front, give a cheer. Presently, through the sweat that ran down into his eyes, he saw Charlie's figure appear as the lad straightened and knew they had entered one of the main roads. Here they would empty their small tub into a ten-hundredweight one as quickly as they could, knowing that all over the pit other men would be doing the same, anxious to catch the cage at the end of the shift. Charlie was only fifteen but a good lad, Ben thought, as the skinny, half-naked figure in front of him began shovelling coal from one tub to the other like a demon out of hell. He hoped his boys, when they came below, would be as good as Charlie.

'Here we go, Ben, mun! That's thirteen ton we've shifted today; not so bad, eh?'

7

Charlie's voice might be squeaky, falsetto one moment and an unnatural bass the next, but he could work! His shovel never faltered in its movement between the two tubs and Ben hastily began to shovel too, until the big tub was packed to capacity. Then he piled his gear on top and began to struggle into his shirt. It was only half on when the tub in front began to move. Ben followed, still bent double, for even here the roof was not high enough for a good-sized dwarf to stand upright, and Ben was a six-footer. He heard voices ahead and thought thankfully that it would be the boy with the ponies; very soon Charlie would be roping their tub on to Jubilee, or Patsy, or Growler, and the men could stop pushing and tugging. The ponies, even old Growler, could each take five or six tubs. If they were lucky they might not have to wait for numbers to be made up.

It was probably because, still bent double, he was buttoning his shirt that he did not immediately realise something was wrong. He was tired, too, after a long and arduous day even by a hewer's normal standards. Holing out was exhausting. The deeper you went the hotter it grew and the more sweat you lost. When he heard a shout ahead he took it not as a warning but as a sign that they were about to attach their tub. Crouched an inch below the level of the heaped-up coal he could see very little. The first he knew of trouble was when the tub stopped short, so that his head collided with it forcefully enough to addle his wits for a crucial second. In that second he should have leaped for the side of the tunnel and found himself a man-hole to crouch in; as it was he hesitated, dazed and in pain.

So he was still on the rails when the tub behind, pushed by another collier who, like him, could not see ahead and had no means of braking in any case, crushed him against the one in front like a nut in a nutcracker.

He heard his own nightmare scream, knew one moment of whitehot agony, and then there was a darkness deeper even than the darkness of the pit, and a silence more profound.

'It's twins,' Nurse said softly to the tall, slim woman who stood in the narrow doorway, looking so like the woman in the bed that no one could have doubted their relationship. 'She's not so well – God knows how she's going to manage with the pair of 'em.'

Megan Pettigrew lowered her already low voice still further, though Ella lay still, to all outward appearances asleep after her ordeal.

'Twins? Both boys? Oh, dear God, if only there was something I could do! Can you come downstairs for a moment, Nurse?'

'I can. Though with the boys everywhere and the front room . . . still, we can go in there for a moment, I dare say.'

Together the two women descended the stairs, though as soon as she entered the kitchen Nurse despatched Annie to sit with her patient.

'Don't say anything, for she's asleep – I've given her laudanum,' she told the girl. 'If she wakes call me.'

She held open the parlour door for Megan. The coffin was on the table, the lid mercifully closed. It arrived at the house already sealed; no one had commented. It happened too often that when a man died down the pit he could not be decently laid out for his family to see and mourn over. Megan, who had heard the story from a sobbing Charlie, knew that what was in the coffin was not recognisable as Ben Fletcher. She had not wanted the body here, but she had only arrived an hour ago, too late to take control of a situation which had shocked everyone by its tragic suddenness. Ella did not even know she was here. Ned Pettigrew was a cattle dealer and came often enough from his home in Norfolk up to Holyhead to see the Irish yearlings and buy for his clients. Megan had not come with him before, but this time, because Ella was pregnant, because it had been seven years since she had been home to the village, because she had no child of her own, she had come with Ned. Not knowing of the tragedy, he had gone on to Holyhead, and would return for her tomorrow or the day after when he had completed his business.

So now the two women faced one another across the small, stiff parlour, with the mortal remains of Ben Fletcher reproachful, it seemed to Megan, because they could do so little for his beloved wife.

'Well, Nurse? What is my poor sister to *do*? She has the three little boys, none of whom is old enough to work, and twin babies who will stop her from working until they are old enough to fend for themselves. I didn't ask — are they both boys?'

'Both boys,' Nurse confirmed. 'The first one was born before she knew, and she named him Hywel. The second one she called Huw, but by then she suspected — she had heard the overman and the shot-firer talking and she knew something had happened to Ben. At first we dared not tell her and she dared not know, if you understand me; but later she knew. No use to lie, when she'd find the truth out quick enough. And besides . . .' She paused, eyeing Megan doubtfully. 'Truth to tell, Megan love, it was in my mind to let the little one go from here. No help to Ella, see, to let a weakly child survive, and she would have the strong one to comfort her. But . . . I couldn't bring myself to do anything right then, not knowing the circumstances, like. So I've let matters rest.'

Megan shook her head, gripping her hands very tightly together. Nurse could not mean what she thought she meant. Perhaps she knew of a home where the baby would be welcomed. She found that she did not want to know more; enough sad and terrible things had happened in the past few hours without adding another to the list.

'Two baby boys. And the others only children, who can do little enough for her. There'll be compensation, though, won't there, Nurse? They won't let them starve?'

'They won't starve,' Nurse said practically. 'But they'll come mighty near it if Ella can't work. If she had just the one child, of course. . .'

The two women stared at one another, the same thought forming in both minds. Megan was childless and longed for a baby; Ella was a widow with one baby more than she could possibly cope with. Though there was a two-year age difference, the girls had been closer than most in their childhood. They had shared everything without complaint — until they had both fallen in love with the same young collier. But Ben had chosen his Ella at just the right moment, for Megan had met Ned Pettigrew and already knew that her feeling for Ben was nothing compared with her love for the cattle dealer who

10

had come to the village to buy some Plas Tegydd calves and stayed because he wanted her.

'What were you going to say, Nurse?' Megan's eyes were shining. 'If Ella would let me . . . I'd have him, of course I would! No one need know; I could leave at night . . . you could put it about that the second child had died. She wouldn't want it known.'

'Why not? Nothing shameful, is there, in letting the child go where he can be better cared for?'

'Perhaps not; but Ella would feel it, I know she would. What do you think? Who should suggest it?'

'I'll see how she feels,' Nurse said guardedly. She paused, eyeing Megan uncertainly, and then continued, 'Truth to tell, girl, there's odd she's been with the second baby. Almost as if she blames him for Ben, though we all know her man was dead before either was born. None too fond of the first one, for the matter of that. Awkward, I do feel, when I put them into her arms and see that look on her face. She's a good girl, but . . . oh, I dare say it's only a fancy.'

Megan looked at Nurse's square, no-nonsense face and her heavy, compact body. A less fanciful person you would have to go a long way to find, she told herself. If Nurse thought that Ella would part willingly with one of the twins, then she herself would make the suggestion. Ned would be in seventh heaven if she brought him a son, never mind that it was no child of his. He liked Ella, had been carelessly fond of his brother-in-law. He would welcome Huw. Or Hywel. Come to that, he would welcome the pair of them, only she knew that Ella would want one of her babies.

'What work can she do, when she's recovered from the birth?' Without mentioning the matter again, both women knew that Ella would want to work, and they both believed she would let Megan take one of the twins. Indeed Nurse, though she did not go more deeply into the matter, knew that she would feel happier once Ella and the younger, smaller child was parted. There had been a coldness in her patient's large grey eyes when they rested on that particular twin which had frightened her. Dislike had been too mild a word for the power of feeling in Ella's glance, and Nurse, who had seen so many babies born and so many brave men die in her forty years of nursing, found herself still appalled by it. If that's what the love of a good man does for a woman I'm glad I'm plain and single, she found herself thinking.

'Work?' she said now, bringing her mind back to the matter in hand. 'Well now, she could work up at the Plas – Mrs Tegydd has a child no more than a twelve-month, and they could be company for one another. And there's the oldest daughter, of course – Kate, her name is. Lovely little girl. The second one's almost as pretty. I'm sure Mrs Olivia could find some light work for Ella, if we explained that Ben died in the Olwen pit. As owner's wife she might feel she should do something.'

'Or she could work at the pit-head and get money worth the earning,' Megan said a trifle tartly. She and Ella had both worked at the Olwen pit before their respective marriages; they thought domestic work was ill-paid drudgery and they were not far wrong. But on the other hand, when one was burdened by a sucking child. . .

'Perhaps,' Nurse said vaguely, 'She'll be at home for some weeks yet; she won't have to make up her mind in a hurry. And in the meantime, Megan, I'll tell Annie to stay, shall I? I suppose you've got to get home with Ned when he comes back?'

'I needn't go at once,' Megan was beginning, when they both heard a commotion upstairs and a shrill, panic-stricken cry from Annie. Nurse ran out of the room, almost falling over Luke, who was pushing a wooden cart round the kitchen on all fours, and stumbled up the stairs with Megan in close pursuit. In the bedroom, they found Ella out of bed and standing beside the cradle. She had picked up one of the babies and was holding it as a mother-cat holds a kitten, except that she held it in one hand by the back of its long flannel nightgown. She was swaying, supporting herself with one hand on the brass bed-stead, and she did not so much as glance round when the two women burst into the room. Annie was standing flattened against the wall, her mouth gaping open, her eyes black with fright. A low keening came from her and her fingers, starfished against the whitewash, were making little, tentative scratching motions as she sought to give herself courage to step forward into Ella's line of vision.

'All right, Annie; she's sleep-walking,' Nurse said briskly. She took the child, or tried to do so, but Ella's grip was strong and she had to use both hands to break it and release the baby. Once she had the child safe, she looked into Ella's half-closed eyes and then patted her arm.

'Back to bed, dear,' she said placatingly. 'The babies aren't hungry yet. They were fed not long ago. Back to bed with you.'

'Hungry?' Ella shook her head very slowly. 'Oh no, they aren't hungry. They've taken it all . . . all.'

She put her hands to her breasts and there was something so desolate in the gesture that Megan found tears rising to her eyes. But she went to her sister's side and guided her back into bed, then tucked the bedclothes round her.

'Ella, are you awake? It's me, Megan.'

Ella nodded. 'I'm awake. I wish I wasn't.'

'Ella, what has happened is the most terrible and sad thing, and I wish I could help you in some way. I'll stay with you for as long as you want, and. . .' her voice shook a little with the strength of her desire '. . . and, if it would h-help, when I leave I'll take one of the twins with me.'

Nurse, standing by the cradle, looked round sharply; plainly she felt that too much was being said too soon. But Megan knew her sister. Ella would tell her if she disapproved of the plan or if she needed more time to think about it.

'Take one of them?' Ella's eyes opened properly and Megan saw that, though they were still drowsy and drugged with pain, there was sanity in them, and understanding. 'Oh Meg, if you took one of them I'd be able to manage so much better! You could take the little one, the one that screams and looks at me with such a satisfied look. I almost hate him.'

'She's feverish still,' Nurse muttered. 'She doesn't know what she's saying.' But Ella ignored her and Megan spared her no more than a quick glance.

'I'll take the little one,' Megan confirmed, holding her sister's hand firmly between her own warm and capable ones. 'I'll bring him up right, just the way that you and Ben would want, I promise. And if you ever want him back. . .'

'No. Once he's gone from here he's no son of mine,' Ella said. A tear rolled down her cheek. 'No child of Ben's either, Megan. Do you understand that? If you take him, it's for good.

13

He's the child of your body, not mine. He's as much yours as though it was you bore the pain of him. I don't want even the thought of him.'

'Right,' Megan said firmly. 'But shall I stay a week or two, Ella? Give you a hand getting yourself back to normal? Ned's coming for me tomorrow but I can easily stay.'

'No.' Again the word was decisive. 'Go when Ned comes for you, Meg, and take the child, and Nurse here will say he died. It's better that way. I've a strange, wicked feeling that God gave me two sons and took my Ben, and it was Ben who mattered, Ben I wanted, not a pair of snivelling brats in his image. If I could give you both of them I would, but I need one of them to make me keep going.'

'You've got three sons already,' Megan reminded her. 'If you want me to take them both I'm sure Nurse would find some story for the village.'

'No. Just one. Ben will understand that I can't bear to see two babies, but he'd reproach me if I let both of them go. You've seen the others? Stan, Dewi and little Luke? You understand why I feel . . . the way I do about the twins?'

'Yes, of course,' Megan said, not understanding at all. 'They're fine boys, Ella.'

Ella sighed and shook her head impatiently. 'Don't you see, Meg? You and I were so close, once, that our thoughts hardly had to be put into words. Don't you see?'

A picture of the three little boys playing downstairs came clear in Megan's mind and, suddenly, she realised what her sister meant. The boys were all neat, brown-haired, brown-eyed children with straight fringes falling across their foreheads. They were not physically like either parent, though she thought, now, that they had a look of their Williams grandfather about them. And the twins? With a guilty shock she realised that she had not really looked at them.

She crossed the room and peered into the cradle, but the afternoon was wearing on and she could scarcely see the small faces in the shadow. At that moment, however, one of them opened a small round mouth and began to whimper; she picked it out of the covers and carried it over to the window. It fitted into her arm as though it had grown there; as though it was the place above all others it wanted to be.

In the fading daylight she looked down at last into the small face, and knew in one horrifying moment why Ella felt the way she did. The face cuddled against her green silk shirtwaister was a tiny replica of Ben's; the hair was his hair, crisply curling, fair, growing into a peak on the broad forehead. All babies have smudges for noses, but this baby would have Ben's nose one day; already it had his mouth, his cleft chin, his breadth of cheekbone. It was such a remarkable, startling resemblance that Megan gasped. She felt almost embarrassed, and then the baby turned its head restlessly against her and once more it was just a little child, vulnerable, soft, needing her, and she wanted nothing more in life than to call it her own.

'Well? Do you see why I can't. . .' Ella's voice broke and she stopped speaking for a moment.

'Yes. I see. Are they both. . .?'

'Will you take him?'

There was pleading in Ella's voice, but she need not have worried; the baby already seemed flesh of Megan's flesh. She put a finger out, tentatively, and touched the baby's tiny fist; the fingers uncurled and grabbed. Megan laughed. The decision was his, and he had made it; he had hold of her and now he need not let her go.

'Huw Pettigrew,' she said softly. 'That's a lovely name, mun! Like it, do you? Think it suits you? Wait till you see your da, then, when he comes to pick us up tomorrow evening — what a surprise we'll have for him, eh? He'll be the happiest fellow in the whole of Wales!'

Two: 1910

'Come on, Jess, let's be having you! The water's starting to boil!'

Ella, calling up the stairs, tried not to sound cross or impatient. Jessica was a good girl, but washing-day waits for no man – or woman – and she knew that her stepdaughter expected to help, even though Ella tried to spare her as much as she could. She had always thought it a cruel trick to start a tiny girl helping in the house, because if she married she would be doing housework for the rest of her life. On the other hand, she could not possibly manage wash-day alone. With four big sons and a husband younger than herself who liked to have his shirts and the rest of his linen sparkling clean, she needed all the help she could get.

She and Glyn had married two years after Ben's death. She knew that some people disapproved, but they had needed one another. Glyn had got a flibbertigibbet of a town-girl in the family way, and the girl had simply marched into his mother's cottage with her two-week-old daughter on one arm and left the child with Mrs Pritchard. To add insult to injury she had referred to Jessica – at the top of her voice so that all the neighbours had heard – as 'your son's red-headed bastard', and had then gone off to London – one assumed – without so much as another word to the astonished father.

Not that Glyn had minded all that much. He was a tall, happy, handsome lad five years younger than Ella, and he had taken one look at his red-haired daughter and declared that she was a better bargain than her mother had ever been.

'Mam'll bring her up,' he had told his astonished work-mates. 'Good little girl she'll be, when she's a bit older. Help around the place, I don't doubt.'

16

Whether he had considered marriage to Jessica's mother no one knew, but Ella doubted it very much. Indeed, she thought that Glyn might never have considered marriage at all — for it was common knowledge that he got his way with most girls — had it not been for her working at the pit-head. He had walked home with her several times, she with the baby on her hip, he chatting easily about his Jessica, but he might not have given her a second thought had he not had occasion to visit her one evening when his small daughter was suffering from a nasty cough.

'Lemon and honey I give mine for a cough,' Ella had said as they climbed the hill side by side. 'Pop round later on, mun, and I'll give you a bottle for the baby.'

He had come round and, as luck would have it, it had been one of those good evenings. The curtains were drawn, the fire roared in the grate and the boys, seated round the tea-table and eating voraciously, had behaved like little angels instead of the devils they could be.

Glyn, she learned later, had had a trying evening. His mother did not much like children and had never ceased to feel aggrieved over the summary manner in which Jessica had been handed over to her. Despite the fact that Jessica was the spitting image of Glyn, she was often heard to remark that they only had the mother's word for it that Jessica was her grand-daughter.

That day Jessica was not a pretty sight. Her nose was running, she was dribbling, and she had been sick over her nightgown. Mrs Pritchard, grumbling, had declined to pick her up all afternoon, so the child had screamed herself into scarlet, hiccuping misery by the time her father got home. And when he picked her up and put her hot, wet little face against his, crooning to her, she was sick again, down his pit-jacket this time, and then wet on his sleeve.

'Doing my best I am, son,' Mrs Pritchard whined when he accused her of neglect. 'Not as young as I was . . . can't manage such a young child. Why not take her down to the poorhouse . . . just till she's old enough to be useful? Folk 'ud understand.'

So Glyn had walked up the road seething, hating his cold house and cold mother, the dripping nappies, the smell of stale vomit and the obscure feeling that he was being unfair to an

17

old woman. And he had walked into what appeared to be domestic heaven. A girl of no more than twenty-seven or eight, who worked twelve-hour shifts, with three sons and a babe not a lot older than his Jessica, yet who could still produce harmony and happiness at the end of a hard day. It was magic — and a magic, Glyn suddenly saw, which he could not only share himself but could also have for his beloved daughter.

From that moment on he courted her assiduously and Ella, worn out, missing Ben, ashamed that she could feel no love for her youngest child, and guiltily aware of her body's needs whenever Glyn touched her hand, was soon in love. More in love than Glyn, she thought wryly sometimes, for things were so different for men. When he wanted warm arms round his neck he swaggered around town, threw some money about and got what he wanted. But Ella, a member of the gentler sex, could only dream and chide herself for dreaming. It was, she knew, wrong to want a man's body, but she, sinner that she was, knew that she wanted Glyn for himself even more than she wanted him as a father and provider for her sons.

Perhaps he only married me in the end because he couldn't get me the other way, she thought now, as she cleared the breakfast table. But it was the only way a woman could make herself plain, and she had certainly done that! She had never actually said that an illicit affair was out of the question, but she had implied it by the way she reacted whenever Glyn's hands slid . . . well, anywhere they shouldn't. And she knew that he hadn't actually wanted an illicit affair — what he had wanted was a home and a wife, though perhaps he had not been fully aware of it at the time.

So she had been mothering Jess for long enough to think of the little girl as hers, and she loved her, she was sure, just as much as she would have loved her own daughter. More, perhaps, because Jessica was such a plain child. She had red hair, like Glyn's only more carroty and less curly, white eyelashes and brows and a good few freckles. Glyn, of course, thought she was as beautiful as the day and spoiled her whenever he was home, but Ella thought her stepdaughter was downright odd-looking. Her hair bushed out, crackling when it was brushed, making her small face look even paler by comparison. That she was clever no one could deny; she absorbed learning as a sponge absorbs water and though she was only seven she had been reading for three years and writing for nearly as long. Everything she read she remembered, and Glyn had great hopes that they might save up and send her to a private school in the town, though Ella could not see this happening. Not whilst Glyn continued to drink, anyway. Colliers working all day in the heat of the pit, sweating profusely, always needed lots of liquid, but most of them drank beer occasionally and made up with quantities of water and tea. Glyn liked beer and drank it, she knew, to excess. Sometimes he came home, ate his meal, and then went straight down to the pub until closing time, returning home clumsy and foolish. It did not do to remind him that Ben had never taken more than he could hold, but there were times when Ella was tempted.

It was because he drank that he hit her, of course. It was strange that a man so easy-going, so pleasant, could be so vicious at times – and to the woman who loved him, furthermore. Ella had grown sadly accustomed to explaining away a black eye, a split lip, an ugly abrasion on arm or knee, for she would never admit that Glyn beat her. Mrs Pritchard, when she came into the house to grumble and whine about her son's neglect or her daughter-in-law's imagined defects, would shoot a quick, sly look at Ella's marked face and purse her mouth, as though the bruises were a sign of some private aberration of Ella's own, or perhaps as though Ella brought the violence on herself by her behaviour.

It might have been easier to understand, Ella thought, if Glyn hit her only in hot blood, when he was ugly-drunk; what hurt her most, perhaps, was that he had grown cunning. He hit her now behind closed doors, or when the house was empty or the boys were in bed.

In a way she was grateful for this, because she had no wish for the boys to witness their stepfather's behaviour. They were growing up. Stan was thirteen and had left school to work at the pit-head, so he could almost be counted as a man. Even Hywel was eight, and she did not think for one moment that her sons would countenance Glyn's behaviour if they knew of it.

She could not begin to understand his violence to her, but

she was grateful that he never turned on the boys. He was a good stepfather to them, easy-going, generous, treating them firmly when they stepped out of line but never hitting, never bullying. So why, dear God, does he have to hit me?

Jess stumbling down the stairs took her mind off the sore subject; she smiled at the child, tutting over her unwashed appearance, then crossed the room and picked up the hair-brush which lived on the old Welsh dresser.

'Here, love, let's get some of them tangles out.'

Brushing Jessica's hair, she hummed to herself, glancing through the low window and catching a glimpse of pale blue sky across which small white clouds were moving purposeful-ly. Good. A fine but windy day was ideal for the washing. Today, as always, she would spend a good few hours just taking the dry linen indoors and putting out the wet. It was easier now that Glyn had bought her a fine new mangle – he was such a good husband in many ways – but even so she dreaded wet Mondays.

'Can I have some breakfast, Mam?'

'Well, you shouldn't, but. . .' Ella cut a slice off the loaf, buttered it, spooned honey on to it, and folded it in half, handing it to her daughter. 'There, never say I don't do nothing for you!'

'Thanks, Mam.' Jessica bit into the sandwich and spoke through her mouthful. 'What'll I do? Is the copper hotting up?'

'It is; I put the water on hours since, and there's sheets in it already. I'll put some potatoes in the sink for you to peel, and then you can clean a cabbage and some swedes; Stan dug some yesterday after chapel. And don't forget, love, to keep an eye out for the water under the door.'

She walked over to the sink and began to put potatoes in the bowl. Behind her, Jessica spoke.

'Why're you limping, Mam?'

Ella was limping because Glyn had knocked her downstairs earlier in the day. Deliberately, of course, but when Stan had come out of his room with his shirt half buttoned to find out what the rumpus was about his stepfather had pretended concern, had announced that Ella had turned her ankle, lost her balance and tripped down the short but steep flight of stairs.

20

'Limping? Didn't you hear me tumble down, when your da was off to work? You sleep like the dead, girl!'

Jessica turned, twitched her hair back and tied a bit of ribbon round it to keep it out of her eyes whilst she worked. She looked at Ella with love and suspicion.

'Did you fall? Or was Da a bit careless, like? Seen how he can push you without noticing, I have.'

Ella turned away so that the child should not see the flush that mounted to her forehead. She had known Jessica was sharp, had wondered if she suspected, but it seemed impossible – the child was only seven, and Stan, who was so much older, had noticed nothing. As the flush died she turned back.

'Well, love, men forget their own strength sometimes. Can you manage in here, now? Don't forget to keep an eye out for the water. I'll give you a call if I need help to get the sheets out.'

It was pleasant outside even though it was only February. A mild, boisterous, blustering sort of day, with yesterday's rain still beading the cabbages and puddling the brick path which Stan had made from the wash-house to the line, yet with the sun shining and the breeze sending showers down from the apple trees and the plum. Glyn was not a garden lover, but Stan made up for it. He kept the family well supplied with vegetables, and there were always a few flowers in bloom except in the very depths of winter. Although it had not been he who had planted the fruit trees, he saw that they were pest-free, pruned them, and gathered the crops when autumn came.

Because the house was built on the side of the mountain the back door came out into a tiny bricked yard no more than four foot by six, and you had to climb half a dozen slippery steps to reach garden level. It made for difficulties on wash-day, because if the copper boiled over the water ran from the wash-house, which was directly above the back door, down the steps and into the kitchen itself. When school was in session Penny-a-day, as they called Annie in the village, had to be employed to mind the kitchen and the fire whilst Ella washed, but during school holidays Jessica helped her mother. She was a good deal better already than Annie, though Ella always felt guilty at asking the child to help. Why, just because of her sex, should Jessica be expected to start her life's work the moment she was old enough to wield a duster?

However, Glyn, though he was by no means a niggardly husband, would have queried paying Annie when Jessica was not in school. So now Ella mounted the steps, glanced at the line from which she had earlier wiped the night's accumulated raindrops, and then went into the wash-house.

It was hot and steamy in there with the copper pouring clouds into the atmosphere and every surface wet. Ella got the washing tongs, great clumsy wooden things, and began to fish for the sheets in the boiling water. She got a good hold on the first one and drew it, dripping, from the suds, then carried it quickly across to the low stone sink. Once there, it was soon joined by a second, and then Ella picked up the bucket which had earlier been filled by the boys and began to rinse the sheets. She was content, in that warm wet atmosphere, because it was a fine day with a good drying wind, because the fire was drawing well indoors, and because in any case dinner on a Monday was always cold meat for the first course with a boiled pudding afterwards. Easy. She reflected, as she worked, that simple things did make one happy. The fine morning seemed to bring spring closer, seemed to push winter further off. And she had resolved that she must make Glyn see that knocking her about was wrong, stupid, and would lead to his own eventual downfall. How she would do it remained to be seen, but having made up her mind she was sure that something would happen which she could turn to her advantage.

The copper began to bubble once more with its new load and Ella picked up two empty buckets and left the wash-house to go to the pump for more rinsing water.

In the kitchen Jessica peeled a mound of potatoes and watched her hands as they slowly crinkled with the wet. At first she was conscientious, peeling the potatoes so that their skins were paper-thin and digging all the eyes out with the point of the knife, but as she worked the potatoes – and, indeed, the sink – became transformed. One particularly fine potato was a mighty liner; she had peeled only half of it so that the peeled half was the deck and the dark half was below the plimsoll line. She narrowed her eyes, noticing that there was a hole, conveniently central, through which the sailors and passengers could get below, into the bowels of the ship. A smaller potato was a tiny fishing trawler and the soap dish was a pleasure steamer. As she dug more eyes out of the remaining potatoes, those eyes, placed carefully in the soap dish, became eager holidaymakers, enjoying their cruise, all rushing to the side when they saw a particularly large whale or a man-eating shark. The peelings did very well for the denizens of the deep, particularly the chunkier pieces.

Presently, carried away by her game, she stood an empty bottle in the sink, where it immediately became a very respectable lighthouse. Or it would have, only it wouldn't stand on the bottom but kept turning on its side with a splash and becoming a floating nuisance, too big for the game, so she stood it on the shore and then began to arrange more potato peelings round it in the semblance of a beach; then since she needed rocks because beaches always have rocks she began to take anything suitable off the kitchen windowsill, finally emptying out a bag of flour to make the sand.

Naturally, since the draining board was covered with wet potato peelings and puddles of water, the flour promptly became satured and bore little resemblance to a beach. Jessica, suddenly realising where she was and what she was doing, leaned right over in an attempt to push the flour bag with what was left in it out of harm's way . . . and fell sideways off the stool on which she was perched, uttering a howl of fright.

The kitchen floor was hard. It was also wet. Indeed, she landed in a good inch of water, and as she scrambled to her feet, sobbing a little over bruised knees and a cracked elbow, she saw that the fire was hissing feebly and the kitchen was flooded. Her clogs, which she had taken off in order to stand more comfortably upon the small stool which enabled her to reach the sink, were actually floating, boatlike, upon the bosom of the deep.

It was a dismaying sight for one a good deal older than seven and to Jessica it seemed the worst thing in the world. She stared, sobbed again, and then seized the broom and began, belatedly, to brush. Uselessly, like a miniature Canute, she brushed and sobbed and brushed some more, but all that happened was that the tide swirled higher, the fire made ominous popping noises, and water continued to flood in under the door.

There was only one course open to her and at last Jessica took it. She waded across the kitchen, opened the back door, and paddled across the yard. Climbing the steps was a bit like climbing up a waterfall, save that this water was warm and soapy, but there was no help for it. Go into the wash-house she must, to make her confession and beg assistance.

It did not occur to Jessica that normally her mother allowed no more than a bucketful of water to boil over before she put things right – not, that is, until she entered the wash-house. The copper had boiled over all right and put the fire out, but that was not why the water was only just beginning to ebb a little. In between the buckets, which were lying anyhow on the hard earth floor, lay Ella. Her breathing was quick and shallow and her face grey and bruised-looking. Jessica flew over to her and knelt down, ignoring the wet.

'Mam! What is it? Are you hurt bad?'

'Oh, Jess, thank goodness you're here! I fell . . . slipped in the wet. I think I've hurt my side. Can you fetch help?'

'Let me help you. . .' Jessica stopped pulling as Ella caught her breath on a sharp cry. 'Oh Mam, I'm sorry! Shall I get Penny-a-day?'

'Yes . . . no, fetch Mrs Dafydd Evans,' Ella said in a small, thin voice which Jessica had never heard before. 'Probably I'm all right, if only she could help me to get indoors. You get Mrs Dafydd, love.'

'Come in, Glyn.'

Mrs Dafydd Evans was a motherly soul who had reared her own children long since and had always been a good friend to Ella. Now she stood in her neat kitchen with Ella's children at the table behind her eating their tea, whilst Glyn stared at her out of his hot blue eyes and wanted to know where Ella was and why his dinner was not on the hob nor the fire burning in the grate. Mr Dafydd Evans was going to tell him, but in her own way and her own time. Eyes in my head I have, she told herself as she ushered Glyn in and across the kitchen to her parlour. Eyes in my head and plenty of sense – I'm not taken in by stories of doors which get in the way or lips which split for no good reason, not me! Master Glyn wants teaching a lesson and I'm the one to do it!

'Well, Mrs Dafydd? What's 'appened to my Ella, then?'

It was cool in the parlour with no fire. Mrs Dafydd kindled the lamp, and then sat down, very prim, on the shiny horsehair sofa with the flowered cushions on it, all embroidered by herself before her marriage. She looked approvingly round the room as she settled her skirt, enjoying the little rosewood piano, the framed prints on the walls, the best china in the cabinet and the soft, thick rugs on the floor. Nice, it was, to have a parlour like this where you could come for weddings and funerals. And to have a quiet talk.

'Your Ella's been taken to the infirmary, Glyn. What's this I hear about a fall? Jessica told me. . .'

Jessica had indeed told her that her mother had fallen twice that day; once in the morning, early, when the men were getting up, and later in the wash-house. Mrs Dafydd had known by the way Jessica had spoken that the first 'fall' had been nothing of the sort. It had been a push. She had a shrewd idea why Glyn had suddenly begun to knock his wife about, but to her way of thinking why he did it was less important than stopping him before it was too late. It could become a bad habit, like, Mrs Dafydd said severely to herself. Never do to let a bad habit go unremarked. But Ella was only young; she did not think of it in quite the same way as an older person.

'The infirmary? But she was all right. She got up at the foot of the stairs. . . a few bruises, she said, that was all.' Glyn's face had whitened and his freckles stood out. His eyes no longer looked hot; they looked decidedly shifty. 'Not hurt, I'd swear to it, Mrs Dafydd!'

'She'll be all right,' Mrs Dafydd said placidly. 'Go down and see her you can this evening, when there's visiting allowed. Probably be back in a week or two, if she mends.'

'Mends? Was something broken? But she was all right, I tell you!' Glyn ran a hand through his crisply curling red hair. 'Went down with a rare old thump, I'll admit, but seemed fine she did when I picked her up.'

'You picked her up? I thought Stan said. . .'

'No, well, she picked herself up, come to think,' Glyn admitted. He got to his feet. 'Right, I'll go now then. Get back to the house, clean up a bit and be off down to the infirmary. Has someone got Penny-a-day to come in till Ella's back?'

'Yes, Annie'll be in tomorrow to see you off to work and get your breakfast,' Mrs Dafydd said. 'Now hold on, Glyn. Ella's hurt her back. Her leg won't work rightly; it may be a while before she can do housework and so on. I think you ought to suggest that she goes away for a few weeks when the infirmary lets her go.'

'A few *weeks*?' Glyn shook his head. 'I couldn't manage without her, Mrs Dafydd; not even for one week! They'll have to let her home, won't they?'

'No, indeed. Better it would be if she got herself well and fit before coming back to all that work.' She paused, eyeing the young man as she, too, got to her feet. 'And then think how clumsy Ella's been this last year. Black eyes, split lips, bruised shoulders and arms . . . well, if she's on crutches God above knows how she might injure herself. Better that she goes and stays with her sister until she's fit to . . . take care of herself. See?'

Glyn, leaving the house with a grateful smile on his lips and murder in his heart, saw only too well. Mrs Dafydd thought it was he who was responsible for those black eyes and bruised arms. If the truth were known it was Ella, and no one else. They had been married six years, yet Ella had born him no child, and people were talking! It was all her fault, the bitch. She'd had fine sons by Ben, yet by him, who was every bit as good a man as Ben, she had not quickened once. His mother told him that folk were even doubting that he had fathered Jessica, saying that Jessica's mother had seen a quick way to get rid of the child by laying the blame at his door. They said that for all his talk and his ways with woman Glyn Pritchard could not give a woman a child, not even a fine woman like Ella who already had a string of sons to her credit. Of course it was all Ella's fault. She must know some way of preventing herself from quickening, for God knew he made love to her on every conceivable occasion. And, being older than he, perhaps she denied him the male dominance which had brought her to bed of four sons when she and Ben were married.

She was always so certain of herself that he had rather enjoyed her changed attitude to him when he first started hitting her, the new wariness which crept into her voice and movements. It was proving who was the dominant partner, he told himself; she might be five years the elder but she was no match for him physically. Yet still there was no sign of a child. And now he had given her a little tap, no more than a love-touch really, at the top of the stairs, and she was in the infirmary and Mrs Dafydd was going on as if he were a secret wife-beater when he was no such thing! Damn it all, a man had to be master in his own house – especially when the woman was older and inclined to be bossy.

He went back to his house. The room smelt of soap, and the fire was out. Someone had laid it, though, with paper and sticks and small knobs of coal; it would not take long to light. However, since he was going down to the infirmary he would not bother to kindle it now.

He stripped before the sink, sloshed cold water into the basin, and began to scrub with the hard red soap. It was a chilly and unpleasant business and it took him ages to get rid of the grime and the coal, but he felt that in a way he was making up to Ella. She was in the infirmary, through something he had done – accidentally, of course – and so it did serve him right if he stood here shivering and raw with scrubbing instead of lolling in a hot bath with Ella hanging towels on the rail ready for when he was clean.

He got into his good shirt and trousers, and then discovered that he was famished. He drank a couple of pints of water, wishing they were beer, and rooted around in the pantry for something to eat. A loaf would have been nice, buttered, but the butter was like iron, so he simply spread jam on a slice and wolfed it down before going upstairs to fetch a tie and some shoes. He would not go into town in clogs.

He hated the idea of returning to Mrs Dafydd's, but knew he would have to do so; he could scarcely go off and leave her with the children without a word. He knocked on her door and she answered it at once. Jessica stood at her elbow. It was dark, and he could scarcely see either face against the golden lamp-glow from the kitchen.

'I'm off now, Mrs Dafydd,' he said awkwardly, 'Could you

send the children home for ten? I'll have to walk down but I'll catch the bus back.'

'The children will stay here tonight,' Mrs Dafydd said. Something in the way she said it made Glyn feel uncomfortable again. What did she think he would do, left alone with the children, for God's sake? 'My Dafydd and me, we'll see to 'em. Make a nice change it will to have them about. Now don't worry, Glyn. I'll see that Stan gets off to work in good time tomorrow when my Dafydd goes, and the other children will be as safe here as in your own home until Annie gets herself organised. Or perhaps tomorrow you'd sooner they went to your mam's?'

That was a nasty dig and they both knew it, since Mrs Pritchard had made it very plain that though her son might have married that scheming Ella the boys were none of her concern.

'Oh, right, Mrs Dafydd. If you're sure they'll be no bother I won't trouble my mam,' Glyn said as she paused. 'Tomorrow I'll get a day off and sort things out.'

'You do that,' Mrs Dafydd said comfortably. 'A day off won't harm, with your wife poorly. You'll come in tomorrow, then, when the boys are up and about?'

'I will,' Glyn promised. 'And . . . and thanks, Mrs Dafydd.'

Lying in her bed in the ward, Ella wondered how they were managing without her. She was in a smallish ward and the beds were clean but the woman opposite smelt appalling and the nurses, though kind and chatty, could only suggest that when visitors came down from the village she should ask them how her family was getting on.

'Don't you worry, girl,' one little nurse said, patting Ella's shoulder. 'Friendly they are, up there, good to each other. And your man works down the Olwen, so they'll see he doesn't want for help.'

It was true, or course, and Ella knew she had no need to worry; not that I'm worrying, I'm just wondering, she told herself, shifting slightly, and then wincing back into stillness once more. By goodness, but she ached! She was a mass of bruises and strained muscles, and she had a nasty burn on her bottom caused by landing, when she had slipped, in a bucket of water that was as near boiling as could be, but she would be all right, or so the sister said. Sister was a caution, the nurses said; always knew better than the doctor. The doctor had said Ella would be better for a week on her back because of the muscle damage but Sister, who nurtured the unfair suspicion that her nice infirmary might come to be regarded as a rest-home for weary housewives if she allowed anyone to linger an hour longer than necessary in one of her beds, pooh-poohed this.

'Tomorrow we'll have you runnin' up and down the ward like a spring chicken,' she said briskly, after the doctor had left. 'Strained your back have you? My nurses strain their backs every day but I don't let them lie in bed!'

'Nasty old cow she is,' the woman opposite breathed to Ella as soon as Sister had rustled out of sight. 'The only time you see her smile is when she sends some poor sick soul tottering out of 'ere. You stay as long as you can, gal. Get the colour back into your cheeks.'

A ribald remark from further up the ward regarding the colour which throbbed painfully on Ella's scalded buttocks was greeted with titters of amusement. Ella, who thought the bed horribly hard, the covers scant and the food appalling, remarked that the infirmary was no place to get fit and well in.

'Once I'm on my feet I'll be best at home,' she told the other women. 'Decent food, a soft bed, and a cup of tea whenever my daughter puts the kettle on, that's what I want.'

Most of the women in the beds were townswomen, and none the worse for that, except that they were for the most part living in slums without decent food or soft beds. They eyed Ella with respect and more than a little envy. Colliery wives, their envious glances said, were lucky, what with the money, the free fuel, and the fact that their husbands usually valued and took care of their women. Living in the Green and down Love Lane in filthy, tumbledown thatched cottages or brick tenements, most of the ward regarded the infirmary as a haven of peace and rest.

So now Ella waited, eyes on the door at the end of the ward. He would come, naturally he would, but in what sort of mood? In front of all these women he would be charming, of course, but she knew Glyn well enough to be able to tell at first glance whether he was blaming her for the fall.

She looked out of the window, but it was dark now; soon he would be here. he wouldn't let her down . . . would he?

He came. He breezed down the ward with a tiny bunch of snowdrops in one large hand, grinning at the other women before settling himself awkwardly on a small stool beside Ella and leaning forward to kiss her cheek.

'You better, gal? Worried, I was, when I got home to find the house empty and the fire dead.'

'I'm better,' Ella said feebly. 'Muscle damage, the doctor said.'

'Ah.' He looked at her as a guilty puppy looks at the person who discovers the chewed shoe. 'Explain, did you? That it was an accident, like? Never a word out of you this morning to say you were hurt bad, or else I wouldn't have gone off with young Stan the way I did.'

It took her a moment or two to realise just what he meant, and then the words which would put him straight were all but hovering on the tip of her tongue before she bit them back.

'Oh . . . it came on later,' she said vaguely. It then occurred to her that once she embarked on a tissue of lies to support his assumption she would almost certainly come to grief. So she added, casually, 'Course, the fall in the washhouse brought it to a head.'

He brightened. His grip on the snowdrops, which had been threatening to sever their heads, loosened; Ella could almost hear the little flowers breathing again. 'Oh? Had a second fall, did you?'

'That's right. I'd been feeling poorly, limping a bit, and I came over fainty and slipped in the water. And when I tried to get up I couldn't.'

'I see. So what's the damage, then?'

Ella laughed feebly. 'Depends who you ask. Sister says it's just a strained back and that I'll be up and about tomorrow; the doctor said he wanted me in bed on this ward for a week before I was moved.'

'A week!' Clearly, Glyn had not expected this. 'Well, Mrs Dafydd's got the children for tonight, and she's fetching Penny-a-day tomorrow morning so's they've got someone to come home to. But I don't know as Annie'll be able to manage, not if you aren't in the house. Jess is a good girl, but too young to do much ... unless you were there, of course.'

'Oh well, I'll be back as soon as I can get.' Ella shifted a little and could not help frowning as pain stabbed her back. 'God, Glyn, I feel bad, really I do.'

'Shall I get the nurse? Or Sister?'

Ella began to shake her head, then groaned and nodded instead. Pain was knifing into her back now, corkscrewing, stabbing. She did not know what was happening but she knew that it hurt!

'Better get the doctor, if you can.'

Glyn hurried off and sent a nurse scurrying for the doctor before returning to the bed. Ella tried to make quiet, comforting conversation but very soon it was impossible to do anything other than breathe deeply and long for someone to come and take the pain away. She could see Glyn's face, sweat-streaked and frightened, but it kept wavering in her vision as tears blurred before her eyes. And then Sister arrived, and a couple of nurses, and they brought a trolley close to her bed and pulled the curtains round her and sent Glyn ignominiously about his business.

'Go and amuse the children up the corridor,' Sister said impatiently. 'We'll call you if we need you.'

The last Ella saw of Glyn was his hunched shoulders and the flush on his neck as he made his way miserably towards the door.

Glyn, kicking his heels in the corridor and importuning every passing member of the infirmary staff, was kept waiting for five long hours until at last Sister emerged from the ward with a couple of nurses and her trolley of equipment. Glyn stepped forward, but he had no need to ask questions. Her eyes raked him, impersonal yet somehow accusing.

'She's miscarried, Mr Pritchard. I don't believe she knew she was pregnant, though she may have had her suspicions.'

'Pregnant? I don't understand.'

Sister stopped, sighed, and then patted Glyn's arm, not unkindly.

'Yes, Mr Pritchard, she's lost a baby son. She was only about four months pregnant – that's a bad time to have a serious fall. The baby couldn't live, you see – not yet fully formed. But your wife's doing nicely, despite her ordeal. She'll be back home with you in a few days.'

'Can . . . can . . .'

'Just a peep,' Sister said, not needing words when his eyes pleaded so hotly to see his wife. 'Don't worry her, just smile and give her a kiss. She'll need to know you don't blame her for the loss, you know.'

'Blame her? I couldn't . . .'

She moved on and Glyn shot through the door and across to the bed. Ella was still on her back and the little nurse was just smoothing the sheets around her. She turned and smiled at Glyn, putting a finger to her lips.

'Gently, Mr Pritchard. She's had a hard time, and if she's asleep. . .'

Glyn would not have woken her for the world, but Ella, at the sound of his name, opened her eyes. They were shadowed, weary, still suffused from her struggle, yet there was a smile in their depths.

'Glyn? There's sorry I am – I didn't know, see? Not that it would have made any difference. . .'

'Sorry, girl? An idiot, that's what you are, if you think it matters! Whose fault was it, eh, if we're being honest? Mine, no other. But there won't be no more of *that*, and I'll keep off the ale . . . you see how it'll be!'

Ella chuckled softly, then closed her eyes again.

'Fine words, love. Now you'd better go, for it must be late. Come down again tomorrow, will you?'

'Today,' Glyn corrected her. 'Yes, I'll be down when I come off shift.'

He kissed her and then walked quietly up the ward between the beds and their sleeping occupants. He had a word with one of the nurses, who agreed with him that it might be an idea to bring a few eggs and some soup to supplement his wife's diet, and then he went out into the darkness. It did not worry him for all through the winter months he and other colliers went to work in the dark, their way lit only by moonlight or starlight or the occasional glow from cottage windows as they went down the street. It was fresh outside after the antiseptic atmosphere of the infirmary, and the stars were brighter for the frosty nip in the air. Glyn strode out, glad to be moving at last, freed from the intolerable strain of not knowing whether Ella was going to die. His Ella! He had loved her ever since they had married, but he had not, until this night, realised how much. It was she who mattered, she who was important – and it would soon go around the village that Ella had been pregnant with his child and had fallen and miscarried of the baby. He did not want other children; it was just the implied slur on his abilities that he had not liked. Now, however, all that would be a thing of the past – Ella had been pregnant by him and but for that fall would have born him a son.

He felt a twinge of regret, but it was brief and soon forgotten as the night wind tousled his hair and he left the town behind him. A child was only another mouth to feed. He and Ella were managing better now that Stan was working, though as yet only at the pit-head. Boys were not allowed down the pit at thirteen, but when he was a year older he could go below and his wages would be higher still.

Over the straggly hedge which separated the sloping meadows from the dusty road a fox barked high and shrill, and Glyn heard the flutter of a bird disturbed from its rest. He felt released, as though he had been trapped into behaviour not his own by feelings of which he was ashamed. Now he and Ella could go forward, enjoying their family and each other, without the feeling that he was not the man Ben was and that the whole community was secretly jeering at him.

The moon, sinking in the sky, reminded him that by the time he got home it would be just about time to set off again, for he must change out of his best clothing, put away his shoes and his good jacket and tie and get himself ready for a day's work. No breakfast, either, unless he made it himself, and though this was by no means beyond him he would scarcely have time to light the fire, cut bacon from the smoked joint, find where Ella had put the eggs, and do all the hundred and one other tasks which his wife did each morning. Feeding the hens and the pig was simple enough, except that yesterday had been wash-day and Ella had probably fallen before she could have boiled up all the peelings and scraps for the hens. They would have to make do with a cold bran mash, which wouldn't help with the egg-production.

He walked quickly, with the sensible, swinging walk of a man used to such exercise, not hurrying, yet covering the ground at a good pace. Even so, when he opened the garden gate carefully, not letting the latch click so that it woke the neighbours, he knew that he would have his work cut out to be ready for his shift this morning.

He unlocked the door and stepped into the kitchen, sighing, bending to take off the unaccustomed shoes and ease his aching feet. He looked at the unlit fire, thought longingly of hot tea, and went over to it, then remembered the little oil stove. That would save lighting the fire. Then, when he came home tonight, even if Penny-a-day had been unable to come, it would be the work of a moment to put a match to the kindling.

He was halfway across the kitchen when he saw something move outside the back window. A practical man, he nevertheless felt the skip of a heartbeat before he rationalised the quick suspicion that there was a ghost out there. It was, of course, the washing, flapping on the line in the starlight, waiting to be got in to be aired before the unlit fire.

He hesitated, weighing up the loss of a day's pay against the grim certainty that if he left the linen on the line it would rain and if he brought it indoors Penny-a-day would probably do something foolish with it. Oh, hell! Peering through the low kitchen window he saw his own and the boys' shirts still flapping out there. They would be in a rare state without a clean shirt to their name for later in the week!

It was tempting to stay off for the one day, just to set things to rights. The owner mightn't mind. Ella had worked at the pit-head twice, before she married. But if he stayed away the fellows would have to wait a whole day longer to learn that he had fathered – and lost – a son. Glyn made up his mind. For the second time in twelve hours he stripped off and soused his head in cold water from the bucket. Then he began to dress in his pit clothes – loose shirt, waistcoat, moleskin trousers, clogs. Someone would get the washing in, see to the children, find time to light the fire. He had news to impart!

Three: 1912

'I wish I were a boy.'

The three Tegydd girls were sitting on top of a load of hay as the cart swayed and jolted its slow way down the steep little lane from the high mountain meadows and into the stackyard of Tegydd Plas. Dot Tegydd, who had spoken, tugged at the thin material of her skirt, trying to persuade it to come down so that the hay stalks would stop sticking into the soft backs of her thighs, but her words lacked their usual conviction this afternoon, because she was so happy. Hot sunshine burned the back of her neck, the delicious smell of the hay was all around, and she was out of doors and working on the farm, her two favourite occupations, if merely being out of doors could be dignified by such a title.

'You look like one, Dot,' Alexandra said lazily from her own comfortable perch. Dot smiled at her older sister. Even after an afternoon in the hayfield Allie looked cool, calm and collected. She was ten years old but somehow she never seemed to get rumpled or crumpled or cross. Her powder-blue dress was covered by a spotless white pinafore and her beautiful hair, which was, Dot thought, the colour of a sun-ripened peach, never blew about untidily or stuck up at the side but lay meekly against her shoulders, curling up just enough but never too much.

Dot, however, glancing down at herself, thought her sister's remark a compliment, for goodness knew she spent long enough trying to act like a boy! This afternoon she was wearing a brief brown dress, much patched, and had her mass of dark, curly hair pulled back with a scrap of ribbon. Bare brown toes wriggled in the hay and she approved her scratched and tanned legs as being thoroughly suitable for a girl who wanted to be a boy.

'I don't see how she can say she wants to be a boy when she doesn't know any,' Kate contributed. The eldest, she was the family beauty, with golden hair, blue eyes and a strong will of her own which kept Alexandra her devoted slave and caused Dot to eye her cautiously. Allie, Dot, knew, was easily persuaded, but Kate was perfectly willing to make everyone's life hell if she did not get her own way, so Dot, her parents and all the servants treated Kate with circumspection. 'Go on, gnome, tell us about boys.'

'I do know some; I know Gwil,' Dot cried, immediately defensive. 'And . . . and I know Father wants a boy and he says, sometimes, that I'm nearly as good, and . . .'

'I'm no *boy*, fach,' protested Gwil, the middle-aged farmhand who was leading Dapple, the carthorse. 'See myself more as a man, I do, what with having a wife and six kids, like.'

'Oh! Well, anyway, a man's only a boy grown up, and there are the village boys, and boys in books, and . . .'

'Dot, stop being so foolish; you've never even exchanged the time of day with a village boy,' Kate said sternly. 'You hang around the farmhands, probably getting in their way, when you would be better occupied attending to what Miss Edenthorpe tells you during lessons.'

'I don't, I'm a help,' Dot said stoutly. 'Father *likes* me to go round the farm with him and he likes me to look like a boy and he thinks . . .'

'Yes, all right,' Alexandra, the peacemaker, said hastily. 'But why did you say you wanted to be a boy then, Dot? Just out of the blue?'

'If I was a boy Father would take me to the beast market tomorrow without a fuss,' Dot said, remembering her grievance with some difficulty, for it was such a lovely day. 'He's going to buy cattle and I do want to go, and I know Mother is taking you two into town to buy material for silly dresses because I heard her telling Edie, and I don't see why I shouldn't go. I've never been and I'm seven going on eight and . . .'

'We don't go down to the beast market,' Kate said loftily, pulling a face at Alexandra's expression of distaste. 'The last place we'd want to go is amongst a lot of horrid, smelly animals. We go into town and have coffee and cakes at a nice teashop and choose material for our dresses, and sometimes we go to Coopers and help mother order biscuits and flour and special sorts of tea and coffee. You could come with us, I suppose, though I daresay you'd be bored.'

'Yes, I would. I want to go to the market,' Dot assured her sisters. 'Father meets all the other landowners, and some pit owners too, and they talk business and prod cows with their sticks and bid at the auction . . . oh, I would dearly love to be a boy and go with him and have a fine time!'

She leaned out at a perilous angle, grabbed a passing branch of honeysuckle, and made it into a crown which she placed for an instant upon her head before snatching it off again and sniffing the waxy blossoms enthusiastically.

'Isn't that the best smell in the world? Or is it the wild roses? I'm never quite sure. Mind you, I *love* the smell in the cowhouse when they've been milking, and there's rather an exciting sort of smell down on the tarmac road when the sun's hot, and then there's the way the kitchen smells on a Sunday when Cook's been roasting chickens . . . what's your favourite smell, Allie?'

'Oh, the perfumed soap Mother uses when she's going to visit her relatives,' Alexandra said, eager to join in this particular game. 'And then there's the smell of those big cabbage roses, the pink ones, when the sun gets on them, and . . .'

'Tomorrow we're having luncheon in town,' Kate chimed in. She and Alexandra were very close, not only in age – there was only a year between them – but in everything else too. Dot, four years younger than Kate, had always known herself to be an outsider in their relationship but usually she accepted her position without a thought. Now, just for a moment, it occurred to her that Kate never gave her a chance to get on well with Allie; she always stepped in, pushing Dot back into the baby sister slot and dragging Allie up to her level. Oh, well! Dot was not particularly bothered, since she was sure that she and Allie had totally different outlooks, but it would have been nice if Kate had let them chat about smells for a little longer!

'Are you? If I went with Father to the beast market perhaps he'd take me to the Wynnstay for luncheon.' Dot sighed as Kate laughed jeeringly. 'Well, you may laugh, but I don't see why he shouldn't, do you, Gwil?'

Gwil was a great ally who frequently stood up for Dot when she needed a champion, and now was no exception. He turned and grinned up at them, red-faced and sweating in the June heat, showing the large gap where he had lost a front tooth years ago during a broomstick fight with his elder bother.

'I reckon the master'll take you down to the beast market tomorrow, Dot, if you ask right nice, like.'

'I always do ask right nice,' Dot reminded him. 'But it hasn't worked yet. Last time, he said, "Out of my way, little frog," and went off with Mr Redman.'

'Ah, but this time may be different, see? Something he said makes me think he will take you down with him tomorrow. Tell you what, why don't you get your Miss Edie to put in a word? Wonderful the way she gets round the master. I've heard you say so many a time.'

'She's very good at persuading him to do what she thinks we ought to want,' Kate corrected. 'And why should she think that Dot ought to go to the market, Gwil? It isn't a very ladylike place, I shouldn't imagine.'

'No-o, but only saying the other day he was that Dot needed a pony to get her about – caught you trying to ride that mare who pulls you mother's gig when she goes visiting, didn't he? – and it's the horse fair this week.'

'Oh, Gwil!' Dot clasped her hands, quite like a child in a story book, then became more natural and flung her honeysuckle wreath with some dexterity over one of Dapple's large, pricked ears, where it hung rakishly, making Dapple look both festive and slightly drunk. 'Do you mean it? Would he really buy me a pony? It's what I want more than anything else.'

'I think he might,' Kate remarked, as Gwil nodded sagely. 'It's the violin lessons. You'll be eight quite soon, too, and it would be a nice birthday present. He and Mother never know what to get you since you aren't interested in clothes. Besides, you get all the things that Allie and I grow out of. I think Gwil's probably right.'

'Violin lessons? What have they got to do with a pony?' Dot pouted as both her sisters laughed. 'I know Father has to let Edie and me have the gig for my lessons, but they were his idea, after all. I didn't want to learn the violin. I quite liked the piano, even if I wasn't very good.'

Gwil, who had heard all about the violin lessons from several sources, turned and grinned at them.

'Hey, I hear you're so good on that old violin, Dot, that the dogs in the village stick their noses up in the air and howl for more. True, is it?'

'It certainly is not,' Dot said with dignity, and then spoiled it by adding, 'I probably sound like a dog howling when I'm practising, but what else can you expect? He won't buy me a violin so I only get a go on it when I'm at Mr Smith's twice a week. And that's not much fun because Mrs Smith always seems to be cooking leeks or cabbage or sprouts and the smell gets into everything. Anyway, Edie said that if I'd been encouraged to play the piano instead of being jeered at I might have done very well.'

'I take it that "he", in this case, refers to our beloved father?' Kate pushed at Dot with one sandalled foot. 'The thing was, you see, Dot, that Father is musical and he couldn't bear to hear you murdering your piano pieces every morning and evening. So he chose the violin, which means that it's only Mr Smith who has to suffer.'

'And his mother,' Dot reminded her placidly, chewing a strand of hay. 'And the dogs, and poor Edie, who has to take me into the village twice a week. Not that she minds, I don't think. She has a friend somewhere who gives her a nice cup of tea whilst I'm violinning away.'

'Yes. So you see what I mean? Father isn't being unkind when he won't buy you a violin of your own, he's being kind. If you had one you'd practise at home and we'd all suffer.'

'Oh, very funny! Anyway, since you haven't heard me playing I don't know who you think you are to say I'm so awful. I might be a genius at it for all you know.'

'Are you?'

Dot subsided. She had suspected for some time that she was not destined for greatness as a musician.

'Well, no. But if I can have a pony . . .' She fell silent, musing on the marvels of actually owning a mount of her own, but before anyone could comment the haywain lumbered into the stackyard and the girls tumbled down, to help hold Dapple and watch the men and boys unload whilst Cobby Jones, the artist who made and thatched the stacks, stood ready. Dot was not strong enough to be of much practical use, so she stood at Dapple's head, but halfway through the unloading Tom Tegydd strode into the yard. Dot immediately deserted her post and ran over to him, tugging at the sleeve of his hacking jacket.

'Father, may I come down to the beast market with you tomorrow? It's the horse fair as well as the market, Gwil was saying, and you know how I love to see horses.'

Tom Tegydd looked down at his plain daughter and grinned at the pleading on her small monkey face. No one knew whether he realised that Dot was as like himself as the two older girls were like his wife – physically, at least. He was not a large man – though so straight-backed and well-built that he looked taller than he was – and he had that gypsyish darkness of hair, eyes and complexion which he found amusing on his daughter. What was acceptable for a man, it seemed, could be totally otherwise for a female! But now he was looking at Dot and smiling, showing the astonishingly even and very white teeth which always won him a second glance. Dot, who knew his moods, recognised that this was a good moment for her request. Something – or someone – had pleased him, and he was approachable as a result.

'Yes, gnome? You'd like to come to the market? I don't see why not. What else did Gwil say?'

Tom's mood could change with mercurial suddenness; Dot hesitated, then decided to make a clean breast of her hopeful half-knowledge.

'We-ell, he did say it was my birthday soon, and then Allie said if I had a pony I wouldn't have to borrow the gig for my violin lessons . . .' She looked up at Tom, half hopeful, half fearful. 'Were they right, Father? Did you think you might look at some ponies for me?'

'I might. The wain's empty – are you going back upalong in time for the harvest tea?'

Hastily, anxious not to offend when a pony seemed a real possibility, Dot rushed up to the waggon and clambered aboard, then turned to Kate and Alexandra.

'Are you coming? Do – the harvest cake is *huge*!'

But Kate was turning away, heading for the house.

'I don't think we'll bother,' she called over her shoulder. 'It's awfully hot up there and we don't want to get all freckled like you.'

'Oh, Katieeee,' Dot wailed. 'Oh . . . well, *you* come, Allie — you love harvest cake.'

'Not if Kate won't. See you later, Dot.'

Dot, settling back on the dusty boards with a resigned sigh, told herself that she would not be happy indoors on such an afternoon, sitting in Mother's cool and shaded drawing room and eating tiny sandwiches and sipping China tea, so she could scarcely blame Allie and Kate, who enjoyed such things, for not appreciating the delights of the harvest tea. And she was used to being alone. With the companionship of the animals and, when she was indoors, of books — for she was an omnivorous and voracious reader — she was never conscious of loneliness.

Even so, she hated the winter months. Plas Tegydd had been built four hundred years ago. Succeeding owners had carried out various alterations, but they had left the big stone blocks and thick walls alone, largely because it would have been impossible to change them without incurring vast expense. So you froze in the Plas during winter. Fires burned in some rooms, but unless you sat almost on top of them you were still chilly on one side. Bedrooms were positively rarefied; draughts like knives whipped across your unprotected shoulders and patches of damp appeared in certain corners, whilst ice regularly formed on your washing water and variegated toadstools had been known to appear in unusual places.

'Some people have rats in their cellars; we have frogs,' the young Kate had once remarked at a family gathering on the Wirral. There had been a shocked silence until someone chose to see it as a joke, and even then the laughter had been uneasy.

Yet Dot loved her home and was, in an odd way, proud of it. Not everyone lived in a four-hundred-year-old castle, but it was not just its antiquity she loved. Despite its chill in winter, the damp which could be just as bad in a wet spring or summer, the inconvenience of a kitchen seemingly miles from the dining room and bedrooms big enough to have a small army encamped on the floor beside the huge old-fashioned beds, there was a friendly feel to the Plas, and a good deal of beauty.

It might not be fashionable to have a timber hall ceiling so far above your head that the curious carving was scarcely visible to the naked eye; stained-glass windows in various distorted forms and shades might not be to modern twentieth-century taste; but Dot could see the beauty of the soaring timber arches, and the glory of the rich scarlets, golds and blues in the stained glass exceeded anything she had seen in a church. What was more, the drawing room was beautifully proportioned; long and elegant with wide arched windows which let in the scent from the rose garden in summer and could look cosy enough when the long red velvet curtains were drawn in winter, even though the fires at either end of the room only served to take the chill off the atmosphere.

The kitchen's nice, too, Dot told herself. It was immense, with huge ranges and long scrubbed wooden tables and a lot of cupboards which were either inconveniently high or even more inconveniently low. It had a weird ceiling, domed and ornately plastered, a little like a vegetable cover or half an onion. No matter how it looked, though, it had one excellent property: it kept the heat in so that the kitchen was always warm. It was usually full of people, too, since although her mother had been forced to let many of her pet schemes drop because Tom would not agree to finance them she had insisted on a good cook and plenty of good food. Tom, who enjoyed his food, raised no objection, so though there might not be maids enough to keep the place clean – and indeed it would have needed an army – there were sufficient servants to see that meals were ample and delicious. To a small and ugly girl whose mother could not see past her plain features and the fact that she was not the longed-for boy, it was important to be able to go into the warm and populated kitchen, perch upon a tall stool, and be fed gingerbread boys and hot chocolate, cream meringues and duck à l'orange, where no one seemed at all fussed that she was neither pretty nor a member of the opposite sex.

Dot knelt so that she could see, round Dapple's ample behind, the summer-rich hedgerows and the thick, pinkish dust of the lane disturbed by Dapple's huge soup-plate hooves. It was a shame, she reflected dispassionately, that her mother could not like her. It meant, naturally enough, that she did not much like her mother, and Olivia needed all the affection she could get. Tall, slim and golden-haired, she was also insipid, indeterminate and lethargic. Her rather round, puddingy face might have been pretty once, but now it was anxious and apologetic. She seldom railed or shouted at Dot, but she often whined and complained, and Dot resented this far more than her father's open criticism, occasional slaps and frequent heavy-handed teasing. Mother gives all her love to Kate and Allie, Dot thought, as the cart lumbered onwards. I don't really mind, because Father likes me best, but . . . it must be rather pleasant to have a mother who likes you.

Of course, there was Edie. Miss Edenthorpe, governess, protector and friend to her three charges, managed to get on well with everyone, certainly with Olivia and definitely with Tom. With her employer, indeed, she was at her best, treating him with just the right mixture of deference and defiance, so that she almost always got what she wanted. Indeed, Olivia was frequently forced to ask Edie to intercede for her with Tom – and Edie always agreed and nearly always succeeded, too, so that Olivia would sigh, 'Oh, Edie, my dear, I can't think how we'd get along without you,' and Edie would smile her sweet, capable smile and tell Olivia that she would do better to be bolder with Tom, more resolute.

'Such things are your right, Olivia,' she would say gaily, smiling her confident smile and taking her mistress's hand gently in her own. 'You must be more forceful with Mr Tegydd, my dear, and then you'll get your own way nine times out of ten.'

Edie was the opposite of Mama; where Mama was tall and slim and somehow frail, Edie was rosy-cheeked, dusky-curled and dimpled. She had a lovely, curvy, generous sort of figure, Dot thought, with a tiny waist and slender wrists and ankles. Her eyes were big and dark and fringed with extravagant curly lashes. Dot had once seen her doing something very odd indeed with those lashes.

It had been winter, she knew, because the fire in the school-room had burned almost down. No one had been up with more coal so she, being the youngest, had been sent in search of a maid who could carry a scuttle up the long flight of stairs and down the even longer corridor. She had been passing Edie's room when she heard voices; a deep, masculine tone and then the lovely, somehow naughty little trill of laughter that Edie gave when she was amused and excited. And then Dot had noticed that Edie's door was not quite shut.

She had meant only to pop her head around it to ask Edie who should bring up the coal. But somehow, as she got nearer and nearer the door, she found herself reluctant to admit she was there, and so she had ended up peeping. Her nose pressed to the wood, she had look through the aperture at the most extraordinary scene, which to this day she could not begin to understand.

Her father had been lying on Edie's bed – that in itself had not seemed particularly strange – and Edie had been lying beside him. Tom was on his back, his head resting comfortably on the pillows, but Edie was supporting herself on one elbow. And even as Dot stared, Tom had seized Edie and pulled her over him, so that she was lying half on his chest.

'Edie? Why won't you . . .'

She had put her face against his then, and turned it so that her long lashes lay against his cheek. And then, slowly and deliberately, she had begun to move her lashes like butterfly wings against Tom's lean brown cheek.

It was very odd. Tom went quite still, and then he grabbed Edie very roughly indeed and there was a commotion and then all Dot could see was Tom's back. Edie was lying on her back and Tom was above her. There was movement, some odd noises and a good deal of mumbling, and then Edie said something in a breathless, sharp little undervoice and Tom said, 'I must, don't you see I must?' and Edie said something else, still very low, and Tom had bounded off the bed and kicked the door shut with such force and unexpectedness that Dot's nose had received a sharp and painful blow.

It ought to have been a lesson to her that no good came to those who crept and spied, but since she was not a particularly curious child all it did was make her measure her lashes a couple of times a week. Mama had once said that Edie was not pretty but she was fascinating, and something in the way she said it had made Kate look at her sharply and Dot think that being fascinating must be a lot more useful than mere prettiness.

After the incident in the bedroom, she realised that long lashes were important if one was to become a fascinator – after all, it had been the lashes that had started the whole thing off. Without them, she supposed that her father would merely have climbed off the bed, wished Edie a decorous farewell and gone about his business. Therefore, if she wanted to fascinate, she must obviously either be pretty or grow her lashes. And since it was plainly impossible for an ugly child to become pretty, she had better cultivate with all her might.

The haywain turned into the gateway of the first meadow and recollections of Edie's behaviour vanished from Dot's mind. All that she could think of was the cut hay and the harvest tea, which two of the maids were spreading out on a white cloth in the shade of a large oak tree in the hedge. Dot could see the huge jugs, the freshly baked bread and the big pats of golden butter with the picture of a cow that the dairy maid pressed on one side with her wooden butter pats. There were meat pies and jars of pickles and a whole ham and a side of roast beef and cakes and two fruit tarts the size of cartwheels and pastries and puddings and – the harvest cake!

Mouth watering, eyes bright with anticipation, Dot raked the hay into manageable bundles and pitched them into the haywain. She could not have been happier had she been Queen of all England . . . and tomorrow she was going with Father to the horse fair!

'Well, which one does my little gnome like best, then?'

Tom Tegydd was jovial, knowing he had an audience, for the horse dealer was hanging on his every word. Tegydd might be buying a pony for his funny little daughter now, but he was also in the market for pit-ponies. There was money to be made there, if you had ponies that were small yet could do the work.

'Oh, I'd like the black one,' Dot said yearningly, and though Father laughed the dealer shook his head. He was an Irish gypsy, with long light brown hair, pale blue eyes and a smile that would charm most women if the blarney failed him. But Dot wanted the black pony and no amount of glib talk could persuade her that it was not right for her.

'Too young. She'd never hold him, sor,' the man was saying.

'Wonderful workers, these little chaps – see the muscles on him – but it's cheatin' you I'd be if I pretended he was right for the young lady. No, not the black, though he's strong as an ox and not even in his full strength yet. But the dun, now . . .'

The dun was a pretty mare, but Dot, who knew more than most girls her age about horseflesh, could see that she was no longer young; she was probably twelve or thirteen, and would not want to trot fast up hills or change her stride at a moment's notice into a long, loping canter. She had been ridden by a woman, the dealer said, as if that was a fine recommendation indeed, but Dot thought it a poor one. Women rode gentle mares at gentle paces along gentle lanes. She intended to take her pony up on the moor and gallop at full stretch and jump hedges, ditches and fences. The black would do it, she could see he would, but the dun? Never in a thousand years.

'Well, little gnome? Which one is it to be? The grey, if you don't care for the dun? Or the chestnut gelding? A nice pony, that – showy, but plenty of good bone.'

Dot set her lips. She knew they would think she was being foolish but she did not care. She would have her own way over this!

'The black. I know he isn't broken for riding, but I could do it, with Jan and Gwil to show me how. And I know he's only a two-year-old, but I'm light enough not to do him any harm, and he'll still have a soft mouth, so I'll be able to handle him.'

The dealer was shaking his head, his glance admiring. You could see he was saying to himself, *Sure and isn't she as obstinate as the devil himself?* but he was too much a dealer to say it aloud.

'No, sweetheart, don't set your wishes on such a one, now, will you? Look at the way his eyes roll when we move – that's no sweet-natured horse such as you deserve. He's scarce felt a rope round his neck until today a week. If you were to touch his back with a saddle he'd have you halfway across Connemara county before you could catch your breath. But the chestnut, now . . .'

'He's got crumbling hooves,' Dot snapped. 'I expect he suffers from laminitis whenever the grass is good.'

'Crumbling hooves? Well, they are a mite dry, perhaps, but nothing that a spot of oil won't cure, and sure the temper of the beast is remarkable and him not yet five years old.'

'He's more than five,' Dot pointed out, lifting the chestnut's upper lip and examining his teeth. 'He's got that mark . . . the Galvayne mark! That means he has to be quite a lot more than five.' Knowledge, picked up from Jan Torch and jealously hoarded, was useful sometimes, Dot realised.

The dealer's pleasant, rather smug expression changed to one of animation. He liked a challenge and he liked selling to someone who knew a bit about a horse, which a good few of his customers fancied they did. But Tom disliked being made to look foolish. He scowled at Dot and gave her a push.

'That's enough; you've said which you prefer but it's my decision. Go and take a look at the sheep or cattle and come back to me here in an hour. Understand?'

Dot, moving away with lagging steps, was so upset she could have cried. She ought to have known better than to show that Tom was about to be cheated, but how could he have believed a dealer over the age of a horse? He had not attempted to look into the animal's mouth, and she thought it was because he did not care whether she had a decent young creature who could be taught her ways or an old break-down who would take the bit between its teeth and bore her to death in a week. It was too bad, really it was. This was supposed to be her birthday present, but was she allowed a choice? Of course not. Now if she had been a boy . . .

She would have hung around the dealer and his stock, hoping to change her father's mind about the black pony, but she had always been sensitive to Tom's mercurial moods and knew instinctively that the worst things she could do would be to interfere again. She made her way towards the sheep pens and hung over the rails above the white and woolly backs, trying to dispel the silly tears which would form and gather at the backs of her eyes. Useless to cry — and, if he saw her, the one way to make sure Tom didn't buy her any pony. After all, it would not be so bad if she was given the chestnut or even the dun; surely anything was better than no pony at all? Yet she knew that, having seen the black, she would never be content with anything less.

'Going to buy yourself a sheep?'

The voice, half teasing, half serious, made Dot jump and

look round. Leaning on the rails next to her was a boy perhaps a couple of years older than she, and he was plainly talking to her. Dot sighed and shook her head.

'No, I don't like sheep much – though these are very nice, I'm sure.' She thought they might belong to his father, since he seemed interested in them. 'What I was going to buy is a pony, but my father sent me away; he's talking to the dealer now.'

'A pony? Lucky, you are, gal.' The boy grinned at her. 'Why do you look as if you'd lost a guinea and found a farthin', then?'

Dot explained about the peerless black steed and the boy nodded, taking her seriously.

'I see. Why not go back, see if your da will change his mind if you wipe away a tear or two?'

'If I go back I shan't get a pony at all,' Dot said positively. 'My father's like that. He's Tom Tegydd and he doesn't like girls much.'

The boy shook his head, then began to whistle quietly between his front teeth in the enviable way that boys seem born with.

'Like that, is it? Likes to make up his own mind? Well, then, we'll go and take a look at the poultry. There's pigeons, bantams, all sorts. And we can take a look at the cage-rabbits and the goats with their kids and the cows and that. Whilst we're gone we'll think up what to say to your da.'

Dot looked up at him. Despite her boast to her sisters, Kate had not been far wrong when she had accused Dot of not knowing any boys. The lads who worked on the farm were young men who took very little notice of her, and the village boys did no more than stare, grin and nudge one another when they saw her on her way to or from the violin lessons. Despite her desire to be a boy, Dot knew almost nothing about the sex, but now she took a good long look at her companion.

He was tough-looking, with scars on his hands, another on his cleft chin, freckles on his cheekbones and the bridge of his nose, and fair hair which curled a bit. He was wearing a patched jacket, corduroy trousers and boots, but despite the patches his clothing was well cared for, and when he saw her staring he grinned again, showing nice white teeth.

'It's all right. No harm in me, see? Got a sister your age at home. I'm Hywel Fletcher. My mam cleans up at your place sometimes. I'm here by meself and I thought we could spend a while taking a look round, but if you don't want to . . .'

'Oh, but I do,' Dot cried, making up her mind in a rush. 'What shall we do first?' She wondered about his mother but brushed aside the sister; she had too many of her own! 'I have to go back to the horses in an hour, Father said, but otherwise I may go anywhere I like.'

'An hour? Plenty of time to see everything. Grab hold of my jacket so's we don't lose one another.'

'There's my father's agent,' Dot said presently, as they saw Mr Redman in the press around the auction ring. 'Oh, he's beckoning. We'd better go over.'

'Here you are, Dot. Being taken care of, I see. Morning, young Fletcher.' Mr Redman nodded to the boy. 'Mr Tegydd's busy, but he gave me some money to see you had a meal.' He smiled at Dot, but handed the money to her new friend. 'You'll find there's enough to feed the pair of you. Glad you've found young Hywel, Dot. He'll see you right.' He turned to address Hywel directly for the first time. 'Can you get her back to Mr Tegydd by two o'clock, lad?'

'Yes, of course,' the boy said. He grabbed Dot's hand and the two of them wriggled through the crowd, emerging near a tent where beer and presumably lemonade were on sale, as well as various sandwiches and pies. 'Come on, we'll go in here.'

Inside the tent, in the dim greenish light, surrounded by the smell of crushed grass and perspiring humanity, the two grinned at each other. Dot accompanied him to the counter, thinking that for a boy he was very nice. There was nothing very special about him, perhaps, save for a jaw both stronger and squarer than hers and a certain jut to his nose; other than that he could easily have been a girl, Dot supposed. Yet having at last made the acquaintance of a member of the sex she so envied she was conscious that there was a deeper difference than she had suspected. This boy did not wriggle or pout or chatter. In fact he did not say much at all, but he had not questioned the trust that Mr Redman had put in him, nor implied that it was not fair to expect him to look after a young girl he scarcely knew. He accepted things with far less questioning than a girl would, Dot concluded, taking the sandwich he held out and starting to eat it. He was a reliable sort of person.

'Beef. My favourite,' she said as the first mouthful slid down her throat. 'And with mustard, too. Is that my lemonade?'

'That's it. The one nearest you.'

Dot bit again, chewed, swallowed, and then picked up the bottle and looked at it doubtfully. It had a glass ball wedged in the neck, and she had never seen one like it before. The boy took it from her, pressed down on the glass ball with a rather grimy thumb, and handed the bottle back just as the lemonade fizzed over, wetting both their hands.

'Manage?'

'Yes, thanks.' She drank and the lemonade fizzed, sweet yet with its own particular brand of sharpness, against her tongue. She wrinkled her nose and sneezed. The boy smiled and took a swig of his own drink, then addressed her.

'Like an old tom-cat you do sound! Drink up and we'll go back to the horses. We might get a word with your da.'

They made their way back to the enclosure and were seen at once by Tom, who waved them over. He slapped the boy's shoulder and chucked his daughter under the chin. He was looking pleased with himself.

'Got yourselves a bite? Good, good.' He nodded to the boy. 'Redman said you're the Fletcher lad and wouldn't mind taking care of Dot here, for an hour. Thankee. Now, Dot, I've bought six ponies, the chestnut and the dun amongst 'em. Which one will you take, eh?'

Dot stared, scarcely able to believe her eyes. There was the dun, the chesnut, a grey, two bays and the black. He had bought the black!

'Oh, Father, you bought him! I'll have the black, please.'

The smile faded from Tom's face. He looked disproportionately cross, Dot thought, considering he had asked her to choose.

'Not the black. He's for the pit. He's too strong to make a riding pony – you heard what the fellow said. Now come, is it to be the dun or the chestnut? Or do you fancy the grey?'

Dot, dumb with disappointment, merely stared at her father whilst tears pressed for release behind her eyes. But her companion was less reticent. He looked at Tom, then at the ponies, then back at Tom; there was a truculent look about his mouth but he spoke quietly enough.

'You've bought the black for the pit, sir? You'll regret it. I know that pony. He won't go between the shafts without a fight; he's a stubborn one! But there couldn't be a better riding pony — his courage is high and he's young enough to train. And won't he look good, indeed, with decent tack on him and his coat curried to black satin? He'll look worth ten times what you paid, Mr Tegydd, sir.'

Dot waited for the explosion, but instead Tom stared first at the boy and then at the pony. When he spoke it was slowly, ruminatively.

'The lad's right. There's breeding there. These dealers . . . tell you anything, they will. My overman usually buys the pit ponies, but since I was spending money on a mount for the child — ' He broke off to hail a tall, angular man leading a leggy roan. 'Carruthers! Have you just bought that creature or are you looking for a buyer?'

'I wouldn't sell a three-legged donkey to you, Tegydd,' Carruthers answered cheerfully. 'This is a better gelding than ever you've had a leg over.'

'Talking of . . .' Tom hesitated and glanced with quick impatience at the children. 'Dot, go and wait for me by the gig. I shan't be long. If the boy's right, you'd better take the black.'

Dot turned and hurried through the thinning crowd before Tom could change his mind. Reaching the gig, where Jan Torch already stood at the horse's head, she clambered aboard and then leaned down to address her companion.

'Thank you *very* much. If it hadn't been for you he'd never have let me have the black. But . . . did you really know the pony?'

The boy grinned and turned away, calling over his shoulder as he went.

'Not the pony, no. But I know a bit about fathers! Bye, miss.'

It was not until he had disappeared that Dot remembered she had not actually given him her name, though surely he must know it, since Mr Redman knew him. And she would meet him again, since he must live in the village if his mother cleaned up at the Plas. She settled down in her seat, glorying in the knowledge that the black pony was to be hers.

Presently Tom joined her, pleased with his day and therefore expansive, even with a small and despised daughter. Revelling in the unusual attention, Dot chattered away, laughed at all her father's jokes and then fell asleep against his shoulder, only waking as the gig rounded the corner of the drive and began to clatter across the uneven stones which paved the drive.

It was late, Edie scolded, putting an arm round Dot and helping her up the stairs, for Dot was still only half awake. It was nice to be fussed over, nice to tell, in a sleep-drugged voice, about the wonderful pony which was to be hers. Nicest of all, perhaps, to fall into her hard little bed with its thin blankets and sleep as soundly as a princess because Father loved her, Hywel Fletcher had been kind to her, and she was the owner of the most beautiful black pony in the whole wide world.

Four: 1914

'Hywel Pritchard, did you hear me? A dream you are, boy!
Come on now, I asked you a question, and I know you've done
the work. I can see it written out from here, so let me be having
an answer, if you please.'

Hywel, jerked out of his dream, muttered an apology,
consulted the page before him, and gave Miss Eliza Jones the
answer she was waiting for. The trouble was, he was mathe-
matically able and by and large the rest of the class was not, so
that he spent a good deal of time dreaming whilst others
wrestled with sums he could do in a few seconds in his head.
But today he knew he was not the only member of the class
with his attention on things other than sums. War had broken
out two months previously, but men were only now drifting
away from the pits to fight for their country. Before Miss Jones
started the lesson they had been talking about the war, the girls
planning to nurse wounded soldiers and the boys seeing a way
out of the pit, which might easily lead, furthermore, to honour
and glory. Most of the fathers would stay here, digging coal,
but elder brothers, cousins, and even the odd friends had gone
or were planning to go. Hywel wondered whether Stan would
leave, but not very seriously. Stan might not enjoy the pit
but he liked the money, and all his spare time was spent growing things; he would realise that his chances of growing
things whilst fighting in France were slight. Dewi, though
only fifteen, was courting. His girl, Sian, worked in the
milliner's shop in town, and they were saving up to get
married. You needed a collier's pay to dream of an early
marriage. As for Luke, he looked even less than his fourteen
years, with a round, innocent face and apple-blossom complexion.

Which leaves me, Hywel thought. I wouldn't mind going, if it's still on when I'm sixteen. Of course it would not be. He was only twelve now. But if the war did continue, or if he looked seventeen or so when he was fifteen, it would be the obvious thing to do.

Actually, Hywel was not twelve for another two days, but he did not give much thought to birthdays. It was on his birthday that his father had died and, though he was very attached to Glyn and thought of him as his true parent, he knew that his mother mourned Ben still. She did not exactly hold Ben's death against him, but she always made it clear, when November 27th came round, that she was not in her happiest mood.

Then there was the business of his twin. Hywel did not know much about it – even whether it was true. It had been one of the things told him by Penny-a-day on his fifth birthday, the one when he had first noticed that although his brothers got a special tea, a trip out, or a cake with candles, all he got was a dry kiss, a present and 'bumps' from his brothers when his mother was out of the way.

'What's wrong with my birthday, Annie?' the small Hywel had asked. 'Luke said to ask for a birthday treat, and Mam just said *certainly not* in a funny voice and went out of the room. Why is it *certainly not* for me, when Luke went on the train for a whole day in Rhyl?'

' 'Spects it's because you was twins, Hywel bach,' Penny-a-day had surmised, giving his hand a little jerk. She was 'helping out', taking him and little Jessica for a walk out of Ella's way whilst she cooked her Christmas puddings. It was a cold day, and their breath puffed out into the air. As they crossed the bridge over the river, Hywel, jumping up, had seen ice on the edges around the rushes.

'Twins? What's them, Annie?'

'Two of you,' Annie said, after deep thought. 'I 'member, when you was born, there were two. And then a few days later there was only you.'

'Only me? What happened to the other one, then? Did he go away? Why did he go away?'

But this question was too much for Penny-a-day, who looked shifty and said she didn't know about that, and how would he like to go into the baker's shop for a warm before they turned for home.

The small Hywel, however, had been fascinated by the thought of twins. There had been two of him? How could that be? Some instinct prevented him from asking his mother but he did mention it to Luke, who shouted with laughter and said that one of him was bad enough and didn't he know that Penny-a-day was simple? However, his father had heard and had taken Hywel to one side later that day, on the pretext of feeding the ducks.

'Look, Hywel,' he said, throwing stale bread to the hungry little flock which hung around the river in winter. 'A good boy you are; don't upset your mam by talking about twins, eh? You see, mun, when you were born you had a brother, born almost the same time – that's twins. Only the other baby boy died. It makes Mam sad to remember, which is why she's quiet-like, sometimes, on your birthday. But I'll give all you lads some money and you can go to the circus in a few days, when Mam's got over thinking about what's past. All right?'

Hywel had been satisfied, but as time went on his dead twin intrigued him more and more. Had he been an identical twin? Just like the image Hywel saw in the mirror each morning when he brushed his hair? If he had not died, what friends they would have been! In the same class, with the same sort of mind, sharing everything: their homework, their scoldings, their treats.

At ten, he wondered whether his twin had been named, and, if so, what. No one seemed to know the answer to that one. At eleven he wanted to know where his twin was buried, and he spent a lot of his spare time going round the small churchyards in the neighbourhood. At twelve, or almost twelve, he realised that the baby had died at the same time as his real father and Mam would not have been able to afford a stone. The baby's grave would be unmarked; one of the small, nameless mounds which were in all the churchyards. His father's grave had a stone with his name on it; perhaps the baby was buried there? If the baby had no name they could scarcely have carved it on the tombstone, and anyway Stan, who could still remember their real father, told him that the owner, Mr Tegydd, had paid for the burial and for the stone because Ben had died in the pit.

He would not have wanted to pay for another name or an explanatory sentence to be added to the gravestone.

Stan knew nothing about a twin though; news to me, mun, he had said when Hywel first asked him. Sure, are you, that you got your facts right, like? Hywel, who was sure, decided to leave the matter. Questions seemed to get him nowhere. The only person who could have told him everything – his mother – did not wish to do so.

Stan had told him about Ben's death, of course, long before he started to search for his twin's grave. Hywel was sure it was his father's death rather than the baby's that Ella mourned. Yet it did not seem fair that she could never look at her youngest son without remembering sad times. Father has been dead for twelve years and I've been alive for that long, Hywel told himself now. Surely it is more important to care about the one who's alive? The dead can neither know nor benefit from caring.

He had a sister now, Jessica, who was only a year younger than himself. He was on good terms with her despite her fierce temper, her cleverness and her closeness to Glyn. They were both dreamers, both country-lovers, and although most of Jessica's spare time was spent helping in the house they went off together occasionally on blackberrying trips or tiddler-catching expeditions. When he did condescend to take his odd-looking step-sister out with him they both enjoyed it.

In another year I'll be down the pit and earning good money, Hywel told himself now, as the teacher began to expound pounds shillings and pence and explain how to work out percentages. Families needed their sons to be earning, and Hywel felt that he, particularly, should try to help out. His arrival had coincided with the death of the provider, and he knew how very hard Mam and the boys had found the two years before Glyn had come along. He could remember none of it, of course, but Stan had told him that their mother had worked at the pit-head, screening the coal for ten hours or more a day, at first with the baby (himself) on her hip and later paying Penny-a-day to keep an eye on him.

Hywel was quite fond of Penny-a-day but he had never forgotten that she was not entirely to be trusted. One of his earliest memories was of Penny-a-day calling for him one cold, dark winter's morning. Usually she came into the house and cooked breakfast or buttered bread for the boys before they went off to school, but on this particular morning, for some reason long lost in the mists of time, she took him off with her.

He rather thought they had been shopping at first, and then, for some reason which again he could not recall, they had begun the long walk over the mountain to the next village. Halfway there they had met a man – or at least he had seemed adult to the child in the shawl on Annie's hip. The man had walked with them and Penny-a-day had talked and laughed and ignored Hywel, who had kept trying to interrupt their talk; jealous, probably, that Annie, who usually talked and played games with him constantly, was giving him no attention whatsoever.

They had been treading a narrow path beside a deep drop, at the bottom of which one of the wild mountain streams ran and chattered over the great rocks which formed its bed. And Annie had undone her shawl and held Hywel out over the abyss.

'Want to go down there, Hywel bach?' she had asked, as her shawl swung slowly back and forth. 'Want to have a bit of a swim in that stream?'

Hywel had been too terrified even to answer her. He had clutched the shawl, round-eyed, waiting for the terror of the drop. And the man, who had wild black hair and wilder eyes, had egged Annie on, almost daring her to do it.

'Say 'e fell, we will. Say 'e ran ahead, tripped up, and fell,' he said. 'G'won, Annie. Let's see how long it takes 'im to reach the bottom.'

It felt like hours before Annie brought him back and tied the shawl about her skinny shoulder once more, but perhaps it was only seconds. She laughed, a little breathlessly, and explained herself to her companion.

'Naw . . . next time I needed a penny or two there would be no one to look after. Got to look ahead, I 'ave.'

He had never forgotten it, though it had never occurred to him to tell anyone. But now, when he was particularly upset by some parental behaviour, he often wondered just how much Ella would have cared. He had the feeling that she put up with him most of the time but that his coming was still so

57

inextricably tied up with Ben's going that she rarely looked at him without remembering.

Outside the classroom the bell for break sounded. Miss Eliza Jones began to rub the figures off the board and reminded her pupils that she expected them to tackle the six sums she had just given them for homework. Hywel, who had dreamed right through the six sums, shuffled his books together with the rest and joined in the jostling mob pushing to get through the doorway and out into the yard. Miss Jones wasn't bad, really, despite a voice which sounded a bit like a sheep's anxious bleat and thick legs. She had gone to the trouble of having a word with Ella, suggesting that Hywel might do better as a clerk in town than down the pit, but no one had taken the well-meant suggestion very seriously. Good money there was in the colliery if you were tough and willing to work hard, and digging coal was a man's job. He'd be on the surface for the first year, but after that the money got steadily better – far better than he could earn in town.

A fight broke out in the doorway. Kev Jones and Dai were thumping any bits of the other that came handy, and Hywel seized the jacket of one and the shirt front of the other and pushed them through the doorway into the chilly, smelly corridor. The three of them fled along the linoleum, through the dark and ill-omened cloakrooms and out into the yard. Hywel had his snap in his jacket pocket – two cheese sandwiches and a wrinkled, rosy-cheeked apple – so he didn't have to waste time fetching it from a coat or hanging around for an elder brother, as some did. Instead, he shot across to where the oak tree grew close to the iron palings. A princely place, he and his friends thought it, and first one out always bagged it for the others.

Only when the four of them were assembled was their food produced. Singer Evans had cold beef, Duffy had a crumbly beef and onion pasty which made Hywel's mouth water, and Porky had cheese. Usually, to give life more variety, each boy handed a sandwich to his left and received one from his right – as good a method of sharing as they had yet discovered – but Duffy's pasty would present problems. Hywel raised his brows at it; there was no need for words.

'Mam's gone to town and my da got me the pasty from the

shop,' Duffy explained. 'Sorry I am, mun, but there's no use repinin'. Shall I halve it?'

'I do love them pasties,' Singer declared; he was not on Duffy's left, but Hywel, who was, declared himself to be passionate about cold beef, and the exchanging went well after all. Duffy's father was the village baker, so Duffy was occasionally given leftovers for his school dinner; though the beef and onion pasties usually sold out, since they were popular with the miners as well as with their children. Singer, on the other hand, was the only son of the local seamstress and since she was not married had been forced to adopt a tough and don't-care attitude which, Hywel suspected, was foreign to his real nature. Duffy was tough too, for anyone whose father was not down the pit had to face a certain amount of nastiness, and Porky, whose mother fed him what she fed his father and expected him to clear his plate, was tough because fat boys were either tough or dead. At least, that was how he had explained it to Hywel when his friend had once asked why Porky felt it incumbent on him to fight every fellow his size in the school.

Hywel himself was tall and strong because his father had been so; in a community where the average height of the men was around five foot five he was already three inches taller than most. If you were different, you had to learn to defend yourself; it stood to reason!

The four boys had been best friends ever since their first day in the babies' class. They rarely thought about it, but now, because there had been talk of the war, they, the acknowledged leaders of their schoolmates, felt that they would have to take the lead. To approve of the war? To say they would rather work down the pit? To look up to the soldiers or to decry them? They ate their food and considered it until Duffy finally broke the unusual silence.

'Like to go for a soldier, I would. Better than down the pit, mun, though there's some won't agree. What d'you say, Hywel?'

'I'd like to go . . . but it'll be over by Christmas, they say. The money's no good, though.'

Duffy raised pale brows; he always looked as though he had just emerged from one of his father's big sacks of flour with his white eyelashes and dusty-white hair.

'Money? That's not the point, mun! You go for the honour
and glory and for the adventure and for the foreign places, not
for *money*.'

Hywel felt snubbed. It was true, too, what Duffy had said;
you didn't go for money, you went to fight for your country.
Nevertheless, if he knew anything about it, the people who had
the most fun would be the owners' sons and the rich farmers'
sons.

'Aye, that's true enough. But if we go, who'll cut their coal
for 'em, eh? Who'll get down there in the dark and the wet and
cut their coal?'

'Someone else,' Singer said practically. 'It won't be me, lads!
Nor soldiering, either. My mam might stop work when I'm
out, or at least not have to work quite so hard. But I don't
fancy the pit, not if I can get anything better. And if the war
does go on, we might get better work because they'll take the
grown men to fight for 'em.'

Hywel nodded approvingly at this good sense and foresight.
His friends were always well worth listening to. Now he
listened to Porky holding forth.

'. . . it isn't so much what we'd like as what's right,' he was
saying, waving his cheese sandwich to illustrate the point. 'I'll
go below, because my da's a getter, but I'll do that after. If it's
still on when I'm old enough, I'll go and fight.'

'Right. Then we're for it, are we?' Hywel raised his hand.
'Who's for the war?'

With only the slightest hesitation everyone put a hand in the
air. Hywel, lowering his arm, grinned. Probably it would never
matter because the war would be over long before they were
old enough to fight, but at least they would know what to say
to the other lads, if anyone made remarks about people who
went for soldiers to get out of going underground. You'd tell
them they were mad for sure; you'd say a soldier's life was
hard as a miner's, every bit as hard, and you'd remind them
that when the war was over and the soldiers home they would
work in the collieries then, having fought for their country
first.

He began to eat his food earnestly and had almost finished
when Porky jerked his arm.

'Howie, you're a dream, just like Eliza says! Don't you see? There's that girl!'

Hywel looked through the railings in the direction of Porky's rudely pointing finger. Yes, there she was, tall, golden, beautiful. Kate Tegydd, the owner's daughter, the object, if she had but known it, of more sexual fantasies amongst the village boys than any other female. Film stars were all very well, if you could get into town to see a cinema show once a month, but the silently mouthing beauties of the silver screen could not compete with Kate's reality. Nor, of course, could your fellow pupils. You saw too much of them, giggling in corners, standing out front being told off, their eyes filling with tears and their stockings wrinkling. Pouting, screaming, swearing when they thought no one was listening, fighting amongst themselves yet presenting a united front against any mere boy who tried to get to know them. A horrible lot, schoolgirls!

'I see her.' Hywel was not very concerned with girls and only showed interest so that his friends would not think him childish. Porky and Duffy were wildly interested. Singer and Hywel, discussing the phenomenon, had concluded that girls were something that struck you soon after your twelfth birthday, like some annoying and unwelcome sickness. The two of them were not yet twelve, so they had managed to escape thus far. Singer had suggested that since they could see the risks inherent in the fair sex they might as well do their best to steer clear of them.

'You warns me if you see signs and I'll warn you,' he explained earnestly to Hywel. 'No need to get soft, I daresay, if only you've got a friend to give you a nudge when it starts coming on.'

'Come to fetch the little 'un from her violin lesson, she has,' Porky remarked now, staring hungrily at Kate's unconscious back. 'Odd that the young kid's so different, isn't it?'

Hywel shrugged, as uninterested in the little 'un as he was in Kate, though he liked Dot's cheerful indifference to appearances and the way she swung down the street beside her sister, sometimes hopping and skipping, grabbing a tree and swinging twice round the trunk, occasionally pulling a face or waving to someone in the schoolyard. Besides, he could tell from a certain salacious note in Porky's voice that he was

61

insinuating Dot was no child of Tegydd's. This was so patently untrue – for Dot had something in her odd little pekinese puppy face which reminded him strongly of Tom Tegydd – that it annoyed him when his friends argued.

'They'll be coming past in a sec; change the subject, eh, men?'

Singer was a natural peacemaker, but the older two would not have disagreed in any event. They wanted to feast their eyes on Kate's beauty without interruption. Everyone stared in silence, therefore, eyes practically on stalks in the case of Porky and Duffy, though they did not embarrass Kate in the slightest since it had never occurred to her that a gaggle of village schoolboys could be interested in her. Dot, attracted by their gaze, did turn and glance at them, then looked away. But not before she had given Hywel a tiny, fleeting smile. He smiled back. Friendly little thing she was, and not half so silly as some. He had a sister of his own, so he felt he could pronounce upon the whole sex without being unfair. He had a girl cousin too, who lived a long way away, in Norfolk somewhere, with his mother's sister. Auntie Megan had a son of about his own age as well as the daughter, who was pretty much the same age as Jessica. Mother, who wrote to her sister and received letters from her about four times a year, had been delighted, so she frequently said, when her sister had given birth to the girl.

'Always the way; one comes along and then another,' she was wont to say with a smile when Auntie Lil or Great-Aunt Ethel came round for a cup of tea and a nice chat. 'Married years and never a sign of a child, then a boy and a girl within twenty months. And no woman a better mother than our Megan.' The aunts and great-aunts all agreed that Megan must make a wonderful mother; as good as you, Ella, they would say, and Mam would smile and shake her head and the talk would veer round to other things.

'Howie, over here, man!' That was Duffy, saving a seat in the back row. Hywel hesitated, torn between a natural desire for a seat near his friends and an equally natural desire for a window seat. If you sat at the back you could talk – whisper, at any rate – pass notes unseen, suck a sweet, Indian-wrestle, scuffle, giggle. But if you had a window seat you could dream, gazing out across the yard and the mean street to the hills which towered above the narrow houses. In summer it was to the hills that he went, to fish, to set traps and to do all the birds-nesting, sheep-chasing and berrying that lively lads do when let loose in the clear remoteness of mountain country. Once you were out on the tops there was no one to see what you did and precious few to care.

In winter, of course, it was different, though you could shoot if you had a rifle, follow the hunt on foot when it met locally, or train a young dog to retrieve for you. But winter games were possibly even better than summer ones. A home-made sledge careering down a steep slope in the snow, faster and faster, until it overturned at the bottom, spilling its burden of woolly-capped, scarved and mittened boys out to shriek and throw snowballs and then toil up to the top of the slope once more for their next turn. Skating, too, on the river, where it widened out into a pool just below the village. Bonfires were more fun in the severe weather, too, and there was nut-roasting and potato-baking in the embers and all the joys of Christmas and the stocking which hung on the brass knob at the end of your bed, so much more fascinating to dream about than to open — though opening was pretty good, as well.

'Right, class. You may sit.' Miss Eliza Jones gave them all her after-luncheon smile, bright and beaming with hope and ambition for them. It would wear a little thin as the thick-headedness of her pupils manifested itself again during the long afternoon, but for now she was still young and optimistic enough to believe that her own enthusiasm could arouse theirs.

Everyone sat with a good deal of scuffling and scraping of chairs, to say nothing of clearing of throats, coughing and turning of pages. Miss Jones stood by the blackboard whilst all this was going on and her smile became a little tighter but did not fade. It would not fade until the class itself, by stupidity, obtuseness and too-obvious clock-watching, dimmed its bright lustre.

'Ready? Now you'll remember, children, that in our last lesson . . .'

*

Despite the freely expressed opinions of her sisters, Dot was not able to ride her pony to her violin lessons, although after two years' hard work he was a biddable and intelligent animal. The reason for this was that her father would not hear of her stabling Matchless in the public house loose boxes, and she would not consider leaving him in the street. So although she rode the pony everywhere else on the least provocation, she was forced to walk into the village for her violin lessons. Kate, undoubtedly for her own reasons, had come to meet her several times just lately.

It was a good walk from the village to the Plas, and most of it uphill once you crossed the bridge over the river, but that did not worry either sister. Country-bred as they were, both took ten-mile treks in their stride and thought nothing of spending the best part of the day on an expedition to visit a lonely farmhouse or a distant beauty spot. To be sure, Kate had walked less since she had put up her hair and taken to being what Dot called 'young-ladified', but she had not lost the habit and when the pony and trap were not available she took it for granted that she would reach her destination easily enough on foot.

Dot, glancing sideways at Kate as they began to climb towards the Plas, wondered just what it was that her sister did whilst she was playing the violin – or attempting to play it – to Mr Smith. Certainly Kate never mentioned meeting anyone or going anywhere; when casually questioned she would say she had walked up to Nain Croucher's place and talked about rheumatism and the curative powers of a poultice of boiled willow leaves slapped on the aching joint straight from the pot. Or perhaps that she had seen Enydd, who had worked up at the Plas for years, and had played with her little boy, now two years old and getting to be a clever lad.

They were turning into the drive between the two huge stone pillars topped with the pair of vicious-looking eagles that had given the small Dot nightmares, and Dot had actually opened her mouth to initiate a conversation which, she hoped, would culminate in Kate's telling her where she had really been, when they heard the trap rattling and the horses's hooves clattering on the hard road surface. Dot's thoughts immediately took a new direction; she hopped and waved, exclaiming as she did

64

so, 'Oh, Kate, it's Edie, coming back from town – we can have a lift!'

'Oh! Well, I think I'd rather walk,' Kate said, and Dot, glancing at her, saw that her sister's cheeks were flushed and her eyes had that tendency to dart about which indicates, if not guilt, at least a guilty conscience. So I was right, she *is* up to something, Dot thought triumphantly as the trap stopped and Edie opened the little half-door.

'Hello, girls. Where have you been? Come along, I'll give you a lift.'

The girls clambered into the trap. Kate, taking her place, immediately appeared to develop a great interest in the passing scenery. Dot saw Edie glance at her sister, compress her lips, and then turn, smiling.

'Well, Dot! You'll be happy to hear that I've purchased your sisters' winter dresses, two each, from Hughie Jones in Henblas Street. That means, of course, that you'll get Kate's golden-brown merino and Alex's light green wool with the braided sleeves and hem. I've got some very pretty pink cashmere, too, if you would like a new skirt of your own.'

'Thank you, Edie,' Dot said politely but without real enthusiasm. At the ripe old age of ten she could not summon up much interest in clothes and was perfectly content to wear hand-me-downs. Kate, on the other hand, adored clothes and was frequently garrulous on the subject. It seemed doubly strange, therefore, that she should not even murmur at the delightful news of two new dresses.

'Your papa also gave me money to buy Kate and Alexandra boots,' Miss Edenthorpe continued, apparently oblivious of the former's presence. 'I searched high and low for Kate when I was about to leave the house but not even Alexandra was quite sure where she was, so the boots had to go unpurchased.'

This time, Dot saw the spasm of pain which crossed her sister's face, but still Kate said nothing. Miss Edenthorpe, apparently unaware of this, continued to chat about clothing, shoes, hairstyles and underwear until Dot simply stopped listening, merely nodding and murmuring whenever her governess paused for breath.

When the trap turned into the stableyard and stopped Dot hopped down first. She held out a hand for Miss Edenthorpe to grasp, and then turned to Jan Torch, already at the horse's head. She was about to ask him how Matchless had behaved in her absence when Kate, at last, spoke.

'What's the use of new clothing and boots, Edie, when we never go anywhere or see anyone? Mother said last year that we should begin to meet neighbours and business acquaintances. Now Father says there's a war on and so we go nowhere and no one comes here, and we might as well dress in old rags for all that it matters.'

Dot, shocked, waited for Edie to tell Kate how selfish and silly she was being, instead Edie smiled and put her arm around Kate's waist.

'I know, my dear. It is very hard. But although there is a war on that's no reason for keeping two beautiful girls closeted like nuns in a nunnery. I intend to tell your father that if he will not entertain at the Plas your mother will be forced to take you to parties and dances in town where you might meet thoroughly unsuitable young gentlemen and wild young women whose acquaintance could do you nothing but harm. Do you think he'll listen to me?'

Kate gave a little skip and returned the governess's hug.

'He will, I'm sure he will! Oh, Edie, if only he would let us get to know other people of our age! Even if he won't invite them here, he could accept invitations . . . Mother says that people *do* suggest that we go to tea, or out for picnics, but Father says we're too young, or busy, or some such thing.'

'Father says they will start gadding when they're eighteen and not before,' Dot remarked, skipping along behind them. 'He says it'll cost enough then without adding to it by letting them start before they're anywhere near marriageable age.'

Edie laughed, but Kate glanced over her shoulder and gave her sister an unfriendly scowl.

'Men don't understand, Dot, and nor do you! If we have to meet people when we're eighteen we shan't know anyone. We'll be terribly out of it. They'll all talk the same language and we'll just sit there and wonder who they mean.'

'The same language? Why? Do they speak Welsh, then? I thought all people like us spoke English.'

'Don't be even stupider than usual,' Kate snapped, but Miss Edenthorpe was kinder.

'What your sister means, Dot, is that she won't know who her new friends are talking about. If you were sent down to the village school tomorrow to join a class you would be rather unhappy at first because you wouldn't know anyone, whereas all the other pupils would have been friends – or, indeed, enemies – ever since they started school years ago. It will be the same for Kate and Alex. If your father doesn't let them meet people now, when they're beginning to grow up, it will be all the harder for them when they do begin to move in ordinary society.'

'I understand *now*,' Dot said loftily, following the others through the side door and into the small cloakroom where they began to shed their boots and overcoats. 'But don't let Father try to make *me* go to parties, Edie, for I should hate it. I'm not going to marry a young gentleman when I grow up. I'm going to marry a horse-dealer and breed horses, and if Father lets us we'll take over the farming side of Plas Tegydd and run it properly, the way it used to be before the family started owning coal mines. I think there's good money to be made out of farming if you do it right. Every bit as good as out of coal.'

'You're a silly little baby,' Kate said contemptuously, throwing down her old patched boots and casting an envious glance at Edie's neat little kid ones. 'What do you know about farming? Or the colliery, for that matter?'

Edie came to the rescue of her youngest pupil for the second time in ten minutes. She took off her last boot, pushed her toes into a pair of fluffy slippers which even Dot quite envied, and then spoke.

'Really, Kate, you are being rather sharp this morning! And as it happens you're quite wrong, for Dot knows more about farming than anyone else in this family except your father. She may know more about modern methods even than he, for she studies all the books that Mr Redman and Mr Evans buy for the good of the estate. And I daresay she knows more about mining than you and Alex put together, for she's often in Mr Tegydd's company when he's discussing colliery matters with his business acquaintances.'

Kate, being Kate, could not bear to find herself in the wrong; she began to argue, Miss Edenthorpe began to grow quietly cross and Dot, seeing that it would be another ten minutes before the gong was rung for luncheon, slid quietly past them and made for the kitchen. It was lamentable, but a fact, that her appetite tended to ignore mealtimes, and right now she just could not wait any longer before grabbing something edible.

Cook, fat and good-natured, with a rolling Cheshire accent which sounded strange amongst her Welsh underlings, greeted her with a smile and a slice of thick pink roast beef on a round of her own delectable bread. As she ate it, Dot considered her morning. She had seen the boy who had helped her to get Matchless, she had very nearly found out why it was that Kate suddenly wanted to visit the village, and she had actually heard Edie pointing out to Kate that she, Dot, knew a good deal about farming. This was a rich reward for all the hours of reading farming books and magazines and publications in the musty, damp old library or in the farm office. About three-quarters of what she read so earnestly passed in at one ear and out at the other, but a little stuck. What was more, she often heard Souse'em Evans and Mr Redman talking. They both thought that her father should spend more on the land, mend the buildings before they fell apart, bring in fresh stock, change policies, try new ideas. But Tom would not; and Dot knew well enough that Tom's main interest was now in the business of coal mining. She had heard Souse'em giving his opinion, once, on why Tom no longer cared for the land, but she had given it little credence, for his words seemed ridiculous. Sous'em had said that her father no longer wanted to enrich his acres because he had no son to follow after him.

'Be different, see, if he'd a lad of his own,' he had said to Mr Redman as the two of them worked on a mare in trouble with a foal too big for her. 'As it is, with three girls to get wed, all he thinks of is how to get money for their dowries.'

'Wrong you are, mun,' Mr Redman assured him, gentling the mare's long, enquiring face as she turned her head to see if anyone could tell her why her foal was so long a-coming. 'Fascinated by the pits, he is. Thinks it his duty to build up the family fortunes by going into coal in a big way. He bought the Roland pit a few years back and it's done well under the fellow he put in to manage it. Now he's talking of getting a bigger place yet; if the Wynd comes up for sale our Tom'll have it if it costs him his last penny.'

'He'd mortgage his land?'

Souse'em had sounded shocked, and Dot, up in the hayloft listening avidly, felt the hair rise on the back of her neck at such a suggestion. She might not know much but she did know that no landowner would ever willingly mortgage his land.

'It's my belief he would, but if the Olwen goes on producing at the rate it has been doing he won't need to borrow. He'll have the money for the Wynd. And it's not everyone, mind, who'd want that pit. Dark place, and I don't mean that the way it sounds. It's always had a bad safety record. There are accidents there every week; the workers are discontented and the management's slovenly. Not a place many would take on.'

At this point the mare had begun to bear her foal and the two men had turned their attention back to the work in hand. But Dot, though she was sure that Souse'em was wrong and her father was not ignoring his land because he only had daughters, could quite see that Tom might feel it was his duty to encourage the collieries and try to make his money that way. After all, when Grandfather had handed over the estate it had been wonderfully rich and productive, and her father, she knew, liked a challenge. The Tegydds had owned only one pit then, the Olwen, and it had been a small pit with few deep seams. A good deal of very shallow work was done, where the miner never actually entered the shaft at all but walked down a drift to his place of work.

Now, of course, the Olwen was one of the larger pits in the area, and the Roland, which had recently been joined to its sister pit for safety reasons, was one of the most modern and up-to-date. Tom was proud of his standing as an owner and enjoyed the meetings in London and Liverpool now coal was needed for the war effort. Yet it was as if he could only concentrate on one thing at a time, and at the moment that thing was the pits. The farms and his land were more of an irritant than a pleasure, something to be pushed aside, ignored, left until tomorrow.

The sound of the gong in the echoing chill of the big hall brought an end to Dot's musings. She had been curled up on the saggy, comfortable chair by the fire where Cook was wont to relax after a meal, but she was off it and across the room almost in the same movement, her mouth still half full of bread and beef. She skidded across the floor, returned a wink from Arthur, who had just finished his vigorous gonging, and made it to the dining room just behind her mother and a whisker ahead of Kate and Alexandra.

There was soup to start with. Dot was not surprised to find she was still famished. Despite her small size and sticklike figure she had an appetite which a grown man might have envied. She eyed the steaming tureen with pleasure as her mother lifted the lid and sniffed the delicate aroma.

'Ham and vegetable, I think – just the thing for a cold day! And Cook has made us some Melba toast, I see! Edie, may I help you to a little soup?'

'Yes please, Olivia – if Mr Tegydd will not be joining us?'

Dot watched as her mother considered for a moment, ladle poised above the tureen. There was a faint colour in Olivia's cheeks and a strand of her thick, pale gold hair hung down over her brow. She looked distinguished and ladylike. Edie, glowing from the cold outside, her thick brown curls shining and her cheeks the colour of rosehips, might be fascinating, but no one could call her distinguished.

'I believe Tom is busy; at any rate, we'll start without him.' Olivia began to ladle the soup and Kate handed the Melba toast, whilst Alexandra passed the butter and Edie wielded the water-jug. When they had all been served and Miss Edenthorpe had said grace conversation became general. Mother was congratulating Edie on the materials she had chosen, and had agreed that it was time Dot had a new skirt – and also time the girls went into society a little more.

'I'm sure you'll persuade him, darling Edie,' she said, finishing her soup and leaning over to squeeze Edie's hand. 'I've asked, of course, but I don't have your sensible way of putting a case, I fear. I often ask myself, my dear, what we should do without you?'

Edie laughed and disclaimed, as she always did, and Arthur came in to clear the soup plates. Another day proceeded on its ordinary course.

Five: 1915

As Dot climbed over the stile and into the birch pasture the first thing she saw was the boy. He was lying on his stomach with both hands apparently immersed in the stream which chattered its way down the steep hillside, to join up presently with the broad river in the valley below. Dot stopped short, wondering what best to do; go on and brazen it out? Go back silently, so that he would not notice her? For she had been crying as she stumbled up the hill, and none of your dignified, ladified tears either but the bawling, snuffling, gasping kind where your eyes get swollen and your face gets puffy, to say nothing of the wetness and the dirt.

It was odd, though, what the presence of another person had done to her grief. Until she laid eyes on the boy nothing but her misery had mattered; it had grown and grown as she climbed higher, until it filled the summer sky and darkened even the brilliance of the sun. Yet embarrassment and curiosity had stopped the tears more effectively than a sympathetic hug could have done. Now, whilst she was still only just over the stile, he looked up and saw her. Dot hesitated. If she took the coward's way out and returned the way she had come he would know that she had seen him and think her rude, and a ninny as well. For he must have heard her bawling as she came across the bracken; even now he was probably hoping that she would not go over to him and start crying again. Boys did not like it if you cried, or so she believed. Nothing drove her father from the room faster than a crying female; she had noticed it many times.

Dot took an undecided step forward, and the boy looked up again and grinned. She recognised him as the boy who had helped her to get Matchless. She knew his name: Hywel

71

Fletcher. He lived in the village with his brothers and sister — none of whom looked at all like him — and their mother was Ella Pritchard, who helped out at the Plas sometimes. Edie had explained that Ella had been married to someone called Ben Fletcher and the boys were his boys, but now she was married to someone called Glyn Pritchard and the girl was a Pritchard. Confusing!

Since Hywel had smiled at her, Dot advanced. She wanted to talk to him because he must like it up here, as she did. You very rarely met the village boys as far up as this. They seemed to like the valley and the town more than they liked the hills. She did wish that her face was not quite so dirty, but perhaps he would not mind; she believed that boys quite admired a bit of dirt. So she kept on walking towards him until surprise stopped her dead in her tracks.

He had been quite still one moment; the next there was a sudden jerk, a flicker of silver, and something wet and shimmering was leaping on the bank. He grabbed it, struck it against a rock, and held it up. He was smiling.

'See? That's the fourth; now if I can get three more . . .'

His hands disappeared into the water once more and as Dot drew nearer she could see the three fish that lay side by side on the bank and the fourth that had just joined them. Brown river trout.

Dot sat down beside him, legs crossed tailor-fashion. She was intrigued by what he was doing and watched his cupped hands, greeny-white below the water, until a fish swam right into them and hesitated there, fins trembling, tail moving slightly, eyes rocking in their sockets the way fish-eyes do.

Hywel stayed very still, and then — so quickly that she could not follow the movement — there was another jerk, a shower of waterdrops deluged them both, and a fifth trout lay, flapping, on the bank.

'There, that's how it's done.' Hywel picked the fish up and killed it quickly with one sharp blow. Only then did he turn to her, a smile starting. 'Hello — you're Dot Tegydd, aren't you? I'm Hywel Fletcher. Haven't you ever seen anyone tickling for trout before?'

'No, though I did know they were trout. We've had them for dinner sometimes. I didn't know they lived in our stream, though. Mother always buys them in town, I think.' Dot wrinkled her nose as a water-drop ran down it. 'I wish I could catch them like that – does it take much practice?'

'Not a lot. Anyone could get them if they had the patience.' He sat back on his heels and rubbed his hands together, then dried them on his jersey. The jersey was old and frayed and lay beside him on the bank. 'I'll teach you one day, if you like, but now I'd best be off down to the village so's Mam can cook these for our tea.'

'Must you go now? Wouldn't it be even nicer if you got another one? Then you could give me an idea of how it's done. I bet no one else in the world could catch fish as cleverly as that.' She hoped the cunning flattery would do what a straight-forward request might not.

'Plenty of people can tickle trout.' He rubbed his forehead with a dirty hand, transferring grime from one to the other. 'Come to think, though, I'm in no rush. Let's see . . .' He glanced, not at a watch as Dot had expected, but at the sun, making its slow way down the heavens towards the distant ridge of Snowdonia. 'Reckon I could spare half an hour, and we might get another fish if we're lucky.'

Dot, noticing the 'we', beamed at him.

'Thank you *very* much, Hywel. Do you work in the pit yet, or are you still at school? And shall I roll my sleeves up or will you show me how first?'

'Can't work underground till you're fourteen, but I'll go down quite soon. I work at the pit-head, screening the coal,' Hywel explained. He took her small paws in his, gently lowered them into the water, and then put his own hands beside them. 'See who gets one first, shall we? Now remember, trout's curious creatures, and when they see your hands and your hands just stay still they come over for a closer look. Once they're in close they'll rub themselves against your fingers. Then you begin to work your fingers very gently along the belly until you come to the fins, and then you find the gills, hook your fingers in, and flick . . .' He sighed at Dot's baffled expression. 'No use I am at explaining, see? Got to show, that's me.'

They waited half an hour, but no more trout appeared. At last Hywel sat back, ruefully shaking his head.

'No use; had our fun for the day, I reckon.' He rubbed his hands down his shirt, offering her the jersey to dry off with, then picked up the fish in his handkerchief. He began to make a knot in it so that the fish would not fall out, and, apparently engrossed, he said casually: 'Why were you crying when you came up the hill, girl? Heard you, I did – I'd no choice unless I was deaf.'

'Crying?' But it would have been churlish to lie. 'Well, there was an awful fuss at home, and I hate fuss.'

'Oh? What sort of fuss? How old are you? Younger than me, because I remember when I was starting school you and your governess and your sisters came into the village sometimes, with you in a big old perambulator. You had a frilly bonnet and long white skirts, and you sat up bright as a button, waving to the school kids.'

'I'm twelve,' Dot said quickly, hoping to distract her new friend's mind from her childish display of grief. 'How old are you?'

'I'll be fourteen in November. Tell the truth, though, because of the war they're letting me go below in a month. You get better pay down there, even if you can't do a man's work.'

'I see; it's so horrible, I suppose, that they pay you more,' Dot said, never having given the matter a thought in her life. 'What do you do when you say you screen?'

'My, you can tell you're the owner's daughter, you know so much!' Hywel's face showed his amusement. 'The coal comes through on long belts and we pick out the slack and the muck so that the stuff that goes through is all good. But once I go below there's lots of different jobs; I could work for the hookers, coupling the tubs together as they fill 'em, or I could work with the pit ponies – I'd like that, I reckon – seeing to them and leading them and so on. Or I could be a door-boy, only I don't think you stay a door-boy long because it's so boring.'

Dot was gazing at him as though he came from another planet. What on earth was a hooker, and how could he help to dig coal by taking care of ponies, and why should a door-boy get bored? But Hywel, deep in his own thoughts, had not yet finished.

'Later on, of course, I could be a stower, or a ropeman or a drawer or perhaps even a shotfirer; but best of all it is if you're a getter, because they earn the most. Mind you, the money's good; it puts you off working on the land when you compare the pay. Besides, there isn't the comradeship on the land. Each man works for himself and his boss, whereas down in the pit you work for each other — your lives depend on it, see.'

'Tell me!' Dot demanded, forgetting to sound properly conciliatory in her thirst for knowledge. 'Tell me what it's like in the pit! I've never been allowed to go down, and I don't suppose I ever shall be. Father doesn't talk about what it's *like*, though he goes on about rates and shifts and overtime and things like that. I like the land best — the farms, the animals, that side of things — so I've never really asked much about the pits.'

She did not add that she had resented the collieries because they took her father from her and forced him — or so she told herself — to spend his money on them rather than on the estate. Once the war is over, Tom Tegydd said vaguely when Dot or his managers questioned the way the place was being allowed to slide downhill, once the war was over and won he would build up his land once more. But now coal was needed for the war effort, and winning the war came before everything else to a patriotic man.

'Well, I can't tell you much since I've not yet been down.' Hywel spoke mildly and patiently. 'I know what the work is, though, since I've three older brothers. A door-boy opens and closes one of the doors as tubs come through. That's all he does.'

'But why? Why are there doors underground? I thought it was just holes and tunnels and men digging out the coal.'

'They need doors to stop the good air rushing back up to the surface and leaving the men with only bad air to breathe. But the tubs full of coal have to get from the faces where the men are working to the pit bottom, where they're pulled up to the surface, so you have to have someone to shut the doors, see?

'I see. And ponies pull the tubs, of course. What would you have to do if you worked with the ponies?'

'Well, I'd lead 'em, see that they got watered regular, feed 'em and groom 'em. Take care of their hurts, generally see to 'em.'

'And I suppose you'd bring them up at the end of each day,' Dot said approvingly, 'so that they can have good grazing in summer and a taste of grass with their hay in winter. I don't suppose they have oats? Though it must be hard work, pulling coal tubs, so perhaps they do?'

He stared at her. The irises of his eyes were goldy-brown and they were surrounded by very white whites. His mouth was a little open with surprise and she saw that he had nice white teeth, too. But she did not like the way he was staring and bristled a bit.

'What's the matter? Don't you get good money working with the ponies? I thought you said . . .'

'It's not that, girl! It's just that every little kid in the village knows that the ponies go down, but they don't come up. They don't need to. They're fed and watered and doctored, too, down in the pit stables. Besides, I doubt they'd go down again willing, once they got up in the real air.'

Dot found her own eyes rounding, her own mouth dropping open a little. Ponies, God's creatures, created to run and jump and roll in the good grass and taste the touch of the wind on their sleek, muscled bodies? Surely no one could be so cruel as to condemn them to a life underground, in the dark, where they could never see the sun, let alone taste fresh grass, feel the wind lifting their manes or the rain-softened ground beneath their hooves? She longed to be able to deny it, to shout at him that her father would not allow such a thing in any colliery of his, but there was that in Hywel's straight glance which told her he was no liar. The ponies were condemned to lifelong darkness by her father as well as by other owners, probably without a pang of conscience or even a thought.

'I think that's the most terrible thing I ever heard,' Dot said slowly, at last. 'Easily the most terrible. What becomes of them when they're old and can't work any more?'

He shrugged, made uneasy by the strength of her feeling. 'Don't know. Made me feel bad, you have; never thought of it quite like that . . . but then there's men die down the pit and all, you know. My own father died the day I was born, digging coal.'

'I'm sorry,' Dot said, sensing his discomfort. 'You see, I do know ponies — as you know, Matchless, my little black gelding, was very nearly taken down the pit – and . . . well, I don't mean to be rude, but I never knew your father, so I can't feel quite the same about him.'

Hywel sighed. He could remember that when he had been a bit of a lad Stan's puppies had been closer companions to him than other children; this lass had not yet grown out of that stage, obviously. She could identify with an animal more easily than with a collier. It occurred to him, as they strolled together down the steep incline beside the stream, that the tales they told about her in the village were probably true; a wild one, wanting to be a boy instead of a girl, ignored by her mother and sisters, sometimes petted by her father, more often jeered at. An unhappy child, the women who worked up at the Plas said. Yet she always seemed happy enough to Hywel when he saw her swinging her way through the village, or trotting past on her pony, or careering down the side of a field where the corn was being cut, swinging wildly at passing rabbits with a stick twice her size.

'It doesn't matter – about my da, I mean. I told you he died the day I was born, so I haven't got much to remember him by. He even spoils my birthday, because Mam's unhappy then, remembering, see?'

They came out of the birch wood and began to cross the fly-buzzing bracken. Then came a meadow, lush with grass, hedged with wild, tangled trees and shrubs which had needed cutting back these five years or more. Hywel pointed to one particular group of trees.

'Hazel nuts; like 'em, do you? Come up here in October and if the squirrels haven't beat you to it you'll find enough nuts scattered around to keep you all winter.'

'I do like nuts; I like most food,' Dot assured him. 'Can I walk down to the village with you, or would you feel ashamed to be seen with a girl?'

'Not ashamed; but better not. Come as far as the bridge over the river,' he suggested, swinging his fish in the damp and dirty handkerchief. 'Better not set people talking.'

'Right.' Dot never questioned a decision she could understand, 'Hywel, why won't they let women go down the pits?'

'Well, they did, once, but now we're too civilised. Dangerous, it is, see, so they won't let young boys go below either.'

'Well, but just to have a look round . . . Imagine it, Hywel, when I'm really old – eighteen perhaps – they still won't let me in the pit to see what it's like. They won't let Kate, even though I suppose she'll own it all one day. It's strange, isn't it? Father prides himself on being a good owner and taking care of his work force and getting the best tools and so on, yet he won't let me go down and see what it's all about.'

'You wouldn't like it much, see,' Hywel told her, as they climbed the gate into the shaggy, overgrown little lane. 'Tell you what, though. I'm going down soon enough; want me to take a good look at everything so's I can tell you about it? Not as good as seeing for yourself, I know, but next best thing.'

'Oh, would you?' Dot sighed happily. 'But once you're working underground will you still be able to get up into the hills? And if you do come, where shall I meet you?'

'I'll be up all right,' Hywel assured her, trying to match his long strides to her shorter ones. 'Always come to the hills and always shall; probably more often, when I'm working below, because shifts are shorter. I'll be up here by half past three most days, if it's fine and if I feel like it. And in the summer I'm up here all day Sunday. As for meeting, name a place and a time and I'll do my best to be there.'

'That would be nice.' They reached a spot where the lane began to wind downhill in a series of hairpin bends. At this particular place Dot always stopped to look over a gate, for from here you had an excellent bird's-eye view of the Plas. Together, she and Hywel leaned on the mossy, overgrown and probably immovable gate and looked down at the ancient house. A fairytale castle, perfect in every detail, beautiful beyond imagining . . .

But was it? After what had happened this morning, would the Plas ever be quite the same again? Tears started to form in Dot's eyes. She sniffed and turned her head away from Hywel but he put a hand under her chin – a hand which smelt strongly of fish – and turned her to face him.

'What *is* it? You tell me what's wrong, mun, and you'll feel a lot better, just you see!'

Dot gave a watery smile at finding herself addressed as 'mun', and then, because she liked Hywel and trusted him, she decided to tell him all about 'the fuss'.

Even as she began to talk, Dot realised that though the story had appeared to start this morning it must really have begun long since, perhaps two years ago, perhaps even before the war started. Things had been not quite right ever since Miss Edenthorpe, helping the girls to clear a high shelf up in the attic, had fallen off the stepladder with the most tremendous crash and landed, bottom first, in a huge wicker laundry basket. Dot could remember the incident perfectly; the diffused sunshine coming through the tiny, dirt-encrusted attic windows; the smell of long-kept apples, of mothballs and old, clean clothing; the velvet dust which lay thick on every available surface; and another smell, the one she always thought of when Miss Edenthorpe referred to the aura of history, because it was such an old and pleasantly *past* sort of smell.

In this quiet scene the shrieks of the girls and Miss Edenthorpe, the crash as the ladder fell sideways, the peculiarly resonant *booiinngg* the wicker basket made as it fell prey to the governess's sudden assault, could not but bring someone running, as indeed it had. Tom Tegydd had heard the abrupt commotion in the attic and had hurried up, burst through the attic door and stopped short, apparently amazed and appalled by the sight of poor Miss Edenthorpe, legs in the air, skirts round her bottom, face all rosy and startled, half laughing and half dismayed as she realised that she could not extricate herself from her present undignified position without a good deal of assistance.

Kate, Alexandra and Dot, of course, had rushed forward, but Tom had waved them back. He had been laughing, with an extra-special gleam in his eye because, Dot thought, he had found their governess less than in command.

'Hold hard, girls,' he had said. 'A captive, I see! Shall we release her or shall we leave her there, to repent of her wicked ways?'

'Wicked ways? Oh, Mr Tegydd, all I was doing was trying to fetch down the old silks and satins in that case on the shelf, so that your wife could take some of them down to the dressmaker in town. You wouldn't leave me here, surely? Do take pity on me, sir.'

'I'm not sure if you deserve to be helped out; and besides, you look very . . . very fetching in that attitude.' He was standing straight above her now and Dot remembered that he had let his eyes wander all over Miss Edenthorpe, from her flushed face and dishevelled curls to the froth of petticoats, the back-turned skirts, and the beautifully slim, shapely legs in their fine black silk stockings. Dot, standing to one side of the wicker basket, could even see a velvet garter with a tiny strip of very white flesh above it — she hoped her father had not noticed!

'We ought to give her a tug, Father,' Kate had said, coming forward. 'Poor Edie — what will she do when it's time for tea? I don't think the maids would want to have to bring it up here for her.'

'That's certainly true; then we'd better have her out of it,' Tom said. He took both her hands in his, but for a moment he did not pull but merely stood there, holding them tightly. 'Now, girls, when Miss Edenthorpe pops out of that basket I fear she may be a little dishevelled, so I think it would be best if you ran downstairs and asked the maids to bring hot water to her room.' He turned to the governess. 'Are you much bruised, my dear girl? I think perhaps you should go straight to bed.'

'I'll go, I'll go!' The three girls had tumbled down the attic stairs to the kitchen. Kate had put a hot-water bottle in Miss Edenthorpe's bed and Alexandra had helped Cook to arrange a dainty tea-tray. Only Dot had wandered back up the stairs, just as her father had begun to descend them, Miss Edenthorpe in his arms. Neither of them noticed the small girl pressed against the newel post at the head of the stairs; Tom's head had been very close to Edie's and he had been whispering, or something, and she had been giving little gasps and murmurs of protest right up to the moment the bedroom door closed on them.

Later that day Father called the doctor and the doctor advised a few days' complete rest in bed. The children visited their governess and thought she looked very well indeed, lying back on her lace-edged pillows with her bright hair flowing loose across her shoulders and her body soft and curved and yielding without its stays and lacings and stiffly starched clothing.

80

To the children's surprise, it was their mother who seemed to suffer most from Edie's indisposition. She looked white and strained and her hair seemed dry and lifeless, whilst her voice, which had been plump and placid and pleased, got smaller and thinner until Dot remarked that it was hard to see who was ill and who was well.

Edie stayed in bed for ten days, and then she got up and Dot supposed that things would go back to normal. Indeed, at the time she thought they had. Now, looking back, she realised they had not. For from that moment on Edie had wielded a sort of power over Tom Tegydd, and it had been easier for the girls and for Olivia herself to get what they wanted, provided Edie interceded for them. On the other hand, they saw less of their father, and less, now that Dot considered it, of their governess, too. When Edie went off to spend a week with her family in the summer, their father went off to a mine-owners' conference in London. Almost as if, Dot thought, he did not particularly care to stay with his family when Edie was not there to amuse him.

Yet she could not really be said to amuse him; or only on rare occasions, anyway. There had been the trip to Rhyl, when Kate and Alexandra had both fallen sick with measles; and no sooner had the last spot disappeared from Allie than Dot came out in a thousand and one of the wretched things. Poor Mother, who had never had measles, was frightened to go into the nursery, so when Father announced that he wanted the girls to go to the seaside to convalesce Mother, naturally, could not accompany them. Edie agreed to go, said goodbye to her employers, and set out with her three charges on the train. They took no maids with them, for Mother did not wish to lose any of her staff, and, besides, Edie said she could manage perfectly well.

Yet the day after their arrival who should turn up but Father, very jolly, in his best dark suit and carrying a small suitcase. He booked into their hotel and, by a strange coincidence, he was given the room next to Miss Edenthorpe's. Though he assured them he was here on business they had a marvellous three days, for he went everywhere with them, took them to the funfair, on a coachride to see Llandudno and the Great Orme, down the promenade to see a Punch and Judy show, around the shops, on the beach donkeys . . . in fact he

81

behaved just as Dot felt a father ought to behave and not at all as he usually did.

He even came part of the way home with them on the train, telling them that they must not let Mother know he had spent so much time with them. She would be angry that he had let his business trip fall through just to be with his daughters.

Looking back, Dot realised that even at the time Kate and Alexandra had given each other knowing looks, though not when either Father or Edie was present. She herself, though she guessed that something was not quite right, was not old or acute enough to guess what it was. She racked her brains to think of a good reason why Mother must not be told of their treat, instead of using her intelligence to wonder why Father, who had never taken much notice of his daughters, should suddenly find them such amusing company.

Eventually, of course, it had struck Dot that Father had come to Rhyl not to see them but to see Edie. At first she had been rather shocked, but after watching the two of them closely it soon ceased to amaze her. Father obviously liked Edie – who did not? – and wanted to be with her sometimes. Equally obviously, he did not want Mother to know, because Mother might not have liked it. But since Edie willingly interceded for Mother whenever she could and used her influence to make life pleasanter for them all, Dot could see no harm in the friendship.

So, as Dot began to recount her tale, she found herself regressing to things which had happened a good while before this morning, so that Hywel would understand. She did not want him to believe Edie had been father's particular friend; Mother had been, if anything, fonder of Edie that anyone else, and with more reason.

Until this morning. They were all at the breakfast table, except for Father who broke his fast far earlier than they as a rule, when Mama had suddenly spoken to Edie in a new, cold voice which Dot had never heard her use before.

'Miss Edie, where did you go this morning?'

'This morning? Oh, I went into the village to see a sick woman; she lives alone, so I thought a visit would cheer her.'

'I hadn't heard old Agatha was sick.' Mother's voice was calm and composed yet Dot, watching her parent's face, could see that the answer had partly pleased and partly angered her. 'Folk who visit Agatha under her own roof usually do so for very different reasons.'

'My dear Olivia, you don't believe all those old wives' tales, do you?' Edie's eyes, which had been lowered towards her plate, lifted to meet her mistress's gaze; there was amusement in them, and a very slight trace of good-natured contempt. Dot waited for her mother to retract her words, to laugh it all off as a joke; she waited in vain. Olivia's eyes remained cold, her voice precise.

'I said nothing of old wives' tales, Edie. I merely asked where you had been and since, to the best of my knowledge, Agatha is not sick – indeed, Peggy said she was at the baker's this morning putting a meat pie in his oven – I wondered why you were there.'

'She wasn't at all well yesterday . . .'

'No, my dear, I'm afraid that explanation really will not do. If you'd been sick visiting you wouldn't have worn a shawl over your head and a ragged skirt and down-at-heel shoes. You'd have gone neatly clad with a basket of comforts on your arm. And you'd have driven down in the dogcart, not gone on foot so early in the morning that most of the villagers were still in bed.'

Kate gasped; it was a foolish things to do and brought her a cold glance from both women, but despite Dot's fears it was apparent that neither protagonist intended to dismiss the girls.

'I'm sorry if it annoys you, that I went early, Olivia, though it really seems to be no one's concern but my own,' Miss Edenthorpe said placidly. 'In fact I chose to go plainly dressed in order not to attract gossip. Old Agatha is thought by a good many people to be a witch, though that's just nonsense; she's no more a witch than I am. She's just a lonely old woman with more intelligence than most.'

Olivia's smile was almost pitying; clearly Edie's answer had not satisfied her, though it seemed eminently sensible to Dot. She looked from face to face, marvelling at her mother's sudden ascendency over the governess; though Edie was smiling too, helping herself to another slice of bread, buttering it, reaching for the honey jar. Her fingers were trembling, however, and Olivia's next words wiped the smile from her mouth.

'I'm sure she isn't a witch, though she certainly knows more than most about the properties of herbs and lotions. You won't object, of course, if I discuss the whole matter with my husband? I shall tell him of your visit and of course include my own theory as to why you went in such an underhand manner.'

Dot thought this threat would be treated with the contempt it appeared to deserve, for did not the entire household turn to Edie to intercede for them, with her father? And she saw that for a moment Edie felt the same, until something in the words her mother had used apparently sank in. She made a quick, nervous, fluttery movement with her hands, though her voice remained calm, even a little amused.

'Certainly you must tell him if you wish, Olivia. In fact, I'll tell him myself. Not that I think it will be of the slightest interest to him. After all, even if I did go to old Agatha for my own reasons, it cannot concern Mr Tegydd.'

'No?' Mama's pale brows arched and she gave another knowing little smile as she began to butter another slice of bread for herself. The little smile broadened until it was almost a grin, but she did not say another word, either to the governess or to her daughters.

The rest of breakfast was eaten in silence, apart from murmurs from the three girls concerning the passing of marmalade and honey and the refilling of coffee cups. But as soon as they possibly could the children escaped to the schoolroom, anxious to discuss what had happened before their governess joined them.

'What was it all about?' Dot enquired of the older two, wide-eyed. 'Why should Edie dress like a poor woman and go to see a witch? I didn't know there was a witch in the village. Anyway, Edie's always telling us that witches and fairies and wizards and magic are just stories for children without a grain of truth in them.' She sighed rather wistfully, for she had been brought up amongst the credulous villagers and had heard many a fine tale of the *tylwyth teg*, the fairy folk, and of the *coblyns* who live in the mines and warn the colliers of danger by their tapping, from nurses and servant girls when she was small.

'An educated woman doesn't believe in the *tylwyth teg*,' Kate confirmed. 'The odd thing is that Edie was frightened when Mother said she'd tell Father – did you see how her hands trembled? I don't think Father worries about witches, but I can quite see that he won't like Edie sneaking off in disguise, like someone out of a fairytale.'

Seeing from the glances that the two older girls kept shooting at each other that there *was* a secret and she was to be kept out of it, Dot went off to the stables. However, it was a chilly, rainy day despite the fact that May was well advanced, and although she tacked Matchless up and led him halfway out of the yard she had nowhere particular to go and very quickly decided that there was little point in both of them getting soaked to the skin. Accordingly, she put Matchless back in his stall and wandered indoors, intending to continue crocheting a browband for him. But she could not settle to anything. Finally, she decided to climb up to one of the high tower rooms from where she might watch the clouds roll away and clear sky approach.

It was a long climb up to the tower-top. Dot laboured on, round and round the spiral stone stairs. Halfway up she noticed with slight surprise that someone had been up here fairly recently; the velvet dust which layered the steps was cleared from the centre of each one. Dot stopped, feeling like Mr Sherlock Holmes, but it was impossible to pick out individual prints; all she could say for certain was that someone had been up and down these stairs a good deal lately. It seemed odd; so far as she knew no one had any business going up to the top of the tower.

It was dark here, but at intervals there was a narrow window, a sort of arrow-slit which had been roughly glazed, through which one could see the surrounding countryside. Halfway up the tower was a room which had once been used to store apples, but which was so used no longer. The smell still lingered; Dot sniffed appreciatively, wondering whether someone was using the room again, but the footprints continued on straight past the door, which, in any case, was locked. The key, she knew, would be on the architrave above it, but by now she was too interested in the footprints to stop. She went on, round and round, until at last she reached the tiny top landing.

Or rather, until she was half a dozen steps below the top

landing, her head on a level with it. For it was then that she heard the voice. It was her father speaking and he was in a royal temper by the sound of it. Dot stopped where she was. Whatever was Father doing up there, where no one came? He could not be alone; he was shouting at someone . . . If they came out and found Dot she would be in deep trouble. What she must do before proceeding further was secure her retreat. It was the work of a moment to fly down the stairs, hook the key down from above the apple-room and unlock the door, leaving it slightly ajar so that she could run down and hide at the first sign of movement from above. Having done that, she went carefully up the stairs again and on to the landing. Father was still shouting.

'I don't give a damn, woman! I won't allow it! How dare you even think of such a thing! You'll leave this house first thing in the morning. Don't argue with me — I'll see to it myself.'

'Oh, Tom!' That was Miss Edenthorpe, her voice heavy with tears. 'You wouldn't cast me off with no character, no means of earning a living, and no one to care for me?'

'Don't be a bloody fool!' That was Father again, still roaring in top register, not caring who heard — except that he must know not a soul other than he and his companion ever came up here now that the apple store was empty. The door was not quite closed and Dot applied her eye to the crack, though with caution. She had not forgotten the last time she had spied on her father and Edie — her nose had been swollen for a week. Now, she could see him taking hold of both Edie's hands and shaking them gently up and down. 'You can't stay here. I couldn't offer Olivia such an insult.'

Edie tried to withdraw her hands. Tears were making her sniffle, or so Dot supposed, for Edie's face was turned away, towards Tom. But she could not get free. Indeed. her attempts were pretty half-hearted.

'Very well, if I must go, I'll go. But I'll kill myself, that's what I'll do, and then no one will know what's happened and my unhappiness will be over.'

'Oh, my poor darling!' Edie was enveloped in Tom's arms, gripped so tightly to his jacket that Dot winced for her discomfort. 'You won't harm yourself. You won't visit Agatha or anyone like her. I'll take good care of you, I swear it. But not here, on my doorstep, where it would cause endless talk and speculation.'

'Then wh-where? And h-how? Oh, Tom, if only you could! If only we could be together somewhere, even the lowliest cottage, I wouldn't mind. I'd make you happy.'

Dot, listening avidly, could only boggle at such crass foolishness. Her father was a proud man, and one, furthermore, who could never relax. He might live in a lowly cottage for a week or two, she supposed, but then he'd start redesigning it, getting an army of gardeners in to replan the garden, going off on his horse to boss people about – for bossing Edie would not make up for all the others who were normally at his beck and call. Happiness, for Tom, lay in working at full stretch on some new project, or tackling a new problem, or dashing off across the country to see for himself how some revolutionary new coal-cutting machine worked. But now he was cradling Edie in his arms, making soothing noises, and kissing the side of her wet, pink cheek.

'Foolish little Edie. As if a cottage would do for my dear one! Come along.' He led her over to the window where, Dot noticed for the first time, there was a huge, cushion-laden, comfortable sofa. This would be interesting, she thought, as her father tenderly laid the governess down upon its luxurious length. She was quite wrong however. For, apart from Miss Edenthorpe's feet and ankles, the couple were now completely out of her view.

'There now; are you comfortable?'

'Oh, yes!' There were sounds of someone else getting on to the couch as springs made their small, sharp noises and cushions sighed in a satiny way. 'Well, if not a cottage . . . Tom, dearest, I'm trying to talk to you!'

Tom's large feet had appeared on the end of the sofa. Although he said nothing, his feet gave an irritable jerk, then settled themselves into a sort of composure once more. Feet in whose mouths butter would not have melted, Dot thought. If feet had mouths. Or, indeed, if butter were available.

'Very well. I thought a little house, dearest, with a maid, and a boy to do the garden and the shoes and so on. You'd probably need a woman to help with the heavy work, but she need only come in three times a week or so. And you might like a little dog. Exercise, in moderation, is good for a woman in your condition.'

Condition? What condition was that? Thrown out of her home and her job? But why did that merit a little dog? And how on earth was Edie to afford a house such a house as Father was describing? Really, men were very naive – or perhaps Edie had been saving up for this moment for years? Except that Mother had once remarked that Edie dressed like a duchess on a servant's wage – and had immediately regretted it, said that no doubt Edie had some private means, and begged Dot to forget her words.

'A little house of my own! Oh, Tom! Could it be by the seaside, do you think? I should so love to live by the seaside. And . . . and you would not desert me? You would come to see me often?'

Tom was squeezing her, Dot decided, since there were various sounds indicative of one person getting to grips with another amongst the cushions.

'My love, nothing would keep me away! Confound these dam' fool buttons or whatever they are!'

A deep, gurgling chuckle from Edie and more shifting noises. Edie's feet turned sideways and Tom's were drawn up. Dot, though consumed with curiosity, still thought it unwise to peer round the corner of the door. If she were caught . . . it was too hideous a prospect to consider.

'They're hooks, dearest; hooks and eyes. Here, let me.'

There was a short pause during which rustlings and the fact that Tom grunted twice caused Dot to entertain the liveliest suspicions. It sounded as if . . . but such a thing could not be, of course. Then both sets of feet appeared again, Edie's in fine black silk stockings and her father's still respectably socked and shod.

'Oh, Tom, my darling, love me!'

'Sweetheart, *how* I love you! It won't do harm?'

Edie's toes wiggled. Impatiently. But her voice remained calm.

'Harm? Of course not. How could you think such a thing of me?'

There were some soft kissing sounds which shocked Dot.

How *dare* Edie kiss Father, even if it was goodbye. She had gathered that Edie was to leave and that Edie would not be too sad to go.

'It's easy to say that, but you did visit old Agatha.'

Edie's silk-clad feet abruptly disappeared. It was plain that she had sat bolt upright and her voice echoed her disapproval of Tom's remark.

'Tom, how can you? I did that for *your* sake. My whole body and soul urged me not to take such a desperate course, but for you, my dearest . . .'

Her voice had descended to a full-throated coo. The small feet slid into view again, followed by a great many noises not one of which Dot could identify and during the course of which feet appeared and disappeared with such rapidity and abandon and in such odd and unusual positions that Dot grew quite dizzy and confused.

The mutterings, rustlings and indeed squeaks and grunts reached a climax and then, gradually, died away into no more than heavy breathing. Both pairs of feet reappeared in conventional poses, looking exhausted and . . . pleased with themselves, Dot thought. Amazing, how such mundane parts of the body as the feet could express such a variety of different emotions.

It was not until then that she realised something. Her father must have rolled his trouser legs up a bit, for at one point she had definitely caught a glimpse of white and hairy leg. What very odd creatures men were to be sure, when they had to roll up their trouser legs in order to kiss and comfort a governess who was being dismissed! Dot, sneaking down the stairs again, tried not to suspect that there had been more to it than that, but the suspicion was there. Fortunately, however, before she could begin to worry, she reached the first arrow-slit and the sunshine was pouring through it from a clear blue sky.

Matchless waited! Dot tiptoed as fast as she could down the remaining steps, then charged across the hall and into the stableyard. She and Matchless greeted one another with characteristic delight, and she jumped into the saddle and headed for the river. Just time, she thought, for a gentle canter before luncheon!

＊

89

'So of course, though I'd heard Edie going on about the little house and the seaside, what I really thought was that she'd talk Father round and he'd explain to Mother that Edie was sorry and we'd all go on as before,' Dot concluded, her voice sinking as she recalled how that particular hope had been dashed. 'Only I was wrong; Father was at luncheon, and Mother, but Miss Edenthorpe stayed in her room and Father told us that she was going away. He said she had been foolish to visit the old woman, no more, but that the real reason she was going was because we were all too old for a governess and she felt she should move on to someone who had younger children who needed her.'

'Fair, that seems,' Hywel said. He was smiling to himself in a manner almost as annoying as the way Dot's mother had smiled when she had heard the news. 'Miss Kate must be sixteen; she can teach you anything you don't know already and Miss Alex can do the rest.'

'That isn't why we need Edie – but do you think it's true, Hywel? Do you think they're sending her away because we don't need her any more?'

'Quite probably,' Hywel said, but he avoided Dot's eyes. They were almost level with the stone gateposts and the drive which led up to the Plas. Hywel jerked his head at them. 'Want to be going home now, do you? Meet another day we will for sure, if you can get up to the tops.'

'No, I'll walk into the village with you and you can show me the witch's house. Will you, please? Is she a real witch, with a black cat and a broom? Does she dance by moonlight and fly over Minera and the Eglwyseg rocks on her broomstick?'

Hywel laughed. 'No such thing, girl! More a wise woman she is. She gathers herbs but does no one harm. I'll show you her cottage, then, but don't you be going to visit her until the fuss over your governess dies down.'

'I shan't go there at all,' Dot decided, skipping along beside him. 'Hywel, I'm not a cry-baby, you know; it really will be dreadful at the Plas without Edie. Worse for me than for the others, because . . .' She hesitated, giving him a quick, sideways glance. She did not wish to shock him nor to alienate him by what she was about to say but she had to tell someone. '. . . because Mother doesn't like me very much. She loves Kate and Alex, of course, but she thinks I'm ugly and boring.'

Once or twice – possibly three times – in her life, Dot had voiced these sentiments before. On every occasion she had been soundly berated and reminded that mothers love all their children equally and that her own mother adored all three of her daughters. But Hywel just sucked in his breath and let it out on a long whistle before nodding slowly.

'Aye, Mam's the same with me. You just have to prove, see, that you're as good as the others any day; then the feeling will come. And if it doesn't, the better person you to have grown up good and straight without it. It's the love you give that's important, I believe, more than the love you get. It doesn't do to worry what folk think of you. Just you get on with being yourself. This governess is fond of you, then?'

'She likes me as much as she likes the others, and she's fair; she sees that I get what she thinks I should have,' Dot said, having thought about it. 'Father likes me, but there's no use denying that I'm *not* a boy, though I try hard to be as boyish as I can, and I don't think he loves girls. I think he's saving his love for a boy. A son, you know.'

Hywel smiled down at her. There was more understanding in his eyes than Dot had ever encountered before.

'A good couple, we are! My mam can't help disliking me a bit because my father died the day I was born and I'd take a bet that your mam doesn't care for you too much because you were a girl instead of the boy her husband wanted. Odd, how things pan out, because my mam was crazy to have a girl; if I'd been a girl I don't believe she'd have held my da's death against me.'

'We ought to swop,' Dot said. She was smiling again and dancing along beside Hywel as though she had not a care in the world. This boy was her friend, the very first friend she had ever had; he was sensible and understanding and he liked her for herself. He did not care that she was little and dark and ugly, he just liked her! He pointed out the witch's cottage when they reached the outskirts of the village, and then his own house, built where the mountain began to slope up so that when he was right at the top of his back garden he could, if he so desired, have spat into his own chimney pot.

When she parted from him – having refused the offered

trout because she did not know how to cook or clean it and thought that fat Cook might take offence if asked to do so for her – she walked alone in the evening glow and wondered just what sort of difference the absence of Edie would really make to their lives. Father might become even more her friend – that would be good. He might agree to let them go to parties and might even have parties at the Plas, which would be good for Kate and Allie, if not for herself. If Mother began to take more of an interest in Kate, then Allie might have a bit more time for a younger sister – and that would be good!

But it was no use conjecturing: one could only wait and see, and in the meantime there was Matchless in his stall, Cook in the kitchen with a great many good things for her to sample, and best of all, her friend. He could teach her to fish, to hit a running rabbit so hard with a billet of wood that it fell instantly dead, to tell a good bird's egg from a bad one, to throw a stone miles up into the blue – a trick which boys seem born possessing and which girls apparently find next to impossible.

And I'll teach him to ride Matchless and to understand about silage and crop rotation and the importance of feeding the land, and why a dairy herd is a good thing but a beef herd less so, she planned, scampering up the drive. It will be awful without Edie – but there are good things coming along to take her place!

Six

Three days after his first meeting with Dot Tegydd, Hywel found himself, in the dawn chill, queuing at the pithead for his lamp. A sure sign, this, that one was considered a man amongst men. It must be admitted, however, that he was glad to be going down with his brother Luke in the same cage. Not that he minded the dark, he told himself, as he crowded into the creaking structure, nor the drop; it was the strangeness, the fact that he had no idea what it was like down there, that was hard to face.

Luke and Stan and even Dewi, the quietest of the brothers, had already warned him to keep away from the side of the cage and to hang on to something, for – though it hardly ever happened – it was possible for the banksman to forget to release the keps, the supporting catches which keep the cage going down steadily. If the engine winder did not realise that the keps were not down and continued to wind, the cage could fall a considerable distance before being brought up short, with a terrible jerk, by the rope. If the rope did not break under the strain, one would suffer no more than minor injuries. If it broke . . . one tried not to think of that.

The gate at the end of the cage clanged shut, there was a moment's pause whilst someone outside asked if the men had been searched and were clean, and then the cage began its slow descent.

It went down into thick darkness, made darker, it seemed, by the tiny lights in their lamps. And it went down fast, much faster than Hywel had imagined, so that for a terrifying second he thought it was in free fall and felt sweat break out, ice-cold, all over his body. It was noisy, though; he could hear the creaking and slamming of the keps as they guided the cage's downward progress, the screeching of the steel ropes, and the sounds of a good many men penned into a small space all talking and laughing and shifting their feet. All afraid, Hywel thought suddenly, as he was, but used to fear, used to hiding it.

When the cage stopped there was another horrible moment when he thought himself not only partially blinded, but stone-deaf. Luke, beside him, opened and closed his mouth and Hywel could not hear a word. He could hear nothing but a pressing silence, to complement the darkness which pressed against the small circle of their lamps.

His hands went to his ears and he opened his mouth to shout that he was deaf, and there then were little explosions in his ears and noise flooded in: the men talking, Luke saying something, the cage beginning to rock a little as the fireman prepared to signal to the engine winder to take it up again. Luke was grinning at him. Hywel, grinning rather shakily back, realised what his brother was saying.

'... should have warned you to put your fingers in your ears. Otherwise you go deaf, the descent's so fast. You all right now?'

'Yes. I was deaf, but when I opened my mouth to tell you it cleared. What do we do now?'

'Wait; for one thing, no use going into the roads before you've got your night-eyes, and for another you haven't been told yet which gang you're working with. Or if you're even with a gang – youngsters often start on the doors, or with the ponies.' The two of them, following the example of the other miners, had crouched down on the ground with their lamps at their feet, but now Luke got up and headed for one of the dark exits. 'See you later, Howie. Good luck, mun.'

It was not more than two minutes before the overman approached him. He gave Hywel a piercing stare, then nodded as if satisfied.

'Fletcher? You're on the doors for two weeks. After that we'll see.' Behind him, a skinny, already filthy boy hovered. The overman beckoned him forward. 'Here's Jim. On the door nearest you, he is. He'll show you where to go and what to do. All right?'

'Thank you, sir,' Hywel said. He followed the lad into what he later knew was one of the main roads, but very soon this

94

way — which was lit, at intervals, by lamps hung on the walls — was left behind them in favour of what looked more like a rabbit's burrow than anything else. It was a little higher inside, fortunately, but still Hywel had to bend double to walk.

'Low it is now, and lower to come,' Jim remarked over his shoulder to his companion. 'Steep too, just now, or they wouldn't need a door. Go careful. Keep your lamp shining in front and watch where you put your feet.' After what felt like about half a mile he turned and shone his own lamp at Hywel. 'Tall you are, mun,' he commented. 'Not realised how tall when I seen you in the street. Keep your shoulders down, now. This bit's where we go down like one of them chimney sweeps in the old days.'

There was a certain horrid aptness in the remark; the tunnel was very low indeed now and it simply fell away from their feet, hell-like. Hywel was glad Jim was ahead, though the warning about the low roof came too late; his spine was already chipped, he felt sure, and certainly there was the warm stickiness of blood running from at least one cut on his back where the roof had proved even lower than it had seemed.

'Nearly there,' encouraged his mentor presently, as the tunnel began to slope less steeply. 'All you got to do is open the door when the tubs come through and shut it behind them. See?'

'Sounds like money for jam,' Hywel said, eyeing the sturdy door as his companion slowed down before it. 'Open and shut the door? Is that all? Nothing to it.'

'Mustn't fall asleep, though,' Jim warned him. 'I'm only on a door for another day or two. Boring, it is, see? Hope I get a near face, I do, because I've a six-mile walk to work every day without another mile or two to tramp below. Still, mustn't grumble.'

'Why don't you go to a nearer pit?' Hywel asked, squatting down beside Jim near the door. 'No need for that walk, is there?'

'No, but we're nigh the Black Wynd and it isn't everyone who'll work there,' Jim told him. 'Got a bit of a broken-down cottage, we 'ave, Mam, me and the five littl'uns. Me da was killed at the Wynd trying to get a mate clear of a fall. The roof came in on 'em both. Mam swore we wouldn't work at the

95

Wynd when we were old enough, not even if it meant a twenty-mile walk.'

'Is the Wynd as bad as they say, then? I thought all the pits were dangerous, but I've heard tell the Wynd is the worst.'

Jim snorted. 'The worst? Three or four accidents every week, mun, to say nothing of the deaths they've 'ad. No one cares, you see. The owner just wants his money, the managers don't give a damn, the firemen turn a blind eye . . . no, Mam was right. Better the long walk.'

'Do any of your brothers work?' Hywel asked, eyeing his companion curiously. Jim was a skinny lad, wearing only a full-sized pair of trousers kept up round his middle with string, an equally full-sized jacket minus all its buttons and most of the sleeves, and a huge pair of clogs in which his grimy feet could be plainly seen.

'Nah! I'm the oldest, the only one working yet. Me mam works, though — uses a rippler and sells what she gets, which isn't much.'

Hywel was silent. He had seen the women with their huge sieves desperately shaking through the slag and shale on the pit banks for whatever bits of coal they could get. It shook him to think that, but for his stepfather, his mother might have been reduced to such straits. But then he remembered that his mother *had* been a widow with young children and she had not sunk that low.

'Why doesn't your mam work on the belts at the pit-head? It's good money, and easier work than rippling.'

'Oh aye, but she's got the kids, see? And she swore never to work at the Wynd or let them have the labour of any of us. They never paid Mam a penny when Da was killed, see? Not a penny. She even had to have his body collected from the pit-head. He had a pauper's funeral, or would've, 'cept his mates paid for a proper good 'un.'

'And couldn't she walk the six miles to us, like you do?'

'Not at first she couldn't. She was having a baby, see? Too fat, like, to walk that far. Tell you the truth, our Phemie — she's nigh on five now — she was born on the pit bank. Mam just wrapped her in her shawl, tied her over her shoulder, and carried on rippling.'

It should have been unbelievable, yet Hywel did not doubt

the truth of Jim's words for a moment. There was that in the flat, matter-of-fact voice which was completely convincing. No wonder the Wynd had such a bad name amongst colliers, if what had happened to Jim's mother was an everyday occurrence, and plainly Jim had no thought of being disbelieved.

'Wait on!' Hywel had been about to speak but stopped short as Jim held up a skinny, blackened hand. 'Hear that? You've got to listen for that, mun, because it's the tubs coming. You get the door open, hold it until the last tub and the drawer – the feller pushing at the back – are through, and then you see it's shut. And that's all there is to it.'

'Right. Where shall I put my snap?' Hywel had heard his brothers' stories of food eaten by rats whilst a man's back was turned, so his own sandwiches were in a tin and his cold tea in a corked bottle, but he found he did not much fancy turning suddenly to find a rat trying to lever the cork from the bottle or the lid from the tin.

'On the hook.'

Hywel turned. Sure enough, someone had shoved a cup-hook into the wall. He had wondered, vaguely, why his tin had an elastic band round it, but now, fixing it round the cup-hook, he knew. Neat! He stood the bottle beneath it and stared at the door as Jim opened it and a couple of tubs came slowly through. There was no sign of the drawer. Then, as the last tub drew level, Hywel saw him. On all fours, with his lamp hanging round his neck, he was shoving with all his might to get the tubs up the incline. He was plainly too breathless to spare much time in talk, but he grinned – a flash of white teeth in a black face – and advised Jim to get down to his own door, since Dewi would only stop there two more minutes.

'Right,' Jim said, getting to his feet and stepping on to the rails, still of course bent double. 'See you later, Hywel. Close the door behind me or we'll lose air.'

'How do I know when it's time to go up again?' Hywel asked, suddenly reluctant to be left alone in this place. 'What about my snap? When'll I eat it?'

Jim paused in the doorway. His face reflected sympathy; it was clear he knew very well why Hywel was suddenly full of questions.

'When the face-workers come through, that's when you

leave. They'll tell you they're the last. And you can eat your snap in the middle of the shift. Ask the drawers as they come past you. Either they'll have a watch or they'll know the time. Some of 'em can tell you almost to the minute. They just know how time passes, seems to me. It isn't so bad if you think of the money. Ta ra.'

Hywel settled down in a miserable crouch by his door. He had thought the pit would be horrible, divorced from the sun and the sky, but this was worse than his wildest imaginings. Now that he was alone he could feel the pressure of the earth all around him, the rocks just waiting their chance to crush him. His lamp cast the tiniest glow, penetrating no more than a couple of feet of darkness; if it went out he would be insane in seconds, he knew it. It was hot, too, and airless; his skin was already oozing sweat and his lungs were working like bellows, at twice their normal rate, trying to suck some goodness from the stale and over-used air.

It seemed like years before he heard again the rumble of approaching tubs and got his door open as the first one came up the incline. Behind the tub the drawer grinned again, but this time no words passed between them. As he disappeared Hywel stared after him; what a hideous way to earn a living! No light could shine ahead for him, doubled up as he was, and his knees must be raw from the roughness of the rails and sleepers, to say nothing of his hands, alternately pushing and scrabbling for a hold, and his forehead, which he was using to shove the tub along faster. Hywel wondered how far he would have to go before he was able to hand the tub over to the pit ponies, and how far the ponies took it before it was tied on to the endless rope and hauled to the surface. It was odd, really; ever since he could remember, the people he had known best had been colliers, yet he knew almost nothing about the pit. What happened to that tub of coal which had just passed him after it left this particular tunnel? How did 'they' know who had got it, sweated for it, pushed it on its way? When it went up, how did 'they' see that the getter was paid for it and not the man on the next face? He knew that men were paid not by the hours they worked but by the amount of coal they cut and the number of tubs which they delivered along their own particular bit of rail.

Most of the men, it seemed, were paid by results; if you were a stower or a packer or a doggie, you earned your money. Boys like him were paid weekly, of course, and he supposed that the higher echelons – shotfirers, deputies, enginemen and so on – would be paid weekly too. But the real colliers were paid for getting coal.

Before he could do more than begin to wonder, however, the rails were vibrating again and he heard the sound of another tub approaching laboriously up the incline. He had been sitting back, eyes closed, spine against the wall, trying to come to terms with what was happening to him, telling himself that he was part of a great endeavour and ought to be proud of it, but now he crouched forward, a hand to the door, ready to pull it wide when the tub was near enough. It came, passed him, went; he closed the door and sat back and, to his horror, found himself fighting tears. Nearly fourteen years old you are, boy, he said fiercely to himself; practically a man grown, isn't it? And would you sit here and cry for the dark and heat, the loneliness and the discomfort of your crouching position, when you had just seen that poor devil crouched double, shuffling on his knees with that unbearable weight supported by his head and scarred fingers? Nothing that anyone had said could have given him the remotest idea of all this, that was the real trouble. The totality of the darkness, the cloying, cheese-smelling bad air, the heat which pressed sweat out of you even when you weren't moving, so that already he longed to drain his bottle of cold tea. He had been prepared for dark, not for pitch; for warmth, not sweltering heat; for low tunnels, not holes through which one had to crawl, at times, on one's belly.

Another rumble made him scrub his eyes fiercely with his knuckles, then pull the door open. Two tubs this time, with a decent distance between and two men pushing and shouting remarks to one another. Stronger, or more used to their work? Hywel could not say, but he felt lighter, less grimly depressed, because of their good-natured chaff. The first man through was Duffy's Uncle Fin. He stopped so that the other could catch up.

'Well, Hywel! How's it with you, eh? A colliery lad now, see.'

'I'm all right, Uncle Fin. I'll be glad when I'm off the door, though. Only a couple of weeks, the overman said.'

Duffy's uncle nodded and braced his head against the tub once more.

'Aye; lonely work, door boy. You'll be better when you're with a gang,' He began to push and the tub squealed into motion once more. 'Off we go, then.'

The second man stopped too, but only for a moment, to inform Hywel that he might as well enjoy being a door boy while he could. At least you didn't sweat the way you did when you were doing men's work. Then he winked and pushed on. Hywel had only just closed his door this time when he had to snatch it open again as another tub rumbled into earshot. This time the drawer, younger and cheekier than his predecessors, was a mate of Hywel's. The two greeted one another, and then Ginger gave Hywel a piece of useful advice.

'Gettin' you down, is it? Don't think about it. That's how I got through the days when I was on doors. Fixed me mind on the greens and blues above, I did. Even now I think about the land, plan how I'll work up there one day.' He began to push once more and his last words came oddly back, echoing off the metal end of the tub. 'Think about them fields and woods,' he bawled. 'Think about what you're under . . . interesting, it is, and takes your mind off the blackness and the thick earth.'

Hywel, closing his door once more and leaning back, thought his friend's advice was sound. He would think about what was 'up there' and take his mind off his present unhappiness. After all, no one could stop him thinking!

Up and up, like a little mole, his mind began to burrow. Through the thick layers of soil and rock and into the real world, popping out, like a mole again, into the broad acres of a big meadow. It was a gentle slope up there, the grass nearly waist-high at this time of year and massed with frail wild flowers. He knew the names of most of them and recited them under his breath; ladies' slipper, ladies' smock, ragged robin, meadow sweet, archangel, harebell. They made a poem in his head more beautiful than any he had laboriously learned in school. In his mind, he walked down the meadow to where the willows leaned over the stream; in their cool green shade he could lie down near the water, hearing its soft lappings and murmurings, with the sunshine shadow-dappled and soft on his bare shoulders, for he would, naturally, be stripped for a swim. He had a hand in the water and was almost feeling its silky coolness on his fingers when the rumble of an approaching tub brought him back below ground. This time he was able to open and close his door cheerfully.

I'll go there when I'm off work, he told himself, settling back against the wall of rock once more and preparing to let his mind roam as freely as his body could not. He would go there, to that very meadow, with its sweet, hay-scented grass, and bathe in that stream.

Much later that day, after he had eaten his cheese sandwiches and his piece of cake and drunk the tepid tea which had come down the pit with him as an ice-cold drink, a strange thing happened to Hywel. Leaning against the wall and waiting for the next tub, he let his mind go again – and found himself in a strange country.

He was not aware, at first, of the strangeness, since he was lying on his back gazing up into the blue sky, feeling the breeze on his cheek and listening, vaguely, to birdsong.

It dawned upon him though, as he lay there, that there was a good smell on the breeze, a freshness which was new to him. Even as he noticed this he realised that the birdsong was different; there were birds here he had not heard on the mountains, with plaintive cries and strong, wailing notes.

He sat up. He was in the middle of what looked like a great flat marsh, and the freshness of the breeze was explained as soon as he looked to the east. The sea! No more than a silver line, it stretched along the flat horizon, from this distance apparently unmoving, totally calm and still. A painted sea with, now that he stared, a tiny painted ship on its surface.

Considerably awed by his own imagination, Hywel looked around him again and saw that a great many cattle were grazing on the marshes, and that though at first glance he had thought himself to be alone there were signs that other people were about. A tiny, reed-thatched cottage was visible, hedged in by a dyke and by sedge. Now that he was staring he could even make out a thin thread of smoke rising from the chimney. It was not only there, it was clearly inhabited.

Hywel got to his feet. He could see, for he had excellent long sight, that there was a garden, some geese, and trees planted about the cottage. Then his attention returned once more to the marsh itself. It was split and divided and divided again by the bright silver lines of ditches and dykes, and on the dykes he could see duck, wild geese and several other birds which he could not identify. The fields, if you could call them fields, were cropped near the cottage, but the rest was grazing land. Some had been used for hay, some were still uncut, and the rest were covered with cattle; big, healthy cattle, all eating steadily.

He had thought himself alone in that vast, bare landscape, but then he saw that there was a flat-bottomed boat on the widest dyke with a man and a boy in it; the boy was poling the craft along, while the man was cutting rushes with a huge scythe. Every now and then he flung a great armful into the bottom of the boat. Hywel wondered why they should cut the stuff, what possible use they would find for it. It might be an idea to walk over and have a word with the people in the boat, find out what they intended to do with the rushes.

The ground beneath his feet was firm enough, but water gleamed between the strong, bright tussocks of grass. He would have to go carefully, though he was suddenly sure that there was no danger here; the cattle would not be turned out to graze if the bog was liable to swallow them down. Nevertheless he kept to the tussocks, reluctant to get his feet wet, until it occurred to him that he was wearing wellington boots, footwear he had never possessed, and that his trousers were of corduroy and not of moleskin.

Even as the thought struck him there was an almighty crash and Hywel, hair standing on end, found himself stumbling to his feet and hurrying to get his door open. Back in the dark, hundreds of feet below ground, he was deeply relieved to see that the tub had been overladen and it was some of its contents falling out which had caused the noise and not, as he had believed, the tub itself crashing into his unguarded door. I fell asleep, he told himself shamefacedly; I fell asleep like any baby and I dreamed a strange dream. I shall never dare let my mind wander like that twice.

After the tub had gone and the door was closed he sat bolt upright, grimly determined that such a thing should not happen again. Nothing bad had resulted, thank goodness —

small thanks to him! After a very few moments however, he found it was impossible to sit and think of nothing; his mind would not obey. He was desperately anxious to return to that marsh, to find out just what those reed-cutters had wanted their cargo for, but there had been something about the dream which, apparently, he could not recreate at will. You could wander in your mind in a place you knew well, and such wanderings did not take you out of yourself. You could return should a pin drop. But now that he was allowing himself to think about it, he found he was puzzled and even a little frightened by the weird clarity of the last dream – if it had been a dream. Could one smell the salt on the breeze in a dream, or see men cutting rushes? Could one feel the spongy turf beneath one's boots, and the rub of the wellington top on the soft part of the inside of the knee? The very feel of corduroy on his skin had been experienced . . . in a *dream*? Still, since he knew very well that it could not have been real, it must have been a dream; the only trouble was that he could not remember ever having been in such a place. Without personal experience how could he have seen it so vividly?

At last he gave up. It was a puzzle and no mistake, but it was unlikely to happen again. He must concentrate on his boring and irksome task. For the rest of the day he worked conscientiously, and when he was told that the shift was over he returned to the cage with his fellow workers feeling that he had earned every penny of his one shilling and tenpence.

That night he tried very hard, before drifting off to sleep, to think about the marshland. But it would not come real in his head the way a place he knew well would come real. It was all there, the things he had seen and noticed, but with that vague mistiness at the edges which characterises a dream, or something simply imagined.

He woke next morning with a dreadful sinking sensation in the pit of his stomach which meant that the day ahead was going to be horrible. He remembered the fear that had clutched him as the cage raced down into that awful dark, the deafness, the sickly popping in his ears as hearing returned. He remembered the bad air, the heat, the cheesy, sweaty oppression of the ominous earth. And then, like a breath of sanity, came another recollection. He remembered lying on the marshes and sniffing the salt breeze. If he could be sure of having that again, the freshness and the coolness and the sheer reality, it would be worth putting up with the colliery. Well worth it.

Huw came in from the marshes early, and wet-pale, because he had had a rotten ugly dream, he told his mother. Being a boy who enjoyed her bit of drama now and then he recounted it with feeling whilst watching Megan make a batch of potato cakes and put loaves of bread to prove by the fire.

'I was lying on my back on a soft bit of grass, not thinking of much, when all of a sudden my mind went off – you know, Ma, the way it does when you're not concentrating. I started to think about last market day, bringing the beasts back from the city, and how if our Sheila's pups are good 'uns Dad says I can take the pick of the litter and bring it up for my own. And then, I don't know – I suppose I fell asleep. Next thing I'm awake and staring, with every hair on my head bolt upright, because I'm buried alive, deep in some damned old tunnel miles and miles under the earth, next to a rickety old wooden sheet thing which I've got to keep opening and closing, God knows why.

'Well, I sit there, trying to wake up, and I can feel the weight of the earth pressing down on me from above and hardness of rocks against my back and the stale air trying to smother me, and it's so real that I feel tears on my cheeks. Real tears, Ma, I swear it! And then I hear a rumbling getting nearer and nearer, and it was scary all right, though I knew it wasn't an earthquake or a rock fall, I felt it in my bones. I knew I must be there to do a job, and the only thing near me was the door, so I reached out towards it to give it a push to let whatever was making the noise through . . . and I woke! All wet with sweat I was and stinking of fear, yet there was the marsh, and the sky above, and a heifer grazing not three feet from me.'

His mother was staring. He could see the whites of her eyes all round the deep brown circle of the iris. She was a beautiful woman with her pale gold hair and clear skin, but perhaps the most surprising thing about her was those very dark, velvety brown eyes where one expected blue or grey. Huw grinned at her, thinking that he must have told the dream well to make

Ma go so pale – and on a baking day, too, when the warmth of the stove had brought such a flush to her cheeks.

'Well, what do you think, Ma? Suffin I ate?'

Because of their mother's lilting Welsh accent and the fact that their father's accent varied according to where he was, neither Huw nor his sisters spoke with a broad Norfolk burr, but of course they used it in school, where to speak without a local accent would have been asking for trouble, children never liking one of their number to be different. Now he dropped into Norfolk because he felt uncomfortable over his mother's continuing silence and the way that her face had first paled and was now rosily flushing. It was only a dream, dammit! He put it into words.

'Hev I frit you, my woman? That's only a dream, gal!'

It brought her down to earth again, from whatever plane she had been inhabiting. She sniffed, wiped a floury hand across her mouth, and began to paint the potato cakes with milk and water to make them shine.

'Dream? A nightmare, more like. And don't talk like that, Huw, if you please. One of the few good things about living right out here, miles from everywhere, is that your bad habits are for the most part your own and not picked up from other children. What's more, you must set the girls a good example; you know what your father says!'

Huw was the eldest child but his sister Helen was barely twelve months younger; then there had been a long gap before the three youngest children, Susan, Sarah and Sybil, put in an appearance. They were neat, dark little girls, as different from fair Huw and fair Helen as could be, but goodness, they were naughty! Susan was four, Sarah three and Sybil only two, for they had followed one another into the world as though anxious to start getting into triple mischief at once, and as soon as they could toddle they were into everything, causing their parents and older brother and sister constant, gnawing anxiety whenever they were out of sight. So now Huw laughed at his mother's strictures and jerked a thumb at the garden through the low kitchen window.

'Me, set them a good example? They wouldn't know a good example if it bit them on the nose – and they certainly wouldn't follow it! Helen's got them on the reins again. If you ask me she

105

only *pretends* to play horses with them so she can stop them wandering off. Otherwise they'd be in trouble, sure as eggs is eggs.'

Megan laughed with him. 'I know, they are naughty; I can't think how I came to have two such good children and then three such bad ones, but they're nice, aren't they?'

'Oh, nice!' It was clear that his mother's mind was now firmly fixed on her three youngest offspring. 'Want some water brought in?'

'Not yet, dear. I'll just get this batch of cakes in the oven though and you can fetch me in some more sea-coal.' Wood was hard to come by on the marshes, and Ned Pettigrew would have scorned to let his wife burn turves as some of the marshmen did, so he and Huw took the horse and cart into the nearest town to buy coal every few months. And sometimes they burned seaweed, so that they rarely went without a fire even when times were hard.

'Oh, right.' He was actually halfway out of the back door when his mother spoke again. She did so casually, yet with an undertone of anxiety which she could not quite hide.

'Huw, love, can you tell me a bit more about that underground place? Don't want to worry you, but it's odd, me being from a mining family and all. You've never thought about the pits, I daresay?'

Huw shook his head. 'Not that I can remember. Perhaps when I was a kid you said something . . . when the letters come from Auntie Ella you might have mentioned it.'

'Mm. I suppose I might have. But there again, I've never been below myself, so it isn't as if I've seen it. Huw, love, would you mind very much telling me again what it was like?'

He found that he did mind, because he could see that it worried her, but he frowned, trying to reconstruct the scene in his head. He did not speak again until he had it clear, or as clear as it would consent to come.

'It was totally dark but for this lamp beside me. Quite a small one, brass I think. The sheet-thing was a door. I can't imagine why there should be a door across a tunnel, but I'm pretty sure that's what it was. The tunnel was low. I could just about sit upright but I couldn't stand, only crouch. And something glinted . . . something on the ground. When

I moved the lamp cast my shadow on something. I can't quite . . .'

'Rails. It 'ud be the rails. They have doors when the tunnel slopes down sharply because of the air. So far as I can remember it's pumped into the lowest point of the pit to replace the foul stuff down there, but if they don't put doors across the roads at certain points the good air comes rushing up again. Yes, that's right. I remember several boys at school were on the doors when they started working below.'

'Yes, but why do the boys sit there? Couldn't the men do it for themselves? It seems a daft way to go on.'

His mother sighed and began to clean down the table after her baking, her cloth making huge swathes through the flour.

'The boys have to be there to open the door for the tubs because there's a man pushing but no one at the front, I imagine,' she said patiently. 'Think, Huw! Then, when the door's open, how could the fellow pushing shut it without the tubs running backwards?'

'Yes, of course.' Huw grinned. 'Why am I dreaming about it, though? It doesn't seem a terribly important thing to dream about!'

'I suppose perhaps because your family have worked there for generations; perhaps all your ancestors were on the doors when they were lads. It's quite likely.'

'I see. One of the teachers in school said that when you dream you're falling it comes from way back, when we were apes swinging through the forest in our mothers' arms, and she dropped us. If you can believe that it's easy enough to believe I can dream about my own family history.'

'Yes. Yes, I suppose it's possible. But I wish you hadn't,' Megan said. 'There's a terrible place, a colliery. Killed your . . . your Uncle Ben, killed your taid, and made the men in our family stunted and small. Brought a good few to their deaths one way and another. I've heard my da say that in places the men lie down flat on their bellies or on their sides to chip out the coal, and then they crawl back to the winding shaft on all fours, like animals. By Christ, I'm glad no child of mine . . .' She stopped short and turned away from him so that he could only see the back of her head, her neck so soft and white and young-seeming, and the pale hair caught up in a big soft bun.

He had never heard her use a bad word or blaspheme and it shook him even more than her vivid word-picture of work in a colliery. He wished with all his heart that he had never mentioned the dream, or whatever it was, for it had done nothing but harm, making his mother remember things she would do much better to forget, bringing it into his head that it was not just a dream but something which had really happened to someone he might have loved.

'Ma? Look, it was only a nightmare, and I'll make jolly sure I never have another like it. Shall we forget it, eh? You wouldn't get me down one of them mines for a million pounds! Even in my dream I hated it. I'm my father's son. We both love the land and the outdoors.'

She turned at that and smiled, wiping tears away with one floury hand, then reached out and stroked his cheek in a rare physical gesture of affection. He gave her a hug, rib-crackingly violent, and lifted her off her feet when she squeaked.

'There, all forgotten, eh? No Pettigrew would work below, so don't even think about it. Is it a bargain?'

She sighed, nodded, and went to the stone sink. She poured water from the tall enamel jug into a bowl and rinsed her hands, then picked up the empty bucket and handed it to him.

'I could do with a bit more water, Huw, love, after you've brought in the coal. You're right. No Pettigrew would work below, and you're your father's son.'

Seven: November 1916

'Another accident at the Wynd, I see.'

Tom Tegydd was eating bacon and egg and reading the morning paper. His post lay by his side plate, ready to be devoured with his toast. Dot, watching fascinated as the food disappeared, thought that her father looked like some hearty, greedy character out of Dickens. She had lately taken a fancy to the Victorian novelist and was reading, half in horror and half in disbelief, of the hard and convict-haunted life led by Pip in *Great Expectations*. Gin-soaked slum poverty was something she had never seen, and the dark and evil purlieus of London seemed a far cry from the town's cautious, chapel-going near-prosperity. Not that anyone claimed to be prosperous in wartime – wages had risen to unprecedented heights but so had prices – yet compared with Dickens's poor they were all doing very nicely, thank you. Sometimes a century, Dot concluded, was a lot longer than a hundred years, especially when it was only seventy or so!

The muddleheadedness of the thought made her smile. She was about to tell Alexandra what she had been thinking when Alex spoke, addressing her father.

'An accident? Where, Father? What happened?'

She was the only person present prepared to indulge Father in light conversation just then, Dot realised. She could see that her mother, who had put on a lot of weight since she became undisputed mistress in her own house, was not in the least interested in what her husband had said. She was spreading butter thickly on the round of bread she had just selected and was eyeing the honey pot with a good deal more interest than she showed in any of her family. Being fat did not suit Olivia; she had managed to look pale and even frail before, and pallor

109

and fragility had carried with it a charm which plump white cheeks, a double chin and fingers whose skin was stretched as tight as little sausages could not rival. It was not as if the plumpness had made her rosier or more prone to laughter. She was still pale, but her pallor was waxy now, and though she often looked self-satisfied there was something rather sly in her drooping eyelids and her small, tight smile.

Kate, of course, would not say a word because she was on bad terms with Father. Once again he had refused a request that she might take dancing lessons in town. He had also refused to allow her to ask Miss Gelda Trehearn to tea; a harmless enough visit it would have been, but Father had said he would not countenance it. Time enough for the girls to enter society when the war was over, he said. Time enough.

Kate had stormed and wept; Mother had sighed and eaten an extra-large box of chocolates whilst the argument raged. But despite her love for Kate she had not supported her daughter, and Alexandra had not done so either. Dot, who was sorry to see Kate's adorable prettiness so obviously wasted here at the Plas, had tried to put in a word for the eminent reasonableness of Kate's wish to have a friend, but this had been a mistake. Once Father had escaped, Kate's wrath had descended on her youngest sister's head.

'Interfering, making things worse,' she had raged. 'When will you learn to mind your own business, Dotty? Father simply assumed that you'd want dancing lessons too. You know how mean he is. He would never agree to pay for an ugly little gnome like you to learn, so you spoiled my chances for nothing.'

Useless to say she would hate to learn to dance. Kate knew very well how she felt. Better just to let Kate say all the cruel things she could lay her tongue to – and they were many and various – and then go away somewhere quiet and tell herself that her sister had not meant any of it. Which was true; it was Kate's frustration which had attacked, not Kate herself.

But now she waited eagerly for Father to answer Allie. Hywel said that the Wynd had a bad accident record; what was it this time? To be in the paper meant that it had been fatal; the *Leader* would not have recorded a run-of-the-mill broken limb or roof fall.

'I told you it was at the Wynd, Alex my dear.' Tom looked at his middle daughter quite kindly over the top of his half-glasses. 'A woman was killed . . . a girl, really. Little fool. These girls think more of a few rubbishy bits of glass jewellery than they do of their safety.' He put the paper down, pushed his dinner plate out of the way and reached for the toast. He buttered a slice, spread marmalade with a prodigal hand, and then began to leaf through his letters with one hand whilst the toast waited. He picked one out; a rich, cream-coloured envelope with a sloping black hand. He stared at it, then put the toast down and picked up his ivory paper knife. He began to slit open the envelope. 'Poor creature, though, for all that. They've not gone into detail, but what a dreadful death!'

'What happened?' Dot said, since her father was now absorbed in his letter. 'How could a girl get killed at the Black Wynd? Girls don't go below even there, do they?'

But her father was smiling, reading the letter, obviously oblivious of them all. During the little silence which followed Dot's question he crumpled the envelope and threw it towards the wastepaper basket, slipped the letter itself into his pocket, and stood up. He crammed the last piece of toast into his mouth, chewed, swallowed, and then addressed his gaping family. Their father never left the table until all the toast was gone and the last cup of coffee drunk. He had scarcely, Dot noticed, taken more than two sips from his very first cup!

'I've a lot to do this morning, so I'll be off now. I'm going into town and probably up to Liverpool, so you won't see me for luncheon or dinner. In fact I may be gone a day or so; I want to see a fellow about shipping coal.' He set off in the direction of the door and it was easy to see he was excited about something, for his step was as bouncy and light as a boy's. 'Dot, take a message to Redman for me, there's a good lass. Tell him I want the sheep he's brought down to the home pastures dipped, and then he's to brand the new breeding stock. That'll keep him busy until I'm home.'

As rapidly as he had jumped to his feet he now left the room, shutting the door so carelessly behind him that it sprang open again. They heard his steps receding into the distance until at last the front door slammed on silence.

Behind him, in the room he had left, no one moved or spoke.

111

Olivia sat there, fingers still sticky from their recent encounter with the honey pot, staring down at the food on her plate as though it had suddenly become repugnant. Kate and Alexandra stared at one another. There was a degree of understanding on their faces, yet Dot could tell they did not exactly know why Father had hurried out, nor why Mother sat so still; they just suspected.

As much to break the uncomfortable silence as anything Dot reached for her mug, drained it, wiped off the resultant white moustache and then held it towards her mother.

'Please may I have some more milk? I'm thirsty.'

But Olivia continued to stare down at her plate as though she had not heard a word. It was Kate who answered.

'Not now, Dot. You can get some from the kitchen later.'

'Why? I don't see . . .'

Dot was reaching for the jug when Olivia moved. She pushed her chair back in slow motion, with a hideous scraping noise on the polished wood blocks of the floor, and then, equally slowly, stood up. She turned and walked towards the door as if she was going to follow her husband's lead and leave the room, and then she appeared to notice the cream-coloured envelope for the first time. It had hit the edge of the wastepaper basket and fallen on to the floor.

Olivia bent and picked it up but did not toss it into the basket. Instead, she smoothed it carefully between her fingers and returned to the table. She sat down, picked up her slice of bread and honey and began, absently, to eat it. Her eyes never left the writing on the cream-coloured envelope and Dot, almost mesmerised, found herself staring at it too.

There was nothing out of the ordinary about either envelope or writing. The writing was neat, copperplate, done with black ink and with care, by the look of it. The capital letters were big and curly, the small letters slightly sloping and distinctive. Dot began to get the feeling that she had seen the writing before — but where, and whose was it? What had someone written to Father that was so exciting that he left the breakfast parlour with his food half-eaten? Whose correspondence could upset Mother so much that she, too, forgot to eat?

But Dot could not think. Kate and Alexandra were staring at the envelope as well, forgetting their own coffee and the ladylike slices of very thin bread they both insisted on. Once, Kate nudged Alexandra, but otherwise they simply sat, like figures in a tableau, waiting for something to happen.

Nothing did. Mother continued to stare at the envelope until she had finished her bread and honey. Then she wiped her fingers and her mouth on her napkin, picked up the envelope and got to her feet. She was standing with the expensive-looking stationery in her hand when Lizzie from the village, who helped out in the kitchen and around the house, came in, her mouth hanging open as it usually did when she wanted to say something. Olivia laid the envelope down on the table.

'Yes, Lizzie?'

'Please, ma'am, if you've finished I'll clear now. I want to get off early for the funeral, like the other gels.'

'Funeral?' Her mother said the word so sharply that Dot actually jumped.

'Yes, ma'am. All going we are, what knew 'er. That poor gel who died at the Wynd's being buried today; a good chapel service for her there'll be and mostly us wants to go. Ewart Evans is running the horse-waggonette from the Public, leaving at 'leven.'

'Oh yes, I forgot. Possibly that was why Mr Tegydd was in such a hurry.' Olivia seemed to have forgotten the envelope, for she walked towards the door, leaving it where it lay. 'Very well, Lizzie, clear right away; you must not miss the wag-gonette.'

As soon as Olivia had shut the door behind her Kate pounced on the envelope. She pushed it into her skirt pocket and the three sisters, Dot at least feeling like the lowest kind of thief, left the room and hurried across the hall and up the stairs to their sitting room, which had, a mere six months earlier, been the schoolroom. It had changed in name only, alas, for Tom had refused to pamper the girls with carpets or comfort-able chairs, but at least it was their refuge, where no one, in theory, could interfere with their ploys.

Kate plumped herself down in the middle of the window seat, gave her sisters a triumphant look, and spread the envelope out on her knees.

'Well? Do either of you recognise the writing?'

Alexandra stared, bent closer, then shook her head, plainly

113

puzzled. Dot stared too, put a finger to her mouth, and then crowed with triumph.

'I do! I recognise it, Kate!'

'You do? Well done! Tell us who wrote it, then.'

'I don't know who wrote it, exactly,' Dot said. 'I recognise the writing, though. It's the writing on the primer teaching copperplate which Miss Edenthorpe used when we were small.'

Kate beamed at her sister.

'You're a clever kid sometimes, Dot. Alex, don't you recognise it now Dot's told you?'

'Well, I see it's very like,' Alexandra admitted. 'But I still don't understand; why should someone use primer writing to address Father?'

'Oh, really, Allie, don't be so stupid! It's you-know-who, of course! You must realise it wouldn't please Mother at *all* to discover that *she* was writing letters to Father.'

'You might as well say Edie straight out,' Dot remarked, whilst Alexandra still looked doubtful and distressed. 'I think she's got a nerve, writing letters secretly to Father and disguising her handwriting so that Mother will be fooled. I don't see why she needed to do it, either. After all, they parted good friends. Surely she could just write straight to Mother, knowing Father will read the letter, and have done?'

'No, that won't do, brat. Since you've found out anyway that Edie's writing to Father we might as well tell you what we know. We believe, Allie and I, that Edie and Papa were fond of one another and that was why Mother had her sent away. Married ladies don't like their husbands to admire other ladies, and there's no doubt that Father admired Edie very much indeed; don't you agree?'

Dot, thinking of the feet in the tower room, agreed fervently. Indeed, there could be no doubt whatsoever!

'And when two people still . . . well, still love, they can't bear to be parted for ever, not even when they know it's their duty. So Edie writes and then Father goes off to visit her. That's what we think.'

Alexandra, who had been staring at the envelope in silence, suddenly added her mite to the conversation.

'It's awfully good stationery, so I suppose Edie is working

114

for a very rich family. Does that mean they allow her to have followers, and don't even suspect that Father is a married man with grown daughters of his own?'

Dot spoke before she thought.

'Oh, no, that stationery is far finer than anything we have. I think Father gives it to her especially to write to him, so he even recognises the envelope. Don't you?'

Kate bounced on the thin cushions and snatched the envelope back.

'Dot, you clever girl! You may be an ugly little gnome but you've got heaps and heaps of brains! I should have noticed that. Perhaps Mother did, and that was why she went on staring at the envelope like a bird at a snake. Has it ever occurred to either of you that Father may have helped Edie to buy a little house somewhere? And that's why he goes away now for two or three days at a time? To see her. That would mean Father has taken Edie under his protection, as they say in novels. Mother probably knows, but can't do anything. How *very* romantic it is!'

Dot, however, gave a disbelieving sniff.

'You've been reading too many love-stories, Kate,' she said roundly. 'As if Father would! Why, he isn't at all romantic. I don't believe he cares very much for ladies, not even for Mother, and certainly not in a romantic way. I'm sure he's dutiful and sometimes quite polite and holds doors open when he remembers and passes the wine when Mother's asked no more than twice, but that isn't at all romantic. I've never seen him kiss Mother tenderly beside her mouth, or go down on one knee and say he wants to save her from the harsh realities of life, or take a rose she has touched to wear in his buttonhole. No, and he doesn't help her out of her chair when she's struggling up after a meal, or hand her out of the gig and kiss her fingers, or . . .'

'Oho, who's been reading romances now?' jeered Kate unkindly, and the three of them giggled at the picture Dot was painting of their down-to-earth parent. 'But what about with Edie? Just you think, Dot, and you might remember the odd little romantic moment.'

'I don't see why she should, when I can't,' Alexandra objected. 'I think you're right, Kate, and Father did like Edie,

115

but I don't think the rest *can* be right. Father is forever telling us how poor we are and how farmers have no money any more and the land is nothing but a drain and a responsibility and though the pits bring in money the government takes most of it away from him. So how could he possibly pay for Edie to live in idleness somewhere? And why would she want to? Dear Edie was always so full of fun and energy. She would be miserable with no one to laugh with and no one to order about and no one to teach.'

Dot waited for Kate to explain it, for surely beautiful, intelligent Kate would have an answer? But she saw that Kate's smooth brow wore a frown; her elder sister was equally at a loss.

'Yes, I know what you both mean,' she said slowly.'Ever since the day Edie left I've wondered and wondered, and yet I still think I'm right. If Edie had a job, her employer wouldn't allow her to see a man who was not related to her. And if she said Father was her brother . . . no, it would never work. Brothers and sisters don't . . . anyway, it wouldn't work. Edie always dressed beautifully, and it was sometimes hinted that she had private means . . . suppose she had some money and Father put up a bit more, and they managed to buy a little house somewhere? That has to be the answer!' She took the envelope and began to tear it into small pieces which she threw into the cold and empty fireplace. 'I can't prove it. I'm not even sure that I want to, but I have a feeling here . . .' she laid a dramatic hand over the region popularly supposed to contain the heart '. . . that I'm right!'

'You're usually right,' Alexandra said peaceably. 'And if you are, though of course I'm sorry for Mother, I do think things are easier for her, don't you?'

'Easier? They're awful. No one to intercede with Father when we want something and Father impatient with Mother almost all the time and not even staying in the room to hear her finish a sentence. If Edie were here she would have seen that I got my dancing lessons and that we could have friends to tea, and she wouldn't have let Father dash off without saying where he was going this morning and I'd have got my new winter boots without a word. As it is, I daresay I'll have to cram my feet into last year's, and they've got huge holes in the soles.'

116

'That's all true,' Dot said. 'I should think Mother misses Edie worse than anyone.'

'Dear me, what a fool you can be, clever though you are,' Kate remarked, promptly changing on to another tack. 'Do you think Mother *liked* having to get Edie to ask Father for a new gown, or a pair of slippers, or a warm coat, when it was her place to have such things? But Mother could see that Father was infatuated and knew that if she tried to interfere her life could be made a misery, so she did nothing. Until Edie walked right into her hands by visiting old Agatha, of course.'

'I still don't see why they were so annoyed,' Dot said plaintively. 'After all, she isn't really a witch. Just a wise woman, and . . .'

'She sells love potions. It's my belief, and Allie agrees – don't you, Allie? – that Edie went to her to get a love potion that would enslave Father even more and that was why she disguised herself as a village woman. And of course Father wouldn't have liked that any more than Mother did, so they got rid of her. Or at least . . .' She paused, plainly seeing snags on every side should Dot start asking awkward questions. 'Anyway, if you find anything out mind you tell us.'

'I might,' Dot said, jumping to her feet and heading for the door. If only they knew how much I already know, she thought smugly. 'Or I might not! I'm going down to the kitchen to find out what happened to that poor girl who died at the Wynd.'

'You shouldn't gossip with the servants,' Kate remarked, but so much with the air of one who expects her advice to be ignored that Dot did not even pause in her flight. 'Whilst you're down there, Dot, just ask around and see if anyone knows where Edie went when she left. She had friends in the village, too – they might know.'

Dot, the door open, turned with a hand still on the knob.

'I'll ask, but I bet no one knows any more than we do. Father's no fool, and nor's Edie. Bye. See you for luncheon.'

As she had said she would, Dot went to the kitchen – and straight through it, having exchanged cheerful greetings with Cook and a couple of maids. She knew the best place for the sort of talk she wanted was in the stables and around the farm.

Besides, she had a message for Mr Redman or for Souse'em, whichever she found first.

As she passed through the great hall she glanced at the big bowls which in Edie's time had always contained fresh flowers, but now, whatever the season, held nothing but the dryness of everlasting ones, dusty-petalled papery things, and wished that her mother got on better with the servants. Then Higgins might bring flowers in from the garden or the greenhouse instead of sending them all to market or simply letting them bloom and die in their beds. But Mother neither cared about flowers nor understood them. She simply took Higgins's word for it when he said 'nothing suitable for the house, ma'am', and continued to allow the dust-gatherers to remain in the bowls and vases.

It did not occur to Dot, hurrying through the great house, that she could easily have done the flowers herself. She was not at all domesticated, and though she would willingly have worked on the farm from dawn until dusk she resented having to so much as tidy her own room indoors. Her sisters said she was useless and idle and Dot took care to nurture this impression, for she had noted an increasing tendency of late to get Kate and Allie to do their share of laundry work, cooking and even dusting. They had little choice. Mother was inept and lazy and apt to remind everyone of her high-born relatives on the Wirral, none of whom had ever lifted a feather duster in anger in their lives; and since Father thought that they were lucky to have a roof over their heads and food in their bellies during war-time, it was doubtful if he would have considered employing so much as one extra maid to keep the house respectable.

That, of course, was another reason why Tom would not allow the girls to entertain or to visit other houses. The comparisons would be odious, there could be no doubt of that; but, worse, the girls who came to visit would carry tales of dirt and neglect back to their own neat, well-run homes. Tom might not care about the Plas, but he would not wish other people to know how he was letting it slide. When he held business meetings here he made sure that a passageway was cleared, so to speak, from his study to the front door and from his study to the dining room. Whilst his guests were present there were flowers in vases, the furniture shone, faded and darned hangings were changed for whatever was best. Dot supposed that the men noticed very little other than the excellence of the wine, the deliciousness and variety of the food they were offered, and the generous way in which the decanter circulated both before and after the meal. They may have remarked on the oil lamps, but so plentiful were these and so brightly did they shine that only someone very pernickety indeed would have regretted gas or electricity.

Of course when the meetings were over things returned to normal. Hangings were taken down, folded in mothballs, and put away for next time. Servants, hired for the party, returned to their distant villages or to the town. The flowers lingered until they died. Only the food remained delicious, since both Father and Mother enjoyed good food; otherwise the magic palace reverted to the one the prince fought his way through a thorn forest to find — a palace, cobweb-garnished, which had been asleep for a hundred years.

Tom would have been surprised to know how much his youngest daughter minded all this — not for herself, but for Plas Tegydd. She felt that the house lifted a proud and beautiful head higher when it was cleaned and polished and decked with flowers, and she hated the Cinderella-like reversion to dirt, dust and muddle which came about so rapidly after the business meetings. Poor darling, she would murmur softly, patting the wood panelling in the hall, poor darling, you deserve to be loved and looked after, not allowed to grow old and hideous. But there was little she could do about it and she could see that Mother cared not one jot — it was not her ancestral home, after all — and that Kate and Allie never even thought about it. They were like a couple of fledglings, perched on the very edge of the nest, eager to try their wings before flying away to make their own nests somewhere else. They had very little interest in the home in which they had been reared.

Crossing the cobbled stable yard, Dot heard Jan Torch whistling as he groomed a horse and hurried into the stable. She stood by the door and cleared her throat loudly until Jan turned and gave her a gap-toothed grin. He was getting crotchety in his old age, was Jan, and nothing annoyed him more than the way she could appear, silently, under his very nose, startling the life out of him. Now he raised the brush quite cheerfully before diving under the horse's belly once more.

'Mornin', Miss Dot! Come to get Matchless fettled?'

'I'll take him out later, I think,' Dot said. Jan was grooming Pride, one of the carriage horses; she took down a brush and approached Folly, who had plainly been out as well judging by the mud on his legs. She bent, saying as a matter of form, 'Can I do this one?' though she knew that Jan was thankful for any help he could get. The war took some of the able-bodied young men, he was apt to say, and the pit took the rest; at the age of seventy he was working harder than ever before, and his life had never been easy. Of course the money was better, too – he had told her many a tale of life before the war when he was young, with a wife and three sons to keep all on ten shillings a week and the rent to pay into the bargain – but as everyone kept reminding you, prices were higher as well, and the agricultural worker, as always, ended up at the bottom of the heap.

'Aye, you might as well.' Not a gracious man, she thought with a little grin, brushing vigorously. It was a dull morning and there had been rain earlier; Folly would need a good deal of attention. Presently she would get the hoof-pick to clear the clag out of his shoes and later she would curry his long mane, but for now her work was cut out just to get his legs free from mud.

'Is Souse'em about?' Dot enquired presently, still vigorously brushing. 'Or Mr Redman? Father gave me a message.'

'Oh, aye. They're in the home pasture, dipping the sheep. Later they'll be branding the new stock.'

Dot chuckled. 'Thanks, Jan. That was the message. Did Father see them himself then, before he went off?'

'No, lass. He were in a hurry, like, see? But if they waited for your father to tell 'em what to do some days they'd best not hold their breaths.' He chuckled at his own joke and Dot, sighing, agreed that Father did not always mind very much what the men did.

The ill-assorted couple worked in silence for a while and then Dot broke it to ask for the hoof-oil. When she was spreading it with the little brush she thought that sufficient time had elapsed to ask Jan a question. Close association with countryfolk had bred in her the realisation that if you wanted a good answer you should not hurry with your query; you should go through all the courtesies first. In this case, you should groom at least one horse.

'Jan, are you going to this funeral at the Wynd this afternoon?'

'No, not me. Didn't know the girl, see? But most of the others will be going. We're lending Dobbin and Boxer to pull a cart or two so's most can go.'

'Oh? The Wynd's doing the funeral though, I suppose?'

Jan was scraping the brick floor with his shovel; the noise faltered, then continued firmly.

'They've got a collection up for the funeral; don't hear tell Carruthers has given anything. Your da's given the men the afternoon; they're having to take French leave from the Wynd, they say.'

'They'll hate Marmy Carruthers worse than ever for that,' Dot observed, beginning to comb Folly's tangled mane. 'They say he's drunk more than he's sober and never goes below to find out what's happening in his own pit. They say his manager buys powder that's been turned down as unsafe by every other owner in North Wales, and that he doesn't allow a search at the pit-head to make sure no one's carrying matches, because it wastes working time.'

'Aye. And now they're saying he near as dammit killed young Kersie with his own hands. All nonsense, but truth there is in it in one way. Wouldn't have happened, see, in a well-run pit.'

'What did happen? All I heard was that she worked at the pit-head and died. I couldn't imagine what could go wrong, though of course I've never visited the pit-head. Father doesn't like women near the mines.'

'Except when they're working,' Jan said, but factually, not nastily. 'Well, it'll be common knowledge soon enough, no matter how they may try to cover it up. Worked next to her aunt, Kersie did, on the endless belt, and her aunt had a shawl same's they mostly do, pinned together with a cameo brooch. Family heirloom, some such thing. The aunt said she valued that brooch above rubies, and the girl knew, see? So when the

121

shawl got caught in the belt it was pulled off and the brooch went too and this youngster, only a bit of a girl, not even fifteen I've heard, she jumped up on the endless belt, followed the shawl which was past praying for, and bent to unhook the brooch. Hair caught in the machinery, see? Dead she was by the time they got the belt stopped.'

Dot shuddered. 'Poor girl! But why was that Marmy's fault?'

'Wasn't, not really. Could have happened at any pit; the Olwen's got the endless belt and all girls born of women are foolish. No, not fair it is to blame Marmy entire.'

'Then why do they?' Dot stepped back to admire her handiwork. 'Just because they hate him?'

'Because the machinery hadn't been tested for many a year and wouldn't go into reverse,' Jan said. 'God knows, mind, whether that would've saved her, but it might, I daresay. Finished Folly, have you? Well, we'll put them out for an hour or two since the rain's stopped. Here, put a halter on him. I've got one on Pride.'

Dot obeyed, trying to rid her mind of the picture of a girl very little older than herself being dragged, shrieking, into the machinery which would kill her because it would not reverse. Quickly, to banish that picture, she asked another question.

'Where did Father go this morning to get the horses in such a lather?'

She happened to be looking at Jan at that point and fancied she could almost see a shutter descend. He concentrated on bringing Pride out of his stall, turning away from her.

'Got a meeting somewhere, I believe. Chester, or Liverpool – he didn't say as I remember. Boggy drove him.'

Boggy was, like Jan, too old for the war or the pit but he was a first class driver. Still, Dot knew that her father fancied his own abilities with the reins and was unlikely to have been driven unless he was continuing his journey by train. Even as she pondered this, Boggy appeared and went over to the end stall.

'Missus wants Clover put in the gig,' he announced briefly. 'She said she wasn't satisfied with the lamb they sent up and she'd visit the butchers' market herself to choose beef for the weekend.' He had been addressing Jan but tugged his forelock on noticing Dot. 'Oh, morning, miss. Gettin' out a bit better now.'

'Morning, Boggy. Where did Father go, this morning? And when are you fetching him back?'

The two men exchanged furtive looks.

'Mr Tegydd went off in the train. Back tomorrow, late. I'm to meet the 9.30 in the evening.'

'Oh? Which 9.30? I mean the 9.30 from where?'

'Dunno, Miss Dot, he only said to meet the 9.30.'

Boggy began to lead Clover over to the waggon shed. Dot thought about following him, then dismissed the idea. She had little doubt that he knew, less that he would not tell her. Loyalty was strong amongst the old workers. They would not give Tom away to her any more than they would have given her away to Tom. They must know where he went and probably had their own ideas about why he went as well, but they would not let him down.

Considering the matter as she shovelled manure into a huge wooden barrow which she and Jan between them would presently push across the yard to the midden, she concluded that Father had probably gone to London, for only in London, that great city, could he hope to hide his Edie. Was London at the seaside? Dot, with a knowledge of geography about equal to her knowledge of love affairs, was fairly sure that it was. No doubt Edie had a dear little house near the sea, shopped each day in Piccadilly and bought all her hams and jars of gentlemen's relish and pickled walnuts at Fortnum & Mason's. Just now she would be waiting for Father, but presently he would arrive, and then what excitement there would be! Dot, kicking manure off her clogs and seizing one handle of the barrow, imagined the scene. Edie stretched out on a coach wearing low-cut white gown and holding an ostrich-feather fan in one hand. Fruit in a nearby bowl, flowers in a tall crystal vase, wine sparkling in a glass. A maid with a dark uniform dress and a spotless white apron to wait on her. And Father, hair water-slicked down but for one romantic curl falling over his brow, in impeccable evening dress, with a bouquet of roses – hothouse, of course – in one hand, kneeling by the couch and saying . . .

Dot's imagination broke down in giggles. Impossible! There

had to be some other explanation for Father's sudden liking for trips away. Tom Tegydd would never go down on one knee, wear a kiss curl or carry flowers! Whatever was going on, she, Kate and Alexandra had surely got hold of the wrong end of the stick!

Blanche Edenthorpe lay back on her lace pillows and smiled at the basketwork cradle at the end of her bed. Her son! Her passport, not only to motherhood, but to respectability, money and position. If you bear me a son, her lover had said, he shall be my heir and you, as the mother of my heir, will be honoured as such. Already he had been generous. She had a nice house in this quiet seaside resort where her 'husband' came and visited her three or four times a month. She and Tom had decided that simplicity must be their keyword if they were not to be found out. They had simply renamed him Elton Edenthorpe, so that when she called him Tom it did not sound too unlikely. Tegydd was a good Welsh name, but unusual; they dared not use it.

During the birth she had been haunted by the fear that the baby might prove to be a girl. Terrible thoughts had run through her mind. She would cast the baby away somewhere and buy a boy-child from some poor woman and pass it off as her own. She would keep the baby covered for the rest of its life and just insist that it was a boy. Tom would never see it other than respectably clothed. No one would!

When the pains were at their height she shocked the nurse by screaming that if the child was a girl she would see it damned before she would admit its sex. And when the baby emerged from her straining thighs she took not one glance at its small face; her eyes were fixed on its genitals.

And it was all right! Unmistakably masculine, the baby lay there, probably ugly, certainly red-faced, wet and blood-streaked, but the boy that she not only wanted but needed, had to have! She had told the nurse that she had been delirious, and pretended a pang of disappointment because you could not dress a little boy in lovely frills, as you could a little girl.

The nurse had given her a very knowing, old-fashioned look, but what did it matter what a mere nurse thought? Or, indeed, said? Now that the boy was born and hers, now that she had him safe . . . but did she mean Tom or the child? She could not have said if her life had been at stake.

Safe! Secure! Verging on respectable! Blanche felt as comfortable as a cat which has got, not only the cream, but the canary lined up for afters. She purred. She was wreathed in smiles. She wrote her letter and got her little maid to despatch it and then she drank nearly half a bottle of the good wine Tom had brought her, and sang songs and fell out of bed and giggled at herself because the relief was so huge, so tangible, that it had to be celebrated and gloated over.

Later, when she was herself again, she wondered about Tom. She knew him as a lusty lover, an impetuous man, an employer. But about his life before she entered it she knew almost nothing. Were there other illegitimate children? Had he had other mistresses? She was sure there had been other women, but if they had borne him children either he had been unsure of their paternity or they had been girls. Odd, she reflected, that she could summon up only pity for his legal wife, but suffer all the pangs of white-hot jealousy if she thought of his mistresses. She adored him, longed for him, would have died for him.

It had been like that from the first. She had entered Plas Tegydd a nineteen-year-old innocent. Eldest child of a large and impecunious family, she had early learned to make do and mend, to housekeep carefully, to turn collars, to refashion hats and retrim them, to sides-to-middle sheets. She had been surprised to find that this huge house was run in a similar fashion to her own small, bulging home, where her father taught school next door and her mother struggled to teach music and bring up her multitudinous flock. Blanche had left home gladly, wanting a glimpse of that better life which she was sure must exist. She had only to look into her glass to know that she was prettier by far than most girls, and she had, in addition, an innocent charm which she determined to cultivate. She wanted to marry well, and was sure that, given the opportunity, she could do so.

Only . . . Tom Tegydd had met her in the dark corridor leading to the nursery, which later became the schoolroom, when she had been working there only a week. He had smiled, stopped, begun to ask her how she was getting on with the children, and then she watched his face begin to change, his eyelids to droop over his eyes, his nostrils to flare, as he took her waist in his hands and drew her close, so close that her high young breasts were pressed hard against his buttoned coat. He said nothing, that was the strange part, and neither did she; she felt her breathing quicken, her heartbeats start to race, and then his mouth took hers.

She did not know how to kiss, but standing there in that dark corridor Tom Tegydd taught her without a word said. She had known, then, that he was an unprincipled rake, a scoundrel in short, to take advantage of his children's governess who could scarcely defend herself, slap his face, or make an outcry. If she did she would lose her job, and jobs were not so easy to find when you were young, pretty, and well taught.

Yet for a rake, for an unprincipled scoundrel, how tender and patient he had been with her! After that first kiss he had released her to go about her business as though it was normal practice to kiss when you met — almost she believed that it must be, so matter of fact was he. Yet with every stolen meeting his kisses led her further along the path that she would eventually tread with him, though she held out for two whole years before allowing him any other intimacy.

And even then, for a long time, though they lay together on her bed they both remained fully clothed, and nothing happened which could have made her ashamed or afraid. He knew, of course, that she was a virgin and he let her choose the pace at which their affair would proceed. It did not occur to her at the time that the pace was all she was allowed to set; he had made up his mind to seduce her, he told her when it was an accomplished fact, on that very first meeting in the darkened corridor, when he had kissed her with such gentle and loving thoroughness.

But she had not known that, she had just gradually grown totally dependent on his loving and his lovemaking. When, at last, lying on her bed one dark afternoon whilst his wife had tea with a friend and his children were busy with their work in the schoolroom, he had let her see that he would take her, must take her, could no longer bear their kissings, cuddlings and strokings which always ended in her soft denial, she had been, if the truth were known, as eager as he. Ripe for seduction these past six months, she had held out against him only for fear that he would take her and cast her aside, or find her less exciting, once he had possessed her, than in his longing imagination.

Their first lovemaking had been so exciting, so perfect, that to think of it could still bring the blood rushing to her cheeks and make her stomach clutch with remembered pleasure. She had feared surrender but when it came it was the most wonderful thing that had ever happened to her. And Tom, who was such a practical man, had sworn it was the same for him — perfection, utter and complete.

She had feared that her power over him, which made him agree to requests couched by her rather than by his wife and children, would wane once he had possessed her. It was quite otherwise; once she was his mistress he did everything in his power to please her. He wanted to be with her all the time. Often and often he would come sneaking into her room in his nightshirt, bare-legged, tumbling between the sheets for no more than a hot and feverish cuddle before he was tumbling out again to return to slumbering Olivia.

She marvelled at herself, for she was a Scarlet Woman, a sinner, an adulteress — or did one have to be married to commit adultery? — yet she felt so good! Round and sweet as a ripe apple, wanting to give, not just to him but to his family, she made their lives richer because of her happiness.

Now, lying in her soft bed, she knew that she had longed for a son because once she had a son, she was certain that Tom would not cast her off. It was not the security she wanted, it was the man. He was, quite simply, her life. Another woman's husband, the father of three beautiful daughters, he was still her life and without him she might as well be dead. But now! Ah, now he would never leave her, never go back to Olivia for good. Now she could stop worrying that one day the knocker would not rise and fall, the bell would not sound, and he would simply never step over the doorsill again, to hurry into her sitting room, take her in his arms, tell her how much he loved her.

No baby could matter to her the way Tom mattered. She had gone to old Agatha to try to get rid of the child within her

127

because she had thought he would cast her off, or hide her away somewhere until the baby was born and then perhaps not allow her to return to the Plas. She could not have borne being away from him for months – he said he loved her wildly, hopelessly, and she hoped it was true but she could never know for certain. All that she knew was how she loved him, and how he had sucked out her soul and mingled it with his, taken her body so that only to his body could it respond, had left her empty, a hollow, aching shell, without him.

He had promised her so many things if she gave him a boy! A dogcart and a pony to pull it; a nursemaid in a smart uniform to push the perambulator along the promenade; a full-time man of all work so that she would not have to do the garden, though as it happened she enjoyed planting, weeding and tidying her small, neat flower beds and lawn.

He had even said he would buy her a bigger house, but that was silly, because this house was perfect; just what she had always longed for without even knowing it until he had led her into it six months earlier. Small, square, sturdy, facing the sea front, it had a red-tiled roof, whitewashed walls and shutters painted blue with hearts cut out of them. It had a small front garden, a shrubbery at the side and a walled back garden where she had noticed such refinements as an espaliered peach tree, a number of blackcurrant bushes and a small but well-maintained greenhouse. It had two reception rooms, a modern kitchen, a scullery and, upstairs, three good-sized bedrooms. There was a bathroom with tiled walls and a deep enamelled bath and up a flight of rickety stairs a small, pointed attic room, warm in summer and chilly in winter, where the maid slept.

She often thought about Plas Tegydd and her charges there; and of silly, weak Olivia who had proved stronger than she had suspected in the end. She pitied them all, poor things, stuck out in the wilds in that great, chilly barn of a house in its huge, unmanageable grounds, with the mountains, which she had always feared a little, looming up behind it, a dramatic backdrop.

The girls would be all right, though. She had a conscience about the girls, because Tom had said girls had no right to land and all his property would go to the baby – if it was a boy. So by giving birth to her son she had effectively disinherited Kate, Alexandra and Dot. It would not affect Kate, she was sure. Lovely, wilful, rather nasty Kate would get a husband without any bother. A rich, handsome man, the sort of man she wanted. She would provide for herself, would Kate.

Alexandra, of course, was a different kettle of fish; she would attract men because her meekness and willingness to bow her head beneath the nearest available yoke would appeal to a good many men who secretly wanted to domineer and lay down the law to a lovely, none-too-bright wife. Her looks were not made the most of, but Blanche meant to see to it, through Tom, that Alex was dressed right, made desirable, before she was loosed upon an unprepared world.

And then there was Dot. Try as she might, Blanche could not help worrying over Dot. So small, so dark, so extremely plain! She wouldn't get a man unless she had a good dowry, and if a boy inherited it all who would see Dot safely married? Clever but not brilliant, she loved only the land and her home. What would she do when Tom broke it to her that he had a son who would inherit? He could give her money, of course . . . but did he have enough to buy a decent husband for an ugly little monkey of a daughter? Blanche doubted it. She really would have to do something for Dot!

Footsteps on the stairs broke into her thoughts. They were his, of course — quick, impetuous, like a boy's. She was smiling when he burst into the room, a huge bouquet of hothouse roses in his arms and a box of chocolates tied with blue ribbon dangling from his fingers. He kissed her, dropped the chocolates on her lap, thrust the roses into her arms and went at once to the cradle. The expression of doting fondness on his face was unmistakable.

'Hello, Tom junior,' he said, bending over and pulling the blankets down so that he could see the small, crumpled face. 'Tom, my lad, it's your da come to see you. Give us a smile, boy!'

Eight: 1917

Hywel and Stan slipped out of the house at five-thirty, because they were on the early shift, and made their way down the street in the starlight, heading towards the pit.

Above them the stars were paling, though it would be a good while yet before dawn came. September smells drifted to their nostrils: colouring leaves, the smoke of fires lit with sappy wood, even the scent of the dew which would be rising now. The houses they passed were silent, darkened, but now and then a door opened and a man stepped out to join the quiet procession making its way towards the colliery.

'A good day it'll be if this sky stays clear,' Stan remarked as their clogs clattered over the cobblestones. 'Thought I might go into town later. There's a play I wouldn't mind seeing. You and Jessica going out?'

'Jessica? She and I haven't been around together since she went to school at the convent.' Hywel glanced slyly at his brother. 'Why don't you ask Cerwyn? She'd like a bit of culture, I daresay.'

Cerwyn Edwards was a teacher at the village school; slim, straight-backed, with her hair in a tiny, hard little knot on top of her head and spectacles perched on her nose. She did her best to seem stern and authoritative, but it was an open secret that she was a gentle little thing really – and that Stan liked her. The trouble was that Stan was shy with girls and Cerwyn with men; Hywel could see that someone would have to do some pushing to get the couple together.

'Aye, I might. What I thought was ... ' Stan grinned shamefacedly at his brother. 'Well, I thought I'd make out I'd got two tickets and then say that Jess couldn't come wi' me, like, and ask Cerwyn if she'd enjoy a trip to the theatre.'

'Cunning blighter. So you want me to see that Jess doesn't blow the gaff? How?'

'Well, if you was to ask her to go up into the hills with you, like you used to, then it would be clear for me to tell any old story. See?'

'I could ask,' Hywel said doubtfully, 'but she'd say no. Even now Mam's working up at the Plas again Jessica steers clear of me. No, what you could do is ask Jess, but pretend I'm going along with you and one or two of the other lads . . . Duff and Porky, for instance. You'd be safe's houses then. You know what Mam thinks about her girl mixing with collier lads! So she'd say no, and you could go ahead and ask Cerwyn.'

'Aye.' Stan nodded. 'That 'ud work. Right; if you don't mind I'll do that. You could come and all, if you want,' he added hastily, making Hywel choke on a laugh.

'You're a mate! But it's all right. If it's fine I'm for the hills.'

'Right, if you're sure.' The two brothers were joined by others now as they neared the pit. Stan lowered his voice. 'If I didn't know better I'd wonder if you're meeting a gal, the way you're up to the tops at the drop of a hat.'

Hywel snorted. Did Stan suspect about Dot, or was it just a chance remark? Not that it mattered. He had been meeting Dot for years now and enjoying her company immensely, but there was nothing sloppy between them. She was a dear, but an odd little thing, looking no more than twelve though she was fifteen, dressing in her sister's castoffs which were always sizes too big, chopping at her hair when the fancy took her with what he suspected from the results achieved might be a pair of rather rusty shears. But you couldn't help liking her. She was so full of joy, always bubbling over with some plan or other.

He heard bits and pieces about her home life from Ella, who was quite talkative about her work up at the Plas – chiefly, he suspected, because she wanted to impress upon Jessica, who was a bit of a snob, that she was not a housemaid but more like a personal assistant to Olivia Tegydd.

'Told her when I started there I'd enough of my own scrubbing and laundering to do and didn't want no more,' Ella was wont to explain. 'So now it's Ella, tack up this flounce, dear, or Ella, could you whisk me up a nice little omelette for lunch, or Ella, I wouldn't trust anyone but you to polish the

131

small table in my boudoir, for it's worth a mint of money and belonged to my grandmother.

'Mind you, though she's good to me she might as well only have two daughters for all the care she lavishes on the little one,' she would go on. 'Better stuff on her back does my Jess have, and she just a collier's daughter, and more attention . . . well, little Dot runs wild. No lessons, no entertainment, no care whatsoever. Yet there isn't a soul in the house who wouldn't bend over backwards to please her. Sweet, she is, and caring. Which is more than you can say for the other two. A shame that she'll never have a chance to do well, with no schooling. Not like our Jessica, as I'm always telling Mrs Tegydd. Our Jessica will go far.

It had been decided long ago that Jessica's brains would not be wasted. Not for her a job behind the counter in Woolworths or working at the pit-head. No, she was to go to University, get a degree, and then teach. Or possibly even go for a doctor.

The men, surging together as the colliery gates were reached, greeted one another quietly. Stan was a hewer now and Hywel filled for him. They were a good team and produced plenty of coal. But Hywel, although he was heading for the pit as fast as his clogs would carry him, was not thinking about work. Because of Stan's words his mind was on the distant hills. He was anticipating his afternoon up on the tops if this day kept its present fair promise. He had it in mind to take his ferrets up to the birch pasture, where the trees grew on the steep slope amongst the tumbled rocks and fast-flowing streams. Here there were a great many rabbit burrows and his jills usually managed to catch at least one animal for the pot.

It was here, too, that he met Dot. She understood that he caught rabbits for food, though it was an excuse to be out in the countryside, as much as anything, instead of digging in the garden, going to chapel or visiting the town. She did not mind his ferreting for rabbits. All farmers considered them pests. They ate the corn – not that Tegydd was growing corn right now – and nibbled the spring crops and ruined banks and hedges. And foxes, which came after the rabbits, strayed into the farmyard and did untold damage there. Only recently a vixen had got into the yard and killed, for sheer spite, half a dozen plump Rhode Island Reds, which had considerably diminished her flock, and had then mauled and left for dead two of the big White Leghorns which laid such large, dark brown eggs. So killing rabbits for the pot was a good idea, and since no one else fished for the dark brown freshwater trout he was welcome to them too, and if he did not pick the mushrooms and the berries and the nuts they would only rot on their stalks.

Once, Hywel gathered from his stepfather's talk, Tom Tegydd had kept his land with jealous care, and then it would not have been all right at all to take his rabbits or his trout. He would not have minded if Hywel had hunted the tops, but he would not have thought much of seeing a collier lad pulling trout out of the stream no more than a half a mile from Plas Tegydd, nor of seeing him bring down the odd pheasant. But now he did not care what you did on Tegydd land, for it was only the pits that mattered, the pits that brought the money in. Furthermore, there was talk that Marmy Carruthers was thinking of selling the Wynd and it was an open secret that Tegydd wanted to buy. He had a stake in the area and wanted to join up the two pits underground, for the safety of them both. Bad management, Tegydd said, had made a bad pit, and with good management and money spent the Wynd could be as good a pit as the Olwen and the Roland. But old colliers shook their heads; the Wynd was a bad pit with a wicked past and a worse future, they said. A deep pit, where the heat was all but unendurable and the air thick with gas. A wet pit, where you could find yourself working up to your waist in water because the seams had been dug in a hurry and the pit props not used decently, step by step, as their own pit props were used. But perhaps Tegydd would not buy. Perhaps he would leave ill alone and concentrate on the Olwen pit and on his vast tracts of land. No one could tell what the owner thought; they dug his coal for him, poached his rabbits and took his trout, and waited. It was all they could do.

Hywel knew that things were not good at the Plas. Dot never said much but he knew she grieved over her father's lack of interest in his land. For all she was only a girl she was a real farmer, with her innate knowledge of what was right and what was wrong with the sort of farming her father was doing now. She had nagged her father about silage; he had given up on it but from her reading she could see that it could be put right instead of simply leaving the silage pits, built at some expense before she was born, to crumble away. She nagged him to buy new machinery – indeed, just to buy machinery – but he would have none of it. Perhaps, in her heart, she was glad, for she loved the horses and the old men who were left had no desire to learn to drive a tractor – they could make a straighter furrow with a good horse and an old hand plough.

'Morning, Hywel, mun.'

Hywel, deep in his thoughts as he stood in line for his lamp, jumped at hearing himself addressed. He turned to grin at Porky, now square rather than plump, standing in line behind him.

'Hello, Porky – you on Queen seam today?'

It was a rhetorical question, really, since Porky filled for Bunny Cross, a square-jawed, square-shouldered man in his forties who was reputed to get more coal per shift than any other single getter. Being his filler, therefore, was no sinecure. Instead of shovelling about twelve tons of coal per shift you probably shovelled fourteen, but it was all money and Porky could take it. I can too, Hywel reminded himself, because when the cutting was easy and the coal decided to oblige, Stan could shift as much as Bunny.

'There you are, lad.' Hywel's filled and lit lamp was put in his hand and the fireman jotted down the amount of oil so that it could be charged against Hywel's pay. The brothers got into the cage, underwent the ritual search for matches, and then heard the bars clang shut and felt the cage begin its descent.

Here we go again, Hywel thought as the darkness closed in and the heat gradually increased. Fingers in ears, he shut out the noise and the speed of movement, until the men began to file out of the cage at the pit bottom. Here the men joked and chatted quietly before dispersing to their various seams. Hywel tried to grow accustomed to the feeling that he was here again, infinitely small and very tender, a creature so wonderfully frail that the great earth around him could crush him in a second, for no reason other than that his presence was irksome, a tickle in its ribs, which one small shift of its mighty rock shoulders could ease for ever.

He thought he could not be the only man present who

suffered this oppression, but no one else seemed to mind. They just chatted, shifted their feet, joked, and waited for their eyes to become accustomed to the dark before drifting off to their respective jobs. You got no money for talking or walking so everyone was eager to get to his stall or face or whatever, but of course it was not just walking; for the majority of them it would be a slithering crawl downhill for the best part of the way, and a slow slither too, with men before and behind, the first holding you up and the second hastening you on.

Despite Hywel's secret conviction that it was the slowest journey ever to the face, they reached it at the usual time and Stan got to work immediately, as did all the other hewers. Tools were unlocked from the bar that kept them safe from other shifts, and a quick, keen-eyed glance in the faint lamp-light was sufficient to see just what had happened since you were here last. Stan slid into his place and at once you could hear the ring and clatter of his pick and the crump of his hammer. The coal came down, Hywel began to swing his big, heavy shovel, the lad working the haulage pushed the tub nearer so that Hywel could fill it the sooner, and another working day had begun.

For a time Hywel worked steadily and almost without thinking of anything beyond the rhythm of the work. Sometimes he found working was good for thinking, but sometimes the thoughts would not come – or not the welcome sort, at any rate. He could not let his mind wander without having frightening ideas – the weight of the rock above him, the way it would feel, crushing down on his head and shoulders, should there be a fall. On days like that he remembered his father's death, imagined he could smell gas, forgot to keep his shoulders down and constantly knocked the vertebrae of his back against the low roofs until the blood stuck to his shirt. On those days he got trodden on by pit ponies, put his foot in excreta and could not see to get it off properly, laid his snap down for a moment without replacing it in its tin and consequently lost it to mice or rats. He usually had a minor accident at such times so that his lamp went out, forcing him to take the long walk back to the pit's eye in the dark so that the lamp could be relit from the fireman's battery. It was horrible, making your way along the narrow seams without light, hitting your head, barking your shoulders against the walls, filled with panic in case you had stumbled into a drift tunnel which had not proved fruitful and would eventually come to a dead end. Pictures of himself, wild-eyed and bearded down to his knees, still lost in the dark in twenty years, might be funny in the broad light of day, but when your lamp was out and you were halfway back to the pit bottom there was just enough gruesome possibility in them to make you wish you'd broken the rules and secreted a match in a jacket seam or the innermost corner of a pocket.

But such days usually manifested themselves early; they were, Hywel thought, one of the reasons for the high rate of absenteeism in the pits. Though he himself usually closed his mind to outside happenings on his way to work, many a miner had turned back because of some rootless, superstitious fear that if he went down the pit that day it would be his last. To meet a woman was considered unlucky by some; others never worked on the thirteenth day of the month, on the day before a family birthday, or on the day someone had been killed or badly injured on the previous shift. It was unlucky to whistle below ground, though you could sing – preferably something religious.

Hywel hated what he called the bad days, but he did not think them unlucky. They were just bad days; he assumed everyone had them. His mother often grumbled that nothing had gone right – her bread had not risen or Mrs Dafydd had got her loaves in early when it had been Ella's turn to go first. The washing had boiled over, or the line had broken and six clean sheets had got mired, or the children had come in from school and eaten all the new bread, or . . . the list could go on and on, on a bad day.

The kids had them too, up and down the street; on the day your favourite hoop disintegrated you could be sure you'd split a clog or get a whipping for work carelessly done, or fall and scrape both knees so that you were left out of the football team. And even girls were liable to bad days; when Jessica missed the bus into town and had to walk to school she got a conduct mark because she was late, and because she had hurried she lost her hair ribbon and was told off for untidiness and dropped her snap crossing the schoolyard and so couldn't eat it, though she was hungry, for fear her friends would despise one who ate food that was not strictly clean and germ-free.

But Hywel was sure, quite soon, that this was not going to be a bad day; quite the opposite, in fact. As he worked a feeling of peacefulness possessed him, and he knew that if he toiled quietly and without interruption he would presently find himself in another place. The Other Place, he called it to himself, because it had been his escape and delight ever since he had started to work below. The Other Place did not open its doors to him because he wanted to go there; it was the one who chose to take him in, not vice versa. He sometimes thought that the more he longed for it the less likely he was to arrive on those flat, sky-reflecting marshes.

It was odd, how he loved it, how totally at home he felt there. Sometimes when he was there it was bitterly cold, the marshes snow-covered, the dykes iced over. A cruel wind swept in from the sea and his fingers and toes ached with the chill. Yet he was always happy there.

He knew it well, now; though he could not go there when he wanted to do so he could imagine it. He did so now, seeing the skeins of wild duck against an evening sunset, the rapid scuddings of the clouds in a mackerel sky, the dance of the gnats on hot summer evenings when they hovered above every oozing patch of marsh-water.

He always saw the cottage but he had never been in it, not even into the garden. There were geese outside it, not actually in the garden, he had discovered, but in a piece of pasture next to the house. There were hens, too; brown ones – Rhode Island Reds, he suspected from his own experience of poultry – and lately he had seen a number of tiny bantams. He thought the girl kept them – there was a girl outside sometimes who was about his own age.

He loved that cottage, and longed passionately to be able to go through the door, to see if it was as attractive as it appeared from his usual vantage point of several hundred yards away. Sometimes he saw the woman of the house putting her washing out or digging potatoes or gathering plums or apples from the rather stunted fruit trees which grew close to the cottage wall. She reminded him of his mother but he knew that this was wishful thinking, because he could tell that the dream-woman, the woman in the Other Place, was a loving mother and he had somehow managed to convince himself that she would love him if only they could meet. His mother had never loved him; that was a fact of life. He got along all right, tried at least not to annoy her, kept his constant longing for affection hidden. It was easier now he was a man grown, of course; no one expected a mother to show love for a son of seventeen. But it had hurt him when she had seemed to turn Jessica against him. He told himself that it was not deliberate, that she was merely making Jessica see that if she wanted to become a young lady, like her new friends at the convent school, she had better not hang around with a collier lad. But . . . it had seemed, at the time, as though she could not even bear him to have someone on his side.

His shovel scraping on the ground as it gathered up the last few pieces of the coal Stan was pushing back to him reminded him that there were sounds in the Other Place but that he never seemed able to speak or to call out. He had stopped wondering whether it was only a dream or not; it was too good, too precious, to try to analyse. He was just grateful for it, longing for its coming, mourning its going.

Stan's pick swung and dug out a narrow cleft into which he forced one of his wedges. It was quite a decent face, this; Stan was working on his knees, not flat on his side. He could get a good swing with the big hammer and now he did so, before beginning to force another wedge in a bit further along. Presently he moved back, ready to deliver the final blow which would bring the coal tumbling. He struck, hard and true, and the great lumps bounced down, sending the men back several feet before Hywel moved in with his shovel and began the smooth, rhythmic movement which he could keep going for hours, the shovel loaded at each swing to its maximum capacity.

Stan grunted and began to hammer another wedge; the lad began to push the loaded tub up the incline; Hywel worked on, his mind waiting, trancelike, for what he hoped was to come.

When the dream came, it was shocking in its difference. The

wind was howling and the cold was intense, despite the thick clothing that Hywel found himself wearing. He was standing on a small area of floor with a fence round him and outside the fence roared and leapt the ocean. He had never been to sea but he knew from distant glimpses at the Other Place that this was the ocean. Waves, green and white, shining and malignant, reared high above the fence, threatened him, blew spume into his face and then sank harmlessly away as the ship plunged, waiting for the next.

Ship? Now that he was over his first surprise he could see that he was on a ship. The floor was the deck and the fence was the ship's rail. Hywel looked around him and wet sprayed him in the face; he licked his lips and they tasted salt. Yes, he was on board ship all right, and behind him was an edifice which he knew or guessed to be the bridge, from which the captain sailed the ship. Looking closer, he saw that all over the ship was equipment which looked vaguely familiar: winding gear, a mass of tarred netting, pulleys. They were familiar because a collier spends a lot of his life being wound down to his work in the cage and wound up again. He walked unsteadily over to the rail and leaned against it, looking down at the fearsome sea and trying to understand just why he was here. This was real, as real as the Other Place, yet obviously it was simply another dream. What did it mean? Why was he here? How could he escape and return to his beloved marshes?

He considered his surroundings. He could feel, through the planks of the deck, the throb of engines below. He looked again at the tangle of equipment and knew that he was on a fishing trawler. He was alone on the deck and it occurred to him that he had probably come up here in order to be alone; below there would be other men, deckhands, engineers, fishermen. He was a person used to solitude. Coming from the marshes as he did he must need it, so he had sought the deck, away from the fug of warmth and food and people which would seem so stifling after a while.

Hywel closed his eyes for a moment, trying to ignore the bucking of the ship and the wail of the gulls soaring above, knifing through the grey sky. When he opened them again he half-expected to find the marsh spread out before him, with a beast's rump no more than a stone's throw away and the smell of the land blending with the salty freshness of the distant sea. The gulls strengthened the impression because they were always on the marshes, particularly when you were ploughing on the leys. But when he opened his eyes the scene was the same. No glinting, many-coloured marsh, no silver line on the horizon that was the sea, no cottage cuddled down low with its thatch pulled down over its eyes against the steady wind. Just the tossing, restless waves and the small deck, the rail which was no protection and the wind singing in the rigging, the engine throbbing beneath his sea boots, the cold biting at his nose, which had somehow managed to escape from the muffler that was pulled right up to his eyes.

Cautiously, against the ship's pitch and toss, Hywel went over to the nearest hatchway, pondered going below and undoubtedly breaking the dream, and then went, instead, back to the rail. Below him the sea swelled, a peculiarly light and translucent green, against the grimy black of the ship's side. Looking ahead, he saw that they were about to run into fog; it lay banked up like a milky white curtain except that, already, fingers of that curtain were reaching out to the ship.

A deep, echoing boom rang out; he guessed that it must be the foghorn. He turned to see whence the sound had come even as a hatchway lifted and an oilskinned figure emerged. Hywel went towards the man. Would he, in these changed circumstances, have a chance to speak to another human being? He realised that this was the first time, in any of his extraordinarily vivid dreams of the Other Place, that someone had come within speaking distance.

The man looked up as Hywel approached and despite the huge muffler Hywel could see the grin start to form, pushing up his cheeks and narrowing his eyes. He opened his mouth but no words came out. The mist, which had been no more than a cloudy breath between them, suddenly seemed much thicker. Thicker yet it grew and still thicker, and then it was black, completely black . . . and then he was bending to his shovel over a glinting pile of coal, back in his own body right down to the familiar gnawing ache across the shoulders which said it was time to stop for a drink of cold tea and some snap. He glanced down at himself; stripped to the waist, his body gleamed with sweat and his clogs had managed to rub a blister on one heel.

All through the dream, he knew that he had continued to swing his shovel. He never knew how long he spent at the Other Place, though he thought that sometimes an hour there was no more than a second or two here. Yet even in that second to go to the Other Place calmed him, filled his mind with peace and hope. Odd that he should feel like that now, because the deck of the ship had been strange to him, even rather frightening. Yet he, who had scarcely seen the sea except in dreams, had felt perfectly at home and even happy on the deck of a small ship, pitching and tossing remorselessly on an alien sea.

'How about a break, mun?' Stan's coal-grimed face split into a grin as he saw his brother nod thankfully. He wiped his sweating face on his arm and backed out of his place, leaning his pick and hammer against the pile of coal. 'A worker you are, mun; never thought you'd shift that lot! Glad of a drink I'll be though.'

'Me too.' Hywel propped his shovel against the wall of the tunnel and picked up his tin. He opened it and felt saliva rush to his mouth at the sight of cold pork and pickled onion butties. Lovely stuff Mam put in their tins, not old rubbish like some got. There was a wedge of fruit cake too, and the bottle of cold tea, which you cursed for its weight and awkwardness all the way down the tunnels on your way to work, was the best of all. No sugar in it, nor milk neither, because what you needed was the slightly bitter thirst-quenching tea itself, to keep you going and to keep replacing what you sweated until you were on land again. Then you could go to the pump and pump yourself a few pints of lovely, ice-cold water, or you could go down to the pub on the corner for a tankard of beer. As Glyn did. Hywel sighed at the recollection of his step-father's weakness, but it wasn't as though Glyn drank too much; it was just that he couldn't let an evening go by without making his way to the Black Horse for a bit of company, a pint or two, and a chat with his mates.

Ella did not like it, but she was sensible enough to realise that it was a weakness that Glyn would not conquer, even if he could. And he was a good husband to her. Hywel had heard from the older boys that Glyn had not always been so, but for years now he had treated Ella like a most precious possession and that was good enough for Hywel. Glyn was kind to the boys, as well, though you could tell from the way he looked at her that he thought Jessica a cut above his stepsons. As she was, Hywel though loyally; lovely girl, Jess. Well, not lovely, precisely, for she was too thin and bony and red-haired ever to qualify for a beauty prize, but she was nice, and many a beauty could not boast that.

All around them men were leaving their work and taking up their snap tins. Hywel squatted down and uncorked his tea and took a swig. It was wonderful, he considered, how most of the men managed to guess at the time even if they did not have watches, so that you could bank on the fact that round about now the whole mine would be free from the ring of the picks and the hammers, free from the scrape and shuffle of shovels, and would only resound to quiet talk, laughter, and munching.

The ponies, too, would be getting their drinks now; he had worked with the ponies for a while when he first came down and liked them, enjoyed remembering how their velvet-soft muzzles would dip below the surface of the water to drink from deeper down; how they would nuzzle into the mangers of food, trying to clear it of the beetles which bred so freely in the dark.

Thinking of the ponies made him remember the mice and rats. They would see it was snap-time and they would be lurking somewhere, just out of lamp-range, bright-eyed, eager, knowing that when the men returned to work there would be a crust thrown down, a few crumbs, a drop or two of cold tea spilt in haste. Hywel himself always left a bite for the mice and he knew that at least half his companions did the same. Bad enough it was to have to come down here for an eight-hour shift. How much worse to be stranded in the pit, through no fault of your own, for a lifetime!

'What are you doing this afternoon, Howie?' That was Porky, eating a huge sandwich which, judging by the smell, was liberally filled with raw onion. 'I'm for town, me.'

'The hills,' Hywel said through a mouthful of pork and pickle. 'Get myself a rabbit or two and some mushrooms, I daresay.'

142

'I get a good long sleep of a Sat'day,' remarked Bunny, devouring a chunk of bread as big as a doorstep with a wedge of white goat's cheese on top. 'First I 'as a bath, 'ot as my old woman can make it. Then I downs a pint, cold as cold. Then I rolls on to the sofa in the front room and snores for five hours solid.'

'And then you go down to the pub for a few more pints and another five hours' sleep,' Porky said, grinning. 'Oh, I've heard about you, Bunny!'

'Me, sleep at the Black 'orse? Never!' protested Bunny. 'Who's been telling you tales, eh?' You're never down there yourself to see.'

'Five-pints,' retorted Porky. Five-pints was the potman at the Black Horse and a crony of Porky's. 'Tells me a lot of things, does Five-pints.'

'Well, he tells you lies,' grumbled Bunny, unwrapping another half-loaf of his wife's good bread. 'Say anything to make folk stare, that feller would. Why, tol' me a week or so back that he'd seen Stan there hobnobbing in the village street with the owner's gal.'

In the faint light from their lamps it was not easy to catch a change of expression, but Hywel could see that his brother had flushed darkly. Stan snorted into his handkerchief to give himself time, Hywel suspected, to think up a story, and then nodded, trying to look offhand.

'Oh aye, I remember. Passed the time of day we did and what harm, even if she does happen to be Miss Tegydd of the Plas?'

'Well I'm damned. I'd never have thought it,' Porky said, winking at Hywel. 'What would a lovely gal like Miss Kate want to hobnob with a collier for, then? Not as I've anything against Stan. He's a good hewer, I'm told, but not exactly one of the gentry.' Porky put on what he fondly imagined to be a high-class English accent. 'Oh I say, old fellow, what's it like working down Daddy's coalmine? Is it ever so dark? That must be jolly for you chaps!'

'She said nothing of the sort, mun,' Stan assured them, emerging from behind his protective handkerchief. 'Asked me if I'd seen her da she did, so I told her he'd gone into the manager's office but would be out in a bit. She stood there, staring at the door and then at me, and so I told her to step inside there, out of the cold. And she said she was quite snug in her big coat and fur mittens so long as she kept moving and could she come with me into the village, just to keep her blood circulating. I laughed and she laughed and she walked into the village with me and then I walked back to the colliery with her, and just as we came abreast of the manager's office her da came out and off she went with him, after saying goodbye to me civil as you please.'

'What did you talk about, mun, whilst you walked?' Alf, another hewer, said curiously. He was a married man with a string of small children and a tiny, precocious child-wife who was thought, with a certain amount of reason, to be fast. Certainly she bred fast, for though she was not yet twenty-one she had mothered a babe every twelvemonth for the past five years; and given the eye to half the village, Ella said contemptuously, and she only hoped that was all she gave. But Alf never heard the rumours and seemed very happy with his seductive little wife and his tiny, active children. He certainly worked hard to support them, for in addition to hewing coal eight hours a day six days a week he kept a horse and cart in which he did furniture removals, carted pigs and undertook any form of work which could be carried out on a Sunday or after four in the afternoon. No wonder he's so skinny, the villagers said, eyeing his large brood, his bedroom-eyed wife and his horse and cart!

But Stan took his question seriously.

'What did we talk about? Why, all sorts. Why her mare gets saddle galls during the autumn, why she won't ride her near the standing stones up on the Maidens ridge, why some clouds bring rain whilst others don't. Commonplace, mostly.'

'Sounds odd. Me and the missus don't talk none of that,' Alf said dubiously. There was ribald laughter at this from two of the younger men, one of whom could not resist the obvious.

'Don't 'ave much time for talk, mun. You're too busy getting yourself another youngster to feed.'

Alf, an easy-going chap, laughed too, but a couple of the older men looked shocked. Loose talk was not encouraged down the pit. God was too near and a neat method of stopping mouths too close at hand. They all think He could strike you dead and bury you neat in one quick movement, Hywel thought, and was shocked at his own flippancy. But as if the Lord would mind them having a bit of a joke with Alf!

'Well, all I can say is, no knowing what your mates get up to these days.' Bunny finished off his last bite of bread, save for a luck-piece which he slung furtively into the darkness, and got to his feet. 'Stan'll be lord of the manor yet, eh, Hywel? What do you think, having a brother who hobnobs with the owner's gal? Not like you, eh, boyo? There's Stan meeting Miss Kate and you meeting a couple of rabbits when her da's back's turned.'

Fortunately at this point Stan decided he had had enough ribbing and began to collect his tin and cork his bottle, getting to his feet as he did so. 'Come on, mun, back to work,' he said, handing Hywel his shovel. And thus everyone was spared the sight of Hywel giggling behind his hand over Bunny's words.

For it had occurred to Hywel as Bunny spoke that he, the youngster of the family, had been hobnobbing with the owner's gal for years and years, ever since he had started work in the pit. Dot was just as much the owner's gal as Kate, even though the villagers did not seem to see it like that. It was she who helped him to set his ferrets at the holes, she who sat chattering beside him as he fished for trout, she who would spot the mushrooms lurking in the long grass at the edge of the pasture and bring them to him to put in his handkerchief.

Not that he had any illusions about Dot. She was the owner's daughter, but she was not treated like his daughter, nor did she act like a member of the gentry. She was not even Miss Dot to most of the men but just Dot, or the littl'un.

Hywel thought that perhaps it was because Dot was so neglected, so little regarded, that he and she got on so well. Ella, working at the Plas, was sorry for Dot. Olivia Tegydd never troubled to hide her indifference to the child and Tom was downright unkind. He called her a dwarf, a gnome, an ugly changeling, and pushed her away when he should have let her draw near. Ella obviously saw no parallel between her son and Tom's daughter – and perhaps it was as well that she did not.

Hywel wondered that her sisters did not take Dot's part more, but to be fair to them Dot never showed the slightest desire to be treated other than as she was at present. She roamed the countryside and the farmland, leggy, wild and undisciplined. Hywel did not think her pretty but he knew that she was neither ugly nor a dwarf; she had big dark eyes with curly lashes, even if her nose was a blob and her mouth on the large side. She should not be called a gnome, though he had to agree that there was something elfish about her. It was a quality of tiptoe expectancy, a wide-eyed waiting for something wonderful to happen which made him think of pixies. She was no longer a child despite being so small and slight. She read long books, used long words, and seemed to be a considerable authority on any type of farming, so that was not why he thought her elfish. It was . . . confound it, he did not *know* what it was. He just knew she was a nice little beggar, a friendly, confiding kid, and he was damned if they treated her as they should. Why shouldn't she have fine clothes and dancing lessons and a place in the carriage when the older girls went to parties? They should let her hair grow so that she could sweep it up into a froth of curls on the crown of her head to give her height, and they should take her about more, let her meet people, allow her to prove herself an intelligent and witty young woman and not the wild child people thought her.

Yet he knew that he did not really want any of these things to come about. Oh, they would happen in due course, and it was right that they should; and when they did he would lose his friend. For the time being, before they decided to start turning her into a young lady, she was his friend and companion, the perfect person to be with, undemanding, amusing, partisan. Whilst he had Dot, he wanted no other. She would become Miss Tegydd soon enough, and without any encouragement from him.

146

Nine

Dot climbed doggedly up the lane, passing by all the temptations, because today she had a definite purpose in mind. The war was over and it had at last impressed itself upon her that her father had not the least intention of spending the money necessary to bring the estate, and Plas Tegydd itself, back into good heart. For years he had blamed the war, for years he had explained that the country needed coal, and now they were in the depression and it seemed that, with no one needing coal, it was even more impossible to spend on the land.

Everyone knew that it was true: the price of coal was dropping and wages must drop to meet them. But although the colliers earned good money, it was for working as hard as a man can work, in fearful conditions, for as long as a man can work. If they wanted them to work longer hours, for less money . . .

She was sorry for all of them: Hywel, her dear friend, his brothers, his father, even his mother, the woman with the grey-gold hair who worked for Olivia at the Plas. But she was sorrier for the land and the men who worked it. Their wages had never been fair. It seemed that there was no such thing as 'good money' for an agricultural worker, and what was more their hours were sinfully long. In the summer the men worked from dawn until it was too dark to see and in the winter half of them did nothing at all because there was no work for them – and no pay, either. How they kept going she did not know. You could not blame the young men for going to the pits. And now, unless things began to improve, working in the pits was not going to bring in the fabled 'good money' which had been the sole incentive for working there.

Lately, she had been forced to think more about her own

position. It had been impossible to continue to think that her lot would improve. She faced and acknowledged the fact that ever since Edie had left her father's interest in herself had gradually faded, until he had become as indifferent to her welfare as her mother was. Alexandra was not the girl to notice. Kate, though she had her failings, would have. But Kate was a married lady now, living in Liverpool with her shipping magnate husband.

She had caught him almost without parental help, too, had clever, ingenious Kate. She had wheedled and persuaded her mother to take her to visit her relatives on the Wirral – just for a week or two, so that she could see them and they her – and during the course of a shopping trip to Liverpool she had caught a glimpse – just a glimpse – of an incredibly handsome young man shopping with a beautiful young woman in Lewis's store.

Most girls would have seen how very beautiful the young woman was, envied her the young man and passed on; not Kate! Kate knew she must seize her opportunities, for no one else was likely to help her. She had been nineteen, extremely inexperienced, extremely unsophisticated. She knew no one in Liverpool who might effect an introduction and was unaccompanied in the big shop save by her mother. But did Kate allow any of this to daunt her? Certainly not!

She had made her way with quiet determination to the counter where the young woman and her escort were examining gloves, and had turned to her mother and said, with ferocity, 'Mother, I am about to faint; be sure you beg that young man to help you.' She had actually indicated the young man she had in mind with a jerk of the thumb.

And then she had fainted. Very beautifully, very elegantly, and almost at the young man's feet; indeed, as she squinted through her long lashes the things nearest her nose – perilously near, she told Dot later – were his highly polished black walking shoes.

It not only worked, it worked like a charm. The young man introduced himself and his sister, and insisted on putting Mrs Tegydd and her child – overcome by the heat – into his very own limousine and taking her back to his father's huge, beturreted house in Crosby where Kate, coming round, very nearly fainted in earnest when she beheld the splendours of the Macmillan mansion.

Being Kate, once she was sure he was interested, she admitted frankly that she had fainted in the store because she had been fascinated by him and had wanted to get to know him. Possibly he was used to female adoration, but certainly not to such female frankness. Then Kate had laughed, and he had laughed too, and she had known, she told Dot, that it was only a matter of time before he wanted her just as much as she wanted him. ,

Dot had never known just what Kate meant by that last sentence. There was little doubt that what Kate had wanted had been a handsome husband, security, and freedom from the stultifying life-style of Plas Tegydd. Dot, looking at her sister's lovely figure, which even the work of a village dressmaker could not spoil, and at that heart-shaped face lit by big, sparkling blue eyes, thought that she could make a very good guess at what was on John Macmillan's mind when he looked at her, but she did not think it was the same feeling at all as that which had made Kate do what she did.

Alexandra was engaged to be married to a neighbour, Humphrey Stott, so she took only the most casual interest in her young sister, and none at all in the fate of Plas Tegydd. She might have done so, for Humphrey was certainly interested in it; he had made it plain that if he ever had the chance he would take in Tegydd's acres with the greatest of pleasure. Dot had heard him discussing it once.

'The house and outbuildings are falling down and must be discounted,' he had said authoritatively. 'But the land could graze more sheep than it does at present, or even more beeves.'

He had said it, fortunately, to Alexandra and not to her father; Alex, who knew nothing and cared less about farming, had murmured that no doubt he knew best, but Dot, who did know about farming, was appalled. If Father knew — and she must make sure he did — there was little chance of Humphrey ever getting his hands on the Plas. Though Father might be — was — neglectful, he would never see his home brought to dust.

Or would he? But it did not bear thinking about, so Dot put it out of her head, and might not have been climbing the lane today but for a chance remark overheard in town the previous week when she had gone to buy some more day-old chicks to rear as layers.

The market was always crowded but that day it had been packed, because there was a horse sale and that always attracted a number of people who did not normally bother to come. Digging her way through the broad and tweedy backs of a dozen farmers, she had heard the words quite distinctly, though she could not, in the crush, see who had spoken.

'. . . over the mountain, above the Tegydd place,' the voice had said. 'God, a revelation it was, mun, coming down that lane and seeing the house clearer and clearer. What's Tom thinking of, to let the place go like that? Not a whole roof, I shouldn't wonder, curtains in rags, stock thin on the ground. All I could do not to rub my eyes and think I was dreaming when I remembered it in old Tom's day. By God, but a generation of Tegydds would turn in their graves like spinning tops if they could see what young Tom has been doing.'

'Or what he's not been doing,' someone else said, in a voice slow and heavy with condemnation. 'All that new machinery for the pits -- though the men don't like it and it doesn't make more money for him -- and that fancy woman of his costing a pretty penny, and now gathering himself together to pick up the Wynd . . .'

But Dot had wriggled on towards the poultry, not wanting to hear more. A fancy woman? But that she dismissed with contempt; she had little doubt that the fellow was right and Father did have a woman somewhere -- God knew there could be little comfort in Mother these days, obsessed as she was with food and with her health -- but it wasn't the reason why her father no longer even bothered to keep up appearances at Plas Tegydd. Was it as bad as the unknown speaker had implied, though, or had he been exaggerating? There was only one way to find out, and as soon as she had time -- for she was working harder now than she had ever done, trying to keep some semblance of order in the house without altogether neglecting the farm -- she would go up to the tops and see for herself.

And at last she was right on the top, the keen wind bringing tears to her eyes and the country spread out before her like a map, beautiful even when there was no sunshine, when the sky overhead was as grey as her mood.

And there, of course, was Plas Tegydd; tiny and seemingly perfect with its domes, weathercocks and tiled roofs standing out against the colours of the dying summer. Yet from here it was possible to see that the land was not as it should be. A few beef cattle, but ground which had been ploughed and had borne good crops gone back to nature, and pasture, neglected, given over to weeds and nettles, with the wicked brambles rampant and great clumps of ragwort triumphantly stealing all the goodness from the ground.

Father said there weren't the men to keep the pastures tidy; he said the stock would do the work for them when he could afford to buy more stock, in the spring, maybe. Maybe not, Dot thought grimly, staring down. Maybe never, not whilst her father was in charge. He must know in his heart what she knew with the whole of her mind – that pasture did not grow good of itself. You had to feed it, fettle it, dig out the bad things to make way for the good. If rabbits ate the young corn you repaired your fencing and took the guns out for an afternoon's sport. You didn't shrug, sigh, and stop growing cereals! When the price of beef dropped, as it was dropping at the moment, you looked for an alternative. You didn't just let your beef herd shrink to only a couple of dozen sad-looking beasts.

Going down the mountain was not the pleasure it had once been when through every gap in the wild and tangled hedge you saw nothing but neglect. When, as you dropped lower, the holes in the roof were easier to see, the rags of curtains at the windows more like cries of reproach, the weathercocks them- selves, their brightness dimmed, seemingly tired of their high perches so that of the four of them three were at half-cock, no longer capable of spinning with the wind.

Plas Tegydd was crying out for help, Dot felt, and she was powerless to give it! What could she do, a girl, plain as a boot and uneducated into the bargain? She would ask Hywel and see if he could think of something. They were meeting later in the day and she would put it to him that unless they could think of a way out Humphrey would probably get the land, raze the house to the ground . . .

Her thoughts stopped short, with an almost physical pain at the idea of being torn from her home. What would she do?

What could she do, come to that? Become a governess? She, whose education had stopped abruptly when she was twelve years old? She probably knew less than the village girls and they never became governesses. Would her father leave her money, or some sort of home, if he was to die tomorrow and if he had already willed the Plas away? Or would he expect Kate or Alexandra to give her a home?

I'd die, rather, she found herself thinking. I'd die rather than leave this place! Cooped up with Kate or Alexandra, unable to leave the house without explaining where I was going and why . . . it would kill me.

By the time she reached this conclusion, she had also reached the stableyard. She looked around her slowly, seeing, as if for the first time, the grass growing between the cobbles, the tall weeds on the midden, the doors, hingeless, propped up in doorways, the gates which no one attempted to open any more but merely climbed over or pushed aside.

She could not bear it. She turned away and ran, ran as fast as she could, down the hill, away from the house. She ran blindly partly because of the tears which coursed down her cheeks and partly because she did not want to see where she went. Into the river, flat on her face . . . what difference did it make if they were going to let her home die of neglect?

When she ran up against someone, when arms went round her and a rough jersey touched her cheek, it was as if she had come home. She hugged Hywel with abandon, breathless and gasping with running and weeping, lightheaded from misery and lack of oxygen.

'Hey, hey, Dot, what's the matter? Come on, you can tell me, love!' He had never sounded more her friend. He was so solid, so reliable, so safe! She wept a little more, into his jersey, and then felt a fraud as her breathing gradually returned to normal and her tears dried. She was crying before she was beaten – she only had to ask Hywel and he would think of a plan!

'I'll tell you. But let's go up to the birch pasture first.'

They walked slowly in the soft autumn sunshine. In the birch pasture the leaves were yellowing but had not yet begun to fall and the moss on the boulders made a comfortable seat. They sat, and Dot told Hywel everything, as she had done before. Simply, truthfully, her thoughts, her fears, what she had heard at the market, what she had seen for herself, what she believed might happen in the future.

Hywel listened without interruption, as he always did. And then he seized on a point that Dot had not considered.

'Why do you reckon he'll leave the Plas to Kate or Alexandra, and not to you? After all, if you aren't going to get married then you're the obvious choice. It would mean there would still be a Tegydd at the Plas, someone he knows understands it.'

'Oh, Hywel, if only he would! B-but he doesn't like me much, you know.'

'So you say. Is he any fonder of Kate? Or Alex?'

'No, I don't believe he is; I think he'd only like sons, and he hasn't got any,' Dot replied slowly. 'He used to say I was the next best thing, and tease me . . . but he doesn't do that any more, so I thought . . .'

'You think the wrong things,' Hywel told her. His brow was furrowed with the effort of putting his feelings into words. 'Look at it this way. He hasn't got a son to whom he can leave his land, and he isn't all that fond of his daughters, so he ignores the land. After all, that will just go to the one who has no home of her own; right?'

'I suppose it's possible, but . . .'

'On the other hand there are the coalmines. They aren't doing as well as they did, but to be fair to your da that isn't his fault. He buys the latest equipment and all the best tools, and he's always willing to have a go at a new idea, provided he can persuade the men to accept a bit of a novelty. Why's that, do you suppose?'

'Well, I thought it was because he enjoys a challenge. Building a place up, being important, and going off to colliery owners' meetings and so on. You see, he's good at that sort of thing. But farming bores him and he really isn't any good at it at all.'

'There you have it,' Hywel exclaimed triumphantly, his voice rising. 'He's doing what he's good at, because it's the only way he knows to make money. When he goes he may leave the Plas run down and the land in bad heart, but he'll leave a mint of money and whoever inherits the one you may be sure will inherit the other. He'll want his heir to have the money to put the place right if she wants, or to continue with the pits if she wants. Now doesn't that sound more natural than all those old bogeys you dreamed up?'

'It does. If only it's *me* he leaves it to,' Dot exclaimed earnestly. 'Now that you mention it, he is letting me get some things done. I had the stable roof repaired, you know, because the rain was coming through on to the horses, and though he grumbled he paid up. The labour didn't cost, because Gwyn and Will did it last winter. And he doesn't object any more when I get the horses shod, or buy more hens out of my egg-money.'

'There, you see? And if you were to ask Kate or Alex, I bet they'd say you could have the place and welcome. They've both got themselves rich fellows. They won't need all the bother of a run-down estate. Come to that, girl, your da might be letting the place go a bit for that very reason. If the house was in good condition there might be a bit of bother over who got it. As it is, neither of them would want the responsibility. Am I right?'

Dot was staring at him, adoration written all over her face, but whether it was for himself or his idea it was impossible to say.

'Oh, Hywel, I *knew* you'd find a way out. You're so clever! I don't know why your mother goes on so about Jessica when you're so much brainier. I bet Jessica couldn't have worked it all out like you did.'

'Me, clever? It's daft you are, girl, if you believe that! Left school at thirteen, I did, not like our Jess, still beavering away at that convent and dead set on going to university. No, you've got it all wrong. Commonsense I do have and why not? But where my brains should be there's just porridge. Thick as two planks, that's me.'

'You aren't. You shouldn't think so little of yourself,' Dot insisted stoutly. 'Hywel, you hate the pit and you hate being a collier; if they start putting men off the way they say they will why don't you try doing something different? Something out of doors. Old Marmy has keepers; why don't you try over there?'

'Because I'm saving up, that's why.' Hywel stood up and dusted dried moss off the seat of his trousers. 'Got a good bit

154

already. When there's enough I want a place of my own with a bit of a garden and a bit of pasture. Got it all planned out. I thought I'd go for one of the shepherd's places — one room and a dirt floor and water from the nearest stream — because no one wants them these days. I'd make me a garden, rear a few beasts, and when I'd got the place running decent I'd take a pony and cart round the villages selling what I'd grown. I'd never be rich, but I reckon I'd be a happy man, and that's rare enough.'

'Tell you what, why don't you hire a room or two at the Plas?' Dot suggested, as they began to search for a likely rabbit hole down which to slip Belle, his favourite ferret. 'I'm sure there are more than enough for both of us.'

'Your da isn't gone yet,' Hywel reminded her with a grin. 'I doubt he'd agree to that plan!'

'Well, no, unless we were married, of course.' She knelt on the ground beside a large, much scuffed entrance hole. 'Will this one do?'

'Probably. We'll put her down and see.' The ferret's long, sinuous body slithered through Hywel's hands, across the short stretch of stamped earth, and disappeared into the burrow. Hywel sat back on his heels and grinned. 'There's your answer — she knows there's rabbits down there, does Belle.'

'Yes . . .' Dot was silent for a moment, staring at the hole. Then she said, without taking her eyes off it: 'If we were married we could both live at the Plas and bring it back to what it should be.'

'If we were married your da would shoot me first and kick me out of his house next,' Hywel remarked. 'Can't say as I'd blame him, either — a penniless collier lad wedding his girl!'

'But what would it matter? My father's always telling me how ugly I am and how I'll never get a husband.' She turned to look up at Hywel, the look of tiptoe expectancy so strong on her small face that his heart smote him. That anyone should speak to her so! 'I know it's true, Hywel, and it doesn't worry me at all, but it would be different for you, wouldn't it? You wouldn't mind that I'm not beautiful, like Kate and Alex, would you? You'd be marrying me so's you could work on land, and have fields and beasts of your own.'

155

'Dot, you aren't ugly.' She was still kneeling by the hole, and he leaned forward and put a hand on either side of her face, tilting it to his. 'You're different from your sisters. You aren't a raving beauty, but you're something more, something better! Whoever marries you will do it because you're pretty and because you make him laugh and want to hug you.'

Their faces were very close; he could see the rose racing over her skin until she was pink from chin to brow. Her eyes shone though, and her mouth smiled, then pulled itself grave, then smiled again.

'Do I do that to you, Hywel? Make you laugh?'

'You do. You've got a sunny face and a way of putting things which often makes me laugh. And you know it, miss!'

She lowered her voice; her eyes, which had been fixed on his, flickered away, the irises hidden by the long lashes.

'And . . . and do you want to hug me?'

Oddly enough, her question caught him totally off balance, though after what he had said he should have expected it. He felt his face flame and swallowed.

'Well, I . . .'

He stopped short, because she had been hurt enough, injured enough, by people who should have loved her. He drew her gently into his arms and hugged her, awkwardly because they were still on their knees. And then, because he knew she expected it, he kissed her. Lightly, teasingly, on the tip of her smudge of a nose.

In his arms, she felt very small and thin; nothing but a collection of light little bones and soft, smooth skin. She felt more of a child than she was, and infinitely more vulnerable. He hugged her again, then held her away from him.

'Well, now you know! And don't ever let me hear you say you're ugly again, understand?'

He got to his feet and helped her to hers; she was still pink, but she looked happier and she kept glancing at him through her eyelashes whenever she thought he wasn't looking. Awkwardly, Hywel pulled the second ferret out of his pocket. She was a good kid, but . . .

'I'll put this one down further up. Hope they don't meet below ground, mind, or they could end up either feasting on their prey or fighting.'

She responded at once, perhaps as glad to get their relationship back on a normal footing as he.

'Oh no, give Penny to me. I'll take her up higher and put her down a burrow. You stay here and keep an eye open for Belle. You know how quick she is.' She walked away from him, up the hill, scrambling, sure-footed. He watched the burrow for Belle, but he could see Dot still out of the corner of his eye without actually watching her. He saw her bend, release the ferret, and then stand and look down at him.

'Hywel? Shall we get married then, one day?'

There was just enough uncertainty in her voice to remind Hywel of her youth and precarious position at home. Anyway, he would tell her no more than the truth.

'Dot, love, you're only fifteen. You've not met anyone much but me. If you still feel the same in five or six years we'll talk about it again.'

'I see.' A pause whilst she continued to eye him doubtfully. 'Hywel — does what you said mean yes?'

He laughed. He could not help it; he had been speaking no more than the truth when he had said she could always make him laugh. And he also knew that impulsive urge to hug her which sometimes came to him when she was being particularly fetching and sweet.

'Oh, Dot! What do *you* think?'

'I think . . . perhaps . . . it does?'

He laughed again. He really could not help it! 'Well then, why ask?' And then, before her questioning could continue, he gave a muffled yelp and fell on Belle, who was emerging from the rabbit hole with a large dead doe gripped between her tiny white teeth, dragging it behind her as a very small St George might have towed a dragon from its lair.

'Hey, she's got a beauty! Don't come down and look, girl, in case Penny comes out. I'll come up and show you.'

The dangerous moment had passed; they were friends once more. Or so Hywel thought, as they collected the ferrets, strung the rabbits together, and set off down the hillside.

Huw was wedged into a corner of the mess deck, trying to write a letter against the ship's pitch and toss. Around him the other hands were playing cards, throwing dice and reading old copies of boy's magazines, whilst an older man knitted industriously and quite without self-consciousness and the cook made very workmanlike string bags which he would sell for a profit once they docked.

Huw had got as far as telling Helen how weird and wonderful were the Arctic seas. Now he was stuck, because although he wanted his much-loved sister to understand what it was all like he did not want her to guess how extremely dangerous it was out here, miles and miles from another ship.

He had known of the dangers when he chose trawling in preference to the other popular winter occupation of farm workers and their sons: working in the maltings at Burton-on-Trent. Ned Pettigrew, as a young man, had gone to the maltings, so he was able to tell his son what it was like. Huw, given the choice, had opted at once for the trawlers. He had never spent much time indoors and could think of nothing worse than being confined in a malting house with the smell of germinating barley in his nostrils day and night. He would not have minded the hardness of the work – humping sixteen-stone comb-sacks did not worry him – but he was pretty sure that the confinement, the heat and the humidity would be more than he could bear.

In part, the dreams had been responsible for his choice. He had never become entirely accustomed to them, and whenever they came they left him sure that they came for a purpose – though what it was he could not say. They were so *real*, so stark, that they could not be simply the product of his own imagination. He might have imagined the dark, the dirt, the smell, but he could not have done it with such amazing accuracy. For he had checked his dreams out after he had begun to wonder about them.

Not with his mother, though; he had never mentioned the dreams to her after that first time. They upset her too much and they made her uneasy; he had seen her watching him and had known that she blamed herself for the dreams, believing they came to him because of her family's long association with the pits.

So he had gone into the Norwich Free library when he was droving cattle from the market there, and had looked up coal mining in the reference section. A lot of what he read was double dutch to him, a lot meant nothing at the time, but even the smallest mention of working conditions, of tools, of the colliers themselves, he found he already knew.

He had told Helen about the dreams and they had wondered whether they would follow him out to the arctic sea or whether they were necessarily connected with the marsh, for he had very speedily realised that they only came when he was working alone out on the leys or droving cattle along the quiet roads, or punting along a dyke with his scythe at the ready to swathe down a good straight growth of rushes.

Oddly enough, after that first fright, he found himself reconciled to the dreams. They never lasted long. He worked in them, worked hard. He felt his sweat running down his bare torso, knew that there was a new blister forming on the base of his palm where the shovel rubbed, tasted the food in the tin, sometimes, when a halt was necessary.

There were others in the pit, of course, but he never spoke to them and they never spoke to him. Sometimes he heard them talking to one another, joking, but though he could hear the words they meant nothing to him. At first he had tried to speak to them, but he soon realised that such a thing was impossible.

He liked the ponies and was sorry when his work took him away from them. On the other hand, he could do so little that he felt ashamed. Where he came from horses were a valuable commodity and were well treated, but in the pits, though the little fellows were well fed, they were, in his opinion, abominably used. Because they spent almost all their lives in total darkness – there was no lamp hanging in their stables and the only light they saw as they worked was the lamp of the man ahead of them – most of them lost their sight quite quickly. He hated their blindness, which was man-made, hated to see their poor shoulders bleeding from the constant collisions with the tunnel walls, their bodies scarred by chains and ropes as they pulled the tubs of coal they would never see out from darkness towards the light.

Most of them died down the pit. They were brought down out of the brightness and the scents of grass and wind, and only brought up in pieces, for when a pony died it was easier to dismember it and take the pathetic little bundle up that way than to try to get the body into the cage.

But the dreams had given him a great admiration for colliers. Crawl on their bellies they might, work up to their knees in water, under abominable conditions, but that did not stop them. The coal was worked for, bled for, but it was brought out, and he knew instinctively that it was each man's pride to cut as much coal on his shift as was humanly possible. As a farm worker on the marshes, as a drover, now as a deckhand on a trawler, Huw knew all about hard work. But no work could be as hateful to a man who loved the outdoors as burrowing in the earth like a blind mole, lying on your side with your head on your jacket, and swinging a pick at a coal face which, when it began to fall, would shower you with tiny splinters of the stuff. A hewer's trademark, those little blue scars all over the face. One day he would hew in the dream, he knew that, but he would not bring the scars back with him, as he did not bring the blisters, the sweat, the dragging ache across the shoulders. His own aches were enough to bear, for hauling the herring was no easy task. But the scars would be there all the same. On his soul? Perhaps.

'What, in't you finished that letter yet, bor? Come on, git a shift on. We want a fourth over here.'

Huw, daydreaming, came back to the present with a jump and grinned at the speaker. Nellie Barton was an immense man, strong as an ox and as obstinate as a mule, the fellows said. Why he was known as Nellie no one knew but it was certainly not because of any tendency to effeminacy; Nellie was a full-time fisherman, not a winter worker, and could out-swear, out-haul and out-eat any two of the rest of them.

'I shan't be a mo,' Huw told him. 'Trouble is, it's difficult to know how much to say — it's to my sister.'

'Oh aye? 'Spect me to believe that? A pretty young feller like you writing to his sister? Some poor gal's breaking her heart over you, Pettigrew, and don't tell me no different.'

'Well, if she is, I'm not writing to her,' Huw said, grinning. 'What do you tell your womenfolk when you write, Nellie? I've told her it's cold, and the food's good, and that's about it.'

'I don't write,' Nellie said simply, shuffling the grimy pack of cards between his two huge hands. 'No need. My home's near enough to the docks, in all conscience. Th'old woman's allus got a meal ready when we dock, acos she can see us as we steam round the breakwater.'

'Well, my sister won't see me until they want me for the spring planting,' Huw said rather glumly. 'So I'd like her to know enough to be interested, but not enough to get scared.'

'Scared? Women don't understand and they're scared regardless,' someone on the other side of the mess deck remarked. 'They're scared of the sea, never mind this part of it. They think we'll get swept overboard or frozen stiff or ate by a shark or dragged under by a giant octopus. If you go tellin' your gal about the dog-fish what snapped clean through your boot she'll hev a fit.'

There was a murmur of laughter, for Huw, new boy as he was, had walked past what he had assumed to be a dead dog-fish on deck and had felt something grab and drag at him. Looking down, he found that the dead dog-fish was still quite lively enough to launch itself viciously at his sea-boot and sink its commendably sharp teeth deep into the rubber. It had taken him several moments to rid himself of his unwanted passenger and his antics had caused great hilarity amongst the other deckies, all of whom had guessed what would happen and, naturally, had not warned him.

'That's what I thought – that she'd be scared if I said too much,' Huw admitted, bending over his letter once more. 'She's working now – on the farm, of course, because she can't get into a town or anything – but she'd love to travel, see the world. I think I'll tell her about the penguins.'

'If you tell her about them, you'll hev to tell her about the iceberg, since they was on it,' Nellie observed wisely. 'That'll send her into a faint, very likely.'

'She isn't like that . . . oh, well, if I tell her how beautiful that iceberg was – it was, wasn't it? – perhaps she won't think about the danger.'

'Oh, ar, it were suffin beautiful,' Nellie said soulfully. 'Death, that's what a berg that size is. But don't let that bother you, young Huw. Jest you think what pretty colours it had.'

'If you don't shut up and let me get on you won't ever get your game of cards,' Huw threatened good-naturedly. 'Will you post it for me when you go ashore, Nellie? I don't suppose I'll get much chance – the gaffer said he'd pay extra if Phil and me stay behind for the turn-around and help clean out and oil the engines.'

'Aye, I don't mind. Come on now, clear a bit of this blooda table, or we'll never get a chance to lay our hands down.'

Huw finished his letter and joined the card game. He was not on watch for another hour or two, so he played half a dozen hands, lost a few and won a few, and then announced that he was going for a blow on deck.

'Can't stay here all day,' he remarked, getting to his feet. 'Too used to being out of doors, I am. Chuck us an oilie.'

It was not sensible to go out on deck alone, but he would not go far, just get out of the hatch and see the stars and feel the chill wind on his face. The ship was heading home now, the cold was nowhere near as intense, the fish-rooms were full. He would go up for a blow, get the fug of the mess deck out of his system, and then he'd spend the rest of his free time in his hammock.

Jock was on watch; he'd be on the bridge. Later, perhaps, he'd have a word with him about getting time off to go home for a few days, perhaps over Christmas. He pushed up the hatch and stepped out into the dark. Stars twinkled overhead, and the keen wind knifed past his face, tugging impatiently at his muffler and reminding him who was boss. Out here the elements ruled, there was no doubt of that. When you docked you'd meet men from trawlers, and out of the half-dozen or so boats someone always reported a death; a chap swept overboard, another dying from exposure, another from a secret hoard of drink he had smuggled aboard. Often the men would shake their heads over the disappearance of a trawler and all her crew. Not in disbelief – they knew the odds too well for that – but in sorrow over the unknown fate of their comrades. You could strike an iceberg and the ship could be gone in seconds. You could hit a floating mine from the War and be blown to smithereens. You could go too far into the pack-ice and the weight and strength of the stuff freezing around you could crush the ship like a walnut in a nutcracker.

I must be mad, Huw thought, as he turned to leave the deck for the warmth and comradeship of the mess once more. Surely I'm mad to choose this for a winter's work, when the farms's done badly over the summer! But he knew it was not madness which had made his choice for him; it had been partly because he hated the thought of the maltings and partly because of guilt. Guilt that it was not he who laboured beneath the earth, digging coal. Guilt because someone, in his own family, had once done the things that he now did in his dreams. He could face the dangers of the mine because they were not real dangers for him, they were only dream-dangers. But out here the dangers were real.

Helen read the letter sitting at the kitchen table, her elbows resting on the scrubbed wooden top and the letter propped up against a jar of winter jasmine from the thin woody shrub that straggled up against the porch. It did not do much outdoors, poor thing, what with the wind and all, but when you cut some and brought it in how it blossomed in the warmth! Its faint, sweet smell gave her a pleasure which the headier perfume of summer flowers never brought. It was so frail a thing and so brave, to put out its buds in winter.

It was a nice letter, as all Huw's letters were. He described things beautifully, Helen thought; so well that it was almost as good as being with him. The immensity of the iceberg, the comical penguins, his mates who teased him, the fish that had leapt at his foot – when she read the words it was almost as good as having Huw beside her, with his slow smile and his tanned face, talking to her.

She was well over halfway before she reached the code-phrase. *I had a trifle of indigestion yesterday.* That was how they had arranged he should let her know if the dreams continued. And they had – she felt, triumphantly, that she had known all along that they would. Because they were so weird, so true from what Huw said, she could not imagine them being beaten back by something as trivial as a change of scene.

That was all he said about the dream, though, because he knew she would let Megan read the letter, as Megan would let Helen read hers when Huw next wrote. And he had long ago explained to his sister that their mother was frightened and upset by the dreams.

'Enjoying it, is he? Poor lad, I didn't want him to go, but you know how it is. Your Dad went after work if they had bad summers when he was a youngster, so nothing would do but for Huw to go as well. Been happier, I would, if he'd chosen to go to the maltings, though your Dad says the danger there is to your lungs and can stay with you all your life. He never went trawling, but he seems to think that if Huw's outdoors . . .' Her voice trailed away, and Helen reached across the table to where her mother sat, peeling potatoes, and squeezed her hand.

'You shall read it for yourself presently. You can tell he's enjoying it, bar a touch of indigestion. Trust our Huw to be thinking of his belly!'

She finished the letter, smiled, and handed it across the table. Megan smiled too, and took it. It was evening and dark outside, but there was a good oil lamp on the table which gave a fair light. Megan tilted the letter and began to read.

Megan, taking the letter from Helen, thought how strange it was that her two elder children, who were only first cousins, should be so alike. The colouring, perhaps, was understandable, but there was more to it than that. Their expressions were so similar. Helen had a small, straight little nose, whereas Huw's was a bit of a beak in comparison, yet when they grinned at you and wrinkled those noses . . . well, they could have been twins.

The thought of twins reminded her of that long-ago deceit. She had never told Huw that he was not her natural son, never told him about Hywel. Once, she had worried over this when Huw had begun to dream about the pit; she had wondered if it were possible that twins were linked in some way so that their thoughts could pass from one to another. But it seemed unlikely. The babies had looked similar on the only occasion when she had seen them together, but she did not think that this necessarily meant that Huw and Hywel were identical twins.

Only think how happy Huw has always been, she told herself, reading the letter. If the boys had been identical twins, linked in their minds in some way, Huw could not have been happy without Hywel. Wasn't that how it went?

She finished the letter, smiled at Helen and laid it down, and because Helen raised her brows and looked enquiring she came straight out with the problem that was on her mind.

'Helen, love, is it true that identical twins can share their thoughts? And that they can only be happy together?'

Helen smiled back. 'You hear all sorts of stories, Mum, but all I know is Jen and Heather Glossmith fight worse than any other kids in school, and I do mean fight each other.'

'Oh! And are they identical twins?'

'Mm hmm. Like as two peas in a pod for looks, if not for much else. Why do you ask?'

'Well, dear, sitting here reading Huw's letter it suddenly struck me how alike you are. It's your ways, I think, more than any actual features. People are always remarking how similar you are. And that made me think about twins.' She began to invent now, since Helen still looked enquiring. 'There were twins in my family, many years ago – I believe your great-grandfather had an identical twin.'

'Oh? And were they inseparable? Or didn't that part of the story get handed down to you?'

'I don't think they could have been, since your great-great-uncle went off to America and never came back to Wales,' Megan said, glad to be back on the straight and narrow once more, for indeed her grandfather's brother had emigrated and had never returned. 'Odd things, families, when you come to think.'

'Oh, I don't know. Our family is rather close-knit and commonplace,' Helen said. 'Look at me – I could be off somewhere, but I'd rather stay here with you and Dad and the kids. And Huw, of course, when he's around.'

'He'll be back in the spring,' Megan told her daughter. She got up to put the pan of peeled potatoes on the fire. 'And then, love, we must think what we are to do with you, for I won't let you stay here and slave on the land like a lad! I know you say you enjoy the droving in summer, but it's not right, not for a lovely young girl like you. You should go and get work in the city, find somewhere decent to stay where they'll take care of you.'

'If you mean domestic service . . .'

'Helen, what a thing to say! No, I don't mean domestic service. That's no life! You're a clever girl, they said so at

165

school. You could work in an office.'

'I'll think about it,' Helen said, beginning to lay the table for tea. 'I'll talk to Huw, when he comes home, in the spring.'

Ten: Autumn 1921

'Dot? Is that you?'

The voice from the bed was faint, but Dot, standing in the window embrasure of her parents' room looking down over the neglected garden, was listening for it and went at once to her mother's bedside. She had grown accustomed to the way sickness had changed Olivia from the plump, rather self-satisfied woman her mother had become after Miss Eden-thorpe had left to this waxen, skeletal-thin creature, but now a pang went through her. Her mother looked no worse than she had yesterday, yet there was a change. The unquiet hands which had plucked and teased at the covers were unmoving now, the frown of pain and the twitching of her lips all smoothed away. Her mother did not look happy, but there was an air of resignation hanging over her which reminded Dot uneasily of animals which had suffered and which had reached the end of their fight. You could tell when you were going to lose a foal or a calf when that look came into their eyes, that acceptance of fate. But Dot smiled down into her mother's face and took her mother's quiet fingers in her own.

'Yes, it's me, Mother. Father sent a telegram to Kate and now he's gone off in the car to fetch Alex. You've been very sick, but you seemed a little better earlier on and he thought it might be a good time to let them come in and say hello.'

'Or . . . goodbye?' Was that a glint of humour in the dull eyes? But Dot shook her head reprovingly even as she wondered at the strange convention which forbade her to acknowledge that her mother was on the verge of death. Olivia, too, observed the conventions in this; until this moment she had always spoken as though it was merely a matter of time before

167

she was up and about again. Had realisation brought acceptance or was it the other way round?

'Really, Mother, what a thing to say! They want to come over before the weather gets severe, I daresay. I know they're coming to us for Christmas, but with you so ill they thought it would be nice to see you sooner.'

'Yes, of course. Is . . . is Christmas very near, then?'

It was early September; outside the windows roses still bloomed and the trees held all their leaves, though some were colouring. Apples clustered on the old, bent apple trees and in church and probably in all three chapels as well they would be holding their harvest festivals as soon as the corn had been carried and stooked and threshed and finally stacked in the yards. It would not be long, now, before the young men who worked on the farms all summer would be leaving to hunt for winter jobs. Once the harvest was in country folk began to think about winter, and Christmas, and how to keep warm and fed during the hungry months. But that would not concern Olivia; she lived from hour to hour now, dwelling often on the past. On parties held in her father's mansion on the Wirral where friends had been entertained by the hundred and the Marchmont girls and their beauty had been the talk of society. On long-ago Christmases, on servants long dead, on friends long forgotten – remembered now by some quirk of the mind's ramblings.

'Christmas? Well, it's not very near, no. But you know how we are. We like to have things planned out well in advance.' Foolish, really, to talk in this way, when they both knew very well that Olivia would not see Christmas. Yet it was comforting, too. No matter where Olivia might be by then, she was still interested in Christmas, in the changing seasons and their continuity. 'I told Kate to bring Cathy and Sarah, but to leave the baby at home just for a few days.'

'Good girl.' There had been some friction when the two elder Tegydd girls had visited last. Dot had hoped her mother had not noticed, but she was obviously mistaken. As it happened, both her sisters had just produced babies, Alex in late May, Kate in early June. Kate had two daughters already; John was her first son, and Alex's boy, James, was the first offspring of the young Stotts.

It was this which had led to the friction. Kate, always a forceful character, had simply pushed Macmillan junior to the fore in everything, seeing to it that he got his fair share — or more — of any adulation going. Alexandra had grown at first querulous and then spiteful as Baby Stott had had his tiny nose constantly put out of joint by her sister. After all, James was her first child and she really did not see why Kate must either ignore him or compare him unfavourably with her own offspring.

Dot, who quite liked children but was not overfond of babies, got cross with her sisters; Tom, who adored boys but apparently did not place a small Macmillan or a small Stott in that category, got crosser. In the end he simply disappeared from the house, leaving his youngest daughter to cope with his sick wife, his disgruntled elder daughters, and the staff, who made no bones about hoping that the visitors would soon leave.

So now, remembering that visit, Dot smiled at her mother. 'Well, it wouldn't do to have them squabbling when you're stuck here in bed and unable to escape.' On the last visit, only two months earlier, Olivia had been up and dressed in the afternoons. Now such a thing was out of the question. How quickly it had happened, Dot mourned to herself, yet how soon one grew accustomed. 'It's a fine day. Shall I open the window wider?'

'No. I feel chilly.' Olivia pulled her blue shawl closer around her throat. 'How old are you, dear?'

'Seventeen. As if you didn't know!' But her mother forgot a lot of things now and as she grew weaker there were whole days when she thought Dot was not her daughter at all but her much younger sister, Dorothy Marchmont. Dot, who was not called Dorothy but Thomasina, a sort of desperate, bastard attempt to name her after her father, disliked her Aunt Dorothy and did not enjoy being taken for her, though she supposed Aunt Dorothy must have been human once. She might have stayed human had she not failed to catch a husband for all her much-talked-of good looks. Now she lived at home on the Wirral with her parents, ruled over by them and always trying to dominate anyone else who came within her ken. She seemed indifferent to the fact that whenever she started on someone that person avoided her thereafter.

Tom, who had little time for any of his sisters-in-law, always referred to her as 'poor Dorothy'. It was only Olivia who called her Dot, only Olivia who now muddled the two of them.

'Seventeen? Older, surely.' A pause whilst Olivia, presumably, unmixed generations in her mind. 'Hmm. Seventeen. Gracious, your sisters were as good as married at your age.' Dot braced herself for the dig that she knew would follow as her mother's eyes slid slyly sideways. 'You'll never marry! Too plain, far too plain. When you were born I looked at you and thought you were a boy because I'd only had beautiful babies before and they'd both been girls. This ugly creature must be a boy, I thought to myself.' The eyes veiled themselves behind the sparse, light coloured lashes, then flickered up to Dot's face once more. 'Good thing you aren't pretty, I suppose, since it means you can look after father for me.'

'I try,' Dot said. Her mother's remarks did not worry her. She had heard them too many times. 'He doesn't grumble over my housekeeping, does he?'

She knew he did not; Tom had many faults, but he appreciated that she was doing her best in most difficult circumstances.

'No, he hasn't grumbled. You do well enough.' The still hands suddenly moved, jerking the sheet. 'Dot, when you're in charge here, you'll see that Father keeps neat and smart, won't you? Don't let him . . . do things carelessly, let the place go down. You'll see to it?'

There was pleading in her voice, though she had not dared to say quite what she meant. Olivia knew very well that Tom took almost no notice of the estate and must have known that he spent freely on good clothing and his personal appearance. What she meant, Dot believed, was that he should not let the estate, himself, and his dead wife down by some behaviour of which she would disapprove. Like, Dot supposed, Other Women. But it would not do to ask questions which she did not want answered. Anyway, Olivia would slide away from being too direct, so Dot answered the question at its face value.

'Father always keeps smart, Mother, but he's lost interest in the estate already, you know that. He's letting me do my best to keep the place running though, and he does make a lot of money out of the pits, which he says he couldn't do if he had to pour capital into the estate. In fact the land is beginning to pay us back for the care we've taken – Souse'em and me, that is – over the past year or two. Did I tell you . . .'

'Yes, I'm sure you did, dear. Where *is* Tom? I haven't seen him for days.'

How her mood changed! Now she sounded like a fretful child, her fingers were plucking at the sheet again and her mouth was twitching. Calm had gone.

'I told you he'd gone to fetch Alex. He'll come up as soon as he arrives home, I promise you. And Ben's been told to meet Kate's train, unless she decides to come by car and arrives earlier.'

'I see. Then I'll order luncheon now.'

'If you wish,' Dot said faintly. This was the most difficult side of her mother's illness, but it had to be faced. 'What would you like, Mother?'

'I'll have some of Cook's cream of mushroom soup, followed by . . . let me see. I'm not terribly hungry, but . . . yes, let it be followed by jugged hare, just a morsel, and some of the young runner beans and a taste of duchesse potatoes. I won't take pudding, I don't think – unless Cook could manage an iced pudding? Something light is needed to follow jugged hare, I always think. Just something very light, with a trace of cream and perhaps a hint of lemon . . . what do you think, Dot?'

'I'll see to it,' Dot said, going over to the bell pull and giving the long satiny rope a tug. 'One of the girls will come up and sit with you whilst I give your order. Do you think you'd like a little sleep?'

'Yes. I'll rest until luncheon arrives,' Olivia said. She turned her head on the pillow and Dot noticed how thin and sharp, how almost transparent, the older woman's nose looked in profile. 'Don't forget, Dot, mushroom soup, hare, and then an iced pudding.'

Dot slipped out of the room, letting one of the maids in and seeing her settled first, then made her way downstairs, wondering about the fantasy world which her mother wove around her diet. For the past few years she had lived for food and so perhaps it was not surprising that she talked so constantly about delicious meals, but people would have thought it very strange if they could have seen her taking the thin gruel which was all her stomach would accept and then congratulating her daughter on the consistency of the gravy, the colour of the jelly, or the splendid richness of the clotted cream.

It is a terrible judgement of the rest of us though, Dot reminded herself as she ran down the stairs. Mother is dying, yet in extremis, it is to a plate of jugged hare and young beans that her thoughts wander and not to her husband or children. She can enjoy the memory of such things more than she can enjoy the memories of her family.

On the other hand, Dot believed it was a compliment that her mother allowed her into her fantasy, for she could not help noticing that Olivia never mentioned food in front of Tom or her elder daughters. Indeed, it was as well that she had not done so, for Dot realised that this might have driven Tom out of the sickroom for ever. Illness embarrassed him and the fact that this was a mortal illness made it no better. In the sickroom he blinked, shuffled, talked too loudly and kept glancing over his shoulder at the door as though he feared it might suddenly seal up and lock him into the room for ever with his dying wife. Had he heard the talk of food he would have believed Olivia to be out of her mind, and that would have scared him even more than her sickness.

Dot swung down the last three stairs and began to cross the chilly, beautiful hall, but before she was but halfway across the tiles the baize door leading to the kitchen quarters opened and Ella appeared with a knitting bag in one hand. She smiled at Dot and brandished the bag.

'Said I'd sit with your mam for a bit, Dot, seeing as cook wants the girl to give a hand wi' luncheon. Brought my knitting I have, see, because I want it ready for when Jessica leaves home. A nice warm suit I'm knitting her, and the jacket's the really tricky part. A bit of time on the fronts I'll need to make it good for when she leaves. Got to be real smart when you're at university, you know.'

'I'm sure,' Dot said politely. She had heard too much about the brilliant Jessica, her marvellous examination results and her flight from the mountains of Wales to the flat and watery acres of Cambridge to want to hear it all over again. Naturally Ella was proud, for it was a considerable achievement for a collier's daughter, but it was difficult for Dot, who had never even been to school, to appreciate just how great the achievement was. Also, she found herself resenting Ella's complete indifference towards her youngest son — an indifference which came close to dislike when you set it against the adulation she showed for her daughter.

'Only the fronts and one sleeve left to go,' Ella said, beginning to mount the stairs. She had a spry and lively step and Dot, watching her, was struck by the fact that Ella and Olivia were about the same age, yet she could never remember her mother climbing stairs like that. She supposed it was because Ella had always been too busy to let her pace slow; until old age did the slowing for her she would continue to be brisk. But Olivia had never had to hurry. Dot waited in the hall until she heard the bedroom door open and then continued on her way. Whatever Ella's faults, she was the most trustworthy member of the staff of the Plas; with her at her mother's bedside, Dot knew she could go out and enjoy a few hours in the open air without any qualms.

As she slipped out of the side door the sweet, apple-scented air blew against her face and she looked up into the mistiness of cloud which, by its blue tinge, showed that it would presently disperse to let the sun shine through. Later, probably after luncheon, they would have a lovely afternoon. Dot took a deep breath and felt all sort of worries and inadequacies fall from her shoulders. Out here she was nobody's ugly little daughter. She was a landowner, even if she did not possess a single rod, pole or perch. If you loved the land and cared for it, she told herself, making for the stables, then you were entitled to take steps to secure the thing you loved. And Tom had made it plain enough to Kate and Alex last time they were here that he had left them nothing besides a sum of money. They did not care; Kate's husband was a richer man than Tom would ever be, and Alex's husband had recently inherited a large sum which he had invested in John Macmillan's shipping company. Money, of course, was always useful, and from things her father had said Dot imagined he meant to leave the income from the Roland and Olwen pits to her sisters and the estate to herself. If he bought the Wynd, perhaps he would leave it to her to help her to finance the estate. But what did it matter? It was a lovely day, she was free for a couple of hours, and her father, bless him, was hale and hearty and likely to live for another forty years at least. With my blessing, Dot thought contentedly, leaning on the stable half-door and surveying Matchless's polished hindquarters with affection. They got on very well now, she and her father. He had become reasonable with the departure of the two older girls and with her own obvious interest in the estate. It was good to be friends — though she still treated him cautiously. He was not predictable.

'Morning, Dot!'

Jan came round the corner from the pigsties, bawling to her above the erratic rumble of his wheelbarrow on the cobbles. His torn cap was tilted at a rakish angle over one ear — a good sign. When it was on straight Jan was not pleased with life.

'Hello, Jan. Anything happening?'

He shrugged and dropped the handles of the empty barrow to scratch the end of his purpling nose.

'Not a lot. Big barn's full, though we didn't have much down to wheat. Ploughed first half of Pedlar's Piece. Want to take a look? Earth's rich as plum puddin', that it is.'

Dot, who had intended simply to take a ride round for the pleasure of being ouside, instantly agreed to go and look at Pedlar's Piece. It had been tough going, reclaiming it from the brambles and saplings, but they'd done it at last. She had it in mind to let it lie fallow this winter and then to put it down to decent grass with plenty of clover and move the dairy herd up there. It was high, but if the earth was good . . .

Tom had agreed to the whole thing, albeit absently, frowning over figures in his large, untidy office, sitting at the roll-top desk that had never, to Dot's knowledge, been rolled down, in front of the window embrasure curtained with long, dust-encrusted red velvet which she had never seen pulled across. Probably if you tried to do so the curtains would come to pieces in your hands, and turn into velvet dust.

'Yes, get it ploughed and replanted if you think it's worth the effort,' he had said when she suggested it. 'More beef cattle, eh?'

'No. Quickest way to lose money farming,' Dot had said incautiously, earning a narrow-eyed glance and a heavy scowl.

Tom had been rearing beef cattle and losing money on them for years. 'I'd like to get a couple of decent heifers and try for a dairy herd.'

'If you get that pasture fit for dairy cows I'll buy you a couple of good heifers for Christmas,' Tom had said absently, his gaze returning to the figures in front of him. 'In fact if it wasn't for the money I need . . . but you shall have 'em for Christmas.'

'Golly, thanks, Father,' Dot said without a trace of sarcasm which, indeed, she did not feel. Kate might ask for diamond earrings and Alex for a fur coat, but she thought that a couple of warm-skinned, wet-nosed heifers would be a much better gift.

So now she began to tack Matchless up, humming to herself and slapping his gleaming black withers as the pony shivered his skin at the touch of the saddle. One day, one day, she would have a famous dairy herd . . . Matchless nuzzled her pocket and she produced the sugar lumps he could undoubtedly smell, fed them to him, kissed his soft muzzle and then led him into the yard. Mounting, she rode through the gateway – the gate had long since rotted away – and up the lane towards the field called Pedlar's Piece. Her mother's imminent end could not be forgotten, but at least it could be pushed to the back of her mind for a few hours. After all, for years she and Matchless had had only each other – and now that she was growing up and therefore useful to her parents it did not mean that she could get along without her pony and occasional draughts of freedom. She caressed his neck as they mounted the hill and the pony broke into a trot, then a canter. They were very happy.

'Would you like another cup of tea, Mrs George?' Dot was doing her best to be a good hostess whilst Kate and Alex, who could have performed the task much more naturally, sat in a corner and exchanged acid comments on their sister's skimped black dress and general diffidence. Not that Dot had heard more than a murmur, but she could guess, from the way they had behaved at the funeral, that she was not in their good books. She did not, however, care. Ella, handing cups, cake, and sandwiches, seemed more like family at this moment than did those two elegantly dressed strangers. Ella saw Dot's tentative movement towards Mrs George Bevin who was talking non-stop in her deep, booming voice to Mrs Enid Bevin and came towards them, taking the cup from Mrs George's grasp without trying to interrupt the volcanic flow of her speech.

'Get 'er a refill, girl,' Ella whispered. 'Needs a drink, gabbing on the way she is.'

Dot, smiling, did as she was told. Then, since everyone seemed to be eating or drinking or both, she turned and searched for her father. All the assembled company were in mourning of some degree or other but Tom, despite a dark suit, a black tie and hair sleeked down with water, did not look particularly grave. He was talking to a fellow landowner, rocking on his heels, occasionally flicking a lock of hair back from his brown forehead and, most reprehensibly, laughing loudly every now and then, seemingly oblivious of the shocked glances this aroused.

Dot, wanting to bring him to a sense of the occasion, went over to him and nudged his elbow. He turned, the smile fading from his face to be replaced by the slightly impatient look with which she was sadly familiar.

'Well? What is it?'

'If you've finished your tea, Father, do you think you ought to speak to some of Mother's relatives? Two of her sisters are here, and . . .'

'No, I oughtn't, and they won't expect it.' He glanced far too obviously at his watch and added, in what he no doubt considered to be lowered tones, 'When are they going, Dotty? I've got work to do. Can't hang around doing the polite all afternoon, you know!'

Marmy Carruthers had a big red face and large teeth – teeth which would have looked equally at home on a carthorse, Dot considered. But now he went darker red and shook his head at his friend.

'Now now, Tom, old feller, no need for that sort of haste, not with your wife scarce underground. We'll get our business settled in a few days.'

'Oh!' Tom plainly did not consider his wife's demise to be any sort of grounds for delaying a business deal. 'You won't want me for three or four days, then?'

'No, old boy. In fact you'll be needed here. Your girl will want . . .'

'Oh, nonsense. She's all right, is Dot. Besides, if you don't need me, Marmy, there's them as do! I'm off to London first thing, Dot; got some business to attend to. Just a day or two and then I'll be back. You'll not miss me.'

'Oh, but Father, there's an awful lot to be arranged here. The girls have come specially, but if you aren't on the spot to tell us what you want . . .'

'Rubbish, Dot! Kate can manage if you can't, I'm very sure of that! You should see that business can't come to a halt just because one woman dies! I'll not say a word against your mother, but you know full well that I've been trying to buy the Wynd for months past and haven't been able to find the capital for such an outlay. I've had all the worry of her illness, and not wanting to be away for long periods . . . but now she's been taken from me I must get myself sorted out.'

Dot could not prevent her lips from tightening as she turned away. Such a mean thing to pretend that his wife's health had prevented him from carrying out business transactions when everyone must know how untrue that was. Tom had been away from Plas Tegydd more than in it even before Olivia's last illness; since that illness he had scarcely done more than put in a token appearance a couple of times a week.

However, there was nothing she could do about it; Tom would go off and expect her to settle all the arguments and to have every trace of Olivia's presence out of their bedroom by the time he got back. He had told her, this very morning, that he would trust her to turn it into what he termed decent bachelor quarters. He had added that this was no disrespect to Olivia, in fact quite the opposite. He wanted no feminine reminders of her presence to make him remember how alone he was now.

Flummery, Dot knew, yet she thought he was right. Better than continuing to live in a room that was more hers than his. It was odd about the Wynd, though. He had been after it for more than two years; there had been talk, whispers . . . yet it was only now, after Olivia's death, that he was able to put into words what everyone had been thinking – that he was buying the colliery.

Dot looked round, satisfied herself that everyone was oc-cupied, and went over to her sisters. They ignored her at first, since they were arguing, in furious undervoices, as to which of them should have mother's engagement ring. Kate might have more money than she knew what to do with and Allie was certainly very comfortably situated, but the betrothal ring had been in the Tegydd family for perhaps as long as five hundred years, possibly longer. It had been re-styled at least twice, Tom had told Dot once when she had remarked on it, but it was still a very valuable antique. It had been passed down from the father to the eldest son's wife in each generation, but now, with Tom and Olivia only having three daughters, no one really knew what would happen to the ring. So Kate and Alexandra, who would watch undisturbed if Plas Tegydd were razed to the ground tomorrow, squabbled over the possession of the great sapphire which had winked on their mother's left hand for as long as they could remember.

'So I feel sure Mother will have left it to the eldest,' Kate remarked at last, and turned to Dot. 'Now that that's settled, have you made arrangements for dinner? I expect it will be just us, staying to dine? I told John we would, and I daresay Allie told Humphrey the same.'

Dot looked across the room to where her two brothers-in-law were deep in conversation. Humphrey was plain, fat and oldish, John young, upstanding and handsome, yet they had a lot in common. She did not care for either of them much, though John's looks had fooled her for a bit into thinking him pleasant enough. In truth he had charm, but did not bother to use it on a young sister-in-law whom he expected to be thrust upon him one day in the guise of dependent relative – or so Dot supposed.

'I've made arrangements for dinner, but I wondered if Mother's relatives from the Wirral might like to stay? Do you think I should get Father to invite them? And as for the ring, surely it's Father you should ask? It's a Tegydd thing. I don't expect Mother had any power to leave it to anyone.'

Kate, who had been staring at her youngest sister quite pleasantly, stiffened and her big blue eyes went cold and hard – harder and colder than the sapphire over which they had been arguing, Dot thought. But no wonder Kate wanted it. She would look so well in it, with her eyes the very shade of the big stone. Today Kate was willow-slim in black silk, with a marvellously soft, rich-looking fur stole in a pale creamy-brown colour round her shoulders and a tiny matching toque on her shining swathes of golden hair. A pity that her expression was not as beautiful as her person, but there was no denying that she was looking extremely nasty. A sneer is not pretty, even upon pretty lips.

'How silly you are, Dot! They didn't want to come, and now they can't wait to get away. I thought perhaps some of Father's friends would have been invited, though. It would be nice for John and Humphrey to have some other fellows to talk to. As well as Father, I mean.'

'No, they won't stay, because Father was talking of going off to London on business,' Dot said. 'I'd like to know where he has to go in such a hurry the very day after Mother is buried. And I'd like to know why he's finally taken the step of buying the Wynd today, whereas before, when I've asked him about it, he's always said that nothing is settled, and he isn't sure whether it would be a good idea, and so on. Yet now he's leaving for London – or so he says – first thing in the morning and when he comes back he's got an appointment with Marmy Carruthers and there's only one thing those two could discuss, and that's the Wynd.' Dot perched on the arm of Kate's chair. 'Well? What do you think? We haven't had much chance to talk yet, but of course tomorrow, when we're going through Mother's things . . .'

'Tomorrow? Kate and I are staying for the will-reading and for dinner, but then we must be off,' Allie said, putting her china cup down so forcibly that the saucer rattled. 'We've got our families to think of. We can't just go gadding off for a day or two any more!'

'I could gad if I wanted,' Kate said sharply, directing a sapphire glare at her sister. 'But I don't, and that's the truth of it. The house is freezing cold and terribly disorganised, and anyway John likes me to be at home. He wouldn't approve of a longer stay.'

'You won't stay? Not even for one night? Oh, but, Kate, there's so much to do sorting through Mother's things. I made sure you'd both stay to help me get things tidy,' Dot said, despair coursing through her at the thought of the long list of solitary tasks ahead. 'You might, really you might! It isn't as if

179

I'll have Father's help, because he's off to London first thing.'

'I'll tell him it's totally impossible for him to go off on business at such a time,' Kate contributed. 'Though personally, you two . . .' her voice sank to a whisper '. . . personally, I believe he goes to see a woman somewhere. And as for buying the Wynd now and not two years ago, it'll be because he needed Mother's money to complete the deal, I imagine.'

It was Dot's turn to look surprised.

'Mother's money? Oh, but I thought it was all spent long ago. I was sure she had no money of her own.'

'Oh really, Dot, how naive you are! Grandpapa Marchmont was a very astute man. He made sure Mother had money which Father couldn't touch. The trouble was, she got almost as bad as Father, and decided she dared not spend freely in case she ever needed it. So there'll be a lot salted away, I've no doubt. And I expect it'll all go to Father.'

'And so it should,' Alexandra said, disposing her black silk skirts more comfortably and giving Dot a sisterly once-over, her eyes going disparagingly from the skimped artificial silk of her dress to the scuffed pumps on her feet. 'Although you could do with some money spending on you, my girl, by the look of you.'

Dot was about to give her opinion of clothing in general when a concerted stir told them that a good many of the funeral party were waiting to say goodbye and leave. Dot, in honour bound, offered the hospitality of her home to her mother's relatives, most of whom, as Kate had said, were eager to be off, though Aunt Mary pressed Dot's hand feelingly and said that if there was anything . . . she had only to ask . . . and Uncle Herbert Fielding kissed all his nieces with more fervour than Dot thought proper or necessary, and assured them that, but for his wife's indisposition, he would have accepted their invitation with pleasure.

'Mr Geraint said there was no need to stay for the will-reading,' he confided, breathing sherry fumes all over the girls. 'Straightforward, he said, no concern of the family's . . . except for direct family, of course.'

'I don't think Geraint should have told anyone until the will was read,' Kate objected, as they stood on the drive waving friends and relatives off. 'I think he's exceeded his duty. I shall speak to Father about it when I tackle him about going off to London.'

But Tom, not for the first time, had stolen a march on them all. When the three girls had changed and were going downstairs to dinner in the dining room, Dot called to Daisy to see if her father was going to dispense sherry in the living room first, as he always used to do when they had company. Daisy, a pretty, flighty little thing who shared an attic room with Lizzie and worked remarkably hard to keep the place fairly tidy, looked startled.

'Mr Tom? Oh, Miss, he left ages ago. Told Jan to bring the trap round soon after tea, and they rattled off down to the main road. Jan came home alone . . . oh, two or so hours since, I reckon. Mr Tom's on his way to London by now, I dessay.'

'The servants always knew more than we did.' Alex hitched her chair closer to the fire and then pulled a face. 'Gracious, log fires are horrid. You either frizzle up or freeze. There doesn't seem to be any alternative.'

'Be thankful Father isn't here; he wouldn't see a fire like that in a grate of his without raging,' Dot pointed out, holding out her own hands to the blaze. It was true that of late Tom's meanness had grown to the point of miserliness; she had often made Hywel laugh with a description of her father sitting over a tiny fire clad in his greatcoat and scarf and gloves and reproaching her, in her skimped dresses and secondhand cardigans, for complaining of the cold.

'I'm not thankful, I'm extremely annoyed,' Kate said icily. She had felt personally insulted to discover that her father had dared to leave the house without so much as a word of farewell when she was visiting him, and she had not been best pleased to discover that her husband and Humphrey Stott did not intend to dine at Plas Tegydd either, but would return to the house for their respective wives at a later hour. John, when reproached, had told her it was business, and that he and Humphrey wanted to take a look at some property on Deeside.

'And fancy Mr Geraint refusing to read the will because Father wasn't here,' Alexandra said. 'After all, we've come all this way . . . it wasn't exactly our fault that Father slipped off.

It was the last thing we expected.'

'I know. But Mr Geraint has gone to see if he can get in touch with Father and ask him whether he'll return tomorrow,' Dot reminded her sisters. 'He went huffing and puffing off to Souse'em's house ages ago, so by now . . .'

A distant clanging made all three girls sit up a little straighter; the front door bell! It would not be their father, of course, but it might be a message from the solicitor. Dot knew that both Kate and Alexandra, though they neither wanted nor expected any money from their Mother's estate, did hope for the sapphire ring. She was sure that poor Olivia had no right so much as to mention the ring in her will, but if it made Kate and Alexandra happier to believe they might inherit the sapphire she supposed it did no harm.

The door shot open; Daisy beamed at them and held the door a little wider.

'It's Mr Geraint, Miss Dot. Shall I bring 'im in?'

'Yes, of course.' Dot moved towards the door to greet this unexpected but nevertheless welcome guest. 'Do come in and sit down, Mr Geraint. My sisters are still here, but Father hasn't returned.'

Mr Geraint, in black still but with a smile now, nodded, murmured greetings, and took the chair indicated, extracting a document from his case as he did so. He took a pair of pince-nez from his waistcoat pocket, adjusted them on his nose, and then looked over the top of them at the three young women. He was smiling.

'My dears, I managed to get in touch with your papa, and I read him the will over the telephone. He gave me permission to come here tonight and read it to you. Shall I begin?'

'I'm very glad for you, Dot.' Kate, about to step into her husband's motor car, patted Dot's shoulder kindly. 'Use the money sensibly, won't you? Get yourself some nice clothes, have a really good haircut, buy shoes with a heel to give you height . . . and who knows, if you come to stay as I'm always urging, you may find yourself a husband yet!'

It was the following day. After the will-reading, both Kate and Alexandra had decided to stay overnight. Now, having endured the hours of darkness in well-aired but sparsely blanketed beds in rooms which, despite Dot's best endeavours, always smelt either musty or damp or both, they were full of condescending kindness. They were very conscious of having done their duty, of having spent three hours the previous evening helping Dot to sort through Olivia's jewellery and of having, this very morning, glanced shudderingly at the two big walk-in cupboards packed with outdated splendour in the way of evening gowns, tatty furs and afternoon dresses.

'Get rid of 'em,' had been Kate's advice, and 'Send them into town for the poor,' had been Alexandra's. Dot could not visualise 'the poor' being grateful for moth-eaten furs and low-cut evening gowns, but she supposed that Alexandra was right; they would probably find the material useful.

Once she would have felt bound to keep the material for her own use, but not now. Now she was the rich Miss Tegydd, for Olivia had left her the huge sum of five thousand pounds.

To do them justice, both Kate and Alex had been honestly delighted; they said she deserved it and must make good use of it and both pressed invitations upon her. Dot, who was already seeing a herd of fine dairy cows grazing upon immaculate pastures, murmured that they were very kind and promised that one day, when things were more settled . . .

'Goodbye, Dot dear. And don't forget, you must come to visit as soon as you've sorted Father out.' Alexandra had accepted a lift with Kate and was already in the car, sitting behind the chauffeur in his dark grey and maroon uniform. 'I know you say you don't like cities, but you don't know anything about them really. All you know is the town. Give our love to Father, and tell him how upset we were to find he'd left without saying goodbye.'

'Yes, I'll tell him.' Dot stood and waved until the car was out of sight, and then returned to the house, to stand dreaming in the study. Five thousand pounds! Enough to buy a small farm, enough to bring in quite an army of workers to put more pasture to rights, enough to build real pighouses, where she could fatten pigs . . . breed them . . . sell them . . . Dreams of farming whirled in her head.

'Miss? Any chance of you coming up again? Me an' Annie can only sort so far, though Ella's doing well with her lot.'

Daisy's little round face in the doorway brought Dot abruptly back to the present. The girls had gone, taking with them a few pieces of jewellery which Olivia had specifically left to them. Not the sapphire ring: it was a family heirloom, Mr Geraint had said a little reproachfully when Kate had asked about it; it was in no gift but Mr Tom's, and he had plans for it.

Dot could see the words *my son* crossing each sister's mind; she even read their gratified smiles as proof that each thought her own son would inherit. People could be awfully foolish — Father had made it clear enough that he did not intend either a Stott or a Macmillan to inherit Plas Tegydd. But that was all conjecture; just now she was needed in her mother's room.

'Sorry, Daisy, I was dreaming. I'll come up right away.'

By mid-afternoon, Dot and her helpers had co-opted others to give a hand, for Tom had sent a message to the colliery and a man had brought it up to the Plas. She had to admit that he had been sensible, too. He wanted all Olivia's clothing to be shared out amongst the staff, and had said that Miss Evans, the seamstress from the village, should be sent for. She was to find out what stuff was usable and what was not. The decent stuff should be made up into dresses, skirts and so on for the staff, at his expense; they should choose what they wanted. Miss Evans, not being directly involved, was to be the final arbitrator. Olivia's personal possessions, too, were to be in Dot's gift; Ella, he had instructed, was to have first pick. Even the jewellery was to go, with the exception, obviously, of the sapphire ring.

Now, with the bed, the chaise lounge, the chairs and the floor covered in clothing, Dot wandered over to the dressing table and began to sift through the jewellery lying there. The better stuff, the string of pearls, the diamond earrings, the emerald cluster ring, the gold and silver chains, had been willed away and were already with the recipients. Kate and Alex had done well there. The heirloom ring lay on its white velvet bed, winking away, waiting for . . . what? Or should it be whom? But the lesser stuff was very pretty. Garnets, turquoises, jade, ivory, some in the form of brooches, some rings, some necklaces or dress clips. Dot knew, of course, that

184

the servants would probably sell what they were given, but why should they not? These gauds and baubles had been bought to enhance Olivia's fair prettiness once; now they would be sold to bring comfort to a servant's home, or they might even be given to a girl to wear as a very special gift. There were some crystal beads which would look lovely on white skin – perhaps Daisy would like them – and the coral beads would look pretty on a young girl, too.

In another tray there were other heirlooms, but they looked pretty dull, Dot considered, beside the sapphire ring. She could not help glancing towards the ring; it meant so much! Whoever got the ring would get Plas Tegydd. She would like to know that it would go, one day, to someone who loved the Plas, as she did.

'How are we doing, Miss Dot?'

Ella, straightening from sorting through a pile of elderly tweed skirts and jackets, passed a hand across her hot forehead and blew out through pursed lips, causing a lock of greying hair to stand comically on end for the duration of her sigh.

'Not too badly, Ella. I'm afraid I'm not doing much at the moment, though. I've got to go through the jewellery, the little pieces, and see which you would like. You and the others, I mean. Have you any ideas? I don't think any of it is terribly valuable, but it's all rather pretty.'

'I'd like something for Jessica,' Ella said at once. 'You choose, Miss Dot. You'll know what a young girl would like better than I could.'

'Well, I will, but I haven't seen Jessica for years.' It would not, Dot realised, be tactful to admit that she had never managed to sort out which of the children she had seen flying along the village street when she was young had been the remarkable Jessica. 'If I were to choose, I think I'd take the crystal beads and the gold ring with the piece of jade set in it to look like a little bunch of green grapes. I'm not saying your daughter would prefer those things, mind, but I like them.'

'Yes, they're the prettiest,' Ella decided, having cast a glance over the tumbled bits and pieces. 'If it's all right, then, they're the ones I'll choose. Lizzie came up earlier and said she'd like that brooch with all the purple twinkly stuff in it, and Annie asked if she could have them big yellow-brown beads.'

'Oh, the amber; yes, of course. I think they're quite good ones,' Dot said, picking up the long, heavy necklace. 'Well, Daisy? What's your choice?'

Daisy, with both arms full of clothing, was about to turn for the door but she paused courteously to reply.

'I'd like the bird brooch, please, Miss Dot. It'll look ever so good with me best hat. And the garnet ring. Cook said as she'd like a bracelet but someone else could choose for her. We settled it between us, miss, that we'd take two small things or one big one. That's why Annie got the beads.'

'That's fine. Ella will see that everyone gets a fair share,' Dot remarked. 'Where are you taking that stuff, Daisy?'

'Down to the stableyard; it's for the workhouse. It's all good heavy material, but most of it's been folded too long for taking apart and making up again, Miss Evans says, so it'll go straight to the old folk.'

'I'm keeping back the newer dresses to work on,' Miss Evans said, looking up from the pile of clothing she was scrutinising. 'There's some blue cotton here, Miss Dot, that 'ud make up a treat for you. And a primrose voile, too. Your mother took great care of her clothes.'

Dot laughed. 'And when would I wear primrose voile? But I'll have the blue cotton, if you think it will suit me. Gracious, what a lot of boots and shoes!'

'I'm having the brown leather boots; fit me as if they was made for me they do,' Daisy said, pushing the door wide. 'And that pair of pale blue shoes with the high heels. Oh, miss, you should see me in 'em! Every inch a lady I look, though they pinches something awful!'

'I bet you do. Well, don't forget. Apart from the jewellery my father set aside, he'll be only too happy for you to have a few things to remember my mother by.' She smiled at Ella and followed Daisy to the doorway, standing with her hand on the architrave as she finished her remarks. 'Ella will sort everything out, won't you, Ella? And can someone tell me whether arrangements have been made for luncheon?'

She had not spoken to Cook since the previous day and it now occurred to her that her father might have told Cook she was no longer needed. If so, Dot said firmly to herself, she would have to disillusion him, for she had no intention of cooking so much as a boiled egg. She had never been taught to cook and did not intend to learn. She had enough on her hands as it was. However, Father would be sure to try for yet more economies if he was truly buying the Wynd, and she did not intend to let him penalise the house or its staff if she could possibly prevent it. Olivia had left him quite a lot of money, and it should be spent, not misered away somewhere, she told herself. But Ella, answering, gave no indication that Cook's importance in the household had changed since the mistress's death.

'Oh yes, Cook's always managed without much help, since your mam was took bad,' Ella said. 'She's using the cold meat left over from yesterday with a nice salad and some sauté potatoes. There was trifle enough left over from dinner last night to last a week, so you know what your dessert will be.'

'Oh, no! People didn't eat as much as we thought they would at the funeral tea, and I told Cook to prepare dinner for a large party as well,' Dot said with a groan. 'Look, let's put the stuff into a big basket and send it down to the village school. The children will enjoy it, and Father isn't back for another day, or so I believe. Otherwise . . . well, you know what Father is . . .'

The women agreed that they knew what Tom was; none of them relished the thought of eating cold meat and trifle for a week or more. Tom liked his food but was largely indifferent to what his daughter and the servants ate. He would speedily rebel over the constant appearance of the trifle on his own table, but would react sharply if it was wasted. Dot could just hear him suggesting that she and the servants wade their way through it for breakfast if need be. They would definitely get rid of the left-overs before his homecoming.

'We're all agreed then, that we'll have cold meat and trifle for luncheon, and then tell Cook to send it down to the village? Good. I'll go down and warn Mrs Ross.'

When the gong boomed, therefore, everyone trooped into the kitchen. The master was away and there was no reason why Miss Dot should not have company to her meal. They all sat down to their cold meats and fried potatoes and halfway through the meal they began to talk about the pit. Dot found herself listening so avidly that she nearly forgot to eat. The servants were used to her being about, and the farmhands, who had also come in for the meal, looked on her, she believed, as one of themselves. Did she not toil with them, understand their problems, try her best to see that they got a fair deal? So the talk went on and Dot listened, not knowing whether she had been forgotten or whether, more probably, they did not care that she was listening, for she had never split on them before and was not likely to do so now. Besides, what they were discussing was fascinating to them all and of particular significance to Dot.

'Mr Tom's good as got the Black Wynd now.' That was Gwil, reaching for another thick slice of Cook's home-made bread. He buttered it, put a generous round of beef on top and bit into a pungent pickled onion. Then, mouth crammed, he continued, thickly, to talk.

'It's all signed and sealed, you know, save for the last little bit. The manager there, Felbrigg, isn't too pleased, I've heard. Thinks the boss'll look into things, mek 'em keep the rules, and that isn't the way Felbrigg made money for Carruthers.'

'No? How, then? I thought 'twas a good pit.'

That was Loopy, who was a good horseman and ploughed one of the straightest furrows in the county. He was called Loopy because he always wore braces but never over his shoulders; they hung in loops down to this knees. Dot considered they had done well to get him to work for them, because he could have gone anywhere. But he was a local man and had wanted to get married, and Tom had a tied cottage vacant . . . So now Loopy worked on the land and his wife came up and did the rough work at the Plas a couple of times a week. A nice, plump little woman she was with a wandering eye which should have been corrected by spectacles, only she never could abide the things. Netta.

'A good pit? It's one of the worst, save that the coal's first-rate. Oh, the Wynd's got all the badnesses; it's wet, it's terrible deep, and it's mortal hot. There's a deal of gas underground, too, though Felbrigg always denies it. Says it's the men not wanting to go into the deeps.'

'Aye, that's all true.' Ted had been a collier, but had lost half a hand in a badly placed blast down the pit. Now he worked on the land when he could and kept a pig and a few chickens up on the moor. He had built himself a sort of cottage – that was the best way to describe it, Dot thought – and managed, somehow, to keep body and soul together. People did what they could because they liked Ted, with his short, stocky body, square, rather pugnacious face and twinkling little eyes. He was reputed to be a devil for the girls, but Dot doubted the truth of that; girls liked him, but not as a lover. He was also a dealer – if you wanted to sell a pony but didn't have a ready market, then you gave it to Ted, who saw to it that the pony was sold to someone, somewhere, at a better price than you would have thought possible. Since he obviously took a commission and people were still well-satisfied, he was a dealer to respect. He cast his eyes now round the table to make sure that everyone was listening to him. 'Worst part is, though, that the coal's all down very deep, so you've a nasty long trek from the pit's eye to your place.' He reached out a long arm for the pickles; very soon now, Dot knew, they would have to lay Ted off for the winter. Even now he was only working three days out of the seven. No doubt he was eating as much as he could against the lean times ahead. Glancing around the table, she noticed that all the farmhands seemed to eat faster and more seriously than the indoor servants, and of course it was sensible that they should. They worked a good deal harder and earned a good deal less.

'Yes, that's right,' Lizzie piped up, leaning her elbows on the table and staring across at Ted. 'Know a feller works there, I do; he says a five mile walk he do have from the pit's eye to his place. A walk that long takes money off of you.'

'The boss'll sort it out, now he's got the place,' Cook said comfortably. 'Annie, get another jar of pickled onions from the shelf, there's a good girl.'

Annie scraped her chair back and headed across the flags to the big walk-in pantry.

'I don't understand, rightly, why Mr Tom wants that place,' she said. 'Old Curruthers is only selling because it isn't making the money it was, so why does Mr Tom want it at all?'

'He wants to join it up with the Olwen, for a start,' Ella said authoritatively. As the wife and the mother of colliers she obviously felt her opinion was worth hearing and the others listened attentively enough. 'My Glyn says that'll save a lot of walking when it's done. And of course you know what Mr Tom is for machinery; there's room at the Wynd for lots, whereas down the Olwen the men say they're cramped for elbow-room when the big machines are talked about. And they say a really good collier steers clear of the Wynd, what with the cheltermasters and all. Mr Tom reckons that if he puts in decent men they'll see what needs doing and they'll work together to get the coal out.'

'So he'll put a stop to the cheltermasters, eh?' That was Ted, between mouthfuls. 'Go back myself, I might, if they did that. No use to try for the Olwen or the Roland, seeing as they're arguing over shifts and wanting to make the men take a five-day week, but the Wynd, run proper, and without none of that cheltermaster nonsense . . . '

Even Dot had heard about the cheltermasters: the old system of paying wages. The money for each gang or group of workers was paid to the cheltermaster, who was a sort of foreman, and it was his job to divide the money up amongst his gang. No doubt some were scrupulous but it was well known that a good few were not; it was an iniquitous system and had never been used in either of the Tegydd pits. Dot was sure Tom would never allow it to continue down the Wynd once he was owner.

'They'll do it, or rather Mr Tom will.' Ella got to her feet and went over to where the kettle was fairly jumping on the hob. 'Make the tea, shall I, Cook? It can brew whilst we eat the trifle.'

'Aye, thanks, Ella.' Cook leaned back in her chair and burped behind her hand. 'Beg pardon. Aye, Mr Tom wouldn't stand for cheltering; some of them fellers would murder their own mothers for a groat, as the saying goes. I've heard tell the cheltermasters charge double rate for lamp oil and tools, too.'

'Well, how can that be?' Gwil, despite having lived in the area all his life, came from a farming family and knew almost nothing about mining. Indeed, when one of his sons had suggested becoming a collier for the better money, Gwil had all but run him out of the house. 'How can a collier be charged for his tools?'

'They aren't his, exactly; the colliers hire their tools from the owner. If they lose 'em or maltreat 'em, they have to pay for 'em. But they say the cheltermasters double up on whatever the owner's hire charge may be.'

'What? D'you mean Mr Tom charges 'em to hire tools?'

Ella, as if becoming aware of Dot for the first time, looked uncomfortable. 'Well, aye, 'course he does. They all do. Tools and lamp oil. That and union money comes off.'

'First time they do come at me to hire a plough, I'm off,' Gwil announced, to laughter. 'Damn me. Always thought farm'ands were badly paid, but at least they don't charge us to use the plough and the sickles and the shovels.'

'Only because they pay so little you couldn't afford it,' Cook said bluntly. 'Now who's going to have seconds of that trifle?'

After the meal, Dot helped the servants to pack the baskets with food for the school, and then headed for the stables. Hywel would be up in the birchwood this afternoon and she had said she would join him there if she could. She had not yet told him of her good fortune and she was looking forward to doing so. There were plenty of other things, too, that she wanted to discuss. It was so good to have a friend like Hywel, constant, honest, ready to listen to woes and make them seem small, ready to counsel, advise, scoff at fears and knock down bogeys. He was the perfect friend. And now, if only he would, they could go into partnership over stock, or land, or even a smallholding, using her money!

Not even to herself could she say how *very* much she liked Hywel; how desperately lost and alone she would be without him. If things had been different, if she had seen in his eyes the look she knew so often shone out of her own . . . but it had not happened, probably never would. I'm plain, she reminded herself now as she went into Matchless's stall. I'm little and dark and ugly, I'm a gnome, and Hywel is tall and golden and beautiful. I can't expect him to feel . . . to feel anything for me, other than friendship.

But still, there was no harm in telling him about the money, hoping that it might make up for her smallness, darkness, ugliness.

Matchless, who loved her, whinnied softly as she began to groom him. She was a conscientious rider and would not have dreamed of tacking him up without first going all over him from top to toe, from the small, pricked ears to the frogs of his hooves. It was how Jan had taught her to look after her pony when she was small, and now that she was old enough to appreciate his feelings she knew that Matchless enjoyed being groomed, having his hooves oiled and worked over with the hoof pick, feeling the careful tug of the curry comb on mane and tail.

'We're going up to the tops, my laddo,' she was murmuring as she worked over his legs, checking them for the loathsome little bot eggs which gave horses such trouble if you did not take them off as promptly as they appeared. 'A nice canter, then a gallop. You'll enjoy it so much on this sunny afternoon . . . '

'Miss Dot, have you got a moment?' Jan's head appeared, tortoiselike, round the edge of the stall. 'The grey mare's sick. I've got a drench that'll most likely do the trick, but it'll tek two of us.'

'What, Maria?' Maria was Olivia's staid old horse, broad-flanked, sweet-tempered, inclined to laziness. 'I thought yesterday that she was slower than usual when I took her into the Shelly Edge for her exercise.' She smoothed Matchless's forelock back, plonked a kiss on the white, four-pointed star, and moved out of the stall. 'Right. I'll come and give you a hand. I was going to take Matchless out, but we can go later.'

Later would be too late for Hywel, she realised, because he would not stay in the birchwood when she did not turn up, but it did not really matter. There were other days in plenty, and when you had good news to impart a little delay only made it more exciting.

Eleven

'That's a good big lot, mun!'

Hywel, his hands still reverberating from the tremendous whack he had just given the wall to bring down a huge piece of coal like that, grunted. Dickie, his filler, was an enthusiastic youngster and was always boasting about Hywel's prowess as a getter, but Hywel was thinking, and did not want to start a conversation with Dickie just now.

He swung his pick at the coal face again, felt it bite, pulled, dodged the coal tumble and then took up a wedge. A nice slit there now to hammer the wedge into, and then he would force another one in a bit further along . . . his eye chose the very spot . . . and in half an hour they would have enough coal down to keep them both busy until leaving-off time.

'Take this one up to the drawers, shall I?'

Dickie's voice, squeaking into falsetto now and again from its manly deepness, promised some time alone, time for thought. Hywel nodded.

'Aye, you do that, lad,' he encouraged. As the wheels squeaked off along the rails he gave himself up to pleasant meditation, though he did not for one moment stop the long, measured swings of pick and hammer at the face.

Today, Jess was coming home. He had been writing to her all term, patiently sitting down in his shared bedroom and writing to tell Jess what was going on. In fact he had been writing to her for over a year, but until late summer his letters had been duty ones and hers scarcely more than notes. However, he had persevered, and it showed that patience can pay dividends because, in the end, he had got what he wanted: Jessica's friendship. At long last her attitude towards him had reverted to the delightful brother-sister relationship they had enjoyed as children, until Ella, with her serpent-in-Eden act, had whispered in Jessica's ear that she was a girl of promise, a young lady at the convent school in town, and that she wanted better than a collier lad for her companion.

Even now, Hywel was not sure why Jessica had changed again, from the remote, uninterested young woman she had become to a warm and friendly person anxious to spend her time with him. But changed she had. It had begun when she had got back from Cambridge at the end of June; had she been bored, perhaps, with village pursuits? There was no telling, but she had certainly shown more interest in him and his doings than she had for many years.

However, it was not until a week before her return to college that the complete breakthrough had come. He had suggested, one sunny September Sunday, that she might like to spend a day in Chester with him. Rather to his surprise she had accepted quite eagerly and they had set off, with sandwiches and an apple each, to catch the train into the city.

It had been a wonderful, golden day, with no breeze, even, to stir the leaves which hung over the river, dappling the sunshine. The two of them had strolled along the river-path, watching the pleasure boats chug past, seeing the hire boats, with young men in boaters at the oars, carrying their burden of pretty young girls with bobbed hair and rouged cheeks further down the river to the meadows, where they would moor and drink wine and eat exotic food from the wicker picnic baskets tucked away in the stern of the boat.

There was so much to look at, so much to enjoy! Under the castle wall artists exhibited their paintings and the two of them had gazed at the bearded and smocked young men, with their paintings and their vivid, untidy girl friends, who strolled about criticising each other's work and trying to appear indifferent to the members of the public who might – or might not – buy.

Jess had been delightful, walking along with her hand tucked into his arm and thanking him for opening her eyes to the city's charms. He had laughed at her, and they had gone into a tea-garden and had a lovely bought tea – Jessica's description – of tiny little sandwiches and scones with cream and jam and slices of delicious almond cake, as well as a big pot of tea and some hot buttered toast which Hywel had suddenly fancied just when they thought themselves sated.

Afterwards they walked further along the bank and threw their sandwiches to the swans so that Ella's feelings would not be hurt, and they had talked. How they had talked! Catching up on years of near-silence, they had talked about university, the colliery, their secret ambitions, their lives. About neighbours, ferreting, the works of Charles Dickens, how to mend a hedge when gypsies have broken it down. About sitting hens and higher mathematics, about the laws of physics and the reason why birds migrate at the summer's end. About what coal dust does to your lungs and what overwork does to your brain.

Finally, when they had talked themselves hoarse, they sat on the train going home and smiled at each other and knew that this was the end of the misunderstandings, the coolness, the silence. Jessica had outgrown her feeling that it was childish and ignorant to want his friendship and he had cast aside his feeling that she had gone out into the wide world and left him behind, the star twinkling in the heavens whilst he, the mole, dug dully underground.

She had only been at home for a couple of days after that Sunday, but busy though she had been, and busy though he had been, nothing could take away their pleasure in this old friendship revived.

And ever since she had gone back, the letters had whizzed across the country; satisfying letters, full of their thoughts and feelings. So when she had written that she was returning for a weekend in a friend's company, to attend the wedding of yet another friend, he had been delighted. She would come to Chester in the friend's motor, she explained, arriving on the Thursday evening, and would spend Friday in the city and Saturday, of course, at the wedding. But she would come home on Saturday evening, spend the whole day with them on Sunday, and would arrange for her friend's motor to pick her up early on the Monday morning. Be sure to tell Mam it's just a fluke because of the free ride in the motor, she reminded him.

It had not been easy to tell his mother that Jessica was coming home for a long weekend, because Ella had promptly and nastily demanded to see the letter. Not possible. He knew at once that if she saw the easy, intimate, friendly letter she would move heaven and earth to put a stop to the correspondence. She'd always been odd over any show of friendliness between himself and Jessica. So he had said that the letter was scarcely more than a note and that he'd destroyed it, and his mother had railed at him and called him a great booby and assured Glyn that Hywel was so half-soaked that he had probably got the whole message wrong and Jessica was not coming home at all.

However, Hywel knew that she believed him in her heart, and watched detachedly as she prepared for her daughter's arrival whilst denying with every other sentence that Jessica would arrive. He had accepted when he was quite small that Ella blamed him for his father's death. But why should she grudge him the affection of a girl who had been brought up as his sister? It was beyond him. So, as he had always done, he simply pushed it out of his mind, worked as hard as he could, and enjoyed his life outside the home where he knew himself bitterly resented.

Now, working away steadily with his pick, he thought about Jessica's Cambridge. She loved the town itself and her life there, but did not think highly of Cambridgeshire, which she described as flat and muddy, all keening wind, stunted trees, and mile after mile of marsh. He wondered, sometimes, if the Other Place was near Cambridge. Certainly it was marshy, but the other descriptions did not fit in the least. He loved it still, but he supposed that for a girl born and bred amidst the mountains, the marshes, especially in winter, might lack charm.

He had always worked hard, latterly because he was saving for his smallholding, but now he did not translate each fall of coal into just pigs, milch cows, or fruit trees. Now, for his sister and friend there must be trips on the river, visits to the cinema, books and pictures. He had always enjoyed giving and he knew that Jessica adored gifts and spoiling and pampering — who did not? So he would earn his money, in some small part, for her pleasure.

He had driven the second wedge in deep and already two vertical cracks gaped. He began to hammer a third wedge in above the other two, seeing the cracks begin to climb and widen, until he judged the moment ripe to stand well back and swing the hammer with all his strength, driving the last wedge in so deep that the coal, in agony almost, must burst from its place on the face to bound and leap in great unwieldy pieces all over the hard-packed earth of the floor.

He got his shovel and began to move the coal. Each of the great, glinting lumps represented . . . what? An hour at the theatre? A trip down the river? A page or two of a leather-bound copy of *Macbeth*? He had no idea. He only knew that he worked as hard as he could for every hour that he was at the face, and that his wage at the end of the week was earned, every penny of it. There was talk of a glut of coal, of the pits having to agree amongst themselves to provide only so much each week. It would be a quota, so they said. But he did not believe that would ever happen, especially now, with winter coming on and everyone wanting a good fire to see them through the bad months. He began to shovel the coal into a heap, sweat gleaming on his back and dripping down his face, and just as Dickie and two empty tubs appeared in the circle of the lamp's rays he got the feeling again. A moment only this time, but a good moment. Just the blue sky above and corn stubble and good earth beneath, with the feel of the plough in his hand, the smell of the turned soil in his nostrils and the gulls' plaintive mewing as they followed behind, battling against the same strong, steady sea-wind which blew his hair into a plume and chilled his hot brow.

Then, oddly, he found he was falling, the earth and the plough rushed up to meet him, something struck his forehead . . . and he was rescuing his dropped shovel and Dickie was reminding him that the whistle had gone but that if they both worked like the very devil and pushed like a pair of oxen they'd make the cage in time to get this last load up to the surface before the shift's end.

In the cage going up, Stan asked him what he'd done to his face. His exploring fingers found a cut just above his eyebrow; it was quite a size, too — a couple of inches long, though not deep. The blood had congealed in it already. It was little more than a long scratch.

'Well, mun?' Stan leaned close, holding his lamp near Hywel's face. 'Clean cut, it is. Been fighting?'

Fighting was not unknown below, but it was rare. Hywel grinned and shook his head.

'No, mun, is it likely? Clouted myself with my shovel . . . or maybe it was a bit of coal flying up the way they do. Truth is I'm none too sure. I was working, see, and you know how you get when you work and it's going well.'

'Aye, I know. Doing anything after work, are you? Evenings are drawing in now, but I've some digging needs seeing to; get pig manure in and then the ground'll improve whilst it lies idle.'

Hywel returned some answer, but his thoughts were far away. Just when – and more important, where – had he received that blow on the head? It was impossible that it could have occurred in the Other Place. Nothing that happened there could physically affect him. Yet he was very sure that he had tripped and gone a purler just as he was leaving the Other Place . . . had that made him trip and gash his forehead against the shovel, or the face, once he was back in the pit?

The cage reached the surface and the men began to stream out, handing their lamps to the fireman as they left. Hywel hurried out with them. If he had struck his face on the coal it would probably leave a blue scar, though not all coal-bites did so. Anyway, what did it matter? It was either the face or the shovel, for one could not come back scarred from a dream!

He began to cross the yard, still in all his dirt, and saw, hovering a little up the road which led to the village, a small, fiery-topped figure in pale green. Jess. His heart lifted and he knew his black face was split by a huge and probably stupid grin. He went towards her but before he could say a word Jessica gave a squeak, grabbed his filthy old pit-coat, and kissed him on the chin, then stood back, eyes like stars. She was wearing a light green suit with tassels and pretty little boots and her thick mass of hair was tied back from her face with green satin ribbons. She looked smart, sophisticated, but her eyes shone with friendship and her mouth was all smiles.

'Hello, Hywel! I say, you *are* black! Better come home and clean up before you kiss *me*!'

'Black you are too, now,' Hywel informed her. 'Don't go touching me, girl. You've already got coal dust on your face, and them gloves will never be quite the same again.'

Jess examined her white gloves ruefully and then tucked a hand into Hywel's elbow. She pulled at him and they began to walk back to the village.

'You're right. Too impulsive I am for the good of my gloves,' she said, turning so that she could speak up into his face. 'However. Glad to see me, are you, Hywel?'

Assuring her, truthfully, that he was very glad indeed, Hywel could not help noticing that despite her smart suit and her elegance, his Jessica was no beauty; she was still too skinny, her hair too carroty and her freckles too numerous. You could tell she was clever, too, because she had a high forehead and a habit of looking at you with mocking intensity out of her almond-shaped greeny-grey eyes which were so cold when she was cross and so warm when she was not.

But beauty did not matter between a brother and sister. You accepted the outer shell and loved the inner person.

'What are you thinking of, Hywel? You look very solemn, whatever it is on your mind.'

'I was thinking I was lucky to have a sister like you, Jess. And don't go getting swollen-headed, because I think you're equally lucky to have a brother like me.'

Jess squeezed his arm and gazed earnestly up into his face.

'That's very nicely put, Hywel, except that I'm not your sister and you're not my brother.'

'Not . . . oh, I see what you mean. But we've been . . . '

Stan, drawing level with them, took Jessica's other hand and tucked it into his elbow, then he spoke over the top of her head to Hywel, winking as he did so.

'Shall we give the littl'un a bit of a lift, then? Come on, mun, we'll hurry her home for tea.'

Jess shrieked as she was lifted off her feet and borne up the hill, but Hywel could tell she rather liked it really, so he too began to hurry until the brothers were running, their squeaking, giggling burden bouncing along between them.

They did not let her down until they reached the gate and then they only did so because the three of them could not pass through it, arms linked. Jessica upbraided them breathlessly, Stan and Hywel laughed at her, and then all three of them disappeared into the cottage.

*

Dot hid in the ditch until all the men had disappeared. She felt sick and cold with disappointment, for she had come all the way down the valley to the gates of the colliery determined to see Hywel and tell him about her inheritance, and look what had happened. That sister of his, that Jessica Ella was so mad about, had turned up out of the blue, in a terribly smart coat and skirt, and had whisked him off with her. She had kissed him, as well, which Dot thought very forward of her.

The trouble was, she could not possibly walk up to Hywel when he had his sister hanging on his arm, so she had been forced to hide until the very last man had left the pit. And to be honest, the friendliness between Hywel and Jessica had startled her considerably; he rarely talked of the other girl, but when he did she had somehow got the impression that far from being friends they were wary of one another. Yet she had run up to him, flung her arms round him, and kissed him. *Was* it Jessica? Or was it some other girl, some wicked creature who had designs on Hywel?

It was chilly in the ditch and thinking dismal thoughts did not help. Dot climbed rather stiffly out and stood for a moment in the fast-fading light, wondering. Then she realised that Stan, who was shy, would scarcely have seized the arm of a comparative stranger and run her up the road the way he had. She smiled. Of course it was Jessica, home from college for some reason and eager for a spree and a laugh. No need to worry. Jessica was only his sister, after all!

This connection lasted a hundred yards up the road, and then another, less pleasing thought struck her. Hywel had never, in all the years she had known him, attempted to take her hand or her arm except, so to speak, in the course of their business. If they were setting traps and she was doing it wrong he would take her fingers in his and show her how to do it right, or he would hoist her over a tall wall or grab her and heave her through a thicket. Once, he had kissed the tip of her nose . . . but lightly, teasingly. That did not count. At least, it did not count as a sign of affection, because it was, if anything, less loving than the kiss he had bestowed on his sister.

There was the rub, Dot realised, mooning up the road and scuffing up the dust with her boots as she did so. She thought of him . . . no, never mind how she thought of him, but he obviously thought of her as a sister! She did not want to be his sister! She wanted . . . she wanted . . .

Somewhere ahead of her an owl shrieked, and Dot's attention focused on it gladly. Useless to speculate on Hywel's possible feelings for her, or on her feelings for him, come to that. After all, what she had come down here to propose was really a partnership more than a marriage — two people who were friends and had the same ambition could surely go into partnership without having to be in love? And anyway, from what she'd seen of it, marriage was not such a marvellous institution. She thought she and Hywel could probably have a very good sort of marriage, both working hard on their farm, without any of that other business — the carryings-on that would lead to babies, and discontent, and eventually, she supposed, to Hywel's taking a mistress.

The sheer absurdity of that last thought stopped her in her tracks again, for a giggle. How stupid she was! True, her father did seem to have a woman friend, or so her sisters thought, but he was the only person she knew to do such a thing. Ella had had two husbands sure enough, but she had only married a second time because her first husband had died. Other than that, all the servants who were married stayed married, as did the farmhands and the labourers who came and went in the summer months. So why on earth did she tell herself that if she married Hywel he would take a mistress?

If you want to think silly thoughts, then think about Kate and Alex, arguing over the sapphire ring which, she was now sure, would be held in trust until Father decided which of his grandchildren was to be granted Plas Tegydd. Or . . . her blood ran cold . . . until he produced a son of his own.

A son of his own? That was silly. Tom was sixty. Not the sort of age to remarry, surely? No, she was being absurd to start worrying about a possibility as remote as her father's bringing another woman to the Plas. She looked around her at the thickening dark; there was a wind but not a hearty, buffeting one. A nightwind, a crafty light nipping wind, touched her cheek with chill and brought leaves drifting down from the trees, dropping them with a tiny crisp flicker of sound on to the hard earth of the lane. Dot, enchanted by the night now that she had made herself notice it, heard the stream long before she reached it, chuckling and bubbling over its rocky bed. She peered through the branches at it and saw a fox silhouetted against the gleaming silver of the water, saw it pause to drink before making its wicked way onward.

Did I shut up the hens? Dot asked herself, breaking into a run and then slowing to a walk again. If she had not done it, Gwil or Ted or Jan would. They approved of her venture into farming and did their best to see that she did not lose by it. It was Jan who had found her a steady sale for eggs – a baker in town who paid rather less than she wanted but bought regularly. And Ted and Gwil had helped her to build up her milk round; no more than eight or ten families yet but she knew it would get bigger and better over the winter. The roundsman who carted his big cans of milk round most of the local villages had to come up from the town, and was not reliable when the weather was bad.

A rustling in the hedge had her stopping to peer into the thickness. It never crossed her mind that it might be a human being, for why should a person lurk in a hedge? People, in Dot's experience, did not do such things. And she was right. It was the cross-looking tomcat owned by Mrs Long at the Black Horse. He had been stalking the sleepy, night-hunched birds, creeping with what he probably fondly imagined was stealth through the thickest part of the hedge, and the rustling Dot had heard was the cat's fall, ignominious and heavy, through the branches, landing with a thud on the dead leaves and twigs beneath the bushes.

'Silly animal,' Dot reproved as the cat wriggled fatly upright, gave her a glare which placed the responsibility for his fall squarely on her shoulders, and nudged his way with what dignity he could muster back onto the roadway. Ignoring her, he stalked away, tail up, legs mincing, feet so light that they did not even disturb the dust. Before he had gone a yard, though, something rustled in the other ditch. Quickly, despite his girth, he turned and glided out of sight. There was a brief scuffle, some swearing, and then Dot heard him squeeze through the hedge in to the meadow on the further side. Safe, over there, from the human laughter a cat of dignity and substance finds so galling.

Amused by the encounter, Dot continued to walk through

the darkening night towards her home. The dark did not worry her, for she knew the lane well, and her eyes grew accustomed to the gloom so quickly that she walked as confidently as if it were broad daylight. As she walked, the exciting thought of her inheritance returned and she began, once more, to plan what she and Hywel could do with the money. I could buy a place and both of us could run it, or I could offer to put my money into stock and equipment and let Hywel rent a smallholding, she told herself, turning into the driveway of the Plas and inhaling the hauntingly sweet scent that one of the fir trees gave forth after dark. She turned up the narrow little path that cut off some of the drive so that she could go indoors through the stableyard; quicker than hammering on the front door and bringing a sleepy servant running, and a good deal less bother for everyone. But she did look back, as she turned away, to where the bulk of the house loomed against the stars. It looked wonderfully romantic in the dark, with almost no hint of its daytime air of desperately hanging on to respectability.

There was a light in the drawing room. It stopped her short, staring. Was Father back, then? But if he was he would not be in the drawing room. He would either be eating, in the breakfast parlour since he would be alone, or in the study. Though of course it was possible that he had popped into the drawing room for a moment just to see to something.

She crossed the stableyard and went in at the side door. In the tiny, flagged cloakroom she kicked off her muddy boots and scuffed into her thin slippers. Then she abandoned her jacket to its fate and made for the drawing room. It would be rather nice to find that Kate or Alex had come calling, though unlikely, in view of the fact that they had only just left. Unless they had realised how unfair it was to leave her all alone here with the work of clearing up her mother's things?

She was halfway across the hall when the drawing room door opened and someone came out.

'Hello, Father! So you're back! What on earth were you doing in the drawing room, though? And you've left the lamp, as well.'

Tom cleared his throat. He looked red-faced and his eyes slid about in a guilty and yet somehow defiant manner.

'Ah, Dot. I was just coming to find you. We've visitors . . . come in and . . . '

Dot followed her father into the drawing room. For a moment she did not recognise the woman sitting sideways on the sofa, facing a small boy in a sailor suit. Then the woman turned to her and began to smile and Dot bounced forward, both hands held out.

'Edie! Oh, Edie, I would never have known you! How are you? Is this your little boy? How very handsome he is. What's his name? And what are you called, now that you're a married lady?' She turned to the small boy, holding out her hand. 'May we shake hands? I'm Dot. When I was small your mother taught me my lessons.'

'I'm Tommy,' the small boy said gravely, staring up at Dot. 'Are you the girl Father said would be my sister and take care of me?'

Dot stared from face to face. As her eyes met those of her father and her ex-governess, both coloured, though Edie's blush was merely a wild-rose flush and her father's a deepening of an already ruddy complexion.

'Father? Edie? I don't quite understand . . . Tommy seems to think . . . '

Tom harrumphed. He looked embarrassed, but also pleased and proud.

'Edie married me yesterday, Dot, and she has come here to be a mother to you as well as to Tommy.'

'Yesterday? I c-can't believe it! Mother only d-died three days ago!'

Dot could not hide her shock and disbelief. Even Tom, thoughtless and selfish as he was, could not have married Edie so quickly! He would put people so firmly against him that they would never accept him again. His name would stink in the nostrils of the righteous and even his workers would despise him. And *why*, for goodness' sake? Why not wait for a year? He must have waited a good few already, since they had obviously been meeting ever since Mother had sent Edie away. The child was five or six and it must be all of five or six years . . .

204

Pennies dropped in Dot's brain with an almost audible clang. She scrutinised Tommy carefully; he looked back at her with deep, friendly interest.

He was a handsome little boy, dark-eyed and merry. A square, obstinate chin, straight, rather thick brows, a wicked trick of making one dimple appear by his mouth though he had not smiled . . . he was the image of her father.

Dot sat down rather more suddenly than she had intended in one of the wing chairs which still had all of its legs and most of its upholstery. She stared at Edie's waistline. Her thickening waistline.

So that was it! His mistress had given him a son, but for obvious reasons Tom had not been able to make sure that he was a Tegydd. Beneath her breath, Dot whispered, 'Tommy Edenthorpe?' and saw Edie give a sigh and a small, reluctant nod. 'I . . . see. And the next child will be a Tegydd?' Again the nod, less reluctant this time, and accompanied by a smile instead of a sigh. Dot turned sharply on her father.

'*Now* what'll we do? If people hear that you married again within a couple of days of Mother's death they'll never speak a civil word to poor Edie. Probably not to you either, Father. As for the boy, and the new baby . . . well, I can guess what local people will call them, no matter how you may hope to force their complaisance. You've ruined them far more effectively than your worst enemy could.'

'I told him,' Edie said. It was the first time she had spoken and her voice, warm, humorous, velvet-soft, had not changed a jot. 'I told him and told him, but your father's an obstinate man. Is there anything we can do to put things right?'

'You must go away again, you and Tommy,' Dot said firmly. 'I'm sorry to say it, but it needn't be very far or for very long. How about Llangollen? Or Chester? You could go for six months, until feelings are less sensitive . . .'

Tom had sat himself down on the sofa by his wife and taken the boy between his knees, but now he frowned and shook his head.

'No, impossible. The baby's due in four months, and it must be born here.'

The three of them stared at each other.

'If the baby's due in four months, then you might as well

205

forget any thought of passing it off as your legitimate heir,' Dot pointed out. 'People will snigger behind their hands, you know. You must let Edie and the child go away and then you must pretend that you've met this charming young widow you once knew rather well. You can bring her back here as your bride and announce that you intend to bring up the children as your own. People will guess, of course, but they won't be quite certain, even if you do give them food for speculation for the next ten years. And there won't be any nastiness, really there won't, Father, towards Edie or the children. They'll say . . . behind our backs, of course . . . that you did right by the young woman. I think it could work out well.'

Tom shook his head, scowling, but Edie was smiling and nodding.

'Dot's right, Tom,' she said gaily. 'What a good thing no one's seen us yet. Tommy and I will leave here first thing tomorrow morning before anyone is up and you can find us a nice flat in Chester for six months. Don't try to persuade me otherwise, for I've no wish to upset people, and it will be easier for the children if things are pleasant. I know you'll look after us, and no matter what other people may believe you and I – and Dot, of course – will know that the child will be born in wedlock and will be your son. Or daughter, of course.'

'There, Father,' Dot said soothingly, getting to her feet. 'How many of the servants have seen Edie and the boy?'

'Only Ben and Lizzie, because I told her dinner for three, and . . . '

'Oh, dear! Did you tell them Edie was your wife?'

'No, he didn't, dear.' Edie's voice was calm. 'I told him that his daughters must be the first to know. I think everyone has assumed I came to offer my condolences on your loss and your father and I met on the train.'

Dot tried to repress a wistful wish that this had indeed been the case, and walked to the door.

'Then that's settled. You've ordered dinner, Father? Perhaps you'd better tell Lizzie I'm in, whilst I go up and wash.'

Upstairs in her room she poured water from the jug into the cracked handbasin and washed briefly, darkening the water with the dirt from her hands and wiping the rest off on the towel. She hurried because it was cold and because her lamp was flickering and faint; she had no wish to find herself half in and half out of a clean dress when the light went out. However by dint of extreme speed and despatch she was halfway down the stairs again before the lamp went out, by which time it did not matter. She took it through to the kitchen, however, because she wanted to make sure all the servants saw that she was on good terms with her father and her ex-governess. Also, she wanted Eggo, Lizzie's daft brother, to fill the lamp, trim the wick and have it in good working order by the time she wanted to go to bed.

Whilst there, telling the staff that Edie was married to an insurance clerk and yes, wasn't the little boy charming, it occurred to her that she had not thought about her inheritance nor about Hywel since the moment she had confronted her father in the hall. So there was good in all things!

'If you'll excuse me,' Edie said at last, when the meal was over and the coffee drunk to the last drop. 'I think Tommy and I will make our way to our room now. He must be worn out, poor child, and I'm tired myself, what with one thing and another.' She came round the table and hugged Dot, then kissed her cheek with genuine affection. 'Goodnight, dear, and perhaps I should say goodbye, for I daresay we'll be off before you're up in the morning. You've been a charming and attentive hostess and a thoughtful and sensible friend – how very well you've turned out!'

'Goodnight, Edie,' Dot said, returning the kiss. 'As for not being up when you leave, of course I shall be, or consider myself a very poor hostess indeed. I'll drive you to the station, if you like.'

'I'll drive 'em myself,' Tom said grumpily. He was now eyeing both his new wife and his daughter from beneath lowered brows, looking for all the world like a Hereford bull who knows he's being teased and infuriated but is not quite sure by whom. Dot guessed that her father's plans for this night had not included his wife's sleeping with their son! 'Why don't you settle Tommy, my dear, and then come down and have a nightcap with me? And with Dot, if she wishes it.'

'No, I won't leave him in a strange house when we've an

early start in the morning . . . ' The sentence crumbled to nothing. Edie tried again. 'Is there an alarm clock we could borrow? It would never do to miss the train.'

'I'll wake you. I get up early to milk the cows,' Dot said, only partially truthfully. In fact, she and Gwil took the milking in turns. 'What time shall I come in?'

'No need. We'll leave at six-thirty and I'll see they're up and about in time for some breakfast before we go,' Tom mumbled. 'Why don't you go and order an early meal, Dot?'

Dot took her dismissal smilingly. She kissed Tommy, then his mother, then her father, and hurried up to her own room. It was only when the door was firmly shut and she had begun hastily undressing that she realised how tense and nervous she had been; now, alone, she was able to relax.

Whew, but it had been a strain, trying to be natural and friendly! She tore her last garments off, cast them on the floor, scrabbled into a long flannelette nightgown which had once belonged to Kate and then to Alex and took a flying leap from her tiny sheepskin rug across the ice-cold boards and on to her bed which, used to the treatment, uttered no more than a protesting squeal as it cannoned into the wall with her as passenger.

It was the work of a moment to claw the bedclothes up round her ears, wrap her body – including her icy feet – in the skirt of the nightgown, curl up into a ball, and summon warmth. It was always the same at the Plas once autumn began; daylight and sunshine might keep the cold at bay but as soon as night fell chill came out of the very stones and the bedrooms began to feel like iceboxes. But the dormouse position had many advantages and very soon warmth began to spread all over Dot until she was cosy, drowsy and comfortable. She let her thoughts wander and found that despite a feeling of outrage over her father's behaviour she would rather enjoy Edie and little Tommy living at Plas Tegydd. Another woman to take charge of the house would be welcome and Tommy seemed a nice enough kid; she liked what she knew of children. She could teach him to ride. Father would be delighted to buy his son a pony of his own once Tommy had learned.

She realised, of course, that the new baby might pose a threat, because Father obviously wanted the child to be his heir. It was a natural enough wish, she supposed. But she would point out all the advantages of giving the baby the collieries, which would bring him in lots of money, and the disadvantages of land and a big, mouldering old house. She was quite willing just to have the house and a part of the land . . . she was willing to help the little one (who might easily be a girl!) to grow to love Plas Tegydd, and to help to build up the land so that his – or her – part of the inheritance would be as good as Dot's own.

She knew that Edie did not love the house, considered it a great white elephant of a place which ought to be pulled down. As the warmth spread and she grew drowsier yet she felt more and more certain that Hywel had been right. Her father would not will Plas Tegydd to anyone but her, because no one but her would want it. No one else would bother to work as hard as she had to make it good. So it was quite safe, indeed sensible, to lie here and dream of the good times to come, when Edie would take charge of the house and the servants and would help her to bully Tom into providing at least the comfort of a sound roof over their heads and windows which neither leaked nor blew out in high winds. And a little boy to play with and teach, and a baby to cuddle and love.

If you had told Dot she was lonely, she would have laughed you to scorn. Nevertheless when she fell asleep at last it was with all the pleasant anticipation of one expecting something very nice to happen quite soon. And that something nice was to be the arrival of her stepmother and her children at Plas Tegydd.

The week following her trip home had been wet, but on the Saturday it seemed as though autumn had relented and was going to give them at least one more day of summer, for when Jessica looked through her bedroom window at Cambridge it was on to sunlight falling through the colouring leaves of the tall elms, which were ruffled by the slightest of breezes.

So she and her friend Pauline took a picnic by the river and sat on the bank beneath trees more gold than green. That was rare here, she knew, for usually by the end of September the trees were stripped of leaves. This year, however, they had managed to hoard their foliage and were now letting it down lightly, curled leaf by curled leaf, so that the movement of them was constantly on the edge of one's vision as they drifted earthwards.

The beauties of nature, however, were largely lost on the two girls, for this was the first opportunity that Jessica had had to tell Pauline about her weekend. It made a fascinating story.

'He's so handsome, Pauline, that you'll faint from sheer envy when you meet him,' Jessica assured her friend. 'Lovely fair hair he has, and though he's below ground at work he's out all the rest of the time – in all weathers, too – so he's lovely and brown. *And* he's got classic features. Tall, he is, and ever so strong, and a nice voice he has, with a bit of a Welsh lilt of course, but deep and pleasant. He's ever so clever, reads a lot, could have any job he wanted. Indeed, he should have gone to the grammar and then to college, except that his mam isn't too fond of him and wanted the money he'd bring in from the pit.'

'I thought he was your half-brother,' Pauline objected. She was a dark-haired, strong-featured girl with an air of knowing just what she wanted, probably the result of being motherless and having to take care of younger brothers and sisters when she was home. Despite, or perhaps because of this, she was shy with young men, and although the opposite sex was a constant topic of conversation between the two of them neither had experienced even the mildest love affair. So Jessica's sudden revelations were as fascinating to Pauline as they were to Jess herself.

'No, we aren't related at all, really. My mam ran off soon after I was born, leaving me with my da. Hywel's story is much more exciting, because his da was killed down the pit the very day he was born. My da says that's why mam – I call Hywel's mam that because she's brought me up – isn't too nice with Hywel. Says she blames him for her Ben's death. Not that I can see – damn it, I've lost the thread. Where was I?'

'You were saying the two of you aren't related. D'you mean to say that your father married Hywel's mother? If that's so, I understand.'

'Yes, that's it in a nutshell,' Jessica said, rather sorry to have been deprived of the opportunity of enlarging on her story. 'So when we were kids Hywel was just like a favourite brother. He was nearest me in age, see. I'm only a couple of months younger than he, and we got on fine. Only . . . well, when I went to the convent school, Mam felt . . . she said it wouldn't do to spend so much time with . . . with Hywel, and I was busy . . . and we grew apart. And she was right, the girls in my school didn't go about with . . . well, with village boys. So between thirteen and now we didn't see a lot of one another.'

'Only at mealtimes,' Pauline agreed. 'Every day . . . but let it pass. Does he like you now? This paragon? This young Greek god?'

'Of course! He always did, but I felt . . . well, never mind that. I don't feel it any longer. We had the jolliest weekend imaginable. He took me to the cinema and up into the mountains after blackberries and wild apples for Mam to bottle. And of course there'll be lots of letters, and I'll write back, and when May comes I'm going to get him to take some days off and come up for the May ball. That'll be marvellous! You'll be able to meet him, and – '

'Go on with you! He won't come! All that way, and only knowing you at the end of it! He's probably shy of English people. And besides, where would he stay?'

'He can find digs in town. They earn good money at the colliery – everyone's always saying how good the money is. He's rather shy, perhaps, but I'll talk him into it, see if I don't.'

'Well, maybe you will, but I shan't hold my breath on the chance,' Pauline said. 'What about Guy? And James Ashe?'

Guy, tall and handsome with a wickedly dissolute droop to his heavy eyelids, had seldom been out of Jessica's thoughts or conversation until her weekend at home. Now she was able to shrug airily and dismiss Guy and James Ashe – blond, burly, a rugger blue – as of no account.

'Oh, them! They were just schoolgirl pashes. I hadn't grown up then or looked beyond my nose. But now I wouldn't go out with either of them if they begged on bended knees.'

'I think you're safe enough,' Pauline said dryly, 'since I suspect that neither of them knows we exist. But you must admit that this business over your br – over Hywel, I mean – is a bit sudden.'

'Love is sudden,' Jessica said dreamily, her unfocused gaze turning the sun on the river into a million shifting points of light. 'Wait until it happens to you. One minute he's just a fellow you've known all your life and the next . . . ' She paused and turned to gaze impressively at her friend. 'The next, he's the most important thing that's ever happened to you.'

'I can't imagine even wanting to feel like that,' Pauline said, unimpressed. 'I'm the most important thing that ever happened to me, not some fellow. And nothing you can say will convince me that the boy-next-door thing is true. I want a total and exciting stranger to whisk me off to paradise, not Philip Conrad Burroughs.'

'Well, not everyone may be as lucky as me and have Hywel for the boy next door, I'll grant you that. When I think what a fool I was all those years, letting Mam influence me . . . At least I've come to my senses now, though. I'm my own woman and I'll do what I know is right for me.'

'You're serious? You want that chap . . . Hywel . . . as more than just a casual fellow?'

'I want him for ever and ever,' Jessica said. 'For my husband, my lover, and my dearest friend.'

'May I wish you every happiness.' Pauline sighed and began to pack the uneaten food – there was precious little – back into the basket. 'Come along. The warmth will go out of the sun very soon and we've got work to do before we go to bed!'

'You saw her, did you? Yes, that was my sister Jessica. You've heard Mam going on about her, no doubt.'

Hywel's answer was clear, his face placid. He and Dot were in the orchard, Dot up a tree because she was the lighter of the two, Hywel at the moment on the ground, picking industriously. Whenever Dot's arms were full she passed her burden gently down to Hywel, for they had long since run out of buckets, even the sort with large holes in the bottom, and it was important that they got every fruit off clean, unbruised and whole. The fruit would all be sold, and the best prices were always paid for apples which had been handled with care.

'It's odd really; I'd got the impression that she was plain, but she's very pretty. Different, too. I liked that thing she was wearing.'

'What thing? Oh, the green thing with the tassels. Yes, it was

212

all right, I suppose. Any more ripe ones up there, or do you want to move to another tree? I've got everything off the lower branches, I think.'

The orchard at the Plas was old, the trees bent and crabbed, but despite their age they cropped heavily in a good year, and this year was particularly good. Disregarding gloomy prophecies of a fearful winter because of the weight of fruit on the trees, Dot had suggested to Tom that this year, if she and a friend gathered the crop, they might be allowed to keep the money. The idea had been met with half-grudging agreement — Tom knew very well that he would never get round to paying casual labour to pick apples and then would never find a buyer — and so the two of them were making good Dot's suggestion.

'I'm nearly finished, but there are about ten right at the very top of the tree that must be picked,' Dot called down. 'Stay there. I'll throw them to you one by one.'

She climbed higher. It was important that they should do well out of the apples, because Hywel would take the lion's share of the money. She was helping to pick, all right, but he would bag them, take them into town, and arrange the sale. She had told him about her inheritance but had only said that she believed she would be getting some money. Suddenly, when she had been about to tell him, all her old doubts had crept in, and she had changed her mind. Father was so tricky. Suppose there was some way in which the money could end up in his hands instead of hers? And it could be ages before she got it. Then there was Hywel, who had shown an undesirable wish to provide at least as much as she did towards any property they bought together. Indeed, he had made it plain that he would buy the property. She might put her savings towards stock or seed or machinery, but he would buy the land itself. The mere sound of five thousand pounds would make him feel that his chances of matching her penny for penny were non-existent. Men were proud. It would never do to let him feel inferior, just because she had had the luck to inherit money and he had not.

'Here, that's the last. Oh no, look at that huge one! I'll just —'

Dot, reaching too far and balancing on a branch no thicker than her own wrist, heard the ominous crack, clutched air, and fell, screaming, through the branches, to land with a sickening

213

thump on the long, unkempt grass at the foot of the tree.

'Dot! You all right, girl?' Hywel's face, bending over her, was pale and anxious. She giggled, knowing that he was having nightmare visions of having to rush in to the Plas and fetch help, then rolled over on to her knees and scrambled to her feet. She was tempted to play crippled for a moment, just to tease him, but she was laughing too obviously. She clutched her back, groaned, and then held out her hand with a princely apple in the palm.

'I got the apple – wasn't that good? And I'm not dead, either, though I feel slightly cracked all over. Come on, which tree's next?'

'You are slightly cracked, you daft thing!' He put a hand on the back of her neck and pulled her towards him. 'You *sure* you're all right, Dot? Went down with the hell of a thump, you did.'

'Of course I'm all right.' She was secretly delighted with the concern on his face, the gentleness of his fingers on her neck, but she ached as she climbed into the big Bramley seedling. It really had been quite a fall, and before they could give up for the day they still had to go all over the orchard and pick up the big piles of fruit beneath each stripped tree. Any other property-owner, she thought ruefully, picking her way between the unpruned branches, would have ladders, buckets and sacks, but not the Tegydds! Their ladders had rungs missing, their buckets had no bottoms, and their sacks had disintegrated long ago. But at least the fruit they picked would be handled with care and windfalls would go for cidermaking, so Hywel should get a pretty penny for all his hard work.

Working steadily, she began to dream about their property. If there was going to be a shared property. If she could persuade him to use her money . . . if she could persuade him to marry an ugly little gnome . . . if she could grow beautiful fairly quickly . . .

It was all ifs, but Dot was used to life being like that. Farming was all ifs. No matter how good a farmer you were the biggest if of all ruled your life – if it rains, if it shines, if it blows, if it snows. The weather. Anyone in Britain who lived by the land was putting his future into the hands of the most unreliable weather in the world. And whatever the weather the farmer or the smallholder or even the gardener never really won. If the weather smiled on you it smiled on everyone else too, so that there was a glut and prices were low. If the weather was foul prices might soar, but you would have a thin crop and so be unable to make your fortune then either. No, you couldn't win, but you could have a lot of fun trying, Dot decided, scurrying down the Bramley and up into the next tree. She began to pick, throwing down the fruit with the utmost care this time, for these apples were rarely seen nowadays and were, therefore, precious.

'What type of apples are these then, Dot? Whoppers, aren't they!'

'Custards,' Dot said briefly. She had been firm with herself until this moment, but now, perched in a convenient crook, she bit into one of the big, yellow fruits. 'Some people call them Long Johns, because of the shape. I think they're the tastiest, most delicious apples in the world. Have one.'

One of the nicest things about Hywel was his ability to see what was important and what was not. Some might have argued that they were still picking, that the afternoon was wearing on, that the custards, being rare, should be saved for the market. Hywel just selected, bit, chewed, and then nodded.

'Aye, that's a good taste. Keep these, shall we? You got an apple loft?'

'Yes, of course. Do you think we ought? They're very nice, but shouldn't we sell them?'

'Too big for ordinary eaters, and folk don't pay the same for cookers. We'll have these between us. I'll take my share home to Mam – we always have a bit of hay in the loft for apples and pears – and I'll carry the rest to your loft and spread 'em for you. You'll need some cookers, too. I'll do them at the same time.' He finished his apple and glanced round at the acres of trees still to be stripped of their crop. 'Reckon we won't miss a tree or two.'

'Good.' Dot finished her own apple, threw the core accurately at a theiving blackbird, and began to pick once more. 'I'll handle these custards with extra care now, knowing I'm going to be eating them all winter!'

Twelve

It was catching sight of the big bowl of apples on the sideboard when Jessica was being what she imagined was provocative under a sprig of mistletoe that reminded Hywel of Dot. They were all playing games around the fire, Ella, Glyń, the boys and their girlfriends and the Evanses from next door. The kitchen was a big room, fortunately, for it was packed with people, and the games, which had begun decorously enough, tended to get wilder and jollier as the cider and home-brewed beer sank in the jugs.

It had been a good Christmas day by any standards, Hywel told himself as he crossed the room to take a custard apple. They had all been pleased with their presents. In a big family like theirs the giving and receiving was considerable, and took a couple of hours between breakfast and morning service. But they had a deal of money coming in, now that Jess was the only non-earner, and that was why they had invited the Evanses, who were not doing so well. Dafydd had grown too tired and slow to continue working underground, and though he had a little pension and a bit put by, things were hard. Without their neighbours they would probably not have celebrated Christmas with much enthusiasm, for their sons had emigrated to Australia years earlier and were no doubt kept in complete ignorance of their parents' frugal existence.

'Hywel! Going to give me a Christmas kiss, are you?'

Drunk too much cider, she has, Hywel told himself, embarrassed, as Jess continued to wave the mistletoe at him, all pink cheeks and starry eyes. He took a bite of apple and turned towards Jess, but Ella was there first.

'Really, miss, what a way to behave! Making your poor brother go red as a turkey cock,' she said sharply. She turned to

216

Mrs Evans. 'I just hope she isn't as bold as that with the young men at that college she goes to!'

'He's not my brother. None of them are. I'm an only child,' Jess muttered, going even redder than Hywel. 'For God's sweet sake, Mam, don't – '

'Jessica, don't you dare blaspheme in my home.'

'Forget it, Mam. She was only messing about.' Stan, the peacemaker, put his arm round his quiet little schoolteacher's waist and drew her over to where Ella stood. 'Right she is, too; no relative of mine is our Jess. Nothing wrong with her giving Hywel a kiss, if she's a mind! Would you like to kiss our Hywel, Cerwyn?'

Cerwyn blushed even more fierily than Jess had and turned her head into Stan's shoulder. He smiled, patted her and turned back to his mother, but Ella was plainly not impressed. She shook her head at him, her fair brows drawn down in a frown.

'No, Stan, that I can't accept. Brought up like brothers and sisters you were, under this roof, and I won't have any . . . any . . .'

'Incest?' Jessica suggested sweetly. 'Don't be so silly, Mam.'

Glyn crashed out a curse and grabbed his daughter by the shoulder, muffling her mouth with his free hand. He had drunk a lot of cider and more beer, and his face was suffused. He shook Jessica wildly.

'How dare you use a word like that before your mam! Apologise to her this moment, my lady, and to everyone else, or you'll spend the rest of the evening in your room. And if the words don't trip off your tongue you'll go off with a beating from me, big though you are. I'll have no child of mine using words like that.'

He meant it, Hywel could see, and he was quite shocked by Jessica's behaviour himself. What on earth was the matter with the girl? She had treated him scornfully for years, mainly because Mam had made it difficult for her to do otherwise, and now that they were older and could see things more clearly they had become friends again. But she must know that Mam would not change; she would not want them to be friends. Hywel was a collier, and Jess was at Cambridge! If she wanted to mess around with one of her . . . . her non-brothers, then

217

why for heaven's sake did she choose him? It would put their new friendship in jeopardy and would only end in tears.

'I'm sorry, Mam, that I used that word. Sorry, everyone.' Jess was a child again for a moment, her new-found adulthood retreating before her father's wrath and her own feeling that she had overstepped both good sense and good manners. Hywel felt sorry for her, but if Ella really thought there was anything between them other than natural brotherly-sisterly feelings she was downright daft. They would both settle down with someone else one of these days. But that was Mam all over. Get an idea in her head and it took more hewing to get it out than he did on a long day's shift!

It was Stan who took the heat out of the situation. He picked up the bowl of apples from the sideboard and held it above his head so that everyone looked up at it.

'Ladies and gentlemen, here we have a bowl of very fine apples. My mother is going into the scullery to fetch out a pail of water and we'll float the apples in it two or three at a time – no, don't bother with the bucket, Mam, fetch out the tin bath – and we'll see who's best at bobbing for apples. I'll give a prize of a shiny gold sovereign to the person who picks out the most apples without cheating or using his fingers.'

A quid? That was wealth unlimited to the Evanses, and probably Jess could use it too, for though Ella sent what she could and Jessica had her scholarship, money was often very tight, Hywel knew. He could see her eyes gleaming with determination to do her best to win the coin. And Stan, who was the kindest and most sensible of men, had another idea.

'Take partners, if you please,' he said briskly. 'Mr Dafydd, would you like to partner wild young Jessica here? And Hywel, you partner Mrs Dafydd. Mam takes Dewi, I'll go with Phyllis here, Luke and da can try their luck together . . . '

He continued to organise them. Mrs Dafydd asked to be given an apple's start since she had false teeth and would probably lose them at the first snap, and Hywel realised that Stan hoped that either he or Jess would win. Then they could hand the money to their partners with the excuse that they were hosting the party.

'Right. Are we all ready? We'll go in order of age and no cheating, if you please. Add your ages together and the oldest goes first. What's this? Mrs Dafydd claims to be no more than sixty-seven. And Hywel's all of nineteen, so that makes . . . ' He screwed up his face in pretended agony of effort. 'Dear me, it's a long time since I was in school . . . eighty-six, is that right? So that's eighty-six years between the couple on my left, ladies and gentlemen, and on my right we have our Jess, same age as Hywel, and Mr Dafydd, who can't be more than sixty-eight? Not seventy-four? That's incredible – a grand total on my right of ninety-three years, ladies and gentlemen, so Mr Dafydd and his fair partner go first. Stand by!'

As Mr Dafydd's balding, blue-pocked head and Jessica's flaming one bent over the tin bath and its provocatively bobbing cargo, Hywel found himself wondering what Dot was doing right now. It was late, but no one went to bed before midnight on Christmas day, so she would still be up. In that long drawing room that Ella had told him about, perhaps, so long that it needed a fire in the grates at either end and was still only half warm. She would have her family around her, including small children, so she would have had a good time even though they would have packed the little ones off to bed by now. But there would still be Kate and Alexandra, their husbands, Tom Tegydd, perhaps a friend or two? How about the governess? Would Tom dare invite her? Dot had told him all about Edie, but he did not think even Tegydd would have brought the woman there for Christmas. At the moment she would be so obviously pregnant that it would embarrass everyone save Tom himself, who never seemed to mind what people thought of him. No, Dot would be with her family and perhaps some friends.

He was still trying to imagine that other party high on the hill above when there was a cheer and a violent splash as Jessica, half-drowned, soaked to the waist, knelt upright with a captive apple in her teeth. Hywel clapped with the rest, and cheered louder than anyone when Mr Dafydd also got an apple. He went through to the scullery and fetched a mop and bucket to clear up the spillage, then filled up the bath again since everyone agreed that it would not be fair to allow the water to shrink away as the game proceeded.

When that was done Stan fetched two more custard apples out of their bowl and dropped them, from a height, into the wildly rocking tub of water, earning more shrieks. Noisy, happy, colourful Christmas! Glyn had bought his wife an oven and she was putting a tray of mince pies in it to heat through. When they were done they would have them with the punch which Glyn and Stan's shy little girlfriend were making. It would be a jolly evening now until everyone was too tired for games and genuinely wanted their beds.

Hywel and Mrs Dafydd took their places, on their knees, on opposite sides of the bath of water. Hywel slipped on the wet quarry tiles and banged his chin on the edge of the tub. Enormous hilarity! Mrs Dafydd and he, both in hot pursuit of an elusive fruit, banged heads – more cheers and laughter. They captured an apple each. Wild cheers and shouts! Dewi was taking bets, which would have made Ella frown on any other day. Hywel ducked again, taking a deep breath, forcing the apple of his choice to the bottom and hard on the side. His whole head and a good bit of his shirt was under water, but he would be up with that apple in time to see Mrs Dafydd give a good old smile any minute now! He emerged, the apple between his teeth, breathless, drenched, grinning, his fair hair plastered down on to his scalp. We're mad enough for anything tonight, he thought, looking with real affection at the assembled company. What a Christmas!

Dot was not in the drawing room, nor even in the kitchen. She was in bed with two glorious stone hot-water bottles, one at her feet and one clutched to her stomach. Her lamp was lit and by her bedside she had a mug of cocoa and a large wedge of Christmas cake. By the cake, nudging it, was a custard apple.

It had not been a particularly memorable Christmas day, Dot reflected, heaving the blankets up round her neck and stretching a cautious hand towards the cake. It was her own fault in a way, because Kate had invited her for the day, Alex had asked her as well, and Father had practically ordered her to go, since he would be spending Christmas day with Edie and the little boy. But it was out of the question. There were beasts to feed, cows to milk, stalls to be cleaned. She could have got one of the men to do it, but their lives were hard enough without her taking away the one holiday of the year to which

220

they felt entitled. Jan was too old, Gwil had a clutch of grandchildren to stay and the other men were either married or going to spend the day with a girl somewhere. And the truth was she could not go for the day to either of her sisters. It would have to be two or three. No, she had not wanted to go, so she had stayed. She had not bargained for her father's decision to give all the servants three days off. With pay, what was more, so he could count it as the Christmas bonus which his wife had paid in earlier years.

Even Cook had gone, and the maids. If things had been different, if there had been a party, Cook and her helpers would have stayed for the day and taken time off later on. But since there was not, and Dot was to be alone in the house, it seemed foolish and selfish to try to persuade any of them to give up the festivities. Lizzie might have stayed, but she was a child really, no older than fifteen, and she would be happier with her family; and Daisy and Annie would go to friends in the village.

It had not been a bad sort of day, though, Dot reflected, taking a big bite out of the rich fruit cake. She had been cold, of course, and rather lonely, but that did not matter. She felt guilty because she had not been to church, but that would have advertised her aloneness and someone would have taken pity on her and asked her back to Christmas dinner, so she had stayed away. Shaming to admit that her sisters would not come for the day, would not freeze for a few hours in the long drawing room just so that they could be together for a while. Shaming that her father could just go off to be with his woman, knowing she had to stay behind to feed and tend the beasts. Yet it was no one's fault but her own, she knew. She could have made arrangements and gone off to Kate or Alexandra.

It had not occurred to either sister that she had no means of transport save for Matchless, and she would scarcely take him thirty miles or more, in the depths of winter, only to turn round after an hour or so and go all the way back! Of course, Kate and Alexandra would cover themselves by saying that they had intended the invitation to be for a week; as if she could be spared for a whole week!

Snuggling down with her cake in her hand, Dot remembered Christmases long past when there had been her sisters, the servants, and Mother handing out presents round the ragged little tree which was all Father could be bothered to bring in out of the woods. But there had been good food, and laughter, and when she was very small the tree had been stupendous, huge, and they had given an enormous Christmas tea to all the estate workers and their children. She could remember it clearly still: the masses of food, the children's shining faces, the games, when everyone charged up and down the drawing room and mothers shrieked to children to mind the fire and not skid on the rugs. There had been keen competition for the prizes and the three little Tegydds had worn silk party frocks, satin ribbons in their hair and satin slippers on their feet, and had helped to hand round the cake and present the prizes. How they had bustled, how their mother had bustled, and how happy and excited they had been!

Remembering could bring a pleasant glow to the mind, but the body, Dot thought ruefully, remained extremely cold. She had not bothered to light a fire in the drawing room, because the closed stove burned brightly enough in the kitchen. She had spent most of the day in there when not actually working outside. She had roasted some chestnuts on the hob, losing half of them, but they made such marvellously loud explosions that she forgave them their abrupt descent into the flames. She had also fried a large pan of cold potatoes, parsnip and sliced onion, and after that she had tried to boil a Christmas pudding, only the horrid thing had not got even half hot, so she had eaten a bit of the outside (the warmest part) and taken a handful of nuts instead.

The house was very quiet when you were alone in it. There were creakings, of course, because old houses always creak, but otherwise it was quiet. Too quiet. Dot wished she had lit a fire in her room, though the chimney was probably blocked with a dozen crows' nests or worse. A fire would have warmed the atmosphere a bit, though, and sounded companionable. She also wished that she had drawn the curtains across the windows before getting into bed. That would have helped to conserve what warmth there was, but she had been in such a hurry to fly into bed that she had not given the great, draughty windows a thought. Should she get up now and shut out the wild and windy night? Too much trouble. Besides, it had taken ages to get her feet warm and to thaw out her hands. If she got out of bed now she'd only freeze up all over again.

She could hear the church clock in the village chiming the half hour. It had been about eight when she came up. Only half past eight, yet it felt like midnight! That was the trouble with being quite alone, time did drag. She reached for her mug of cocoa, heard a sound outside like someone knocking, snatched her hand away and knocked the drink over. It puddled the floor, then slid sideways and soaked into the wedge of cake still uneaten and now uneatable.

Two large tears formed in Dot's eyes and trickled down her cheeks. For a moment she just lay there, and then the wind, gusting, blew her door open.

Shock made her scream thinly, though she knew very well that it was only the wind. It often happened in conditions like these. It was silly to feel afraid, even for a moment, she scolded herself, but now that she thought about it she had never spent a night alone at Plas Tegydd before. If Lizzie had been here, or Cook, or Father, she could have told herself that it was they who made the boards creak, the doors move, the curtains sway with sudden violence as a gust knifed through the ill-fitting windows. As it was, she was forced to keep reminding herself that old houses always behaved like this, and to tell herself not to be such a fool. This was her home. No one could be afraid in her own home!

The door, which had blown open, blew shut. Dot gasped, feeling her heart suddenly leap, hammering, into her throat. Then she jumped out of bed, clearing the cold boards with the force of her bound and landing on the sheepskin rug. She snatched up her scattered clothes, teeth already chattering, but did not attempt to put them on. Now that she had moved she noticed that the tree nearest the window was nearer than she remembered; a skeleton arm with long, twig fingers was close enough to scratch and snatch at the panes, to force an entry, to reach out and . . .

Dot rolled her clothes into a ball and shot out of the room and down the stairs. Halfway to the kitchen – her destination – she realised that her eyes were shut and opened them defiantly. This was her home. Nothing about it could frighten her. It was as dear, as familiar . . .

Ahead of her someone jumped out from behind the hall stand, someone with a white face and huge staring black eyes and spiky hair. A mirror! How stupid she was . . . but her heart was banging once more, her palms clammy. Oh, God, where was the kitchen door? She had left her lamp upstairs but there was enough faint starlight coming through the high stained-glass windows for her to see about her. Did she have to pass any more mirrors, though, to reach the green baize door which led to the kitchen regions? Ridiculous, but she could not remember . . . did people actually die of fright? Useless to tell herself that it was only half past eight, that she had been almost alone in the house many times and a good deal later than this, too, even though she might never have spent a night alone here before. She had to get to the kitchen, find the fire, light a lamp, and then rediscover normality. Otherwise they would find her here, whitehaired and gibbering, when they got back from their Christmas break. It might serve Father right – well, it jolly well would serve him right – but it would do very little for her!

She reached the kitchen at last, without encountering any more mirrors, and burst into the room, slamming the door behind her. She noticed at once what she would never have thought of in normal circumstances – that the back door had not been bolted. It never was, or not by Dot, and it was always open in the morning when she came down, but just now this seemed madness. She flew across the kitchen, shot the bolt with a hollow thud, and then returned, slowly, to the chair in front of the stove. Her legs were jelly and her heart was beating like a fallen fledgling's, but she was in a warm room, with a locked door between her and the night and a fire to cheer her up. Very soon she would regain her equilibrium.

Now that she was in warmth and light she began to feel better, though distinctly sheepish. What an idiot she had been! She was still trembling a bit and her thin cotton nightgown was damp with perspiration. She would just get warm and then she would put her clothes on over her nightgown. She held out her hands to the stove – and something moved in the yard outside. In a moment her heart was lodged in her throat again and she was on her feet, eyes fixed on the low, uncurtained kitchen window. Oh, God . . . but it was no use appealing to a higher authority when she had not gone to church that morning – the first Christmas morning in her entire life that she had not gone to morning service. If she had gone this would never have happened, she thought confusedly. The better the day the better the deed. If you did not go to God's house on His very own birthday, how could you expect him to come to yours when you were in trouble? In the wildness of her fright she told herself that the devil had probably been lurking round the house that morning and had noticed her defection, leaping to the worst conclusions. If he thought her truly wicked and had come to get her . . . could the devil get through a locked door? Wasn't there something about a threshold spell? She seemed to remember that no evil creature could enter your house uninvited. Dot began to hurl on her clothes over her nightgown in any old order. She could distinctly hear the sound of someone – or something – barging round the yard; at least she would face her Maker – or worse – fully dressed!

Her head had just emerged from the neck of her pink wool jersey when part of a face appeared at the lower pane. Her scream this time was full-blooded and as the face jerked away, eyes rolling, she caught a terrifying glimpse of horns. It was! It was the devil come to get her! Dot grabbed the poker in one hand and the shovel in the other. She was shaking but grimly determined to fight for her soul, her body, or any other threatened part. That evil thing out there was real. It might be someone dressed up or it might really be the devil, but she was not going to cower in the kitchen waiting for it to get her. She was going to open the back door, make the sign of the cross, demand Godly protection – and bring the poker down hard on the head of her uninvited visitor!

By this time she realised that only action would help her fear. She flung the door wide and the wind promptly slammed it almost on her nose. She staggered back, giggled, spluttered, then laughed aloud. Laughter, she discovered, brings a kind of bravery of its own with it. She opened the door again more cautiously, staring out into the blackness. She could see nothing, so she wedged the door open with a log of wood and then, still armed, walked suspiciously out into the night.

The devil proved to be a very frightened heifer, wearing ample evidence of how she had got into the yard on her horns.

Hedge decorated them. She must have burst through, the little monster, no doubt hoping to find something eatable in the garden. Why she had done it tonight of all nights though, when Dot had given all the beasts an extra feed, was anyone's guess.

Relief sent poker and shovel clattering on to the cobbles. Dot, giggling, put her arms round the heifer's neck and started to untangle the branches of quickthorn from its horns. Stupid creature, what a fright it had given her! Now she would shut it in the stable with an armful of hay to keep it quiet and in the morning she would deal with the injured hedge. She remembered, now, that she had put the heifers in the near pasture because it was going to be she who carried their feed out to them both today and tomorrow and it was a shorter distance to walk. Foolish, because the hedges in the near pasture were weak to start with and heifers are born curious, but at the time it had seemed sensible.

She dealt with the heifer and then discovered that she was shivering. She crossed the yard again at a brisk trot, entered the kitchen, slammed the door and found that she did not much want to be inside Plas Tegydd. She would rather spend the night in the stables with the heifer, or in Matchless's stall. At least they would be company. She simply could not bear to be in the house, alone, when all of a sudden it had stopped being a home and had become eerie, menacing. Its long and probably unstained history was no longer comforting. Undreamed-of ghosts might lurk, happenings occult or murderous might have taken place even in the once-cosy kitchen. If she went upstairs and fetched blankets she could snuggle down beside Matchless quite happily.

Halfway across the kitchen she stopped short again. Oh, damn it, she did not want to go upstairs for blankets. She did not even want to have to cross the big, echoing hall to fetch coats from the cloakroom. And she would look an awful fool in the morning if one of the men came early to work and caught her sleeping under a pile of hay in the stables. She was wearing a full-length nightdress under the grey wool skirt that Kate had passed on to her about five years ago. She had no stockings; goodness knew where they had gone. She had probably dropped them on her flight down the stairs. And as for shoes . . . well, she did have her ancient slippers, which were better than nothing.

Outside, the wind whined, and then she heard a noise in the hall. Not a creak, more of a long groan. The hair began to prickle erect all over her head even as she reminded herself that it would be the wind, pushing the drawing room door open and closed as it had done a thousand times before. But logic was no good to her; she wanted to get out and she wanted to get out now!

Before she knew it she was standing in the middle of the yard, the wind whistling round her and a light rain falling on her face. Her bare legs were icy and she could feel the wet cobbles through the holes in the soles of her slippers. She crossed over to the stable and then discovered how very dark it was in there. Of course she knew that those rolling eyes belonged to the heifer – she had shut it in herself – but they could equally well have belonged to Old Nick. She would be perfectly safe with Matchless, her dearest friend after Hywel, but there was a lot of dark stable – and the heifer – to pass before she reached the pony's stall.

Irresolute, she stood in the middle of the yard, her hair slowly getting flattened to her head by the rain. Where could she go? It was not late, though it felt it. Who would accept her presence, without question, dressed as she was and at this time in the evening? One of the farm workers? Well, they would, but she would feel she was letting herself and her father down by appealing to them. A neighbour? Too far away. Someone in the village? Ella was a motherly sort of woman and Hywel would welcome her, but could she bring herself to go down there and practically beg for admittance? It would be the most awful acknowledgement of failure. No, she could not possibly . . .

There was a thump and a wild, petulant roar from the stables and Dot found herself flying down the road towards the village, her slippers sliding off at every step, her hair standing on end. Only the heifer, turning too sharply in the narrow stall and catching her horns on the partition. Yes, she *knew* it was only that, but even so she did not feel she wanted to linger in the yard any longer. She was still running as she rounded the corner of the lane and hurried over the bridge, the wild pattering of her slippers nothing compared with the roar of the water and the thunder of her heart.

In the village she slowed. What should she do? Just walk up to a door, tap on it, and ask for admittance? In daylight she surely knew which house Hywel lived in, but now? Suppose she chose the wrong door and found herself face to face with a stranger? But if she could find the right house she would not actually have to throw herself on their mercy. All she would have to do would be to wish them a merry Christmas and say she'd come to ask Ella if she could possibly come up to Plas Tegydd next morning for an hour or two. And of course they'd ask her in. Out of politeness. Wouldn't they? Ella did not know she knew Hywel, so she would have to be careful not to treat him with particular friendliness, but that would not prove an insuperable problem. She would say hello to everyone, smile, and then go and sit by the fire and explain . . . no, it would not be a good idea to explain. She would go to the door, gain admittance, and then play it by ear.

She stopped outside the house she believed to be Ella's; it was brightly illumined and there was a great deal of noise coming from the tiny slit of open window. Dot clicked the latch and walked up the path, then hesitated again, her hand raised to knock. Should she? Or would she rather go home and face the heifer or whatever it was in the stable, and spend the night huddled up under a thin covering of straw? She knocked peremptorily enough to be sure of being heard even above the din coming from the house. And she was heard; silence fell, there were murmurs, shuffling, a shout of laughter, and then footsteps clicked across to the door. It opened. Light and warmth streamed out, together with a glorious smell of cooking and a feeling of happiness and good fellowship so intense that it was almost tangible.

'Yes?'

Dot gulped and stepped forward.

Thirteen

The girl facing Dot in the doorway was not much older than herself, a thin girl in a cream-coloured dress with brown and gold embroidery round the wrists and hem. She had been smiling when she opened the door, but now her greeny-grey eyes stared challengingly and coldly at the visitor. She repeated her monosyllable.

'Yes?'

'I'm sorry to disturb you,' Dot said nervously. 'But I wonder if I could have a word with Ella for a moment? She's your m-mother, isn't she?'

The girl continued to stare, but called over her shoulder: 'Mam? It's someone wants you.'

'Bring her in, girl.' That was a man's voice, deep, friendly, a little impatient. 'Ask her in, then we can get on with our game.'

Odd, how the red-haired girl was scrutinising her! But at the man's words she stood aside, jerking her head impatiently, and Dot, in her old slippers, came uncertainly into the room.

It was a big room, a kitchen, and it was both jollier and more crowded than Dot had imagined a room could be. Paper decorations garlanded the ceiling; there was holly and mistletoe all round the picture rails and behind every ornament; the fire roared up the chimney so violently that a chimney blaze seemed imminent; and everywhere there were people. They were all dressed in their best new clothes – probably Christmas presents – and no one else had hair like a badly combed sheep's, or down-at-heel slippers, or shabby jerseys and skirts. Dot wished desperately that she had managed to get at least a coat. But here she stood, ice-cold, unkempt and coatless.

Also, she realised, stared at. The cynosure of all eyes, that was Dot. There was not a person present who was not staring, and Hywel's eyes were almost popping out of his head. Dot could feel a blush beginning to burn across her face and neck. She felt hot for the first time that day. She stood there, her eyes on her terrible slippers, and wished the floor would open and swallow her up. She even wondered what it would be like to be dead.

Ella saved her. Ella's voice, normal and matter of fact, penetrated the fog of shame and misery which had surrounded Dot like a cloak.

'Well, if it isn't our Dot! You look cold, my dear. Come over by here.' Hands caught her, directed her to the fire and to Ella. Ella put an arm round her, pushed her on to the sofa, sat down beside her. Ella's hands chafed her own small, chilly ones. Ella began to boss people about, telling this one to fetch their guest some hot punch, another to bring a hot mince pie and some of them chestnuts over here; another still – incredible kindness – was ordered to run up to Ella's room and fetch down that cardigan Aunt Phoebe had knitted her for Christmas. It was lovely and warm, she assured Dot, and both she and Aunt Phoebe would be honoured if Dot would like to slip it on for a few minutes, just until she warmed up.

Once she had provided her guest with hot punch, mince pies, chestnuts and the fluffy softness of the angora wool cardigan, Ella seemed to feel that she could ask some questions.

'Dot, love, why did you run down here without so much as a coat? You've not quarrelled with your da, have you? And where are the girls – Kate and Alexandra? Why didn't they stop you, or make you put something warm on? Not being nosy, see; just concerned, I am.'

Dot risked a peep around her. Courteously, everyone was pretending to mind their own business but, being Welsh and therefore curious, each person had one ear almost visibly stretched towards Dot. Hywel was the only one who really did not seem to be taking the slightest notice; he was sitting on the arm of the chair in which his sister Jessica sat, talking to her in a low voice. A pang of bright green jealousy shot through Dot's heart. She sat up straighter and raised her voice a little, though she still kept it decently low.

'I've not quarrelled with my father. He isn't at home, and the girls aren't either. I got the most awful fright. One of the heifers broke out of the lower pasture and wandered into the yard and I went out to drive it into the stable and left the back door open. The kitchen got cold and the fire went out and when I went back indoors I thought someone might have sneaked in whilst I was gone – some old tramp or a gypsy – and might be waiting for me . . . and the lamp was out too. Oh, and then when I was halfway across the kitchen a door slammed somewhere in the house – the wind, I expect – and I just didn't feel I wanted to stay there alone another minute. So . . . so I came here.'

'It's good that you felt you could come here,' Ella said, at her most motherly. 'But, Dot, I thought your sisters would be with you, sure as sure! Or did they come over, and then your da have to take them home again? Is that it? Will they be back tomorrow?'

Dot, rapidly regaining her composure, shook her head and grinned.

'No. I've been alone all day. I don't mind – or I didn't, rather. Cook and the girls went home to spend Christmas; after all, there was only me, and I can rustle something up for myself. Kate and Alexandra did ask me to go to them for the holiday but I couldn't – didn't want to, either. Someone has to see to the beasts, you know, and I have to take my turn at the milking. I thought I'd be all right. I quite looked forward to taking care of myself, but it was the h-heifer and the c-cold and the d-dark . . .'

To her horror her voice began to wobble and the last few words ended with a distinct sniff. Hywel, who had seemed to be taking no notice at all, was suddenly on his feet, standing in front of the sofa, shielding her from the curious eyes. He bent down and touched his mother's shoulder.

'Mam, how about a game of charades? Then you and Miss Dot can have a comfortable chat by the fire.'

'Good idea, Hywel.' Ella's approval brought Hywel's shy smile into being. 'Dot and I will have our chat and get warm, and then we'll see about joining in. What did you have for your dinner, girl?'

'Oh, I told you, I can take care of myself. I had a fry-up – cold potato and parsnip – and then I tried to heat up the

Christmas pudding only it wouldn't warm through . . . I'd have been all right if it hadn't been for the heifer.'

'You mean that was your Christmas dinner? You had ponchmipe, like a cottager?' Ella's voice was incredulous; she tutted. 'And there was us with a fat old goose, and a ham and a saddle of mutton . . . you should have come earlier, my dear child, you should indeed!'

'Yes, I should; you cook the best mince pies in the world, I think,' Dot said, eating eagerly. 'As for ponchmipe, I like it, and so does Father. We often have it when Cook is off for the day because it's easy to make and filling.'

Ella sniffed, but one of Hywel's brothers, the eldest one who had once been kind to Kate, stared at her, then shook his head wonderingly and headed, with the rest of them, for the door leading into the little hall.

'They'll take sides out there,' Ella said, 'and then one group will come in and sit here to act as audience and guessers, and the others will act out a word, syllable by syllable.'

'I know; we used to play,' Dot said, just as half the company came back noisily and merrily into the room. The red-haired girl was one of them and so was Hywel. Hywel was talking, but the red-haired girl spared Dot a cold, inimical look before taking her seat at the opposite side of the room. What have I done? wondered Dot. But she did not think it could be much. She had only just met the red-haired girl!

When the first group had done their acting, with considerable hilarity, and the two groups had changed over, Dot ventured to question her hostess.

'Ella, is that pretty red-haired girl your daughter Jessica? The clever one?'

'Yes, that's our Jess.' Ella sounded smug. 'She is pretty, isn't she? Clever, too. Of course there are people who don't admire her style, say she's too thin, too different-looking, but we think her very pretty. The family, I mean.'

'Yes, I can imagine that some people might not see much beside her glorious hair. I've seen her several times when she's been home from Cambridge.'

'Down, dear. Down from Cambridge, not home from Cambridge. They say things differently, it seems.' Ella laughed comfortably. 'I'm always making mistakes like that, but Jess

232

doesn't mind. She's a good girl, is our Jess.'

Presently the group came back and it was Hywel and Jessica's turn to act out their word. Dot, who had been fighting an urge to lay her head on Ella's shoulder and go off to sleep, was unaccountably wide awake and very interested. She enjoyed the play-acting, laughed with the others and called out guesses, and tried not to watch Hywel too much or too obviously. Nevertheless it was interesting to see him with his own people. He was unchanged, though, in most ways. Kind, humorous, quick-witted, with the sort of reactions which meant that he was there with an answer almost before you had got out the question. Of all the brothers, she thought him the most handsome, for his fairness and his height set him apart from Stan, Luke and Dewi, who were all brown-haired, brown-eyed and stocky. They said in the village he was like his father – Ben must have been a good-looking man! This suspicion was confirmed when they were all told to take their places for a bite of supper. Ella, ever thoughtful, invited her guest to visit her bedroom for a moment to tidy her hair and have a bit of a wash, and up there, tucked away on a chest of drawers covered in photographs, Ella pointed out her wedding portrait. One glance was enough to show Dot that the bridegroom was not handsome, greying Glyn with his bright, roving eyes and his freckles. It had to be Ben, because he was so like Hywel.

'Weren't you a lovely bride?' she said, conventionally, only discovering after she had said it that it was true. Ella had been radiantly beautiful; not even the ugly old-fashioned headdress nor the skimped, cheap gown could take away that radiance. How happy she must have been! Yet she loved Glyn, Dot thought, and was proud of their daughter. In fact, Jessica was easily Ella's favourite child. She was very like her father in colouring and perhaps even in temperament, though Dot felt that she could not judge the latter from their short acquaintance. Rumour had it that Glyn drank too much but that otherwise there was no harm in him. Judging by the malevolence in the glances being shot at her by the sprightly Jessica, the same could scarcely be said of his daughter!

'Happy, I was,' Ella said softly. 'But then I'm happy now, with my Glyn.' She sighed, then straightened her back. 'Come along, now. Let's be getting down to our supper and a bit more fun.'

Downstairs, Dot ate an excellent meal and then joined the rest of the party, first in a sing-song round the piano in the front room, and then in a game of consequences which had the younger ones shrieking with laughter. After that it was the maddest game of musical chairs she had ever dreamed of, with far too many participants, far too little room, and so much noise that the street outside must have rung with it. But then the party began to break up. Mr Dafydd and his dear little wife said their goodbyes. People began, regretfully but nevertheless finally, to gather up their things, wrap themselves up in their coats and scarves, don their hats and gloves. The family tidied, made up the fire, pushed the chairs back to their proper places and began to wash up the last few dishes.

She would have to go; there was no question of spending the night. The little house was bursting at the seams already. A cousin from Gresford was sharing the boys' room, the little schoolteacher who seemed to be Stan's girl was sleeping top-to-toe with Jessica, and the couch was occupied, it now appeared, by Glyn's brother, Uncle Joseph, who had come all the way from Rhuddlan — walked he had, see — to spend Christmas with his relatives.

Dot was in the middle of murmuring her thanks to Ella whilst trying to sidle unobtrusively towards the door when Hywel came over, smiled at her, and spoke to his mother.

'Bet you've told her she can't sleep in that great barn of a place all by herself, haven't you, eh, Mam? I thought me and Luke would walk her home and have a shakedown in the kitchen, so's she wouldn't feel there was no one there if she woke in the small hours. What d'you say? I've got a coat here so she won't freeze going home.'

'It's awfully good of you, but I couldn't put you to so much trouble. Besides, the house'll be freezing cold by now,' Dot said earnestly. 'If you wouldn't mind walking me to the gate . . . or better still, if I'm honest, to the back door . . . I'll run indoors and go straight up to bed and sleep like a top until morning.' She had already decided to try to sleep in the stable for what was left of the night; indeed, she would have crouched beneath the hedge rather than face that dark house alone. But perhaps Hywel guessed how she felt, for he held out a great big coat, many sizes too large for her, and began to wrap her up in it.

'Look, we're not useless. We'll soon get your fire going and see to it that you've a decent warm room to come down to in the morning. Now no more nonsense, and you shall be allowed to bring us a cup of tea when you want us to get up.'

Dot joined in the family laughter and then stared down at her feet, fringed now by the hem of the huge coat.

'Look, it's awfully good of you. If you really don't mind . . .'

'It's a good idea, girl,' Ella said warmly. 'I wish we could offer you a bed here, but you see how it is. Unless you'd like to sleep on the scullery floor with the beetles . . .'

'I wouldn't dream of it. And I think you've got the best family in the world, and the nicest sons,' Dot said, bestowing her warmest smile on Hywel and Luke. 'Thank you both very much, I'll bring you more than a cup of tea. You shall have bacon and eggs when I wake you!'

'And ponchmipe,' suggested Hywel. They were still laughing over this when Jessica spoke up. She had already put on a blue cloak, with a hood which she pulled up over her bright hair, and though she addressed Ella Dot knew that the words were aimed at her.

'Mam, there's no need for Luke to go along. Spoil his evening, it will, for he wants to take Sally home, you know he does! I'll go, and keep Dot company for the night. More fitting it is to have a couple of girls together in a big old house than two lads and her. Hywel can walk us up there and bed himself down somewhere, and me and . . . and Dot can share her room.'

'Luke doesn't mind, Jess. He'll go with Hywel.'

'Of course he minds, Mam. He wants to see Sally home and spend half an hour telling her goodnight,' Jessica said impatiently.

'We-ell . . .' Ella, for some reason Dot could not fathom, did not seem keen on the new idea. She glanced from her tall son to her daughter and back again. 'Not stay there the two, will you? No need, there is, if Jess is to keep Dot company.'

Dot bit back a fervent desire to say she would sooner keep company with a viper. Anyway, it was not true. She thought

Jessica pretty, knew she was clever, would have liked to get to know her, but it was only too plain that these feelings were not reciprocated. Even now, when a warm and friendly smile or even a glance would have eased matters, Jessica could not bring herself so much as to look at Dot.

'I think Hywel should stay,' Jessica said quickly. 'Who's to bring me home tomorrow morning, Mam, but my own brother?'

The silence that followed was not only awkward, it was one of those silences which seem to teem with unspoken comments. Yet no one said a word. At last Hywel broke the silence.

'Who indeed? But no need for me to stay, as Mam says. I'll see the girls safe and warm up at the Plas, and then I'll come home. But I'll be back at eight, in plenty of time for that breakfast, and afterwards I can walk Jess home.'

Luke was smiling, an engaging, gap-toothed grin. He addressed Dot for the first time.

'Willingly I'd have gone with you,' he assured her. 'But I do admit I enjoy walking Sal home.'

During the good-natured chaff which followed this remark people began shrugging themselves into their coats and taking their leave. Hywel, putting on thick gloves and a huge muffler, offered an arm to each of the girls.

'Hold on to me, and I'll have the pair of you back at the Plas in no time,' he instructed them. 'Good at running, are you?'

The girls did indeed have to run to keep up with his long strides. He slowed down, complaining that the pair of them, filled with Christmas food, were enough to tether any man to the earth. Hywel was in a singing mood, a shouting mood, and Dot, who had seen her father several times when he had taken too much drink, guessed that Hywel's inroads on the hot punch had removed a good few inhibitions. She was feeling very happy herself, swinging along on Hywel's arm and trotting to keep up with him as they began to climb the hill, though she had probably drunk less than anyone. She peeped around Hywel and saw Jessica's face, bleached by moonlight – for the rain had stopped – her curls dark against the pallor of her skin. Jessica was holding Hywel's arm very tightly, possessively almost. It was clear that she did not intend to let her favourite brother go messing about with some old Tegydd girl from the Plas!

Thinking about it, Dot still could not understand why someone should feel that way about her brother. Jessica must know that he would find himself a girl of his own one day. But there. People were strange; you could not account for their odd ways. And presently there was the Plas, dark and forbidding, and there was the back door, still open, and the two girls stood outside whilst Hywel, who seemed to have a cat's ability to see in the dark, went into the kitchen, found the lamp, lit it, and then, by its light, beckoned them inside.

'Bright enough for you? Brrr, it's cold. The fire's not gone out, though — it's just died right down. I'll give it a rattle . . .' he suited actions to words, sending ash all over the three of them in a fine shower, making Dot giggle again '. . . and put on a bit more coal. Give it ten minutes and you'll be warming your hands at it.'

'Well, we'll be very warm and jolly in here, the two of us,' Jessica said vivaciously as the fire began to glow and then to roar. 'What a pity you aren't stopping, Hywel. But be a good boy and do as Mam says. Scuttle off home when she calls. Think of you, we will, when we're having ourselves a hot drink and a bite to eat.'

'You're welcome to do so, except that I shan't leave until the hot drink's been served,' Hywel said equably. 'What's bitin' you, Jess?'

Jessica shrugged. Her eyes gleamed and her mouth was tight with annoyance; what a companion, Dot thought apprehensively. I doubt she'll throw me a word all night! However, she did her best to pour what oil she could on waters which seemed troubled only to Jessica.

'Look, Hywel, there's no need for either of you to stay here the night, really there isn't. I'll build up a good fire and pull two of the chairs together and spend the night in here very happily. You and Jess can go home now.'

'No indeed,' Jessica said. She had obviously not planned to be sent home, unwanted. 'No, it would be mean to leave you here alone. Anyway, I like the thought of spending a night up at the Plas. Very posh it'll sound when I tell the girls.'

'It may sound posh, but I'm afraid it really isn't,' Dot said rather apologetically. 'What's more, I have to go out very early to deal with the stock. At least it's Gwil's turn to milk the cows tomorrow. All I have to do is muck out and feed.'

The Tegydd milk-round covered quite half the village, yet Jessica stared. Plainly it had never occurred to her that the young lady of the house mucked out the cows!

'You milk 'em? Wouldn't know where to start, me!'

Hywel was busying himself collecting crockery from the big Welsh dresser against the far wall. Dot pushed up the sleeves of her borrowed coat and went over to cut some bread. She spoke as she worked.

'Oh, you'd learn soon enough. People are all different, though, don't you find? You can do lots of things I can't. Stands to reason, because we lead such different lives. I can do nearly everything on the farm, but I'm not very good in the house, and I couldn't work with books and my brain, like you do. I've never even been to school!'

'You haven't?' Jessica sounded incredulous. 'But then you had a governess. You're probably clever really. Not that it matters, when you've got money and position and all that. And this marvellous house, of course.'

Dot narrowly missed her thumb with the bread knife, swore, and laughed. She had cut six thick slices off the loaf and now she took the first over to the fire.

'I'll make some toast. Jessica, if you stab a piece on a fork you can share the fire and it'll get made quicker. What were you saying? Oh yes, money and position and a marvellous house. I think you'll find you're rather out there. I don't run this place jolly nearly singlehanded because I like the challenge, you know! My father makes a lot of money from the pits, but he doesn't spend any of it on this place, or on me, or on the land even. As for the house, it was marvellous once, but not in my time. Now it's more like a crumbling ruin – you wait until you see it in daylight!'

'I've heard Mam complaining it's been run down,' Jessica admitted. 'But I thought that was just . . . just comparatively. When I was small we used to see you and your sisters in the village and you always looked splendidly rich to us.'

'Did we? I can't think why! Well, yes, I can, of course. It's silly to pretend we weren't a good deal better off than most.

We had ponies and once we had a seaside holiday. We were treated like well-to-do farmers' children. But now . . . the truth is that Father won't spend. He sees that good food is provided because he likes it, but apart from that I do the best I can. Hey, your toast is burning!'

'Kettle's boiled,' Hywel remarked as the two girls sighed over the cindered patch on Jessica's bread. 'Cocoa, is it? And that toast, and some cake and mince pies and a chunk of this apple tart . . . that'll set you up for the night and me up for the walk home. Where are you going to sleep?'

'Oh, down here, if Jessica doesn't mind,' Dot said quickly. She had no desire for brother and sister – particularly the sister – to see her bare, damp bedroom, and the miles of corridor were still something she would sooner face in daylight. 'We'll be really cosy down here, if you could just fetch us some blankets, Hywel, from the chest on the upstairs landing.'

'I will. Are they likely to be aired, though?' Hywel asked. Dot laughed but said on second thoughts they would probably do better to get what they could out of the airing cupboard up behind the fire. She and Jessica rooted through this and came out with half a dozen thin blankets and a couple of pillowcases which, Dot said triumphantly, they could fill with cushions from the drawing room. Having made all their sleeping arrangements for the night, for there were two large, winged armchairs by the kitchen fire and they could have one each, they drank their cocoa and ate their supper. Then Hywel rewrapped himself in his muffler, caught up his gloves and made for the back door.

'I can't thank you enough, Hywel,' Dot said as the door swung open. It had begun to rain again and the kitchen, in contrast, looked very snug. 'We'll have a good breakfast waiting for you at eight.'

'Never mind that. Many a rabbit and a trout I've had from this place. About time I paid your da back. I'll give you a hand to muck out, and all.'

Jessica grabbed Hywel's sleeve as he was about to leave; she was pouting, but merrily.

'Aren't you going to say goodnight to me, Hywel? There's unfriendly you can be. Mam isn't here now, you know, glaring at us! Take care, and don't go falling in the river!'

'Is it likely? Goodnight, girls.'

Jessica closed the back door, shot the bolt, and then came rather disconsolately back to her chair. Then she sighed and smiled at Dot.

'Nice, isn't he? I'm glad he isn't my brother, for all Mam tries to play up a relationship which doesn't exist. These blankets are thin, aren't they?'

'Yes, very. Why do you say Hywel isn't your brother? I suppose a half-brother isn't quite . . .'

'Half-brother? No, girl, now it's you got things wrong. Hywel's not related to me at all – and nor's Mam, for all I call her that. My own mam went away and left me, so Da married Hywel's mam and we were brought up as one family, like; but that's all there is to it.'

'You're not his sister! Not even half, or a cousin or something!' Light broke dazzlingly. 'Oh, I *see*!'

'No, I don't suppose you do see. Tell you what, I'll explain when we're all cuddled down with the lights out. Easier to talk when it's dark, I think, don't you?'

Dot had no experience of girlish confidences exchanged in either broad daylight or darkest night but she did not intend to say so. She nodded hard.

'Much easier. We're not taking any clothes off, are we? We'd only be cold – the fire will die once we're asleep.' She giggled. 'And I'm still wearing my nightgown under this lot, come to think, though I did hoist it up when I came to your door.'

'A fright you did look,' Jessica said bluntly as they cuddled beneath their covers. 'Not so much as a scarf on you, girl, and your hair all tangled. Nearly shut the door on you, I did, only it is Christmas.'

'Yes, I daresay I did look a bit wild,' Dot said. 'The truth is . . .' and she related the story of her Ghastly Experience, from the moment she took fright until she ran out of the stable and headed for the village. Jessica laughed until she cried.

'Oh, Dot, no wonder you wanted someone to stay with you here! But you'd rather me than the fellers, wouldn't you? I mean, you and I can talk and that. I know you know Hywel. Don't try and pull the wool over my eyes, now – it's clear as the nose on your face. You kept looking at him when you thought no one was watching. But you wouldn't have wanted him stuck in your cold old spare room now, would you? Better me, eh? So's we can have a bit of a chat and a laugh.'

'Much better,' Dot said comfortably, if not entirely truthfully. She had reached the disastrously painful stage in her relationship with Hywel when to have him under the same roof was joy unparalleled, but she knew what Jessica was driving at. And she did not want Jessica — or anyone else for that matter — to know how she felt about Hywel.

'That's good. Shall we have the lamp out?' Dot, being the nearest, snuffed the lamp and the two looked at each other rather shyly in the fire's glow. 'That's better. Easier to talk, I always think. The fact is, I'm going to marry him, see, so when I saw you . . . well, I did wonder. He writes to me and he'd mentioned one or two things — the apples, meeting you up in the hills — and I couldn't but wonder, could I? Only you're not at all what I thought, not a bit stuck-up or grabby, and I reckon you're too busy working on this place to start getting ideas about marrying? I'm right, aren't I?'

'By and large, yes, you're right,' Dot admitted. 'But — don't think I'm being horrid, but Hywel and I have talked from time to time and he's never mentioned marrying you. Or anyone else, for that matter,' she added hurriedly.

'Oh no, he wouldn't. It isn't his idea yet, but he'll come round to it,' Jessica said. 'He's slow to change, is Hywel, and he's thought of me as his sister for years, so I have to keep reminding him that I'm not. There was a row before you came, over that very thing — I wanted him to kiss me under the mistletoe and Mam said it wasn't right and Hywel just sort of stood there, going red. Mam doesn't much care for Hywel for all he's her own flesh and blood. I don't know why. I suppose some people just don't like others. I think that's why he won't stand up and tell her he'll do what he wants.'

'He may not tell her, but I reckon he'll do it all the same,' Dot observed sagely from her own nest of blankets. 'He's neither to lead nor drive when he's made up his mind, your bro — sorry, your half — no, sorry . . . Gracious, what *do* you call yourselves?'

'Oh, friends. We'll be lovers one day, though, just you wait and see. I used to be influenced by Mam, though, that was the

241

trouble. She told me it wouldn't do me any good to be seen with a collier boy, so I stopped going about with him. And then one day when I came back from Cambridge I found I was in love with him. Weird, isn't it? So now I shall be very charming and sweet to him and not try to make him kiss me for a bit, and he'll fall in love with me before he knows it and we'll get married. See? Then I'll teach until we've a bit of money put by and he can come out of that wretched colliery and do a real job in town. He's clever, is Hywel. He could be a solicitor's clerk or work on the railways. He could have gone to college, like I did, but Mam wouldn't hear of it and he didn't seem bothered.'

'You don't think you might fall in love with someone else?' Dot asked cautiously. 'Because I don't think your . . . Hywel, I mean, wants to work in town. He likes the land a lot, and animals, and farming.'

Jessica nodded reluctantly. 'Yes, I know. But if I do fall for someone else it won't matter, and if I stay true to Hywel he'll fall in love with me and he'll want to do what will please me, I suppose.'

Dot opened her eyes at this naive outlook but did not comment. It was plainly impossible to point out to Jessica that if one wanted to please the loved one it should work both ways. She claimed to be in love with Hywel yet there was no mention of her changing to please him!

'I think love's very important,' Jessica continued, oblivious of Dot's astonished amusement. 'I suppose it's because I'm a love-child – did you know that? My mother and father weren't married; he just met her in town and gave her a baby – me – and then she ran off and left me with him. Or with him and my nain. I daresay you'll think my real mother was no better than she should be, but I think the way my da behaved made up for all that. He made me a love-child, if you like! Many a fellow would have denied the baby, but not my da. He *surrounded* me with love. I'm sure he married Mam for me, and that's why love is so terribly important to me.'

'I think,' Dot said slowly, after a thoughtful pause, 'that love is important to most people. You say it's important to you because you had so much of it, but I think it's important to me because I had so little. Did you know my parents wanted a boy, when I was born? Mother never could care for me because I was such a disappointment. I think she knew she would only hold my father by giving him a son. And Father doesn't much like girls, though there was a time . . .' She stopped, struck by a sudden thought. Of course!

'What? There was a time . . .? You can't start something and not finish it! I've told you the secrets of my heart, like being a love-child and wanting to marry Hywel.'

'Well, all right then. It's just occurred to me that my father seemed to be resigned to having no son and to rather like me because I tried very hard to be boyish, until about five years ago. Then he got bored with me and I couldn't understand it, it was so sudden. But just now I remembered that five years ago the woman . . . his mistress, whatever you call it . . . she had a son, his son. And it was *then* that he stopped liking me a bit.'

'Golly! So you really have got a half-brother!'

'Yes, I suppose I have. Not a word to a soul, though, because now that Mother's dead Father's married his . . . the person I told you about, and he's going to bring her back to live in a few months, when people won't think badly of him for re-marrying.'

'Golly!' Jessica repeated. 'Will you like that? Having someone you don't know as your mother and the little boy here as well?'

'I do know her. Do you remember . . .'

'The governess!' Jessica's squeak was triumphant. 'Of course! There was a lot of talk – I think there probably still is – about your da and her. Well, so he was true to her all those years and now that he's free he's married her. I call that truly romantic!'

'Not for Mother it wasn't,' Dot reminded her friend. 'It must have been hell, half-knowing and yet unable to do anything about it. Still, I don't blame Edie. She was only young, and I expect Father swept her off her feet. I believe older men do. As for not wanting her, I *do* want her – wouldn't you? Someone to take care of the domestic side of things, someone to keep Father not only happy but at home, too. And the boy seems a nice kid. He'll be fun to have around the place as well.'

243

'You've met him? Golly! Do you think it will stop your father being so . . . well, so careful with his money, having them here?'

'Yes, I suppose I do, though I haven't given it much thought, to be honest. But when Edie was here things were easier. She didn't let him ignore the house the way he does now. When she's in charge she'll do a better job on his purse than I could. She'll not live in a tumbledown home, I feel sure.'

There was another pause before Jessica spoke again.

'Then you won't feel supplanted when they come? You really are looking forward to it?'

'Yes, I am. Truly. And now I think we'd better settle down and try to get some sleep, or we'll shock Hywel with our haggardness tomorrow morning.'

Fourteen

If Boxing day did dawn, and Dot supposed that it had, few people could have noticed, for when she and Jessica were woken by a knocking at the door and she ran to open it the rain was coming down so heavily that it looked as though a river had been diverted in its course to pour down the window panes and waterfall from the gutters. She could not see Hywel at all clearly in the grey and rain-slashed light but she dragged him indoors; indeed, on such a day she would have dragged anyone in, she told herself, even Old Nick, to get him out of the downpour.

'Phew! Swimming I am, girls.' Hywel was clad in a long mackintosh and he carried a big black umbrella but he was still soaked, his hair clinging wetly to his head. He would have stood his umbrella outside, but Dot cried out that she would stand it in the sink, so he handed it to her before beginning to divest himself of his outer clothing and the great wellington boots on his feet. 'Morning, Jess. You decent?'

Jessica answered in a sleep-thickened croak that she was fine, and then sat up and exclaimed at the slowly growing lake in which her brother stood. Hywel, grinning, shook his head at her and drops flew across the room.

'I told you, I had to swim here,' he pointed out righteously. 'All very well for you, tucked up in your blankets. There's some who got in last night drenched and are drenched a second time before you've even surfaced! It didn't keep you awake, I take it? Thundering so hard on the tiles it was when I got in that I'd a job to get off to sleep.'

'We talked till quite late,' Dot said, perching on the corner of the kitchen table and watching as Hywel detached the roller towel from the back of the door and began, vigorously, to dry his wet hair. 'It's a good thing we stayed down here. There's a leak in the corner of my bedroom which . . . oh, mercy!'

'What's the matter?' Hywel rehung the now sodden towel before turning to her. 'I know you've not fed the stock or mucked out, but it's early yet. I'll give you a hand and likely Jess will too, so the work will be done before you know it.'

'It isn't that,' Dot said hollowly. 'It's the leak! I keep a . . . a receptacle under it as a rule and I always make sure it's in the right place if it looks like rain. Only last night I was down here.'

'Aye, and sleeping like the dead, I'll warrant,' Hywel said. 'Want to go up and take a look now, or wait until after breakfast?'

His voice sounded wistful; it was clear that he could have demolished eggs and bacon, strong tea and probably a loaf of bread and a pound of butter without even pausing for breath. But Dot knew how her roof could leak and what havoc it could cause.

'Look, if you'll start things off down here, Hywel, you and Jess, I'll nip up and deal with whatever I find. With the sort of rain we've had all sorts of leaks will be going strong. I bet the one in the tower room's filled up, and the one over the blanket chest on the upper landing, though that shouldn't have overflowed.' She was making for the door as she spoke but when she left the room Hywel was close behind her. She pulled a face at him and shook her head. 'No, don't come, Hywel. I can cope now I'm awake.'

'I'll come with you and help, Jessica can manage breakfast.' He was looking amused. 'What do you mean, *that shouldn't have overflowed*? The whole point of a leak indoors is that it's overflowed, surely?'

'Well, yes, but I didn't actually mean the leak itself, I meant the tin bath. Some places are really bad, you see, so we keep buckets or baths under them all the time, and then if they do overflow and we can't keep up someone has to try and find that particular bit of roof or guttering and mend it or clean it out or something. The men do their best, but we don't have any terribly reliable ladders . . . it's scary crawling around on the roof without knowing how you'll get down again. My room, needless to say, isn't leaking where it can be reached to mend. At least, you'll see for yourself in a moment.'

In the faint greyish light the stairs and passages were still gloomy, but last night they had seemed worse than merely gloomy to lonely Dot. The mirror was there still, but how different it looked when it reflected a pink and smiling face. Doors might creak and swing, but what did it matter when you had a six-foot-tall coal hewer close behind you to keep you safe?

They were only halfway across the big square upper landing, however, when Dot gave a groan.

'Oh, damn, it really is a cloudburst! Look!'

'I see.' Hywel eyed the rising flood which was creeping across the floor towards them with some surprise. 'Well, no wonder the bath couldn't take it!'

There against the wall was the carved oak blanket chest and on top of it, a brimming tin bath. Into it streamed a tinkling waterfall; out of it streamed an equally musical flood. It was no longer containing the water, it was merely passing it on, and not only was the blanket chest saturated but the floor was inches deep and the level was rising. It would not be long before the water took to the stairs!

'I'm afraid you're right. It was too much to expect of even the biggest bath. Look, if you take hold of the tub by one end I'll grab the other, and we'll carry it to that window and tip it out on to the garden. That's what we usually do.'

'But usually, I trust, before it's as full as this,' Hywel puffed, as the two of them hefted the bath. He gasped as they lurched and he was showered with cold water, then grinned as Dot was doused on the return swing. 'Used to this, are you? Fond of it, maybe? Duw, it's an odd old place to live, isn't it?'

'No it is not! Any roof's entitled to leak when it's more than four hundred years old.' They stood the bath down and Dot wrestled with the window catch, then allowed Hywel to open it for her with a blow so hefty that a piece of putty, insecurely attached, popped out into the downpour. 'Now if only we were the same height this would be easy.'

'It's easy anyway. No, stand back, girl, I can manage this part.' Hywel picked up the bath, rested it on the windowsill, and then tipped it in a glittering arc down on to the garden below. 'Hope there's no one passing by!'

'I doubt if they'd notice with the rain so heavy already.' Dot took the now empty bath and trotted back across the hall to replace it on the blanket chest. 'Now I'd better go and take a look at my private and personal leak.'

'Sounds rude, that,' Hywel commented, but Dot was suddenly filled with agonising apprehension. Suppose she opened her bedroom door and a wall of water six feet high rushed out? Suppose the water had rotted the floor and when they opened the door there was just a great, gaping hole? She hesitated, hand outstretched, scarcely daring to touch the door-knob. She looked down, but there was so much water on the landing that if more was running out from under her door she could not possibly have told.

'Come on, Dot. Nothing to be afraid of, is there?'

At his words, Dot hastily pushed the door open. It was bad, of course. The water was inches deep in here too. And then, behind her, Hywel gave a shout of laughter.

'Well, would you look at that! Strange craft to find in a young lady's room!'

The clogs she wore for yardwork were floating, and so were her empty cocoa mug and the tin plate with its burden of soggy Christmas cake. But there breasting the tide, magnificently bobbing, was the receptacle which Dot usually placed beneath the leak. An outsize chamber pot, regally decorated with pink and yellow roses, it circled leisurely on the flood, now floating towards the bed, now towards the wall and now, as the opening of the door made another destination possible, it came bearing down upon them, heading for the as yet unvisited lake on the upper landing. Dot had a fleeting vision of it trundling gently down the stairs on a sort of waterfall and finding its way out into the great world; then she joined Hywel in helpless laughter.

'But we'll have to catch the leaks,' she said presently, after they had mopped their eyes and composed themselves. 'It'll have to be something a good deal bigger than that pot if this continues.' She nodded towards the window, where the rain still beat vainly – so far – against the panes. 'There's a hip-bath in Mother's room, an enormous thing. If you could give me a hand we could bring it through.'

They were still trying to reduce the water, as helpless as

Lewis Carroll's seven maids with seven mops, when Jessica came cautiously up the stairs.

'I heard you laughing a moment ago,' she said accusingly. 'And I can't cook, so I haven't started anything. I'd only make a mess of it. Couldn't Dot come down and show me how, even if both of . . .' She broke off, eyes widening as she saw the extent of the flood. 'Oh, gracious, no wonder you didn't come down sooner!'

'Might as well give up, I think,' Hywel said. 'Like trying to stem the Red Sea, it is.' He went to the open window and wrung the towel he was using over the sill. 'Maybe if we tried to brush it down the stairs . . .?'

'We'll try after we've eaten,' Dot said, throwing her own towel down into the lake which lapped at her feet. 'We'll work better on full stomachs. Oh, but then there are the beasts to feed, and you two will want to get home. Gwil can give me a hand, I daresay.'

Clattering down the stairs behind her, Hywel snorted.

'Oh, sure. We'll go home and sit by the fire and have a good meal now, and you'll be up here by yourself brushing water and mopping and emptying buckets and baths. That's what friends are for, to desert you when you really need 'em.'

'But it's Christmas, and you work terribly hard getting coal. You need your free time,' Dot said. 'I can't let you spend your holiday working here!'

'Can't let us? You try to stop us!' Jessica was beaming. 'Great fun it is, playing with water – you'd have the rest of the family up here if they knew. Come on, let's see who can eat the most bacon and eggs. Won't the animals wait for a bit whilst you have some breakfast?'

In fact the question never arose. As they re-entered the kitchen the back door opened and Gwil, a sack over his head and another over his shoulders, erupted, dripping, amongst them. He showed little surprise at finding his mistress entertaining in the kitchen and as he threw his sacks in the general direction of the sink he grinned at them all.

'Morning! Can't say good, can I, when it's raining cats and dogs! I've fed the stock, Miss Dot, for I couldn't see you gettin' round to it this morning, and I milked earlier, as we'd arranged. Ted took the churns off soon's I finished so I told him to keep the lids on or he'd find himself selling watered milk. The master said to bring in the fuel, so I come to see what's needed.'

'Gwil, you're worth your weight in gold,' Dot said fervently. 'Sit down and I'll make us all some breakfast. Then, if you could muck out, the rest of us will get on with brushing the water out. We're flooded, as I daresay you've guessed,' she added, putting Gwil in the picture.

'Aye, I thought you would be,' Gwil said phlegmatically. 'Never known rain like it. The lane's like a river,' he added with all the ghoulish pleasure of a countryman to whom every natural disaster means a chance to go one better than a previous horrible happening. 'I'll mark the barn door as I go past, shall I?'

'Oh, don't say the yard's going to flood,' Dot cried. 'It's too soon to mark the barn door, surely?'

'Too soon? Past the ten-year-ago mark already, though the barn's sunk a bit on the side nearest the pond,' Gwil informed her. 'What was the river like, mun, when you came by?'

'Roaring,' Hywel said briefly. 'That's a thought – Jess, would you stay here another night if the servants can't get back? It's not just likely, it's bound to happen if the river goes on rising. Come to that, we might have a job getting back ourselves.'

'Will the master be home tomorrow?' Gwil went over to the sink as the appetising smell of frying bacon filled the room, and began to pump water over his hands. When they were clean he tried to dry them on the roller towel, grimaced at its sodden state, and went over to the table and began to slice bread. Hywel and Jessica exchanged startled glances, but Dot obviously found nothing strange in the farmhand's being so at home in the kitchen, for as Gwil put bread on to the plates she slid a large, orange-yolked egg on to each slice, following it up with crisply spitting bacon and some fried tomatoes she had conjured up from somewhere.

'No. And, as Hywel was saying, he might not be able to get back the day after that. He's in Chester, I believe, and the river there can flood . . . we'll see. Not that it matters once the servants come back, because Father has almost nothing to do with the estate now.' Dot dished up the last fried tomato, pushed the plates towards her guests and joined them, sitting down heavily on a kitchen chair and then jumping to her feet again with a cry. 'Oh, damn! I forgot the tea!'

'I'll get it.' Jessica had watched Dot's confident handling of the frying pan with awe, but now she left the table and busied herself with the heavy pot. 'See? I can be quite practical too, sometimes.'

'My word, a real little marvel you are,' Hywel said affectionately. 'Made that tea like a real expert, you did. When you can milk a cow and stem a flood you'll be Dot's equal, I daresay.'

'I haven't stemmed the flood yet,' Dot reminded them through a mouthful of bread and bacon. 'Gwil, you ought to see my room, and the upstairs landing. Oh, *oh!* I've had a perfectly awful thought!'

'What is it?' Gwil asked, chewing, obviously unmoved by her shriek. 'Your room and the landing have flooded before.'

'Yes, but not like this. Gwil, I didn't think – the back stairs! That's why it hasn't come pouring down into the front hall.'

'Why?' Jessica asked. 'I don't get it.'

'Well, no, you wouldn't. But the house is built on several different levels. Once you pass my room you go down three stairs to get to the rooms on the other side, and then you go down another three to a servant's room with all the bells from the bedrooms in it, and that room has two doors and you go out the far door and there's a teeny little landing and a bathroom and toilet and the back stairs, which come out in the scullery.' She gestured with her fork 'Through there. That's lower than this, so the water wouldn't come in here.'

'Well, if it's come that way it should brush out easy enough,' Gwil said, eating steadily. 'Quarry tiles through there and a step down into the yard. Probably running out of the back door this very moment, girl.'

Dot, who had sat bolt upright, relaxed again and lifted the cosy to put her hand reflectively against the side of the fat brown teapot. She snatched it away again, held it against her cheek, and then began to pour herself more tea.

'True. We may brush it through without too much . . . oh, lor!'

'Disaster after disaster, and most of 'em imaginary,' Hywel remarked. 'What now, Dot?'

'The spare room's next to mine. The spare room's decent . . . almost,' Dot explained with a sigh. 'There's carpet on the floor and curtains round the bed and frills round the dressing table. Oh, and there's a fancy footstool embroidered by my great-great-something or other and a firescreen and a little desk that Father once said was worth a mint of money . . . Heavens, he'll go mad if anything's spoilt.'

'Sit down and eat your breakfast,' Hywel said firmly. 'Why should your da go mad, Dot? After all, he's taken so little interest in the place that he didn't even get anyone to mend the leaks. They've been there long enough, from what you said. He leaves you here all by yourself to cope with whatever comes along, he doesn't even arrange for a servant to stay to keep you company, and if the whole place got flooded or burned down or destroyed he'd have no one to blame but himself. Lord, it makes me boil just to think of it – if you'd been upstairs, how could one skinny, undersized little lass like you have managed to empty that bath into the garden? Forget it. Any trouble he's brought right on his own head.'

'You're right,' Dot said. 'I'll just nip up the back stairs and . . .'

'Sit down and finish your breakfast!' The roar, coming simultaneously from three throats, made them all laugh, but Dot did sit down again. It was so nice to be with friends, and they were right: it was no fault of hers if Father went off and left her alone and they had a flood.

'How about some more food?' Hywel had swung the doors of the stove open and was spiking a slice of bread on his fork. 'Who's for toast?'

Everyone was, and soon the four of them settled down to steady eating.

That night Dot lay in her own bed in her own room, examining the situation from every angle. She had had a thoroughly enjoyable if unorthodox day. Jessica and Hywel had worked side by side with her all day and by teatime the water had been banished, though it continued to drip into the various receptacles they had found to receive it. They had enjoyed picnic meals after that excellent cooked breakfast, but the food had been none the worse for that and when, at five, Lizzie and Annie had turned up, having made their way somehow across the swollen river, Jessica had wanted Dot to return to the village and spend the evening with them. But this Dot did not feel she could do. She was tired, she had jobs which she must do before she could go to bed, and she knew that if she had gone she would have worried all the while in case the rain started again and prevented her from getting back to Plas Tegydd that night.

She liked Jessica very much, which was odd, considering that they were both intent on capturing – or did she mean captivating? – the same young man. But Dot, who had never had a girl friend – one could scarcely count older and unsympathetic sisters as friends – was revelling in the delights of having actually talked to someone who was not a member of her family – talked intimately, with confidences exchanged, little jokes understood, about the things which could only, she supposed, interest another girl of about your own age. The peculiar affairs of the old, the way one felt, what one wanted out of life . . . no one, before, had ever cared how Dot felt about these things; now someone did.

Hywel was more than a friend to her and she loved him; she no longer had any doubts on that score. But she would not have dreamed of talking to Hywel as she had talked to Jessica. Whenever he had gone out to help Gwil or to empty baths and buckets she and Jessica had started again on what she supposed was girl-talk. Easy, intimate, their discussions ranged over all the things that mattered only to them: friends – she had few; makeup – she had never worn any; clothes – she had none, or none worth discussing. Yet the talk had never been strained or one-sided, for Dot had plenty of opinions which she had never before had the chance to air.

She had known very soon that if Hywel had to marry anyone but her, she would rather it was Jessica. Her altruism had not reached the stage of mental willingness to hand him over, but at least if the worst came to the worst she would like the woman he wanted to make his wife. Not that she believed for one moment that Hywel would marry Jessica; the dream was totally one-sided. As things stood, she was sure Hywel preferred her to Jess as regards marriage; if she could only grow beautiful, or perhaps elegant and fashionable . . . but she did not think he would marry Jessica, who was, in a small way, all three.

She mentioned none of this to Jessica, of course. Friendship was too new, too precious, to risk a jarring note. They would write to each other when Jessica returned to Cambridge – that had been agreed almost without discussion. During the rest of Jess's vacation they would meet, go to town together, look at the shops and visit the cinema. They might even take a train to Chester and go to the theatre there, where Jess had spent many happy hours and Dot had never been. Oddly enough, despite the fact that she had been born and bred there, Dot soon realised that Jessica had no close friends in the village and was as eager as herself for their relationship to continue – indeed, to blossom and grow.

It was strange, when you thought of it, how things turned out. A disastrous Christmas day, ending in a flight from her beloved home in fear and trembling, had ended very happily. She had known Hywel for years, but now she knew him from a different angle: his home angle. Not only that, but she had seen him at Plas Tegydd, very much in command, telling everyone what to do and doing plenty himself. He would fit in here, if they ever . . . if she ever . . . if he asked her . . . if only, if only! And her friend, her new friend, her best and only friend? What would happen to Jessica, if Hywel married Dot? But Jessica had chances of meeting people which could never be Dot's; she moved in a society where it was perfectly possible that she might meet someone far more suited to her than Hywel was, and in those circumstances she had as good as said she would not hesitate to leave Hywel and his farming hopes alone.

Now that is odd, because she's two years older than me, yet she's got no more conscience about hurting people than a baby, Dot told herself. And she was a city girl at heart. Or even if that was not quite right, she was certainly too lively and adventurous to settle down without complaint to life on a smallholding, with very little money and almost no entertainment save what you could provide yourself. She said she would teach – but for how long? And when she finished teaching, would she really be content to settle down to raising a family? She was exciting, ambitious, and very clever. Probably her feelings for Hywel were just a whim, which would not last once she got back to Cambridge. She had told Dot how differently she had felt about Hywel only a year ago; feelings which sprang to life so suddenly could die just as quickly, Dot felt. Her own feelings, of steadily increasing dependence and affection, were, she was sure, quite different. To leave Hywel would be to tear up her roots, and Dot was a firmly rooted and faithful plant.

Having worked out to her own satisfaction that, first, Jessica did not really want Hywel, and, second, that even if she did she was not the right person for him, Dot turned her attention to the differences between the two of them. Jessica was exciting and glamorous, with a marvellously slender figure and long legs. Dot was small, dark, and rooted in the soil of just one spot. Jessica's hair was a flame of beauty. Dot's was . . . well, it was just dark. Jessica's eyes were big and green and sparkling. Dot's were . . . oh damn it, damn it, damn it . . . Dot's were just dark!

However, Jessica did not have enough money to buy anyone a smallholding; a mean thing to think, but true, nevertheless, nor did she hope one day to inherit Plas Tegydd and its broad acres. Hywel might not know about her five thousand pounds, he might have his doubts about her inheritance, but they were cards on her side which might, in the end, prove just as potent as brilliant hair and long legs. Sighing, Dot turned her face into the pillow and was soon asleep.

She was woken by someone opening her door with a crash and stumbling across the room. Before she had done more than sit upright, her nocturnal visitor had crashed across the foot of her bed, swearing richly and breathing fumes of alcohol over her. He lay supine for a moment, and then sat up, still swaying, and peered suspiciously around him.

'Father! What on earth. . .?'

'Yesh, 'smee. Come to ta' c-care of m'lil gal. Come to shee . . . see . . . come to make sure Dot's not bin washed away by th'awful rain.' He hiccuped so loudly that it sounded like a

255

shot being fired. He had been carrying a candle and by some miracle he had not dropped it when he fell across the bed. Now, in its light, he blinked around as though searching for the perpetrator of the enormous hiccup. 'Wha'ss that? Wha'ss that, I say? Come to ta' care of li'l Dot, li'l Dotty.'

'That's very kind,' Dot said, wavering between laughter and annoyance. 'But wouldn't it do in the morning? Why not go to bed now, Father?'

Tom frowned round, then rubbed the side of his nose with one finger. He looked sly and somehow stupid.

'Only came 'cos Blanche made me,' he announced lugubriously. 'Said it looked bad, said people 'ud talk, say things. Fat lot I care,' he added indistinctly. 'Been talkin' about me for ever, I tol' her, but she pushes me out, into the rain and the col', without a thought for my health or my 'vanced years. So I tooka bottla brandy off the si'board.' The sly look was now much in evidence. 'Yes, took it, I did, and swigged it and swigged it and swigged it and swigged it till the bottle was hempty.' He paused, cocking his head interrogatively. 'Hempty? *Hempty?* Sounds very pecu . . . peculi . . . sounds very odd, that.'

'It's all right,' Dot said, nobly keeping a straight face and hardly letting her voice waver at all. 'I expect Blanche was right, Father, and it's better that you're here with me. The house did flood this morning and if it rains very much more the river will be over its banks.'

'Yes, yes, made me come, out into the col', all on me ownio,' Tom continued as though she had not spoken. 'Go back to your daught . . . daughter, tha'ss what she said, go back! That girl's keepin' the place warm so's my li'l boy can tek over. You shou' appreciate what she's doin'. If your girl din't care, what would my boy 'herit, when the time comes?' He laughed squeakily and ran a hand through his hair. ''Strue, I tol' her, 'strue, every las' word, so back I came to see my li'l Dot.'

Dot, sitting up in bed, was as still as if she had been turned to stone. What had he said? Taking care of . . . no, keeping the place warm for . . . she could not bring herself to put it into words, not even into thoughts. The slurred mutter could not have meant what she had thought. But he was rambling on again, about how Blanche had made him leave. She must find out!

256

'Father, who am I keeping the place decent for?'

He giggled again, then leaned over and tried to pat her head, or perhaps her shoulder. She could not tell because he missed both and patted the wall instead.

'Why, for Tommy, li'l Tommyo. The leg . . . the secon' one'll get the money an' the pits and mos' of the land, I daresay. But pore li'l Tommy, wha's he goin' to get? Just Plas Tegydd, that's all, an' my li'l Dot's gettin' it nice and keepin' it warm for him, so she is.'

She had heard enough. Huge shudders were shaking her, but of course he would not notice, drunk as he was. She lay down. Carefully, as though if she moved quickly she might crack and splinter into a thousand pieces. She said, very loudly and clearly: 'Get out of my room.'

'Whassat? Whassat you say?'

'Get – out – of – my – room.'

In her whole life she had never spoken to him like that and it sobered him, at least partially. He stared at her, the candle wobbling in his hand as he held it high to examine her features. And then he shambled to his feet and left the room without another word. She heard him stumbling along the corridor to his own room, heard the door bang open, swing, creak. Even heard him fall on to the bed. She wondered whether he would set fire to the bedclothes and destroy the whole house, but since she neither smelt smoke nor heard shouts she supposed that he had either snuffed the candle or, dropping it, ensured that it snuffed itself.

Presently, stentorian snores rent the air. Bubbling, unattractive snores. Dot, lying as still and cold as a marble statue, found herself hating the snorer with a most unfilial hatred. So he would give Plas Tegydd to his bastard, would he? And thank her for taking good care of it for the kid? Well, he would discover his mistake soon enough. As soon as day dawned she would leave the house and its drunken, hateful owner and find Hywel and tell him that they must find a place *now*, so that she could move in right away. She would get her five thousand pounds from the family solicitor. She would not spend another night under this roof where she was expected to work to build the place up for a five-year-old who had never even lived here!

She could not sleep; bitter thoughts would not permit it. She could not help going over and over in her mind the things she had done for Plas Tegydd, to find herself not only disinherited but thought of so little account that her father could sit on her bed and boast of what he had done. He had not believed she had enough spirit to go, to leave the place to the tender mercies of himself and his bastard. He thought she would stay and continue to work like an unpaid labourer for him. Well, he was wrong! Let him try to run the place on nothing for his sins; he would wish her back then!

The night passed incredibly slowly. When at last the sky streaked with the grey promise of another rainy dawn, Dot was glad to get out of bed. At least if she was moving she was not forced to keep going over and over in her mind what had happened to her. She took her clothes and tiptoed down to the kitchen, to dress in the warm before the stove. Down there, in the rosy glow of the firelight, she began to wonder if her father could have been play-acting, not meaning a word of what he had said. Perhaps it had been the drink speaking and not Tom Tegydd?

But a little thought convinced her that *in vino veritas* was not just an idle saying. Her father did not often get really drunk, but when he did he spoke the truth. Unpalatable often, but nevertheless the truth as he saw it. Useless to pretend to herself, as he would doubtless pretend to her if she asked him, that he did not intend to disinherit her. He would think up some story to convince her that she had misunderstood him because he would never, when cold sober, make the mistake of letting her know what he planned. But she knew he had been telling the truth; he intended Plas Tegydd for Tommy. Her home, her place . . . but no use dwelling on it. She had had her eyes opened, and would not continue to strive in the belief that she was working for her own future. Now she knew the truth she could Take Steps.

Once dressed, she cut slices off the loaf, toasted them and ate them hungrily. She had a lot to do today! She would ride Matchless into town and find the family solicitor who was dealing with her mother's will, and she would explain that she wanted the money – her money – immediately in order to buy a small property. She would like a local property if possible, but if not she would be willing to go elsewhere. In fact, if she could afford it, it might be better to go down on to the Wirral where the land was richer and more easily cultivated.

But she knew in her heart she would not willingly go away. These rounded hills, with the mountains towering in the background, were a part of her. She would stay here if she could.

Out in the stables tacking up the pony, she continued to plan her day. First the solicitor, next to see property and finally to find Hywel. She would be far happier if he would agree that they should join forces and buy their smallholding together, but in the circumstances she had already made up her mind that if he felt it was too soon to do such a thing she would buy anyway, on her own. It should be quite straightforward. Only the other day her father had come to her with a paper to sign so that she might get her money more quickly. He had explained that Olivia had tied up her funds in various ways . . . shares, investments and the like . . . but that it was possible to get Dot's five thousand pounds extricated from the rest, if she would prefer it that way. She had said she would, so the money should be easy to obtain.

She did think, a little guiltily, that perhaps she was being unfair to Tommy, but that thought did not survive for long. Tommy was five, but in a mere ten years he would be fifteen, a young man. And then how would he like it if half-sister Dot tried to tell him how to run the property that would one day be his? Or might already be his, come to that. Tom would be nearly seventy by then. Even if she had wanted the hassle, she knew that it would not be fair to Plas Tegydd. No property could stand the tug of two masters. If she loved her home and liked the boy, then she should go now, whilst she still could.

She heard Gwil in the milking shed and went through to see him, tying Matchless up outside. He grinned at her, assuming she had come to give a hand, and for a moment she was tempted – after all, they were her cows; she had reared them from calves, spent all her time and energy and a good deal of her precious money turning them into first-class milkers. Surely she could stay for a moment, help with the milking, and tell Gwil that she would take the herd – and himself – with her, when she went? But she did not know where she was going or with whom; better leave it until she was sure.

'Oh, Gwil, I won't give you a hand because I'm off into town and there are a few things I want to do first. Is there anything we need, by the way? I'll be back late, probably about four.'

Gwil considered, then turned back to the cow he was milking and leaned his head against its smooth belly.

'Not a thing, Miss Dot, unless you want to order more cattle cake? But enough we do have for a week or two yet.'

'I won't bother, then. Cheerio, Gwil.'

Leaving the milking shed she mounted Matchless, kicked his sides, and turned out of the yard and into the lane. It was not raining, but it was cold and overcast and she was glad she had thought to put on her thick old cloak and the woollen mittens which Ella had knitted her for Christmas. Lovely to have warm hands. As she rode, her heart rose with the unseen sun. A terrible thing had happened to her but she was young and life was an adventure. Everyone should have to make his own way in the world; she had believed she was doing so by trying to bring Plas Tegydd back to prosperity, but of course she had been building on very ancient foundations. Probably Tegydds had been letting the Plas rot and bringing it back to good heart every other generation since time immemorial! It would be good for her character and for her farming to have to start quite literally from scratch.

Plas Tegydd was high and the town was on the plain, so even when you had ridden right down to the highway the the town was still far below you and in full view for half-a-dozen miles until you, too, reached the plain. Today it was wreathed in the smoke of many chimneys and beneath the grey and lowering sky was not a pretty sight. Even so, she hummed to herself as she rode. She would no longer repine. She would make the best of what she had. Imagine, she told herself, what you would be feeling like if mother had not left you five thousands pounds! She could imagine it only too well, the gloom and despair, for even with her savings and Hywel's combined they could not have bought a decent place. Renting was all very well, but she knew Hywel did not want to rent, and by herself, of course, it would be impossible. Her lot could have been immeasurably harder.

She reached the outskirts of the town and knew at once that something unusual was taking place there. There were crowds and crowds of people, all in their best clothes, heading in the general direction of the beast market. And then she remembered the big cattle sale which was held each year on 27th December. Despite all that had happened, that was today! She smiled at the people nearest her and rode on, feeling a stir of real excitement. Jolly lucky! She would see the solicitor and then, if she found a place she liked, she could look around, choose herself some decent beasts to start her new herd. If the solicitor did not know of a suitable smallholding, what was more, with so many people in town there was sure to be someone wanting to sell land, or a house with a few acres, or both!

As she stabled Matchless behind the Wynnstay it crossed her mind that she might meet her father here later. He hated to miss a good cattle sale, though it was not for the sake of the stock that he enjoyed it. He liked meeting other landowners, of course, but for the last ten years or so that had been a mixed blessing. What he really enjoyed was meeting other owners and talking about collieries. And now that she had thought about him, she realised that he might well be down here today, doing any final business he had in connection with his purchase of the Black Wynd. She assumed the sale had gone through; certainly he talked as if it had.

Dot found she did not want to meet Tom. Treacherous Tom Tegydd. But he would have one hell of a hangover, so he would not be out of bed too early. If she left the solicitor's office before eleven she should be safe enough from the most embarrassing encounter, which would be actually inside the office, so that he would – might – guess what she was doing there. He would know that soon enough, of course, but she preferred that he discovered what she had done when it had become a *fait accompli*, rather than when it was still in the delicate planning stage.

The solicitor's office was on Pen-y-Bryn, not too far away. She walked briskly up the hill with its small, sloping houses on either side, finding his office without difficulty since she had visited it several times with her mother or father. The ground floor was a milliner's shop. As she climbed the stairs to the first floor a doubt shook her. The milliner's shop had been closed; suppose Mr Geraint was having an extended Christmas holiday? She did not want to talk to any of his clerks.

But she should have guessed that, with the cattle sale on, Mr Geraint would not risk losing business. The clerk in the outer office sat her in a chair and then went through to see his employer, coming back almost at once with the news that Mr Geraint would see her now and asking if she would like a cup of coffee, since he was about to take one through for the solicitor.

Dot accepted the coffee, for the outer office was very chilly, but when she got into Mr Geraint's room it was lit by a bright fire and looked cosy and pleasant, with coloured prints of fox-hunting on the walls and studio portraits of his wife and their children in silver frames on his desk. He stood up when she entered, a tall, stout man who looked rather like a farmer himself with crinkly grey hair cut very short, pince-nez glasses on the end of a bulbous nose, and a square chin. He was wearing a tweed suit and gaiters. Was he trying to look like a farmer, Dot wondered, amused.

'Good morning, good morning,' Mr Geraint said heartily, shaking her hand. 'It's little Miss Tegydd, come to ask after her investments, I'll be bound. Come in with Papa, have you, to the cattle sale? There's plenty for a pretty young thing to do apart from examining cattle. My wife always comes in on market day, though she says you must keep a sharp eye on your handbag.'

'I don't have a handbag,' Dot said, taking the chair that Mr Geraint had indicated. 'Actually, Mr Geraint, I've come about the money I've inherited from my mother, the five thousand pounds. I wonder if it would be possible for me to have it right away? I want to buy property, and now is a good time for buying and a bad time for selling.'

He looked astonished and something more: embarrassed? A tide of scarlet suffused his face and Dot thought that he must be younger than he looked, for surely an elderly man could not blush like a rose?

'Your inheritance? You mean ... you mean your five thousand pounds? You want it to buy *property*? I don't quite understand you, Miss Tegydd.'

Danger can sometimes be scented. Dot felt sick with apprehension and with what she knew in her heart was to come. She wanted to turn and run out of this room which had suddenly become threatening. Damn it all, she had seen the will, heard Mr Geraint reading it, knew that five thousand pounds existed. So why on earth could he not understand her simple request and hand it over? Just what did he mean?

'My mother left me five thousand pounds in her will, Mr Geraint. Is that correct?'

The tide of colour retreated. He nodded, staring at her.

'Yes, yes, you've got that quite correct, my dear.'

'Well, I'm glad we agree on that, at any rate!' She was smiling, trying to sound jolly, self-confident, but she felt as though she stood on a small tussock of grass surrounded by a quaking quagmire. 'As you know, I haven't yet received the money, because Father says things take time, but if possible I'd like to have it soon so that I can buy property. As I'm sure you know, farming land is selling very cheaply at the moment, so my money would buy a decent little place. I've worked very hard up at the Plas, but the time has come when I would like to work for myself, which is why I've decided to move on. Mr Geraint, is there any reason why you should not release the money to me? I know I'm under age, but Father said Mother had specified that I might have the money immediately and that I might spend it how I wished. So, unless I have it wrong . . .'

'No indeed, Miss Dot, you've grasped it all adequately. But my dear young lady, don't you remember that your father has recently bought the Black Wynd pit?'

'Oh, did he? He talked about it a lot but I was not sure he'd actually gone ahead and done it. However, I don't quite see what that has got to do with my inheritance.'

'Why, Mr Tegydd used that five thousand pounds to make up the purchase price! There was a paper, signing over the money to him – the signature appeared to be yours. I had no idea . . . but surely you knew? If you are suggesting that I withdraw the money, such a thing is impossible, quite impossible. He was short of cash, you see, having most of his money tied up in the pits and in machinery and so on. He needed that money . . . I made sure you'd signed . . . I thought, naturally, that you knew, had read . . .'

Dot could not believe what she was hearing. She frowned

down at her hands, lying quiet on her lap. The quagmire was moving now with a vengeance!

'I did sign a paper, but I thought . . . Father said it would give me control of the money sooner . . . I didn't read it. I thought . . . '

Her voice trailed away. What a damned, bloody little fool she had been! Not to read a paper! To put her signature on anything Tom had given her would have been foolhardy but over a matter of money . . . she must have been mad. He had held the long legal document so that she could scarcely see anything other than a lot of heretofores and thereafters and he had told her to sign it or her money would be endlessly delayed.

He had lied to her. He had not been content to take Plas Tegydd from her. He had had to have her little inheritance as well.

All of a sudden the blood which filled her body seemed to drain away, leaving her light, faint, white as snow. Mr Geraint's voice came from far off. The room was turning, the fire was no longer warm but stifling hot. She staggered to her feet. She must get out of here!

She took two steps towards the door and felt her knees crumple. She hit the oilcloth lightly, with the tiniest of clatters, barely having time to notice disapprovingly that it was an ugly and unpatterned shade of brown before darkness enveloped her.

Fifteen

It was as if all in a moment she had lost everything, had been stripped and cast into the world naked and alone. When she came round Mr Geraint's concerned face hung above her, scarlet with the effort of getting her up from the floor and on to the hard little chair. She had explained – untruthfully – that she had come straight into town without breakfast and that she would be all right once she had drunk the cup of coffee and eaten the piece of bread and butter which 'the boy' had fetched up for her. Then she had sat patiently on her chair, sipping the coffee and listening to Mr Geraint explaining how safe her money would be in the Wynd, what an excellent investment it would make, and how the sum involved would double and treble under her father's ownership. She nodded, sipped, nibbled the bread and butter, and when he seemed to be running out of steam and she thought that she could get down the stairs without again making a fool of herself she finished off the coffee and the bread and butter and stood up to take her leave.

She thanked him for his kindness, apologised for her foolishness in fainting on his nice floor, and begged him to say nothing of the affair to Tom. He agreed at once. She could see that he had guessed that her signature on that document had been obtained by trickery and was horrified and embarrassed by the knowledge. She could see, too, that he would do nothing, probably could do nothing. For both their sakes he would not mention her visit.

Once out in the street, she joined the throng heading for the market. But how different her feelings now from those of earlier in the day! Then she had been a person of property, about to offer the man she loved a share in a dream. Now she was a beggar, with savings very much smaller than Hywel's, wondering whether she dared suggest that he give up a well-paid job in the pit so that he could marry her and set up home with her in a tiny, rented smallholding.

When she had thought that she was offering Hywel a handsome dowry and the prospect, one day, of being lord of Plas Tegydd as well as her own small, plain self, it had not seemed wrong to suggest marriage. His acceptance would have seemed reasonable — sensible, even. What he had been offered was a choice between Jessica, who was brilliant and fascinating but whom he did not love ('not yet', whispered Jessica's voice in her remembering ear) and a nice little farm, with Plas Tegydd to follow some time in the future. She herself had merely been a make-weight, like those mockeries of chocolates in the boxes of sweets her mother had been so fond of. A plain piece of dark chocolate shaped to look a little like the real thing, popped into the corner of the box to make the weight up to the one pound stated on the wrapping. She had pretended to herself that the box of chocolates was a little extra and that it was the make-weight which mattered. Now she acknowleged that it had been the other way around; the box of chocolates was the reason Hywel might have taken her for his wife. With no chocolates, only a fool would glance twice at the make-weight!

So what to do? Creep back to Plas Tegydd and accept the place Tom had suggested, as caretaker for his bastard son who would one day push her out? Go to Mother's relatives on the Wirral, who cared not one jot for the Tegydd connection? Cast herself on Kate's mercy, or on Allie's? She realised she was walking along the High Street now, shaking her head to try and shake away the problems which confronted her and probably looking like a madwoman to passers-by. Hastily she crossed the pavement and examined the window of a chemist's shop. She saw none of the tastefully arrayed bottles, jars and tubes in the window, but she felt calmer for stopping and presently she dug her hand into the pocket of her skirt and found a sugar lump and a florin. Good; she would go back to the Wynnstay and have a hot cup of coffee, or possibly a sandwich, and consider her next move. And then she would take a look round the market and give the sugar lump to some

266

pony or other. They would be selling a lot of horses today and she always liked looking them over.

Halfway up the High Street, though, she met a farmer she knew trying to herd sheep into the narrow entrance of Charles Street. He had a young dog, he explained rather breathlessly, who did not yet know his commands perfectly and had grown stupid and frightened with all the traffic and the people. So Dot helped him, and it took her out of herself for a little and gave her back her sense of perspective.

'You're a good lass,' he said as they reached the pens and could relax. 'Wish I'd a daughter like you – you'll make a fine farmer. And that's a thing I never thought I'd say about a woman.'

I am a good farmer, she found herself saying, as she walked amongst the stalls and the pens. Suppose I do go back to Plas Tegydd and work terribly hard and make a good bit of money? Surely then Hywel would let us marry, and . . .

Her mind wanted to carry on with the dream, but it was no good. The magic had gone out of that particular brand of escapism. She had believed in it, and then all in a moment she had been forced to face a great many unpalatable facts and none of them would disappear now and let her plunge back into fantasy. Hywel did not love her, and, if he did not, then she could not let him take her on without even the hope of the Plas one day. It would not be fair. It was not his fault that she loved him with all her heart and soul; he could scarcely be held responsible for being so totally lovable.

However, there was one faint hope. Hywel might not be in love with her, she might have no money and no prospects, but there was one thing she had which no one, not even her father, could take from her.

She was a hard worker and she had a way with animals. She could build up a milk herd from nothing and she had plenty of good, novel ideas where farming was concerned. Perhaps he might want her truly as a business partner? It would be horribly humiliating to have to go to him now and ask him whether he would like to marry her and work together, but it would have to be done. If he said no, and she was sure he would say no, then she would go away, seek her fortune somewhere else. With Kate? With Alexandra? With Mother's relatives? She did not know. She just knew she could not stay at the Plas without even the hope of escape. Alone, she could never save up enough to buy a smallholding.

Hywel was on the early shift, so Dot went back to the Wynnstay. She was leading Matchless out on to the road preparatory to mounting when a dark little man with bow legs and twinkling eyes suddenly deserted the three tweedy farmers he was talking to and came over to her.

'I know that pony! Wouldn't I swear now that he's a yearling I sold here nine or ten years ago? Have ye had good use out of him, ma'am? A lovely little feller and one of me own rearin' — aren't I sure of it as I'm sure the moon will rise tonight? Ah, there's breedin' there, and blood!'

Dot, who had learned a good deal about horse-dealing since the day she and Matchless had first fallen for each other (she was sure the feeling was mutual and Matchless had never given her cause to doubt it), laughed and continued to manoeuvre the pony so she could mount, but she did not deny the man's words. He was, after all, betting on short odds to accost a local girl riding a handsome pony at one of the biggest horse sales for miles around. And anyway he might be speaking the truth — she knew that Matchless had been bought here, she believed he had been Irish bred, and she even remembered the dealer who had sold him as dark and small.

'If you ever want to get shot of him, me darlin',' the man went on, 'then aren't I the feller to give you the good price? Ah, a lovely colt he was, and hasn't he made up just as I said, into a glowing, coal-black beauty?'

'Thanks, but no thanks,' Dot said, mounting at last and riding away down the road. But the man had planted a seed in her mind that might later bear fruit. Now she simply rode along, trying to pretend that everything was going to come right, that she would ask Hywel to marry her, he would say yes, and they would live happily ever after.

She reached the pit just as the men were streaming out off the early shift. Folk said how hard it was to recognise a man beneath his pit dirt, but Dot knew Hywel at once. Not only was he taller than the others, with a certain something in his walk, but he wore, for Dot, a special glow. She could have picked him out of a far larger crowd, no matter how he was disguised.

She waited until the men began to disperse outside the gates and then led Matchless up to him; he saw her, smiled, said something to the man beside him, and then fell back and came over to her.

'Hello, Dot, what brings you here? Your father's home. He came down the pit this morning, talked to us all. He's in high fettle because he's bought the Wynd . . . he had a few words with me, in fact.' He looked more closely at her and his tone sharpened. 'What's happened? What's the matter?'

'Well, I . . . ' She stopped, suddenly unable to voice her woe. How could she bring herself to tell him that there was no future for them, that even the unnamed sum of money she had told him about had vanished into her father's capacious – and rapacious – pocket?

'Here, come down here.' The pit was nearly a mile from the village, and one of the lanes which wandered up into the hills led, eventually, to the main village street. They entered it, and once they were well clear of the pit he put an arm about her waist. 'Come on, tell me what's happened.'

'I'm not going to inherit the Plas, not ever. Father came in last night, drunk, and told me he's leaving it to Tommy. Tommy's Edie's boy, the one I told you about.'

'He wouldn't do that,' Hywel said. He sounded shocked. 'No man would do that, Dot! The place is yours by right of birth and because of the work you've put into it. He wouldn't let his love-child take over, not whilst you're alive to have it.'

'He will. He was plain enough; he even thanked me for keeping it in good order for his little boy. There was no mistake.'

Hywel muttered something in Welsh which Dot pretended not to understand. Calling names would help no one, after all.

'All right, he may mean it now, but I'll bet you he won't do it, not when it comes to the point. And you've got your little bit of money from your mam, and I'm saving hard! When I've enough money, if you're still of the same mind, you and I can have that place.'

'Can we? Then . . . could we get it now, Hywel? Even if we

269

have to rent and not buy? Money . . . money takes time to come through, you see, and after what Father said I don't want to have to go back there. But if you would help me, rent a place . . . '

'Certainly I will, you know that.' The hand on her waist tightened slightly. 'But not right here and now, Dot, not so soon. God, girl, you're seventeen – women of your class don't become farmer's wives at that age, particularly when they've met no one, gone nowhere. Folk 'ud say I'd taken advantage of your being brought up the way you were and they'd be right! If you really won't stay at home to go to Miss Kate or Miss Alex. Meet people, find out just what it is you really want. Then, when you're eighteen, if you're still of the same mind we'll talk to your father. But now we'd certainly not get his consent.'

'His consent?' Dot stared up at him, confused. 'What on earth should we want with his consent? Kate wasn't much older than I am now when she married and no one talked about consent then!'

'My dear girl, there's ignorant you are!' He was laughing at her, but kindly. 'So far as I know it, you've got to be twenty-one before you can marry without your da's consent; that doesn't just mean you, that means the highest and lowest in the land. Didn't you know?'

'But . . . if we had a place . . . if we just moved in together . . .' Dot stammered. Hywel pulled her to a halt and caught Matchless's bridle just above the bit. He turned her round so that she could look at his face as he spoke.

'They'd take you away, make you a ward of court – and I'd lose my job, my self-respect, the lot! Look, everything comes to him who waits, and I've got a bit of news for you which may make the waiting easier. Your da's bought the Wynd and he came down today to ask if any of his hewers would work for him at his new pit. He explained, see, that the Wynd's got a bad reputation and consequently the best workers go elsewhere. Their safety record's rotten as well and he wants that put right, only he knows they can't do that unless they get new workers. They've got the existing firemen and deputies and so on – your father thinks he can work all right with them – but it's the colliers he wants. Paying double rates he is for the right men. So I saw him, told him I was prepared to

270

work devilish hard, and he said I was on and could start Monday.'

'At the Wynd? Oh, but you mustn't! It's the most dangerous pit in the area, and wet . . . there's gas . . . oh, Hywel, promise me you'll never work there!'

'It's been bad, I grant you, but it'll be good now, with new men and better management. As for gas and wet, I daresay it's no worse than the Roland and the Olwen. Anyway, I gave my word to your da, so there's no point discussing it, but don't you see what a good thing it is for us? I'll get the money together in half the time – less, if I work a few double shifts – and then we can buy our property. With your bit of money and my savings it could even be before you're twenty-one!'

She forgot that her inheritance was no more, that she needed to escape from home right away. She grabbed Hywel's arms and shook him hard. All that mattered, now, was that he should promise to remain where he was in the Olwen pit, should not move to the ill-omened colliery which had been haunted by bad luck and accidents since its very beginnings. Her own future – what did that matter, compared with his life?

'No, Hywel, you mustn't work at the Wynd. It's bad, and I have a bad feeling about it. I'll do anything, I'll go away and leave you alone, I'll move in with Kate or Allie, if only you'll promise me faithfully that you won't go down the Wynd. Please, please, Hywel, swear it!'

Hywel looked embarrassed, uneasy.

'Come on, girl, be sensible! Think of the money! In two years, if I slog at it, we can get that farm!'

Dot threw her last argument into the balance. No matter that it was a lie. She would make it come true, somehow, if only he would agree.

'Look, I'll work on Mr Geraint, get my inheritance now, and you can buy a place with it. I won't bother you. We'll wait until I'm twenty-one, but you could be making a go of the place right this minute, almost.'

But he was shaking his head, frowning.

'As if I'd take your money! No indeed. But you go to your sister and stay at least a year and if you still want to get that farm . . . '

She could only stare at him as he continued to assure her that what he was going to do was for the best. When at last he ran out of words tears were standing in her eyes.

'You mean it? You'll go down the Wynd? Nothing I can do or say will stop you?'

She was sure, at that moment, that if he loved her even a little bit he would take pity on her, not do what must distress her so terribly. But he was shaking his head, his mouth and face determined.

'If there's a risk, love, it's one I'm prepared to take. I'm a man of my word, too, and I gave your da my word I'd hew for him, down the Wynd. I can't go back on that.'

She could not understand. Her father would have given his word one minute and retracted it quite cheerfully the next. Why did Hywel have to treat him differently from the way Tom would have behaved had the situation been reversed? She sighed and wiped her eyes with the back of her hand and Matchless, bored by all this apparently fruitless talk, nudged her in the back so that she tipped forward and landed on hands and knees in the mud. Hywel laughed, pretended to smack the pony's nose and picked her up. He held her for a moment, but Dot was sure she knew why: he wanted the discussion to end amicably, but he was probably longing to get home to his tea and a bath as well. She was being a nuisance. It had not escaped her notice that when she had offered to go away and leave him alone he had not denied that this might be in the back of his mind.

She had lied to him, too. Now that it was no use any longer she wished she had not lied, not pretended that the money was still there. It had done her no good. She was adrift on a sea of trouble, for Hywel did not want her, not even with her non-existent five thousand pounds.

'All right, Matchless. You're bored, and it's time we stopped hanging about here.' She swung herself into the saddle, ignoring Hywel's hand outstretched to help her. She did not need help from anyone. If she was alone, then she would *be* alone! She settled herself comfortably in the saddle, picked up the reins and clicked her tongue to her pony, wheeling him round to overtake Hywel and ride ahead of him into the village street. Over her shoulder she said the last words she would speak to him for a long time.

'I'm sorry, Hywel, if I embarrassed you. I didn't know what to do, and I thought I owed it to both of us to make sure how you felt. I'm going away now. You won't be troubled by me again.'

'Troubled by you! Dot, love, you've been my good friend . . . '

But she had urged Matchless into a canter and Hywel's words were drowned in the clattering of the pony's hooves. A good friend! That sounded cold when put beside words like lover, wife, darling. But at least she knew where she stood. Hywel thought she should go away so that she could meet someone else. Father did not really want her at all except as an unpaid farm worker and estate manager until Tommy was old enough to take over. Very well, she would make them both happy, but not by going to Kate's house to be bossed around and dressed up like a monkey and made a fool of. She would go far away, where no one would ever find her, and nurse the hurts they had inflicted, and become strong and independent and free of them all.

As she rode she became filled with icy determination. She would show them all, and survive despite them! But not here; she did not trust herself to remain hard and cold on the day that Hywel took his bride to church, nor to see her home ill-managed without weeping. Yes, and what was more she would not come home until she was rich – rich as Croesus! She would come back in a long motor car with a chauffeur in grey and maroon, and she would show them by . . . by . . . yes, that was it! By then her father would have reduced Plas Tegydd to a rambling ruin and himself to penury and she would buy Plas Tegydd back!

The new dream kept her happy on the journey back to town.

' . . . you've been my good friend and my dearest love for years.' Hywel's words petered out as he saw she could no longer hear him. He sighed, then began to walk homeward. Women! He had always thought Dot a sensible little thing, but she was as bad as the rest. She did not know the meaning of logic, or the sacredness of one's given word. And as for buying a farm with her money — he would be little better than a kept man if he agreed to that!

On reflection, he was glad she had not heard herself called his dearest love, true though it might be. It had crept up on him gradually, his feeling for her, and he was not yet sure of it himself. Was it love? He did not think it was love to want to take care of someone, shield them from the world's hurts, but that was how he felt whenever he was with Dot. And lately there had been another feeling, too. On the few occasions when he had held her in his arms he had wanted very badly to hug her harder, to make a fuss of her, but ever since the flood at Plas Tegydd he had been uncomfortably aware that there were powerful feelings in him which he was having difficulty in checking. Just now, when he had turned her to face him, had held her waist in his hands, he had become aware of a strong, pulsing urge to pull her so close that their bodies blended together, and then to . . . to . . .

He supposed, shamefacedly, that he wanted her. Hywel was not experienced in any but the most casual of boy and girl kisses, glances, touches, but he had walked into the wash-house only a few days ago and found Stan and Cerwyn there. It was all perfectly respectable, perfectly proper, for they were engaged to be married and they had, when all was said and done, only been kissing. But there had been something in the way Stan's fingers had tightened on Cerwyn's hips, something in the way their lips clung and moved, which told Hywel like a shout that they were two people in love who wanted to belong completely to each other.

But his own inexperience was nowhere near at total as Dot's. She had not even had the doubtful advantage of the dirty talk which schoolboys delight in. Hywel could not have remained ignorant of the facts of life even if he had wanted to, not with ten children living in a three-bedroomed house just up the road. What those children did not know — and pass on to their friends — was not worth knowing. Then there were all the stories and jokes, the back-of-the-bikeshed experimentation, the girls who mysteriously enlarged, gave birth, were derided, and then returned to the fold, probably to marry a lad everyone knew.

Dot had had none of this. Jessica had told him, only

half-jokingly, that though only two years separated them she had felt them divided, at times, by centuries, so little did Dot know of life. And this untouched child wanted him to steal her away, to marry her or just to live with her, against her father's wishes, on some tiny, rented smallholding somewhere up in the hills. It would be a crime to do any such thing until she had looked around her a little!

He reached the village street and glanced up and down it, but of course Dot and Matchless had gone long since. He sighed, his hand on the gate. Should he go in search of her, tell her that he would not desert her? But she knew that – he had said it! When you're twenty-one . . . when you've had a bit more experience of life . . . when my savings are bigger . . . Yes, he had told her that they would marry and have that little farm, and she must not think herself unwanted!

He went through the gate and up the short path and paused again, a hand outstretched to the door-knob. Girls set great store by being told things, he knew that. He had never actually asked her to marry him, had never actually told her he loved her – if he loved her. But then if he ran after her, caught her up, he would only say things which would make it impossible for him to insist on her going to stay with Kate. He did not want her to go away, he wanted her to stay right here, near him, but that was just sheer selfishness. He must let her go and then welcome her back – if she came back – with open arms and, if possible, with the prospect of marriage and their own place.

He opened the door and went inside, straight through the kitchen and scullery and out the back door, and there was Stan in the wash-house with the door open and wreaths of steam making him almost invisible. In winter they bathed in the kitchen but now, with Jessica home, Mam had banished them to the wash-house. More decent. Though why Jessica could not be sent into the front room whilst they bathed in the warm was more than he and Stan and the others could fathom. Spoilt, that was what his sister was becoming, but it was not for long; another fortnight and she would be off and they would be having their baths in front of the kitchen fire once more.

'Here you are, mun. I've poured clean water for you.' Stan

was already wrapped in a towel, eager to get back to the warmth of the house. Hywel shouted his thanks as his brother scooted for the back door, then threw off his clothes: the rough shirt, the tattered jacket, the filthy moleskin trousers and the clogs. Mother-naked, he stepped into the hot water.

Lovely! He luxuriated in the sensation for a moment, then grabbed the square of carbolic soap and began to lather himself. When he was covered with suds he ducked under to rinse before standing up, reaching for the towel and beginning to rub. In five minutes he was ready for the rush across the back yard and in at the door.

After the steamy, dark wash-house the kitchen seemed beautifully warm and bright. Jessica had come in and was just taking a tray of fat currant buns out of the oven. Hywel felt water rush to his mouth. He padded, barefoot, past her and as he did so she turned, grinned and made a grab for his towel, laughing with her head thrown back and her eyes narrowed to slits as he squealed and clutched.

'Shy as a girl you are, Hywel! Go and get decent before Mam gets back.'

'Is she out? How about giving me a bun, then, to eat whilst I dress?'

'I might.' She stood very near, smiling up at him, her eyes green and wicked in the lamplight. 'What'll you do for me if I give you a bun? Do I get that Christmas kiss I was after?'

'You'll get a bang round the ear if you don't give me a bun,' Hywel said threateningly. 'Come on, just one!'

'We-ell . . . ' She was almost leaning on his chest now, he noticed with some alarm. She slid her hands up his bare arms, over the swell of his muscles, until her fingers were resting on his shoulders. Hywel stood very still. What the devil was she playing at? She slid her hands round his neck and now her body was pressed so close that, through the towel, he could feel the shape of her. He tried to move away, hot with embarrassment, but she simply followed him, her face raised to his, her mouth trembling a little.

'What's the matter, Hywel? Give me a kiss, mun, and you can have all the old buns!'

'Stop it, you idiot!' His voice, thank heavens, came out firm and sensible, not all little and trembling and hot, the way it felt.

276

He might not know much about women or their ways, but he was sufficiently shrewd to know that it was not just kisses Jessica was offering, pressing herself up against his towel-wrapped body in that shameless way.

'What's the matter, Hywel? You frightened? Come on, kiss me – you'll find you like it!'

Abruptly, Hywel stopped being embarrassed and became amused. She sounded just like a cinema-vamp, all innuendo and sultry promise. He laughed and caught hold of her, giving her a hard shove which sent her back against the sink, the sultry promise wiped clean away to be replaced by annoyance and a shade of the embarrassment from which he had been suffering.

'Who do you think you are, little sister? Salome? Or Delilah? Or just Pearl White, star of the silver screen?'

He did not wait for her reaction but took a bun, sauntered across the kitchen and began to climb the stairs. At the top of them he turned into the room he shared with his brothers and took his ordinary clothes off the foot of the bed. He began to get dressed, thinking what a devilish day it had been so far, what with work being interrupted so that the old man could talk to them about the new pit, then Dot getting on her high horse and riding off in a temper, and now Jessica acting like a loose woman out of a play. And the rest of it was not likely to be much better, for, though he was free now to go out and up into the hills, what was the point? Dot was upset and hurt, and anyway if he met her he would only compound his sins by telling her all over again that she should go and stay with Kate and spend her new-found wealth on herself; she could buy hats and things, he thought vaguely. Of course she could go up there alone and take a look at the rabbit runs, or put a ferret down, but the thought of such solitary pastimes on a cold, overcast day had little appeal. It would have been fun with Dot, of course, but without her it was not worth leaving the warm house.

He tucked his shirt into his trousers, buttoned up, slid his feet into old slippers and made his way down the stairs. To his relief he heard Ella's voice floating up to meet him. She was grumbling about the number of people in town because of the market, the crowds on the bus. He could hear Jessica's lighter voice answering, teasing, and wished for a moment that he could speak to their mother like that. Well, he did try, but he rarely won a gurgle of laughter from her, as Jess just had. It was probably because they were both females, he told himself as he re-entered the kitchen. A man had to be careful what he said to a woman.

' . . . met your friend Dot as I was coming home,' Ella was saying. 'Riding that black pony of hers like a Valkyrie, heading for town. Heaven knows where she's going in such a rush, I said to Mrs Dafydd, who was sitting by me, but Mrs Dafydd says that on market day you can pick up many a bargain, so probably she was off to buy a pig or two, or maybe even another dirty goat, though I hope not.' The goat had not been a success; in its extravagant fondness for Dot, who it appeared to think was its mother, it had become adept at finding an open door and nipping into the house. Nipping, Ella had said darkly, was by no means all it did.

'I'm going up to see her tomorrow, so I'll find out,' Jessica said. She did not glance round as Hywel joined them but he saw a tiny flush steal across her cheek. Good, so she felt she had made a fool of herself. Perhaps that would stop her from doing it again! 'It's odd, though. You know how Dot loves Matchless. You wouldn't think she'd ride him hard downhill, would you? It's dangerous, that.'

Hywel felt a faint breath of unease; riding hard downhill? That was not like Dot at all. Suppose she had an accident? It would be his fault, for upsetting her, for not telling her how he felt.

'Well, she was riding downhill and riding hard, too,' Ella assured the younger woman. 'I'm working at the Plas tomorrow morning, so we'll find out what was wrong. Ah, Hywel. Are you going out?'

Again that slight feeling of unease; should he catch a bus into town, find her? But he was not dressed for town, and even if he went, and managed to find her, what was he going to say that could not be said equally well tomorrow?

'No, I'm not going out this afternoon,' he heard himself saying. 'Those buns look good.'

'Yes, she's made a nice job of 'em,' Ella said, unpacking her shopping bag and tutting over the contents. 'The price of cheese — it would have made your nain drop dead in her tracks. As for what they've the nerve to ask for a bag of potatoes . . . well, just glad I am we grow our own. Butter a few buns, Jess, and we'll try 'em whilst the kettle boils.'

In the warm kitchen with the good smell of baking and the lighthearted chatter, it was easy to forget that small figure riding off on her black pony, to push her and her worries — largely imaginary, he felt sure — to the back of his mind. But he could not quite banish his unease. Every time he stopped talking he was aware of it, the unwanted guest, the skeleton at the feast.

Tomorrow, when I come off shift, I'll go straight up to the Plas and we'll talk the whole thing through again, he reassured himself. Tomorrow. That's plenty time enough.

PART TWO

Sixteen

'She *sold* 'em? The whole herd?' Tom, sitting at his desk and nursing his second hangover in two days, muffled a groan and squinted up at Gwil through bleary, bloodshot eyes. 'Now what's she up to? Mind, she's not like most women. She'll have some scheme in mind. She's always saying she wants to improve the stock. She may have had a chance at a better herd, going cheap. Hasn't she said? And who's bought 'em?'

'It's Tim Evans; he farms over Caergwrle way. A bill of sale he's got, made out all proper and signed by the auctioneer, so we'd know it's all right, and a letter from Miss Dot, just a note saying it's all above board. I thought like you that she'd seen something better . . . only they was lovely beasts, and she was fond of each and every one, so she was, loved 'em like kids. So I thought I'd better 'ave a word.'

'You've not seen her this morning? I wonder if she's ill? She's always down before me as a rule.' Tom reached over and tugged at the bell-pull, then turned back to Gwil. 'Odd, that.' He rubbed his chin, wincing at the sharpness of his bristles, for he had not been able to bear the thought of shaving yet. 'Did she sell anything else, d'you know?'

'Mr Tim said she'd sold the pigs, but not to him. Said arrangements had been made with . . . ' He stopped speaking as the front door bell jangled. 'There's someone now. I daresay we'll find out pretty soon what she's up to. Shall I . . . ?'

'No need. Lizzie or Annie will go.' They heard feet hurrying across the hall, the low murmur of voices as the big oak door swung inwards, and then the heavy tread of masculine boots. There was a tap on the study door and Annie's head appeared.

'Feller to see you,' she announced without finesse. She shoved the door wide. 'Here, go in.'

283

A farmer known slightly to both men entered the room. He held out a hand and shook Tom's vigorously, nodding to Gwil.

'Morning, morning! Come for the pigs I have; Miss Dot said to come early.'

'Which pigs will that be? We've several sows, some in-pig gilts, some baconers and about twenty piglets . . .' Tom began uncertainly, but was interrupted.

'The lot, mun. Sold the lot, Miss Dot did. Said she knew I'd tek good care of 'em, which I will, and we shook hands on the deal. I've the bill of sale here . . .' he held it out, '. . . and a bit of a letter, in case anyone queried what she'd done, she said.' He looked diffidently from master to man. 'I thought it would be all right since it's common knowledge that Miss Dot do run the estate.'

'Aye, that's right,' Tom said, his voice ringing false even in his own ears. 'Very go-ahead is our Dot. You mentioned a letter . . . '

The letter was produced but Tom felt he could not read it in front of the farmer without admitting his complete ignorance of Dot's extraordinary behaviour. He put it down on his desk, therefore, and got out a bottle of sherry so that they could drink to the deal, then he took the farmer into the yard to point out the sties, though Gwil knew more about the pigs and their needs than either of the two men. Only when at last the pigs had been herded into a large and shiny motor-van did Tom feel he could return to his study, his head now banging like a trip-hammer, and open the envelope.

The letter was quite short.

Dear Father, I need some money since you have so kindly disposed of my five thousand pounds for me – I saw Mr Geraint today and he told me what you had done – so I've sold my cows and pigs. I had to do it because I needed the money, but anyway I would not have left them with you. You would not have treated them right and it would have been unfair to Gwil. You'll guess by now that I've gone and won't be coming back. I'd say not to worry only I know you won't worry a bit. Yours sincerely, Dot.

Tom stared at it for a moment, then turned to the postscript.

P.S. Gwil is to have the in-pig gilt called Penny for his own, also the hens and the bantams. I told Mr Geraint this and he will tell Gwil and also give him a paper I've signed so that Gwil has written proof. A piece of paper can be very important.

Tom had been standing up when he started to read but he found himself sitting down behind his desk again with no clear notion of having moved at all. What a daughter! Undutiful child, to send him a hurtful letter like this, selling all the stock and simply announcing that she was leaving home. How dared she – what on earth would Blanche think when she got here and found no Dot to help her? Blanche was equal to most things, but not to running the estate, and he was far too heavily committed to the collieries, particularly now, to take an interest in the land. The place and the stock would no doubt fall into disrepair; it was too bad of Dot!

Not that there was any stock, he remembered. Belatedly, Tom realised that it had not been her own pride that Dot had salvaged by her hard and dedicated work on the estate, but his. He had been holding his head up amongst his fellow landowners of late, for they could see that the place was being pulled together at last and never dreamed that Dot was doing it alone. Of course, he had always intended to get to work on it, when he had the time and the inclination, but in the event it had not been necessary. Dot had come along and without his having to spend more than a few pounds she had begun to drag the place out of the dismals. She had reclaimed pasture he thought lost to the wild for ever, she had manured and ploughed and sown, and then she had reaped and sold. She had saved up to buy a few chickens when she had been only a little thing, and from there it had grown without his having to lift a finger. She had sold eggs to buy a sickly bit of a calf that no one else wanted, she had reared that calf and paid to have the heifer serviced by a neighbour's stud bull. Then she had bred the calf, bought another one, reared some baconers and used the money they brought for a fine heifer, bred with the heifer . . . it had gone on and on, under his nose, until the place had been running properly for the first time in years.

He picked up the letter and read it through again very

285

carefully, and his heart, which had sunk into his boots, lifted a little. She was annoyed with him because he had invested her inheritance in the Wynd, that was the trouble. Foolish, misguided girl to doubt him. She would see her money doubled, nay trebled, before three years were out. Of course, the way she had brought on her herd, she might have thought the money better invested in the estate, but that was just moonshine! There was money in coal, lots of money; she would benefit from his foresight in the end.

He thought some more, sitting at his desk with the letter spread out in front of him. Damn it, he had not taken the money without a great deal of thought — he had needed it! He was short of cash — many people found themselves in the same position these days — and then poor Olivia had died and he had been flush enough to go through with the deal for the Wynd without having to do anything thoroughly unpleasant, like selling land or his stocks and shares. Only he was five thousand short and though he had sold the house in Rhyl he had been forced to buy another, in Chester, for the duration of Blanche's stay there. So it had seemed foolish not to take advantage of Dot's money, which would just lie in the bank otherwise, wasting away.

The door of his study, bursting open without so much as a tap, dragged his attention away from the letter. He thought for a moment that it might be Dot and prepared a reproachful, fatherly expression, but it was only Ella. She looked flushed. What was the matter with everyone today? If only people would tell him when something was wrong, instead of selling cows and pigs and running off without a word, giving him no chance to put things right!

Ella, however, came straight to the point.

'Where's Dot?'

Tom blinked, then tried a scowl. It felt a good deal more in character, right now, than a smile. He deepened the scowl until he could scarcely see Ella through the thick undergrowth of eyebrow which had descended over his eyes.

'Dot? What do you mean, woman?'

'You know very well what I mean — your daughter, Mr Tegydd. Where in heaven's name is she? She's not slept in her bed, you know.'

Blustering would be best. Tom proceeded to bluster.

'Really, Ella, that's no way to speak to me. And what's more . . . '

'Don't you *Really, Ella* me! You've treated that child shamefully and now you've driven her away! Yes, she's gone. I daresay you think life will be easier without her, but you're wrong, and you'll pretty soon find out.' She was dragging her apron off, not bothering to untie it; he heard the strings tear and winced. He had paid good money for that apron! 'No decent woman will work up here, Mr Tegydd, without little Dot. And when you bring your fancy woman here there's many as won't speak to you at all, lord of the manor or no lord of the manor, pit-owner or no pit-owner. Particularly when I tell people how you drove your own flesh and blood to run away from you with your wicked selfish ways!'

One bit of that diatribe could not be allowed to pass. Tom blinked his bloodshot eyes, put a trembling hand to his head and told her what he thought.

'My fancy woman? I don't know what you mean, and I think, Ella, that you forget yourself.'

'Oh, do I? Do I, indeed?' She had always seemed a friendly, sensible woman but now she had turned without warning into a shrill-voiced scold! She came over to the desk and he was hard put to it not to shrink back, so like an avenging angel did she seem. 'If you've hurt Dot, then you'll suffer for it. The wicked and ungodly always suffer in the end and you'll be no exception!'

'Hurt her? My little girl? I've never raised a hand to her in all my . . . '

'There's worse ways of hurting a child than a smack.' Her apron was off now and she hurled it down on the desk, hiding Dot's letter, which was probably something to be thankful for. 'Send my money down to the village with Lizzie, if you please. I shan't be coming back here no more.'

She slammed out of the study, leaving Tom, holding his sore head, to remember all the cutting and truthful things he could have said, had he only thought of them in time. Now it was too late. She had gone – for ever, it seemed. Good riddance! They would get on very well without her. The other servants might have to work a little harder but he could always offer them more money . . .

An hour later he had been visited by Annie, Daisy and Lizzie – together – and by Cook and the gardener – separately. They all announced, in their own way, that they would not be working up at the Plas after today. Cook, a stout person with a moustache on her upper lip and the strength of an ox, had been particularly difficult. She had seemed about to descend to physical violence, and, though Tom had told himself tremulously that no gentleman would ever hit a woman, the thought of holding himself back had not been his chief worry at the time. Cook had picked him up by one shoulder and had actually held him inches above the floor, like a newborn kitten, whilst she reiterated that Miss Dot had been an angel to all of them and had made their lives worth living and that if he'd harmed a hair on her head or harm came to her because of his turning her out of the house . . .

Idle to keep repeating that Dot had left of her own accord, because Cook was not only angry, she had taken a nip or two of cooking sherry, judging by the choleric colour in her cheeks and the way she slurred her words. He judged it best – for he did not wish to have to hit a woman, even a woman with a bristly moustache and the strength of an ox – to simply hang there in her grasp, agree with everything she said, and hope she would soon go away, leaving him more or less intact.

Anyone would think, Tom told himself plaintively when Cook had left, that Dot had spent the last ten years or so defending the servants from his wicked wiles. Did he not pay them? Provide them with aprons and scrubbing brushes and so on? Had he not tried to be polite – well, fairly polite – and friendly towards them? Always a smile and a bluff greeting, no matter how busy he was. Well, nearly always.

And then, just when he really was beginning to wonder how he was going to manage, he was struck by the Great Idea. It did not matter now whether Blanche was pregnant or not, because there was no one here to criticise and it did not look as though anyone in the village had any intention of exchanging a word with him again. He would drive to the station, catch a train for Chester, and persuade his dear one to return to the Plas with him. They could close down her little house and bring her small staff back here with them! She had someone called a general who was a very good cook, a girl of fifteen who obeyed the general's every command, and a young man who did the garden, ran errands and looked after any work too heavy for the general and the girl. Yes, they could *all* come here. It would just show those tight-mouthed villagers who was the boss and who could manage very well without them. Fortunately the madness which had carried away the indoor staff had not affected the farm workers. It would have been difficult for the latter, who mostly lived in tied accommodation, to give in their notice, but Tom chose to see it more as a masculine understanding. Comforted, he put on his greatcoat and his thickest muffler, made arrangements for the trap to be prepared, and then strode up to his room to throw a few things in a bag. Blanche would not want to come, he quite saw that, because of her pregnancy and because of putting backs up. Also, she had a good doctor in Chester and had made all the arrangements for the birth to take place there. His confident feeling that he only had to mention it to bring Blanche and her entourage scuttling on to the train with him shook a little as he thought of these things, but his resolution to chance his luck did not falter.

He left as he had planned, whistling, cheerful, even going so far as to tell Jan, who drove him to the station, that he expected to return next day, probably with a party of people.

Alas for confidence and high hopes; next day he returned alone. Blanche was sweet, sorry for him, regretful. But firm as the rock of Gibraltar. She would not go to Plas Tegydd until the baby was a few weeks old and she would have no scandal.

Dot woke because there was sunshine, and she loved a sunny day. Not that she got up, because the alarm had not gone and for some reason the bantam cocks, who were extremely noisy when you considered their size, were not crowing their little lungs out. She lay for a moment curled into a warm ball with her toes inside her nightdress and her nose nearly on her knees, dreamily contemplating the day ahead. First she would do the milking because it was her turn, then she would feed the poultry, then . . . A strange noise brought her up short. A car or a lorry, turning into the yard at this time of morning? What on earth . . . ?

One glance round the room and she remembered the miles between her and Plas Tegydd, the cows that had been sold, and the pigs, and her pony. She felt so bad about Matchless that she could not bear to remember him as he had been led away. He had looked back over his shoulder and her heart had nearly broken; her one and only, her true friend! She had had him for ten wonderful years and now she had sold him to Mr Christian Markwell, for his ten-year-old daughter. She had wanted to give him the pony, for he was a kindly and sensible man and a good father, but he told her, very gravely, that you never gave an animal away if you wanted that animal to be valued.

'Always sell and always ask a good price, love,' he had advised. 'You want someone to treat an animal like nothing, you give it away and that's what'll happen. Now I'll treat Matchless like you did, because I paid good money for him.'

After she had let Matchless go, there had seemed no point in staying; she had nothing, any more, to stay for. So she had fled, by train because she knew no other way, and she had ended up in this high attic room in a city big enough to make her living in.

It was a horrid room, which went without saying. She ought to try to see good in it, especially today, which was the first of January 1922, but she could not deny what her eyes told her. Greying whitewashed walls, a tiny, never-used fireplace, a washstand made of raw looking pine, a narrow bed, a rag rug. That was just about it, unless you counted a couple of framed texts on the walls and the cheap gingham curtains at the window.

Through the window she could see the curve of the street, which was called, oddly, Castle Meadow. It was that which had attracted her to it, the country name. And Norwich was a country city. Not that she had found Norwich; the city had found her. She had got on the first train which had come chugging into the station, got off at Chester, got on another train and journeyed on for hours and hours. When she left that one, she was in a small town in the middle of England, and one night in a cheap boarding house and an hour's walking around had been enough to convince her that she was unlikely to find work here and even unlikelier to find fame and fortune.

Next morning she went back to the railway station and

again caught the first train heading away from her home. It had been going to Norwich and when it drew in to Thorpe Station she enquired of the porter, who told her that this was a big city and that she would very likely find work and somewhere to live here. He was not a local man – he was Irish – and hearing the familiar voice was warming to someone who was beginning to feel very far from home.

She did not yet know whether he was right about finding a job, but she had had no difficulty in getting a cheap room. It was over a greengrocer's shop, and Mrs Pointer and her husband let three rooms. There were other lodgers, therefore, but as yet Dot had not met them. She had only wandered, in a dazed kind of way, round the city, making sure that she was right to try here before moving on.

Having thought herself up to the present, Dot got out of bed, shivering as her toes touched lino. It was cold, but no colder than her room at home, and she could stand on the rag rug whilst she washed. For her modest weekly rent she was provided with breakfast and an evening meal, but, since breakfast was only thin porridge, tea and thick bread thinly buttered, she did not in the least mind missing it. Come to that, she would not have minded missing the evening meal. How could a woman murder food the way Mrs Pointer did and yet apparently remain oblivious of the fact, Dot wondered, putting on her grey skirt and fawn jumper. She was sleeping in her vest and knickers since she had not as yet acquired a nightgown, but today she would spend a bit of her fast shrinking capital on some clothing. Otherwise Mrs Pointer, whom she had already privately stigmatised as extremely nasty, might get suspicious. She had mortally offended Dot on their first meeting by enquiring whether Dot had run away from school, making it clear that she thought her lodger to be a mere child.

Some clothes, a nightgown, an alarm clock so that she did not again oversleep . . . Dot ticked the items she would need off on her fingers as she hurried down the stairs. Once she had a job – like Queen Victoria she refused to admit the possibility of defeat – she would need to be up on time or she would not keep it long. Not that she was likely to oversleep again, of course; today's late waking had been the result of four days of very real mental anguish and a good deal of unusual travelling and walking round city streets. She was jolly glad she had settled on Norwich – or it on her – because, as she had thought, it really was a country city. Country people with broad country faces thronged the streets and there was a big market – two in fact. One sold fruit and vegetables and was there all the time, the other was a beast market like the one at home but a bit bigger, and was only open on certain days – she did not yet know which. She supposed that somewhere she might find slums and ragged children, big city squalor, but as yet she had not done so. From what she had seen, she was willing to give Norwich a try.

Popping her head round the kitchen door, where assembled Pointers and lodgers ate, she saw Mrs Pointer standing in the middle of the room consulting what was probably a shopping list. Her skinny little maidservant who looked permanently underfed was standing apprehensively in front of her, twisting her hands in her apron. It was clear Mrs Pointer was complaining about something she had missed, for she was saying: ' . . . should be the best part of a pound left, my girl!' as Dot entered.

'Morning, Mrs Pointer; morning, Ethel,' Dot said cheerfully. 'Nice morning, isn't it?'

Mrs Pointer smiled, but the smile never reached her eyes. 'Good morning, Miss Evans. You've missed breakfast. I'm afraid I never serve . . . '

'It's all right. I decided I needed the rest and I'm not hungry. I'm going out now, but I'll be back later, in good time for your evening meal. What time is that served, again?'

'Six,' Mrs Pointer said, visibly disappointed that Dot was not going to take issue with her over the missed breakfast. 'Six on the dot, mind.'

'Right.' Dot made a mental note to keep an eye open for more congenial lodgings, smiled at the maid, and headed down yet another steep flight of stairs which led out on to the street. A good thing she was not looking for domestic work, if Mrs Pointer was a typical mistress. Awful to have to work for someone like that.

As she emerged from the door a tram thundered past, seeming to Dot to be running almost on the pavement. Horrid, and such a shock to the system so early! There were trams in the town, of course, but they did not seem to penetrate very far into the hills, presumably because there would not be enough passengers to set against the expense. Once the tram had gone, however, she sniffed appreciatively at the cold morning air. She was late all right, but perhaps because it was New Year's day there were not many people about and the air tasted fresh and unused. Nice. Another tram, a lot slower, could be heard coming from the opposite direction, grinding up the hill, and she glanced towards the sound, to smile delightedly as a large flock of sheep appeared, a dog bunching them together, plainly being herded out of the city and towards some country village or farm. Being held up by the sheep was obviously annoying the tram driver, who leaned out of his cab to exchange sharp remarks with the shepherd, both speaking in accents so strange that at first Dot could not understand a word. Then she heard the shepherd say, 'They'm doin' the best they can, you duzzy fule,' and she smiled to herself. An independent man, obviously; not one to bow to the indignation of a mere tram driver. His sheep could hold up every tram in the city for all he cared!

She turned right and went towards the castle and its gardens. When she reached them she decided to turn right again, down Davy Steps, and go straight through on to the wide street which fronted the market. She had expected it to be called Market Street, which would have been logical, but it was called Gentleman's Walk. She shook her head as she hurried along. It was all so odd and unexpected; she was in Davy Place now, but she had just passed a crooked little street called Back-of-the-Inns. Thank God for Prince of Wales Road. At least that was ordinary enough!

Halfway down Davy Place there was a lovely big shop with an enticing window. *Ashworth & Pike*, it said in curly gold letters across the glass. Inside were beautiful cakes and at the back, though it was rather dim, a tea-shop. Already there were people at the tables, eating and sipping coffee. Dot swallowed. A country girl, she had a big appetite and her stomach was already grumbling softly to itself over its missed breakfast. Should she go in and have hot buttered toast, tea and a boiled egg? Or if not an egg, for it was a little late for breakfast, one of those large and delicious looking cakes?

Dot wavered for a moment, then sighed and entered the portals. Best look for work on a full stomach, she told herself, giving the waitress her order.

Three hours later, tired and more than a little depressed, she decided that the reason why no one wanted to employ her was her appearance. People took her for a child of thirteen or so and did not want to pay her a living wage. She had meant to buy some clothes today anyway; better get them now, change into them, and then see how she fared.

She looked around her; her job-hunting had taken her up to All Saints Green – another odd name for a street – and right in front of her was a very imposing edifice, all gables and beams and arcaded front. She crossed over the busy road and discovered as she had thought that the shop sold clothing. She looked in the windows for a moment, then decided that she might as well take the plunge. Sensible things, she told herself as she entered the shop. Dark and sensible.

An assistant came over to her; they smiled at one another and Dot, a little flushed, for this was her very first clothing purchase, began to outline her requirements.

Thirty minutes later she emerged from the shop, her old clothes in a neat brown paper parcel and her new things on; she now had a very high opinion of Buntings and their staff, for when she had explained her requirements the young lady had been helpfulness itself, even to advising her that nice though that particular skirt was, Miss could get the same effect for very much less money by trying this one.

Now, neatly arrayed in a black skirt, black long-sleeved blouse with white collar and cuffs, and silk stockings, she felt quite capable of buying shoes which would enhance the impression of sombre elegance she wished to convey. She bought the shoes and changed into them in the shop, shoving her old ones into the paper bag the assistant offered, and then, fully equipped, she returned to the Walk. There had been a restaurant there where she felt sure she could get a meal without having to spend too much money. Her purse felt a good deal lighter after her wild expenditure of the morning. It would not be sensible to spend more than she had to – but she was terribly hungry!

She went over to the restaurant and hung about for a little, watching. It seemed that you could have pretty well whatever you wanted and you could pay as much or as little as you liked. The customers were mostly men but there were women at the tables here and there, and the food did look good! There was a menu chalked on a board on the wall and it seemed cheap, too.

Finally, deciding that she stood no chance of finding a job with her mind absorbed in her hunger, she went in and slid into a seat. Having settled herself, she slipped off her coat, then discovered that there was a big coat-rack near the door. Better hang it up. No point in taking up more space than she had to; she had already realised that the room was crammed with tables and that people tended to eat up and go, not lingering over coffee or a cigarette. Obviously the proprietor made his money from selling a lot of food cheaply. He did not want customers to be too comfortable!

She had hung her coat up and was on her way back to her seat when a man accosted her. 'Two chops and roast,' he said briskly. 'Make it snappy, eh, nippy? Got to see a man about a dog in ten minutes.'

Dot frowned and was about to ask what he meant when a girl with a loaded tray elbowed her way past, looked at Dot and also addressed her.

'Come you on, gal, don't just stand there agawpin'! Fetch me two spotted and custard and a full house, will you? You've got no orders of your own, I suppose?'

They thought she was a waitress! Dot looked at the other girl and saw that she, too, wore black with white collar and cuffs. She had a little muslin apron on, though, and a small cap perched on the back of her head. Dot's thick dark curls might, she supposed, have hidden the cap. At first glance her lovely new clothes probably looked very like the waitress's.

Even as she wondered how to tell them, the waitress realized. A hand went to her mouth, then she grinned at Dot. 'I'm sorry, miss; whatever was I thinkin'! If the gentleman hadn't spoken to you . . . '

The young man, also grinning but a trifle red about the gills, was pulling Dot's chair out for her.

'I'm sorry, too, to take you for a nippy. But they wear black and they're all about your build – they have to be small and slim to get between the tables – and I was fooled for a minute. What's your order, now the girl's here?'

'Oh . . . custard and a full house,' Dot said wildly, without glancing at the list on the board. 'It doesn't matter. I wish I *was* a waitress, actually. Why did you call them nippies, though?'

'A full house is egg, bacon and sausage. It don't go too well with custard,' the waitress said kindly. 'Tell you what. The beef stoo and dumplings is good today. Shall I bring you some of that?'

'Oh.' Dot felt her cheeks flame. 'Sorry! What's a spotted, anyway?'

'Currant pudding. You know – spotted dick. Some of that for afters?'

'Please.'

The waitress went off and the young man sat down opposite Dot. He had a newspaper and his expression was friendly and interested.

'You from the country? Your voice isn't city – it isn't Norfolk, for that matter. Work in an office, do you? Or just visiting?'

'Well, neither. I'm searching for work, actually,' Dot began, when a small, harassed man in a black tail suit with a drooping carnation in his buttonhole came up to them. He carried no tray yet it was clear that he worked in the restaurant. The manager, perhaps?

'I'm sorry, miss, you was taken for a nippy,' he said. 'However, I can't deny you're the very build. My young lady who mistook you said she didn't think you'd take offence if I asked you a question: are you looking for work?'

'Well, yes . . . '

'Ah! We've been let down, see. There was a young lady to start this very morning, interview over, wages set, hours agreed. But she never turned up. Would you like to finish your meal and come along to my office? Then I can explain what's what.'

'Certainly,' Dot said as calmly as she could, though inside

she was in a ferment of excitement and – it must be admitted – panic. Did she want to work here? It looked great fun and everyone seemed happy and friendly but she had seen how the nippies flew about their work. No need to wonder why they were called that. One moment in the restaurant was enough to make it plain. But the young man was smiling, congratulating her, and presently the friendly waitress came along with her order and Dot tucked into a most delicious stew and thought the dumplings – a type of food which had not come her way before – thoroughly delectable. Presently the girl came back with her pudding and the young man's bill, but when Dot asked for hers she was informed that it was 'on the house, 'cos of the error'.

'That was good,' Dot said, pushing her empty stew plate away and starting on the pudding. 'I wonder what it's like, being a nippy? I've never even been a waitress. I wonder if I could do it?'

'They're fussy who they employ,' the young man admitted. 'You've got to be fast, see, but neat-fingered too. It in't everyone who can do it. The pay's heaps better than a waitress usually gets, though – that's why you don't get much change-round of staff. Nice, that.' He watched, fascinated, as Dot cleared her plate. 'I say, you were mortal hungry, weren't you?'

'Yes. I usually am.' Dot pushed the plate away and stood up. 'Thanks for the information and for your company. You'd better go and see that man about that dog, hadn't you? If I get the job I'll think of you.'

'Yes, it's time I was off. And if you get the job you'll see me most dinnertimes. I usually eat here.' He stood up too and held out a hand. 'Good luck! Not that I think you'll need it. You look the part, and if you wait on table as quick as you polish off food you should be a cert for the job.'

Dot shook his hand, thanked him again, and set off for the back of the restaurant. If they gave her a chance she would prove to them that she could work better than any other girl they had ever employed, she decided. She would like to work here!

'Then if Castle Meadow's the wrong place to live, where's the right one?' Dot, cleaning down tables after the noon rush, addressed her new friend, Jane. 'I didn't choose old Ma Pointer, you know. I just took the first thing offered.'

'Well, you've been there a month, for all your talk! Get out, my woman, before you're old and grey and don't have no money for the move. It's ever so much cheaper if you live out of the city, though it costs a bit in tram fares in winter. In summer you can walk – or bike, like I do, if you've got a bike by then.'

'I wouldn't mind,' Dot admitted, sweeping her cloth across the glass table top and grimacing at the quantity of food which came off it. 'Where do you live, Jane? It's difficult for me because I don't know what's what, so I could easily answer an advert and find myself in the back of beyond somewhere.'

'Earlham Road. I live with my aunt, but there's a widder-woman with a dippy son two doors up and she's got a room to let. Ever so nice she is, but people get put off by Horatio. Would you mind him? There in't no vice in Horry, mind, that I'd swear.'

'I wouldn't mind him,' Dot said, with comfortable memories of dippy Annie and even dippier Alfie back home. Both of them were easy to deal with if you were prepared to take explanations at a snail's place and repeat most things twice. 'Does she do dinners?'

'Sunday, you mean? Not as I know, but I'm sure she would, if she took to you. She does a worker's breakfast and a high tea six days a week, I do know that.'

'It sounds fine. How much would she charge, though? Mrs P. has her bad side – I've yet to discover a single redeeming feature, come to think – but she is cheap.'

'Mrs Blishen may not be cheap, but she's a jolly fine cook. And there's ever such lovely country no more than half a mile further down the road. And you do moan about the traffic; there's none to speak of up our way and it's so quiet at night you can hear the owls hooting down the wood,' the temptress said craftily. 'Go on, Dot, give it a try, eh? Come you home with me after work and you can take a look at the place and meet Mrs Blishen.'

'We-ell . . .' Dot was longing to change her lodgings, yet she clung, perversely, to the only place she knew. Her horrible, chilly, smelly little attic room had become, if not loved, at least familiar. To uproot herself again would be a lot harder than Jane realised.

'Oh, come on! It'ud be fun. We could walk to and from work together, catch the same tram . . . you've not asked how much she charges.'

'Go on, then. How much?'

Jane named a sum which made Dot whistle.

'Gosh, so little? Old Ma Pointer charges me half a crown more than that and no meals on Sundays.' She moved on to her next table, for both girls had been working steadily as they talked, and emptied the ashtray, pulling a face at the cloud of fine ash which rose from the slop bucket as the dog-ends cascaded in. 'Right, Jane. I'll come back with you after work, then, and see this lady. Come on, I've finished clearing. Let's lay up for teas before the rush starts.'

Walking up the pasture towards the birch wood, Hywel saw, through the light flakes of snow which were falling, a fox slinking through the dead bracken and stopped to watch it. It was unaware of his presence, since the wind was blowing towards him, and it was not hurrying because it was carrying a dead bird in its mouth and the weight and the snow slowed it down. After a moment Hywel realised that the bird was a bantam, a little cock bird, its brilliance already tarnished by death. That would be one of Dot's. She was the only person hereabouts who kept bantams – though of course they were hers no longer since she had given them to Gwil. It was a hard winter up here in the hills. The fox must have taken the bantam in full daylight, which was unusual; but of course it would have a mate hidden away somewhere, probably in cub, so it would need all the food it could get.

He stood very still, watching the fox but thinking of Dot. He missed her horribly, as he had always known he would, but before, when he had envisaged her going away he had thought she would stay with Kate or Alexandra. Then he knew she would keep coming home on visits, she would write to him, they might even meet in Chester or perhaps in the town. He had never dreamed of this total and complete silence.

It was like having a limb amputated, he thought, watching the fox's slow progress. When you lost a limb it was gone and you could neither see it nor touch it, yet it ached all the time and you missed it all the time, even when you were working, chatting with a friend, or sleeping. He knew about the pain of a lost limb through old Picky Ned, who had lost an arm in a colliery accident and who was now potman at the Golden Lion; he knew about losing someone you cared for because he had done just that. He had lost Dot, and through his own fault.

He dreamed of her often. Usually she was in trouble of some kind which he could not help with, so that he woke sweating and shouting. Stan, who shared his bed, was getting fed up and no wonder, but there was nothing he could do about it. Until she came back or got in touch he could not help worrying about her, awake or asleep. She was so young, so sturdily, touchingly innocent! Anyone could take advantage of her, because she expected people to behave well, or she could be penniless, starving somewhere, perhaps forced into marriage with some horrible old man who wanted her body . . . Hywel had never thought of himself as being a particularly imaginative person but now he realised that he was. Imagining horrors was a forte he very much regretted but, where Dot was concerned, you would have had to go a long way to beat him.

The fact that he had told her to go haunted him. Of course he had not meant it, had not intended her to do anything other than go to her sisters for a short stay. But had he seriously thought she would go to Kate or Alexandra? No, of course he had not! He had felt it was his duty to try to send her away but he had expected to be defied, expected her to stay and, eventually, to insist on marriage.

The truth was that much though he wanted Dot and dearly though he loved her, he did not want to marry anyone; not just yet. Eventually, yes, but like most young men he wanted a taste of real freedom first. Dot knew he wanted the farm but it had not occurred to her that before he was tied to the land he would like to travel a bit, see other parts of the country, find out how other farmers farmed. He had wanted to do those things untrammelled by marriage or property. It was only then, when he had done his roving around, that he wanted the farm and a wife. But by running away she had spoiled his dream. He no longer wanted to do anything other than find her and keep her safe somewhere. Travel, without her, would be dull, their little farm would be boring. She had, he supposed, spoiled his life.

It was true that at times he felt downright angry with Dot and would, had she appeared before him, have given her a right good telling off – before that enormous hug that he had taken to dreaming about. She had upset the even and agreeable tenor of his days, she had turned his world topsy-turvy, she had given him more worry and heartache than he had imagined it was possible to suffer. She had done badly by Tom Tegydd too, which was a damned good thing in Hywel's opinion, but nevertheless Tom was suffering. He was living pretty well alone at the Plas save for the lackadaisical attentions of a brassy-headed piece who lived in town and had to be paid generously to come in daytimes. She flung together a meal now and then, dusted when she felt like it, and had no qualms about telling anyone who would listen that in her opinion the old man would do better to move out and go and live in Chester with his fancy piece instead of staying on at the Plas for a mere three nights out of the seven and pretending that things would come right soon.

There was gossip about him down the Wynd, too. He did not seem to care so much about the work. He had ordered new coal-cutting machines but, when the men said they did not want them because they would take the hewers' work away in time, he had made remarkably little fuss. Mind you, they said, that might be just his cunning, because the machines would be working soon despite the objections.

The fox had stopped. Head up, it was staring into the hedge in front of it. Did it sense danger? Or the presence of another creature? Or was it the hunting instinct, roused by the sight of a bird hopping from branch to branch, picking off the tiny, dried-up haws?

As he watched, the scene before him began to move and blur as if a sheet of water was between him and it, and he knew he was going to the Other Place. He still went there often and it seemed that the older he grew the more acute feelings and scenes became. What was more, he had come to realise that he was not the only one to have these experiences. Now and then he would be working, or setting his ferrets on a rabbit, or dreaming and fishing, and he would suddenly see things extra-clear, as though his perception had been heightened by a considerable degree. Beauty became, for those moments, almost unbearably lovely; ugliness unbearably horrible. He knew – or believed, rather – that at such moments the other chap was with him, seeing what he was seeing, feeling what he felt.

It was damned strange, to put it no stronger, yet it neither frightened nor worried him. He liked it. It was like having a close friend who could see your point of view not only figuratively but literally too. Knowing that there was some-one, somewhere, so akin to him that he could slip in and out of his thoughts was good, not bad. He was sure it was a man, because of the things being done. Ploughing, reaping, trawl-ing, tramping . . . they were all the sort of things a man did, not a woman. Besides, the feeling of total identification would not have been possible had they been of different sexes. He did not know why he was so sure of this, but he was. Men and women might be alike, but their minds, their thoughts and the way they reacted to situations came from a differentness so fun-damental that the exchange which he and his friend from the Other Place took part in would have been quite impossible.

It was winter now, so he half expected to find himself on board the trawler when the blurring cleared. He thought he would feel the line cold and slippery between his fingers, or the wind tearing the hair off his head, whilst he watched one of those remarkable, blood-red and gold sunsets which can only be seen to full advantage at sea. But this time it was far simpler and he was on land, walking along a road he knew well which stretched across the marsh. He was in a line of men, and he was one of them. He was carrying something on his shoulder and he felt a pain of loss so sharp, so poignant, that he could have groaned aloud. Before him, another man bore the same weight and his heavy boots crunched over the frosted furrows of the road's thick mud a pace ahead of Hywel's.

He was carrying a coffin. It was heavy, and it contained someone he loved so much that it was as if a knife twisted in his heart because the person in the coffin had gone and could never be recalled. Beside him, keeping pace with him, was a

302

girl, younger than he, fair-haired, her eyes swollen and her face blubbered with weeping. The weight of the coffin dug into his shoulder, the chill in the air had frozen drops on his cheeks; he could feel them there, wanted to wipe them away but could not.

The girl looked sideways at him, then smiled tremulously and reached up a hand. Rough wool brushed away the frozen drops. Because she was so kind and he knew they shared the same heartache the tears started again and for an instant he looked into her eyes and thought she must know he was there too, and then before he could blink he was staring at the rustling hedge into which the fox was just disappearing and feeling the wetness of tears on his cheeks.

For a moment two pains mingled, the pain of losing Dot and that other, deeper loss, and then, astonishingly, he felt easier because at least he knew Dot would return, that he would see her again. The person who had weighed so heavy on his shoulder weighed heavy on someone else's heart, because they would never meet again in this life.

Thoughtfully, Hywel pushed his way through the thick, frosted bracken, scarcely noticing now the beauty of the petrified undergrowth or the icicles hanging from the hedge. Why did he feel better, because of that shared moment of sadness? It was as if someone had said to him, *She's gone, but not for ever; my loss is for ever*; and it had done him good, made him count his blessings.

Dot would come back; suddenly he was not hoping for it, he was waiting for it with complete certainty. She could not stay away, because Plas Tegydd was her life. She would have to see it again, have to be very sure there was no future there for her, before she would push it right out of her mind. She had left on impulse and in such a hurry that she would, one day, be forced to return. He found himself devoutly hoping that it would be soon, though; that she would not let too many years elapse before she came home. Life without her lacked an edge, a sharpness of taste, that she had given it in abundance.

Is this love? he asked himself, retracing his steps when he had examined his empty traps. Can that be what love is – one's life losing a dimension because one small, irritating girl had left one's orbit? He had no idea; he just knew he would give everything he possessed to have her back.

Seventeen

Spring was well advanced, Dot thought contentedly as she waved goodbye to Mrs Blishen and mounted her rickety old bicycle. She had wondered how she would bear to see the spears of daffodils and crocus pierce the earth and the buds appear, break, blow, knowing that all this was happening at Plas Tegydd too. Without her. But she did bear it because, strange though it might seem, she was happy in her new life. To be sure she told herself it was an episode and that when it was over she would find herself miraculously restored to Plas Tegydd and fortune, but that was not the only reason for her enjoyment. She had been bitterly lonely, kept from people of her own age for the first seventeen years of her life; she had been denied love. She had believed herself to be undersized and ugly.

No more. How could she, when she was surrounded, at work, by girls who were equally small and slight? She had heaps of friends, too, and what was even more surprising, when you thought how her parents had bemoaned her lack of attraction, she had admirers! Men liked her and wanted to be with her, and that was heady stuff for one who had been constantly criticised by the very people who should have loved her best.

It was not only men who liked her; Mrs Blishen liked her too. Olivia had not been a motherly woman and Miss Edenthorpe, though kind, had always been remote, but Mrs Blishen was a natural mother who longed for a daughter of her own. She took Dot to her bosom, fed her like a queen at weekends and would accept no payment, knitted her a garment called a spencer to wear under her uniform when the weather was cold, and generally mothered her.

Dot blossomed. She still missed home and Hywel horribly, but she managed to put both out of her mind for long periods. She rode out into the country as soon as the weather allowed it, talking to her bicycle as she had once talked to Matchless, and was much impressed with the Norfolk countryside. Not the scenery perhaps, for she was born and bred to the hills and thought the flatness and the east wind unfortunate. It was the richness of the land, the crops one could raise on such fertile soil, which tempted her to start saving for a piece of good Norfolk earth of her own. Her fingers itched to plough here, to sow and to reap, to see a herd of her own cows grazing on these lush pastures. She never lost sight of her ultimate aim — to return to Wales and buy Plas Tegydd — but she could tell that if she bought land here first, and made a success of it, her eventual return home would be in the nature of a Triumph.

It was not easy to save, though, with so much, all of a sudden, to spend her money on. Her friends expected her to buy clothes and makeup as they did, and to go with them on the spree. She found that she adored the cinema and the theatre, that she loved dancing, enjoyed listening to band concerts in the Castle Gardens on a sunny afternoon, and entered wholeheartedly into the sparking and flirting which young male customers expected a pretty young nippy to take part in.

Sometimes, dressing to go out in her pretty room on Earlham Road, Dot would look at herself in the round mirror which Mrs Blishen had hung on her wall and wonder just who she really was. Was she Dot Evans, who lived here, or was she Dot Tegydd, who came from North Wales? It was not the name which mattered of course, though she had denied the name Tegydd because it was Tom's name; she wanted nothing from him, not even the loan of his name. What mattered was the person. Dot Evans was so different, so much more *alive*, when you compared her to Dot Teggydd, dreaming her life away in her ancient home, working like a slave on the land, never thinking of rebellion. Never thinking of a bloke either, the girls at work would have said if they had known. My, hasn't that Dot changed! Now she thought of her name as a loan because she saw that despite what her father had said she would marry. Jim Tolworth gave her boxes of chocolates and took her to the cinema whenever she would go; Randolph Barnard hung around outside the restaurant with half a dozen eggs or a nice piece of ham for her to take home for her tea (Mrs Blishen appreciated them even more than Dot did herself, for generous though she was to her lodger times were still hard when you were living on a widow's pension and bringing up a mentally retarded son). When Dot helped Ernie, the manager, to carry the takings to the bank there was a bank clerk with a kiss-curl and a dapper little moustache who always gave her a specially warm smile.

But now, riding along beside the spring gardens and beneath the budding trees, Dot had more exciting things to think about. Maisie Phillips had invited her home to have tea the previous Sunday, and Maisie lived outside the city, at Eaton. Meeting Maisie's parents and three younger sisters had been pleasant enough, but whilst she wandered round their large, rambling garden and played with their dog and admired the neat rows of vegetables which were already beginning to come up, she had seen, over a hedge, a dreadful, wild tangle of rough ground.

'What's that?' she had enquired, only to be told that it had been a decent little medder once, but now it was let go, because the feller that owned it was dead and his widder din't want the bother.

Would she sell? Dot had wondered out loud, and the answer had been that the widow would undoubtedly sell, except that the meadow was so surrounded by smallholdings and little patches of garden that none of the people with money to spare for land would want it.

But I want it, Dot reminded herself now, with rising excitement. I want it badly! My savings aren't what they should be, not yet, but one day . . .

She was still dreaming about the piece of land when Jane cycled up alongside her. Dot jumped and swerved when Jane shouted, because her mind had been miles away – in Eaton village, to be precise – but she soon came down to earth when Jane started talking.

'Dot, I meant to come round yours last night, but what with one thing and another . . . guess who come round ours?'

'Claud?' suggested Dot, knowing that this was more like a

certainty than a guess but not much caring. She liked Claud.

'That's right. And guess what he asked me!'

'To marry him?'

'No, of course not, fule!' Jane's bicycle veered as Jane leaned over and clumped her friend's shoulder. 'It was much more exciting than that! He wants us to go out with him. Saturday night. Him and Tolly, I mean.'

'Lovely. But where?'

'To the fair, on the cattle market. There's always a fair here at Easter — you bin to many fairs, gal Dot?'

'Not many. Well, none. But is a fair on at night-time?'

'Not half it is. You'll hear the din for miles around. And Saturday's the best night of all because there's a big horse sale on Saturday morning and the farmers and their families come in from miles around and quite often stay over and go on the fair later. A fair's more fun when you can scarce move,' she added.

'It sounds like a good evening,' Dot said. 'Tell Claud I'll be glad to go with Tolly. What about getting home, though? Shall we cycle?'

'No indeed. I already told Claud they could take us home in a taxi. We don't want to have to rush to catch the last tram. We'll be quite tired, mind, because it must be our busiest day, pretty near, Easter Saturday. There's so many farmers in with manure on their boots that it smells more like a cowshed than a restaurant come five o'clock.'

'I don't mind. Are they meeting us straight from work? What time did you tell 'em?'

'Half six, I said. Just time to put a dab of powder on our noses and get out of uniform; I hate going out on the spree in that old dress.'

The two girls reached the Walk and wheeled their bicycles round the side of the restaurant and into the little yard at the back. Dot reflected that even if she had wanted to mope over being far from home she would scarcely have time to do so! What a life, eh, she told herself. All go from morning to night. And don't I enjoy it that way!

By half past six that Saturday evening Dot and Jane were ready

307

for anything. They had changed, Dot into a grey skirt and pink jumper with her light grey coat on top and Jane into mauve wool, they had powdered their noses, and now they emerged from the side gate to find their swains ready too, and raring to go.

'We're going down to Deacons for a fish supper,' Tolly told Dot as she slipped her hand into his elbow. 'Then we'll go straight to the fair; fancy a meal, do you, old partner?'

'Yes please,' Dot said hopefully. She had just eaten a very substantial tea at her place of employment but she was, she told herself, a growing girl. More food seldom came amiss. 'Jane said to wear sensible shoes, so I have.'

Tolly glanced down at her small feet in their flat-heeled working shoes. Usually she wore high heels when they went out together. He smiled at her.

'Good idea. You're so little they'll probably charge you half-price for everything. Come on!'

The four of them repaired to Deacons where large plates of fish, chips and peas were bought, smothered in salt and vinegar and rapidly devoured, accompanied by large cups of tea and thick bread and margarine. Dot ate everything within reach, and then leaned back, replete.

'That was lovely. Thank you very much. I just hope I can walk down to the fair after all that food.'

'If you can't we'll roll you there, like a hoop,' Claud teased. 'Once you've been whirled on the roundabout and jiggled on the cakewalk and whizzed down the chute of the tall tower it will have moved down a bit and you'll be crying out for cake and candy floss.'

Dot protested, Jane mocked, and the four of them set out, bound for pleasure. It was dark already and long before they reached the fair they could hear the music, loud and raucous, and see the lights glittering feverishly against the frosty night sky.

Dot loved the fair. The noise, the packed humanity, the excitement, brought out a noisy, gasping, fun-loving Dot – a third person, one who was neither quite Dot Tegydd nor Dot Evans.

She had never been nervous of trying new things, so she was duly jiggled on the cakewalk, whirled round on the painted horses and whizzed down the chute. She did this last three times, and was only lured away by Tolly's promises of more excitement to come.

Next, armed with candy-floss, they tried their luck at the shooting galleries, dart throwing and shove-ha'penny. They won, of course, for were they not young, keen-eyed and steady-handed? The girls had their arms full quite soon, Jane with a pink plush rabbit, a garish dressing-table set in vivid blue silk and an outsize lollypop, whilst Dot grasped a doll with a pert little celluloid face and a dress made of dyed feathers and a bag of toffees. But they had not yet sucked all possible amusement out of the fair, so they left the stalls where you tried your skill and went back to the amusements.

They went on the ghost train, Dot shrieking with the best, through the hall of mirrors which was voted pretty tame, and then into the tent which contained in one half the fattest woman in the world ('They in't seen Mrs Cripps, thass clear,' Dot heard someone mutter) and in the other the snake woman, who had a couple of small but clearly alive pythons on her person.

'Now let's have a go on them dodgems,' Jane suggested, shouting half because you had to shout to be heard above the din and half because she felt like it. 'I bags drive!'

The four of them charged across to the dodgems just, as luck would have it, as the last customers began to vacate the small cars. Tolly and Dot ran, hand in hand, across the slippery floor. The air was blue with cigarette smoke, with the smell of the fuel which kept the fair running and with the noise – noise so loud had to be visible, Dot felt, as she spotted a car about to be vacated and screamed to Tolly to go right, go right!

Tolly went right, towing her behind him, and Dot cannoned violently into a tall young man with a girl hanging on his arm who had just left another car. He turned to apologise, Dot turned to say it didn't matter . . . and said nothing. For a split second she simply stared.

Hywel! Here, hundreds of miles from home, in the middle of the dodgems rink he stood, looking down at her. For an instant she saw – or thought she saw – dawning recognition in his

309

eyes, and then he said, 'Sorry, love,' and hurried off the floor, taking the girl with him.

At this moment Dot found herself swung off her feet and seated, rather roughly, in the passenger side of the dodgem car. Tolly was teasing her, saying she had nearly lost them their ride and to punish her he intended to drive. He had intended to do so all along, she realised, but she could only smile at him and twist round in her seat, trying to see where Hywel . . . that fellow . . . had gone.

'What's up, Dot? Don't keep staring over there – you lost something?' enquired Tolly presently, as he handed his money over to the boy who swung on the front bumper of their vehicle. 'We'll be off any moment. You want to keep your eyes open for me, so's we don't crash into anyone else.'

Dot knew very well that he had every intention of crashing into as many people as possible during the next five minutes, despite his virtuous tone.

'I thought I saw a friend,' she said breathlessly, turning eyes front once more. The chap had completely disappeared into the vast crowd. It had not been Hywel of course, just a remarkable resemblance. Folk said everyone had a double. Well, she had just seen Hywel's. Still . . . 'Perhaps we could have a look round, Tolly, when we get off here?'

'Course we could; anything you like, Dot,' Tolly assured her. But though he was as good as his word they saw no sign of the tall young man who had, for a moment, looked so very much like Hywel.

Hywel could not sleep. He lay awake, staring into the darkness, trying to ignore his brothers' snores, desperate to get to sleep so that he could stop his mind from dancing its unending jig round what had happened earlier in the evening.

He had worked a double shift, that was the trouble, he told himself. Already tired but wanting the extra money, he had agreed to stay below and work in another man's place.

The other man, fortunately, had a good place, not too deep, where the getting was easier. Hywel had been working away quietly enough, but feeling terribly tired, and then all of a sudden he had slid into the Other Place, and it had been very different from his other visits.

The noise hit him first: music blaring, people shouting, a vast crowd of folk all talking and laughing at once. And the movement was strange – fast, skidding, uneasily jerking. And then he took a good look round him and he was in a bumper car on a fair, with a girl sitting beside him. She was sitting forward so that her long hair fell over her face but he was pretty sure that it was the girl from the marshes and even as he looked the car slowed down and stopped and he and the girl jumped out.

The floor was very wide and shiny and he was excited, happy, glad to be here amongst all the people. He turned as someone cannoned violently into him and opened his mouth to apologise and then stood stock still, staring.

It was Dot! Slap bang in front of him she stood, with her own apology fading from her lips and recognition . . . affection . . . dawning in her eyes. It was unmistakably Dot, with her snub nose, her tatty fringe of curls over her forehead, and the big mouth smiling and faltering and opening a little in her shocked surprise, to show her small, uneven white teeth.

He lost it then, it slid away from him, though because he tried so desperately to stay it happened strangely. It was like being carried away from a scene by force – dragged backwards, he thought. The fairground simply receded until he could see it dwindling to nothing, being replaced by blackness. And then the blackness was no longer total – he could see the reflection of his lamp in the black diamonds of the coal face, his hands, black already, gripping his pick. And even as he was stunned by the despairing realisation that he had lost her, his new filler's voice, bored and slightly peevish, reminded him that it was time for snap.

He had worried and worried over it for the rest of the shift, like a dog worrying a bone to get at the marrow. He should have been delighted to see Dot, to know that she was well and happy, but if the truth were told he was not. At first, he worried because the Other Place had always been remote from reality. If Dot was there, though, that meant that it was not just a sort of vision but a physical place which anyone might visit. Or, if it was just a sort of vision, might it not mean that Dot was . . . was dead?

He did not continue to think that for long, though. A

fairground was too earthy to belong to a vision, either of this world or the next! What worried him now was the look of happiness and excitement on Dot's face before she recognised him. She had been with a fellow, and they had been holding hands! He could not pretend to himself that she had been happy and excited because of his presence; she was happy with that other lad.

And Hywel resented it. It was easy to dream of her return — but suppose she returned with a husband and family? He had always thought her a fetching little thing but now he realised that others shared his feelings. Clearly, Dot was no longer unappreciated; that fellow she'd been holding hands with had known a good thing when he saw one.

Which is more than I did, Hywel acknowledged ruefully now, lying very still in bed and hoping that Stan would not be woken by his wakefulness. I sent her away, or as good as; now I'm daring to feel aggrieved because she's found happiness! Go to sleep, you great selfish idiot, he counselled himself. Count sheep, or lumps of coal, or the money in the bank, but go to sleep! You've worked a double shift, you're tired out, yet tomorrow you'll still be expected to turn up for afternoons! Dammit, man, I *order* you to get some sleep!

It was, however, easier said than done. The night was stealing towards dawn before he slept at last.

Everything that happened, Dot concluded afterwards, happened because of that trip to the fair. It was a . . .whatsitsname . . . a thingummy . . . a catalyst, that's what it was. It changed everything.

There could be no doubt that thinking she had seen Hywel had upset her equilibrium, because after that she never stopped thinking she saw him. It had happened a lot at first, but she had known, then, that it had to be an illusion and it always had been. A head had turned and it had not been his head, a shoulder had lifted in a shrug and she had known at once that it was not his shoulder. She had grown accustomed to ignoring sudden sightings because they always ended in disappointment.

But not this one, not this time. This time the chap had been so very like Hywel that a face-to-face encounter had not stabbed her with disappointment but with a wild, unreasoning hope. So of course, though she knew it had not been Hywel, she began searching for him everywhere.

That alone might not have mattered, though it was a painful business. What did matter was that their first day back at work after the holiday the manager, Ernie, asked Dot to go out for a meal with him. And Dot refused.

'It's awfully kind of you, but I couldn't, really,' she had said, adding disarmingly, 'I do think you're a bit too old for me really, sir.'

'Why couldn't you keep your tongue between your teeth?' moaned Jane when she found out. 'Ernie's ever so sensitive about his age and he'd taken a real shine to you, gal! You should've told him you and Tolly was going serious. He'd have understood that and not taken it personal.'

'I'm sorry. I didn't mean to hurt his feelings,' Dot said, genuinely distressed. She did not much like the manager, who was quick to find fault and slow to praise, but she respected him and admired his abilities in running the place faultlessly.

'Hmmm. Being sorry may not be enough. Just you toe the line, gal, for a week or two, until he's got over what you said.'

Dot had meant to do it, too, only three days later, as though to prove Jane's point, Dot thought she saw Hywel again. She was carrying a heavy tray laden with customers' dinners at the time and she dropped the lot, flew across the room, and found herself confronting a total stranger.

Ernie appeared like the demon in a pantomime, apologised to the customers, set two waitresses to clear up the mess and two more to make good the orders, and sacked Dot on the spot. No amount of pleading, no promise of an explanation, would change his mind. He simply repeated that she was sacked, without a reference, and then he marched out of the restaurant, his little black legs going very fast, like Charlie Chaplin's, and locked himself in his office.

There had been no choice but to go, and by that time Dot was in a temper because he was being so totally unreasonable and unfair and all the staff knew why. So she had a little weep, said goodbye to all her friends, and then hesitated in the back doorway. Her bicycle was there, but did she really want to cycle home and admit total defeat? It was early, only two o'clock; suppose she went job-hunting first? After all, she was an experienced waitress now, and should have no difficulty in getting work. And she could always fetch her bicycle another day, or even ask Jane to ride it home for her. She knew that Jane, having grievously overslept that morning, had come in on the tram.

She would do it! With the decision, some of her depression lifted. After all, she was doing something – she might even be bettering herself if she got a really good job. She returned to the restaurant where Jane, tearful still, was clearing, and asked her to ride the bicycle home. Jane agreed, and said that Dot was to be sure to come round as soon as she could that evening and tell her how the job-hunting had gone.

'I'm sure I'll get something,' Dot said, buoyant again. 'Wish me luck, girls!'

They did, fervently; Dot was universally popular with the staff. It never occurred to any of them, however, that it was perhaps not the most sensible thing in the world to go job-hunting in the middle of the afternoon and still in nippy uniform, thus plainly proclaiming that she had been summarily dismissed.

As ill-luck would have it, it was a wet afternoon, too, with the rain falling steadily and the cold east-coast wind blowing fitfully. A lot of Dot's natural ebullience had drained away after two tearooms had told her they were fully staffed, thank you. When these refusals were rapidly followed by others she began to feel downright miserable, and to see herself, out of work and starving, forced to take to domestic servitude in order to keep body and soul together.

Down came the rain, round and round trudged Dot. Her shoes were soaked and a sole came loose, her hair became wild witchlocks; even the stout grey gabardine began to leak at the seams.

Her spirit finally broke at a workmen's cafe down by the river Wensum; she knew they wanted a waitress because there was a notice in the window saying so, yet when she entered the place the beefy proprietress took one look at her and said they were suited, thanks.

314

Dot stamped out, stood on the pavement for a moment, and then, with a sob, headed back towards the city centre. She must have gone a hundred yards before she realised she had company. Literally dogging her heels was the most pitiable mongrel imaginable. Small, starved, and with a skin disease which had caused large tufts of its brown and white fur to fall out, it slunk along with its nose almost touching the backs of her calves. When she stopped it shrank back, yet there seemed to be, in its liquid dark eyes, a look which said, *you won't harm me*; *we're both down on our luck*.

'Hello, old fellow.' Dot searched her pockets but found nothing but a sugar lump. She held it out doubtfully but her new companion was long past pride or fussiness. He did not snatch but he took it with undisguised eagerness, gulped, and looked hopefully at her still outstretched hand.

'My, you are hungry. What can I do with you, though? Mrs Blishen's got a heart of gold but I doubt she'd welcome another mouth to feed – especially with me having to tell her I've lost my job.' She sniffed and the dog, emboldened by her tone and by the sugar lump, wagged its stringy tail and cocked an ear. Only one; the other, drooping from some fight or encounter with a missile, drooped still.

'However, if you'll wait a second . . .' Dot turned back to the workmen's cafe. When she reached it she did not tell the dog to wait, as she had intended, but opened the door and beckoned. The dog, after a second's hesitation, trotted in. Even her company seemed to have given him hope, for she saw that he carried one ear permanently cocked now, and his eyes were bright.

'Git that blooda dawg outa here,' the proprietress said in a belligerent tone as soon as she saw who Dot was. 'Go on, git it out!'

'I will. But give me a couple of ham sandwiches, would you, please? And a meat pie, I think.'

A desire to sell her produce warred with a natural hatred of stray dogs; concupiscence won.

'Two 'am, one pie, that's a bob,' she said, snatching the money and pushing the food across the counter. 'Now git 'im out!'

'We're going,' Dot said loftily, heading for the door. 'We

315

wouldn't stay in this horrid place even if you *did* want a waitress!'

The woman, incensed, followed her to the door gobbling like a turkey, but Dot and the dog were well up Prince of Wales Road before she started to shout.

'Now we'll go to the Castle gardens,' Dot told her small friend, who could smell the food in the white paper bag she held. 'We'll get into one of those shelter places so we're out of the rain, and you shall have the best dinner you've had for ages, by the look of your ribs.'

The two of them repaired to the gardens, the dog sticking so determinedly close to Dot that he banged his nose constantly against her legs. It was easy to find a seat, for in such a downpour the place was pretty well deserted, though every now and then someone hurried through, muffled and gumbooted, taking a short cut no doubt.

'Here we are!' Dot sat down on a drenched wooden seat in the doubtful shelter of an open-fronted rustic pavilion. 'Which will you have first, dear sir, ham sandwich or pie?'

The dog did not seem to care which came first; probably he would have devoured the paper bag with as much enthusiasm as he showed for the piece of sandwich Dot handed him.

'Good, was it?' The dog, crowding close to her knee, indicated that it had been more than good. 'Want another bit?' His eyes, fixed on the bag, shone and his tail trembled. The second half of the sandwich went down, if anything, quicker than the first.

It was not until the dog had finished his repast that her own miserable state struck Dot again. What could she do for the poor little creature, other than feed him and then walk away from him? Or try to walk away from him. He polished off the last crumbs of the pie and then sank down beside her, resting his slight weight against her leg, regardless of the good-sized puddle in which he sat. He sighed, yawned, and then settled down with the air of a dog who has found food, a friend and a future. He began to lick his disgustingly dirty tummy and as he did so Dot saw, just in advance of his nose, a flea, creeping, quick and dark, through his patchy fur.

Naturally he would have fleas. And doubtless worms and nits and lice and every other pest known to dog. But she could buy some powders and there were lotions . . . the dog, as if he knew she was thinking about him, reached up almost absently and licked her hand.

It was her undoing. Dot began to whimper, then to sob, and then to cry in good earnest. It was so unfair! She could do nothing for this little waif because she had no money, or not enough to promise him – or herself – the security they both needed so desperately. If she took him in, bathed him, powdered him and fed him, she would build up love and trust and then, inevitably, let him down far worse than if she had never bought the sandwiches and the pie, never fed him.

The dog, sensing her distress, stood up, whined, looked at her with his head cocked, and then jumped on to her lap. Even through her tears she had to smile; he was filthy and wet and flea-ridden, but he was warm. And when he nuzzled up to her, trying to lick her chin, she knew that she could not desert him, not now. They would go home together, face Mrs Blishen, persuade that good woman to take on another stray, and then, somehow, Dot would get work which could support them both.

She was still at the sniffling, dry-my-eyes stage when someone spoke.

'I say . . . excuse me, but can I help? I can see you're upset – is anything the matter?'

Startled, she looked up. And up. The tallest young man, sheltered by a vast umbrella, stood before her. Dark hair, dark eyes, a deep, gentle voice. Hastily, Dot grubbed for a handkerchief, failed to run one to earth and regretfully wiped her eyes – and a good deal of nose – on her grey gabardine sleeve.

'It's all right, thank you. It's just the depressing, horrid rain.'

'Oh, the rain! Yes, of course.' He sounded amused now, and not at all believing. 'Is your little dog hurt?'

'He isn't . . . well, he's mine now. No, he's all right.'

'Then what is it? Lost your job, or your lover, or your week's wages?'

His voice was so encouraging that Dot found herself confiding in him without in the least meaning to do so.

'It's my job. It wasn't fair. He sacked me because I dropped a tray, but lots of girls drop trays from time to time and they don't get sacked. Only he asked me out and I wouldn't go and

317

the girls said I was a fool and I'd be in trouble. I thought I'd get somewhere else easy as easy, because nippies are the best, but no one wants me. I've tried everywhere. And then this poor little dog followed me, and I've fed him, but what about tomorrow? And . . .'

'You're a nippy?' He sat down on the seat beside her, regardless of the wet, and took the dog off her lap. 'Now that *is* interesting! Have you thought of trying the Royal Pavilion? For a job, I mean.'

'He's awfully dirty,' Dot said apprehensively as the dog's filthy paws scrabbled for a hold on her companion's clean fawn mackintosh. 'The Royal? Oh no, I wouldn't try there. It's the best restaurant in the city. They don't have waitresses, anyway. I've heard the girls talking about it. They only have waiters and they have to be the best. But if they wanted a kitchen worker, I suppose I could try them. Why?'

'Well, it's possible that they want some help, evenings,' the young man said. 'I'm on my way there now. Want to come along with me and see what they've got? I know the staff and could introduce you.'

Thoughts of white slave traders whizzed through Dot's head and were dismissed. This young man would do her no harm – look how good he was with the dog! But how could she possibly turn up at the Royal soaked to the skin and draggly and with the dog in tow? She looked doubtfully up at her new friend. He was smiling, apparently not noticing or possibly even not caring that the dog had already covered the skirt of his mackintosh with muddy rosettes.

'Going to trust me? Come on, then. I won't bite you, and if you think they might not appreciate the dog I can assure you they'll think he's mine, particularly as I shall carry him.' He examined the dog's small, pinky-brown pads. 'He's done enough tramping the streets for a bit. Once he's got some more food inside him and has had a good rest he'll be able to outwalk the pair of us, but for now he can ride like a lord under my arm.'

Dot laughed but stood up as he did.

'I didn't know that was how you carried lords! Of course I'll trust you, and thank you very much for offering to accompany me. If I could get a job – any job – I wouldn't mind asking Mrs

Blishen if I could keep the dog at her house. She's my landlady,' she added as an afterthought.

'And you are . . .?'

'Oh, sorry. I'm Dot Evans.'

He held out a hand, which Dot shook; they smiled at each other.

'And I'm Carlo Peruzzi. Evans is a Welsh name. I thought you didn't sound Norfolk born and bred exactly. I'm from Italian stock, of course, as you probably guessed.'

'That's exciting. Were you born here or do you long for the sunny south?' Dot was so wet that turning her coat collar up or getting under his umbrella were pointless exercises, but she did them both.

'No, I wasn't born here, but I came here when I was no more than a year old. You see, Mamma is from the north of Italy and Pappa is from the south. It won't mean much to you, I daresay, but there's quite strong feeling amongst Italians against inter-marriage between north and south. It simply isn't done – and there is real Romeo and Juliet feeling against marriages, what's more. So when my parents fell in love they realised it would be better to move right away from Italy. They tried Spain for a year – that's where I was born – but they soon decided that they would be better off here, so they came to Norwich, Pappa to work as a chef and Mamma as a kitchen maid.'

'And do they work there – your parents, I mean?'

He laughed. 'At the Royal? Well, they own it.'

Dot gazed up at him with some awe. A restauranteur!

'Gosh! No wonder you knew about jobs there. What do you do? You don't look like a chef, but . . .'

'I'm an insurance salesman. To tell the truth I'm not keen on kitchen working conditions – the heat and all the people. I like to spend most of my life out of doors, which is just what I do.'

'I see. And you think your parents might take me on to work in their kitchens?'

'Something like that. We turn right here – we'll go in the back way. Pappa's easy-going, but he wouldn't wish me to take the dog through the restaurant even when it's closed.'

'He isn't exactly an advertisement for a place,' Dot admit-ted. 'Do you live with your parents?'

'No. I've a ground-floor flat with a garden just off Unthank Road. It's . . . it's more convenient for me. Here we are!'

They had entered a small courtyard and even in the rain it was an attractive place, with pink and cream paving stones, bay trees in painted tubs and two old-fashioned herbacious borders gay, now, with spring flowers.

A blue-painted door, obviously left open to allow steam to swirl out of the kitchen, also released the murmur of voices and laughter from within, and Dot followed Carlo over to the doorway, eager to see into the room beyond.

The two of them stopped for a moment whilst Carlo shook and furled his umbrella and, as they stepped inside, the people in the room – and there were a great many of them – turned and stared. Immediately a buzz of uninhibited comment and criticism broke out.

'Oh no, not another!'

'Eet ees Carrrlo, another one he has!'

'Wot's this, then? Don't tell me, it's another milkman's 'orse!'

Did they mean the dog, or herself? But before she could do more than blink and smile uncertainly, a huge man in white with a chef's hat perched at a rakish angle on springy black curls surged towards them, a large hand held out.

'Ees Carlo, come 'ome. Wotta you got thees time, Carlo? Not just a little dog, eh, but a pretty younk lady, too. Well, well, well!'

'Er, this is Miss Dot Evans. She's . . . she's a friend. And it isn't what you think! The dog belongs to her, doesn't it, Dot?'

More cheerful, friendly jeers greeted this remark, coming mainly from a number of young men, obviously waiters, who were lolling about in shirtsleeves.

'Oh, sure, Carlo. We'll believe it, thousands wouldn't. Pull the other one.'

'Honest to God, Carlo, why bring it 'ere? It's too skinny to make a meal for the clients!'

'Che spaventapasseri! Cosa intende dire, Carlo?'

To this last Carlo replied in the same language, but briefly, so that Dot did not fall into the trap of thinking herself the subject of the conversation, and then he turned to her at once.

'I'm very sorry, Dot. How rude you'll think us! Napoleone

wanted to know what I was up to and the answer is that I am up to nothing whatsoever. Now Dot, let me introduce you.'

There were a lot of foreigners in the kitchen, Dot concluded, as the names rolled out. Ciro was the chef, Domenica, his wife, the pudding chef. There were half a dozen waiters — Napoleone was one of them — and a head waiter, Albert, who had a cockney accent and a face like a monkey. There was Sandra who peeled the vegetables, Leandro who was under-chef and who would one day take over from Ciro . . . this caused much amusement and some comments in Italian which made the unfortunate Leandro blush like a beetroot . . and little Emilio, everyone's friend, who did odd jobs and who was sometimes allowed to wait when a regular waiter was away. And all the time the introductions were being performed everyone's eyes were fixed on Dot. It was uncanny, like suddenly finding oneself on stage at the Hippodrome with no act prepared and one's oldest clothing on.

'And now that you know all our names, I'll tell you, folk, that Miss Dot's a nippy. Or rather, she was . . .'

There was another of those mocking mutters, and Albert repeated his remark, though *sotto voce*, about the milkman's horse.

'I thought . . . you know Pappa was saying he was short-staffed for evenings, so I thought . . .'

'Ay-yi-yi, Carlo,' interposed the chef, 'your pappa would never employ a waitress! A woman pudding chef he thinks immoral, only my Domenica did he employ from desperate need!'

'No, I didn't mean her to wait . . . dammit, Ciro, give me credit for *some* sense! But someone has to make up the plates and whip cream and sprinkle sugar and I heard Pappa say that Mrs Ridgeway had left, so when I knew Dot had lost her job — through no fault of her own, Ciro, honest to God — I thought he might give her a try. What do you think?'

Ciro shrugged. He did it with his whole body, and even his face shrugged too, his eyebrows climbing, his eyelids screwing themselves tightly shut, his mouth pursing, even his cheeks bulging out with the strength of the shrug.

'Oh, Pappa say, Pappa say! Go ask Pappa, see what he say now!'

'Look, thank you very much for trying, but . . .' Dot began, turning back towards the door, but Carlo was having none of that.

'Now look what you've done,' he said angrily to the astonished chef. 'There's no harm in asking Pappa, is there? Has he already employed someone? Is that what you mean? Because if so . . .'

'No, no, no! I'm sorry, mees.' Ciro's dark eyes were eloquent. 'But eef you are waitress, why bother to work in kitchen? It seem a waste. Nippies are so queeck, so clever, that surely someone will want you?'

'Perhaps, but . . . we'll go and see Pappa now,' Carlo interrupted firmly. 'Come along, Dot. They won't eat you.'

Carlo shepherded Dot across the kitchen and into a narrow hall at the back, then up a flight of stairs. As they climbed he told her that at this time of day his parents would probably be relaxing over a cup of tea – a bad English habit they had picked up, he added with a grin – so it would be a good moment to catch them.

After the dingy staircase she expected the flat to be plain, dark and dull. Instead she emerged on the landing and stepped straight into opulence. The hall had highly polished, brightly coloured tiles scattered with rich looking rugs, there were oil paintings on the walls, and directly facing the head of the stairs was a huge mirror in a gilt frame of such elaborate beauty that she could have spent a happy hour just picking out the various figures and embellishments. Even in the glance she was allowed she noticed cherubs holding gilt bows above their heads, birds flying with garlands looped from their beaks, beautiful Greek goddesses holding baskets laden with fruit, and a number of tiny monkeys swinging from trees.

Unfortunately she took time, at that point, to look into the mirror. A ragamuffin looked back, her drenched curls plastered to her scalp, her gaberdine mackintosh a wreck of its former self, her shoes squelching. Dot stopped short, a hand flying to her mouth.

'Oh, Carlo, I can't . . .'

'Rubbish.' He still had the dog in one arm but he walked across to the nearest door and pushed it open, announcing loudly as he did so, 'Good afternoon, Mamma, Pappa. I've brought someone to meet you.' He had Dot's arm in a firm grip by now. 'Come on, Dot!'

Dot took a deep breath, squared her shoulders, and marched into the room.

It was a big room which seemed smaller than it was because it was so crowded with furniture, knick-knacks and ornaments. Every wall was hung with paintings of various sizes and the floor was not only carpeted, but covered with rugs as well.

Mr Peruzzi sat in a winged armchair with a cup of tea in one hand and a book, open, in the other. He wore a pair of round, surprised-looking spectacles which were perched right on the end of a magnificent nose. He looked at his son and Dot over the glasses, then his gaze focused on the dog. He groaned and put his book face down on his lap.

'Mamma, Mamma, another one! Knowing what we think he bring another one for our approval, eh? Carlo, when will you learn . . .'

His wife interrupted him. She glanced once at her son, once at the dog, and then her small black eyes had fixed themselves firmly on Dot.

'Hush, Arturo. Do you not see we have a visitor? Introduce your little friend, Carlo my dear.'

'A visitor? If this is another way of saying the milk-man's . . .' But at this point Mr Peruzzi seemed to see Dot properly for the first time. He got ponderously to his feet, laying his book down on the arm of his chair. 'Introduce the young lady, Carlo.'

'Of course, Pappa. That was what I came here to do! Miss Dot Evans, my parents. Mamma, Pappa, my friend Miss Evans.'

'Ah! How do you do, Miss Dot. Carlo, take Miss Dot's wet coat and your own into the kitchen and ask Maria to dry them out for you. And then come back here . . . without that dog, if you please . . . and we'll all have some tea. Better tell Maria to bring two more cups and some more toast.'

Dot waited for Carlo to explain that the dog was hers and that she was an out-of-work waitress, but she waited in vain. Whilst their son was pursuing his errand his parents made small-talk and when Carlo returned he at once proceeded to pull the wool over the Peruzzis' eyes.

'Dot's a nippy, Pappa, which is why she's dressed like that,' he said, sinking into a chair and gratefully accepting a cup of tea from his mother. 'She was at a loose end, having an unexpected afternoon off . . .' (how true, Dot thought dismally) '. . . and we fell to chatting and of course found we had a lot in common. So I thought I'd bring her back for a nice cup of tea and then I'd nip up to my old room and put some dry things on and we'd go and see a film.'

'Oh, but . . .' Dot began, but was silenced by an imperious wave of Carlo's hand.

'You're worried about your dog. Dot's dog isn't too well. I'm going to take care of him for her, get him fit again,' he said in an aside to his mother. 'Well, don't worry. Mamma will look after him whilst we see the film and perhaps have a meal, won't you, Mamma?'

To Dot's astonishment, Mrs Peruzzi agreed enthusiastically that she would enjoy taking care of the little dog.

'And I expect Pappa would like to ask you questions about your work, for we went, once, into your restaurant and were very impressed with the way such small girls carry such large trays – and so quickly! Pappa, I'm sure Dot would be pleased to explain how she was trained.'

This was a bit of a facer since Dot's training had consisted entirely of the practical work of waitressing, but she managed to give sensible replies to Mr Peruzzi's eminently sensible questions. He shook his head sadly over some of the cooking methods Dot described but admitted that, whilst not haute cuisine, they undoubtedly filled a need.

'And bellies,' his son said, twinkling at Dot.

'Don't be vulgar, Carlo,' Mrs Peruzzi said, twinkling too. 'And just where were you thinking of eating, after this cinema trip?'

'Oh, somewhere quiet, with good cheap food . . .' began Carlo, smiling at Dot, only to be cried down by his mother.

'Here is best – and for you, cheapest,' she reminded him. 'We should be delighted to give you dinner in the restaurant at our table. What time would suit you?'

'If we go to the Regent the film ends at ten, so we could be

324

back here by a quarter past,' Carlo said. 'Now, Dot, if you've finished your tea, I'll get one of the waiters to nip out for a taxi to take you home. You'll feel more comfortable changed out of your uniform, no doubt, though your coat will be dry by now.'

Not a word, all this time, of her jobless state!

In the taxi, she reproached Carlo for not telling his people the truth and reminded him that she needed a job badly, but though he looked a little hangdog it was clear he was not repentant.

'They were so pleased to meet a nippy, how could I tell them you wanted a job?' he said plaintively. 'They liked you, that was easy to see, and anyway I've thought of something else. I've heaps of friends in the catering trade, truly I have, and any one of them would give you a job on my recommendation. Just tell me where you'd like to work . . .'

'The Inglenook tearoom,' Dot said with what she imagined would be dismaying promptitude, but he smiled gently and nodded.

'Easy. I'll speak to Miss Rodway tomorrow. I promise you, Dot, that you shall have a good job by tomorrow lunchtime. If, of course, you stop nagging me about it and enjoy the film – and your dinner!'

'That's all very well, but I'm a *sacked* nippy, don't forget, with no references.'

Carlo waved a lordly hand.

'That's nothing. I shall explain that you left because the manager made unwelcome overtures to you. People will understand. Don't you believe me when I tell you tomorrow will see you in a job again?'

'I'm not sure. You said I might work for your parents,' Dot reminded him, but he shook his head at her, his eyes laughing though his mouth was grave.

'Silly Dot. It would not have been a good idea at all. I'll tell you why, one day!'

At noon on the day following her meeting with Carlo, Dot got a job as a waitress at the Inglenook tearoom. It was only a small place and the work was by no means tiring, but the pay was as good as that she had been receiving as a nippy and the

325

uniform a pretty pale green dress and a muslin apron which was all frills, so she was not too discontented with her lot. To be sure she missed her friends dreadfully at first, for the Inglenook only employed two waitresses, herself and a rheumatic elderly lady by the name of Anna Crump, whose conversation, at first, consisted almost entirely of complaints about her health and the state of her feet, which needed – but did not get – the constant attentions of a chiropodist. Corns, bunions, hammer toes and fallen arches haunted Miss Crump and soon began to haunt Dot too, but she was a good-natured girl and took care to save Miss Crump's feet – and rheumatic joints – all the running about she could, whereupon Miss Crump, able to move slowly and spend more time with her feet up in the kitchen, began to improve and to talk of other things. She was a cinema enthusiast and knew everything about the stars' private and public lives, and she was also a keen royalist, able to talk for hours about King George, Queen Mary, and their various offspring, greatly admiring the Prince of Wales and able to tell anyone who was interested every detail of his recent tour of India.

And Carlo was always there; escorting her to the cinema, taking her to dances at Samson & Hercules House, buying her little presents. Mrs Blishen had not seen Dot's dog until Carlo had made him presentable, and when she did that good woman took him to her heart, spending so much time exercising him during the day when Dot was working that the little chap speedily became as attached to her as he was to his mistress. Dot, christening him Chappie because that was how Mrs Blishen referred to him and seeing her pet pampered and valued, knew how much was due to Carlo's benevolent interference and was grateful. He was so kind, was Carlo, so disinterestedly good.

She believed in his disinterest for a month, until she discovered by chance that her wages at the tearoom were half as much again as those paid to Miss Crump. Enquiries elicited the fact that Mr Carlo had been very pressing about giving her employment. Miss Rodway had been happy to oblige, for a younger pair of feet would improve her business no end, yet she could not dream of letting Miss Crump go. So when Mr Carlo had offered to pay half her wages . . .

When tackled, Carlo had gone bright red, gazed at his toes for a moment, and then come out with the truth.

'The moment I saw you sitting there crying on that cold old seat, with Chappie on your lap, I knew you were the only girl for me,' he told her earnestly. 'Only . . . I've always been shy with girls and I knew I'd never dare ask you out. Or only by pretending — to myself as much as to you — that I wasn't interested in you as a girl but only as a person to help. And then when we got back to the Royal I knew that if you worked there you'd be with all those handsome young men . . . and it would have been awkward for me to dance attendance on you without Ciro and the others guessing. Yet I couldn't bear to let you go in case I lost you, so I approached Miss Rodway.'

'Oh, Carlo, you're so good and kind. Why on earth don't you have more self-confidence?'

He grinned, reddening.

'I do! Good God, woman, how could I sell insurance — and do very well at it — if I didn't have self-confidence? It's only with women that I get all flustered, and then only if I'm . . . well, interested in them. I can sell insurance to housewives — indeed, I do it every day — without turning a hair. But it's taken me until now to pluck up courage to ask a girl to marry me.'

They were in the Castle gardens and spring had given way to a soft and balmy June. Dot turned and stared up at him. There was a tree in full bloom behind his head and someone, somewhere, was singing the Skye Boat Song.

'What did you say?'

He smiled and his arm, which had been round her waist, tightened a little.

'Will you marry me, Dot?'

'Gosh! You don't want to marry me, Carlo! I'm little and plain and only a waitress . . .'

'Stop denigrating yourself, silly, and answer a civil question. I don't know why I'm such a fool as to ask. I should just grab you, sling you over my shoulder, and carry you off — but I'm asking. Yes or no?'

'That's not fair. You aren't a bit romantic. You should say . . .'

He let go of her waist and turned away from her, and she realised that he was not really feeling a bit light and teasing, the

327

way he was acting. This was a solemn moment for him and she was in danger of spoiling it.

She tugged his arm.

'Carlo, look at me! Yes please, Carlo, I'd like to marry you very much.'

They were married quietly, in a register office, because Carlo was a catholic and she was not and it seemed best. Mr and Mrs Peruzzi were so delighted that a girl they had liked from the first was to be their son's wife that they would have agreed to the couple's getting wed on top of Ben Nevis, Dot believed, in order to have the knot tied between them.

Dot never asked herself why she was marrying him, because she knew the answer would be the wrong one. She was fond of him, she admired him, she enjoyed his company, but never for one moment did she tell herself she loved him as she had loved Hywel. However, she believed that they could make a good life together and that, in time, she might come to love him. She would certainly do her utmost to make him happy.

She had known before they married that his pet hobby was the rescuing and tending of stray animals. She had not, until her marriage, realised the extent of it. They decided not to have a proper honeymoon, since Carlo returned to Italy for a month every September and wished to do so this year as usual, to introduce his bride to his many relatives. But they did get away for a pleasant five-day trip to London.

It was not spoiled by the fact that Carlo brought in the cab from Liverpool Street Station an emaciated tom cat with three legs and a gangrenous stump, but it would be idle to pretend that the cat's indignant and ungrateful presence enlivened their stay. Carlo was intent on curing the cat; the cat was intent on escape. Consequently, it ranged up and down the room yowling and whining throughout their wedding night. In fact, at the most tender and difficult moment, when Dot was surrendering her virtue and thoroughly puzzled and a little upset by Carlo's sudden transition from gentle lover to savage brute, her cries and the cat's were almost indistinguishable.

After the honeymoon the three of them returned to Carlo's flat and its canine and feline occupants. The cats were clean,

328

the dogs housetrained, but the place still smelt and Dot, though an animal-lover, did not like it. Oddly enough, Chappie did not like it either and after a mere three-day stay he ran away, back to Mrs Blishen and Horry, who did not keep a menagerie but had plenty of room in their hearts for one small dappled mongrel.

Sometimes Dot rather despairingly thought of following suit, for Carlo never considered when he picked up a stray. A greyhound, a spiteful and vicious brute who hated all women and Dot in particular, was brought home with a broken leg; its owner had intended to have it put down but Carlo had insisted on buying it and carting it home. Flash, as he called it, had never lived in a house and though he respected the kitchen, where he was fed, he regularly urinated on any old post, door-lintel or indeed temporarily stationary leg which he found around. He had formed a violent affection for Carlo and, since he was a jealous creature by nature, he would not allow Dot to so much as caress her husband's cheek without a low, menacing growl and Flash's immediate presence between them.

Carlo thought this funny; Dot did not. In fact after a month the only member of the menagerie she would not have turned out without a qualm was Dobbin, the milkman's horse. He was a huge, gentle elephant of a creature who lived an undemanding and pleasant life in the old stabling at the back of the house. He had summer grazing not too far off and Dot walked him down there whenever the weather was fine, talking softly to him. Sometimes she rode on his broad back, though this always made Carlo nervous since Dobbin had never been anything but a milkman's horse, but Dot poohpoohed any thought of danger. As she informed her spouse, cart horses on farms are never broken to a saddle, but a child of two is safe as houses perched on their broad backs.

Dobbin was hired out from time to time to people Carlo could trust and the money thus earned helped towards his keep. Every now and then Carlo would find a dog a good home. But other than that the menagerie grew and grew, and though at first Dot put up with it she soon realised that she would have to put her foot down or be swamped.

So she told Carlo that she could not continue to run his

animal farm. It was getting overcrowded, and that, in its way, was as cruel to the animals who lived with them as it was to Dot herself.

Carlo, always willing to listen to reason, listened, thought about it, and saw her point. He said that he would, in future, only bring animals back in order to fit them for a new and better life, and he would make contacts who would help him to find new homes for his strays.

Dot did not expect him to abide by his promise, but there she wronged him, for Carlo was a man of his word and he was also practical. He must have wondered how they were going to manage, once he started bringing in a new animal most weeks, and probably, Dot thought, she had only brought to a head a problem which had been hovering at the back of his mind for ages.

Two months after their marriage, with the flat respectably containing only four cats, two dogs and the young couple themselves, Dot thought that nothing could have been nicer than her life. She had learned to cook so that she could give Carlo good meals. She did not have a maid, because there was no need for one, but she did use a laundry so that her husband's shirts were always immaculately clean and starched. Every morning, after she had seen him off, adequately breakfasted, she put the dogs on their double lead and took them round the block. Then she went home, changed into a grey suit, or a skirt and blouse, and caught a tram down to the Royal Pavilion, where she helped her mother-in-law, or shelled peas for the chef, or laid up the tables for the waiters. It kept her busy and bustling and it gave her some pin-money of her own, but best of all it stopped her from too much thinking. After luncheon she helped in the kitchen again until about three, and then went home so that she could clear briskly through the flat, get Carlo's evening meal on the stove, exercise the dogs again and return to the flat to change into a pretty dress and to serve up the meal.

As the months passed she began, increasingly, to enjoy Carlo's company and to pine less for home and Hywel. Summer meant that they were out of doors most evenings and all weekends, animals needed less rescuing in the brilliant weather, and Carlo obviously found her a most satisfactory wife for he never came home late, always wanted her company, and made love to her very nearly often enough to satisfy Dot.

She loved her new life, but most of all she adored lovemaking, that delightful physical exercise which had never come her way before. It was so *good*, to find herself capable not only of rousing Carlo to heights of passion hitherto undreamed of, but to climb those same heights herself. They often laughed, now, about the three-legged tom – long since decamped – who had honeymooned with them. Carlo talked of getting a little house in the country and Dot dreamed of it almost as much as she dreamed of Plas Tegydd, for though she knew it was wrong, tried very hard to keep it at bay, dreaming of Plas Tegydd was a great comfort. She told herself that if Carlo did buy a place in the country then she would no longer need to dream of the Plas, to see in her mind's eye those rolling acres, to wonder what Father was doing with them. She could have a big vegetable patch, a pig-sty with a pig or two in it, pehaps even some hens. She had wondered about getting some hens in the garden attached to the flat, for it was big enough to keep half a dozen happily occupied scratching about on the thin, dog-abused grass. The only thing that stopped her was the fear that her husband would refuse to eat the hens when they stopped producing large and respectable eggs and would start a geriatric hennery in the garden, where old and useless birds might come to eat corn and die in peace. He would doubtless bury them, with full military honours, when they eventually died of old age.

It worried her rather that she had married a man who did not see that animals had been put on God's earth to work as well as to play. Cows in a field did not delight him; he only worried that they might not be as happy as the day is long. Their milk yields were a matter of total indifference to him, and if Dot began to talk of such things he accused her of forgetting that God's creatures had as much right to the earth as she.

Yet he ate meat with a hearty appetite, whilst deploring the wickedness of slaughtering little calves and baby lambs for the sake of their flesh. When she put to his mother, however, that Carlo's actions and feelings were inconsistent,

Mrs Peruzzi smiled and shook her head.

'Ah, but he feels with his heart and eats with his head! He is very naive, very sensitive. One day, Dot, he'll become like the rest of us, but not quite yet.'

A fortnight before they were due to set off for Italy, Dot was sitting on the kitchen table, dreaming in the sunshine, when Carlo came through the front door with a large bouquet of roses in his arms. He put them down on the draining board and came and lifted her off the table, kissing her mouth as he did so.

'Darling! I'm early, you see, with some flowers. Do you like them?'

Dot, who had coloured, looked at him for a moment without speaking, then gave a small, strained laugh.

'Roses? What on earth . . .?'

'Don't you like them? I just thought they'd cheer the house up a bit. They smell lovely, too. I always think the red ones smell good. And I wanted to ask you to be a good little wife and have a friend of mine to dine tonight.'

'Of course I will. I thought . . . but who is it? Randall?' Randall worked as an insurance salesman for the same company as Carlo. The two young men were good friends and frequently met to discuss business. But this time, it appeared, it was not Randall.

'Randall? Whatever made you think of him? No, my love, it's not Randall. Incidentally, why are you wearing that pretty dress?' He frowned. 'Don't say . . . have you seen Mamma this morning?'

'Yes, of course. I went there . . .' she hesitated, then continued, '. . . after I'd seen the doctor.'

'What's the matter with you?' Sitting on the table she had looked the picture of health, and even now, though her colour was high, he could see that she was not ill. 'Go on, Dot, stop smiling like that and tell me what's been happening.'

'I'm having a baby,' Dot said. It was difficult to sound thrilled or delighted because she and Carlo had never exchanged so much as a word on the subject of having a family, so she had no idea whether he would be pleased or dismayed.

'A baby!' He sounded, above all else, astonished. 'A baby? Are you sure?'

'Well, yes. The doctor did a test and says it will be born in February.' She pulled a face. 'Horrid time of year, but there isn't much else to do in February!'

'Caramba!' He was beginning, she decided, to sound pleased as well as surprised. 'I say, will this stop us going to Italy?'

'No, of course not! So you see when you walked in with those roses I thought you knew all along.'

'Roses? Oh yes, of course. The roses.' He went over to the draining board, picked the bouquet up, and laid it reverently in her arms. 'There you are, darling, specially for you because you are so clever and you're going to have a baby!'

He now sounded thrilled and delighted, Dot decided, which made it easier for her, because she had not, at first, felt either emotion. What she had felt, she decided dismally, was trapped.

'Well, that's the best news . . . look, we must go round, tell Mamma and Pappa . . . you've not told them? No, sweetheart, I was sure you wouldn't. We'll go round and tell them and have dinner with them and then we'll go to the theatre – would you like that? – or out somewhere. Dancing! You like dancing! We could go dancing . . .'

He was gabbling with excitement and Dot, laughing, held a hand over his mouth to gain a moment's silence.

'Oh, Carlo, shush a minute! Who are we having to dine this evening?'

But he waved an impatient hand at that and began kissing her neck and the side of her face.

'Dinner is with the family,' he said against her cheek. 'No one else is going to come here, because we're going out. It was just a fellow I know, but I'll put him off. You can meet him some other time.'

Accordingly, that evening the four Perruzzis, old and young, dined together and drank healths and got very excited and more than a little tipsy. Mamma Peruzzi had a little weep and Pappa Peruzzi had tears in his eyes and eveyone was very congratulatory and very kind. Dot drank champagne and warned everyone that she would probably have a girl because girls ran in her family and Carlo said he would rather have a girl first and the waiters sang as they waited and made rude jokes in Italian which Dot did not fully understand even when Carlo translated in a whisper.

It was all great fun and very lighthearted and when she got home and into bed and settled down she should have been the happiest young woman on earth.

But instead of happiness, she promptly became a prey to black despair. Without even knowing it, she realised now, she had been telling herself ever since her marriage that this was all a delightful way to spend some of her years of exile, but that when she felt the time was ripe she would go back . . . and here the old game of entering Plas Tegydd as conqueror began again, only this time it was Dot and her rich husband who came back and took over.

It was only now, with Carlo's child quickening within her, that she realised she had never for one moment really either expected or wanted to take Carlo back to Plas Tegydd. He would be totally out of place and completely useless and horribly unhappy there. When she had dreamed of Dot and her rich husband she had seen, not Carlo, but Hywel, inexplicably raised to riches in order the better to give bone and blood to an otherwise pretty insubstantial dream.

She had been foolish to think that she could simply walk out of her marriage, she told herself. Baby or no, you could not do that. Yet she knew now that she would have walked out of her marriage with very few qualms had Tom sent for her with promises of Plas Tegydd and sufficient money to bring it back to its former glories. She was very fond of Carlo – he was her dear husband and lover – yet she would have left him simply because nothing that had happened to her since she left Plas Tegydd had been absolutely real. It had all been slightly dreamlike. All the time she had been living here, working, marrying, arguing, kissing and making up, she had thought of it as an interlude which would be over when she chose to end it.

But a baby! That would make a difference. You could not just walk out on a baby! She could not even take it with her without all sorts of complications, because it would be Carlo's baby too!

Poor Dot looked down the years to come and felt a great big sob rise up in her chest. They would never live in the country, she knew that now; Carlo was a child of the city and in his heart it was what he wanted. She would spend the rest of her life here, bringing up a child, making do with parks and gardens when she wanted the hills, the mountains, and the clean, cold sweep of the moors. Making do with Carlo, when she wanted . . . yes, she still wanted Hywel!

Beside her, Carlo's steady breathing told her that he slept. He had eaten well and drunk more deeply than usual, and had gone to sleep as soon as his head touched the pillow. Dot could have screamed, so lonely and deserted did she feel, but instead she grabbed hold of as much of Carlo as she could, wrapped her arms and legs round him in a strangling hug, and began to kiss his neck. When he showed an irritating tendency to mutter, groan, and go back to sleep, she bit him, and quite hard too, so that he woke on a shout.

'Aargh! Oh, oh, ouch!'

'Carlo? Are you awake?'

Carlo rolled over and sat up on one elbow. In the dim light Dott could see him uneasily fingering his neck.

'Awake? Well, I am now. Whatever happened?'

'I was having a nightmare and I think I hit out. I'm sorry,' Dot murmured. 'Oh Carlo, I was so frightened! It was an awful dream, really it was.'

'Poor kid,' Carlo murmured, but perfunctorily. 'Go to sleep, then, love. I'll take care of you.'

He lay down and Dot promptly burrowed against his chest.

'Carlo? Do you love me?'

'What? Go to sleep, darling. Carlo's here. I'll take . . .' His voice trailed off and Dot jabbed a cruel elbow into his chest. This might not be the one place on earth she loved, Carlo might not be the man of her dreams, but there was one thing he could do as well as anyone she knew!

'Carlo! Wake up! Do – you – love – me?'

Carlo woke; he lay there for a moment, gathering his wits, she guessed, and then he rolled over and his arms went round her. He chuckled sleepily, but there was understanding in his voice when at last he spoke.

'Oh, I see – *that's* what you mean!'

Eighteen

'Pass me a couple of wedges, Dickie.'

Hywel and his boy were down deep – and at the Wynd you could go damned deep. He and Dickie were working in water, and the air was none too good. Gas was thick in it, so that you found yourself breathing fast and shallow to avoid drawing the stuff deep into your lungs, and that of course meant that you tired quickly. Every shift down here felt like two.

'Here you are, mun.'

Dickie passed the wedges and Hywel began to knock the first one in with heavy, deliberate blows. The coal down here was good, almost worth the awful effort of getting it, and his savings were increasing nicely, thanks to a lazy overman who had decided to set double shifts. Tom Tegydd found out, though, and he promptly stopped it. He said – and rightly – that you didn't get the best out of a man doing double shifts because he couldn't work at full stretch with every muscle crying out for a rest. Instead they paid overtime for working nights, and since night was the same as day down the pit, and he slept in the day with everyone out of the house, it suited him. Then there was weekend work, and Sundays on double time, so if you were reliable and did not mind working all the hours that were available you could make a pretty penny.

Tegydd had been doing well with the pit, improving all round. He would have got on to the overmen and the shot firers, the people who made it a dangerous pit, Hywel thought, but for his own personal tragedy. That had taken it out of him all right, he had not seemed the same man, after. He had left the pit to itself and the overman who worked the same shifts as Hywel, Ned Jarret, was a fanatic when it came to coal getting. He was making a reputation for himself so that he

336

could get a manager's job, the men reckoned, and that meant he was willing to take risks with other people's lives to send his output soaring.

Hywel swung his hammer and the wedge went right in. Yes, Tegydd was not the same man. Losing Dot had started the rot, but losing the woman he'd married and the baby she was carrying seemed to have knocked all the stuffing out of him. He'd gone round for days like the living dead, Ella had said, after the tragedy. Of course she'd gone back to the Plas to work when the new Mrs Tegydd died in childbirth; as much to look after the little boy as anything, she claimed, but it was not that, not really. Tegydd had sent the boy to his wife's people within a couple of weeks of her death. He had no time for him, he told Ella fretfully, and he put a big notice in the paper about the second Mrs Tegydd's death and an appeal to his daughter to return.

Hywel waited, sure that Dot would come. But she had not; perhaps she had not seen the notice or perhaps she was so busy and happy in her new life that she no longer wanted to come back.

The second wedge was hammered in and as he struck the last blow the coal fell. He stepped out of range. It was a good fall, and when it had stopped coming down he seized a shovel and he and the boy began to move the coal out of the stall and nearer to the tubs. Bent double like this they were nearer the gas, because gas, being heavier than air, was always thicker the lower you got. Dickie coughed and straightened to gasp some better air into his lungs for a moment.

'There's a lot of gas down here, mun.' Dickie sounded worried. 'Don't like it, me. Nor working in water, though there's no harm in that, I daresay.'

Hywel grunted. He did not like working in water either, but it was ankle deep in the stall and the more coal you got the more water, it seemed, replaced it. You had to scrabble around below the surface to get the last few pieces of the precious coal out, and that meant that when you were back on land again you would find your skin pitted with scars where the coal chips had flown deep into water-softened flesh. Even your clogs got slimy and unpleasant working in water, and of course your socks were sodden, if you wore such things. Dickie did not, being only fourteen, but he was a good 'un with the shovel and getting stronger every day. It was tough on him in one sense to work in such conditions, but on the other hand the coal was not hard to get and they were always pleased, at the end of each shift, by the number of tubs they had shifted. Apart from that, of course, the Wynd was a bad place to start a lad off, because he might think that the bad ways practised here were normal. Dickie, however, came from a mining family and knew very well that more care should be taken all round. Now he cleared his throat and went over to the tubs, pulling them near the big pile of coal which he and Hywel were building up.

'Start putting it into the tub, shall I? I wonder why the airways don't work as well here as they do in the Olwen? My da says the airways there take most of the foul air away. I told him they don't always check the lamps as we go off and he said to shut my mouth. Have you noticed that, Hywel?'

'Aye. Carelessness like that costs lives.'

It did, too. There was only one certain-sure way of telling which colliers were working on a given shift if something went wrong, and that was by going to the lamphouse and checking the lamps. If a man's lamp was missing then he was down; if it was hanging on its hook then he was at home. But Jarret did not think this was at all important and the manager, Frewin, was new and more involved with the books than with the men. In normal times, the men themselves would not have stood for it. They would have shown their disapproval by leaving the Wynd, and then someone would have started asking pertinent questions. But now, with almost every other pit on short time, men thought twice before moving from pit to pit as they once had. The money was good here, but more important the coal was a special sort. There had been no suggestion that the work force at the Wynd be cut — nor their hours, though at the Roland and the Olwen and other pits too the men were only doing a four-day week.

That was why Stan had moved here. He wanted to get married and he could not do so on a four-day week, so he had come up to the manager's office and obtained a job as hewer without any trouble at all. Hywel's work-sheet was enough to convince them that any relative of his was worth having, Stan had told his brothers, and that had more or less started the rot.

First Stan, then Luke, now Dewi. All strong men, all welcomed. And his mother blamed Hywel for enticing them away from the safe pits – not that he had had any say in it. She scarcely spoke to him now, slamming his meals on the table, putting his clean clothes up in his room without a word, never letting a murmur of thanks escape her when he handed his keep money over at the end of each week.

It upset Jessica, of course. She had tried reasoning with Ella, tried pointing out that Hywel had had no hand in what his older brothers did, and the only result had been that once Jessica was safe back in Cambridge again Ella had accused him of turning the girl against her.

'My only girl, dearer to me than any of you, and you tell lies about me, try to twist the truth . . .'

'I didn't tell anything or twist anything,' Hywel had said mildly. 'Jess saw how you are with me.'

'Oh yes, and why am I like that? Why, tell me that!'

'I don't know, Mam. I've never known.'

At that point, when Ella's voice had started to climb and Hywel had thought, apprehensively, that they were in for either pot-throwing or hysterics, his stepfather had intervened, a thing he rarely did, for Glyn, now that he was in his fifties, loved peace.

'Ella, if your older boys are such ninnies that they go on the word of a boy four years and more younger than they, you should be ashamed of the way you've brought them up. As for lies, Hywel has told none – I'd take my Bible oath on that. Jessica's my daughter. If I think she needs protecting I'll do it, I won't ask you to interfere.'

It had cut Ella to the quick, because she could not blaze back and call Jessica hers. She had flushed darkly, pinched her lips tight, flared her nostrils, and stalked out of the room.

Jessica was making it clearer and clearer that she wanted Hywel, which was one reason for Ella's cold dislike. All through Jessica's vacations she walked round, Mam did, wanting to stick a notice to Jess's head which read *Too good for a collier*, but because she could not do it she simply grew crosser and crosser, until it all came out in a fearful shouting and temper tantrum. Or had. Last time Jess was home, at Easter, Mam had appeared to notice for the first time that

Hywel was not encouraging the girl to throw herself at his head – quite the opposite. Not that this made the slightest difference to Jess, of course. She continued to wheedle and flirt and attach herself to him regardless of his insistence on their relationship. He had not gone to the May ball either last year or this, but he had not felt it incumbent upon him to stop taking her to the cinema and the theatre, or for river trips or long hikes; by this time he could see that he would be in the wrong with Ella whether he behaved well or ill, so he might as well behave naturally and enjoy Jessica's company without a nagging conscience.

Since she had gone back to college, though, he had twice taken one of the village girls to the cinema and once to a hop at the village hall, and he had written and told Jess what he had done. Best not let her think he must have his eye on her because he never took others out, he decided.

Today, before he came on shift, he had got her reply to his letter. *Doing well, our Hywel,* she had written. *Soon have you normal as the next. Don't think I mind you taking a girl or two out, because I'm glad you can enjoy yourself, man. But just remember I'm going to marry you, will you?*

Thinking about it now, he could not stop grinning. She had no shame, that was a fact, but she was a nice girl, one whose company could only give him pleasure. He had no intention of marrying her, but if that was how she wanted it there was nothing he could do, save to keep assuring her that he did not intend to marry anyone yet.

'The tub's full to the brim, Hywel, don't put no more on!' Dickie's voice, slightly alarmed, brought Hywel back to the present with a jolt; he had been about to add to the conical pile, when to do so would have led to a spectacular spill-over. He straightened, a hand going to his back.

'Fool that I am, Dickie, I was dreaming over it. Right you are, we'll have that one emptied. How many've we done?'

'More than we should,' Dickie said complacently. 'Think back, have an add.'

Hywel thought, then grinned in the flickering lamplight.

'Aye, we've shifted more than usual. Reckon we'll call it a day. Take these to the endless belt, and then we'll go have a word with Stan or one of your mates.' He rooted round and found his watch, staring at the tiny black figures. 'Damn, there's near two hours to go before the shift finishes.'

'We could go up the airway, get ourselves a drink and be home before the bell rings,' Dickie said longingly. 'Ever been out that way? I have, when you've not been here . . . when I've been on doors or ponies or something.'

'Through the *airway*?' It was not a route which men took; the airways were there strictly for ventilation purposes. When you thought about it, though, men had dug them, so there must be room for a man to pass in and out through them.

'Aye. There's one comes out above your village, nice and handy. Couldn't do it at most pits, of course, because of your lamp, but here where there's no check it's easy. You just walk in tomorrow morning with your lamp under your jacket, get it out as if you'd just taken it off the hook, and get into line for the cage. Simple.'

'Above my village, eh? But that isn't much use to you, Dickie.' Dickie lived further down the mountain.

'No, but I'll put you on the right road and then I'll go off the way that I use. Mine comes out further down. We'd best take these tubs up to the ponies first, though.'

'Right. I'll push, you pull.'

Hywel hung his lamp round his neck and began to push. It was hard work, for the tunnel was as steep as the side of a house and the tubs were both overflowing. Ahead of him he could hear Dickie grunting as he heaved. Damn it, where were the ponies? At least they had harness and could pull. They did not have to push, on their knees, as he did.

'How far to the ponies?' he called ahead. 'This is devilish!'

'Aye, it's about two hundred yards like this,' Dickie panted. 'Wicked steep, ain't it? No pony could keep a footing, see. That's why they don't start 'em down here.'

It took ten minutes of solid toil to reach the main road, where they fastened the tubs on to a line of others. A pony and a boy were waiting to haul them up to the endless belt.

'Right. Now let's find that airway,' Hywel decided as the boy and the line of tubs disappeared into the darkness. It would be no use returning to the pit bottom and declaring you had dug enough for one day. Hywel remembered horrified talk, years back, of a man getting badly mangled at the Wynd and being rushed to the pit's eye by his friends. The overman would not let the cage be used to take him up because they were carting tubs. Not until the end of the shift would the cage carry men, and by then it was too late and the injured man was dead. He would probably not have survived in any case, but the slender chance of life had been stolen from him by that overman's refusal to let him go up in the cage.

'Here we are.' The two of them had retraced their steps, but had not dived into the steep tunnel which led to Hywel's stall. Instead they took the main road until Dickie stopped by an airway. 'This one comes out where I said. See you to-morrow.'

'Right. Where's yours, then?'

'Oh, not far. I'll be home before you!'

Dickie disappeared and Hywel began, gingerly, to climb up the steep and narrow airway. It was unlit, of course, but so were most of the side roads, and although horridly steep the climb was well worth it when Hywel saw light ahead. Present-ly, bursting into the blue and green summer in a tiny copse high on the mountain, Hywel thought it quite the nicest thing about the Wynd, that escape route. When you were below you thought about what was above you all right, but you never really managed to get it sorted in your mind. Now, standing on the edge of the copse, he could see the village in the valley and Plas Tegydd above it. He was a five-minute downhill run from a hot bath and a meal!

He turned to take a last look at the airway from which he had emerged, and noticed how very clearly he was seeing everything. The hazel trees showed up sharply against the sky, the grass was emerald green. Turning again, he saw the village as someone's bright toy and Plas Tegydd as a newly painted castle, just finished, the weathercocks of purest gold, the roofs burning with brilliant colour.

He looked around carefully, sure that the fellow from the Other Place was with him and looking too, although he had not been conscious of the other presence whilst he was scrab-bling up the steep slope of the airway.

'So you're here, are you?' he said out loud. 'Interested? It's an airway. Leads all the way from the heart of the pit out above the village. Rather good, don't you think?'

But it was going, almost as if he had talked it away; the feeling of vision intensified left him, and for a moment he felt the lack as a great loneliness.

But that was foolish if you like, because he was used to being alone on the mountain, especially since Dot had left. So he began to whistle and to step out briskly, moving with sureness down the steep meadow in which he had found himself. Within a matter of minutes he was level with Plas Tegydd, looking, as he always did, to see if he could see Dot, though certain, as he always was, that she would not be there. After that he crossed the bridge and was in the village, a full hour before he should have been back. Glyn would be home because he had been on an early shift, but Ella would be up at the Plas and the other boys would, he supposed, still be working as well. They were all of them in a higher part of the mine where conditions were better but the coal was slower to come down, so they would need the extra time to dig in order to get the right number of tubs.

It was only moments before he was walking down the village street, and very odd it seemed to be alone there in the afternoon quiet, when normally he would have been tramping up the dusty road with his clog-clatter unnoticed among the noise made by a score or more other workers returning home.

He went up the path, opened the door, and grinned at Glyn, patiently peeling potatoes at the open window which overlooked the garden. Glyn grinned back and flourished the knife.

'Back early, eh? Well, I won't tell no tales. Or I won't if you give a hand here, any road.'

At about the same time that Hywel escaped into the sunshine, Tom Tegydd sat in his study at the Plas, tapping a pencil against his teeth and frowning over the figures spread before him on the desk. Not that he was thinking about them, for he was not. The Olwen and the Roland were holding their own and the Wynd was doing very well indeed. The terrible pain of loss which he had suffered had begun to ease after a year of inward mourning. Tom was not the man to wear his heart on his sleeve.

What worried him now was his own situation, here at the

343

Plas. He was not by nature a celibate and he had recently begun to long for a woman in his arms again. Not a wife, never that, not after Blanche, but just a woman. On the other hand, he was terrified that, if Ella and the rest of his staff discovered that he was using the services of the town whores, they would leave. That time before Blanche had moved in was a desolate memory still, as was the time directly after her death.

He had scarcely believed it when the doctor told him she was dead, and the newborn babe with her. She was so young to die! But young though she was she had taken his life and turned it into something valuable and precious and the fact that she was no longer with him had turned it back again into sackcloth and ashes. No, worse than that, because before he had met Blanche his life had been satisfactory enough. He had just not known it could be wonderful, every moment eagerly anticipated and enjoyed. And to go from that to less than nothing . . . it had seemed unendurable at the time and it was devilish hard still.

He would never forget her. He would never take another woman to his heart, though he fully intended to take one to his bed. Blanche would understand. She would realise that he wanted a woman in a perfectly normal and respectable sort of way, really. Only there did not seem any chance of getting one, so what to do?

Tap, tap, tap. The pencil bounced along his still strong teeth and Tom frowned and thought. If he was completely honest with himself, he did not really want a town whore in the slightest; might not even be able to take advantage of one if he had one! What he really wanted was a warm comfortable woman up here twenty-four hours out of the twenty-four, to see to the house and the housekeeping, to ensure that his shirts were darned and ironed. And washed. To talk to him, too, so a housekeeper would not do.

To go to bed with him? It would be nice, but . . . to his astonishment he discovered that the bed part was by no means essential. He wanted to be *wifed*, if there was such a word, without the necessity of any emotional husbandly response from him.

If only . . . if only what? If only Blanche had not died? If she had not died everything would be wonderful still, but she had and that was not going to be undone by wishing. If only Dot had not left? Yes, that was better. Dot could be brought back, if only he knew where the devil the girl had gone! He had tried advertisements in the press, he had even got an agency to search for her, but to no avail. She had disappeared as completely as if the earth had swallowed her up.

Tom laid his pencil down on the desk and put his head on his arms. God, he was lonely! If he had been an imaginative or sensitive man he might have put two and two together and thought about the loneliness he had forced on his youngest daughter. No parties, no dances, no meetings even, because he had not wanted the trouble of entertaining. Then, when she grew up, nothing but hard work on the estate – and ill she had been repaid for that hard work, by his unfortunately voiced determination to leave the estate to Tommy.

Tommy! The child had gone and he was glad of it. Blanche's parents had taken the boy willingly, for a large sum of Tegydd money was paid over each month and would be until the lad reached his majority. Blanche would have wanted to know her son was financially safe, but she had never approved of his avowed intention to disinherit Dot.

So what should he do? A housekeeper could be the answer. Oh, she would not be able to talk to him in the evenings, help him with the books, discuss the estate; that was what he wanted his Dot home for. But in other ways she could make his life a lot pleasanter. Tom drew a sheet of paper towards him and began to jot down a few ideas for an advertisement which would be placed in the *Leader* that very day. He would have to phrase it most carefully, but he was sure he could do it!

An hour later, his wastepaper basket brimming with failed efforts, he flung the pencil across the room and scowled at the sunny afternoon outside. What a life! It was impossible to put into words exactly what he was looking for without getting all the locals on his back again, preaching morality, having his name called in church and chapel, or so he understood, as an ungodly person.

He got to his feet and jerked at the bell-pull. Might as well have a cup of tea and a bit of cake whilst he thought. If only that wretched girl would remember her duty to him and come home!

*

345

'Do you want to feed the ducks, pet? Hop out, then, and throw some bread.'

Dot got a brown paper bag full of bits of stale bread out of her shopping basket and handed it to Paoletta. She helped her small daughter out of the pushchair and stood and watched as Paoletta dropped small pieces of dry bread at her own feet.

Throwing was plainly not Paoletta's strong point and presently, because the ducks were ignoring her so totally, Dot began to give her a hand, swinging the baby's arm rhythmically, letting go the piece of bread she held herself, until the ducks came quacking over and began to grab the food.

'There! All gone. Did you like that, pet?'

Paoletta nodded enthusiastically, with that look of total trust and happiness which only young children can wear. She was sixteen months old and although she could say Mumma and Dadda the rest of her chat was still at the gabble-gabble stage, when only someone as besotted as the Peruzzi family could have believed any of the words made sense.

She was not a pretty child, but Dot told herself that she could not have loved a pretty child the way she loved her daughter. Paoletta was not the possessor of a mass of curls, big blue eyes or pearly teeth; in fact teeth and hair were as yet thin on the ground, but her hair was very fine and would no doubt be a mop of black curls one day; and her teeth, all four of them, must doubtless multiply. She was a very thin little girl, too, with none of the delightful chubbiness of her contemporaries, but she had a charm all of her own which came from the appealing, three-cornered smile she gave when she was very happy and the way the big dark eyes, whilst staring at you, could be seen to be very slightly crossed. Why this should be attractive Dot had no idea; she just knew that it was so and was glad for her daughter's sake that she had charm. God knows I had little enough, she thought sadly, lifting Paoletta back into her pushchair and strapping her safely in. I could not even captivate my own parents, let alone strangers! Paoletta enslaved not only her doting mother and father, but her grandparents, the entire staff at the Royal Pavilion, and a host of others. Neighbours, friends, visiting tradesmen, all fell for the tiny, skinny little creature who always had something to say for herself, even if it was said in gibberish!

Dot had always had the unstinted love of her in-laws, but now she had their admiration as well, for had she not produced the most beautiful granddaughter in the world? And was she not about to produce another one? So small, Pappa Peruzzi had exclaimed when Carlo told them the news, but so prolific!

She and Carlo had decided that they must move out of the flat, and now they had a small house on Valentine Street. It had a tiny front garden, a respectable back one, and plenty of space for children to play, particularly now that the odd animal department, as Dot called it, had been moved on. Voluntarily, when they decided to take the new house, Carlo had offered to keep his animals elsewhere. He had a friend, it appeared, who had been abroad but was now back in Norwich. The friend had taken a house with a range of stabling at the back big enough to house all the odd animals, even Dobbin. Carlo could visit them daily, but they would no longer actually inhabit the same premises as the young Peruzzis.

Unfortunately, Dot did not like Carlo's dear friend Crispino. She found it difficult to be pleasant to him, for he came visiting so often and had a manner towards her, half patronising and half placatory, which she found hard to stomach. Furthermore, she had been mortally offended when he had been dining with them one day about two months ago. She had happened to mention the forthcoming event and, as it also happened, to be watching him at the time. When Carlo, seeing that Crispino had not fully understood the information, enlarged upon it, she had been privileged to see an expression compounded of horror and disgust flit across his face. It was not the sort of reaction she had expected and it struck her forcibly that she had not been meant to see it, for seconds later Crispino was crying out with astonished delight at the news that his friend was to be a father for the second time.

'Let us drink to the possibility of a son,' he cried, raising his wine glass. 'What could be nicer? Unless it was another daughter. Just like Paoletta, of course.'

'Ah, there could never be another like Paoletta,' Carlo assured his friend with fatherly prejudice. 'Paoletta is unique.'

Naturally Crispino agreed with this, but that did not lessen

Dot's dislike, and the emotion was fostered by the elder Peruzzis' attitude.

'Crispino is not a good influence on Carlo,' Rina Peruzzi told her daughter-in-law. 'Always we have trouble with Carlo when Crispino is about. They were the same as little boys — Crispino pushed Carlo to do what he dared not do himself. Bad, he is. Bad, bad.'

'Well, boring,' Dot admitted. 'I'll do my best to see they don't get up to any mischief together now, though.'

Sometimes she wondered just what the two young men could get up to, what with their respective occupations and Carlo's full married life, but nevertheless she did her best to see that Carlo was not thrown too often into Crispino's company.

'Mummummum . . .' chanted Paoletta, bouncing up and down on the seat of the pushchair and pointing with her forefinger at the yacht pond. 'Mummummumm . . .'

'Yes, that's right, darling, pretty boats. Does Paoletta want to stand on the edge of the basin and watch them sail round and round?' Paoletta managed to indicate, by bounce and gobbledegook, that she did indeed want to watch the yachts, so Dot lifted her out of the pushchair and balanced her on the concrete rim, careful to keep a tight hold of so precious a possession. They stood there for five minutes or so, a pretty picture had they but known it, Dot in her full pink cotton dress with her bobbed brown curls blown back by the breeze, and tiny Paoletta, in a paler shade of pink, with her fine hair in a plume on her head and her eyes sparkling with excitement. Then Dot lifted her down and, as she did so, felt the newest Peruzzi stir sleepily within her in his warm, pre-birth sleep. Oddly enough, feeling Paoletta's small body firm and strong in one arm and having the new baby's movements against the other reminded her that she was not the only member of her family with a baby. Blanche Tegydd would have a child about a year older than Paoletta, and she, too, might be pregnant again by now.

I wonder if she had a girl as well, Dot found herself thinking as she strapped Paoletta into her chair once more. I wonder if she's going to have another, as I am, and is as sure as I am that this next child will be a boy? Not that it mattered much, for all that was in prospect for a son of hers was eventually to take over the Royal Pavilion.

The honesty of this thought, coming unbidden into her mind, shocked her more than a little. Did she think, then, that a restaurant which had taken the family two decades to build up was not worthy of her son? The answer, of course, was that to Dot, even after three years away, only the land and its nurturing was a future worth fighting for. And she was sure that any son of hers would feel the same. Paoletta, dearly though she loved her, would never have to think like a boy, plan like a boy for the future. The very fact that she was so loved would save her from the fate that had been Dot's — Dot had grown to love the land because she had very little else on which to bestow the warmth of her affections. But a boy . . . naturally a boy would expect an inheritance other than a restaurant!

Thinking of Plas Tegydd was always dangerous. Now, as she walked, Dot found that she was thinking of a particular corner of the loft where the dusty hay lay thick and where, as a child, she had been wont to lie, looking up through the gaps in the tiles at the deep blue of the sky above, fascinated by the occasional glimpse of a swift's wing, or a tiny fragment of fluffy cloud, or a flying leaf, curled and brown, taking off from its parent-tree in autumn.

One day it had rained on her through that hole in the tiles; and it had been at that moment that her hopes and plans for the future had crystallised into real determination. I'll mend that hole when I'm grown up, she found herself thinking, and all the other holes in all the other roofs at Plas Tegydd. I shall mend them all!

It had seemed an ambition well worth the nurturing when she had been eight or so; it was still, in Dot's opinion, a sensible and good thing to want to spend your life doing.

'Mummummumm . . .'

Paoletta was pointing to a thin, gypsy-looking woman, standing by the swing boats, selling balloons. Dot wanted one nearly as badly as Paoletta did, so they walked over and purchased a fine red one, which Dot looped round her daughter's little thin wrist.

'There, darling, something for you to watch all the way home! Isn't that a lovely balloon?'

They set off once more and Dot found herself wondering

about other people at home. It was odd that she had never, until this afternoon, wondered about the others. Annie and Lizzie, Daisy and Jessica, Stan's quiet girlfriend Cerwen. Were any of them married? Did any of them have children? Suppose . . . suppose Jessica had married Hywel and was now the mother of his child?

It was such a shocking and painful thought that Dot stopped dead in her tracks. Paoletta, waving her wrist to see the balloon bob, turned and stared up into her mother's face. She began to talk, chattering wildly, bobbing the balloon more than ever, but her mother remained still, silent, staring into space.

Hywel, married, and the father of a child! He had everything, then; the land, the mountains, and what he wanted, for he would not have married Jess unless he was sure. A knot of sick longing, an ache of homesickness combined with a sudden sense of desolate loss, started in Dot's stomach. She had thought herself immune, saved from such feelings by Carlo's love and by the child, but it was not so. Perhaps she would love Hywel, and regret his loss, until the day she died. She knew she would always long for Plas Tegydd, but she hoped that domesticity and her husband's comforting presence would dull the ache in time. She had congratulated herself that already it was easing, but the truth was that she usually kept her mind in check, did not let it wander back to Wales and her one-time love.

All-time love. That was the trouble. She was not a person to simply forget and pass on. She was, in her fashion, faithful.

'Mumma!' Paoletta was bouncing nineteen to the dozen now. 'See, Mumma? Bawoon, bawoon!'

That brought Dot back to the present with a bump. She looked into the small face, full of uncritical, trusting love, and began to smile and take notice once more.

'Paoletta, you spoke! You clever, *clever* girl! Just you wait till Daddy hears this!' Dot broke into a trot, pushing the pram ahead of her. 'Daddy's best girl can talk just as well as Mummy can!'

When Stan and Hywel reached the pit a party of visitors was

about to go down, so they had to wait, standing uneasily by, whilst two ladies, looking rather ill-at-ease in bright blue overalls and white hats, and three men, looking only marginally more comfortable in their protective clothing, climbed into the cage.

'Who's them?' someone asked, but apart from the probably erroneous information that one was said to be a duchess and the other Lady something or other no one ventured a guess.

'Don't know why they wants to go below if they don't 'ave to,' one of the men remarked as the cage returned for them. 'Damned if I would, if I didn't have to. But at least our Tom isn't in the selling line. He's never sold a pit yet. Reckon he's showin' off all that mechanical stuff he's got down in Queen.'

'I wonder what they think of it?' Hywel said, as the men clambered into the cage and waited whilst the side was slotted into place ready for the descent. 'I wonder how it strikes 'em. Do you remember how you felt, Stan, first time down?'

'Aye. Not a thing you forget.' Stan, a man of few words, settled his back against the bar and then they had perforce to be silent as they whooshed horribly fast into the dark limbo, to arrive safely, clanging, at the pit bottom.

'You still on the stall near me?' Stan asked as the two of them headed for the main road. 'Have our snap together, then, shall we?'

'Right, we'll do that.' They were still walking upright, but would not be able to do so for long. Hywel paused for Dickie to catch up with them. 'Morning, Dickie.'

'Morning, Hywel.' Dickie had broadened out in the last year, Hywel thought. It was odd how it happened; one day just a kid and the next a chunky-shouldered youth, whose voice had settled comfortably into deepness. He would be hewing for himself in the not too distant future, but in the meantime they were a good team. Stan and Hywel hewed, Dickie and Prowler Jones shifted the coal and took the tubs up to the ponies, besides seeing that the stowers worked on their tunnels and did not just leave them to chance, for in a pit where the bosses' only preoccupation was getting the coal you had to look out for your own safety. Packing the walls with waste rock and keeping the ceiling up with pit-props was not a job that the hewers, fillers and drawers could do, not if they were to get the coal; that was the stower's work.

The men reached a side passage, considerably lower than the main they had been on until now, and one by one they entered it, wriggling through the first short bit on hands and knees, then rising to a crouch and walking doubled up, almost like men but probably more like apes. In front of them four more men who worked on the Brassy seam were chatting. One of them, old Fred, was telling a tale of some sort, so Hywel, Stan and the two fillers moved closer the better to hear it.

'What are you on about, Fred?' Stan asked, as they caught up. 'You telling us who those visitors are who went down in the cage before us?'

The little old man with his blue-pocked face and hairless scalp nodded, twinkling a grin at them.

'Aye. Won't send me round wi' parties now, not if they's wimmin along.'

'Why not? Come to think, you always used to take visitors. You had a nice line in chat, they reckoned in the offices.'

Fred chuckled. He had been at the Wynd for thirty years, which made him the longest serving collier there, for it had always been considered a pit that was good to leave when you could afford to do so.

'I was just tellin' Tucker here. Took a party down, see, a twelvemonth ago. It was all serene at first. Told 'em what the boss wanted me to tell 'em, took 'em where the boss wanted me to take 'em. Then one of 'em, very posh with a whinnying sorta voice, said, "That's what we were supposed to see, my good man, but what about all them other little 'oles, eh? What we've been a-passin' without so much as a peep? I'd like to see one of them." So of course I thought he'd only complain about me to the boss if I didn't give 'em a show, so I dived off down the next road I knew would hold 'em, and they follows, doesn't they, like so many rabbits down a burrow, with their lamps held anyways.'

'You'd stuck to the mains, the lighted roads, till then, I suppose?' Hywel could not help smiling at the thought of a visitor's being taken into a side road. 'I suppose they didn't appreciate your kindness?'

'I wouldn't say they were ungrateful, exactly, but I wanted 'em to get the atmosphere, see, so I told 'em to stop where they was and put their lamps on the floor by their feet – they was already stooped, they weren't small to start with – and then I said, "Now listen very careful, ladies and gents," and acourse they listened, thinking to hear machinery working, or birds singing for all I know. But we all know what they heard, lads!'

'Aye.' If you paused from your work you always heard it; the creaking, the dripping, the sudden inexplicable sharp little cracks, the mutterings.

'Well, I made 'em listen for a moment or two, till it began to get 'em – you know how it does.' The men nodded, a trifle shamefaced; they knew all right. When the earth talks a miner listens, for who knows what warning it may have for him? 'Aye, we all listen. And then I said to 'em, "Now you've heard what the miners hear; the earth, talking to us. She's quiet now, almost chatty like, just tellin' us not to irritate her, to go careful like. But if you're ever down at three or four in the morning, on the night shift, then you'll hear her wake. She has a different voice then, that warns you she's in a naggy, craggy kind o' humour. Then she don't whisper, like she's whisperin' now, she mutters and grumbles and turns over in her waking, and makes many a roof fall and a slide. Not a big, dangerous one, mostly, just a little'un, to remind us that we're trespassin', like. We're in her place and at her mercy." '

'Fancy talk,' Stan said, irritated at the hollow tone old Fred was using. 'What happened then, Fred? Did they tell on you to the boss?'

'Naw! Well, leastways, not then. But one of 'em fainted clean away, a big, broad feller with a 'tache what he'd spiked out wi' wax. I had to throw me bottle of tea in his face 'fore he'd come round.'

The men laughed and Fred chuckled squeakily.

'Aye, fainted clean away, big as he was. But what did for me was the cold tea, 'cos he felt he'd been made to look a fool in front of them wimmin what was with them. So I got called into the gaffer's office and he was a-laughin' away behind his hand when he thought I weren't lookin'. But he said, "No more takin' visitors round, Fred, you put the wind up 'em with your talk," and that was that. Not that I mind, seein' you good as lost a shift.'

'Aye, true. Best move on, then.'

The men made their way to their stalls and began work. Hywel started to size up the best way to attack the face, but whether it was old Fred's story which had made him uneasy, or whether it was something else, he felt a coldness at the back of his neck despite the heat. When the time came for a break he and Dickie made their way over to Stan's stall, sat down and got out their snap, and presently Stan and Prowler joined them. Prowler was a thin, pale man who looked as if he had outgrown his strength; he suffered from pimples and boils, which did not enhance his appearance. But he was a good deal stronger than he looked, and a quick wit and ready laugh made him popular with his fellow workers.

As Prowler opened his snap tin he glanced round, sniffed, then raised a brow at Hywel.

'Smell that? Gas again. And it was powerful warm in our stall, eh, Stan?'

'Think it was gobfire?' Hywel suggested. It was not unknown for the gob – the worked-out part of the mine – to burst into spontaneous combustion, and this could be extremely dangerous if it either exploded or managed to burn its way through to the present workings. However, Stan shook his head.

'No, there's too much gas about for that. If it was gobfire there'd be an explosion. Reckon it's just heat from being so deep. I hope.'

'Gas was bad on our last stall,' Hywel remembered. 'It isn't so bad where we are now, though. What about you, Davie?'

Davie and Clipper, his drawer, worked further yet down the narrow tunnel. Davie shrugged.

'Hot, it is, and the air bad. Always is in Candle Deep,' he said in his slow, heavy voice. 'When I gets 'ome I falls asleep in my dirt before the missus can get a meal on the table or the bath before the fire. Always so when you're working in bad air.'

'They ought to bring the canaries down, I'm thinking,' Dickie said uneasily. 'All them other tricks with a lighted

354

candle and so on are too dangerous. But a canary now . . .'

The men all knew that there were a dozen caged canaries behind the lamproom, but Stan shook his head.

'Which canaries, mun? Dead they've been these three months. The management just let 'em starve, poor little blighters. Old Frewin's too mean even to feed a little bird if it doesn't dig coal.'

The silence drew out as the men munched. Dickie broke it.

'Wish I hadn't come here! Me da talks about the Olwen often. Clever they are there, to see that no one comes to harm, or not more harm than's natural for a collier. But here they don't seem to care for owt but the getting.'

'Aye, but Olwen's on a four-day week,' Clipper reminded him. 'Can't tell when it'll go down to three. We get good money and plenty of hours here.'

'True. If we live to spend it.' Stan finished his food, clipped down the lid of his tin, and stood up. 'Come on, Prowler. Let's go to it.'

Hywel and Dickie got up as well. 'Aye, we'd best get on,' Hywel said, attaching his tin to his belt once more, where it was out of the way and left his hands free. 'Got another few tons to shift before we're off, eh, Dickie?'

Despite the break, however, Hywel's uneasiness persisted; in fact it grew. There *was* something today: an extra heat in the air, the smell of gas stronger than usual, the mutterings of the earth as she stirred more ominous.

Then there was Stan's remark about the canaries. Stan had not wanted to work in the Wynd, but he did want to get married and a young married man could not afford to work only three or four days a week. Of course Cerwyn was working too, saving up for her wedding, but when she stopped they would be dependent on Stan's money, and he wanted that to be regular. Because he had not wanted to come here, Stan seemed more observant than the rest. He saw and commented on the behaviour of shotfirers, overmen, enginemen . . . anyone who was in a position of trust and who, in Stan's opinion, abused it. Down the Wynd, Hywel realised, there were a great many people like that. And there was carelessness of course, because they knew that checking up would be minimal. Hywel himself had been given a nasty turn only a week or so back by one of the shotfirers. The man had come along to Hywel's new stall to start it off by placing some explosive and had completely ignored the strong smell of gas which Hywel commented on. The fellow pushed his explosive into a crack and lit the fuse, and then he, Hywel and Dickie had retreated to a safe distance. Hywel watched as the flame crept along, lit the explosive, and instead of merely igniting it ran twenty, thirty feet along the tunnel, brilliant blue and orange, roaring and screaming, making the passage, for thirty seconds, into a narrow mouth of fire. And then, as abruptly as it had come, it was out. Blackness remained.

'What in heaven's name . . .' Hywel had gasped and the shotfirer, pale beneath the grime, had looked guilty and sheepish.

'Didn't notice the crack ran right along, see, when I pushed 'ome the charge. Gas about, too. Probably coming in through that crack. So I lit the charge and it blew back. All right now, though. Dead's a doornail.'

'Aye, as the three of us might've been,' Hywel returned grimly, walking over to the stall. He remembered the faint, sulphuric smell of burned out gas and the overheated rock and the speed with which it had happened. If you had been further up the tunnel, where the flame had sped, you would not have stood a cat in hell's chance of escaping serious burns. It had leapt that twenty or thirty feet in a split second and Hywel had not been fooled by the brevity of it, either. Whilst it lasted that flame would have had the skin off you.

But the shotfirer was turning away, going off to get a hard piece of face down for someone else.

'Take care I do, as a rule. Freak conditions it was, see?'

Now, swinging his pick at the face, jarring his teeth in his head when he did not make sufficient allowance for the hardness of the rock, he wondered how long he should stay down here. Jessica wanted him out, she said, by the time she came home for good, at the end of the summer. That was impossible, though. Until he had saved enough he could not afford to leave the Wynd, and the chances of being taken on at another pit when they were working short time were almost nil. No, it would be a year or two – or three – yet.

If Dot had been here, of course, it would have been different.

He thought he would have accepted her offer of some of her money for a little place, but it would not have been just the money. The two of them working together could easily have made good on what he had saved. Jessica, charming though she was, would be useless on a farm or a smallholding – and anyway, he did not want to marry Jessica. It was true that he turned to her more and more, though, because he was so confoundedly lonely. Missing Dot, hating the work in the pit, seeing no future for himself but either grubbing beneath the earth or working alone on a farm, he had naturally turned to the girl who vowed so constantly that she was deep in love with him. Whether she was or not he had no means of knowing, but her friendship, at least, was precious to him.

At first Ella's stony-faced resentment about that friendship had worried him, but no longer. His attitude to his mother had subtly changed, almost without his realising it. He worked as hard or harder than his brothers and stepfather, he contributed as much to the household as any of them. He helped Stan in the garden, he gathered fruit and nuts when they were in season, he went out into the mountains and trapped rabbits, caught fish, worked in the hayfields at harvest and brought the money thus earned home. Yet he was not good enough for Jessica, not good enough for her heart's darling!

If Ella only knew it, she was almost prodding him into asking Jess to marry him, just to prove that he was capable of taking care of her. But he had not yet reached this point. He knew he did not love her and could hazard a guess that when she realised he intended to have that farm he talked of come hell or high water she would be deeply disappointed and probably very unhappy. She was a pretty thing; she enjoyed having people around, and compliments, and work for her mind. She would go mad, stuck away on a smallholding with only himself and the animals for company.

'Full tub, Hywel, mun. I'll just take this up to the main. Shan't be long.'

'Right. I'll fill the second one by the time you get back.'

Hywel leaned on his pick, watching Dickie out of sight, then he began to work once more, hitting in the wedges, choosing the precise spots where the coal seam was weakest and would respond best to his blows.

But his mind would not take time off; the minute he got into the rhythm of work his brain began to tease its present, most pressing problem. When Jessica finished with college and came home, he would have to make up his mind once and for all what their future was to be — whether they had a future, together. He might not be in love with her but he was attracted to her, and it was pretty tempting the way she damned near offered herself to him on a plate the moment they were alone! His mind toyed with the idea of tasting the fruit before he bought, but he banished such thoughts, horrified. It just went to show! Nain Pritchard had once let slip that Jessica's mother had been no better than she should be — in fact she'd called her a real little tart — so although Jessica was well brought up and knew better than to count herself cheap, there was in her sufficient of her mother to mean that she could not pass by the man she wanted without giving him the glad eye, brushing shoulders, knees or fingers, making it plain that she was available. Had it been possible, Hywel thought with a wry grin, a notice reading *I'm yours* would have lit up in her eyes every time she glanced in his direction. But since it was not possible, she merely used age-old feminine wiles to say exactly the same thing.

Dickie's return brought his mind back to the present again. He had got quite a pile of coal down. Now he turned and began to shovel it into the empty tub.

'Dickie, would you marry a girl you'd known all your life if you didn't think you loved her? Or would you wait on, in case either of you met someone else?'

'Jessica, d'you mean?' Dickie was sharper than most, Hywel reflected, or else he had not managed to keep the friendship quite the dark secret he had supposed. 'Oh, aye, she's a pretty girl, and clever too, like you, Hywel. But can she cook and keep house? I'm sure she'd satisfy you in other ways, mun. As for love, not too sure about that I am, never having been that way inclined.'

'I don't mind much about cooking; women learn once they marry, I suppose. Anyway, she'll be home soon enough, but we couldn't wed for a good few years, so she'd have plenty of time to learn household things. I don't reckon to marry for three years at least — possibly four.'

'I don't see your Jess waiting round for you that long,' Dickie said, again displaying amazing shrewdness. 'If she's made up her mind you've had it, mun. She'll truss you up and cuddle you down and before you know it you'll be married.'

They both laughed at that, and then settled down once more to the steady rhythm of their work.

Jessica had been so happy in Cambridge that the thought of leaving there, never to return, made her want to die. Well – she amended the thought, which seemed a trifle theatrical – it made her want to cry and hit out at someone. In fact the only way she could face leaving was by telling herself, and anyone else who would listen, that she and Hywel were going to become man and wife before many months had elapsed.

Marriage! Delicious anticipatory thrills ran all over her at the mere thought. Being in love with Hywel had cramped her style a bit at college, so she had only indulged in the very mildest forms of lovemaking, and this seemed unfair since when she went home Hywel showed no desire whatsoever to increase her experience. However, she was not ignorant of the meaning of marriage – or not very ignorant, anyway. It all sounded great fun and she was sure that, with the right partner, she would enjoy marriage even more than college. It was just getting Hywel to see this eminently sensible viewpoint that was proving difficult.

The train rattled through a tunnel, plunging the carriage into temporary darkness. Never mind. Every turn of the wheels brought her nearer home. Not that she could get straight home. Cross-country journeys were always bad, and she had at least three changes before she stepped out at the General and knew herself home for good. She had written to Hywel asking him to meet the train but she knew it depended on what shift he was working. If he could he would be there but if not then one of the others would be waiting. Perhaps Ella or, best of all, Glyn.

She adored her father. Next to Hywel I love him best in the world, she told herself now, gazing out at the summer countryside rushing past, the mysterious, hidden countryside that can only been seen from a train window. Woods, deep and thick, banks jewelled with wild flowers, ponds dreaming beneath the sun far from human habitation, rabbits grazing fearlessly, not even looking up as the monster roared past. They clattered over a level crossing and a child, fat fingers starfished in a wave, sunbonnet slipping over one ear, little socks disappearing into little sandals, waved violently. Jessica waved back and was whisked away, to see a pony, pretending panic, kicking up its heels and galloping away from them whilst cows grazed and chewed the cud and whisked flies away with their tails.

Very rural, Jessica thought, yawning. She was not attracted by nature, though she was sure it was very pretty, since everyone said so. Once, when she was small, the family had gone to Rhyl on a charabanc outing. They had gone round the shops, walked up and down the fascinating prom, spent their money in amusement arcades and eaten a lot of unsuitable food. They had also picnicked on the beach, had donkey rides, and gone round the harbour in a motor boat.

Hywel had scarcely seen them all day. He had rolled up his trouser legs and gone off, way down to where the sea glittered provocatively on the horizon, and had not returned until the charabanc had honked for him. He had scrambled aboard, dreamy, sandy, sun-kissed, with a handkerchief full of shells and pebbles and a mind so full of the wonders he had seen that he, silent Hywel, had not stopped talking all the way home.

He was a strange fellow, but she loved him so much! She knew of course that he had some absurd idea of buying a farm – who ever heard of a collier turned farmer? – but he had never experienced how exciting and delightful life in a town could be. Once he had seen for himself how stimulating and interesting one became in response to the challenge of living with intelligent people he would change, she was sure of it. It was not as though he were not intelligent himself. He was, even more so than she. At school he had been effortlessly at the top of the class in every subject and the teachers had wanted him to try for a scholarship, but Mam had been adamant that they needed the money he would bring in from the pits, and Hywel had not argued. Perhaps he felt he had had enough of school. He had simply left when he could and begun working.

She herself had been different; appalled by the boredom of

domestic work, horrified at the thought of working in a shop or above ground at the colliery, she had clamoured for the chance of a better education and, once installed at the convent, had worked feverishly to get her scholarship to Cambridge. Loving it had meant that her degree had come more easily, but even so she had worked very hard. She had entered into everything, too – had acted on the amateur student stage, sung in their choirs, debated in debating societies, flung her cap over the windmill during mass rag, made a fool of herself for charity, sold kisses at a summer fete for the local children's home. It had been a wonderful time, an unforgettable time, and she could not but regret its passing.

Yet she was going home, and would probably get a job somewhere in Denbighshire too; possibly even in the town, if it were offered. She was voluntarily returning to that stultifying miner's cottage in the narrow-minded little village where she had been born. Why? Why? No one else who had done well in college intended going home for a job. But since the job, if she got it, would be in town she would be able to get lodgings there, which would be preferable to going back to her cramped bedroom under the roof, to the overcrowded, noisy kitchen-life lived by everyone in the village.

She would not do it, of course, would not live away. If she did she would halve her chances of marrying Hywel. Her instincts were those of a hunter; she wanted Hywel and knew she could persuade him that he wanted her too far more effectively if they were living under the same roof. There would be opportunities . . . Ella worked up at the Plas most days, so there would undoubtedly be times when she and Hywel would be alone in the house, and then . . . who could tell?

Do you intend to trick him into marrying you? she asked herself, and smiled guiltily in answer. Of course she did, if that was the only way. She knew she could make him blissfully happy, so why let a little thing like the fellow's reluctance to commit himself come between them?

The train began to slow and Jessica dragged her mind reluctantly from a picture of herself in white floating down the aisle on Hywel's arm. Although of necessity limited by ignorance, the next scene of her fantasy – the bit where she

361

undressed in a hotel bedroom with a four-poster bed in the background whose green silk curtains provided a perfect foil for her red hair – could not be rushed. It needed time and quiet, and since this was the first of her changes and she would presently be jostled by farmers, schoolchildren and housewives in their rush to get off this train and on to the next, she would postpone the bedroom sequence until later. Anyway, she knew she should rethink the nightdress situation before indulging in that part of her daydream again. Something said by a college friend had led her to infer that nightdresses were not much worn on wedding nights. This was not only shocking, it seemed terribly basic and unromantic to Jessica; she had no objection to a goggle-eyed bridegroom's catching a glimpse of a rounded breast (in profile, she rather thought) or even the outline of a creamy thigh, but otherwise she intended to be shrouded not only in mystery but also in white lace. He would, she felt sure, appreciate what he suspected was there far more than what he could see with his own eyes.

At this point the slowing *tickety-boosh, tickety-boosh* of the train turned into a cross and cackling clatter as they ran over the points, and then came all the usual sounds of brakes being applied, steam screaming out, and the roar as they drew up between the small station buildings. Since she was alone in the carriage – though about to join a far busier train than this slow one from Norwich to Peterborough – she had to let down the window, open the door, and cart all her belongings down herself, standing them on the platform until the pile was complete, when she had to pick them all up again and stagger across to the other side where, presently, the next train would come fussily in. Because the train had not been full she had weighed the delights of solitary travel against masculine baggage carriers, and had opted for the former.

She did not have a long wait before the train approached, slowed, and finally drew in beside the platform. Jessica used her smile to persuade one of the farmers to heft her luggage on to the rack, sank into a corner seat, used her smile again, and then, despite the other people in the carriage, lapsed into dreaming once more.

'Alone at last,' the dream-Jessica breathed to the dream-Hywel. She was wearing a smart cream-coloured jacket with braided pockets and a straight skirt . . . no, that was wrong. She had seen a perfectly divine dress in a magazine which would do far better. She was wearing a lavender-coloured coat with dark fur collar and cuffs, and a little matching hat, pulled well forward, gave only an intriguing glimpse of her brilliant hair and pale, aristocratic face. I shall have got rid of my freckles by then, Jessica informed her conscience, which baulked somewhat at this description. Beneath the coat, which she proceeded to peel languidly off, was the special dress, with its box pleats, wide reveres and tiny patch pockets. It was in a dreamy shade of jade. It had short sleeves, showing off her perfect white arms, and round one wrist she wore . . . she wore the solid gold charm bracelet which Hywel had given her as a wedding gift.

She jangled the bracelet and gave Hywel a melting glance which was met by one of wonder spiced with lust. It made her feel quite hot, so she yawned, glanced at the bed and began to peel off the jacket . . .

Oh, confound it, I'm wearing a dress, Jessica reminded herself crossly. No one can peel off a dress seductively. You have to pull it over your head, showing underwear and silk stockings and things, and looking just like a rabbit being skinned. Hastily she replayed the film back to the moment when she stood in the palatial bedroom, the green silk bed-curtains framing her gleaming red hair, and took off the smart cream-coloured jacket . . .

PART THREE

Nineteen: 1925

Dot was watching for the postman. If anyone had noticed they might have thought it strange, for she had been married for four years and had never yet received a letter.

But this was soon to change, or so Dot hoped. With the birth of her son, christened Tommy for her father, who would never see him and would not care if he did, her longing for some connection, some link, with Plas Tegydd had been well nigh unendurable. And so, two weeks earlier, she had written to Jessica. She had addressed it to the village and had put 'please forward' on the envelope, just in case.

She said nothing to Carlo, partly because she had never told him anything about her family or friends but more because their relationship was not the thing of joy that it had been. Sometimes it was not even a relationship. They lived together but their lives scarcely touched.

She believed now that his initial affection for her had been no more than the feeling which made him pick up strays all over the city. He had seen her weeping, with the dirty little dog in her lap, and one half of his mind had seen her as a waif whilst the other half had noted the dog, known that he needed a wife, and decided that she would do.

He indignantly denied it, of course, was probably not even aware that he had taken such a decision, but the longer they were married the more Dot began to believe it. Also, he had been lonely. Crispino had gone to Italy, Carlo believed for good, and his loving parents had refused to have his animals anywhere near their beautiful home. One way and another Carlo, who had never thought of marriage, began to see the advantages of a wife.

When she put this viewpoint to Jane, however, Jane had

laughed and told her that in her opinion nine out of ten marriages took place not because the people concerned were really meant for each other, but because at the precise moment that they had crossed one another's path, each had been ready for marriage. To someone.

'You were the same,' she told Dot. 'You'd lost your job, you didn't know when you'd get another, and Carlo came along like a prince in a fairy tale. He was very good-looking, very kind, and he liked animals. Just at that moment you *needed* someone like Carlo, just as he needed you, so don't go thinking it was a marriage of convenience on one side only!'

Dot could see the truth of that. Yet now, after four years, acknowledging that there had been faults on both sides did not make up for the emptiness, the way the marriage limped rather than ran smoothly. It was not only Carlo's fault, but the fact that Crispino had become a third in everything they did had not helped Dot to be a better partner – quite the opposite. She resented his presence, and even more Carlo's absence when he and Crispino went off together. The fact that Crispino was apt to remark, 'Just like the old days!' with a malicious glance in her direction as he led Carlo away did not help matters. The old days, as far as Carlo and Crispino were concerned, were better forgotten, or so Mamma Peruzzi hinted when she and her daughter-in-law had a heart-to-heart.

Of course Mamma Peruzzi noticed that the atmosphere was sometimes strained, but she pretended nothing was wrong and made an even bigger fuss of her grandchildren than before. Tommy was not a bit like Paoletta but he was very like Dot. Small, dark and ugly, he lay in his cot, scowling when he had a dirty nappy, a tummy ache or a tooth coming through. The rest of the time he smiled, a wicked, gummy grin which made Dot's heart ache with love for him.

She had mentioned to Carlo that she did not think Crispino's constant presence was good for their marriage and he had flown into one of his rare rages, shouting that he had known Cris all his life and did not intend to turn him away just because she was jealous.

'I give time to my work, to my animals, to my friend and to my wife and family. That should be enough,' he had shouted.

'Bedtime's the only time you give to me,' Dot screamed

back. 'That's the only way I interest you now!'

She had written to Jessica because she wanted a link with home. She had friends here, good ones too, and she had had few enough friends in Wales. She had barely met Jessica before her flight, but even so it was to Jessica that she wrote. Who else was there, when it came down to it? Her sisters had more or less severed their connections with Plas Tegydd when they married and left, and she had a shrewd suspicion that they would not approve of their father's second marriage. Never mind that it made him comfortable, gave him someone to care for him. They would not think of that. They would think of their consequence, the awkwardness of having a half-brother younger than their own children, and they would draw further and further away from Tom. Anyway, she had never much liked either sister, when it came down to it, so why should she appeal to them now?

But Jessica was not only a link with home, she was a link with Hywel. It had worried Dot that she must give away her married state, because she felt obscurely ashamed by what she had done, which was absolutely ridiculous however you looked at it. Hywel had not wanted her. He must have been pleased when she obeyed him and went away, so why on earth should she feel that she had been disloyal by marrying and producing children? Yet the feeling persisted, and in the end, though her letter was friendly, she gave Jessica far fewer details than she would have done had she not visualised Hywel reading it.

This morning Dot was quite busy about the house. Carlo was coming home to lunch, a thing he did not always do, and she intended to make him a hot meal in another desperate attempt to set things right between them. Naturally, just as she was in the middle of rolling out pastry and cooking the meat for his favourite steak and kidney pie, Tommy began to grizzle and then to bellow. Dot swore, washed her hands clean of the flour and fat and plucked Tommy forth. As she had guessed, he was dirty, and she had him laid out on the kitchen table like a small fat turkey ready for stuffing when the letter-box clicked once. Since Carlo received very little post at home, she was sure that it had to be from Jessica. Unable to bear waiting, she whisked her son up from his undignified position into one scarcely better, and rushed to the front door.

It lay on the mat. *Mrs Dorothy Peruzzi*, it said on the light blue envelope in neat, slightly sloping handwriting.

She bent and picked up the letter. Tommy muttered, hiccuped and began to wail. Contrite, she returned to the kitchen, propped the letter on the dresser, and began, with the speed and ease of long practice, to wash the baby's small bottom, to dry him, to talcum him, and then to wrap him neatly in a clean, warm nappy. He was all done up and about to be returned to his pram when she remembered she had not used cream; and she had been about to put him back in the pram without his stout rubberized knickers.

Dot and Tommy returned to the kitchen. Taking a deep breath, she began all over again, and presently, despite secret fears that it would take for ever, Tommy was clean, clad and quiet and she was opening the blue envelope.

It was, she saw with pleasure, a long letter. That was nice, because her letter to Jess had been pretty short. She skipped through the pages, still not reading but only counting. Seven! Not bad. Jessica had nice small writing, though it was clear enough. Dot went out of the kitchen and turned left into the high-ceilinged living room. Sitting down on the sofa, she leaned back and began to read.

It began with news of Jessica's own life at Cambridge, what she was doing now – which was teaching at the convent school in town – how she enjoyed it, and a little about the children in her care, and then it grew more personal.

> *Hywel and I are determined to marry, though Mam is unhappy about it and makes us miserable by pretending it's immoral. We think we'll marry before Christmas, though Hywel teases me by trying to say spring weddings are prettiest. I want the Christmas wedding so we can get into a little house and be all cosy for the winter.*

Dot laid the letter down on her knee for a moment. Funny how her hand was trembling. It must be the thrill of having a letter from the village after all these years. It could not be shock because Hywel was going to marry her friend. She had known Hywel would marry one day, and that Jessica wanted him. Considering she was married herself she could scarcely grudge

Jessica her lover. She stilled her fingers and, when she felt a little calmer, picked up the letter and read on.

Mam's up at the Plas again, working for Mr Tegydd. Did you know she stopped for a while after you went off? She said he'd driven you away with his carryings on! But after the poor thing died, Mam said to let bygones be bygones and they went back to work – Mam and Annie and Daisy, that is. Lizzie couldn't. She's got a dear little baby now. No husband, of course. [Why not? wondered Dot.] *They miss you dreadfully up at the Plas. You ought to let your da know you're alive and well, but I won't say anything unless you ask me to.*

There was not a lot more: idle chat about a little house she'd seen, a story about the school Nativity play, an aside about another teacher who had as good as made a pass at her. Then heaps of love from her friend Jess, three crosses and a post-script.

Don't let it be four years again before you get in touch, Jess had written.

Dot laid the letter down and looked around her drawing room. She was so lucky. She had so much! The baby asleep in the crook of her arm, the Persian rug Carlo had given her, the cut glass bowl full of oranges and grapes, lit, at this moment, by slanting rays of sunlight so that it sparkled and shone, beautifying the window embrasure in which it stood.

There was love here, too. The volumes in the bookcase had been specially chosen and were all Dot's favourites; the oil painting above the fireplace was a mountainous view so that she should have something of her own place about her. Even the curtains, rich dark blue velvet, had been chosen by her.

So what a fool she was to cry just because she could no longer dream of a homecoming which included a reconciliation with Hywel! Absurd to think even for a moment of throwing this away. Carlo had loved her once, and if only she could view his friendship with Crispino with a little more complaisance would probably do so again. Their estrangement had as much to do with her as with him, partly because she had never, in her heart, got over loving Hywel. So in a sense it was doubly unfair that she should expect Carlo to give

371

Crispino up when she would not – could not – tear Hywel from her heart.

Presently, Dot picked up the letter again, a slight frown on her brow. What was that bit about the poor thing dying? She read it over, then laid the page down again the better to think. Ella had left the house because of Father marrying Blanche, that was clear enough; that was what Ella had called his 'carryings on'. Yet she had gone back there to work after 'the poor thing died'. It had to be Blanche. She must have died in childbirth. How absolutely awful for Father, to say nothing of little Tommy.

She felt tears slide down her cheeks and moved her head so that they should not fall on Tommy – her Tommy. But with Blanche gone and the baby, poor little thing, on his hands, surely her father must need her dreadfully badly? She looked again at the letter. There was no mention of the baby, so it was possible that it had not lived either. If that was so, then Dot thought she really should go home. Oh, not for good. She could not do that to Carlo or her in-laws. Just for a short stay, to help sort things out.

Just to see how the land lies, you mean, her more honest self reminded her. Just to see what the chances of inheriting would be now. She did not think her father would let the place be passed down to Tommy Edenthorpe, but she could be mistaken. Surely, now, Tommy would inherit the pits? Especially if he was being the prop of her father's old age and showing an interest in things.

The letter came in for another perusal, but this time she drew a blank. There was nothing in the mild, gossipy sentences to indicate that her father was missing her. *They miss you dreadfully up at the Plas* would seem to indicate that it was the staff and the farm workers more than her father.

There was, of course, one way to find out exactly what was happening and what would be happening in the future. She could write again to Jessica and ask. Dot stood up cautiously and Tommy grunted and butted her with his round, hard little head. She stayed very still, however, and presently the baby sank into deep sleep once more. He had had a bad night, and though he was usually a difficult baby, slow to sleep and quick to shout, he was obviously feeling the effects of his earlier wakefulness, for when she moved slowly across the room and began to mount the stairs he gave no more than a sleepy mutter.

The lowering of the baby into the cot was a bit tricky, but Tommy slumbered on, never even stirring when she pulled the covers over him. She tiptoed downstairs, went into the study where she and Carlo shared a small desk, sat down and pulled a sheet of paper towards her.

Presently, mind made up, she tested the pen on the blotter, squared her elbows, and began to write.

Jessica was surprised and delighted to find her letter answered so promptly, and so fully, as well. The first letter from Dot had been no more than a note, simply saying that she was well and living in Norwich in a dear little house. She mentioned a baby but said nothing about her husband from which Jessica had, not unnaturally, concluded that there wasn't one.

However, the second letter was longer and much more detailed. She had not merely used the name Peruzzi to disguise her unmarried state, she was married to Carlo Peruzzi. She seemed to be having a lovely sort of life. It came over in the letter as all sunshine in the park, meals out at a fabulous restaurant owned by her in-laws, and theatre visits.

There were descriptions of various local places which Dot obviously thought would interest her friend, descriptions of her son and daughter (Gracious! Two children!) which Jessica skipped, and an interesting bit about a new play she had seen and an exciting film at the local cinema. There were some questions thrown in, as well. Had Mr Tegydd mentioned his missing daughter? How did Jessica think Dot would be received if she came back for a visit? How was Father coping with Tommy, and must she suppose that the baby her father's second wife had been expecting had died at birth? She was very sorry, but would not write to Father since it was far too late to express condolences, though she did think she would try to come up for a short visit.

Jessica could be heedless, and thoughtless too, but she was a good friend and she was fond of Dot, even at a distance and with so much lost time between them. However, she did not think it a good idea to write back at once; better wait until she had some news of her own to impart. Having boasted about marrying before Christmas it would be as well to get some sort of date out of Hywel, or she might be made to look a fool. In her heart she had not thought that Dot would write again, but now that she had Jessica would do her best to have some exciting news to impart when she next wrote.

She took another look at the letter, however, and decided that part of it at least called for a prompt answer. She found a coloured postcard of the church in the town and wrote briefly on the back, then dispatched it. *Everyone will be thrilled if you come for a visit*, she said. *I didn't know about the baby. Who is Tommy? Will write soon. Your loving Jess.*

As for the letter, Jessica thought about telling Hywel or Ella that Dot was fine and had written to her, and then remembered that Dot had not given her permission to do so. Instead, she put the letter right at the back of her underwear drawer and forgot all about it.

'Trouble with this time of year is not seeing daylight 'cept at weekends,' grumbled Stan as he and Hywel let themselves out of the house and went round the back for their bicycles. When you worked at the Wynd it was not sensible to walk to work. With a bicycle, though coming home was hard uphill slog, going was great; you just coasted most of the time, with your feet out of harm's way and the pedals going round like windmills in a gale.

Stan had been married a month now and the cottage, not far up the road from his old home, was beginning to look very homely. Because Cerwyn was still working, Stan always let himself quietly out of the house and came round to his mam's place for breakfast and a chat. Cerwyn caught a bus into town now, having a job at the same school as Jessica, so though she would get up during holiday times and see Stan off, during termtimes she slept on, scurrying off to work herself with no more than a cup of tea inside her, for it was not worth while lighting the fire when they were both out all morning.

The management of the Wynd rarely met with the Fletcher boys' approval, but it was easy-going about shift changes provided the right number of men were working when it needed them. Everyone had been asked to take a cut in pay because coal was not as quick to sell as it had been, but the Wynd had taken the smallest cut of any local pit and the men were still working a six-day week. Part of the reason for the willingness to allow men to choose their shifts, Hywel thought, was the steady drift of men away from the mine. And there was the absentee problem. With rules so lax and accidents correspondingly common the men, superstitious as a breed, had become more and more uneasy. They took notice of any tiny sign that this might be the day the Wynd had the big one. Tegydd's interest in the pit had waned to the point where the management did as it wished and the owner merely drew the money. Sometimes Hywel wondered if Tom Tegydd knew what went on, but it did not signify; if he knew he did not act, and things went from bad to worse.

However, Hywel was hoping to be out of it by summer. In his bank in town nestled very nearly enough money to buy that smallholding. After Christmas he would begin putting feelers out, discover what was available and what sort of price was likely to be asked. It was a good time to buy. Farmers were going bankrupt all over the country and land was as cheap as it was ever likely to be, yet folk were still reluctant to purchase. They were afraid of competition from the cheap beef, lamb and pork which was being imported from the continent and the colonies, but Hywel was sure he could cope with it. However, he would go on working at the pit until the smallholding was actually his, and any extra money he earned would go towards stock, seed and implements.

Cycling along in the dark, Hywel let his mind dwell fondly on the year to come. 1926 would see him a farmer and a free man, no longer tied to the colliery and life underground. It was a thought which had kept him going ever since Dot left, had saved him from despair when he had begun to realise she was not going to come home.

'What've you bought our mam for Christmas, Hywel? Cerwyn chose a lovely coat and mittens. Real nice – wait till you see 'em. Of course it's easier for her to buy stuff than me, now she's in town, with Jess. You doing your own shopping this year, or is Jess getting stuff for you?'

'Oh, I'll get Mam something in a day or two.' Hywel was aware, suddenly, that he did not want Jessica to do his shopping for him; time enough for that if she did ever manage to drag him to the altar. He was a bit shocked to find that he had such thoughts. The girl was taking it for granted that they would marry, and he had done little enough to dissuade her. Besides, he was fond of her. It was not as if there had been any word from Dot. He knew there had been none, because Ella had mentioned that Tegydd was always asking, casual-like, if anyone had seen or heard from her. Even strangers got the tale. You had to hand it to Tegydd. The story did not show him in a good light yet he was quite prepared to tell it, to admit that his girl had run away, just to try to get news of her.

They reached the foot of the mountain and turned up a rutted track, a short cut to the colliery. Talking was difficult here because of the rough terrain, so they bumped along for a moment in silence before reaching the better surface of the real road once more.

'A day or two? There's only three shopping days left, mun. Better let Jess get 'em. You could give her a list. That's what I used to do before Cerwyn and me got hitched.'

'I could, I suppose, only . . .'

'Look, mun, if you think it'll give her ideas you're barking up the wrong tree, because she's got 'em already. Are you going to pop the question or has she already asked you? If so, I'm damned if I know what you said, you're acting so coy!'

'Asks me every second day, but I never give a straight answer. It isn't that I'm not fond of her. But marriage is a bit different. Not sure if I want to marry at all, see?'

'There's no one else, though,' Stan observed as they swung through the colliery gates. 'Never seen you take much notice of any other girl.' The whites of his eyes glinted as he looked sideways at his younger brother. 'Well, unless you count little Dot Tegydd, years ago. Had a feeling, I did, then, that you liked her.'

Hywel felt most peculiar, partly as if someone had pulled the skin off him and exposed the most sensitive nerve in his whole body and partly as if a burden had been lifted from his shoulders. As they swung off their bicycles and chained them beneath the shelter, he turned to grin at Stan.

'I've never told a soul how I felt about young Dot, not even her. But I liked her a lot. If she hadn't run off . . .'

'Aye, I wondered about that, too. No reason for her to run off, was there, mun? No reason that involved you, I mean?'

Hywel did not misunderstand him. He shook his head positively. 'No, nothing like that. Only a kid she seemed, see. We'd talked a lot about marriage but it was all tied up with me wanting a smallholding and it got to sound more like a partnership than a marriage. She wanted us to have the smallholding together, and that would have meant marriage for sure, in a place like this. The trouble was she wanted to buy it with the money her mam left her, before I'd got my share saved. Yes, and she came and met me out of the colliery one day, all in my dirt I was, and asked me straight out if I'd buy a place, or even rent it, and marry her then and there. I told her you have to have permission to marry girls who aren't twenty-one, and anyway she'd done nothing, met no one. All she knew was me, a collier, and she'd known me since we were both kids. So I said go to your sister for a few months, meet your own class, and if you feel the same at the end of it we'll talk again about marrying. That night she ran away.'

'Phew!' Stan whistled softly into the darkness. 'Not your fault though, mun. I've heard Mam say it was that same day she found that her da had taken her inheritance – stole it, I'd call it – without her say-so and put it all into the Wynd. No wonder she ran off!'

They were walking towards the line of men waiting for their lamps, but Hywel stopped and stared at his brother.

'Took her inheritance? That can't be right. She offered it me to buy a place. She pressed me to take it and get something right away.'

'Aye, that sounds what she would do. She must've been desperate, see, to get away from her da, after she found out what he'd done and that he was bringing a wife and a kid home. Mam says Tegydd told her that same day that he was disinheriting her, leaving her out altogether, quite apart from having taken her mam's money. You were her last hope of staying, in a way. If you'd agreed in principle, see, it's my bet she'd have persuaded you to rent and then come out with the truth. She knew you pretty well. She'd know you wouldn't agree to marry her unless you genuinely wanted to.'

'You mean . . . she did say something about renting . . . I wouldn't, I told her it was too soon . . . ' He groaned, putting his hand over his eyes for a moment. 'Duw, why didn't she tell me she'd no money? I'd have rented a place – she could have moved in whilst I saved . . . '

'Yes, but she'd never have known if that was pity, would she? She believed herself to be a pauper . . . well, she was, pretty well. So she couldn't trick you into helping – no, not trick, but persuade you into it – by letting you know what had happened.'

Hywel groaned again; it seemed to come deep from within him, from a part of him that was sore and raw now with the knowledge of what he had done to her years ago and could not, now, undo. Unless he could find her? He had always been sure she loved him, but had thought it the result of ignorance, of simply not knowing anyone else. Now he thought that love does not happen like that. It isn't such a surface affection. Or Dot's had not been. She had loved him truly, as he loved her. She would have waited for him had he given her the slightest encouragement to do so. He took a lamp from the fireman without a glance at it and stepped into the cage, eyes unfocused, mind so deeply engaged in thought that he scarcely noticed where he was.

God, but he had let her down! It had not been his fault – he had not known what had happened – but he would give anything, right now, to be able to live those few minutes again. But of course no one could re-live the past, undo the harm done. You might do your best, but it would leave a scar – and he could not even do his best.

The cage began its descent; it could not have dropped faster or further than Hywel's heart.

'Nearly didn't turn in today, you know.'

Dickie, eating his snap, addressed Hywel through a mouthful of beef sandwich. Hywel, grinning, took a swig of cold tea before replying.

'Oh, no? And why not this time? Was it just the holiday getting so close, or some other reason?'

'What, Christmas? No, as a matter of fact . . . '

Dickie was off; another story of wildly circumstantial happenings, in this case apparently centring round an owl out after prey which had barely missed Dickie's left ear as he came in through the colliery gates. Hywel, chewing a bacon butty, nodded at intervals and winked at Stan, also solidly eating. Dickie was a good lad and seldom missed a shift, but he was always on about missing, as though it were a dream he could not, as yet, afford to put into practice. He had told Hywel several times that the moment Hywel wanted a farm worker Dickie would apply for the post. 'Strong I am, and handy,' he had said. 'A good deal worse you could do, mun, for your land.'

He could do with some open-air life, too, could Dickie, Hywel thought now, for though the boy was strong he was also pasty-pale. When Hywel was off work he went into the countryside and got fresh air in his lungs and colour in his skin, but when Dickie was off he went into town with his mates, to the cinema, or to the pub. Hywel liked the lad, but could not see him working on a farm, especially with wages as low as they were, and almost no employment in winter.

Dickie's story came to its dramatic conclusion and it was time to finish their snap. Tins were closed, bottles corked, and the men began to disperse, though slowly, for no one was in a hurry to get back to their work so near Christmas.

'There's a funny old smell,' Stan remarked as he and Hywel and their lads walked along the narrowing seam. 'Sulphur – something like that. Smell it?'

Hywel sniffed and admitted that there was an odd smell.

'Probably Dickie's feet,' Prowler joked. 'Hywel says they smell like hell, and hell smells of sulphur, I'm told.'

'Oh, aye? And who d'you know who's been to hell?' jeered Dickie over his shoulder as he and Hywel made for their own stall. 'Half your family's going, I know *that*, but which one's been there and back to report, eh, mun?'

It was then that they heard the noise. Deep and far off, a growling, rumbling roar which did not stop or quieten but increased in intensity until the men could scarcely bear it, could not hear each other speak, could only stare round them, waiting for some sign of what was happening.

Hywel wanted to run but he restrained himself and grabbed Dickie's arm. No point in rushing off in the direction which might well prove to be the most dangerous; much better wait and see. His hair was erect on his head, his body wet with the sweat of terror, but despite this he stood still and compelled Dickie to do the same, both with lamps held high so that they could see whence the danger would come.

The lamps were not needed; Hywel heard or perhaps felt Dickie's scream, saw his pointing finger. The boy was shouting that they must run, he could read his lips, but neither of them moved. Ten feet further along the tunnel there was a brilliant line of light, just as if a long crack of fluorescence had appeared against the dark.

It happened in slow motion; the tunnel wall bulged out and out, the brilliant light grew brighter and brighter. He and Dickie were still rooted to the spot when the wall gave, and the light engulfed them.

Stan saw the rat before the noise began. He and Prowler had reached their stall, and when he picked up his hammer and a wedge, there, sheltering behind it, was a big grandaddy rat. In the lamplight it looked enormous, with a ginger ruff and the quick, beady eyes of its kind. But what made Stan go cold was that it took not the slightest notice of them. It seemed unaware that it was watched, and before either man could move it had reared up on its back legs and put its head on one side, like a circus dog begging for scraps — or someone listening to a sound, far off.

'What the hell . . . '

Stan backed out of the stall, pushing Prowler behind him. There was something uncanny about the rat's indifference to them, its intentness on something they could not see, which appeared to completely override its normal fear of man.

Then they heard the rumble . . . and even as it reached their ears the rat darted past them and headed down the tunnel.

'Follow it!' Stan yelled to Prowler above the increasing din. 'Follow it, mun! Reckon it knows where the trouble's coming from. Shift yourself!'

They flew along the tunnel, the roar increasing like an

express train behind them, but at the first bend Stan, like Lot's wife, glanced back. Behind them the tunnel was a mass of flame. Hot air, smelling of sulphur, stung his eyes and invaded his nostrils. He hesitated, tried to turn back and was hauled on by Prowler.

'Come *on*, mun! Don't want to roast, do you?'

But he had to drag Stan another ten or twelve feet before Stan saw the uselessness of turning back. They ran together, bent double, along the passage and Stan's heart hammered out the words that he was saying aloud, though the din was so great that no one could have heard a word.

'My brother's back there! My little brother's back there!'

Glyn, working down the Olwen, heard the explosion as he finished his snap, though the pits were four miles apart. They had never been connected, though it was probably still Tegydd's intention to do so one day. He and his stepson Luke were on the same shift, for Luke had recently left the Wynd, and both stared around, thinking that a disaster was about to descend on them, so loud was the noise.

'Better get to the pit's eye,' Glyn roared, and set a sharp pace. All over the mine men were hurrying to get back to the cage and in the main roads they met others, who had been working in different seams.

'Yours?'

'No, God be thanked. Yours?'

Heads were shaken. Glyn suggested that it might be the Roland, and they put on more speed, for they could not do anything until they reached the pit bottom and could telephone the offices to find out what had happened.

The men crowded to the pit bottom and the cage was brought down. No one knew what had happened nor where, but most thought it unlikely that the Roland had been affected. A skinny lad, dancing on tiptoes with anxiety, came nearest.

'Could it be the Wynd? Me da's there. He says there's gas, but they use naked lights. The men aren't searched for matches, and some of 'em light up a pipe after their snap. Could it be the Wynd?'

He was comforted and hushed: it was most unlikely; the

Wynd was a long way off; not to worry, it was probably an almighty great fall in one of the gob tunnels, a worked-out tunnel which had been sealed off. Sometimes fires started in such tunnels and could be a nuisance; this one might have blown its seal, which would account for the noise. The boy's voice quieted but his eyes showed the whites around the irises. He pushed his way to the cage, his shrill voice rising above the mutter of the mature men.

'Could it be the Wynd? Me da's there – me da's there!'

Ella knew it was the Wynd before most of the village. The villagers hurried to the Olwen and the Roland, met men streaming up, and were told, then, that it was not at either pit; but Ella was at the Plas and she answered the door to the man who had come up from the Wynd.

'Where's Tom?' he said, his breathing heavy, his face scarlet with exertion, but before she could tell him that *Mr Tegydd* was in the study he had pushed past her, pounded across the marble tiles, and shot the door open without, Ella noticed disapprovingly, so much as a knock.

'There's been a bad 'un at the Wynd,' the man said. He spoke very thickly and fast, so that the words all ran into each other. 'Down Candle Deep. Probably gas, but there's fire now. Can you come?'

Tom had been sitting at his desk reading, a far cry from the days when the only books he ever read were account books. He had a pair of glasses on his nose, and pushed them down to stare at his unexpected visitor over the top.

'At the Wynd? Oh, my God! How many are hurt? How did you get here?'

'Don't know. Gilligan dropped me at the drive-end. He's gone right back – said I was to bring you at all costs.'

Ella stood in the doorway, white to the lips, as the men pushed past her. So it had not been thunder, that roar she had heard earlier! She followed the two men, saw Tom snatch his coat, and reached for the nearest though it was none of hers. She had a boy down the pit. Her eldest son was down the Wynd. She had to get out of here right now and go there. Possibly the owner would offer her a lift. He turned and saw her, and surprisingly reached out and squeezed her hand.

'Take Ella with you — she's got family who work there. Get the trap put to — I'll take Hotspur and go cross-country.'

Ella, in her borrowed coat, was in the stableyard before she remembered that Stan was a married man now. His wife should be told. Yet was there any point in going all the way down into town and worrying Cerwyn stiff if Stan was alive and well? True, he worked down Candle Deep, which was where the explosion had happened, but that did not mean to say he was among the trapped or injured. If there were any. But she did not doubt it, not in her heart. That rumble would have been ominous enough coming from the Olwen or the Roland, but to hear the explosion in a pit a good four miles further away . . . well, it was not to be taken lightly.

So she rode down to the colliery in the trap with the messenger, and it was not until she climbed down and went to join the watchers round the winding house that she remembered she had another son, who worked at the Wynd too and was down there as well, in Candle Deep.

Huw was at the Christmas fatstock show. He had spent more money than he should have done on a young bull he hoped he would give him some decent calves next year, but he could not go home yet. Helen worked in the city now, and he would take her back with him when he went. She did not finish work until after five, however, so he planned to go to the cinema this afternoon and see *Huckleberry Finn*. He had enjoyed all the Mark Twain books as a lad, he had enjoyed the *Tom Sawyer* film, and he expected to enjoy this one too, but fearing to be thought childish he would go by himself and only mention it to Helen if she asked.

At just after eleven he decided to go into the Bell for a drink and a sandwich, and then he would arrange with the bull's owner for the animal's transport back to the marshes. He was standing at the crowded bar waiting to be served when the bar-room wavered and vanished and he was in the colliery, where the Other Feller worked. As he looked round him he saw the side of the tunnel bulge, the crack appear, running faster than light as far as the eye could see, and then his whole vision was filled with flames. He could feel them hot on his face, even, as he could feel the sweat of fear drying on him and the vomit of cold terror rising in his gut.

He must have fallen. Someone was helping him to his feet, taking him over to a settle, sitting him down. It was all right. He was back in the pub; there was even a pint of ale in his hand. But he was still shuddering all over. He must get home, back to the marshes! A terrible thing was happening to the Other Feller . . . to him . . . to them both? But even as he wondered he knew that it was happening to him, to him, to *him*! He did not understand what was happening, but now, half mad with terror and the agony of limited knowledge, he knew that he would – must! – talk to his mother about it. That fire! The heat! And he had gone, pulled out, left the Other Feller to face that hellish inferno.

With his brain he knew that it was no fault of his; he had never been able to control his comings and goings when he was with the Other Feller. But with his heart and his emotions he felt that he should have done something to help. He should not simply have left to return to the total safety of a pub possibly hundreds – for all he knew, thousands – of miles away.

He got up presently, still shuddering, and set off on the journey back to the marshes. He forgot the bull and his appointment with Helen; all he could think of was the fire and the cruel, underground dark. He must get home, he must!

Twenty

They had heard the sound of the explosion in town but Jessica, in her quiet classroom with two dozen little girls working away at their books, simply assumed that it was distant thunder. The clouds overhead were grey, certainly; she had thought them laden with snow, but she had obviously been mistaken. Cerwyn was the same; they met to catch their bus home, neither of them having given the noise another thought. Not long now, only another day, and then it would be school holidays! Today was a half day, so they caught the two o'clock bus and chatted animatedly about their work and the holiday to come all the way back to the village.

Jessica's bag was laden. She explained to Cerwyn that since Hywel had not bought a single Christmas present despite her nagging she had finally decided to buy them for him. She had chosen nice things, she thought, and if Hywel did not agree it was his bad luck. Surely he would rather have gifts to exchange than not?

Cerwyn was a satisfactory sort of person to talk to. She said she was sure Hywel would appreciate Jessica's forethought and asked, with a twinkle, if Jess had bought her own gift from Hywel as well. Jessica had not quite had the courage to do that, but she intended to hint heavily about a couple of things, and to point out to Hywel that if he chose to buy her the ring in the middle of the jeweller's window in Lambpit Street he would really be saving money, for it would be a Christmas present and an engagement present too.

He would laugh, she thought, look rather self-conscious, and then either ask her to marry him or change the subject. She could not be sure which, but she fancied that this time he might ask her. He had come near to it a week or so back, and then something had happened – she could not remember exactly what – and he had not referred to it again. Oh, yes, now that she thought, it had been on a walk up and over the mountain. Coming home they had been looking down on Plas Tegydd and Hywel had been talking about his future when she, like a fool, had remarked on the fact that one of the weathercocks on the house below them was still spinning in the wind. It had been a small enough remark and she had tried, afterwards, to get him back to the point, but it had been impossible. He had gone off at a tangent about landowners never selling land and that had been that. Her interest had waned. Ceasing to listen, she indulged, instead, in a daydream in which a young teacher at her school took the starring role instead of Hywel. Just to teach him. Not that it had, of course, since he knew nothing about it, but still . . .

She and Cerwyn chattered away, commenting quietly on the fact that despite a three-day working week most of the women on the bus had laden baskets. Everyone who could saved a bit, and even if you were on the social people in the village would see you right at Christmas. It was always so in a mining community. If people couldn't afford turkeys this year they would manage a capon or, if not a capon, something a bit special. You might not run to bright paper streamers from the shops but the kids would pick holly and mistletoe in the woods and make some bits and pieces in school, and there were apples and vegetables from the garden . . . Everyone would have a good Christmas.

'Have you decorated your place?' Jessica asked, as she and Cerwyn left the bus and drew level with the older girl's cottage. 'We've got holly and mistletoe up, and a few streamers the boys made when they were small.'

'We're doing ours tomorrow, when I get back from school,' Cerwyn told her. 'Stan will be off work, so we can do it together.' She put a hand on the latch, then stiffened like a pointer. She was looking at the window. Unlit. 'Why, Stan must have gone round to your place. He's always in as a rule when he's on earlies.'

'Perhaps he went up the woods to gather holly,' Jessica suggested, for now that she looked there was no light in her house either. 'Mam must be working late at the Plas . . . but

Hywel should have been off shift by now. In fact I daresay he and Stan have gone off together.'

Cerwyn nodded and went up her path. Jessica hurried on to her own path, went up it, and opened the door.

The house was empty. She knew it as soon as she stepped over the threshold. It was cold and there was an echoing quality to her step which told her that no one else was in. Puzzled, Jessica looked round for some clue as to the family's whereabouts, but there was nothing. No food was in preparation, no fire lit, no coats hung on the hooks behind the door.

No coats – so they were all out! Da had been on earlies, and so had Luke, though Dewi would be working, of course. Mam should have been here . . . what on earth was going on?

Jessica left the house again and looked up and down the street. Now that she thought about it, several of the houses were unlit, but two doors further up there were lights in the Edwards' place. A lot of lights.

Jessica went to their door and would have knocked had it not been ajar. She looked round it, a Christmas elf in her poppy-red coat with its collar turned up round her bright hair and brighter face. She smiled at the Edwards parents, both retired from work but with a clutch of large sons all in the pits. They smiled back, but with a degree of discomfort she was quick to notice. Only one of the sons was present, and he was obviously getting ready to go out, for he was sitting on the sofa pulling on the first of a pair of stout boots.

'Hello. What's happened?'

Jessica's question seemed to surprise them; eyes and mouths rounded but no one answered.

'There's no one at my house,' Jessica expanded. 'And their coats are missing – they've all gone out. Where, d'you know?'

'Aye, love. To the Wynd. There's been a bad 'un there. Down Candle Deep.'

'A . . . an explosion?'

'That's right. And a fire. They want rescue teams, see. That's where our Peter's off to now.'

'Candle Deep? That's where Hywel works!' Jessica came right into the room. 'Is he . . . does anyone know who's hurt, who's come up?'

'No. You'd best go down with Pete, love, and see for

yourself.' Pete, putting on the second boot, looked up and gave her a small smile. He was a very large young man indeed. Jessica had heard him called steady and reliable and believed both descriptions. 'A good few women are down there, see. Your mam's one of 'em.

'Oh, yes, because Stan . . . heavens, Cerwyn!'

She would have run down to Cerwyn's little house, but she was forestalled. Mrs Edwards came over to her, put a gentle hand on her arm.

'It's all right, love. My Sidney's took her down there. On his motor bike, same's Pete'll take you. She'll be there by now, like as not.'

'Oh. Thank you very much.' Jessica knew she must have gone very white by the worried look in Mrs Edwards' eyes. She smiled at the older woman. 'Don't worry if I'm pale. I shan't faint or anything. But it's been . . . well, a shock. I'll feel better when I'm down there and can see for myself what's happening.'

'Going right now I am,' Peter said, getting to his feet. 'See what we can do to help, like.' He led her round the side of the house, to where his motor bike stood. He wheeled it out into the road, twiddled something, spun something else, and then there was a roar and he was grinning at her. 'Ever ridden pillion before? No? Well, all you've got to do is hang on tight and lean when I do. Right?'

Jessica nodded and climbed on to the pillion seat, closing her eyes as the bike began to gather speed down the steep hill.

Afterwards she supposed that it must have been an exciting ride; the speed alone was exciting enough. She could remember the howl of the wind and its cold breath knifing her cheek, pulling her hair back in a plume of rippling red, numbing her ears and nose. She could remember her fingers aching with the cold but continuing to grip Peter's jacket, as he had instructed. She could remember the grey sky and the pale ribbon of road unwinding before them faster than an adder could glide. And then she could see the pit, the lights on because dusk comes early on winter afternoons, and a darkness which she did not understand until they were close enough to see that it was a great concourse of people. Silent people, save for a sound not unlike the breaking of small waves on a shingle shore: the murmur of quiet voices and the harsher sound of women sobbing.

Peter skidded to a halt and Jessica climbed off, knowing that she was stiff, iced into position, and would find it difficult to walk. Peter must have guessed how she felt, for he stood the bike up on its stand and then came over and took her arm.

'Come on, let's find your mam,' he said.

It was impossible to pick anyone out in the crowd, however, let alone to reach them. A woman near them was crying quietly and holding a tiny baby in her shawl; she had two toddlers at her knee and they were crying too, dismayed by their mother's grief, Jessica supposed. She knelt down and picked the smaller child up, cradling him in her arms. He was a dirty, unkempt little boy of three or so, smelling of stale urine and thin beneath his man's cut-down jacket, but he rubbed his rough little head under her chin as a cat might and ceased his thin wailing.

The woman turned and spoke.

'My man's down there. First work he's had for five weeks. Been living on the social, we have, and then 'e got this offer to stand in for someone else. I was that glad, I went out and bought the kids bread and jam, and fresh milk for the baby – I was *glad* 'e'd gone, because I knew how it irked him not being able to provide for us. I thanked God 'e'd found work in time for Christmas. Like a present, it seemed.'

'Maybe you were right to be glad, and he'll come up presently and kiss the kiddies and go off home with you,' Jessica said hopefully. 'They don't know what's happened yet, do they?'

'No, but whatever it was, it 'appened in Candle Deep. That's where 'e was working. There was another explosion earlier, quite a small one, and some of the fellers come up and said they'd all get blown to kingdom come if it kept 'appening and they wanted to seal off the level.'

'Seal if off?' Jessica could not help her voice rising. 'Oh, no. They can't do that. My fellow's down there, and my brother. Surely they wouldn't . . .'

Peter came and joined her. He put an arm around her, then bent and picked up the older child. He held it gently, moving with a rocking motion as he spoke. A good man, Jessica realised. A gentle, kind man, and one she had never looked at twice because he did not have a face like a Greek god and curly fair hair.

'They won't seal it off whilst there's a hope of getting a man out alive that way,' he said, his deep voice reassuring. 'Here, take the little one, Jessica. I'll go over to the offices and see what I can find out. They'll be sending another rescue team down in an hour or so – I'll be going down then. And remember, if they seal a tunnel that's not like sealing a level. Stay there.'

He pushed his way through the crowd, and Jessica saw him stop to speak to someone, gesturing back over his shoulder in her direction. Presently, her mother came towards her, with Cerwyn. They both looked ill.

'Jess, love, I'm sorry I didn't leave you a message, but I came straight here from the Plas. Your da went down with the first rescue team. Trained, he's been, so he says, and of course Dewi went down and Luke is to go next. Your da comes up in twenty minutes or so. He'll tell us what it's like down there.'

'Mam? They'd been down Candle Deep a week or two. Were they down there today? Were they?'

'Not too sure, I am,' Ella said uneasily. 'They've not come up, but then they wouldn't, see? Not whilst there were men trapped. They'd stay down until they'd done all they could.'

'Yes, of course. They wouldn't . . . ' Jessica turned away, unable to finish the sentence. She was sure that both Hywel and Stan had gone down to stalls in Candle Deep; there had been no talk of the face being worked out or of different stalls being allocated. And if they were there, what chance would they have of escape?

As she moved, there came another sound, similar to the noise she thought was thunder but bigger, closer, more frightening. It was a low, grumbling roar which deepened until it sounded like a train entering a tunnel, then began to mutter into the distance as the train got further and further away. Only this was directly beneath their feet and it was no train. It was another explosion, a nearer one judging by the shouts from the men near the shaft and the way they scattered.

A second later, the hot air engulfed them. Jessica, her face still chilly from the ride on the motor bike, felt the furnace blast of the explosion's breath and hugged the children to her, ducking her chin into her coat collar. All around were exclamations, cries, children's screams. And then she heard Ella, her voice shrill, repeating something over and over.

'Glyn's down there, and Dewi, and my Stan. They'll be cindered by that heat, my men will. Glyn's down there! Glyn's down there!'

Around her, a cry was being taken up. 'Get the men out! Get the rescue team out before they go the way of the men in Candle Deep! Get our men up!'

An under-manager, Eifion Rees Jones, stood on a coal tub and shouted to the crowd. His face, lit from below by the lamps, looked other-worldly, earnest.

'Listen, my friends, that explosion was some way off, your men should be in no danger. The new shift will be going down shortly to work through the night whilst your men come up to get some rest. There have been several explosions, but all a good way from here, and there's a fire – fire usually follows an explosion. We fear that some men must have been injured and may be trapped. We can't withdraw the rescue teams until we're sure we can't reach survivors. Indeed, the men wouldn't come up whilst there's a fellow-worker who might be alive and could possibly be rescued, you know that.'

'Where's the owner, then?' a tall man shouted from the back. 'Where's Tom Tegydd? Got any explanation, have he, why his wonderful pit should start to explode and trap men in Candle Deep? Any good reason, do he have? Deepest pit round here, and that's the lowest level, Candle Deep.'

'Mr Tegydd's with the rescue team,' the under-manager told them. It occurred to Jessica that under the dirt he was looking ten years older than he usually looked. Last time she'd seen him he had been neat and dapper in a suit and pearl-grey waistcoat, fat Mrs Rees Jones hanging on to his arm as they shopped round town. Now he could have been a collier, so dirty and tired did he look.

'You mean he's below?'

'That's right. Went down as soon as he reached the pit. He and a few of the older men have gone right along, as near to Candle Deep as they can get. They're trying to see whether they can get round the roof falls and testing for gas.'

'Taken the canaries?'

There was derisive laughter from a group of miners waiting near the shaft to take their turn to go below. One of them called out: 'Dead them poor little buggers have been these twelve months. Might have told more than you wanted to know, eh, Mr Jones bach?'

Someone said, low and aggressive, 'Shut your bloody gob unless you want trouble after,' and someone else contributed, 'Hope they've got a decent light, mun. Our Tom'll be needin' his pipe and some matches to have a smoke.'

'Aw, c'mon, don't be unfair! He can light 'is bloody pipe at the fire,' someone else shouted. The under-manager turned quickly towards the miners and they fell silent. No use recriminating before they knew just what had happened.

'Who said that? No one flouted rules down this pit, and you all know it. Why, even shot-firing never took place when there was gas about as it does in some pits.'

This was too much for anyone to swallow. There was a low mutter of rage from the crowd and one of the miners opened his mouth, but before he could say a word a bell clanged, there was a whirr and a clatter of machinery, and the cage came up out of the depths. The crowd surged forward. What they expected to see no one quite knew, but it was certainly not what they saw.

The cage was full of boys, scarcely one of them over fourteen. They tumbled out, white-faced beneath the coal dust. Mothers rushed forward. Jessica saw a lad she knew well from the village, Caw Prydd Jones, stumble out of the cage into his mother's arms. Caw had a laugh like a crow, but he was not laughing now. He was shaking, trying to talk without crying, whilst Mrs Prydd Jones led him away from the crowd and the winding house, her arm around his narrow shoulders. He was gabbling fast as he passed Jessica, anxious to talk about his fearful experience.

'Black's pitch, Mam, except for the flames,' he was saying, between sobs and deep breaths of the cold air. 'The 'eat was awful. Near fried, I was, and scared! The flames just roar along the tunnels at you. Mr Tom the owner was down there, Mam, and he was crying like I were and his good shirt all torn and filthy. I see 'is nails, all broken and blackened where he'd clawed at one fall as if he could get through it 'imself and reach the lads on the other side. They say there's one place you can 'ear 'em crying and scrabbling at the rock face and coughing. The gas is terrible bad, Mam.'

He was gone, led off into the crowd. Jessica stood, holding the children close, trying not to let her mind function. Think of the night sky up there and the stars you cannot see for clouds, remote and alien, looking down on our small troubles. Think of the poor canaries, dead on their perches before they could warn the miners about the gas. Think of the brave men who will fight the fire, put it out, rescue their comrades.

Don't think of the man you love, the hands you love, scrabbling helplessly against the weight of rock and coal through which they cannot possibly hope to penetrate. Don't think of the lungs of the man you love fighting the coal dust, the heat, being horribly slowed and finally stopped by the seepage of poisonous gas. Don't think . . . don't think . . . don't think.

When the new rescue team arrived, Tom was sitting at the entrance to the main road, his knees drawn up, his head resting on them, his hands across the top of his head. He was filthy, worn out, terrified, but he had refused every effort to make him go above and take a rest. When he had heard of the tragedy it was as if a veil had been torn from before his eyes. The pit had been a bad pit with a bad reputation and he had bought it and put good men in it, because he believed that with good men it could become a good pit again.

And then what had he done? He had let his personal sorrow over Blanche's death kill men as well as innocent youngsters, for that was what it would amount to, from what he had seen. He had persuaded miners to come here because they knew of his work in the Olwen and the Roland, had seen how safe and modern those pits were, had believed him when he said he would make the Wynd just like them only better.

He had done none of it. Because his woman had died he had let his interest in the pit die too. He had known about charges badly placed, dangerously fired, but his overman had argued that they brought down good coal so he had done nothing to stop it. He knew that tunnels were dug and then not properly packed, that roofs were not propped the way they should have been. He had winked at the practice of employing men to dig the coal, shovel the coal, cart the coal, load and unload the coal, when at least half those men should have been employed in safety procedures.

He had known that ventilation was poor, airways were blocked by minor falls, rails laid carelessly. He knew that when an accident happened someone was sent to check that rails were laid properly, with sleepers and fish-plates, or that tunnels were blocked off or roofs propped up. This was done so that an enquiry would find no incriminating evidence, not to save lives. It was done to save coal, which meant to save money.

He had never bothered to get the Wynd linked to his other pits, though he had intended to do it. He had not taken the advice of some of the older men, when Candle Deep began to bring out such good coal, to sink another ventilation shaft. He had not bothered with gobfires, even when men warned him of the danger of gas now that they had gone so deep. He had known, as had all his management, of the gas in Candle Deep; he had meant to do something . . . why in God's name had they all done nothing? Why had they let it come to this?

'You all right, mister?' A young, concerned face hovered before him, the skin barely touched with dust, for this must be a chap from the new rescue team. 'You want to get above, now, mate; have a bath and a meal. We'll cope down here.'

Tom stood up. His legs would hardly hold him. He muttered something about going now and went off in the direction of the cage. He had not the slightest intention of leaving the pit, but he could not stay there, sitting on the ground, too tired and depressed to move. The firemen had cabins near the pit's eye. He would go down there, get a drink – they had flasks of tea – and then get someone to take him as near Candle Deep as they could go, see whether they could possibly find a way round, or start trying to dig a way through.

As he walked, he told himself that it really was only a mighty explosion and a big roof fall; once they could dig through it they would find the men on the other side, some perhaps injured but mostly alive and well. They could not consider moving out until they had brought the colliers up.

If it was just an explosion and roof fall, he promised God, he would make very sure that all the rules were obeyed down here in future. No one would smoke, they would abide by the rule of a lamp to a man, they would buy more canaries, spend money on making the place as safe as a pit could be. Please God let it be just an explosion, just a roof fall!

Peter stayed with the man until he shambled off towards the pit's eye, then set out after his mates who were already on the main road. One of them, Tinker, looked round and grinned at him.

'Well, what did the old devil say? Blast your eyes? Tell you to mind your own business?'

'No, of course not. Wore out, he was,' Peter said, rather surprised. 'Been down here since the start, I reckon, and missed the cage when it went up last. He'll go up with the next lot, doubtless.'

'Oh aye, do you think? Who was it, eh?'

'Elderly chap from another colliery, likely. Didn't know him. Why?'

Tinker grinned and bit off a piece of chewing tobacco. With his jaws working rhythmically he spoke.

'That's the boss, the owner. Tom Tegydd.'

'It never was!' Peter stopped short. 'Nay, Tink, he was filthy. His shirt was torn . . . I've seen Tegydd many a time. Dapper chap, always looks ruddy faced . . . ' His voice trailed away. He was picturing again the worn face, the bright dark eyes fogged with tiredness. 'By God, you're right! It was Tom!'

'Aye, told you so. He were a good chap, once. Trouble is he bit off more'n he could chew here, so he left it to management.' Tinker shook his massive, shaggy head. 'They say there's nowt so good for the land as the master's foot; same goes for collieries, I reckon. If the owner don't come down, see for himself, then others won't bother. Ah well, he's down now. Let's go to it.'

The men continued cautiously, holding their lamps high, nerves strung taut as violin strings. They were ready to duck into a man-hole or to turn tail, to stand and fight their way through a rock fall if there seemed to be life beyond, or to go round another way if it was impassable. Ahead of them the road stretched, blue-hazed, smelling of sulphur, with the occasional rock lying on the track to show that a disaster had struck.

They could hear a roaring, mind. Fire? Aye, but a way ahead, Peter told himself, and then they rounded a bend and there was the long stretch of the tunnel, diving downwards, and there it was.

It was like looking into hell. The flames were licking up the tunnel towards them, orange, scarlet, fluorescent blue. And the heat! Now and then there was a louder roar and the flames seemed to be blown towards the rescue team. Their heat preceded them, scorching eyebrows and lashes, singeing hair, blistering skin. They were forced back, unable to stand against it and knowing the uselessness of defiance.

When they were back round the corner, old Dafydd Evans, who led, roared at them that they would go back to where the road forked and try going the other way this time. They might be able to get round the back of the fire, and so into Candle Deep.

'If we could get there the fellows who're trapped could do it too,' Peter said to Tinker, but Tinker shook his head.

'It's not that. Anyone capable of moving would be out now, see? It's them as is injured, or trapped by rock falls, who'll be lyin' waitin' for us. Come on, mun.'

They hurried back to where the tunnel forked, took the right-hand way and went down once more into darkness and appalling heat. This time the fire was no surprise, but its violence was. White-hot, the air crackling with such heat and danger that no one had to be told to retreat. They nearly killed themselves in their haste, for either the heat or a gas leak dislodged a good segment of the tunnel roof and it came down just ahead of them; the first man skidded to a halt barely in time and the rest piled up against him.

'Dig,' Dafydd said briefly. 'Fast.'

There was no need to say more; it was clear what would happen if they did not move fast. They worked like madmen and were through in a moment, hoofing it down the road once more towards the pit's eye. A hundred yards and they were helped on their way by another explosion and a blast of hot air which must, Peter thought, have carried them fifty yards before it dumped them, higgledy piggledy, in a heap at another road junction.

They picked themselves up and tore for the eye. No one doubted what they must say, and old Dafydd voiced it once they arrived. He grabbed the manager by the collar and spoke directly to him so that there could be no misunderstanding.

'Call the men off, will you! Then seal Candle Deep and seal it good. If that fire reaches the main tunnel, and it's coming now, then it'll have the whole mine in three hours. No one down there could have a cat in hell's chance, I tell you. Seal it, mun.'

'But we've got firefighting equipment coming from town, and we've . . . '

Dafydd still had the man by the collar; without another word he turned, still gripping the manager as a mother cat holds a kitten, and half-dragged, half-carried him back the way they had just come. When the other members of the team would have accompanied him he waved them back.

'No, mates. You know what it's like. Our friend here must learn.'

The two of them disappeared down the road and the others went over to the firemen's cabins to explain what had happened.

Tom Tegydd was there; he had a brandy flask in one hand and his eyes were glittering. His face was still drawn but no longer hopeless; he was certain they could succeed.

'Seal the main road down to Candle Deep? Men, you couldn't seal off the last hope of your mates . . . ' he was saying, when the door of the cabin opened and the manager staggered in. He looked odd. Peter realised that his hair had been burnt right off his head and his eyebrows and lashes were quite gone. His eyes, pink-rimmed and painfully bloodshot, peered at Tom, then round at the men. When he spoke his voice was a dry and breathless croak.

'Fire's . . . too . . . fierce. Must . . . seal . . . the road.'

Behind them, Dafydd loomed. His pit jacket was smouldering and his face was grim.

'Order it sealed,' he said quietly. 'If the men aren't out in three hours there won't be one left alive. I know. I've seen fire before.'

397

Peter saw that Tom, who had only stared at the manager, accepted the grim old collier's word without question.

'No chance, then? Right, we'll seal the main, but we'll have a go at reaching them later, when the fire's burned down a bit, and mebbe we can fight it from a different angle. We've maps ... plans ... of the workings, haven't we? We'll get 'em out ... '

Now the men were no longer a rescue team in the old sense of the word, for they must seal off the main down into Candle Deep. They knew it and worked fast, but it was a grim and dreadful task and they were glad to leave it when it was done. They went up in the cage with Tom Tegydd and into the offices, where women armed with teapots and jugs of milk were pouring out mugs of their brew for the teams.

'It's good to know it can't get no further,' Tinker said with satisfaction as he drank the sweet tea. 'Only the manager and the clutchman down now, and they'll be up ... '

A tremendous explosion rent the air, followed by a long, whistling squeal which made Peter's blood run cold. He stared at Tinker.

'What the hell ... ?'

They were running to the shaft, elbow to elbow, dreading what they would see.

'Seal's blown,' Tinker told him. 'Another explosion, most likely. They'll have to close this shaft, now, until the fire below burns itself out.'

The cage creaked into view, mostly blown away but with enough of it left to hold the two figures who crouched on the floor. One was the clutchman, who must actually have been in the cage when the explosion happened; the other was what was left of the manager. He had obviously been blown into the cage – or what was left of him had. Peter turned away, shuddering, but Tinker moved forward, compelling the younger man to accompany him.

'Come on, mun,' he said gently. 'Get the clutchman to the office. Been through a lot, he has. I'll bring ... the body.'

Peter, helping the clutchman out of the cage, glanced sideways and saw Tinker holding the manager's body in his arms like a baby. Or rather the manager's torso, for his head had been blown off. The heat had sealed the bleeding but the sight was so terrible that Peter could not bear to look. Tinker walked ahead, his ghastly burden firmly grasped, and Peter stumbled behind, tears running down his face, half carrying the clutchman. They made for the offices. Most of the waiting women had gone home long ago – it was full dark – and all the men had gone. It was a dangerous place to be and they could do no good here.

There was one girl left, though. The girl from up the road, Jessica of the flaming hair. Peter helped the clutchman into the office and sat him down, then went back to Jessica. He tried to grin at her but knew it was a poor effort.

'Might as well go 'ome, girl,' he said, and realised that his voice croaked as Dafydd's had. 'They'll make another attempt down the other shaft, but it'll be too hot right now. They'll have to leave it till morning. A fresh team then, it'll be, and they may have the luck to get through.'

'Home? Yes, I might as well. Mam went when Da and Dewi came up safe, so she could get their baths and tea and see 'em to bed. They won't bring anyone else up this way, then?'

Peter walked her, very slowly, over to where his bike was parked. He held it steady and motioned her to climb on to the pillion seat, then he revved the engine, shouting above the din.

'No, love. They've sealed the main tunnel. Someone will have to go down again tomorrow, though, to put another seal on, because this one blew off. The way to reach them is the back way. Don't worry too much. If there's anyone left alive down there we'll reach 'em in the morning.'

The sky was paling in the east as they rode home and the stars seemed dull. As they came up the hill Jessica saw that a mist had formed below them, on the plain, thick as milk. The taller buildings of the town and the tops of the spoil pits seemed to float on it, rearing black and mysterious out of the mist, even appearing to move and shimmer in the starlight.

Tomorrow was nearly here. Tomorrow they would send more men down the mine and they would find Hywel and Stan and all the others. Alive and well. Possibly injured a little but alive and well. They would find them. Pete was talking as if they would find them. They must find them! They were so young, so alive! Stan had been married such a short time, his wife loved him so much . . . There were two hundred men

399

missing, someone had said, and that meant two hundred wives, or sweethearts, or mothers. God was a loving God. He knew how hard the miners worked, what chances they took with their lives every day of His week; surely He would not let them die? If He loved His creation, why would He pen them under the earth, stifle them with His gases, crush them with the weight of His rocks and earth? He knew how many of them scratched a living three days a week, paid less and less. Surely He would not punish them further yet?

The bike stopped outside her gate and Jessica stumbled off it and up the short path to the front door. It was opened by Ella, who must have been watching for her. She took Jessica in her arms and Jessica gulped, sobbed, and tried to pull herself together. She looked over her shoulder at Peter, still astride his motor bike.

'Will you take me to the other shaft tomorrow?' Her voice trembled and there was a catch in her breath. 'Will you? Please?'

'I'll take you. I'm leaving eight o'clock.'

'I'll be there.'

She was inside the warm kitchen. Her father, still filthy, was asleep on the sofa. Her brothers, Luke and Dewi, equally filthy, were asleep in the two armchairs. No Stan. No Hywel. Oh, *God*, no Hywel! How could she go on living without Hywel?

She walked across the room and up the stairs like a sleep-walker. Ella followed her, talking gently about a hot drink, something to eat . . . but she had got past hunger or thirst. She slumped across her bed and made no attempt to help as Ella struggled to get her out of her thick coat, pulled off her sturdy boots and warm mittens. She moaned a little when her mother swung her legs up on to the bed and began to pull the covers over her, but she made no other sound at all. Her eyes closed through no volition of hers, but she heard Ella moving about the room, pulling the curtains, hanging up the poppy-coloured coat, getting out fresh undies and laying them on the chair. Then Ella was tiptoeing out of the room and the light behind her lids faded as her mother went down the stairs, taking the lamp with her.

When it was dark and quiet she opened her eyes once more,

and stared unseeingly at the ceiling. Ella must be nearly down now. She heard the creak that the third stair from the bottom always gave. Well, she knew she would never sleep, she just knew it, so she might as well resign herself to lying here all night and worrying.

She was asleep before the line of light had disappeared from under the bedroom door.

Twenty-One

Huw got home late, because he had missed a train, but it was still light when he walked through the back door and saw his mother placidly cooking. The girls were all still in school, which was a blessing, because if they had been here he might have found it difficult to say what he must to his mother.

All the way home, in the train and walking from the station, he had been haunted by what he had seen, and afraid of what he might yet see. It had been terrible, those flames and the heat from them, but he was sure there would be worse to come. Usually, once he came back from being with the Other Feller, apart from the odd moment when he wondered about it all he never thought about it again, but now it did not once leave his mind and he knew with utter certainty that what he had witnessed had not been the end of the incident. Somewhere, the Other Feller was still going through it, and even thinking about it brought gooseflesh up on Huw's skin and had his hair prickling erect.

It was not easy to tackle Megan, though, because he knew how much it would upset her. Yet he was sure she had some knowledge of this matter which she preferred – for her own good reasons, no doubt – not to pass on to him. Would she do so when he explained what was happening to him? Surely she would!

'Mum, I want a bit of a chat. Can you leave off that cooking and come and sit down for a while?'

She had not guessed, so he must look much as usual; she glanced up at him, enquiring, unworried.

'Can't we chat whilst I work, Huw, love? I'm making a steak and kidney pudding for tea and that takes some cooking. It can't be done all in a rush.'

402

'All right. But . . . it's important, Mum. You will listen hard and try to understand, won't you?'

'Of course. When have I ever done anything else?' She had diced the meat and peeled and chopped the onion and now she was making the suet pastry. He went and stood by the table, watching.

'That's true. Mum, do you remember when I was quite a kid I had a dream about a place . . . you said it was a coalmine?'

Her busy hands were still for a moment, then continued their work. They moved less quickly now, though, pausing every time either of them spoke.

'Yes, I remember. It worried me at the time because I'm from a mining family and I thought I might have given you those dreams or whatever they were, and I knew you disliked them.'

'Yes. But I didn't always dislike them, because it wasn't always down the mine that we went. Sometimes it was into mountain country, very beautiful, sometimes up on the moors – they're lovely too, aren't they, Mum? – and sometimes it was into town, to the beast market or the fair or whatever.'

The hands were still now.

'We?'

'Yes. Me and the Other Feller. I don't know what to call him because names never come into my . . . dreams, only they aren't dreams. Anyway, names never come into it. I came to realise that I go to the Other Feller, to where he is, see.'

She was staring at him. She looked a little frightened. Then she started working her pastry again and her eyes dropped.

'Yes?'

'I went there this morning. I was in the bar of the Bell, having a drink and a sandwich, when all of a sudden I wasn't in the Bell at all, I was in the mine.' He swallowed, the recollection almost as frightening as the experience. 'And there was a terrible noise, and a fire, and the Other Feller, he was trapped, Mum!'

He had raised his voice without realising it, so vivid the picture in his mind, but Megan waited, sprinkling flour over the ball of pastry.

'It wasn't a dream. It was real. Somewhere it's really happening. Where am I dreaming about, Mum? It may be terribly

403

important that you tell me, because . . . I'll have to go to him. I think . . . '

'It can't be real! It can't be happening now!' Megan looked really frightened. She had stopped making pastry and her hands were clutching each other like two terrified children. 'No, Huw, it comes from the past. Sure of it, I am. It happened long ago!'

'You're wrong, Mum. It's happening right now. Whilst we stand here and talk there's men . . . '

It came again. Without warning, without so much as the wobbling, under-water effect, he found himself underground. He was trying to hurry, pulling another fellow along behind him. The noise was ear-splitting and ahead of them a great rock came bouncing down out of the wall, rocking to a stop in the middle of their road. He . . . the Other Feller . . . jumped over it, urging the man behind to hurry. And then he was staring at his mother and the kitchen was calm and warm about them.

'Huw? Are you all right, love?' Her voice was sharp with worry. 'You're ill. I can see you're ill!'

'I shall be ill if you go on pretending!' His voice was sharp, too, because he had thought her so sensible. Could she not *see* that it was killing him, not knowing? He could not let the Other Feller suffer alone if there was any way to reach him!

The scene before him changed again: just darkness this time, and noise, and his own heavy breathing. What had happened to the other man? He must be ahead, or far behind. He was scrabbling up a steep tunnel, narrow, bare. No pit-props, no rails, just dirt all around, and rocks pushing their great noses out of the walls of the place, and his body one long ache.

It was a nightmare this time and no mistake! The darkness cleared for a moment and he was back in the lighted kitchen, but seeing everything from a different angle because he was lying on the floor. He opened his eyes and there was the kitchen table, seen from beneath, and his mother's feet, and . . . they disappeared. He was struggling along in the darkness. His lamp had gone – where had it gone? – and he must go, now, by feel. He inched onwards, moving upward, through heat and incredible noise and pressing, pulsating fear. He did not think about the kitchen, nor about the woman making

404

pastry, he just struggled on like a dumb animal, knowing that hope lay ahead and death behind.

Hywel took one horrified look at the wall of flame roaring towards them, and then he grabbed Dickie's hand and made the younger lad run towards it! Dickie gave one hoarse shout, tried to drag free, and then they were both cramming themselves into the airway that Hywel had remembered, pushing and shoving to get as far up it as they could, with the roar of fire behind urging them to greater effort.

Dickie's lamp had gone but Hywel still had his, so he went first and his lamp lit the way ahead. The airway was narrow, boy-width rather than man-width in many places, and when a big rock stuck out into the passageway they were sometimes wedged, like corks in bottles, for heartstopping moments. Hywel had visions then of becoming fossils until the end of time, but they always managed to free themselves somehow, and wriggle on.

He did not know how long they had been travelling nor how far they had progressed when the second explosion roared around them. The sound booms triggered off a fall, and they were pinned down like butterflies on a board, Hywel by the legs, Dickie by the shoulders.

'You all right, mun?' Hywel called, twisting round and heaving his legs free, and saw Dickie's black face split by a grin.

'Oh aye, fine – unless you count half Denbighshire resting on the small of me back.'

But he wriggled and kicked himself free, and they were pressing on when the worst happened. Another explosion ripped the air, coal dust thickened it, and as the two of them clung to the sides of the airway the floor of their retreat simply disappeared and there was the fire again, whitehot flames fringed with all the reds and oranges of hell.

Hywel heard his own scream as he scrabbled frantically for a hold, but he heard not a sound from Dickie. He only saw him fall, like a blackened, curled leaf, into the inferno. One moment he was there, the next he was gone, his body devoured within a second.

Even as Hywel scrabbled away from the gaping hole he saw the edges begin to crumble. Sick horror sent him up the next reach in record time, and though the tunnel grew steeper here he forced himself on, clutching at the ground with hands raw and bleeding, his head and shoulders banged and scraped until he knew he must be a mass of wounds. But he was getting further from the fire, further from certain destruction. He might die anyway, probably would, but he could not face death by burning; he must keep on and upward.

His lamp had gone when Dickie died; he continued to crawl on into total darkness, lying on his belly in places, literally inching along. He was in a poor way when the fourth explosion occurred; all he could find the strength to do was to curl up, knees in belly, hands round head, and wait, and hope.

He was curled thus when the world fell on him, and he knew no more.

'In another minute I'd have told him, I swear it.' Megan, white-faced, sat on one side of her son's bed whilst Helen, equally pale, sat on the other. 'Oh, the wickedness there is in the world — why should my boy suffer for that other when he's suffering of his own to bear?'

Helen had come in a couple of hours earlier to find her mother kneeling beside Huw's prostrate figure, trying to bring him round. Between them they had got him to bed and Megan had told her daughter what had happened, though she had not as yet said more than that she believed Huw was having some sort of brainstorm, and was dreaming of her old home in Wales, and of her sister's family who lived there. To be sure Huw had been running a fierce temperature, but now he was deathly cold; Helen had made hot bottles and packed the bed with them, but he was still chilly, his brow dank.

'You'd have told him what? That he was dreaming about your family? I don't see that it would have done much good, Mum, nor that not knowing could harm him,' Helen began, and then shook her head lovingly at her mother's distraught face. 'Look, you're worn out and worried sick. Go downstairs, make yourself a cup of tea, and have a warm by the fire — it's awfully cold up here. By the time you've done that Huw will have come round and everything will be fine.'

'Well, I'll bring a cup up,' Megan decided, getting off the bed. 'Got to visit the ty bach, I have, or I wouldn't. Shan't be two ticks.'

When her mother had gone, Helen took Huw's hand, and it was still too cold. She frowned. It was worrying. It was not like her sturdy, self-reliant brother to be taken ill like this. He stirred and she stroked his cheek, then wondered whether a nip of brandy would help. Her mother kept a bottle for just such an emergency, hidden away in the sideboard downstairs.

She was on her feet and halfway to the door when Huw spoke. Low at first and then louder. She listened, but it made no sense, and that frightened her. She said, 'What did you say, Huw?' but he did not reply. Then, just as she turned back towards the door, he spoke again, loudly and clearly. In gibberish.

Helen had had enough. She turned and fled down the stairs, shrieking for her mother at the top of her voice. The three younger girls, gathered round the kitchen table doing their homework, stared, open-mouthed, but Helen went to the back door, opened it on to the dark, and shrieked again.

'Mum! Come at once! I think Huw's gone mad!'

Megan had boiled the kettle, made the tea, and then thrown her old coat round her shoulders and set off down the garden to the ty bach. Everyone hated using it in winter. She had to fumble for the latch because in her haste she had forgotten to pick up the lantern they used on dark nights. However, she got in, sat down, and searched around with her hand until she found the bundle of newspaper squares tied together with string. There were plenty, so that was all right. Many a time she had found herself stranded out here without paper, and that could be pretty nasty; you had to sit and shout until someone heard you, or take desperate measures.

The roof of the shed was not a good fit, and through one corner you could see the stars. If the rain was driving you could also get wet, but this evening there were only the stars, sparkling frostily through the gap. Megan found herself wondering if Ella was looking at those same stars and what her sister would say if she knew about Huw's dreams. She tried never to think of Ella in connection with Huw because she had done as her sister had commanded: she never acknowledged to herself or to anyone else that Huw was anything but her beloved son. Even now, she was sure the dreams were nothing to do with what had happened in that low-ceilinged bedroom twenty-three years ago.

Her daughter's shriek took her completely by surprise and startled the life out of her. She leaped off the seat, dragging her drawers on anyhow, hurled the door open and ran up the path, forgetting the cardinal rule of the ty bach, which was always to close the door on quitting it. Helen stood framed in the doorway, her hair lit from behind by the lamp.

'Mum, Mum, come quick! Huw's woke, but he's talking nonsense, complete gibberish. I think we ought to get the doctor!'

Megan was into the house and halfway up the stairs almost before she had drawn another breath.

'What was he saying, love? Was he calling for me?'

'No, he was . . . there, he's at it again. Can you hear him?'

She could. As the moaned words came to her she felt as though iced water was pouring down her spine. Superstitious fear kept her rooted to the spot.

'*Rwyf yma! Tyrd ataf fi!*'

Slowly, Megan mounted the rest of the stairs. As she entered the bedroom she said, to Helen just behind her, 'He's speaking Welsh, love. It's not nonsense.'

'Welsh? But we can't speak Welsh! What does it mean?'

'It means, *I'm here; come to me,*' Megan said slowly. She bent over Huw, stroking his brow. He continued to repeat the Welsh phrases for a moment, then his voice slurred to nothing. Megan turned to Helen, trying to keep calm, not to panic.

'God, what have I done? I should have told, only I was afraid . . . I'd promised, you see . . . we must bring him round now. No use waiting for a doctor.' She began to shake her son violently. She had been very wrong to keep the truth from him, once he had explained what he was going through. I knew it then, she told herself bitterly, trying to bring Huw's mind back from wherever it had gone. I knew, but I couldn't bring myself to admit that a thing so strange could happen. *He knows*

408

what's happening to Hywel. His brother's in trouble, and he has the right, no matter what I may have promised Ella, to know why he has these experiences. Suppose he could help? Have I the right to deny him the knowledge that might save lives? She knew she had no such right, that there are times when old promises grudgingly given are best forgot.

She shook him again and at last he began to stir.

'I can hardly believe it!' Huw was sitting on the sofa now with a cup of tea in his hand. His sisters were clustered round. 'I have a twin brother — the girls aren't my sisters, they're my cousins — and you think that Howard and I can share each other's experiences because we're twins. Is that right?'

'Yes. Except that his name's Hywel, not Howard. I would have told you before, but Ella — that's your real Mam — made me promise not to. Ashamed, she was, of what she did, and as for your father and I, well, we loved you so much, see, that we wanted to go along with it, pretend you were our real child. We had you from a few days old . . . oh, Huw, you couldn't have been dearer to us, I promise you that!'

'Haven't you proved it in a thousand ways, Mum? Don't be daft. You're my mother and Dad was my father and that's all there is to it. Auntie Ella could never be more than a stranger, not even now I know. But the dreams . . . they aren't dreams, of course. I always knew they weren't. So Hywel's in danger, real bad danger.'

'Yes. And he's calling through you, poor lad.'

For the first time she told Huw what she and Helen had heard him saying, and saw his eyes widen, knew the feelings which were coursing through him. Yet even so his reaction surprised her.

'Well, I'll go then. What's the time? Any chance of getting a train today?'

'You're going? Oh, but — Huw, love, I wouldn't stop you if I thought there was the slightest chance, but from what you've said the lad's been in a pit disaster. How can you possibly help? There's trained men for emergencies. They've got firefighting equipment, knowledge of the roads and airways, what's possible and what isn't . . . you couldn't do no good! Anyway, think of the time it would take you! Winter it is, and all but Christmas. You get in touch with the mine, that's sensible, and tell them Hywel's alive but trapped . . . '

Her voice died away beneath the critical stare of five pairs of eyes. She smiled, then gave a little giggle.

'Aye, I suppose it would take some swallowing. But how'll you get there? And what'll you do when you reach the place?'

Huw shrugged. He stood up and went over to the door, taking his coat off the hook.

'Don't know, but it . . . the mind business, I mean . . . it's a bit like being in a one-way telephone. When Hywel wants to come through he'll do so, and he'll show me, somehow, where he is. As for getting there, I'll borrow Eddie's motor bike. He wants me to buy it, so I'll try it for a week and fork out the money at the end of it.'

'In this weather? You can't ride it all that way!'

Helen had been smiling to herself, but now she laughed aloud. She looked remarkably pleased with events, Megan thought.

'*Cousin* Huw's been riding that bike on the sly for two years, Mum, so I daresay he'll manage to reach North Wales on it. Besides, they take 'em on the train, so he could probably ride for a bit and then catch a train the rest of the way.'

'Bright girl!' Megan waited for Huw to look hurt over his new relationship being thrust down his throat, but he was grinning at Helen.

'That's just what I'll do: ride and tie, you might say.'

'Well, you won't set out tonight,' Megan was beginning, when she saw that Huw had the door open. 'Not tonight, surely? Tomorrow morning, early . . . '

'Tonight.' His voice was indulgent but firm. 'I can get good mileage under my belt tonight and catch a train tomorrow. Tell you what, put me up a flask of tea and some sandwiches whilst I go and sweet-talk Eddie into lending me his bike, and then if the girls can fetch me down some clothes and Helen can pack a bag I can be off almost at once.'

'Yes, of course.' Megan was being sensible now, accepting the need for speed. Huw had said an explosion and fire. If he did not hurry it could easily be too late. As he went out through the door she turned to her daughters.

410

'Right, bustle round, girls. Let's see that your . . . let's see that Huw gets away in good time.'

The motor bike was not new and it needed loving handling, but Huw had been riding it, as Helen had said, for quite long enough to understand its little vagaries. And setting out at night was exciting, with the frosty stars above and the dark and the wind trying to find a way through all the coats and scarves and mufflers and goggles with which his person was bedecked.

He was going to be sensible, too. He rode for miles without stopping, but when he did stop it was for a rest, and that meant finding a haystack, digging himself into it, and sleeping until the light woke him.

He did not dream. Hywel's life had never come to him in dreams, but as soon as he woke, frowsty and thirsty and cramped, he began to urge his mind back to the pit and his twin. At intervals throughout that long day, as he heaved his motor bike on and off trains, rode for a while, stopped at cafés for snacks and hot drinks, he tried to get through, but always without success. Darkness was all that seemed to appear, though once or twice in the train, when he was relaxed, he found himself re-running old pictures of places he had gone with the Other Feller, and he thought that these re-runs probably had some sort of reason which as yet he could not fathom.

The second night he found himself still with fifty miles to go. Reasoning that he would not be able to do much searching in the dark, he got a bed in a hostel just for the night, explaining that he was visiting relatives so would be up and away as soon as dawn broke. They quite understood, so he paid his night's lodgings, had a meal, filled his flask and went to bed, where he slept soundly until morning.

There were flakes of snow falling when he mounted the bike, but not enough to worry him. He had to keep his eyes open for signposts, of course, but even so as he drew near his destination he found that he remembered scenes he knew through the Other Feller, and when he reached the village itself, with the

411

steep cobbled road winding up between the miners' cottages, he felt a double jolt of recognition.

He had been here before, but had never known! It was his birthplace. It was on to light flooding in from one of these mean streets that I first opened my eyes, he told himself. In one of these narrow, stone-built houses I gave my first cry. In a little room with a view of these humped hills and gleaming slate roofs I was torn from the Other Feller.

It was a poor place, perhaps, yet the houses were not unattractive. They seemed to have a cared-for look and they were clean, unmarked by the coal that had built them. Behind them he could see gardens, bare now but neatly tilled, and trees, frosted into beauty. He wondered what the houses were like inside, yet he had no real desire to visit one. The urge to find Hywel had increased as he neared the village, and now that he had actually arrived he felt he should give his mind peace and quiet so that Hywel could get through to him. If he was still able. It worried him that the Other Feller had shown him only darkness on the journey down from Norfolk. It gave him nothing to go on, no hint of his brother's whereabouts. He knew, dammit, that it would be dark below ground. It was no use to show him where Hywel lay!

As he stood in the grey morning street a woman came out of the houses with a teapot in her hand. She wore a blue wool dress, probably a Christmas present, and a voluminous apron, and her hair had been tightly curled into tiny sausages all over her head. She poured the tea-dregs over the roots of a rosebush by the door, then stood for a moment, staring out across the street up to where the hills reared, dark and clear-cut against the cloudy sky. Quickly, before she could retreat again, Huw went over to her, wheeling his bike.

'Excuse me . . . ' he began, then realised that his voice was muffled by his scarf and pulled it down to his chin. 'Excuse me, but can you direct me to the pit?'

'The pit? Several there are, hereabouts. Let me see. There's the Olwen, the Roland, the Wynd . . . '

'The Olwen, I think. The one where the explosion happened,' Huw said, and was rewarded at once by a quick lift of the head as she gave him her full attention.

'Oh no, not the Olwen. That was the Wynd, the Black

Wynd.' She jerked her head towards the road he had just come along. 'Black Wynd's that way, four or five mile back. You can't miss it.'

He thanked her and turned his bike, then hesitated. She could not be mistaken, yet he had the strongest feeling that he was wanted *here*, not four or five miles down the road. He turned back. She was staring at him.

'I'm sorry, but are you quite sure that there wasn't an explosion in the Olwen? My relatives mostly work down the Olwen, and they were involved in the disaster, I believe.'

She had been standing by her front door, but now she came down towards the gate; her eyes glittered with interest and she stared at him hard, though she could make out very little under his gear.

'Relatives, is it? Now who might that be?'

'The Fletchers. Ella Fletcher that was is my aunt.'

She hissed the breath out between her teeth and shook her head sadly, but still with that air of intense curiosity he had noticed from the moment he had mentioned his relatives.

'Fletchers. Oh, there's sad. They was down the Wynd all right, or some of 'em. One's been found dead. You'll be wanting the Fletcher place, then . . . '

He shook his head, pulling up his scarf to cover his mouth, a feeling of nausea coming over him. Could she be right? Was that why he saw only darkness when he shared the Other Feller's mind now? But even as the thought occurred he dismissed it. Impossible! The Other Feller lived. He was as sure of it as he was of his own heartbeat, his own steady breathing.

'I'll go to the pit,' he said thickly, through the scarf. 'Good afternoon.'

She called after him, something about there likely being no one there on such a day, but he ignored her, the motor bike making so much noise that he could scarcely be blamed for continuing on his way. He roared along, downhill all the way, saw the colliery wheel standing proud of the bare-branched trees on his right, and came to the great wrought-iron gates.

They were closed and bolted, but he could see through them. He peered, then dismounted once more, wheeled his bike close, and rattled the bars. Surely there must be someone here! It was not, to the best of his recollection, a Sunday!

He saw movement after his third attack on the gates and an old man, curved and slow as a tortoise, crossed the yard and came close enough for him to see the thinning white hair, the rheumy eyes, the blue scars on his face and the frailty of his body. All the while they talked, the watchman — for so he proved — was coughing. Not loudly or obtrusively, just a small disturbance which shook his thin frame so that he had formed the habit of pressing one hand against his jerking ribs as if to ease his breathing.

It shook Huw; if this was what mining did to a man, then the sooner the Other Feller took to doing something else the better! But the old man spoke, in Welsh at first, then, at Huw's blank expression, changing to English, and Huw learned that 'There iss no work here today, and only a skellington staff other days, mun, since the hexplosion.'

'I see. But can you tell me exactly where the explosion happened? I'd been expecting to find burned out buildings, yet it looks quite ordinary. Was the fire far from the shaft?'

'Aye. The roads go many miles, mun. Why, it could've been a good four mile off, where the gas first lit and blew. They say there's bodies lying under Tegydd that won't ever be brung out.'

'Under Tegydd? The village?'

'Aye. And the Plas, too. Know it, do you? You cross the bridge and go up the road and the Plas iss on your right. Great big 'ouse, a deal of land, but there's dead men lying under it.' He leaned closer to the gate and lowered his already slight voice so that Huw had to strain to catch the words. 'Neglect there wass at this old pit, though to cover it up they do try!'

'And there's no one here now, except for yourself?'

The old man nodded, then shook his head, confused by the ambiguity of the question in a language which plainly did not come first to his tongue.

'No one here but for me. Why would there be, on such a day?'

But Huw was already getting back on his motor bike to return to the village. His instinct had been right, then. He was needed, not at the shaft, but probably even beyond Tegydd. As he rode, much slower this time for the way was steep and the bike elderly, he pondered the question. He had thought to get someone to take him down the pit and then to follow his own feelings in his search for Hywel, but now, it seemed, he must find some other way. Were there ways into a mine other than down the shafts? There must be, or he would not feel so strongly that he must leave the pit-head behind and seek the Other Feller in the mountainous country above the village.

Presently he reached the village, apparently dead to the world still, though the morning was going on. Huw crossed the bridge and decided to leave his motor bike here, leaning against the parapet. Presently, he knew, the lane would grow both too steep and too rough for riding, and so far as he could recall he would soon have to leave the lane altogether and climb over a stile. The bike would be safe enough here.

He had walked only a few feet when what he had just thought jolted him. How did he know with such certainty? Oh, it was clear enough why he knew the lie of the land, but how did he know that the way was over the stile and not on and up the rugged, narrowing lane?

Instinct, he decided, and then he glanced to his right and saw the Plas, a fairytale castle with onion spires and golden weathercocks and great grey stone walls. A winter jasmine poured its delicate yellow flowers in a flood around a door and over a window, and somewhere a horse whinnied and stamped its hooves. It was a fascinating house, with its air of lost grandeur, but Huw knew he had no time to speculate about it. His subconscious wanted him to cross the stile, but if he was to get further he must keep his mind a blank receptacle for his brother's use.

Suddenly, he was there, he was with the Other Feller. In the deep dark, with his face pressed into the cold gravel and his breathing very light, very shallow. There was pain in each intake of air. With the slight rise and fall of his rib-cage he felt its sharp stab a dozen times in a dozen different places, yet he continued to breathe.

He could not move his head, yet suddenly he could see – not light, nothing nearly so definite, but a lessening of the deep and velvet dark. He sensed a greyness, even a breath of clearer air than the sulphurous, dank stuff he was drawing into his lungs.

He struggled to see where he was but all he did was return himself to the lane just as into the Other Feller's darkened, pain-filled mind came a picture: emerging from a hole or

415

tunnel into the light and warmth of a summer's afternoon. There had been birch trees dancing, dappling the sunshine with leaf-shadows.

Huw came to a halt, fists clenched, and fought to remember. Birch trees. Birch trees, and a brilliant afternoon. Birch trees. Someone had told the Other Feller . . . someone had said that if enough coal had been hewed and one wanted to go home without waiting for the cage . . .

Suddenly, as vividly as that shaft of remembered sunlight, he remembered, too, where he must go. An old tunnel through which he had scrambled all the way from the workings below had emerged in that upland meadow with its copse of birch trees. He thought that his one visit to the place must have been the Other Feller's first visit too, because Hywel had stopped and taken a good look around, imprinting it on his memory. Their memory. Why? Had it been a wisp of foreknowledge, or was it merely luck? At any rate, it was a way in and he was close to it. He must keep his mind open!

He came to the stile and climbed over it; flakes of snow kissed his face but he ignored them. He was playing a deadly game of hide-and-seek and he knew he was getting warm. His long knowledge of that other body, just breathing, of that mind, just functioning, told him that this life-and-death game was also a race against time for which he needed every shred of his concentration. If he did not play it well enough that body, just breathing, would imperceptibly cease to breathe, would chill, would stiffen. And that lovely mind, so near now, physically as well as mentally, to his own, would imperceptibly cease, too.

He reached the sloping meadow, though he doubted it for a second, so different was it now, in December, from that day in June. But it was the same; there was the copse hiding the tunnel entrance. He approached and began to tear at the rampant brambles, his strong farmer's hands not minding the thorns, his strong farmer's boots relishing and aiding the destruction.

And there it was, the tunnel through which he knew the Other Feller had emerged on that summer afternoon. Very low, very narrow, but by no means impenetrable. He dropped to his knees and crawled inside and then stopped; there was a terrible chill here, a smell of sulphur and a feeling of nightmare. He had not thought to bring a light and some of his experiences – albeit secondhand – in this mine had been recent and terrifying. Could he bring himself to go forward, into that thick dark, not knowing what he might find? His body blocked the light already, only a few feet in; he could see nothing ahead, he could find himself falling into space and he would be unable to do a thing about it. He was sweating and shaking, yet still he crawled on. His heartbeats were deafening and his hands slipped wetly on the rock floor. Should he return, fetch help, a light? But he knew very well that there was no time. If he lingered, indecisive, it would be too late.

He went on, into the dark. It crossed his mind that rescuers must have known about the tunnel and might have searched it already, but he knew this was just idle speculation. He crawled on. The tunnel was going downhill quite steeply now and the floor was gravelly, uneven. As he slid his hands forward he was pushing tiny fragments or rock ahead of him and they made a little skittering noise which he found faintly reassuring.

Suddenly, the skittering stopped. Huw stopped too – had the tiny pieces of rock reached the abyss that he feared? Or a wall? Or . . .

His hand went out cautiously, feeling for a crumbling edge, and touched something cool and smooth. He knew at once that it was another hand, and, with his heart suddenly full to bursting, he shouted with exultation and flung himself down beside his brother and put both arms round him and hugged him, feeling a purity of relief and love he had never experienced before and probably never would again. The Other Feller was here, and alive! They were together at last, and in that moment Huw knew Hywel would live because he had reached him before that terrible moment when his breathing would begin to falter, to slow . . . he would get him to a doctor or a hospital, despite the difficulties ahead, because at that moment he could have borne the weight of the world on his shoulders for his brother's sake. And not just for Hywel's sake, but for his own too. Inextricably entangled, one unconscious and the other exalted, they lay on the cold earth, their bodies close for the first time for years, two halves of a whole, twin cockleshells, two people who could share one mind.

Presently he tugged at the Other Feller's shoulders, but he

did not move. Huw felt around and found that a rock fall was pinning Hywel to the ground by the hips. His fingers traced the fall up to the roof, but there were no huge boulders, it was earth and clay and small stones. It was possible to move it.

Huw got to his knees. Working in the dark, with infinite care for his brother, he began to shift the stuff, working quickly and neatly with a collier's skill. It seemed to take a lifetime, but it was really only twenty minutes before he breathed the stuffy air from the pit and pulled at Hywel's shoulders again and felt him slither free.

Uphill he toiled, then, pulling the good weight of the Other Feller after him. In the dark, unable to see, he had to go slowly and carefully, to ignore the salt sweat stinging his eyes, the bumps on elbows and knees as he collided with rocks – and, worst of all, the dreadful feeling that he was getting nowhere, that he had taken a wrong turning and would continue for the rest of time to back up a narrow tunnel in the pitch dark dragging an increasingly heavy weight behind him.

But he emerged at last, and pulled the Other Feller out under the grey winter sky. Breathless, panting, exhausted, he still felt, faintly, that sense of exultation as he turned to look for the first time at his brother's face.

His ruined face. Crushed, bloodied, smashed. Once, it might have been like looking into a mirror image; impossible to tell, now, how alike they had been. But breath came faintly from the bruised and swollen lips and once the lid of his right eye fluttered.

He should have been shocked; perhaps he was, a little, but he was sure the state of the Other Feller's face would not affect his eventual recovery, and that was what mattered.

It was still snowing, though not hard; lazy flakes drifted down, touched grass or tree, waited for the next. When they landed on Huw's hot face they melted at once, but when they landed on Hywel they stayed for a moment. Huw brushed them off with almost superstitious fear – his brother was so cold! But at least it galvanised his weary limbs into action. He managed to get the Other Feller on to his shoulders by dint of holding Hywel's wrists and heaving himself first on to his knees, then into a crouch, and finally upright, and then he began the long trek down the mountain.

Several times he thought he would never make it. His whole body was so exhausted and overstrained that knees and elbows shook violently and after quite a short distance he found that he had to stop and rest every ten paces, though he dared not release his burden. His breath was coming in sobs and he was perilously close to exhaustion when he reached the gates of Plas Tegydd; he stood with his forehead against one of the gateposts, welcoming even such an unconventional means of support, and prayed, not for the first time that day, for the strength to go on.

His prayer was answered, though not in quite the way he had imagined. He heard a clatter, and then a man driving a pony trap emerged from the stableyard. Even in his stupor of weariness Huw realised that this was possible help. He moved back from the gatepost and heard an exclamation, heard the pony being adjured to 'Whoa!' and then hands were lifting his burden from him, his back cracked with relief, and he could turn to the newcomer.

'Need a hand? Shooting accident, is it? I'll get him into the trap and drive the pair of you down to the infirmary. Looks like a hospital bed is the best place for you both!'

A clipped, Welsh accent. Huw, still trembling violently, watched as his brother was arranged on the floor of the trap and then smiled at his rescuer. A smallish, neat man with iron-grey hair and very dark eyes, dressed for an occasion of some importance judging by the crispness of his white shirt and the well-tailored dark suit he wore. A gentleman farmer? But it scarcely mattered; he was Providence.

'I'll be all right. I'm just tired — he's a weight! It wasn't a shooting accident, though. Reckon he was in this here mine disaster I've heard about.'

'A chap from the Wynd? But you came down the mountain. You must have been . . .' The man shook his head doubtfully, glancing from Huw to the Other Feller, supine on the floor of the trap. 'Well, tell me as we drive, eh? Your friend's in a poor way.'

They were both in the trap and moving briskly over the bridge before either spoke again, and then it was the older man. He glanced sideways at the bridge parapet, then at Huw.

'That your motorbike? Thought so, since you're in biking

clobber. Well now, whom have I the honour of addressing? And who's your friend?'

It struck Huw forcibly that the truth, if he told it all, was going to lead to amazement if not downright disbelief, so he paused, marshalling his thoughts, before he spoke. He would not lie, particularly to this man who had helped him without a second's hesitation, but he would arrange his story to sound a little less far-fetched than the bare facts.

'Well, sir, I'm Huw Pettigrew, Megan Pettigrew's son. Megan's sister to Ella Pritchard. I came down to visit and I heard about the disaster, so I reckoned I'd just walk up the mountain to an old tunnel my cousin Hywel had mentioned in his letters, see what I could see.

'I heard a noise, like, a bit of a groan and that, and so I doubled me up and wriggled down, and after a bit it got steep and I near turned back only I heard the noise again. And there was my cousin, as you see him.'

'The airway! I wouldn't have thought it possible that a grown man could have got through it after all these years. Well, it's a miracle, that's what it is. So it's Hywel Fletcher? Marvellous, marvellous. We've heard so much bad news that to hear some good is like a tonic. One out of three hundred may not sound much, but when you've believed them all dead it lifts your heart that even one was spared.' He shook his head and fished out a big white handkerchief, blowing his nose resoundingly whilst still holding on to the reins with one hand. 'If you knew the bad news I've had to pass on to relatives and such lately . . . ' He put his handkerchief away and brightened. 'Think, though, going to your poor Aunt Ella with news like this – that her son, which was dead, is alive again!' He paused again, glancing almost shyly at Huw. 'You won't mind if I tell her? You see, I had to tell her when Stan's body was recovered . . . though you found him, after all. The job of telling her Hywel's alive should be yours, by rights.'

'I couldn't,' Huw said truthfully. 'I've never met my Aunt Ella, you know. I arrived earlier than I said, so I've not even been to the house yet. Thought I'd just take a walk up the mountain first. In fact, I hadn't told her I was coming, so she'll be surprised to see me at all.'

'Right, right.' Suddenly the man shot out a hand, grinning

broadly now. 'Forgot myself! I'm Tom Tegydd, Huw. Nice to meet you.'

'We seem to have passed over the formal bit,' Huw said, shaking the proffered hand. 'Hello, is this the infirmary? It's big, isn't it?'

They had left the road, which was absolutely empty, and swung into a gateway; the size of the building alone, Huw thought, would have given its identity away even had he not had Tom Tegydd alongside him. The older man drew the trap to a halt and looped the reins over a post, and then the two of them carried Hywel carefully into the entrance hall. It smelt of disinfectant and of hot food, but Huw barely had time to absorb any sort of impression before activity flurried forth. Nurses and a doctor appeared as if by magic, and as Tom Tegydd told the story he was able to keep in the background, still in his muffling motor-bike clothing, watching to see that the Other Feller was going to be treated right. And it was soon clear that he was; every face beamed, though, as Huw knew, the Other Feller had been badly hurt and was weak from lack of food and exposure. Yet to have come alive out of Candle Deep was miracle enough.

'Like findin' a hundred pound!' one little nurse said to him, as she bustled about. 'And on such a day!'

They examined Hywel in the entrance hall, right there on a trolley, then took him up to the ward. The doctor came up to them, smiling, rubbing his hands.

'Strong as an ox, that one. Can't tell the full extent of the injuries yet, of course, but he'll mend. Come back tomorrow, when he'll probably have regained consciousness, and we'll tell you more.'

'Can I take a look at him before I go?' Hywel asked shyly. He had heard himself described as the invalid's cousin rather ruefully, but he knew it was for the best. Too many people would be hurt if the truth ever got out.

The doctor nodded.

'You do that. Come back later, if you like, but he'll be well looked after, you may be sure of that! Dear me, after all this time to get a man out alive is like a miracle to us all.'

He bustled away, a small, overworked, weary man in a stained white coat too large for him and down-at-heel shoes, but to Hywel he might have been an angel, so confident did he seem that the Other Feller would be all right.

He and Tom Tegydd were led into the ward by a nurse, and Huw went straight to the bed and took Hywel's hand. Was it his imagination or did that other hand return the pressure of his? No, it was not imagination. Huw spoke quickly and low.

'Look, Hywel, I'm just going to see your mum and pa, tell them you're safe, then I'll come back. Will that be all right? Can you wait?'

As if his brother could do anything else, all bandaged and washed and laid out flat like a corpse! But Hywel understood; the fingers in Huw's moved slightly and his eyelashes shivered on his cheeks. Hywel would be all right, but he wanted his brother to return. Huw patted the Other Feller's shoulder, tucked the hand back under the sheet, and turned to Mr Tegydd.

'I'll come back to the village with you, Mr Tegydd, if you'll be going that way, then I'll come down here again. I'll stay with him, I think, until he comes round.'

'Aye, I'm going back to the village. Nothing would stop me, not with such news to tell,' Tom agreed. 'It occurred to me just now that Ella and Glyn will be worried sick if they've seen your bike and no nephew!'

'They weren't expecting me,' Huw said. 'Once I've said hello I'll come back down to the infirmary on the bike.'

'Aye – there'll be no buses running today or tomorrow, of course.' The pair of them were outside the infirmary now and getting back into the trap. Tom clicked to the horse and the equipage moved off towards the open gates. 'You'll not mind if I tell your aunt and uncle? I've had so much bad news to impart that it'll be wonderful to see smiles instead of tears.'

'Yes, of course,' Huw said. 'As I said, they're strangers to me, you see. I've not met them before that I can remember. I hope they're at home.'

'At home? Where else would they be? It's a time for being together, under your own roof, and the morning service has been over these two hours.'

Tom turned the horse into the roadway and Huw, glancing idly in through a front bow-window, saw the family, paper hats on their heads gathered round, a table spread with a gleaming white cloth loaded with food.

It was only then that he realised the significance of what Tom and the nurse had said. It was Christmas Day!

'That house, it is. Shall I go in first?'

Huw smiled and nodded. Mr Tegydd was like a child, lit up from inside by excitement at the thought of what he would presently reveal. Huw followed, feeling increasingly apprehensive as the older man led him up the path and knocked on the door. He realised that he was shaking like a leaf. His heart was hammering in his throat somewhere and sweat was pouring down his neck. This was the house . . . he had been born here! He heard footsteps clicking across quarry tiles. Presently the door would open, and he would meet the woman who had given him life. Hywel, the Other Feller, had spent nearly a quarter of a century living in this house!

A woman opened the door. He knew at once that it must be Megan's sister, because of the likeness. Beautiful women the pair of them, though he was prejudiced enough to think Megan's mouth sweeter, her eyes the more gentle and understanding.

Mr Tegydd was in full flood, walking into the room, arms going like windmills as he told them that Hywel had been found, was going to be all right . . .

Huw was scarcely listening; absently he was taking off his motorcycle gear because the room was warm and because one did not come into the presence of one's mother for the first time wrapped up like an Egyptian mummy. He turned to hang his coat on the hook behind the door and turned back, to find himself the cynosure of all eyes. Even Tom's narrative had faltered and stopped. For a second Huw was completely taken aback. He had not even spoken. Why were they all staring at him like that? And then, before he could speak, Ella came towards him until barely a foot separated them.

'I knew it! Where've you been hiding whilst we've all been mad with grief, and your good brother dead, burned dead, down Candle Deep? I knew it! God has taken the righteous from amongst us and left you still here, like the bad penny you are!'

The silence was shocking. Two younger men stared, horrified, and an older man with greying, reddish hair started towards her, then stopped short. But the only girl in the room shot across to him and threw her arms tightly round his neck.

'Hywel, my darling, don't listen to her! It's a miracle, a wonderful Christmas present, to have you safe!'

He could not even speak to her. The older woman's words were gnawing at his soul. That so much hate could fester in one human heart was almost incredible. What harm it must have done her, over the years. What harm it must have done the Other Feller!

Tom Tegydd was as shocked as the rest, but he was not gentry for nothing. His voice fell, coldly, across the silence.

'This is not your son, Ella; look again! Your son is at death's door in the infirmary, but the doctor thinks he'll pull round, thanks to this fellow.' He turned to pat Huw's shoulder. 'This chap saved the boy from certain death, I think he deserves more than an exhibition of bad manners and worse. Was that outburst shock, Ella? I hope to God it was, and that everyone present can bring themselves to forget what you said.'

Ella had fallen back, her hands flying to her face, hiding it. 'It was shock,' she muttered. 'Glad I am that our Hywel is alive, but who is the other? He has Hywel's very face!'

'Your sister Megan's son.' He turned to the girl, and Huw saw that she was slim and red-haired, pale now with the shock of finding herself cuddling the wrong fellow, no doubt, but pretty in an odd kind of way. 'Jess, why don't you put the kettle on, offer us both a cup of tea? It's cold out, and maybe we need something to take the taste out of our mouths.'

'Yes, of course. Then this is our cousin?' She smiled at him, then went across to the fire, pulling a blackened kettle onto the hob. 'I would shake hands with you, cousin, but foolish it would be when I've already given you a good old hug!'

The tension might have eased a whisker, but it still held Huw, like a fly in amber, standing near the door. One of the boys moved, looked at the other, then came over, a hand outstretched.

'I'm Dewi; that's Luke. You're very like our brother – I expect you were surprised when you saw him, weren't you? You did find him, didn't you?'

'That's right.' Tom Tegydd was anxious to bring things back on to a more normal footing. 'Apparently Hywel had mentioned the airway to Huw here when they wrote, and when Huw heard about the accident it occurred to him to wonder whether his cousin had made use of the old escape route. He went up there this morning and found him, just inside the opening, pinned down by a roof fall.'

'Writing letters, is it?' Ella's voice. 'Not a word to me, oh no, not a word. Deceitful. And so like him to go behind my back.'

'Mam, if you say one more word against the man I'm going to marry I shall walk out of this house and never come back.' The red-haired girl was no longer pale, she was flushed and bright-eyed. 'There's wicked, to talk like that.'

'You're not marrying a collier when you could marry anyone,' Ella said, her voice rising. 'It isn't decent. You've been brought up like brother and sister. I won't see you throw yourself away . . .'

'If you will not shut your mouth, Ella, I will shut it for you,' the elderly man said between his teeth. 'Jess is my daughter and she'll marry who she pleases. I've done my best to father Hywel these twenty-odd years and a better boy never breathed, so take your knife from his back this moment. Shame on you, and the boy lying in a hospital bed!'

The silence that followed this pronouncement was broken by the clatter of cups and spoons as Jessica made the tea. Ella did not seem to be at all abashed by what had been said but stared across at Huw with an inimical expression in her eyes. She hated him because he was like her son . . . no, he was forgetting. She hated him because he *was* her son and she could tell no one! She had hated him years ago and she hated him still – what a burden it must have been.

'Come on, cousin, here's a hot cup of tea. Drink it up, and then we'll sit down and you can tell us all about finding Hywel,' Jessica said, putting the cup into his hand. 'You can sleep in Hywel's bed tonight. We could probably even manage clean sheets, eh, Mam?'

Huw was thirsty; he took the cup of tea eagerly, lifted it to his lips, and then put it down again, untasted. No! He would not accept even water under this roof, where the feeling of hatred ran so hot and high in his mother that she could bring herself neither to welcome him nor to give him a little bit of a smile. The tea rocked in the cup, so hard had he banged it down on to the table, but he ignored it, taking his coat from the door and beginning to dress for the cold outside.

'You stay here, Mr Tegydd, and enjoy your cuppa. I'm off again down to the infirmary. You can see it's best.'

A hubbub broke out as the family — except Ella — tried to persuade him to stay.

'You'll sleep here, won't you, mun?' the man he knew must be Glyn Pritchard said anxiously. 'Come back here tonight, eh, when things are quieted down. I promise you a real welcome this time — ashamed we are of . . . of harsh words said.'

'No, but thanks for the offer,' Huw said, opening the door. 'It would be better if I found myself somewhere in town for a night or two; nearer the infirmary, more convenient.'

He left, closing the door firmly behind him, but it was opened a moment later by Mr Tegydd, still looking red about the gills. He hurried after Huw and stood by him as Huw began to mount his motorcycle down by the bridge.

'A dreadful thing, dreadful! I thought her a good woman — a bit impatient, a bit quick-tongued, but otherwise a good woman. She hates the boy, of course, and you, so like him . . . but no excuse, is there, for cruelty and bad manners. Will you come back with me up to the Plas, and accept my hospitality whilst you're in North Wales? Glad I'd be to make you up a bed.'

Huw thanked him and mounted the bike, but shook his head as the engine roared and raised his voice to be heard above it.

'I think not, sir, thanks all the same. I'll be better in town, near my . . . my cousin. He needs a friend, with a mother like that.'

Tom shook his head sadly but agreed, and Huw waved and rode off down the village street towards the distant town. The snow blew into his face and starred his goggles, but he felt warmer than he had done in his mother's firelit kitchen. He was going back to the Other Feller!

Back in the firelit kitchen, the first-class row which had started as soon as Huw walked out was assuming gigantic propor-

426

tions. Jessica was screaming at her mother, Ella was screaming at Glyn, and Glyn was telling her and anyone else who cared to listen that his girl was a good girl and he'd thank Ella to keep her nose out of his daughter's affairs.

'Nothing wrong with Hywel! A collier same's me and Luke and Dewi,' he bellowed, loud enough for them to hear two doors off. 'If he wants to marry Jess, and I don't doubt he does, then he shall, and nothing you can do or say – you've a wicked tongue, Ella – will stop them.'

'I'll marry Hywel as soon as he's out of the infirmary,' Jessica shouted every time she thought she might be heard. 'I want to marry him worse than ever now, after what he's been through. Worse than ever!'

'You'll be wasted on him. Not an ounce of sensitivity or thought for others,' wailed Ella.

'Leave my girl alone . . . '

Dewi and Luke, peaceable young men, stood by the fire feeling the warmth of it on their broad backs and wishing themselves elsewhere. After one particularly vituperative exchange they caught each other's eyes and moved as one towards the door. They took down their duffle coats, slipped them on, and disappeared outside without anyone's noticing their defection. Behind them, the noise of the room soared again as Glyn shouted Ella down and Jessica's voice rose above the older ones. The neighbours were openly at their doors, but no one said a word to the two young men; the women simply went inside, no doubt continuing to watch between their twitching curtains, and the men went back to their big fires and Christmas dinners. Dewi and Luke stared round them, then went down the path and out into the street.

'Pub?' Dewi asked.

Luke looked at his watch, then nodded.

'Aye. Then the 'firmary.'

'Right.'

The two brown heads bobbed down the hill, turned right at the cross and disappeared into the Black Horse.

Afterwards, the doctor admitted to Huw that he had not been as confident as he had seemed when they first brought Hywel in.

427

'But good psychology it was, to tell myself and everyone else that the boy would make it,' he told Huw. 'He'd lost a lot of blood, and his temperature was much too low. Yet I thought he'd pull through in spite of everything.'

'And he has,' Huw finished for him. Huw knew as well as the doctor that the Other Feller no longer inhabited the shadowed valley he had lingered in for several days after he had been taken to the infirmary. 'I wouldn't say he was cheerful yet, but he's getting so he can laugh again.'

'True. Always better he is when you're with him. Pulse stronger, heartbeat stronger, and the man himself stronger.' The doctor was a little dark man from a remote village in Anglesey, with a deep look to his eyes and a sing-song lilt to his voice. 'Close in the spirit you are to your cousin, Huw bach.'

There was a question in his voice, but Huw, with Glyn standing near, could not let anyone down by admitting the truth. He nodded.

'Aye, only cousins. But we are alike, I believe.'

'Aye, like twins,' Glyn contributed, all unconscious of the irony of his words. 'Not *now*, of course. Daresay you wouldn't know they were cousins save for the hair and the height being similar, but before – Duw, they must've been as like as peas in a pod.'

'Really? Well, I'm telling you, mun, right now those two share strength.'

Share strength. An odd choice of phrase, but Huw knew that it was a good one. When Hywel had been really bad, at his worst, with a raging fever from lying so long on the cold ground and his mind wandering all over, only Huw's touch could quiet him. Once he had astonished Huw by saying quite clearly as he arrived by the bed, 'Well, if it isn't the Other Feller!'

Huw had felt an overwhelming desire to sit on the edge of the bed and howl like a five-year old at that, and he knew why. He loved his brother, but he could not possibly love from the same depths of deprivation as Hywel; his life had been so good! His parents adored him, his sister Helen and he had always been the warmest of friends, and his little sisters idolised him. And still he felt that his love for the Other Feller was as deep as his love for his family. But what must Hywel

428

feel? Disliked by his mother, liked but not defended by his stepfather, accepted by his brothers. He had needed Huw desperately.

Oddly enough, Hywel had known what he thought, for when he did sit down and take the other's hand in his Hywel had spoken in a husky mutter.

'I did have Dot, you know,' he said, incomprehensibly to Huw. 'Right from children, only she went away. And I had old Stan too, only . . . '

Huw did not know whether Hywel knew that Stan was dead and he had no intention of breaking the news now. He shook a reproving finger, therefore, and then remembered that Hywel would not be able to see it. His eyes had taken a good deal of punishment and, though one was uncovered and Hywel could distinguish light and dark, he could not pick out small movements or recognise faces, nor for that matter tell a man from a woman.

'Don't forget me, Hywel, when you're counting up your mates,' Huw said. 'I was always there rooting for you, and you for me.'

'Aye. Fond I was of you, even before we met. And of the Other Place.'

'And me. You must come and visit me on the marshes and see it all properly, same's I've seen you and your place now.'

He had told Hywel, as soon as his brother was well enough to take it in, that they were twins. Hywel had not been particularly surprised; he had just accepted it, the way he accepted everything that happened to him these days. Passively. But now he raised an eyebrow.

'See? Call this seeing, mun? Good as blind I am, and how in hell am I going to work when I can't pick out my hand before my face?'

'Your sight will be OK, the doctor said. You'll see darned nearly as well as I can out of one eye, and you might even have some sight in the other. Give it a chance. You'll work all right . . . that is, you'll work above ground. Below . . . '

'Oh, I don't intend to go below again. I've been saving for years for a place of my own, a little farm in the hills. Ages ago Dot and I – Dot's the girl I told you about – thought we'd share a place, only she's gone. I can afford something . . . but I don't know whether I could run it, not seeing too well.'

'I know what you mean. But Jessica wants to marry you.'

He had not meant to say it. The relationship between his brother and the red-haired girl puzzled him, though in one way he understood it perfectly. He had always felt rather guilty over the warmth he felt for Helen; she was a year younger than he and his sister, yet he liked her better than any of the girls he had taken to village hops or the flicks, and it had worried him how much he enjoyed and sought her company. It had seemed, not in any way wrong, but somehow cissyish to want to be with one's sister.

Now that he knew they were only cousins, though, he intended to do something about that! He was pretty sure Helen felt the same about him, for was she not twenty-two years old and uninterested in any one boy? And pretty as a picture, he thought fondly; they didn't come prettier or sweeter than *Cousin* Helen!

What puzzled him, therefore, about Hywel and Jessica was not the relationship so much as the lack of it! They had never believed themselves to be brother and sister; Jessica, though no beauty, had a certain attraction; yet Hywel had obviously remained pretty well impervious to her charms. Equally obviously, Jessica was head over heels in love with his brother.

There was Dot, of course, but Hywel had never said he loved her in a marrying sort of way. Huw had the impression that he had simply been fond of her – a childhood sweetheart whose attractions had not stood the test of time? Perhaps. If this was so, Jessica had not slipped into the place she vacated. Yet despite all this it seemed that Hywel was not keeping Jessica at arm's length. He might not show lover-like ardour in her presence, but neither did he repulse her, apparently. She had talked about marriage, Hywel admitted, and, though he denied having shown any enthusiasm, neither had he told her that she was talking through her hat. So now, the remark about Jessica having slipped out, Huw waited with considerable interest for Hywel's reaction.

'I know she does – half the village knows that poor Jess is set on marrying beneath her, as Mam would have it. In some ways it might be a good idea, since it would take two of us, really, to work a hill farm. In other ways, though, I don't think it would do at all. She doesn't have the faintest idea what hard work it would be, for a start. Nor does she realise that I'd stick to it no matter what and wouldn't dream of giving in to her and moving into town to work in a bank or a clothing shop. If I thought she'd really be happy, mind, I'd go ahead with it tomorrow. Why not? There's no one else and I don't think there ever will be.'

'Well, see how you feel when you leave here,' Huw said after a short pause. 'You know, I've never asked you about Dot. I know you liked her a lot years ago. Is she that little dark girl you used to spend time with up in the woods and on the mountain? The one that moves like quicksilver?'

It was amazing to see the smile that lit his brother's face, the way his whole expressoin softened.

'Yes, that's her. Of course you'd have seen her once or twice, I suppose. She was . . . special.'

'Then why don't you write to her, ask her to come back? Why did you let her leave without telling her how special she was?'

Hywel frowned and shook his head.

'I can't get used to the idea that you don't know every last thing about me and mine! Dot run off, see, more than four years ago. Wanted to get married, she did, but she was only seventeen, and . . .'

He told Huw the story, ending with, 'So you see, she's gone far from here. Loved the place she did, but her da and I drove her away between us, and she's gone for good now. Used to think she'd come back, I did, but that hope's faded too. No, she's gone.'

'Why on earth? Hywel, she could walk in tomorrow! Women are strange creatures. I bet you . . .'

'No, mun. You don't know Dot, and I do. The Wynd disaster was splashed across every paper in the land, right? Couldn't have been in the country and not known, eh? I'd swear by my life that if she knew she'd come back here so fast her heels would catch fire. Wouldn't be no stopping her, I promise you. A loving little thing, Dot, and though it's natural enough that she'd bear a bit of a grudge for what her da and me did to her it wouldn't last years, not with Dot. She'd come flying back to make sure we were all fit and well. That's why

I'd marry Jess if I thought it was the right thing to do. Dot's either dead or so far away that she wouldn't have heard about the Wynd and couldn't come back if she had.'

Poor old boy, he loved her, Huw mourned wordlessly. It was wicked and wrong that his life should have been so blessed and his brother's so bereft. Was it possible that Hywel could find happiness with Jessica? After all, she adored him; perhaps for his sake she would become a good wife for a hill farmer. He knew that he would worry endlessly about his brother if Hywel really did buy a farm in the back of beyond somewhere and move into it alone.

'Well, probably you're right. So you think about Jessica, and make up your mind whether you're going to make her the happiest woman on earth when the spring comes!'

Both brothers laughed. Both felt more like weeping.

Twenty-Two

'I told you all she needed was a couple of months of sunshine!'
Pappa Peruzzi, beaming from ear to ear, took Dot in his arms
as she climbed down from the train and whirled her around,
then kissed her cheek resoundingly. 'You are better, eh, my
little one? Recovered from the pneumonia?'

In mid-November Dot, worn out by the demands of two
young children, had fallen a prey to bronchitis and had been
quite ill, but the pneumonia was a polite fiction between
herself and her father-in-law. It had begun when Carlo had
made it very clear that her illness was more of an annoyance
than anything else and had taken the opportunity to move
Crispino in, on the grounds that his friend could help him to
cope with his sick wife and all-too-healthy children.

Crispino had not been much in evidence at mealtimes, save
to eat heartily, or at bathtimes, save to take baths himself. He
kept pretty well aloof from the domestic side of the household,
but it was perfectly true that he kept Carlo amused. In the
evenings they played cards, talked, and read aloud to each
other, whilst Dot fretted in bed, sure that her children were
being neglected.

Carlo got a nanny in to deal with the children, and a maid
took over most of the care of his sick wife. Nevertheless,
Crispino remained very much in control of the spare room. He
took to ordering the meals, and the maid, Lucy, came creeping
up the stairs to complain to Dot that she could not manage Mr
Crispino's menus on the money that Mr Carlo gave her and the
young gentleman did make a lot of work and she really had not
thought she would be cooking and cleaning for quite such a
large family, as well as nursing, and she didn't want to upset
anyone but she would be giving in her notice come Friday.

Dot's recovery had been far slower than she would have expected. After two weeks in bed she was still pale, listless and terribly depressed. Her marriage was on the rocks, her health, which had always been extraordinarily good, was tottery, and her children cried more than they laughed.

The day the maid finally gave notice and Carlo accepted it with careless indifference, Dot crawled out of bed, dressed, and tottered into the nursery. Paoletta was at kindergarten, which she adored, but Tommy lay in his cot, red and blubbered with crying, his nose running all down his face and the pillow by his head wet with vomit.

Dot's heart missed a beat. Babies *died* if they were put on their backs and swallowed their own vomit! She snatched Tommy up, stood swaying by the cot for a moment whilst the child's howls died down to no more than a sleepy grumble, and then set shakily off downstairs. There was no one in the house, the overworked maid having gone off shopping, she discovered afterwards. It was a Friday and Carlo had taken a day off, so the maid had assumed he would look after things in her absence. Instead, the men had gone off to see the stray animals at Crispino's place, obviously never giving a thought to the baby upstairs in his cot, or the wife who lay sick.

Too weak to feel the rage she would later know, Dot rang for a taxi and climbed into it with Tommy, blanket-wrapped, in her arms. She went straight to the Royal Pavilion and her parents-in-law.

Or rather, to her father-in-law, for Pappa Peruzzi was alone. His wife had gone Christmas shopping — it was, by this time, early December. He had taken one look at his pale and wan daughter-in-law, another at his exhausted grandson, and had swept them along to the kitchen, having rung down to the restaurant for assistance.

Without having to explain anything, Dot found herself tucked up in bed with hot water bottles at her knees and feet and the doctor summoned. The baby lay beside her, cooing now despite a dreadful headcold.

'We will say to Mamma that it is pneumonia,' Pappa Peruzzi said, when the doctor had been, prescribed, and gone. 'We will say that too ill you were for Carlo to cope. Yes, dearest, I know full well that most of this is Carlo's fault and he does not deserve that I should shelter him thus, but you would not wish to break Mamma's heart? And then, when I can, I will speak severely to my son and show him the error of his ways. Paoletta shall stay here too. Mamma and I will take good care of them both, and you shall quietly get better for our sakes, and for Carlo's sake, because he must be at his wits' end with you so ill. That will be why he went out and left you and the child.'

Dot only had to say one word, but she felt several would do better.

'Crispino. He's been staying at our house ever since I got bronchitis. They went out together to feed Carlo's animals.'

'They did? To feed those . . .' Pappa Peruzzi, perhaps fortunately, broke into impassioned Italian at this point, ending with two sentences in English. 'You will take a holiday whilst I get Carlo to realise what he has done. You will go to Italy, with the baby.'

'Oh, I couldn't!' But the thought of it brought a smile to her lips and a faint sparkle to her eyes. Just the thought of the warmth and the gaiety, the pleasant people, the admiring young men who never seemed to find her boring and apparently enjoyed giving her Italian lessons, was enough to make Dot feel that perhaps recovery was not beyond her. And it would be so good for poor Tommy's cold and Paoletta's tendency to wheezy chest coughs. If I went, and came back able to fight them, I could easily get Crispino sent back where he belongs and begin to enjoy life with Carlo again, she thought optimistically. Oh, think of the blue sea, the fresh oranges growing on the trees, and the sunshine! She loved her northern Italian relatives, but the southern Italian ones were even nicer. Kind Aunt Lidia, fat Uncle Venanzio, jolly cousin Rodolfo! The northern relatives said the southern ones were idle and feckless . . . but it was not true! Living was easier in some ways, but they were very much poorer and toiled hard on their land.

But suppose she did go? And suppose she came back to find Crispino firmly established and Carlo willing to do without her and the children? The answer popped, unbidden, into her head. If that was the case, no one could blame her for leaving Carlo and returning to North Wales, taking the children with her.

It was like a tonic. Just the thought of going home . . . She knew that, despite the fact that North Wales, in December, would be cold, snowy and bleak, to see it for a day would do her more good than a month in sunny Italy.

She had never thought about leaving Carlo before, but once everything had been arranged and he had come, chastened, to take her and the children to the station, she knew that such a seed, once planted, would take some uprooting. It would be his fault. He had made her unhappy; had made it clear, furthermore, that as far as he was concerned she counted for less than his stray dogs and cats – and considerably less than his friend Crispino. Even so, she should not be thinking of leaving him as some sort of reward!

All the way to the Peruzzi's home in Sorrento, on the long and tiring train journey through France, across the alps and right down the length of Italy, she found herself thinking guiltily, *if he is no better when I get home again, then it will serve him right if I go home.*

All through the long, lazy, sun-kissed days in Sorrento, the thought hovered, giving her intense pleasure. *I have paid for my children by my devotion to them and by being a good wife to Carlo. If, however, he repays me by treating me like dirt and bringing his friend to make an uncomfortable and unwanted third, why should I not leave him?*

Even now, in her father-in-law's warm embrace, she was conscious of the same old thought. *If Carlo has not done as his pappa says and cast Crispino out, then I shall feel justified in returning to Wales.*

She could not say this out loud, however.

'I'm fine now, Pappa; and Tommy's cold has quite gone, and Paoletta's chest is as clear as a bell,' she said instead. 'How is Carlo?'

'He wanted to come to the station, but one of the directors of his company has come down for a day to talk to the salesmen. Carlo is going to give him lunch at the Royal,' Pappa said with pardonable pride. 'Such a good boy . . . so grateful that you have recovered from your pneumonia! A new leaf he is overturning, a new life starting from this day. No more will you be troubled by that wretched fellow – and Carlo is most sincerely sorry for the way he behaved.'

If my heart sinks a little, then I am a very wicked person, Dot told herself severely as the taxi carried them back to Valentine Street. And how ridiculous that I should want to return to Wales, which would be admitting that I'd failed at my marriage! I should be very glad and happy that Carlo is going to give our marriage a chance.

When they reached the house she felt shy; she got out of the taxi, watched Pappa pay the driver and help him bring out the suitcases, and then walked up the short front path between the big hydrangea bush on the left and the tangly lilac on the right. It was nice when the door opened, though, to show the hall scrupulously clean and bright, flowers on the half-moon table and a new and pretty maid smiling a welcome.

'Good morning, Mrs Peruzzi. I'm Pearl Beckett and I've come to take care of you and help in the house and look after the children,' she said all in a rush. 'Mr Peruzzi said you needed cosseting.'

Dot laughed; impossible not to feel warmed at such a sentiment, and she did look a pleasant, efficient young thing, too.

'I feel marvellous, after such a lovely holiday,' she said, shaking the young woman's hand. 'It's very nice to meet you, Pearl. I'm sure we'll get along well. I expect you can guess that this is Tommy' – she made Tommy wave a hand – 'and this young lady is Paoletta.'

'Yes, ma'am. Would you step into the drawing room for a moment? I'll get the cases in and then serve coffee and biscuits – they're all ready in the kitchen.'

'I can make . . .' Dot began, but her father-in-law, about to step into the taxi to return to his place of work, shook a reproving head at her.

'Now now, dearest. Just you go and sit down and your coffee enjoy,' he called. 'Mamma and I will see you tonight.'

Not displeased at the thought of sitting down in her lovely room, Dot opened the door . . . and found herself whisked up in a pair of familiar arms and hugged tight to a familiar chest.

'Dot, darling! Oh, it's marvellous to see you again. You've no idea how badly I've missed you!'

Dot looked up into Carlo's handsome, rather sensuous face, and made a discovery.

437

'I've missed you too,' she said, trying not to sound too surprised. 'Oh, Carlo, it's good to be back!'

'Did you have a good time? How was an Italian Christmas?'

'Wonderful to both. We had some lovely presents, and we've brought some back for you, too. Now tell me about Pearl. She does seem a treasure. Where on earth did you find her?'

'Oh, that wasn't me, love, that was Crispino! He's very sorry he was so selfish, thinking of nothing but our friendship – he admits that he has been jealous of you, thinking you wanted to push him out – and he was so remorseful when Pappa spoke to him that he said he would find you a really good girl to take care of you.' Carlo looked at her anxiously. 'It does not annoy you that he found Pearl? He was afraid it might.'

Dot had always been generous and her heart melted at the thought of Crispino, who hated domesticity, searching for a maid – he was a snob, too, and disliked what he would have called the Lower Orders – so she banished some slight misgiving over the immediate introduction of Crispino's name into the conversation.

'Not at all. I'm very grateful to him,' she assured her husband. 'So long as he remembers that I'm your wife and enjoy your company every bit as much as, if not more than, he does, we should all get along very well.'

She thought she spoke no more than the truth; surely Carlo would realise now that a good friend had a place in his life and a wife had a place too, and one could not be allowed to take over the other the way Crispino had tried to? But she had not bargained for the strength of Carlo's feelings for his friend. A week after she arrived home, Crispino came for a meal, scarcely spoke more than the merest commonplaces to his hostess all evening, and when the time came for him to take his departure peeped out through the front door, announced that it was snowing far too heavily to make the long trek out to Eaton village practicable, and reminded Carlo that he had an appointment with a client very early next morning.

Dot waited for Carlo to tell his friend that the snow was nothing much and the appointment not until ten anyway. Instead, Carlo unhesitatingly offered Crispino the spare room and Dot knew that the monster had not been slain, but merely slightly wounded.

She went, depressed, to bed.

Though she had blamed both young men for Crispino's overnight stay, it really was scarcely his fault that the weather worsened. Outside the windows the snow lay six inches deep, a foot, two feet, three. It would have been difficult for Crispino to have got out to his home and back again night and morning, and, when Carlo offered the hospitality of his roof for as long as the weather remained bad, Dot felt she could scarcely object.

On this occasion, too, he was a much nicer guest, showing Dot the charming, amusing side of his nature instead of, so to speak, spending all his time with his charm turned towards Carlo and his cold back towards Carlo's wife. They played cards as a foursome in the evening – for Pearl was a nice girl and enjoyed a hand of cards now and again – sat round the fire chatting and roasting chestnuts in the embers, and sometimes when Carlo had to do his paperwork Dot and Crispino would play word games, or struggle with the crossword puzzle.

The strange thing was, though, that Crispino never seemed to want to go to bed. As the hour grew later he grew livelier, and quite often it was only Carlo's insistence that took them off at last.

Dot was wiser now; she smiled, kept a lively expression on her face, and refused to let Crispino bundle her upstairs, on the grounds that she worked too hard and must be tired, but really, she knew, so that he and Carlo could have heart-to-heart chats until the fire was long dead and the room chilly.

It was often a nuisance, but she kept reminding herself that the bad weather would not last for ever. Soon it would clear, Crispino would go home, and she and Carlo would be able to go to bed by ten if they felt like it.

In the meantime, she made very sure that she was an ideal hostess for two young men with similar interests. She catered for their tastes in food, occasionally took herself off for an evening with Jane or one of her other friends so that they could be alone, sometimes sent them out for a drink whilst she stayed in with Pearl and the children. The only thing she would not do — and she did not really know why she would not — was allow herself to be packed off early to bed.

And there was no doubt that it worked. Carlo was loving to her, proud of her. Crispino frequently forgot that he did not really like her very much and joked and teased her, obviously enjoying her company. Dot began, cautiously, to believe that her marriage had a future.

The snowstorms and blizzards ceased as suddenly as they had begun. For ten days it was fierce beyond their door, and then Dot drew back the curtains one morning to gentle but persistent rain. Warm rain, what was more. The thaw had come, and soon green grass and perhaps even the noses of the crocuses she had planted last October would begin to show. And Crispino went home, presenting Dot with a large bowl of miniature tulips for her front windowsill and an even larger box of chocolates. Carlo joined her in waving the young man off and then turned to her and kissed her ear.

'He's a grand fellow, and I'm happier than I can say that you've made friends at last,' he said. 'But I'm bound to admit that it's nice to be just the two of us again!'

Dot's heart warmed, but she said teasingly, 'The two of us, Pearl, Paoletta and Tommy, you mean!'

They had three happy days after that. Crispino left on a Friday, and they spent the weekend quietly pottering round the garden and taking the children for walks in the park to admire the yachts on the round pond and to play on the swings.

Monday went by as Mondays were wont to do. On Tuesday Crispino came back.

Dot could not believe her eyes when she saw him coming up the hall with a suitcase in his hand.

'Morning, Dot, my love,' he said breezily, in his light, rather affected voice. 'Don't worry, not another marathon stay like last time. This is just for a night or two. We've got company directors coming down this week and that means early morning meetings, so we thought, Carlo and I, that it would be easier if I were on the spot. We'll entertain them to dinner in the evenings, you see, and I wouldn't want to have to get all the way back to the village when I could walk home with Carlo.'

Carlo had gone to work without a word on this score. Dot put her hands on her hips. She felt that they must get the whole business cleared up once and for all.

'Easier for you, perhaps, Cris, but not for me! You know very well that the directors come down once a month — do you expect to move in here for two or three days every month? Right through the summer and everything? I don't mean to be inhospitable, but it does rather complicate my life, you know!'

Crispino put his case down and headed back to the front door.

'Discuss it with hubby, darling — I think you'll find he's in favour,' he said lightly. 'See you tonight.'

Despite Crispino's confident prediction, however, Carlo was not pleased. On the other hand, he would not tell his friend to move out again.

'I'll speak to him after the meetings,' he said, tugging at his earlobe. 'He's being silly. I don't understand him!'

If he did not understand Crispino, however, Dot was beginning to have a shrewd suspicion that she did. And that very same night she was as sure as she could be.

After dinner Carlo did some paperwork, and then at ten o'clock he stood up, stretched, yawned rather artificially, and held out a hand to Dot.

'Ready for some shut-eye, love? I've got a hard day tomorrow.'

'Yes, fine. I'll just make up the fire so that Cris doesn't freeze.' Dot gave Crispino a tight-lipped smile. 'See you in the morning, Cris!'

'Good God, Carlino, you can't be off already!' Crispino used the diminutive caressingly, completely ignoring Dot. 'Come on, I'll play you a hand or two of cards.'

'Not tonight, Cris.' Carlo yawned again. 'See you in the morning.'

Upstairs, they peeped in on the children, as they always did, then went quietly to their own room and began to undress hurriedly, for it was cold, though the bed would be warmed through by the hot-water bottles Dot had put in earlier. Carlo did not seem to want to talk; Dot guessed he was feeling guilty about leaving someone downstairs who was, after all, their guest. However, if Crispino intended to act like a member of the family, he would have to get used to being treated like one, too.

Once in bed and warming up nicely, Dot slid her arms round Carlo's neck and kissed his ear.

'Well, this is one place we can be by ourselves, even if . . . no matter how many guests we have!'

Carlo laughed, turned and kissed her, and then proceeded to make himself comfortable for the night. Dot realised that this was the usual procedure when Crispino was staying. She had noticed that Carlo did not usually make any overt show of affection at such times, but it was only now that it occurred to her that they did not make love in the privacy of their own room either when Crispino slept – or did not sleep – next door.

This filled her with a mixture of amusement and righteous rage, and also with an urge to be cuddled. She took a deep breath, hooked a leg over her unresponsive spouse's hips, and began to nibble his ear, breathing her warm breath into it and pushing her body against him. She would not allow Crispino to dictate celibacy to either Carlo or herself. If necessary she would seduce Carlo, husband or no husband. It would not, she reflected, be very difficult!

It was not difficult at all. A mere two minutes after she had started the most intimate and insidious caresses she could bring to mind, Carlo was quite literally all over her, kissing, squeezing, tugging her warm nightgown up, struggling out of his own pyjamas.

They were happily naked and deeply engaged when, without warning, the door shot open and a beam of light shone across the bed. On the empty side, fortunately. Dot, who happened to be underneath Carlo at the time, fought free of the entanglement which, seconds before, she had been encouraging like billyo, and sat up on one elbow. She longed passionately for the nightdress which Carlo had flung down on the floor on top of his striped pyjama trousers. The jacket, she saw, decorated the dressing-table mirror. But wishing did no good, so she faced the light and the dark figure behind it, doing her best to look like someone roused from a deep and innocent sleep.

'Yes? What is it?'

'Why, Paoletta, what a bad girl you are to run into Mummy and Daddy's room like that without even knocking!' Crispino's voice was higher than usual and had a tremor in it. 'She woke me up, my dear, because she wanted a little tinkle and couldn't find her chamberpot. I was under the bed trying to fetch it out when she ran through here.'

'Really? With the lamp in her hand? And with no encouragement?' Dot was too angry and embarrassed to mince words.

'Well, I was right behind her, of course, trying to catch hold of her. And of course I knew you weren't asleep. I'd heard you ... talking ... through the wall — aren't the walls *thin*, my dear? — so we arrived more or less together. Of course if I'd had any idea she meant to come through to you I'd have prevented her.'

'Oh, we don't mind the child in the least,' Dot said, trying not to emphasise the word *child* too strongly. She could just make out Paoletta's small figure at Crispino's elbow, and addressed her directly. 'Your potty's under the bed, love. It may have got pushed back a bit, though, when Pearl cleaned through today.'

'Well, I don't know, I'm sure. God knows I *looked*.' The tremor had left Crispino's voice and he was beginning to sound maliciously amused. He must have seen the nightgown and the pyjamas and be well aware how difficult their situation was, Dot realised. 'Wouldn't it be better, Dot darling, if you came out and found it for us?'

Carlo, with typical male cowardice, had dived beneath the covers at the first click of the door; now an eye appeared and a muffled voice spoke.

'If the child wants to pee, take her to the toilet, Cris.'

'Oh!' This simple solution had plainly not occurred to Crispino. 'That's all very well, Carlo old fellow, but what about later on? We don't want any little accidents, do we?'

'No. So let Paoletta go along to the toilet at once, before she puddles on our carpet. Off you go, Daddy's favourite Polly!'

Dot reprehensibly giggled. She saw Paoletta turn and disappear and then the light receded and their door slammed shut.

For a moment there was silence, and then Carlo said, 'Phew!'

'I know. Designed, I imagine, to stop such carryings-on once and for all.'

'Too right. Sorry, love, but . . . goodnight.'

Dot grabbed a handful of Carlo's hair and pulled until he flopped over on to his back. Then she sat astride his stomach, still holding his hair in an iron grip, and started to butterfly kiss his cheeks with her eyelashes. When he gave a snort of laughter she began to do other things which stopped him laughing almost at once. And they didn't only speed up his breathing, she thought with satisfaction a moment later. She slid down from his stomach until their mouths were on the same level and began to kiss him in the most arousing way she knew. Presently, it was no longer hard work. He had forgotten Crispino's sudden appearance, he had forgotten that their bed was young and lissom no more. Soon it was creaking like a wooden ship in a gale, and Carlo was saying how much he wanted her in a clearly audible voice, to which Dot added a few groans for good measure. In fact, considering that her uppermost thought throughout the next few minutes was how Crispino would be hating all this activity, it was a wonder that she managed to enjoy herself at all.

When they lay sated at last and she threw a damp arm across his wet chest and told him how wonderful he was, Carlo said that she had put into words his very thoughts.

'Poor old Cris,' he whispered presently (too late for whispering, thought Dot exultantly), 'all he needs is a woman of his own. If he had a wife like you, Dotty . . .'

Dot pretended to agree, but she did not think that Crispino would have much use for a woman of any kind. The anger in his voice, the way he had slammed out of the room when Carlo took her side, had confirmed all her suspicions. Crispino was *one of them*, like the gentle little unfrocked clergyman who used to come into the restaurant twice a week to befriend a customer or two. He had no interest in the waitresses. She did not intend to see Carlo become *one of them* too! Having outwitted Crispino, she would allow no further pussyfooting. She and Carlo would make very sure he did not stay with them again, save in dire necessity.

If Dot thought she had won, she was speedily disillusioned. Next morning she explained to Carlo that after what had transpired she would not entertain Crispino overnight again, though he was of course welcome to share a meal and spend the evening.

Two days later she had a message from Carlo.

'Meeting in London tomorrow,' it said. 'Staying the night with Crispino so we can leave on the early train — less bother for you. Much love, Carlo.'

'Daddy's going to London with Uncle Cris, darling,' Dot said as she walked Paoletta to kindergarten, with Tommy sitting up in the pram and hurling his teddy and his woolly ball out on to the pavement at regular intervals. 'He'll be back tomorrow, I expect. We mustn't expect Daddy to be with us all the time, must we?'

'Other people's daddies are,' Paoletta said. 'I don't like Uncle Crispino much. I don't like him at all! I hate him!'

Unerringly, as children will, she had gone straight to the heart of the problem. She did not waste breath blaming Daddy's job or Daddy's bosses, she blamed Crispino. Dot tried not to join in this crescendo of feeling, however.

'Well, Daddy only spent the night with Uncle Cris. I expect he'll be home tomorrow night.'

'Will he bring Uncle Cris?'

'I don't know.' Thankfully, they had reached the kindergarten. Dot bent, kissed her daughter, and waved her out of sight, then returned home, wondering what she ought to do.

Carlo *knew* how she felt about Crispino's encroaching ways, though she had never put into words her conviction that he was *one of them*. When this trip to London had been planned she had begged him not to let Cris talk him into allowing him to spend the night in Valentine Street. He had deliberately gone against her wishes, though not directly. He must have known it would make her bitterly unhappy, but that had obviously counted for nothing against the wish to please Crispino.

What on earth should she do? Appeal to her in-laws? They would probably send her off to Italy for a month again, and heaven knew where she might have happened by the time she got back! Once, she had planned to go home, but now, having settled into the house in Valentine Street again, she was loth to take so drastic and final a step. She would think about it this morning and then, after lunch, she would go down to the kindergarten and pick Paoletta up and they would go and visit Mrs Blishen. Her old landlady had remained a firm friend. She and Dot frequently exchanged visits and had lunch or tea with one another. What was more, because she had been managing alone with Horry for so long, she was both broadminded and practical. Mr Blishen had been fond of a bit of fun and a pretty face, so her marriage had not been a bed of roses, and when he left she had worked in factories, in shops and even, once, as a domestic, so her experience was wide. She would consult Mrs Blishen!

Arriving home, brisk and windswept, for there was a gale blowing, Dot found Pearl sitting hunched up in a corner of the kitchen clutching her middle. Though strong and willing, poor Pearl did suffer cruelly at certain times of the month and this, it was clear, was one of them. Dot put the kettle on for tea and a hot-water bottle, saw Pearl take aspirin tablets, and then packed her off to bed.

'You'll be fine by lunchtime if you rest now,' she told her. 'Otherwise you know how it is. You'll be ill all day and most of the night too.' Pearl went off clutching the bottle and a cup of hot tea, and Dot settled down to the housework. She was glad, in fact, to have vigorous physical work to do, because it made it easier to think. She had decided just what she would say to Mrs Blishen by the time she had washed and wiped up the breakfast dishes, and was feeling very much better by the time she had scrubbed the kitchen floor. Standing up to view the gleaming wet quarry tiles, she reflected that it was a good thing she enjoyed hard work, otherwise her lot would have seemed insupportable. But . . . she had married Carlo, she had known when she did so that she did not truly love him, so she must do the best she could now to patch things up.

She turned away, and a feeble voice from the head of the stairs announced, 'Please, ma'am, I've been ever so sick. Could you bring me up a glass of water?'

Pearl's bad days frequently followed this pattern, so Dot tiptoed across the kitchen floor, ran a glass of water, and was about to tiptoe back when she realised how foolish she was being. It is in the nature of a housewife's work that the moment she washes a floor she will need to cross it a dozen or more times before it can dry. She must do what Pearl always did and spread newspapers.

Under the sink was a pile of old papers kept for just such a purpose. Dot spread them out, reading them idly as one will, humming to herself, gradually laying a good path to the door, then to the back door as well. Then her humming – and her heart – faltered. A headline caught her eye.

WORST PIT DISASTER FOR YEARS, it read in letters two inches high. BLACK WYND IN DENBIGHSHIRE EXPLODES; HUNDREDS FEARED DEAD.

Dot knelt on the floor, forgetting all about Pearl's glass of water. Wet was seeping into the paper, making it difficult to read, but she could make it out well enough. There had been a series of gas explosions at the Wynd, she read, and all the miners working on the level known as Candle Deep had been killed outright, burned, gassed or trapped. Her own name leapt out at her: Tom Tegydd, the owner, says . . . and a few words of conventional regret, promises of an enquiry, mentions of gas and gobfires, of the bravery of the rescue teams who had worked unceasingly, and so on and so on.

As soon as she finished the article she looked at the top of the page; it had happened weeks ago, before Christmas! It must have been on everyone's lips for ages, but she had been in Italy, and by the time she returned it had been stale news, seldom thought about and never mentioned. It had passed into history until it was resurrected here, on her kitchen floor.

Feverishly she dragged out the rest of the papers and searched for ones with more up-to-date news. There were no earlier papers, but the later ones printed their gradually diminishing reports, first in a corner of the front page, then inside, then further and further down. She read names of men she knew, she read their words as they talked to 'our reporter', telling of comrades trapped, gushing gas, fires which raged like the infernos of hell.

She knelt where she was until she had read every last word on the matter and then got to her feet, her heart hammering in her throat and her head banging in sympathy. The final total had been nearly three hundred dead, and Hywel had worked in that dreadful, ill-fated pit! She had to know, she must know, what had happened to him! She knew her father was alive, though he had been down the pit with the rescue teams, but so many others were dead . . .

'Ma'am . . . have you forgotten my drink of water?'

It was poor Pearl, croaking away at the head of the stairs! Dot ran across the kitchen, grabbed the glass of water and shot up the flight with it, losing a good bit as she went. She thrust the glass into Pearl's hand and spoke with frantic haste.

'Pearl, I've got to go home right this minute. I've had bad news! I'll be gone . . . oh, a day or so, I suppose. Take care of the children for me – fetch Paoletta from kindergarten . . . and tell Mr Carlo that he must stay here until I get back. All right? Or on second thoughts, just in case Mr Carlo finds himself too busy, would you take the children down to the Royal? My parents-in-law will take good care of them for me.'

'Yes, of course, ma'am. Will you let Mr Carlo know . . . dear me, there's Tommy crying!' The poor girl had drunk the last drop of water eagerly, and now she turned and headed for the nursery. 'I'll have him in bed with me, ma'am, if you don't mind. I can't face going back and forth, not full of aspirin and aches like I am.'

'Oh, poor Pearl!' Dot flew into the bedroom and grabbed the surprised Tommy from his cot. 'I'll take him with me. He's a big boy now, aren't you, darling? You'd like to go on a choo-choo train with me, wouldn't you? I'll sling some nappies and things into a bag and we'll be off.'

She was as good as her word. She dressed Tommy in a woollen suit, his blue reefer coat and a warm woollen helmet, dragged mittens on his hot and resistant hands and sturdy little shoes on his small feet. He was fifteen months and walking very well, so they set off, hand in hand, down the road with Dot carrying the bag, but after a few yards a bus swooped up beside them and they jumped aboard.

'One to Thorpe Station, please. Do I have to pay for the baby?'

After that there was no time to think, for they arrived at the station just as a train was leaving which could take them some of the way. Dot ran, with Tommy in her arms and the bag bumping along behind on its strap, and they caught the train with no time to spare — it was already moving as Dot hurled herself, the baby and the bag into a carriage.

It was a tedious cross-country journey involving too many changes, but somehow she and Tommy weathered them all, and at last they were in the train which would carry them all the way to the town. The scenery outside the windows gradually became more and more familiar, and Dot began to grow excited and apprehensive and to wonder what sort of a welcome she would get.

She was not going to stay long, of course; that would scarcely be fair to Carlo. She would ring him up at the office tomorrow morning and let him know where she was and tell him when she would be coming back. But it would serve him right to be the one to worry a bit, to wonder where she had gone and how long she would be away.

She had not looked away from the window at all, save to glance at Tommy, who was fast asleep beside her. Now, at last, she saw in the distance the faint blue of the mountains. She was unprepared for the great leap her heart gave and the way tears flooded to her eyes and ran down her cheeks. Home! Oh, how she had missed it, without even admitting to herself how much! How she had hungered for mountains, even whilst admiring the marvellously rich and fertile soil of the flat Norfolk countryside. As the train got nearer and nearer to the town, it occurred to her that she was about to change not only her name, but her entire being, for she had been Dorothy Evans, then Dorothy Peruzzi, and now she would go back to being just Dot again for the duration of her stay. She did not know when she had made the conscious decision not to reveal that Tommy was half Italian, but she knew her father and his prejudices. She would think up some story . . . she could go back to being Dorothy Evans, say she had met a good Welshman and married him, or she could just avoid saying anything about her husband. It was no business of anyone's, after the way her father had treated her.

As the countryside grew more and more familiar, so the

pleasure and the ache of anxiety increased. Oh, wonderful to be home! But what would she find here? What had happened at the Wynd, and to whom? She could not bear the thought that she lived in a world which did not also contain Hywel, somewhere, doing something. She could not bear it, so she would not even consider it. She sat back in her seat and willed herself to patience.

The bandages came off and Huw told his brother that he was handsome as ever. Folk would be amazed to see two such good-looking devils. Hywel grinned, but Huw could see he was not believed. Not that his brother could see for himself what had happened to his face. The scarring where the rock had ripped from browline to chin was livid still, and it bisected his eyebrow, eyelid and eye as well as his cheek and jaw. Muscles and nerves had torn like paper, and, though they had knitted to an extent, as yet Hywel's facial muscles could not actually work, so that the right side of his face did not move, not when he smiled nor when he wept. Immobile, his mouth drooped, his eyelid drooped, his cheek seemed flaccid. His right eye was sightless; you could not see much of it for the lowered lid, yet it gleamed scarlet, disconcerting, when he moved his head and something within caught the light.

It had caught his upper lip, that rock, so he found it difficult to drink from a cup. He let liquid dribble down his chin and was embarrassed and upset when he found out. His right arm and hand, too, were criss-crossed with scar tissue, deeply purple, slow to pale. But that did not matter. It was Hywel's face that mattered. Folk who knew no better might think at first glance that he had had a stroke. It worried Huw deeply that someone might hurt his brother by being startled, possibly even repelled, by the injuries to his face.

But he had not worried about Jessica. Still, the feeling that they had something in common, that they both loved someone who had been brought up as a sibling, made him assume that Jessica would understand as he would. She was coming to see Hywel around teatime, she had promised the previous day. Hywel had finally brought himself to ask her to marry him and she had said yes, so they needed time together. Huw planned to leave when she arrived, and watched for her.

She appeared in the doorway of the ward. By the grace of God he said nothing, continuing to talk steadily to his brother, but he watched her, saw her face.

She came down the ward; she was smiling, animated. She got close enough to see the extent of the injuries, the way eye, cheek and mouth were affected. Huw saw the luminous skin pale, the eyes stare, and then colour rush up into her cheeks and a hand fly to her mouth. He went on talking in his slow, measured Norfolk voice as she backed away, shaking her head. He did not falter as she turned and fled, though he longed, for a moment, to go after her, slap her head until it rang like the empty vessel it was, shake some sense into that shallow little mind. How could she, the little bitch? How could she hurt Hywel so?

Not that Hywel knew, of course. His sight was not sufficiently strong to know when someone reached his bedside, let alone when they were walking up the ward. Presently, he asked what time it was and Huw told him, and then his tea arrived and Huw helped his brother to find the cup, and put the sandwiches, one by one, into his good hand, remarking jocularly as he did so that no doubt Jessica would be along in a moment.

'Again, mun? Oh, I don't think so. One look was enough – surely you could see that?'

Huw stared at his brother.

'See it? But you can't see that well, my old beauty, and we both know it! D'you mean your sight's coming back?'

Hywel was grinning with half his face, but it was a defiant and shaky grin.

'No such luck, mun. With your eyes I did see it, same's we used to. Lovely and clear, too. Our Jess coming down the aisle, going first white and then pink, grabbing her throat . . . running out. Oh, aye. I saw it just like you did.'

Words would not come. Huw took his brother's hand.

'Don't worry, Huw. Horrible I do look, no doubt. Poor girl, don't blame her. She's too young to be told that beauty's only skin-deep! Besides, better to know now than later . . . imagine marrying someone who couldn't ever look at you without a shudder! For the best it is.'

Huw touched his brother's jaw with a bunched-up fist; a pretend clout. Tears were running down his cheeks but he forced his voice to remain calm, even a little amused.

'Now that's enough of that. We're too much alike for me to let that go! You might look a bit rough now – well, you do, to be honest – but it's nothing that time won't mend. Scars pale, muscles knit . . . you don't want to think she did it from not liking it. It was just the shock of seeing you looking different. She'll probably be all over you tomorrow.'

'No. I wouldn't want it. Only thing I regret, mun, is my little hill farm. No chance, see, without someone to give a hand. But there, once I'm out of here perhaps I'll find someone . . .'

'You're sure, my old beauty, that you really don't want marriage? If she was to agree, I mean?' He saw Hywel's nod. 'Well then, there's something I've been wanting to suggest for many a day, but didn't like to because of Jess and your hill farm.

'Our place has got big, a good deal more than I can handle, though we managed well enough when Dad was alive. But we're remote, see, a good five miles from the nearest village for one thing, so workers aren't easy to come by. I was wondering, not liking to suggest it, but – are you set on a hill farm? You wouldn't care to try a bit of marsh farming? Just until you've got your sight back and can see what you're buying, say? Mum would be so grateful, and my sisters too. You know what girls are – they don't think farm work does their complexions much good! I don't take much money out, but we'd share everything . . . what's the matter?'

Hywel's face was working, one half of his mouth screwing up, one half of his brow furrowing. One eye, the good one, was brighter than usual and his fingers were gripping the cup hard enough to crush it to shards, it seemed to Huw.

'You're sure I could be useful? I'm strong, I can . . .' His voice faltered to a stop and he stretched out a hand to put down his tea whilst he regained control. The cup missed the table and tea went everywhere. Huw got up and began to mop, but Hywel hit the side table with controlled force.

'By God, what did you go saying that for, mun? A bloody great clumsy useless hulk, that's me. Never be no good to you – never get a thing right. I'll manage, I'll . . .'

'You'll come?' Huw took his own cup of tea and put it into his brother's hand. 'Here, stop whining. You only spilled a drop. Now come on, give me a fair answer; will you come home with me?'

'Thought I'd knocked it all over the show,' Hywel muttered. He took a drink, then put the cup carefully back on the side table. He sighed. 'You're sure I'll be able to see well enough to do a job, give a hand?'

'I'll swear it on a whole stack of Bibles if you'll only agree to come back and live with us.'

'Right. It's a deal. If I find I'm no good to you I shan't stay, so I won't be taking advantage. Shake!'

Solemnly, the two shook hands.

Throughout all his time in North Wales, Huw had never again been to the house in the village, nor seen his mother. He no longer thought of her as his mother. She no more deserved the title than would an animal who devoured its own young. He disliked her with sufficient intensity to make him chary of meeting her in case it showed in his eyes.

But they came to the station to see him and his brother off, the whole family. Luke and Dewi carried the big trunk containing all Hywel's worldly possessions, and it did not weigh all that much. Glyn had brought him a letter from Tegydd saying that he would be paid compensation for what had happened to him, and a packed meal to eat on the train. They were taking the journey slowly because Hywel was still not fit, so they were leaving on an afternoon train and only going sixty miles or so that day. Huw had telephoned ahead and arranged a boarding-house room which they would share for the first night.

Ella came over to them. She must have nerved herself up for this meeting, must have guessed how Huw hated her; you had to admire her courage in some things. She touched Hywel's hand and he must have known her touch at once for he stiffened defensively.

It hurt her; wicked she might be, but that tiny movement of rejection still hurt.

'I . . . I've come to wish you happy, Hywel, bach.' She

almost muttered the words. 'It's best to start afresh, the way you are.'

'What way, Mam?' Hywel's voice was strong and clear. 'Hideously scarred, is that what you mean?'

'No, no . . . I'm sorry, I meant to be so . . . I mean since you and Jess have decided not to marry it's better to go far away.'

'I see. So that she can remain here and not feel guilty every time she sets eyes on me? Is that what you mean?'

'Ashamed of her I am,' Glyn said gloomily. 'Blowing hot and cold, mad to get you one moment, fighting shy the next. Ashamed.'

'Don't be.' Hywel smiled lopsidedly in Glyn's general direction. 'Better that there be truth than lies between people. Always be fond of Jessica, me, but that doesn't mean marriage would ever have been right.'

'Perhaps not. Had her head turned, see, by the very people who ought to know better.' Glyn glared at Ella, who glared back, and Huw saw that their marriage, which had been a good one, would never quite recover from what had happened. Sad. But once Glyn had seen what his wife was capable of he could probably never feel the same.

The train came in, busily, noisily, with a great slamming of doors and pushing and shoving of luggage and people. Huw chose them a quiet carriage, put their luggage up on the rack, and then turned to the farewell scene taking place outside the train. Because it was only February sunset came early and today had been fine since early morning. From here he could see the mountains, white-browed still, with the lower slopes clear and above them a brilliant sunset. Red and gold, it streaked the sky as the sun plunged into the cloudlets that would hide its actual slide beneath the horizon.

Another train had drawn in on the opposite platform. He saw, without interest, people get off and make their way to the grey stone station building. Some were farmers, others gaitered shepherds back from market, the odd housewife. And a girl with a baby in her arms. A lovely baby in a scarlet helmet and blue reefer coat. The baby waggled its hand and Huw waved back, but the girl and her precious burden were tiny; they were swallowed up in the crowd which was surging towards the ticket collector and the town.

'Well, mun, all the best, is it?' Luke. 'Write, we will. And you?'

'Thanks, mun. I'll be all right. I don't know about writing; we'll see.'

'Goodbye, boys, goodbye!' And then the train was starting and drawing away, the waving grew more and more furious, the shouts began to sound small and forlorn. He saw a figure up on the bridge, leaning over, waving, crying. Long red hair framed a pale face, the mouth drawn down, the eyes tear-stained.

Huw pulled the window up and returned to his seat next to his brother.

'Jessica was waving as we came under the bridge.'

'Aye?' Not even Huw could tell, from his face, what Hywel was thinking. 'Glad I am that she came. No use regretting what happened. She'll be crying, I daresay?'

'Well, yes.'

'Aye. A great girl for what people think, our Jess. Let herself down, see, by running out of the ward that day. She'll regret that moment more than most. If she'd thought, she could have carried it off then and broke it to me later, but she didn't think. Ah, well, she'll forget it soon enough.'

'True.' They sat for a moment in companionable silence, then Huw said, 'Like me to tell you what we're passing?'

'No need. Tell you what, that old doctor wasn't so far off. Getting better, my sight is. Can't see·faces yet, but I can tell you . . .' he paused to stare '. . . brown and white cows . . . might be Herefords, grazing on something thrown down for them . . . parsnips?'

'Hywel, you crafty bugger!' Huw was delighted and it showed in his voice. 'How long háve you been able to do that?'

'It's been coming a bit better every day, but I didn't fancy saying in case it was some kind of fluke. Tell you what , we'll play a game, shall we? I'll tell you what I think I see and you tell me when I'm right or wrong.'

It might have seemed childish, but the game kept them absorbed for the whole journey.

Twenty-Three

She remembered the station as being both smaller and quieter than this, but then on the few occasions she had been here before, she had been either much later in the evening or earlier in the morning. Now, with a train going out on the opposite platform and people pouring off the train she had been on, it was almost confusing. But one thing was not; through a gap in the fencing she could see the mountains, white-browed, and above them a brilliant sunset. She stood still for a moment to watch it, and felt Tommy squiggle in her arms as he waved to the train opposite, about to depart. But then they were carried along by the impatient crowd, squeezed past the ticket collector, and spat out on the paving stones beneath the smart green and cream wooden canopy.

'Well, Tommy, here we are!' Dot lugged her bag across to where some taxicabs waited. She bent down to the first one and addressed the driver.

'I've run out of money, but I can pay when I reach my destination. Is that all right?'

The driver, a small, weaselly-faced man who looked vaguely familiar, grunted and indicated the back seat.

'Good enough, I daresay. Where do you want to go, now?'

'Plas Tegydd.'

The man screwed round in his seat the better to stare, then a slow grin spread across his face.

'The Plas, eh? Would you be Miss Dot?'

'I wou . . . I mean, yes, that's me.'

'Thought I recognised you, miss! Only seen you a couple of times, mind, when I come up to the Plas on business with your Da. I'm James Lewis. Worked on the books at the Olwen, I did, then moved over to the Wynd about a year back.'

This was luck — or was it? Dot's heart began to hammer with enough fierceness to make her breathless. But she had to ask!

'I see — then you'll know most of my friends who worked in the pit, I daresay? I've been abroad so I've only just heard about the disaster. Could you tell me, please, if the F-Fletcher brothers are all right? The one I kn-knew best was Hywel F-Fletcher.'

'Oh aye, I know the Fletcher lads all right; not well, mind. We don't know the colliers so well when we're in administrative. And anyway, after the disaster I started this . . .' he indicated the taxi cab. 'Couldn't face all the worry, what with court appearances and post mortems. And awful identifications there were, made your blood run cold.'

'Were any of the Fletcher brothers hurt?' Dot said, trying to ignore the salacious tone in which he spoke. 'Can you remember if . . . if Hywel was hurt?' She could see that he looked doubtful and added, 'He was going to get married before Christmas, I believe.'

The narrow brow cleared, then clouded.

'Oh, *that* one; aye, I remember that one. One of the best they said he was, strapping strong chap. Married a school-teacher, would that be the one?'

'Yes.' She could not elaborate on it. Her whole soul was listening for the words she wanted to hear, dreading the words she could not bear to believe.

'Dead. The wife came up — pretty little thing — identified him by his belt and his snap tin. That was usual, see. Not much else they *could* identify.'

'You're sure? I mean were they sure it was him?' Her lips were so cold and stiff that she could hardly force the words through them. All along she had felt sure in her heart that Hywel had survived; now to have this little man so certain he was dead was a knife in her breast. 'How could they be sure, if . . . if . . .'

'If the body were badly burned, which it were,' the taxi driver said promptly. 'Well, only because of the belt and the snap tin, like. But not often it is that a man will swop a belt, see? And most hang the snap tin on their belts. Keeps it out of the way of their hands and the tools they get their coal with.'

457

'I see. He married the schoolteacher, you say. Is she still in the village?'

'Strange you should ask that. No, went away, she did, to a school a long way off, in Yorkshire somewhere. Best to get right away, perhaps. And yet in a way she was lucky, that girl, because they say two hundred men still lie in Candle Deep. No one can identify a man down there since they've sealed the level.'

As if by common consent, they both stopped talking then and Dot watched as the road neared the village, turned over the bridge, became a lane, an overgrown track . . . and there was the Plas.

Hollow victory, to be back and Hywel dead! His going had sucked the colours from the mountains and the glow from being in her own place once more. She climbed wearily out of the taxi and trailed her bag behind her, bumping it carelessly across the drive and up the steps to the front door. She rang and a maid appeared, her cap awry, a dust-smear across her brow. Behind her the house looked like the Sleeping Beauty's castle after the hundred years; she could see cobwebs on the beautiful timber ceiling and dust lay thick and soft on the marble tiles.

'I'd like to see Mr Tegydd. Please pay the taxi driver,' she said curtly. In her arms Tommy began the mutter of waking which usually presaged tears. The maid stared, then led her across the hall to the study door. She said, 'In there he is,' and turned without more ado to return to the kitchen.

Dot tapped on the door and then opened it. Tommy began to grizzle. Her father was sitting at the big desk, writing something in a book. The room was reasonably neat and fairly clean, that was the most you could say about it, and a fire burned in the grate. Tom himself was neither neat nor clean, however. He had always been well turned out, but now he was shabby. Shabby-genteel perhaps, but nevertheless shabby. His jacket was patched, his trousers faded, his shirt not even clean, and he had loosened his tie which had managed to get round under his ear. He had developed a pot-belly which did not suit him, and there was a bald patch on top of his head. By his hand was a whisky glass, by the glass a half empty bottle. A soda siphon stood within reach. The smell of stale spirit and stale air was not pleasant.

Dot took all this in whilst her father continued to write, staring apathetically down at his work. Then he said, quite sharply, 'Put the logs near the fire, girl, or how do you think they'll be dry enough to burn?' and looked up.

'Well, why . . . my God, am I dreaming?' He got up, and she saw that he was shaking. 'It's Dot, isn't it? You've come home!'

'That's right.' She moved further into the room, trying out a smile. It felt natural to smile at the old reprobate. She had loved him so much when she was a little girl!

'Is that . . . it's a baby!' He sounded absolutely delighted. 'Well, well, well, and a boy, I'll warrant! What's his name?'

'I called him Tommy, after you. Oh dear, he's going to start bawling, he's had an awfully long day.'

'Tommy. Tommy Tegydd junior.' Her father tilted his head as though to consider the name and Dot, who had opened her mouth to contradict him, did not speak. Time enough for that. 'Well, well, Tommy Tegydd and my little Dot, come to take care of the old man, eh? Or the old place, at any rate.' As Tommy started to cry in good earnest his grandfather picked up the whisky bottle, poured a drop into a glass, and came and took the baby from her. Before she could say a word the glass was at Tommy's mouth and Tommy had guzzled, coughed, and smacked his lips loudly. He then burped, turned his head into his grandfather's disgusting old jacket, and proceeded to snuggle down to sleep.

'Best medicine for a crying child, especially if it's got the wind,' Tom said complacently. He was holding Tommy as though his arms had been specially made for just such a task. 'Sit down, my dear, and tell me what's been happening to you. You'll stay?'

'Ah, now, I haven't come back because I need anything – or anyone, for that matter. I've come back because I've been abroad and I've only just heard about the disaster at the Wynd. Father, I'm most terribly sorry. You must have gone through a dreadful time. If I'd known earlier I'd have come at once.'

'That's what I thought.' He had waved her into a fireside chair and sunk into the matching one himself. 'When they splashed the news of the disaster over every paper in the country I said to myself she's either dead or so happy she

459

doesn't care about us any more, but I didn't think it was the latter. I thought you were dead. Ah, dear me, and there you were, you and the lad here, off enjoying yourself abroad. Or have you been living abroad? Was that it?'

'No, that wasn't it. I'd been rather ill with bronchitis and I'd got friends in Italy so I went to stay with them until I got rid of the thing. Then I saw an old paper and I got straight on the next train which would bring me here.'

'Mm. You should have come as soon as the lad was born. I wouldn't have blamed you; you should have known that! Why, my dearest wish has been for a Tegydd heir and you've gone and produced one without a word to anyone – a fine boy, too.' He looked dotingly at the small, slumbering face in the crook of his shoulder. 'Yes, he'll have the lot – the mines, this house, all my land. And since you're his mother it'll be left to you, in trust for him, one day.'

With those words he had undone all the bitterness, all the harm. But she could not let it go at that.

'Father, what about Blanche's boy? The other Tommy? I took it for granted he'd inherit.'

'No. He isn't a Tegydd, you see; he's an Edenthorpe. I sent him back to her family after she died – you knew she died? – and I go and see him once a year, but he's all Edenthorpe. Even got that awful accent . . . and the old lady's vulgar ways. I'll leave him an annuity but no land, nor the pits. They'll go to my laddo here.'

'Father, a quarter of an hour ago you didn't know Tommy existed; who was your heir then?'

He shrugged, smiling down at the child.

'Oh, who knows? You, if you were alive; possibly one of Kate's brats if you were not. It didn't matter; nothing has mattered since you left and Blanche died until this evening when you walked in with the child. Umm . . . you will stay, won't you? You won't just disappear again?'

'No, I won't do that. I don't know about staying, though. I've got . . . well, commitments.'

She meant a husband and a daughter, but she could not say it! If she did he would not hold Tommy so lovingly in his arm, smile so fondly upon the sleeping face. And it was a small enough deception; she would not need to tell him just yet.

460

Later, perhaps. Or not even then? Why should she tell him, take away his happiness — and her son's chance of inheriting Plas Tegydd? All she and Carlo could give him was the Royal Pavilion one day and their little Victorian double dweller. She knew that Tommy would want more than that — he was her son! Her boy would want land and an ancient house and a family name; Carlo could give him none of those things, but she could! It did not matter a jot to her that everyone would believe the baby to be illegitimate. If it made him the Tegydd heir it would not matter; she could bring him up here, watch him grow, teach him about the land and the crops and the beasts that throve in hill country. They could be so happy!

'Commitments? If you need money . . .'

'Oh no, nothing like that.' She twisted her wedding ring uneasily, and the little engagement ring; it had been all Carlo could afford at the time and she had thought it beautiful, with its tiny diamonds and the pale emerald like a fairy's teardrop. Now, she thought it was a good thing that they had not been able to spend much money on a ring, or Tom might have guessed her secret. As it was, he plainly believed she wore both rings for respectability. Wronging her sadly, but there!

'Then if it's not money . . . are you happy, wherever you've been? Happier than you were here?'

Her head shook. Ah no, she had never been happy, truly happy, divorced from this place, though at the time she had felt content enough. If only things had not changed! But with no Hywel, what would her future be? Better to work hard here and build the Plas up for her son than fade away in Norwich, with a husband who did not really love her, had married her for all the wrong reasons. It was just . . . she could not desert Paoletta! She adored her daughter. The thought of not seeing her for weeks was cruel to contemplate. Turn those weeks into years . . .

No, she could not possibly stay. Well, not for ever. But for a week or two, or three, it would do her good to be back here, and it would do Carlo good to know that she was not always at his beck and call.

'I was very well content when I first went, because of . . . well, you know why, Father. But I soon began to miss everything — people, the countryside, the house. I knew you'd let it go to rack and ruin – you really have, Father; it's disgraceful – and I couldn't bear the thought of it, so by and large I tried not to think. However, I made a life for myself, lots of friends, and a very nice little home. I came back on impulse, because of the disaster, but I've got a feeling that I should have been making tracks in this direction quite soon in any case. I was so horribly homesick, and . . . well, I think children need country air.'

'You were in a city? Yes, I thought you'd probably go to London. I put advertisments in the national papers, but I daresay you never read them? No, I suppose youngsters don't much, these days. Wanted you to come back, you see. And now you have – it's like a dream come true.'

'I'm glad you're pleased to see me, Father. But I'm not back for good. I shall have to go again in a week or so.'

'This time, Father, I shall stay on my terms, and they'll be quite specific.'

It was two weeks after her return to the Plas. She and Tom were in the study, comfortably settled on opposite sides of the desk. She had known within a day that she would never willingly go back to Norwich and leave her father and her home behind her, but she had been far too shrewd to let Tom know this right away. She had not told him until this morning, and then the relief and jubilation on his face had convinced her that she was doing the right thing. But she had trusted Tom too easily once. She would not do so again. This time she would have it in writing!

'Of course, of course! I'll have Mr Geraint draw up a contract if it will make you feel safer.'

'It will, but you won't have to do anything of the sort, since I'll draw it up myself. If you'll forgive my saying so, Father, you were always a man of whims. If you met some pretty young thing tomorrow and in nine months' time she had a child by you, Tommy and I would be cut off without a shilling, I've no doubt. It's happened to me once. I won't see it happen again.'

'It won't happen again. And you shouldn't speak in that coarse way, my dear, even to me! Nine months later, indeed! As if I would, at my age.' He pushed his chest out and grinned,

462

however, giving her a sly glance from above the spectacles which he occasionally wore when doing close work. 'Of course I *could*; to be honest, I thought very seriously of taking a mistress after you left and Blanche died – I didn't seem able to manage, somehow. But . . . you'll be amazed, one of these days, to find out how being in love with someone like Blanche can affect you. I couldn't summon up any enthusiasm for another woman, not the prettiest, sauciest, naughtiest of them all. To tell you the truth, even work and making money lost its appeal. Until you walked through that door with me laddo, I didn't have a thing worth living for and I knew it, though I tried to tell myself different.'

'Poor Father.' Dot put her arm round his shoulders and gave him a hug. 'I do like the nurse you've got for Tommy, she's sensible and kind, but we need more staff. You know that, don't you? This place is going to sparkle, because no child of mine inherits a ruin if I can help it, and anyway, it grieves me to see the Plas so run down. I love it as I love my child, and I feel responsible for its welfare, and that goes for the grounds and the farm and all the land, too, so as you can see we're going to get things straight as part of my bargain.'

'Good, good!' Tom was eager now, seeing that Dot would be more likely to stay if she was immersed in estate business. 'What else?'

'I want Souse'em back; he was a very good man. Not Redfern. He was good too, but we aren't big enough for him any more. Souse'em will come, though; someone down in the village told me he's out of work and drinking anything he can lay his hands on. He'll help all right, and be glad to.'

'Yes, I can arrange that. Oh, by the way, I met Ella in the village this morning and told her you were back. She was thrilled – said she'd pop up some time and see you. I wish she'd come back to work here again, but she doesn't feel she can, not since the accident.'

'Oh, it will be nice to see Ella,' Dot said. 'But I shan't know what to say . . . about her son being killed, I mean.'

'Yes, dreadfully sad, and it doesn't do to remind her about the younger one. That was a miracle – I don't suppose you know about it, do you? Young Hywel getting out of Candle Deep through an airway?'

The room whirled around her. Stars appeared and burst in coloured rain. She had *known* he was not dead! She had known it!

'No, I haven't heard. Tell me.'

He told her the whole story, and Dot could not prevent her cheeks from flaming, nor her eyes from sparkling. 'I'd like to see him again,' she said, when the story was done. 'It's been years. I expect he's changed.'

'Well, love, you can't see him. He's left the area. That young red-haired girl he was going steady with has gone too; probably wanted to get married well away from the mother.' He then completed his tale by relating what had happened when he and Huw had arrived at Ella's house.

'And you think he and Jessica went off somewhere to get married? But he was so keen on having a hill farm, Father! Perhaps they've just gone away for a while so that Hywel can recuperate.'

'Possibly. But Jessica didn't strike me as the kind of girl who'd enjoy hill farming. Still, you can be mistaken in people. Now how about coming into town with me tomorrow morning and getting this contract of yours drawn up?'

She agreed to it and ignored the nagging ache of guilt and sadness because she was denying her daughter. She loved Paoletta and missed her very much, but the child would be well looked after, and Carlo adored her too. And she had got Tommy. It was no use fretting. She would have Paoletta with her in a year or two, when Father was so accustomed to Tommy that he would never want to let them leave. In the meantime, she must simply throw herself, body and soul, into the redemption of Plas Tegydd.

She knew, now, that Hywel was alive and probably married, but she found that even the latter no longer hurt her. To know him alive was sufficient. The guilt over deserting Paoletta would dull in time. It simply never occurred to Dot that she might be subjecting her daughter to a very similar childhood to her own, a childhood of loneliness and deprivation. Carlo loved his little girl, she told herself, and the Perruzzis adored her, and Pearl doted on her. Oh, Paoletta would be fine!

*

'Put it down at once and go straight up to bed! I declare, you're the most difficult child I ever had to deal with!'

Paoletta stared solemnly at the new housekeeper. There had been so many of them since Mummy had left, each one, she thought, nastier than the last; but Mrs Goudge was a real beast. Paoletta could do nothing right. If she was happy, singing away to herself, she was noisy and thoughtless, ignoring Mrs Goudge's poor head. If she was quiet she was a deceitful brat planning mischief.

'Why? You said I was to . . .'

But nothing made Mrs Goudge madder than being told she was wrong, though she must have known that she had told Paoletta to pick up all the bits of cotton and the pins which she, Mrs Goudge, had scattered all over the drawing room carpet.

'Polly, I said get to your room and I meant it. If you want to see your daddy when he comes home . . .'

Paoletta was out of the room and up the stairs before the sentence was finished. She did so love being with Daddy whilst they ate their evening meal, had a game of cards or read to each other, and then, after her bath, she would go downstairs in her nightdress and Daddy would brush her hair one hundred times and say poems to her as he did it. Lovely! When they were doing her hair, Mrs Goudge was not allowed to come interfering into the drawing room, and a good thing too!

Uncle Cris always found the housekeepers and they were always quite fat, usually fair-haired and very very plain. The first one had had a real snout, just like a pig, and hair on her chin too, which glinted when the light fell on it right. She had not lasted more than a few days, because Gran had come round visiting and had seen Pigface washing her feet in the sink. Ugh! Out she went.

Then they had tried another plump one, only she was quite pretty really and had no hairs on her chin. She had upset Uncle Cris by going to his bedroom in the middle of the night (no doubt she had mistaken his door for the toilet, Paoletta charitably supposed) when he was staying with them. Uncle Cris had stamped and wailed and finally had wept real tears and had tried to hug Daddy, who was not having any of *that*! So Uncle Cris went home and the second housekeeper disappeared. The third had been old and very crotchety; she had left when Daddy discovered that Paoletta was doing most of the washing and wiping up, scrubbing the kitchen floor and generally saving the third housekeeper's poor back. The fourth one got drunk on Daddy's whisky on her birthday – she said it was her birthday but Daddy said he doubted it – and the fifth one was the detestable Mrs Goudge.

Unfortunately Mrs Goudge did not have whiskers, a snout or old age. She was old to Paoletta but possibly not more than forty. She kept the house lovely and clean, Paoletta could see that, and she cooked lovely meals effortlessly – even Paoletta's lunches, when Daddy was not on hand to see, were delicious and temptingly served. But her horribleness was much better hidden and much more horrible than her predecessors'. She was sly, punishing Paoletta and making her life a misery, but only when Daddy was well out of the way. Paoletta was waiting for her to make a mistake, but she had not done so yet. She was for ever starching his shirts and darning his socks and doing all the little things that the other housekeepers had tended to skimp, and this meant that Daddy was less critical over Mrs Goudge.

Even Gran thought that Daddy had found a good person to take care of him this time. Gran did not see Mrs Goudge taking Paoletta to her kindergarten, walking too fast so that Paoletta had to run and got a stitch in her side, and then grabbing Paoletta's arm and towing her along by it so that the joining bit, the hinge part at the top, was sore and achey for the rest of the day. She was clever about bruises, too. They showed. So her pinches and cuffs were always either applied to places not commonly on display, or hard enough to hurt but not to mark.

At first, poor bewildered little Paoletta had spent her days and most of her nights wondering when Mummy was coming back. Then she wondered why Mummy had left her – what had she done that was so naughty that Mummy could go off and leave her, yet take Tommy, a crybaby if ever there was one? Sometimes Daddy said he thought Mummy would come back one day; at other times he thought she would not. Gran and Grandpa put advertisements in the papers and went to and from the police station in the hopes that Mummy might have lost her memory and presently be found and brought home.

They blamed Crispino, and so did Paoletta, but Daddy said that Cris was his only friend and had stayed true to him after Mummy had proved false.

Mind you, when Crispino had moved in, Daddy had not liked that one little bit. Late one night there had been a scene and Daddy had roared at his friend to go home and stay home. The ill-feeling had not lasted, but Paoletta did not think things had ever been quite the same between the two men.

Paoletta's little room was chilly, but she took a blanket off her bed, wrapped it shawl-fashion round her shoulders, and got out her locking diary. Daddy had given it to her for Christmas and every day she unlocked it, taking the key out from under the squeaky floorboard where it was hidden, and wrote a short entry. It had to be short, because writing was a new skill and her letters were still very large, but she could manage a word or two. She was keeping track on the evils of housekeepers, and this present one was known, simply but forcefully, as *wiked wich*. Today she announced that ww – it saved space – had smaked P for doin wot she was tole. On the opposite page she drew an exciting picture of P weeping in her bedroom. Then she coloured it. Then she locked the diary away and got out the Giant Book of Fairy Stories and began to read. By the time Daddy got home the fairy stories would have transported her to so many lovely places that she would look, once more, like his happy girl.

It had not occurred to her that she might complain of housekeeperly behaviour to Daddy or to Gran and Grandpa. One did not tell on grown-ups. It was a useless task, or so she believed.

And presently, because Daddy was late, she climbed into bed and fell asleep, to dream that Mummy came back and sent Wiked Wich packing. There was a smile on her face for quite a minute when she woke.

It was a far cry from the pit to working the land, a further cry from the swelling hills of North Wales to the Norfolk marshes. But Hywel had known those marshes for ten years, and even though he had been unable to choose where to wander they were not strange to him. What was strange was meeting the people he had sometimes seen from afar – his aunt, his girl cousins, even a visiting farmer or a wildfowler or a bent old man cutting rushes. They did not know Hywel, but he knew them all right.

But the welcome he got from Megan more than made up for any strangeness. She had a motherliness that her sister lacked, and was not ashamed to show it. Her first words had warmed him. She had met them at the door, hugged her adopted son, and then hugged her nephew, with a naturalness which made the gesture not only acceptable but desired.

'Well now, if I say you've grown a bit you'll think me mad, but when I last held you in my arms you were a little bit of a thing no more than a few days old. I loved you then. I would have taken you with Huw, here, but it was more than my sister could bear to have both her boys gone from her. So I've spent many an hour wondering about you. No better present could I have than Hywel himself come here to live.'

It was a harsh winter, too, and yet he and Huw seemed to find something to do every day. Huw had not been exaggerating when he said that the work was too much for him. He really did need someone else to keep the place going. Even now, with the stock kept deliberately low, for there was not the grazing for them with the marsh under snow or iced over, there was work. Huw had converted one meadow to pigs and geese, and they needed feeding, cleaning out, sometimes doctoring. Then the beasts that were still out on the marshes wanted food taking to them: great bundles of the hay, sweet-smelling still, which Huw and the girls had cut out on the leys in the summer. And there were the small tasks like milking the cow, collecting the eggs and feeding and cleaning out the poultry which had to be done every day, regardless. After a week the family was wondering aloud how it had ever managed before Hywel came, and Huw was talking of buying sheep when spring arrived.

'We din't bother before. Too much trouble, and none of us knew about sheep. But you say you do, old partner?'

'Aye, a lot I did pick up as a lad – and kept the knowledge green, too, by talking to the shepherds. Oh, I'm not denying you can work hard with a poor flock. They seem to delight in disease, I reckon it's that great greasy fleece hanging in all the muck, but once you've got 'em clean you keep 'em clean, and then they can be real money-spinners. Lambing, shearing, grazing till they're fat, then selling off the lambs you don't need, dipping, putting them to the ram . . . you'll find yourself employing labour before you know it, and able to afford it, too.'

'We'll help,' Susan volunteered. Hywel had had difficulty at first sorting the three little girls out and had taken to calling Susan, his favourite, Senior Baby. Now he ruffled her brown fringe, tugged at a tiny pigtail, and told her that she really would be useful come the spring.

Middle Baby Sarah promptly reminded all and sundry that she already helped; she was quite domesticated and regularly made scones and cakes which Megan and Helen were too busy to do. The Baby, Sybil, was still too young to do much, and since she worked hard at school and showed great promise, her teachers said, she was allowed to get out of a good deal of the domestic work.

Helen, of course, was only home at weekends. She had a job, and a good one too, as secretary to an important man in a big insurance office in the city. Everyone was proud of her, particularly Huw, and Hywel thought her a very nice person, though he did wonder now and then why someone so pretty should still be unmarried at the age of twenty-two – and not only unmarried but without a boyfriend.

Today, Hywel was chopping wood. Trees did not abound on the marshes so what wood you had was husbanded carefully, but they fetched coal and there was a pile of peat turves waiting to bank the fire at night if the weather warranted it. He was singing as he worked, stacking the wood up into a neat pile and thinking with pleasant anticipation of the rest of the day ahead of him. After their midday meal he and Huw were going to drive down to the coast and pick up some more coal from the docks; it would be his first visit to the shore and he was looking forward to it. Huw had taken a gun out early, before breakfast, and had come home with a brace of wild duck, so that was dinner tonight catered for; Hywel had seen Megan, eyes tear-filled, peeling onions, and he was very fond of wild duck, roast in the tin and flanked with onions and potatoes cut small so that they crisped to a delicious golden brown. Megan had a way with gravy, too, that brought the water to your mouth.

They always had their big meal in the evening, because the baby-brigade were at school ten miles off and could not get home at noon. He and Huw fared pretty well. A cooked breakfast, a large snack when they went in mid-morning — usually bread and the crumbly cheese Megan made from their own milk, with a couple of big pickled onions on the side or a great pile of pickled cabbage — then a meal around one o'clock: again, nothing cooked in the oven but quite often what Megan called hasty-stew and a couple of big, floury dumplings apiece, with thick slices of fruit loaf to follow.

But what really mattered, of course, was acceptance and love, and these were things which the Pettigrews had given to Hywel in full measure, and little enough he had done in return yet, save to work as hard as he could. But later, when he bought the sheep — he was determined that it would be he who bought them — then he would really be able to show his gratitude. No, not gratitude. That would be a poor return for what they had given him: his love.

'Please, miss, I did what you said, I did.'

'So you did, Pauline.' Jessica sighed, took the blotched and stained sheet of paper from the desk and tried to find it beautiful, because the child had tried, though all too obviously without success. 'You must remember, Pauline, that though neatness is not all-important, it does help. And when you learn a poem, it helps if you remember it not just as a jumble of words, but as consecutive sentences. Then, when you write it down, you don't get . . . well, such a muddle of words.'

'Yes, miss. I'll remember.'

Jessica walked back to her own desk on its raised platform, with the blackboard at the back. She had fled from the pleasant convent school in the town to this big city school, because she had not wanted to live at home after the way she had behaved. Her deep guilt feelings, she supposed, had driven her to apply to a church school set in the Liverpool slums rather than to a grammar school. She did not feel she deserved clean, intelligent children after what she had done to Hywel.

She still felt ashamed whenever she thought about it — how could she have let him down like that! If she had only shown a bit of commonsense she could have carried it off, pretended not to mind, and then gradually let the relationship cool. But no, at the sight of . . . Her mind squirmed away. Even when she had gone to wave the train off she had been glad she had not been near enough to see Hywel properly.

If he had never been beautiful, she told herself, she would not have been so disgusted and repelled by his terrible face. It was the contrast, especially with Huw sitting by the bed, still the owner of an almost identical face to that which her lover had once possessed. It had pointed up the differences, made it twice as hard to bear.

She had tried to go back to the hospital afterwards, but once she had spoken to Huw and found out that Hywel knew she had been and gone it seemed pointless. And even Mam — Mam who hated the thought of her liking Hywel, let alone marrying him — had been reproachful.

'Foolish it was to show so clear that it was his looks that mattered to you,' she had said. 'Do you no good, love. Why couldn't you have bit your tongue, said a few sweet things? God knows when I didn't want you to, you did it time and again.'

'Mi-iss! Oh, mi-iss, Ser-ry's tek me 'er-ribbing.'

Once she would not have been able to understand what the child was talking about; now she knew that Sarah had taken Maureen's hair-ribbon. She frowned and stood up. Fortunately her height and pallor made her quite an imposing figure, for some of these tough kids from the slums did not have much time for teachers.

'That's quite enough of that, Sarah, Give it back at once, please.'

Chastened, Sarah handed it over and Jessica took her seat behind the desk again.

'Get on with your work, please, girls. When you've finished copying down the poem you learned just put your hand up and catch my eye and I'll come and see how well you've done.'

Once everyone was busy, she could write a bit more of her letter. She wrote every few days to Mam, because though she felt she could no longer live at home it did not mean she could not keep in touch. She visited often, and not only her own home. There was someone in the street who understood, who did not despise her for turning Hywel down after his accident. Not that anyone ever said outright what they thought, but she could guess! They could not punish her more than she was punishing herself. Stuck up here in a tiny terraced house, living with a woman who took in dressmaking for a living and her docker husband, sharing their meals and scurrying into their bathroom to wash, only to find the place dripping with lines of washing and all the filth of the docks around the handbasin. And the food was awful. If she'd had lobscouse once this week she'd had it five times. Mrs Bagnold was a heavy smoker, too; if you went into the kitchen and saw her making pastry with the cigarette dangling out of the corner of her mouh and the smoke going up in a straight line, past the eye she kept permanently screwed closed in case it should get in the way of her fumes, you could not help wondering where the ash went. Not that I wonder, Jessica thought, stabbing her pen into the inkwell, a good inch of it was interred in that sponge pudding we had the other night. Ugh!

Yet in spite of everything, she was happier than she deserved. Liverpool was such a marvellous place to be if you had a little money, and thanks to her cheap lodgings she had more than most. She could go to the theatre or the cinema, take a big ship and go across to Ireland for a weekend, meet people at concerts and art galleries, enjoy the museums, the big shops and the restaurants where they served the sort of food Mrs Bagnold could not even dream about.

She felt guilty about that, too. She had driven Hywel away from his beloved hills to wherever it was that Huw lived. He would be cooped up in some little cottage with a crowd of cousins who could not possibly like him because of the way he looked, and who could not remember him when he had been beautiful, as his own family could. He would be miserable, she was sure of it, and she had come here meaning to be miserable too.

It seemed, however, that unhappiness would not come just because you deserved it. And because she was so happy, and was going home at Easter to see . . . all her friends in the village, she decided to put a postscript on her letter.

Can I have Hywel's address, please, Mam? she wrote. *I think I ought to write to him from time to time to tell him how I'm getting on and to see how he is.*

'Mi-iss! I've done, miss.'

She looked up and there was a veritable forest of arms, all waving. Trust them to finish quickly just when her attention was elsewhere. She smiled at them, however, and they smiled back. They adored her, of course; children always did. She stood up and moved down the room towards them.

'Well done, all of you. Now I wonder who's got every word right?'

'Look, m'dear, aren't you being a bit foolish? I want to buy the boy a pony, I've said I shall, and yet you keep on saying that it has to be the one you sold — what, seven years ago! You know what dealers are. He was a sturdy little beast, a good ride for a younger than I, and since I'm all of twenty-four — or shall be Or dead, to put it bluntly.'

'Don't be so defeatist, Father. He was about five years younger that I, and since I'm all of twenty-four — or shall be later this year — he'll only be nineteen. Think of Grey Nell, and Dobbin. They both made thirty; Matchless is in his prime still. Wherever he is.'

'Yes, exactly. Wherever he is! When Tommy's four I'll get him a pedigree Arab; a grey, I think. And then . . .'

'Father, you don't understand! Tommy's only a little kid, he doesn't need a pony right now. I want Matchless back for *me*.'

They were in the tack room. Even the smell brought Dot's childhood flooding back into her mind. She touched an old saddle and slid her hand across the darkened, polished leather, down the straps to the stirrups, worn thin but still good. She had sold Matchless to Mr Markwell and he had promised to take good care of the pony, so now she was home almost her first action had been to go over to the Markwells' place and ask if she could buy Matchless back.

But seven years is a long time. The child who had owned the pony was a child no longer. At university down in Cardiff, they told Dot proudly. And Mr Markwell had died of a heart attack three years ago. The groom knew that Matchless had been sold, but he was not sure to whom. He had promised to put the word about, and had no doubt that the pony would be traced, in time.

'I'll buy you a horse, girl! What do you want with a pony past his best? You need a decent mare, about fifteen hands, with some turn of speed and a showy canter. We'll go down to the horse fair at Easter and I'll get you something good.'

No talk of pedigree Arabs for a mere girl, Dot thought with an inward grin. Not that she wanted an Arab – she wanted Matchless!

'Thank you, Father, I'd like that. I haven't explained very well, probably, it's a question of doing what's right, really. I never should have sold him, he'd been a good pony to me, but I had to. Now I'm back, and I owe him something for all the happy years of service he gave to me. It worries me that he might be owned by some little brute who kicks him up steep hills and doesn't worry about his having the best hay in winter and a decent piece of pasture. I want him for himself – not just because he's a good pony.'

'Ah, I see.' Tom looked round the tack room, and perhaps he thought of his own childhood pony, for his expression softened. 'But you'll have the mare? Good, good. We'll put the word about at the fair over Easter that you're after the pony you once owned – all black with a white star under the browband, eh? – and I reckon we'll get news sooner or later.'

'I hope so.' Dot had been cleaning tack when her father joined her. Now she took down the next bridle from its hook and tutted over the state of it. Green where it should have shone silver, dank and mouldy where it should have gleamed with polish.

'That's settled, then. Now when are you coming down to see the pits with me? Not the Wynd, if that worries you, but you should take a look at the Olwen and the Roland.'

'It doesn't worry me. I just hate the thought of it and I hate the pits and I won't go down them,' Dot said obstinately, as she had said several times before. 'I keep telling you I'm not afraid of the dark. I'm not scared that the whole place will collapse on me like it did on . . . on the men in Candle Deep. I don't approve of coalmining and I won't go and peer at what goes on down there. I should be disgusted by it all.'

'Well, I'm telling you, you should go down. Where do you think the money comes from for all these improvements to the Plas? The pits, of course. And the men would appreciate it. Most of 'em know you'll be the owner when I pop off. If there's things you disapprove of, maybe we could change 'em.'

'I disapprove of men having to dig coal, and you aren't likely to change that,' Dot pointed out. 'It's no use, Father. Perhaps I read *At the Back of the North Wind* and *The Princess and Curdie* at an impressionable age; but mining, goblins and disaster seem to go together in my mind.'

'All right, I won't press you now, but you'll have to change your attitude one day, my dear. Shutting your eyes to a thing doesn't mean it goes away, you know.'

'No, but it means you don't have to look at it!' Dot picked up another bridle and slung it across her shoulder, then another, and hung it over her arm. 'I'm going indoors to the kitchen to see if cook has any bright ideas on cleaning leather. Saddlesoap just isn't making any impression on the mould!'

Twenty-Four

'What's he like, the feller that lives with you now?'

Cath Blount was a pretty, wispy brunette with the sort of stick-like thinness which attracts some men and repels others. She was perched on the corner of Helen's desk making a paperclip chain whilst Helen typed on steadily, finishing an urgent memo for her boss.

'Hywel, you mean? And I wish you'd find some other way to phrase it. He doesn't live with *me*, he lives with the family. He's . . . he's very nice.'

'Oh?' Cath's overplucked brows rose into an even higher arch than their owner had intended. 'You don't sound too keen, to me.'

'I am, really. Only . . . he and Huw are so close! When I go home at weekends now I feel pushed out. You wouldn't believe how Huw's changed. He doesn't need any one but Hywel. The two of them even think alike. I've seen one turn to the other at the exact same moment and come out with identical sentences! Really! It's uncanny!'

'And once you knew that Huw wasn't your brother you thought you and he might make a go of it.' Cath's voice was sympathetic, though you could hear her curiosity. 'What's gone wrong?'

'Nothing. Only we never talk any more. There's never a chance. The two of them are always together.'

'Hmm. I reckon, my woman, that your Hywel needs a gal!'

'I don't see why! He had one, and when she saw him after the accident she ran out on him. Perhaps one's enough.'

'One like that, you mean. He needs a gal what'll like him for himself, not for what he was. They coming in for the cattle market at Easter?'

'Bound to be. I said I'd go home with them and help drove the animals they buy back to the marshes. Why?'

'Well, catch a later train,' Cath advised, 'and you and I can take them lads round the fair. Or they can take us, if you like the sound of that better. Who knows? This feller interests me.'

'Who, Hywel? But you haven't even met him!'

'True. Let's remedy that, shall we?'

As the two girls were talking, Huw and Hywel were sitting opposite one another at the kitchen table, working on their book. It was large, with a ring binder and loose leaves, so that each could get on with his own idea and compare notes afterwards. Except, as Huw once remarked with a rueful grin, that their ideas usually turned out to be identical. They were making a plan for a proper pig-house which would hold a couple of score of pigs. When the drawings were finished they would compare them, take parts of one and parts of the other, and the final drawing would be an amalgam of their ideas. On the sofa the Babies were sitting side by side, industriously crocheting. It was the craze of the moment, and Susan, who had begun to crochet a table-centre, had already achieved a large tablecloth and looked like going on, as Huw said, until the immense piece of work could serve as a roof for the house should the need arise.

Hywel had finished his pig-house, and started to jot down various bits and pieces of information about sheep. He and Huw intended to go to the cattle market on Easter Saturday and buy themselves the nucleus of a flock. He would pay. It was all arranged. It would be his best opportunity so far to help build up the farm and he was looking forward to it.

Huw and his father had done wonders, though. From a tiny cottage with reed thatch and cob walls they had made what was really a substantial farmhouse, and from a few water-logged acres they had drained and bought and expanded and seeded until they had one of the largest farms in the area.

Too big, though, to manage alone. And Huw had been diffident about employing a man in case the place did not justify it. It was not only a matter of paying out wages; if you intended to employ full-time farmworkers they needed accommodation and, as yet, there was only the farmhouse.

'We'll start building next spring, then, if this here business with the sheep come off,' Huw said absently. The three little girls scarcely raised their eyes from their crocheting but Megan, knitting by the fire, gave a little smile. They were at it again, one speaking and the other only thinking. Uncanny until you got used to it.

'Aye – time enough. Go for a double-dweller, shall we?'

'Good idea.'

Hywel began to flick back through the pages of their book. They were very proud of it. Neatly arranged with graphs and explanatory paragraphs, the past history of the property and their future hopes were all put down on paper. Ned would have scoffed, but Hywel had an orderly mind and enjoyed seeing it all laid out. Reading about it, he could see it as it really was. A piece of good farming which he and his brother would make, not just better, but the best. He wished he could bring Dot here, show her what it was possible to attain. Ned and Huw had done it without the benefit of owning vast areas of land, too. What might Dot have achieved if only she had stayed!

He remembered that he had seen her in the Other Place, once. It had been at a fair. Just suppose that he and Huw should go to the cattle market next Saturday and have the luck to meet her at the Easter fair afterwards! He imagined taking her small hand, giving her the biggest hug in the world, and explaining that he was living here now, on a farm out on the marshes. A picture of her as he had seen her then filled his mind: laughing, tousle-headed, emerging from the crowd with flushed cheeks, pulling some fellow by the hand. Catching his eye, her own filling with incredulous joy and excitement – and then losing her, being whisked back to his own life.

'Would you like to go on the fair after we've bought the sheep, Huw? We can pen the beasts at the station and catch the last train home.'

'Who mentioned the fair, mun?'

They grinned at each other; their thoughts still tended to flash between them, tiny pictures, so that speech was seldom necessary.

'If you're thinking of going to the fair, you'd best drop Helen

478

a line.' Megan said. 'After all, she's staying in Norwich an extra day so she can help you with the sheep.'

'I'll phone her from the village when I go in for flour,' Huw said. 'She'll like the fair.'

'Ask her to ask a friend along to make up a foursome,' Megan suggested.

'What, for me?' Hywel grunted. 'I shouldn't bother.'

'No, we're all right as a threesome,' Huw agreed. 'She might bring some ghastly woman we didn't take to.'

Megan shook her head at them, but did not stop knitting. 'Have it your own way. One of these days . . .'

After she had got the three youngsters to bed and banked the fire with turves, for it was still chilly first thing, Megan went outside to check that her hens were in their house and safe from foxes, that the geese were in the shelter which Hywel had made for them, and that Joel, the ancient brown and white sheepdog, was in his kennel. He was a marvel at herding cattle, was Joel, but he was getting too old to manage by himself. They would have to buy a pup whilst Joel still had sufficient energy to train a younger dog. And sheep were not like cattle. Though she could not imagine Joel hurting any farm stock deliberately, he might grow impatient with sheep and nip a bit too hard. He was getting rather crotchety in his old age; he could do with a younger dog to run ahead, round up the heifers which decided to take a wrong turning. Young things were all the same: they liked a bit of a challenge. A young dog would take hard work in its stride.

She came back indoors to find the boys ready for bed as well. Huw was putting everything tidily away in the makeshift filing system which Helen had made for them. Hywel was pouring boiling water on to cocoa powder and sugar, having ferreted in the pantry for the homemade oat biscuits which they usually had last thing. She watched them fondly but with a certain amount of exasperation as they moved quietly around, getting themselves ready for bed and preparing for the morning. So sensitive to each other, these two, but thick as two short planks, sometimes, when it came to outsiders.

Not that she could ever think of Helen as an outsider. A

bright, loving, intelligent girl who had worked as hard as a boy when she had been Susan's age, droving cattle, learning how to capture a frisky calf with nothing but her wits and a length of rope, teaching herself to swim in the cut – no, Huw had taught her, but still, she was the only one of the girls to learn.

She had been a real tomboy, had Helen. And then Huw had gone off on the trawlers and she had been sent, at considerable expense, into Norwich to a special school where a girl could learn shorthand, typing and book-keeping. She had done well at school, and better at the business training college. It was too far to go in every day so they had paid for her to lodge with a nice family, and then she had got herself a good job. When she did come home, she was changed, altogether different. No more the untidy child with the long fair hair wind-whipped about her face, her brother's trousers on her bottom like as not, and on old shirt of her father's doing service as a blouse. A young lady now, with shining nails and hair done up in a bun on the back of her head.

Huw changed, too. Independent before, he became fiercely independent after his time on the trawlers. Strong, quiet . . . she had almost said silent, but that would not have been true, for he had always talked non-stop to Helen.

It was an odd coincidence, really, but Megan had realised she would have to tell Huw that he was only Helen's cousin and vice versa about a month before events did her telling for her. They had spent half a dozen years apart, only meeting for a couple of hours at weekends and sometimes not even that, for months together. And Megan noticed that as their characters and appearances had developed, so had their attitudes to each other. There was a warmth, a *specialness*, which singled out their relationship, showing that it was no longer merely the sibling affection which both had taken for granted. Megan had thought that though neither was aware that they were not brother and sister, in some mysterious way their bodies knew.

It had been strange to see them so tender to each other yet all unknowing, never dreaming that such tenderness does not normally exist between brother and sister. Or did they? She had fancied a difference, an awkwardness, between them just before Huw went off to Wales.

And then they knew, and she waited for them to tell her that they were in love. And nothing happened. Huw came home with Hywel, and the relationship between the two lads seemed to override anything else. Helen seemed to be regarded by both Huw and Hywel as a good friend and no more, and Megan, who loved all her children, could see that it was not so for Helen. She loved Huw still with all her loyal and faithful heart, and was bitterly hurt by his apparent neglect.

But how to put this right? Perhaps she had been mistaken. The love she had seen might, she supposed, have come only from Helen. If so, there was nothing she could do about it. On the other hand, could not Huw give what had once been a warm affection a chance? Could he not have agreed to make up a foursome, so that he and Helen could pick up their friendship where they had laid it down last year?

'Night, Mum.' They chorused the words. Hywel had never called her Auntie Megan after his first greeting. She had told him that she would answer to anything he chose, and from that moment he had called her Mum.

'Goodnight, lads. Who's on early milking in the morning?'

'I am.' That was Hywel.

'Right. Give me a shout on your way out, there's a good lad, and I'll have your breakfast on the table by the time you're through.'

'Eh, she's a good woman, salt of the earth,' Hywel said, grinning. 'Bring you a cuppa I will, for that.'

He would, too. She smiled at them both, then shooed them up the stairs. In all her happy married life, she and Ned had always been last up those stairs and she would not change now.

Alone, she pottered about checking on the porridge, the side of bacon, the supply of eggs and the freshness of the bread. Only when she heard the boys talking as they climbed into bed did she, in her turn, mount the stairs.

It was hard, being a widow. If Ned had been here she could have discussed everything with him: Huw's feelings for Helen, Helen's for Huw, Hywel's possible loneliness. What they should do about his meeting people. Whether Susan should be allowed to join a ballet class. Why the geese had stopped laying. Whether to build a cottage so that Huw and Hywel could have more help.

481

She opened her bedroom door and laughed to herself and tried not to notice how bitterly cold it was. And lonely. You're just a stupid woman, Megan, she scolded, beginning to undress. The boys are good boys and work their hardest to see you have no worries. They'll sort out their own salvation, all three of them. Just you do what you've always done – keep a good home for them, decent food and a warm hearth – and you won't go far wrong. She climbed between the cold sheets and laid her head on her cold pillow. Uselessly, she missed Ned every hour of every day that she lived, though she never let it show. What good would it do to go round with a long face and her heart on her sleeve? It would only make others miserable. But sometimes, when she'd had a long and tiring day and sleep would not come, she would look down the long vista of years ahead and wonder what she had done to deserve such protracted punishment.

'Well, that was money well spent.' The brothers leaned over the side of the pen looking down on the eight yearling ewes they had just purchased. 'You're sure they're good'uns?'

'Sure I'm sure.' Hywell grinned. 'And that ram's a beauty, mun! Next spring we'll have the biggest and best lambs the marshmen have ever seen, just you wait. Look at her!' He pointed. 'Back as broad as a dining-room table and a fleece a foot thick. Shan't regret this moment, us. It'll be worth buying that bit of land and reclaiming it, hard though the work will be. And don't forget what I was telling you about growing for seed.'

'You mean the high field? It's an idea, but a bit of a gamble, isn't it? Still, I've always been a gambling man myself. We might as well have a go.'

Hywel had always been a reader and he had not changed. A few weeks previously he had read an article on growing clover for seed if you had a smallish field where the soil was sufficiently rich. He had gone up to what they called the high meadow – though the name would make a cat laugh, he just wished the folk at home could see it. It had to be all of fifty feet above sea-level and they thought it prodigious high! But it was a good piece of land and well sheltered from the bitter east winds by a thick hedge on three sides and a deepish wood on the fourth. He had cut a sod, smelt it, touched his tongue to it, eyed the grass which already grew on it, and decided that it would do very well. Coming back down, he put the suggestion to Huw, and they had been mulling it over in every spare moment since.

'Aye, I'm the same. Where we meeting them girls then, Huw? It must be nearly time.'

Huw consulted his watch. 'You're right. They said at the big nippy restaurant on the Walk. We'd best set off. It's not such a long walk, but I want to go into the gents and clean up a bit. Or we could go into the Bell, I suppose.'

'Can we? But the bar won't be open yet, will it?'

'One track mind you've got, bor! It's a hotel. We can go in there, get ourselves cleaned up in their cloakroom, and go out again. Damn it, they won't mind, we spend enough money there as a rule on market day.'

'Yes, of course.' Hywel had seen the farmers at home strolling in and out of the Wynnstay as if they owned it. 'Go there then, shall we?'

'Sorry we're late, but we had to clean up a bit. By the time we'd got the sheep penned we smelt like old rams ourselves.' Huw kissed Helen's cheek and smiled at her companion. 'Hello! I'm Huw, and this is Hywel.'

'I'm Cathy Blount. Helen and I work together and she said you wouldn't mind if I came along with you tonight.'

'You're welcome.' Both young men shook hands with her, and then they took their places at the table opposite the girls. 'Ordered yet, have you?'

'Not yet; but I'm ready to eat a horse! I'll have steak pie, chips, peas and gravy.' Cathy was reading from the board. 'Tea, of course, and bread and butter, and then apple crumble and custard. Yes, that'll just about fill me up.'

'Do you think it's wise to shovel all that grub down when we're going on the fair?' Helen asked, laughing. 'If it comes up again . . .'

Groans all round, but the waitress was beside them and so they ordered, then turned to surreptitiously sizing one another up once more.

Hywel could see that Cathy was not his type, but also that she would be good fun, so that was all right. A bit hard on Huw, mind, to have to go round with his sister . . . no, not his sister, his cousin . . . but he could see that Huw was not at all interested in Cathy. And the fair wasn't exactly the sort of place which only lovers could frequent. You went there to have fun, not to be alone together.

So the four of them talked and laughed and ate and Hywel tried to tell himself that they were only going to the fair, that nothing much was likely to happen to him, apart from winning a few fairings and getting all giddy.

Yet, as the meal progressed, he could feel unbearable excitement building up inside him. Suppose she was there again? Suppose he saw Dot?

They caught the last train, as they had arranged, and it was a late one too, because of its being market day. They saw Cathy off on her bus before herding the sheep into the cattle truck which would be attached to their train when it pulled in, and presently they found themselves a carriage and sank into the seats.

Hywel had not seen so much as a sign of Dot, but they had all had a good time, which should have been all he expected. He was sitting in a corner seat with Huw, Helen opposite him, and he was rather touched to see that Helen's mouth bore traces of the pinkness left behind by candyfloss and her cheeks the sugaring of doughnuts. She had always seemed remote, very sure of herself, but she had been charmingly natural at the fair, screaming on the rides, jumping up and down when the brothers were trying their luck, colliding with Huw when she had rushed away from a reflection in the hall of mirrors, so that he had been forced to grab her before she banged into something more breakable!

Yes, all in all a good evening. Of course he had hoped to see Dot and he had not done so, but that did not mean she was not in Norwich somewhere. If she really was here, he would find her sooner or later. Fate was an odd thing, but surely, if she was near, he would know? One way or another he would find her, or she would find him. She was older now, more mature. Surely she would realise that by telling her to stay with her

484

sister and meet other men he had not meant go for ever? He was a patient man, he told himself, and would give it six months; if she had not appeared by then he would start putting notices in newspapers, asking questions everywhere he went. After all, he must be nearer her now than he had been for years, so it stood to reason that their paths would cross. Norwich was a country city with a fairly small centre; he would make a point of going in more than once a month, as he and Huw had been doing, and if she was there he would find her.

Presently he fell asleep and dreamed of Dot. They were at home, on the sunny uplands, with the country spread before them like a map and so beautiful that it brought tears to his eyes even in the dream. Dot was wearing a ragged sweater and jodhpurs and she was sitting, tailor-fashion, on a low shelf of rock, absorbed in the art of plaiting straw into corn dollies. She looked up when he spoke to her and grinned at him and he found himself thinking, *How nice that she isn't all larded with paint, like that Cathy girl*, and promptly woke, as though remembering someone he had recently met was sufficient to make him realise that he was only dreaming.

Blinking, he looked around the carriage. Huw and Helen were both sleeping soundly, their two fair heads leaning together a bit like bookends. Now that Hywel could look into their unconscious faces he could see that the likeness folk remarked on was very superficial. Helen's hair was golden, glossy brown with streaks of blonde at the temples. Hywel admired her regular features and her skin was clear and unfreckled, but she was too quiet and restrained for him. He liked a girl to be noisy sometimes, bubbly all the time . . . he liked Dot.

Helen stirred and opened those smoke-coloured eyes which could not be said to be either blue or grey because they seemed to change with her mood. She rubbed her face with both hands, thrust her fingers through her loosened hair, and then turned and blew into Huw's face. He screwed up his eyes and muttered protestingly.

'Come on, old partner, the station's coming up. The train's gone over the points at the junction.' She shook him, laughing when he groaned and tried to escape. 'No use. You've got to wake up, Huw!'

485

The train's slowing and stopping woke him, aided by Hywel's letting the window down and the cold air in. The three of them bundled out onto the cold platform beneath the stars, Huw having to be steadied before they could set off for the cattle truck. By the time they reached it though, they were all alert enough – which turned out to be just as well.

They had not brought Joel with them for obvious reasons, and though they intended to buy a new pup they had not yet done so. Three of them, Hywel had declared, should be able to cope with eight ewes and a ram.

'Herd 'em out through the side gate. Don't bother with the ticket barrier,' Huw advised, coming fully back to consciousness. 'We don't want them still on the platform when the train moves.'

Perhaps it was because the ewes were in lamb, or perhaps they, too, had been asleep and were still more than usually muddled, but they could not have behaved more badly had they been taking lessons. They eluded Helen and invaded the waiting room; they dodged around the ticket barrier, ignoring the invitingly open gate; they barged against the wooden seats and even tried to climb back into the train. When it began to pull out six sheep still remained on the platform. Hywel suffered from the lively fear that the stupid woolly-heads would fall on to the line and break their stick-like legs, but in this at least he wronged them. They could see only a great pit, deep and dark and strange, once the train had gone, and they sheered away from it with such promptness that Huw, Hywel and the porter were able to guide them out on to the road without their realising it.

Unfortunately, having attained the road, their flock set off – at the sort of shambling run sheep favour – in the wrong direction.

'It's a good thing the cold air woke us up,' Helen panted as the three of them set off in pursuit. 'I'm getting a stitch in my side!'

'You go home and get to bed, my woman,' Huw said breathlessly. 'We'll manage, Hywel and me.'

Hywel, however, was beginning to get the measure of his new flock. He shook his head. 'Don't you dare go off and leave us, love,' he shouted back as he began to try to outflank his charges. 'You can bet your life no one will have closed a gate on either side of the road and they'll try to charge into every field but the right one. Numbers counts when you've no dog and your sheep are more wool than brain. Three of us might just do it. Someone to drive 'em forward, one to guard the left side and another to guard the right. See?'

They saw. Gradually they got the sheep to turn round in a bleating stampede and hurry up the road towards the farm, the ram with them. He made no effort to cherish all these bleating females which had suddenly come under his protection, neither did he lead, but, as Hywel breathlessly remarked, it was a good job that he did not take unkindly to being harooshed along an unknown road in the middle of the night.

'Nasty, an angry ram can be,' he told them. 'Still, this one seems pretty resigned, wouldn't you say?'

Fortunately it was a moonlit night, and a beautiful one too, Hywel realised as they came, after vicissitudes too numerous and horrible to mention, to the marshes. Mist hung over the dykes like wreaths of white smoke and the moon picked out the patches of water, turning them silver, making the frosted reeds shimmer magically in its rays. This did have one disadvantage, however: the shadows were so black that you felt you could have picked them up and put them in your pocket; and once someone – or some sheep – got into shadow it was very difficult to see them.

Sheep, furthermore, are not connoisseurs of beauty. These sheep merely saw in the marshes a chance to threaten their new owners with yet more broken legs. Swaying enormously under the twin burdens of extended bellies and enormous fleeces, they bounded through every passable gap and set off, ignoring the dangers of deep pools, uncertain ground, shivering marsh patches and the dykes themselves. Hywel, anxious for their new possessions, wanted to follow his flock and teach them the error of their ways, but once they were near enough to the farmhouse Helen and Huw made their own feelings plain.

'Let them kill themselves if they want,' Helen said. 'I'm sick of all creatures cloven-hooved. They have devil's feet! I want my bed!'

'Me too, but perhaps I'd better go and sort 'em out,' Huw said, staring out across the marsh. 'What do you think?'

'Well, be all right they will, I daresay,' Hywel admitted. 'Not as foolish as they seem, sheep. Besides, short of taking them to bed with you, what can you do when they're determined on risking their lives?'

'If Huw takes them to bed, Hywel, then you may come in with me,' Helen said, linking her left arm with one brother and her right with the other. 'I don't think they'll kill themselves, not when they're in lamb. Mothers don't do things like that.'

'Oh, all right,' Huw said, giving in because that was how he felt as well, his brother surmised. 'But don't you blame me, together, if we find 'em all legless or drowned come morning.'

'Not a word from either of us, I swear,' Hywel said, winking at Helen. 'You think they're fools, and I another for buying 'em, but you'll see. They'll take to the marshes like ducks to water, and learn quicker than we could teach 'em to tell good land from bad.'

He guessed, of course, that the reason Huw was anxious was because he, Hywel, had paid for the flock. It worried Huw that he might lose his brother's money, though he saw how important it was for Hywel to feel he had a stake in the place.

'One day you'll want a place of your own, no question,' he had said. 'When you pull out, old partner, I want you to be able to take a good bit of cash, enough to buy you a decent little farm. At the moment you won't even take pocket-money!'

'No, because I've got my compensation and all I've done so far is to work a bit and have my board and lodgings free,' Hywel explained.

'A bit? Call that a bit? All right, but we've got to get the financial side of it sorted sooner or later.'

The three of them, tired, weak from laughter but very happy, reeled into the farmhouse in perfect harmony with one another. Despite knowing that they needed their beds, they put the kettle on, made a hot drink, got out the biscuit jar and the cake tin and toasted their toes by the turved-down fire. At last, however, the tea drunk and the biscuits and cake reduced to crumbs, they tidied, washed and wiped up and made for the stairs. At Helen's door Huw suddenly stopped, holding Helen by her elbows, looking down at her. Hywel stopped too, and kissed Helen's cheek even though his brother did not release her. Huw seemed awkward, speechless. He was asleep on his feet, Hywel thought compassionately, and embarrassing the poor girl.

'Come on, Huw, mun, say goodnight and let's all get some shut-eye. That poor kid's worked like a slave with the sheep tonight. She needs her sleep.'

The poor kid slanted a venomous look at Hywel before laughing and patting his cheek.

'That's very true. We're all tired,' she said lightly. 'Goodnight, boys.'

The brothers made their way to their room. It was a pleasant place, with one bed alongside the window and another against the opposite wall so that each had plenty of space for his own things. Hywel got undressed to his shirt and drawers and climbed into his bed. He and Huw exchanged a few words on the sheep and the fair, Hywel admitted that Cathy was not really his type, and then they settled down.

Hywel slept at once but woke later and knew, in that strange way one does, that despite even breathing Huw was not asleep. He was fretting about something, Hywel believed, but what? The sheep?

'Huw?' he said softly. 'Are you awake, mun? What's up?'

There was no sound from the bed below the window. It must have been the sheep and Huw did not want to say. Hywel settled down again and slept soundly until morning.

Twenty-Five

Next morning when Hywel woke his first thought was for the sheep. He got out of bed and tiptoed to the window, glancing down at Huw as he did so. His brother was sleeping like the dead, almost certainly because despite his silence when Hywel had spoken he had been lying awake for hours, worrying about their new acquisitions. Hywel lifted up the edge of the curtain. Dawn had broken, though the sun was not yet up. It would not be long, though; a clear sky and a brilliant colour in the east meant that today there would be a sunrise instead of just a lightening of the clouds; perhaps spring had come at last!

It was not Hywel's morning for milking, but he found he was suffering from a thirst that needed about a gallon of tea to quench it, so he set off down the stairs, his clothes in one hand. He would poke up the fire, set the kettle on the hob and dress. By the time he was respectable the kettle would have boiled.

Downstairs the kitchen looked as it always did with the curtains pulled; intimate, different. He always felt that seconds earlier hobgoblins had been sweeping the dust away, setting out milk for the cat, sitting on the sagging armchairs and chatting. The kitchen knew, but it would not say. Instead, it seemed to almost resent the first one down, the spell-breaker.

Hywel pulled the curtains, letting in a flood of early morning light, poked up the fire, and went over to the sink and picked up the dipper. He pumped some water, drank, reprehensibly, straight from the dipper, then rinsed it, refilled it, and took it over to top up the kettle. Then he began to dress.

Small actions occupy the body whilst leaving the mind free to wander where it will. Hywel's mind covered a good bit of ground whilst he pottered, and he was quite surprised to find that the kettle had boiled and the lid was jumping, the heated hob hissing.

He made a pot of tea, poured himself out a big mug, and settled down to drink it. The room was warming up nicely now, the fire lighting it, painting the whitewashed walls with pink and gold. Outside, though, the dawn wind would be stirring the frosted rushes, touching the cat-ice on the edge of the dyke, bringing the ducks winging in from their roosting places. He had a second mug of tea and decided to go and check up on the sheep – any excuse to get out there. He could take a gun, see if he could fetch down a duck or a goose. It was far too early to wake Megan, especially as it was Sunday, and even Huw would not come down to milk for a while yet. He would put on his duffle and go out and see what was what; there were bullocks about a mile from the house which had been brought in for fattening. It would do no harm to take a look at them whilst he found the sheep.

He went to unbolt and unlock the door, then stopped short, frowning. The door was unbolted and unlocked, yet he knew very well that he had done both small tasks before they went upstairs. Megan said there was no need, but there were always tramps and sailors going home and gypsies, and when you lived so far from any neighbours it was as well to take the elementary precaution of locking the door.

The front door, of course, was almost never unlocked but he felt he had better just check.

He went out into the hallway but the heavy front door was locked and bolted, the bolts pretty well rusted into place. He made a mental note to check them some time, then walked back through the house. Odd! But one of the kids might be up and off out on some mischief.

Outside, there had been a hard frost and it was still cold despite the clear sky. Hywel shivered; it was nearly April, but the weather had not yet begun to warm. Huw had warned him that he would find the marshes cold. The wind came straight from Siberia, he had boasted; you had to be tough just to survive!

Megan called it bracing, or fresh; Hywel at this moment thought it was just bloody cold, mun, and stepped out. He had a muffler, but when he put it round his face it got wet from his breath, so he preferred to wear it around his neck; now he sank his chin into it and went to peer in at Joel, curled up in his straw in the kennel.

Joel half wagged his tail but made no move to get up; his rheumaticky joints did not much like early mornings. Hywel went across the yard to the milking shed, but no one had brought the cows in, so he peered into the stable. Broom and Bess, the big Suffolk punches, turned to peer back at him, their mild eyes enquiring. Bess was almost asleep still; he could tell by the way she turned back to face her manger as soon as she recognised him, moving a great, shaggy hoof with a clink on the iron-hard ground and shifting her hindquarters into a more comfortable position. He moved out of the stable. The horses worked harder than any other animal he had ever encountered – everything was a challenge to them, and they actually seemed to enjoy pulling – but they did deserve their rest.

I'll have Suffolks when I've a place of my own, he was thinking as he crossed the back yard again, heading for the gate this time. This was the back of the farmhouse, but it was much more important than the front which edged the lane. It had been carved out of the marshes, and the gate led over a sturdy wooden bridge which spanned the deep dyke. It had to be a sturdy bridge because all the stock went to and from the stables and sheds by that route; it would have taken far too long to bring them out and around by the lane.

The gate had not been properly latched. Oh ho, he thought to himself, someone has been wandering then, it was not just an urgent visit to the ty bach. Chamberpots were the rule at night, but if one needed something more commodious it was understood that you would pad down the stairs, get hatted and coated, and use the two-seater out in its neat little shed.

However, you did not need to unlatch the gate to do that. It must be Sarah. Middle Baby was a great wanderer and she had a friend, an old wildfowler who took her out in his boat and always sent her home with a duck or a clutch of eggs or a few cabbages from his garden. Doubtless she had gone off with Larkin.

As he crossed the bridge Hywel glanced at the water. As he had thought, cat-ice again, but it would clear soon enough when the sun got up. The light in the east was glowing, pale primrose now, the line of the horizon steel blue. It would be a nice day. Perhaps they could go down to the coast, fetch a cartload of seaweed so that when they ploughed the high meadow they could turn it in, nicely chopped, to lighten the soil.

Before him the marshes stretched as far as the eye could see until they reached the shore. They were criss-crossed with dykes, some big enough to carry a sizeable boat, others so narrrow that he could jump across them. The sheep, he thought, would have made their way to where the grazing was best, though at this time of year, with the grass as yet growing so slowly that it scarcely counted, they would have to make do with thinner fodder than that which they would enjoy in May. Their diet would be supplemented with the hay that Huw had packed away in the barn: sweet, light-coloured stuff from the broad leys which his brother had harvested almost unaided last year. He strode on, avoiding the oozing hollows and the deceptively green patches. Give it another month to six weeks and the grass would be shooting up, and all their stock would fatten and flourish.

He was soon able to pick out the sheep. They had not, of course, stayed where they had been left. In the long watches of the ice-cold night they had made their way to a hollow some way from the house, where the grass was still fairly plentiful and they were sheltered from the wind partly by the lie of the land but also by a thick copse of gorse which had taken root on the raised side of the hollow, making good protection for stock. As he got nearer he could see them clearly, grazing away with their fleeces silvered with frost and their breath and the warmth of their bodies making a mist which hung around them so that they looked like ghost-sheep save for their constantly moving jaws.

Hywel went down amongst them – not distressing them at all since they simply moved a little further off and continued to graze – to check that they were all there and none the worse for their journey. As the sun eased up to the horizon and the light strengthened he saw that the sheep were every bit as good as he had thought them yesterday. The fact gave him great satisfaction. Just like dining-room tables with wool on, he thought, eyeing their sturdy, square-shaped bodies. If they could just drop similarly strong and well-fleshed lambs they would rear them, too. He hoped he would be around when they began to bear, but sheep very often gave birth at night. The farmer who had sold them to him had said the ewes had another week to go, but they were so thickly fleeced that it was difficult to judge. I'll bring them in in a day or two, Hywel told himself. These will be their first lambs; they need someone standing by. They're too precious to be allowed to give birth out on the marshes by themselves.

He climbed out of the hollow again, brushing against the gorse, yellow starred with a few defiant blossoms. He found the bullocks without difficulty, having had a shrewd suspicion where they would be, and the heifers too. They were looking good, though not as good as they would look when the grass began to grow. The community on the marshes might be scattered, but every man jack of them had one overriding interest at this time of year – the coming of the new grass. They looked to the Pettigrews, the neighbours did, to give advice, for Ned Pettigrew had been one of the few well-to-do marshmen. Not that they cared! They did not want to improve on what they did, they just wanted to do it as well as their fathers had done, but they agreed the Pettigrews had some sensible ideas as well as lots of new-fangled and therefore foolish ones.

The neighbours thought Hywel was quite mad, though.

'Sheep?' old Mr Haydock had said scornfully yesterday, when they met him at the market and told him they were going to buy ewes. 'Did yu say yu wor a-buyin' sheep?' He pronounced it *ship*, which confused Hywel for a moment. 'Well, bors, yu'll ketch a cold at that! Sheep in't niver done nawthin' but poor on these hare marshes. Unhealthy critturs, they git everything they kin, plus foot-rot!'

'Yes, but only if you forget that . . .' Hywel began, but was briskly interrupted. Mr Haydock had not lived to be eighty just so's a young taffy could teach him his business.

'And not oonly foot-rot. There's maggot and hid-itch and Gawd know what beside! Men with suffin' to 'em give up on them critturs yares agone.'

'Well, we're only buying half a dozen,' Hywel said soothingly. 'If we've made a mistake it won't break us. And we'll have the lambs, since they're all due to give birth soon.'

'Ha!' the old man snorted and shook his head sadly at such innocence. 'You'll lose more'n half the lambs, I dessay, and them ewes will give some disease to your cattle! Bound to happen; bound to!'

'I expect you're right. Now, what are you drinking?'

That was sensible talk, apparently. Mr Haydock's rheumy eyes brightened, his tottering limbs straightened, and after a shrewd glance at Hywel's tweed coat he announced that a whisky with a ginger wine went down well at this time o' year.

Huw had told Hywel that the marshmen knew they would never make much money if they just continued to fatten other men's breeding, and that was why, originally, they had tried sheep. But ignorance and the fact that cattle could simply be turned out onto the rich pastures in spring and ignored until autumn meant that the sheep, who could not, had not done well at all, and the marshmen had given up in disgust on a creature which was forever ailing and needed time and money spending.

Now, having seen for himself that the cattle were all present and correct, he pushed through an admiring circle of heifers, all of whom hoped he had brought them out a load of hay – presumably very well hidden on his person – and were edging nearer and nearer in the hope of a share in his largesse. He was making for the bank of the big dyke, from where he would have a bird's-eye view of the marshes.

He took his time as the sun rose behind him, scanning the terrain. There was the farmhouse with a curl of smoke coming from the chimney stack; the fire had burned through by now, he supposed. The red of the sunrise was reflecting in the windows and even as he watched he saw a pane of glass flash gold as someone – Huw, probably – opened a window and then closed it again. He watched the house for another moment or two but nothing else moved, so he let his attention return to the marsh.

Nothing moved here, either, save for the beasts wandering slowly, heads down, cropping as they went, and the birds circling overhead. There were always birds: wild duck, wild geese, herons, curlew, sandpipers. And the gulls. Huw had told him that when Broom and Bess were harnessed to the plough the birds would gather in their hundreds, circling, mewing, descending on the newly turned earth in raucous, noisy groups, arguing with every other bird of the air over every insect which moved in the rich, plum-dark soil which reminded Hywel of Christmas pudding.

Usually there would be someone out, perhaps on the dyke, perhaps in the rushes or, far distant, out to sea, but today there was no one. No one cutting reeds nor fishing nor sculling along in a boat. No one stalking the wildfowl which he could see far off where the dyke spread into a lake. Only Hywel and the wind stirring the rushes and the smell of the sea.

Hywel turned and ran down the steep bank. The sun was so low that it was difficult to make much out in that direction, which was probably how he had come to miss the footprints the first time.

For now that he was facing towards home and was on a lower level, he saw them. Leading past him, out towards the distant sea, was a line of footprints in the soft marsh, lit with an eery brightness. The hair prickled erect on Hywel's neck and goosepimples came up on his arms. How had he managed to miss them? And why did they shine like that? Closer inspection solved the puzzle. The footprints must have been made earlier, for the shine on them was the whiteness of frost. They would not have been visible when the whole marsh was frosted, but now the sun had cleared the surface and the frosted prints stood out clearly against the greens, browns and purples of the marsh.

Hywel bent over the prints. They were very small and narrow and had been made by someone light, too, light as a fairy, running over the ground, scarcely sinking in at all. And then he remembered that when she, whoever she was, had been running, the ground had been too hard for her to sink very far. So much for fairies! But it was not Sarah; the prints were too big for her little feet. This was an adult, he thought.

They led away from the farmhouse and Hywel had been heading back in that direction. He glanced at the building. The curtains were all drawn back now and Megan would be getting breakfast. Huw would have started the milking, Susan would be collecting the eggs, there would be the rich smell of bacon and the sound of it spitting as it was turned in the pan, and Megan had baked yesterday . . . He was hungry; should he go back?

He stood, torn by indecision for a second, then set off towards the sea in the wake of the footprints. He would find out who was out so early before his breakfast; waiting thirty minutes or so longer would sharpen his already keen appetite.

But he must hurry, for as soon as the sun was high enough the frost in the prints would disappear and they would be very hard to see. Now almost an old hand at the marshes, he did not kid himself that he would find someone easily if they wished to remain hidden. Though the marshes looked so flat they were not; there were hollows deep enough to hide a man and clumps of bramble as well as the gorse and the deformed-looking willows, so like old men until the leaves bean to sprout with their clear yellow-greenness, when they became young girls combing their tresses over the clearness of a marsh pool.

The footprints were heading for just such a clump of sallows, he saw, standing by just such a pool. He went steadily forward, but carefully and quietly too; who was it, hiding beneath the willows? There were sprites on the marsh at night, or so they said, and he himself had seen mysterious lights, though Huw said it was only marsh gas. But miners as a breed are superstitious and Hywel was no exception. He would go carefully.

He reached the trees and someone hidden by them started singing. That was enough to make anyone feel a bit odd, hearing that small, clear voice singing in the sunrise, with the willows bearing, not leaves yet and frost no longer, but a thousand diamond drops. And the wind from the sea was bringing not only the smell of salt but the sound of bells as Sunday service was announced from half a dozen little churches and chapels.

His imagination expected a mermaid, sitting on the little jut of pale sand with her tail curled under her and a comb poised above her rippling hair, and the reality was not so far off at that. A girl sat there with her back to him, staring out to sea and singing. She was sitting on the roots of a willow tree, her knees hugged up, her chin resting on them. She sang a sad little refrain in a warbling voice, softly and almost absently, as one sings when one believes oneself alone.

Hywel cleared his throat and the girl turned sharply, with a swing of her long, golden-brown hair, and it was only Helen, the song faltering on her lips and a half-smile stealing across to take its place.

'Hywel! Goodness, you made me jump! What are you doing here? I thought it was your turn to milk this morning.'

'No, it's either Huw or Susan. She takes a turn at weekends now. Didn't you know? Lovely it is to lie and know someone else is out in that cold. She's a good kid. I was on yesterday, see – that's how I know it isn't me.' He ducked under the willow branches and a shower of drops pattered down on his head and shoulders, their coldness making him gasp. 'Come to that, what are you doing here?'

She shrugged, uncurling her legs and stretching them out in front of her, shaking her hair back from her face. It was very fine hair and seeing it for a moment with the sun shining through it made him think of Jessica's flaming mop. But he blinked and it was just Helen and it occurred to him that Helen's hair was long, fine and rather limp, Jessica's curly and springing. Yet Helen's hair was beautiful and Jessica's was not. Odd, that.

'Me? Oh, I often come here. Why not? It's so pretty, and you're well hidden, too. It's not easy to hide comfortably on the marsh.'

'No . . . except in summer, when the grass is high and the reeds are too, and you can lie down and let someone walk within a foot of you and never know you're there.'

'That's true.' She looked at him curiously. 'But you've never been here in summer, Hywel, so how do you know?'

It was his turn now to evade the question as, he was very sure, Helen had evaded his a moment earlier.

'Just guessing. You can tell the lie of the land, winter or summer, if you use your eyes and your intelligence.'

She did not pursue it, any more than he had pursued her reason for wanting to hide. Every child knows the answer to that one, anyway. It's important for a child to have a place where other people cannot find you.

'I see. Hywel, are you happy here? Don't you miss your mountains?'

'Yes, I miss them; not painfully, mind, nor urgently. They'll

498

wait for me, and in the meantime this . . .' he gestured around him '. . . this is good, and I'm very happy, working the land. Have you ever been to Wales, Helen?'

She shook her head. She was drawing patterns in the hard damp sand with one forefinger. They were all swirling, circular patterns. There was no meaning to them; they were just something to keep her fingers busy whilst her mind pursued its own thoughts. She was worried by something, he guessed. But what?

'No, I've never been more than thirty miles from home. Huw told me how lovely the country is though, when he came back. Well, beautiful he said. All great mountains and hills and plenty of trees . . . I thought you must miss all that. If you could farm there, would you go back?'

Hywel shrugged; there was something in these ordinary questions which made him feel uneasy, a prickling between his shoulderblades as though . . . but it was ridiculous. Why should Helen wish him away? It was his cursed imagination, like that business about the mermaid.

'I'd like to go back one day,' he said slowly. 'Only thing is, I'd dread the loneliness. Lonely I was, see, but didn't know it. When you've had someone close, then you understand how lonely you were before. My mam doesn't care for me, my da died when I was born, my favourite brother was killed down Candle Deep. And then how could I go back, and make things difficult for Jessica? She's so fond of Mam and of the village, yet I can't see her staying there, not if I were near.' He paused; he knew that Helen knew he and Huw were twins, but did she know about the other business? 'There's a closeness between Huw and me which . . . has he ever mentioned me? Before the disaster, I mean.'

'Yes.' She breathed the word very softly, watching her finger as it drew in the sand. 'Yes. I knew about you long ago, Hywel. Huw told me.'

'There's wonderful close you must have been,' Hywel said, his voice touched with envy despite himself. 'No one I could tell I did have, see, except for Dot, and I couldn't explain, so I said nothing. Awful lonely I was when she went away.'

'And then there was Jessica, of course. Going away too.' Without looking at him she leaned over and took his hand.

'You've known a couple of silly, unworthy girls, but that doesn't make us all bad, Hywel! You must meet people, go places, make up for all those lonely years. There are decent girls you could meet, get to know.'

'Not Dot!' He said it quickly, urgently; he could not bear that anyone should think Dot had left him for the wrong reasons, nor that she was not a darling! 'Dot was different. It was my own stupid fault she left, see? If Dot were home . . .'

'Yes? Would it make a great difference? Would you not be lonely?'

'Lonely? With Dot?' He laughed, pleasure at the mention of her name flooding through him. 'Oh no, cariad, no one could be lonely with Dot about! As for me . . . well, Dot meant more than either of us knew at the time. But it's no use wishing; she went and they've heard no word from that day to this.'

'Oh. Tell me what she's like.'

He told her, sparing Dot's blushes not at all, though she would have been gratified to hear how very pretty she was, how witty, how clever, how unendingly dear.

'She's quite small then, and dark? Have you ever met Alice Haydock? I think you should – I'll arrange it. We'll go to the Saturday hop at the village hall next weekend. You can meet her then.'

Hywel was touched by her concern; he patted her shoulder, then stood up.

'That's nice. Right, it's a date, and so's breakfast. You coming back now?'

'No, I'll stay a bit longer,' Helen said. 'Don't tell them where I am, will you? I don't want breakfast. I took some bread and jam and had a drink from the dipper as I came through the kitchen, but I'll be in for the midday meal.'

'Right. I'll tell Mum that if she asks. I say, look at that sky! Blue isn't a good enough word for a colour that deep and lovely.'

He left her then, not looking back in case any one should see him. He was shyly delighted to feel that he was beginning to know Helen, and was deeply affected by her kindness and sympathy. If it made her happy to matchmake he was quite willing to humour her. After all, she was his cousin – and when she had been making all those swirly patterns in the sand she had not just done so to avoid having to look at him; it had been to hide the fact that she had been crying.

Halfway back across the marsh he met Huw, striding along in rubber boots with his coat open and a song on his lips. The sunshine was bringing out the best in everyone. But Huw was heading rather too near Helen's clump of willows for Hywel's liking; a fat lot she would think of him if he let her be discovered when she had asked him not to tell where she had hidden herself away. So he stopped Huw.

'Hang on a moment, mun. If you're off to check on the sheep I've done it. I counted them earlier and they're all fine.'

'The sheep? Oh no, it wasn't the sheep, I guessed you'd see to them.' Huw tried to edge past. 'It's the cattle I want to check up on. I've not counted them for a week.'

'They're fine. I'll take them down a load of hay later, but they're all on good ground, grazing away.'

'Ah, that's the bullocks. I meant . . .'

'The heifers are all right as well. They mobbed me, though, wanting their ration of hay, so we'd best get them some after breakfast. Have you had breakfast?'

It occurred to him that Huw looked hunted, though he could think of no reason why.

'No. But it's a grand day. I think I'll take a walk first, freshen me up.'

'I'll come with you.' Hywell fell into step by his brother, whose brisk steps seemed suddenly to have slowed to a snail's pace. 'As it's such a fine day I was wondering if we could take a cart down to the coast afer dinner? We could all go and collect seaweed, and then have a wander. Take a picnic, I daresay, make a trip of it. What do you say?'

'Good idea,' Huw said, though without much enthusiasm. 'Well, I think I've walked enough for one day. We might as well go back and get our breakfasts.'

Together, they turned towards the distant farmhouse.

Late that night, when Megan was clearing up downstairs and all her chicks were in their nests — how disgusted Huw and

Hywel would be, she thought, to know that that was how she thought of them – she heard a muffled noise coming from Helen's room. It sounded, to an experienced motherly ear, like sobs which had begun as sniffles and worked up to bawlings which a pillow was failing to stifle. Megan climbed the stairs, tapped on Helen's door, and walked in.

'It's only me,' she whispered, closing the door softly behind her. 'Come on, now, darling. Tell Mum what's happened.'

Helen was quiet for a moment, and then she pulled a hanky from under her pillow and blew her nose. There was almost no light in the room and Megan had no intention of bringing in her candle, which she had left on the landing outside. It was easier to weep and talk in the kindly dark.

'Sorry about that. It's Huw and Hywel. They don't need me, Mum. It wouldn't matter, only . . . well, I love Huw and I was pretty sure he loved me! He wrote me beautiful letters from Wales, telling me how we'd have to get to know each other as cousins and forget about the brother-sister bit . . . he said he loved me, I told him I loved him. And then he comes home, wrapped up in Hywel, and scarcely has time for more than a smile in passing! And . . . and today . . . he . . . he stood me up! I w-waited and w-waited and he never came!'

'Give them time, Helen, darling. It's all so new to them. They have a very special relationship, you know. It must be like losing your memory and then finding it again . . . oh, that's not right. It must be such a weird and wonderful experience that there's no parallel I can think of. But wonderful though it is, the novelty of it will wear off and Huw will come back to you.'

'I don't want him if Hywel's always going to come first,' Helen muttered. 'It would be awful, Mum, to be perpetually second to a twin brother! And anyway, I think he's fallen out of love with me – if he was ever in it, that is.'

'You're wrong – well, I think you are. He looks at you very lovingly when you aren't looking, dearest! I'm sure he'd like to talk to you alone, but he won't hurt Hywel, you see – the poor fellow's been hurt enough. I'm sure you agree.'

'Oh yes. If that's all it is – but how can I find out, Mum? When I just never get him to myself for five minutes?'

'I think we'll have to be a bit devious,' Megan said thoughtfully, after a moment. 'You can't trick Hywel, because he'd step down hastily if he suspected he was in the way. But I'm afraid Huw will have to be tricked.' She frowned, absently stroking her daughter's hand. 'Aha, I have it! You will miss your train back to the city on Monday evening.'

'Will I? What good will that do?'

'Well, we'll all come to the station to see you off and you'll miss the train. Huw will offer to drive you into the city in the trap and I'll encourage him to do so, but I'll insist that Hywel comes home with me to do all the bits and pieces of work about the place. How's that?'

'Would you? Oh, Mum!' Megan could almost hear the smile, and she could see the whiteness of it even through the dark. 'If only it works!'

'Oh dear, I'm terribly sorry!' Helen tried to sound truly contrite, though inside she was all satisfaction. 'I ran, truly I did, but the guard didn't see me and the train just went straight on out of the station! I'm always nearly missing it but this time I really have!'

Helen was standing by the trap, her suitcase in her hand. Huw held the reins and Hywel sat beside him. Both were grinning.

'Don't you worry, my woman; I'll get you back to the city tonight. You'll be a bit later, but though Dobbin's no speedster he can go at a good steady pace for miles together. How about it, Hywel? Fancy a ride into the city?'

'Boys, don't you both plan to desert me,' Megan cried at once. 'You can drive us home, Huw, and then you must leave Hywel to help me get things cleared up for tomorrow.'

'Yes, that seems fair,' Huw began, but Hywel pointed out that they could easily stop off with Megan now, do their various jobs, and then drive Helen back a little later.

'No, dears, she'd be too late for her landlady's liking,' Megan said, repressing a desire to shake Hywel. 'Jump up, Helen, and we'll quickly go home and you can drop us off. I'd love a trip into Norwich too,' she added, to show Hywel that she understood how he felt. 'But there's always a lot to do on a farm, especially after a holiday weekend.'

During the drive back to the farm, Helen and Megan chattted and the boys were silent. Helen had the uncanny feeling that they were *thinking* grumbles about her stupidity in losing the train and her selfishness in wanting to go home now, when the pair of them were not free to take her. But she ignored the thought, jumped down at the gate, helped Megan to alight, and then climbed into the seat that Hywel had just vacated.

'I *am* sorry,' she called, as the two of them went round the side of the house, no doubt to find the babies up to some mischief. 'I won't keep Huw a moment longer than necessary.'

The trap was lit by a swaying lantern fore and aft; in the glow of the lamps Megan stood and waved until her figure was swallowed up by the darkness. Hywel had gone in at once and had not come out to wave them off. Was he annoyed? Helen doubted it. He would be working now, conscientiously doing the tasks that he and Huw usually divided between them.

The two travellers were silent for a few moments. Helen glanced sideways at Huw and felt a pang of dismay; he did not look at all pleased to have her to himself for once, in fact, he looked rather glum! Probably he was thinking of the long and lonely journey home, she thought guiltily, with no one but Dobbin to talk to, but he had not minded that at one time! Once he had asked nothing better than her company, and would have faced a good deal more than an hour or two of solitude to get it. Yet now it was all so different. And suppose he did still want her, in a sort of threesome? One woman, two men, one mind? She could not help giving a muffled snort at this, since her own mind had somehow been missed out of her calculations, and Huw immediately glanced at her and smiled.

'What was that about? You seemed very quiet at the prospect of being alone with me all the way to Norwich!'

'I thought the boot was on the other foot,' Helen pointed out. 'You seemed to want Hywel to come along!'

'Oh, well. We're close, Hywel and me. We could've talked about the farm driving home. Same's you and I could have talked going into the city.'

'Not with Hywel sitting here,' Helen pointed out. 'For one thing it would be rude, and for another we've been having three-way conversations all weekend and we haven't said very much, have we?'

'Well, no, I suppose you've got a point there. But things aren't easy, not now.'

'Why not?' Helen, glancing across at him in the flickering lantern-light, could not help reflecting how very handsome he was, and how dear to her. 'Why should having Hywel living with us make things difficult between you and me?'

'Well, it's kind of complicated. But . . . remember when Hywel was just the Other Feller, how we used to nip in and out of each other's lives and thinkings without really knowing how or why? Just because we're living under the same roof doesn't mean it's stopped, you know. In a way it's stronger, because when I think I'm thinking something that's special to me, it turns out I'm only thinking it because I've picked up his thought, like tuning in to someone on a wireless set!'

'Golly!' Helen could not help sounding dismayed, for that was how she felt. 'You mean if you started thinking about me in a . . . well, a lovey sort of way, Hywel could pick it up? Could even . . . well, be there? Share what we're . . . share what . . . I mean . . .'

Her voice stammered into silence. There was a long pause. Dobbin's hooves clip-clopped along the hardening road surface and the wind nipped at the only bits of Helen it could reach – her nose and eyes. The rest of her was well muffled up against the cold, but her nose felt like an icicle and her eyes were running. She wore woollen mittens and a muff, but even so her fingertips were chilly. She looked at Huw's bare hands gripping the reins and felt for a moment in her own cuddled up fingers the icy grip of the wind.

'Huw, your hands must be freezing. If I lend you my muff . . .'

'My hands don't feel the cold, but if they do get a bit chilled, like, I drop them on to my knees and they warm through quite quickly. Now you see Hywel would *know* that, and I'd know if his hands were cold. It makes things hard.'

'You mean he's always in your mind, like a spy? That he can pop in at any moment? What you're trying to say is I might be kissing you, I might *think* I was kissing you, but it might be Hywel. Is that right?'

505

'No! You don't understand. We don't *spy* on each other, we couldn't, even if we wanted! When we were kept apart we . . . oh, I don't know, we stepped into each other's lives a bit, I suppose. I saw what Hywel was seeing and vice versa. But never, I swear on my life, never at any sort of awkward or intimate moment. Good God, girl, what a ghastly suggestion!' He brooded on it, eyes steady on the road ahead, brows frowning. Suddenly the frown cleared; he looked sideways at Helen and his voice, when he spoke, was low, teasing.

'Anyway, who mentioned kissing? Do you want me to kiss you?'

Their eyes were locked; Helen could not have looked away for a fortune and she was sure Huw felt the same. The horse's broad rump jogged up and down, the movement caught her eye even though she could not move her gaze from Huw's. She swallowed; oh, God, what should she say? It wasn't fair. If she said yes she was a brazen hussy and if she said no she was a liar!

'Yes, please.' A little whisper which came, surely, from someone else! Huw let go the reins and they lay loose on the horse's back. He cupped her face in his hands, pushing her muffler down and slipping his fingers inside her hood. His hands were not cold. They were warm, vibrant, strong on her skin. She shivered deliciously, feeling that she had waited for this moment all her life and now that it had come at last she should let herself enjoy it. His face came nearer, his eyelids were drooping and his mouth was making a shape which was strange to her; a little frightening, more than a little exciting. His lips brushed hers, a tentative touch, then returned, claiming her mouth. His arms were round her, straining her close, and he was kissing her in a way she had never imagined possible, until they drew apart by mutual consent, both breathless and treembling.

'Golly!' Helen took Huw's hand and held it between both hers. 'Oh, Huw, do you feel the way I feel?'

'Yes.' Annoyingly, he did not ask how she felt but took it for granted that she loved him and wanted him. 'But you've got to realise, Helen, that I'm not quite like other blokes – nor's Hywel, of course, but it doesn't matter to him, not yet – I'm closer to my brother than most. If I was asked to dinner by Hywel and his missus years in the future, I wouldn't be able to

506

think *Hell, that boring woman*, because he'd know. See?'

A great light dawned on Helen. She squeezed his hand and laid her cheek against his sleeve.

'I see more than that! I see why you've avoided me, why you haven't even tried to see me alone! If you did he'd know and you think he'd be upset and possibly even a bit jealous. Is that right?'

'Well, it's a bit more complicated than that, but you've got it more or less right. He'd be hurt, Helen. He'd know that though I'm enough for him he really isn't enough for me. I want you as well. And just at the moment, because of the scarring and his mam as he calls her and that woman, that Jessica, he can't take any more hurt. See? So I think we ought to stay apart until we can sort him out.'

'Well, that won't take long,' Helen said determinedly. She picked up the reins and handed them to him, though Dobbin jogged on still at the same steady pace, obviously needing little or no guidance from above. 'Don't you see, Huw? You've got a girl, and Hywel needs one! All we've got to do is find him a girl and we shall all of us be fine.'

He stared at her for a moment, then a wicked grin spread over his face. 'Cathy Blount! So that was why she came along!'

She laughed with him. 'Well, I certainly didn't bring her so that you could take a fancy to her! It didn't work, anyway. Cath just wasn't your brother's type. But he mentioned a girl, so I got him to describe her. She's small and dark and . . . oh, kind of cheeky, I suppose. So I said I'd introduce him to Alice Haydock at the dance next weekend, and he laughed and said rightyho.'

'You're a witch! But if it works it would be marvellous for Hywel as well as for us. He needs love.'

Ahead, the road plunged between high banks and on top of the banks the trees grew so close that they mingled their branches overhead, turning the road into a dark tunnel. Once they were under the trees they could only see by the light of their lanterns. Dobbin slowed and began to pick his way delicately down the slope. Helen snuggled into the hollow of Huw's broad shoulder.

'Isn't this nice? Just the two of us. That's how it should be, Huw, and it will be too, once we've fixed Hywel up with a girl of his own.'

Huw, putting an arm about her shoulders and agreeing, felt that he must remind her Hywel had a mind of his own and was stubborn as a mule into the bargain.

'He never wanted to marry that Jessica,' he confided. 'But she had spent years persuading him and the girl he did love had left him so it seemed the sensible thing. It wasn't, of course – it never would have worked even without the accident. So now you may find he's a bit resistant to your sex.'

'I like a challenge,' Helen said. 'And I've got heaps and heaps of friends all hunting for a gorgeous farmer like Hywel. I shan't despair until he's worked his way through the lot!'

They were still laughing when Huw drove into the outskirts of the city.

PART FOUR

Twenty-Six: June 1928

'Mum! Mummeeee!' Tommy's face appeared round the corner of the barn where Dot and Gwil, filthy, hot and secretly enjoying themselves hugely, were trying to find out just what was stopping the tractor from taking the hills in its stride.

'Yes? What is it, pet?'

Dot wriggled out from beneath the vehicle, grabbed Tommy, bestowed an oily kiss on his cheek and slapped his bottom. 'Come on, Sunny Jim, cough it up! I thought you were helping Taid with the harvesters' tea?'

The men were haymaking. It was a big job now and an important one, because they needed all the hay they could get. Dot had built up a fine herd of dairy cows and already Tegydd farm butter and cheese was a name to be conjured with. Her father had not been best pleased at first; he said that the English might be proud of having it said they were a nation of shopkeepers but that he, a Welshman, did not intend to swell their numbers. Dot kept tactfully silent about the children's rhyme concerning Taffy's propensity to steal legs of beef! It was not just idle chatter, that, either, for it was not more than a century ago that her own disgruntled ancestors, living on the Wirral, had spent as much time chasing the Welsh sheep and cattle rustlers who crossed the Dee estuary at low tide as they did farming. However! Tom might not have thought much of it at first, but now he was like a peacock when the farm produce was mentioned; his chest stuck out, and he almost fell on his back, so proudly did he strut.

It probably helped to reconcile him to being not-quite-but-almost a shopkeeper that the mines were not going as well as they had. Short time, low prices for coal, the awful seven-month strike last year which had almost broken him, in heart

511

as well as pocket. Then, when he could not bear to go near the pits and see them empty, he had enjoyed watching the milk being processed and the workers busy. Now that the men were back, though — earning less, poor devils, for doing the same work — he was happier. Though it was a blow that the Wynd had been forced into a four-day-week because of the quota system.

Tommy, fidgeting at her knee, brought her back to the present.

'I am supposed to be getting the tea,' he said in an aggrieved voice. 'I would of been out, if only Hawkins hadn't caught me. I say, Mummy, what are you and Gwil doing to that poor tractor?'

To prevent himself from falling into the error of standing still, her son now stood on one leg, twisted the other round it, flapped his elbows against his sides like a hen trying to fly, and hissed through his teeth. Dot giggled.

'All right, all right, you want to go! But give me the message first, if there is one.'

'Course there is. There's a lady to see you. She's in your room.'

Dot had her own study now, where she tackled — with distaste — all her books and accounts. It did not have a telephone, yet, but she was trying to get her father to install one, and it had most other things. A smart typewriter, pale grey with dark green keys, a couple of filing cabinets, two desks — one for her and one for Maggie Evans, who had started coming up to the Plas to give a hand whilst she studied shorthand and typing at the secretarial school in town and was now working full-time for the Tegydds — and of course a swivel chair for guests, standing on a pale grey carpet. There was a modern fireplace with an efficient fire which warmed the room very well, and an old-fashioned clock on the mantelpiece with a sweet ring of chimes which sounded on the hour, the quarters and the half. Dot was very attached to her room and if she had to be indoors she liked to be there, but it was not a place where the staff would normally put a social caller. Since this was a Saturday and the caller female, it seemed unlikely that she was here on business.

'In my room, darling? How odd.' Dot wiped some of the

grease on her hands off on her dungarees, then cast a wistful glance at Gwil, still immersed in the mysteries of the tractor. 'I'm sorry, Gwil. You'll have to struggle on alone for a bit. I'll come back to you as soon as I'm free.'

'Don't worry, Miss Dot, I've found the trouble.' Not all the hinting or even ordering on earth would persuade the older farmworkers to call Dot by any courtesy title, though Miss Dot was rather inappropriate when she was constantly attended by her small son.

'Oh? Anything much?'

'No. Dirt in a connection and a lead rusted up.'

'Ah, we thought it was something like that, didn't we?' Dot adored meddling with engines but she did not know one end of a point from the other, so she usually kept such remarks vague. 'Well, if you've done perhaps you could clean up, and then take the tractor up to the field in time for tea. No doubt they'll find a use for it when you've all eaten.'

She headed for the side door, Tommy close behind her. They went indoors and Dot began to clean up in the little cloak-room, now provided with a washbasin, several towels, and a toilet.

'Why my room, old boy? Hawkins usually puts people in the drawing room.'

'Dunno. Can I go now, Mummy, and find Taid? There's a cake with icing on and Philly's gone up too. I saw him sitting on Pluto looking ever so high.'

Pluto was an ex-dray horse, a huge elephant-like beast, and Tommy's friend Phil was tiny. Dot laughed and gave him a loving shove. 'Yes, of course, you run off. Give Philly my love and tell him to eat lots and lots of tea, then he'll get big, like you.'

Dot regretted the harvest tea, which she adored, but trusted that whatever the woman wanted she could be got rid of fairly quickly. Plas Tegydd was doing very nicely, but they would never turn down business – perhaps she owned a shop and wanted farm butter and cheese? However, she would get through it and then hurry up to the harvest field. She had always adored al fresco meals and loved them still, with their romantic overtones – the cloth spread in the shade of the hedge, the men sitting down together: gypsies, lord of the manor, agent, farmworker; they would all share their harvest tea. Everyone armed themselves with a well-foliaged branch to swish the flies away and everyone drank the tea from the big enamel jugs and ate the still-hot Welsh cakes, spread thickly with farm butter and strawberry jam, the slices of bara brith topped with crumbly brown sugar and thick cream, the cheese scones spread with a tangy layer of marmalade, and the great veal and ham pie, the eggs set deep in the meat like yellow eyes.

She opened the study door, a polite smile on her lips. The woman sat in the swivel chair, studying a book on farming which she had taken from the bookshelf by her side. She was facing the window and had not heard the door open so her back was to Dot, but Dot did not need to see more than the flaming hair to know who it was.

'Jessica!'

'Dot, darling!'

She jumped up and held out her arms, then the smile faded as Dot hung back. Dot laughed.

'Oh, Jess, it's wonderful to see you, but . . .' She held out her oily hands and indicated her dungarees. 'I daren't even shake hands, let alone give you a big kiss and a hug as I want to do! I'd muck you up so dreadfully.'

Jessica was elegantly turned out as always. She wore a close-fitting olive-green suit with a ruffled blouse beneath it. She laughed at Dot's oily hands, though, and seized them in her own clean-gloved ones, then drew Dot closer. They both kissed air near each other's cheeks, as undemonstrative people will.

'There, now we're both oily,' Jessica said, stepping back. 'Oh, Dot, it's been a long time! We're getting quite old . . . I'm twenty-six so you must be twenty-four . . . and when I heard you were back and had been for a couple of years I could have wept! All that time and me not knowing! I wrote to that place in Norwich, but there was never any reply, so I stopped trying. Oh, and your little boy's *lovely*. I quite wish I had one of my own. I remember that time you wrote you said you had a child. And a hus . . .'

Dot put a finger on her lips. 'Hush, darling. That's not . . . well, I'd rather you forgot it. I have. I live for now, not yesterday. Look, I'll ring for some tea and then we can settle down and have a lovely long talk over old times and what we've been up to. How does that sound?'

'It sounds lovely.' Jessica sat down on her chair again with a little bounce that made Dot's eyes prick. She had not seen her friend do that for nearly seven years! 'I say, you've made some changes!'

'True.' Dot pulled the bell. Neither of them spoke until the maid arrived and Dot asked for a good tea to be brought to the study for the pair of them.

Presently the girl returned with a laden tolley and Jessica stared. She waited until the girl had left, however, before speaking.

'Dot, you're so grand, just like I imagined you would be all those years ago! And you must have heaps of servants to get that trolley ready so quickly.'

Dot, pouring tea, shook her head. 'I'm not grand, but I'm working at it. It's the harvest tea, so all cook had to do was scoop a bit of this and a bit of that out of the baskets, sling it on to plates, and send the girl up with it. But things are getting organised, I agree with that. Do you still have milk and sugar, like me?'

'Oh, please. Two lumps. And . . .' Jessica got to her feet and bent lovingly over the trolley. 'Can I fill a plate? I'm starving.'

'Yes, do. I'll do the same.' The two girls piled their plates, took their cups and pulled their chairs close. 'Isn't this nice? You've no idea how I've missed talking to someone of my own generation. Oh, I should have said how shocked and distressed I was to hear about Hywel – I hope he's completely recovered?'

'Oh yes, I should imagine so,' Jessica said cheerfully. 'I haven't seen him since then, of course, but Mam writes to her sister – he's living with his cousins – and she'd say if he wasn't all right. I asked her for his address once. I thought it would be nice to write, but she wouldn't give it me. She's funny, is Mam,' she added a trifle self-consciously.

Dot's heart began to speed up.

'Then you didn't marry, you and Hywel?'

'Good God, no! Oh, I suppose when I wrote to you . . . yes, I remember, I was thinking of marrying, but I . . . we, I should say . . . decided we wouldn't suit. So I went off to Liverpool, teaching, and Hywel went off with this cousin; he's with him

515

still so far as I know.'

'Is he married?'

She had not meant to ask the question direct and felt her cheeks burn, but it had just slipped out. Fortunately Jessica did not seem to think it an unusual question.

'I don't know. No, he can't be, because Mam made some very acid comment about Hywel having played the field – that was two Christmases ago – but now he seems to have settled down at last with someone called Anna – or was it Alice? Yes, I'm almost sure it was Alice.' She pouted. 'That's enough about Hywel. Aren't you going to ask about me?'

'What about you? Honestly, Jess, you radiate happiness and . . . and satisfaction. Who is he?'

Jessica laughed on a tinkling trill.

'It's really weird. When you hear you'll be *astonished*. I've been away from home for two years, I've been out with lots of young men, yet I'm marrying a man from the village!'

'No! Anyone I know? Have you been courting all this time? Or is it someone who you met in Liverpool?'

'You're very clever,' Jessica said approvingly. 'Cleverer than you know, in fact. It's Peter Edwards; big he is, but dark-haired. Not very good-looking either. But I love him. He was good to me when . . . well, at the time of the Wynd disaster. He wrote to me when most of the village wouldn't so much as look at me if they met me in the street. Hypocrites. Peter was a collier, but he was a cut above the rest and came up to Liverpool when they started the quota and short-time working because he wanted to better himself. He took a degree in engineering and of course there we were, both from the same village, so we met . . . started going out . . . and now we're marrying. In two weeks, at the parish church, and we'd be glad it you'd come.'

'Yes, I'd love to,' Dot said at once. 'I saw your mother in the village a week or two back but she didn't say anything about a wedding. Well, to tell the truth she doesn't say much to me now. Just good morning or good afternoon, depending.'

Ella's strangeness had hurt when she had first come home, but she grew accustomed to it. Apparently Ella's husband, Glyn, had left her for some brassy little bit he had picked up in the course of a drinking bout in town and Ella could not forgive him. Not that he wanted forgiving; it appeared that he and his twenty-two-year-old mistress were perfectly happy, living in a flat over a fish and chip shop in St George's Crescent.

'Oh, well, Mam's always been strange,' Jessica said light-heartedly. 'Ever so pleased about me marrying Peter, she is; offered to have the reception at her place, but we've hired the church hall. It'll be quite smart,' she added rather self-consciously. 'We've been saving hard and lots of our friends from Liverpool will be coming. I've arranged for Stevens to cater, so the food should be good.'

'And the family too, I hope,' Dot said, cunningly. 'They'll all be there, won't they? I daresay even those cousins that Hywel's living with would come if you asked them. And Hywel wouldn't miss it, I bet.'

'Oh, he won't come. I wouldn't invite him – it would look as though I was asking for a present. And anyway, he's in thingummy . . . East Anglia, miles and miles away, much too far to travel. For all I know he may have kids, too, that he wouldn't want to leave.'

'Oh? But you said just now he wasn't married.'

'Did I? No, I don't think he is, but he's going steady with this girl, Alice or Edith or whatever her name is. And of course if I asked him I'd have to ask that other chap – Huw – and I don't even like him. He kept pinching his mouth up and disapproving of me. I wouldn't invite him to my wedding if he was a royal duke!'

Dot giggled to take some of the tension out of the conversation. 'You daft thing, Jessica! I shouldn't think anyone would invite a royal duke to their wedding. They'd be quite over-shadowed, and it is supposed to be the bride's day! Tell me, after the wedding where will you live – and how will you live? I mean will you work, or just laze around?'

'Oh, I'll work. Didn't I say? Peter's got a job at the Wynd, a full-time job of course, doing things to engines. Your da's always been wild about engines and he remembered Pete from before, and gave him the job. So I thought if he can do it . . . and I went and visited the nuns at the convent in town and told them I was moving back and that I was about to become a married lady. They thought about it for ages – kept shooting little, slanty looks at me and giggling – and then they said I could take up the position of teacher of English to the lower school, starting next September the tenth. And since it's June now, and they break up on the fifteenth of July, that's absolutely ideal.'

'I'm happy for you,' Dot assured her. 'Where did you say your house was?'

Presently, when Jessica had told her all about the darling little house and the neat garden and the hens she intended to keep, she asked Dot how her life had gone since she had returned to Wales.

'If you don't want to talk about the other bit, we won't,' she said obligingly. 'I expect you've a young man?'

'Several, but no one special,' Dot admitted. The new-found attractions which had come to light in Norwich had not simply disappeared on her return home. Her father, she knew, had great hopes of Andrew Fairweather, because his land marched with theirs; she rather liked Stuart Stanford, but then he was feckless and would undoubtedly be nothing but a charge on the estate were she to marry him; and the other contender, Dick Michaels, had gone down in her estimation because he did not like children.

'Several? Well, you always were a fetching little thing. I used to think that was better than being ravingly beautiful in the long run,' Jessica said frankly.

'Ravingly beautiful? Really, Jess, for an English teacher you could learn a thing or two. And I take it you're thinking of yourself when you use that particular phrase?'

'No, indeed. I'm not ravingly beautiful – what's wrong with saying that? – but you must admit I make the most of what I've got.' Jessica touched her hair and smoothed down the silk jacket of her suit. 'Come on, what else? Everyone's talking about you and saying what a marvellous job you've made of the Plas. That's how I came to know you were home since Mam never said a word.'

'It'll bore you . . . but here goes.'

Dot launched into the saga of the dairy farm, the reclaiming of vast tracts of land, the new machinery, better farming methods, additional workers. But long before she had finished Jessica had interrupted.

518

'Oh, by the way, what happened to your black pony? I *did* envy you that pony. He was so romantic-looking — and you had him so well trained. I remember when I was quite young I was sitting by the window in the schoolroom and you'd been into the village for something and left the pony outside the railings. You came out of the one of the shops and just whistled . . . I never could whistle . . . and that pony trotted right up to you! I thought it was marvellous.'

'Yes, he was wonderful,' Dot said reminiscently. 'But I sold him to a chap over by Caer and when I came home and wanted him back they didn't know who'd got him. I asked and asked, and then the groom at the Markwells' came over here one day and said he believed the old boy had sold Matchless to someone over Corwen way who had a crippled child. So of course I couldn't try to take him back from a child who needed him, and I gave up the thought. Father has bought Tommy a dear little Shetland pony, a bright chestnut with a pale mane, but he'll never be like my Matchless.'

'No, I can understand that. Hywel used to say you and that horse were close as brother and sister.'

'We were. I loved him dearly. But I couldn't take him from a crippled child even if I could trace him.'

'True enough. Dot, are you really not going to marry? I should have thought you'd need a husband, with the little boy to bring up and this great big place to run.'

'No, I can manage quite well by myself, thanks,' Dot said cheerfully. 'Father asks, sometimes, but I don't let it bother me. If I met the right person I suppose I wouldn't hesitate, but I haven't, not yet. Or rather,' she added, natural honesty getting the better of her, 'I did meet someone, once, but it never came to anything.'

'Oh? Anyone I know? I remember Stan once said to Hywel that he'd always wondered about you and him. I didn't hear him saying it, but he repeated it to Cerwyn and I was listening. Of course I knew there was nothing in it, Hywel was such a softie that you wouldn't have wanted *him*, but I did wonder what had set Stan off on that track.'

'He was not a softie, whatever that might mean, and I most certainly did want him,' Dot said curtly. 'It was him . . . he, I mean . . . who didn't want me. Anyway, that was years ago. I was a kid of seventeen. I hadn't met anyone else. That was one reason I went away, because Hywel said I should meet other people.'

'You went away because *Hywel* said . . .' Jessica clutched her brow. 'I must be dreaming! The whole village knows you went away because your father decided to leave the Plas to someone else and took your inheritance and put it into the Wynd without asking. Don't tell me they got that wrong too!'

'No, it was right. But if Hywel hadn't urged me to go and stay with my sister . . . if he'd said he wanted me here, then I think I'd have soldiered on through all the other business.' Dot took a deep breath, exhaled slowly, and then went on with determined brightness, 'So there's good in everything, because if it hadn't been for Hywel telling me to go I'd never have had Tommy, and I love him very dearly.'

'That money . . . the money your father put in the Wynd . . . must have made a lot more money by now,' Jessica said thoughtfully. 'They talk about the Wynd when they're lecturing about colleries and coal at college, Peter says. It's because it has a very good type of coal, I believe. Bless me, Dot, you aren't only lady of the manor (is there such a thing?) but a coal baron as well! Do you rush round the pits interfering and making them buy new machinery, the way you do here?'

'No fear! I think coal mining's evil, and I hate it. I don't want to profit from money got with men's lives,' Dot said scornfully. 'I've never been down a pit and I'll never go down, either. Once I didn't have any pride, Jessica, just a yearning for love, but now I've learned a thing or two. People don't respect love, but they respect pride! I was fond . . . very fond . . . of Hywel, but I wouldn't go running to him now even if he only lived a mile off. All I'd get would be a punch in the face, very likely . . . oh, I don't mean literally. Hywel is far too polite and kind to do that, but he'd punch me just as effectively by showing me that he'd forgotten me! And I'm the same with the pits. I've always despised money got from mining, I've always said my farming will pay for Plas Tegydd to be made good again, and I'll stick to it.'

'That sounds more like pigheaded obstinacy than pride,' Jessica said, looking pensive. 'What about those fellows you

520

mentioned? Does pride come into the way you feel about them?'

'Yes. But I am really considering marriage, so though I shan't pip you at the post I may not be far behind you. Actually I'm going to the midsummer ball at the Myddeltons – you know, over at Chirk Castle – in a week or so and all three of my admirers will be there. The one I rather like, the one Father rather likes, and the one we both thought highly suitable and exciting until he told me he didn't like kids. It's a very romantic evening. Perhaps I'll succumb to a surfeit of champagne and the moon on the battlements, and accept someone's proposal. If I do I'll let you know.'

'Right. I'll keep you to that.' Jessica stood up. 'I'd better be going now, Dot. I've got a lot to do when I get home, but how would you like me to get you Hywel's address? I could, easily. Mam isn't what she was. She hides letters away in the oddest places, like some old jackdaw. I could easily find it and copy it down and pass it on to you. After all, you liked him once. You might enjoy keeping in touch.'

Dot stared at her friend, her whole body aching with temptation; but suppose he really was about to marry this Alice person? Or suppose he really had forgotten her? Suppose he simply told her to leave him alone, to forget him as he had forgotten her? She cringed at the thought. She had been so hurt by him all those years ago, she had done such a good job of putting him right out of her mind, learning to live without him, that it seemed downright foolish to put it all at risk again. Just one letter and she could find her hard-won contentment vanishing in longing.

'Well, I don't know, Jess,' she said slowly. 'Tell you what. You find it if it isn't too much trouble and give it to me some time. But I won't promise to write, because I'm not too keen on letter-writing. I'll put it away in my desk and if the urge to know what he's up to gets too strong I'll drop him a line. How's that?'

'Grand. Look, do you ever come into town of a morning? We could meet for a cup of coffee and I could show you the bridesmaids' dresses and that. It would be a bit of fun. And then I could give you the address.'

'Right, that's a date. When?'

'Well, how about next Wednesday? Sharp at eleven in the Copper Kettle.' Jessica was crossing the room towards the door but she halted when she reached it, a hand on the knob. 'Dot, I've done some bad things in my life, far worse than you know. Why is someone really good, like Peter, prepared to take me on? I try very hard but I'm shallow and fun-loving and attention-seeking and conceited and . . . and yet Peter likes me.'

'There's no accounting for tastes,' Dot said with a twinkle. 'You told me just now that I was stubborn, and I think perhaps you're right. We'll both try to improve ourselves, shall we? Then the men of our choice won't have to stoop quite so far to raise us up!'

'Oh, Dot, it does me good to laugh!' Jessica opened the door just as Tommy, flushed and excited, hurtled across the hall. 'Gracious, here comes the Flying Scotsman from the look of it!'

Tommy, who had been emitting ear-piercing whistles, looked gratified, but made straight for his mother.

'We've had the tea and you never come up,' he said shrilly. 'Taid ate all the bara brith, every bit. He's going to be as fat as a pig. And Gwil let me ride down on the tractor. Better than poor Philly on that old horse.'

Dot sighed, kissed him, and then hoisted him into her arms.

'There speaks a child of the twenties, more interested in a smelly old tractor than a beautiful, noble animal,' she said ruefully. 'Come along, young man, it's time for your bath, and then bed.'

'Why does you call me old man one minute and young man the next?' her son enquired craftily. 'I'm either old man or young man, I can't be both. Why don't you stay down here and explain it to me?'

'Oh, sure, and I was only born yesterday too,' Dot said, giving Tommy the giggles. 'Jess, darling, can you let yourself out? This . . . this middle-aged man needs a bit of attention.'

'Of course, darling. Don't forget, Wednesday at eleven.' Jessica disappeared through the front door, closing it behind her, and Dot and her burden began to mount the stairs. Halfway up them Tommy became a tractor with engine problems, and Dot said that if he would just shut up she would give him a horsy-ride on her back. She would not be so obliging for a mechanical monster.

'I'll pretend you're not a horse but a tractor,' Tommy declared, once he was being piggy-backed. He gave a shriek of laughter when she protested that he was cheating and threw himself back so violently that only a miracle saved them both from descending the stairs a good deal faster than they had climbed them.

'I don't know how I stand you. You're harder work than the whole farm – including the tractors,' Dot declared when she stood in the bathroom doorway. Peggy, the faithful nursery maid who had been with them ever since they arrived back at Plas Tegydd, had already run the bath. 'Come on, my lad, get those filthy clothes off and into the water before I count ten, or . . .'

'Taid's coming,' shouted a deep voice from the stairwell. 'You'd better be in that water before Taid reaches the bathroom or you'll get a smack on the bottom instead of this lovely lollypop!'

Tommy promptly threw himself into the water with a tremendous splash. He was still wearing his little vest, but since it was very dirty indeed and covered in tickly hayseeds it could only benefit from the ducking. Tom Tegydd arrived on the scene, his grandson disappeared under the rocking water, the nursery maid protested that Mummy and Taid were more trouble than a dozen children, and Tommy, a little over-excited, threw water.

Another bedtime had begun.

In due course Jessica handed over Hywel's address. Dot looked at it longingly but decided she would not write yet. She was so busy! And then there was the midsummer ball – suppose she decided that an advantageous marriage was what she wanted and needed, rather than the faint chance of a love-match? The fact that she was legally married to Carlo worried her not at all, since she assumed – wrongly as it happened – that since she had given her name as Dorothy Evans and not – ugh – Thomasina Tegydd she was not married at all. Carlo had married a myth, in fact.

Several times in the days that followed she picked up the piece of paper with the address on, and very nearly wrote. But not quite. She would take up a pen, pull a pad of paper towards her, and then decide not to act precipitately. She had offered herself to Hywel once and he had turned her down. She had reached a stage, now, when a merciful numbness had more or less taken the place of the yearning she had felt for him; did she really want to deliberately poke at the wound, start that dreadful, gnawing agony of loss up again?

The date of the midsummer ball approached, and then arrived. Her father was going too, along with most of the county, and he looked very smart in a new dinner jacket with a frilled shirt and a velvet bow tie with which Dot nearly strangled him before she got it right.

Dot wore the prettiest evening dress: an earth-brown slip with a floating gauze overdress in a light chestnut colour. It suited her very well, emphasising the deep, rich tones in her hair and making her creamy skin and dark eyes look excitingly contrasted.

'Well, Tommy?' Her son, sleeping-suited and angelic, had been allowed downstairs to see them off, with the nursemaid in attendance. 'Don't we made a lovely couple?' She took her father's arm and curtseyed, to Tommy's great amusement. 'What are you laughing for? I think we look . . . like . . .'

'You're a princess and Taid's the king,' her son announced. 'Bring me back a magic balloon!'

Dot could never go to any sort of social function without bringing back a balloon, having done so on a previous occasion. She laughed down at him, then kissed his cheek and went out with Tom into the beautiful June evening and got into the hired car which would take them to Chirk and call for them again when the ball was over.

Dot felt that by telling Jessica she would probably make up her mind between her suitors at the midsummer ball she had, in a way, committed herself. And not before time, either, she knew well. So she would definitely decide, tonight, which of them if any she intended to make the happiest man on earth.

Arriving at the castle, Dot and her father went under the high arch and into the central courtyard to find it full of people, most of whom they knew. Everyone was in evening dress, and most of the women had chosen carefully and looked lovely. Pinks, pale blues and whites predominated. Dot was glad of her brown and gold draperies, especially as several of the older women wore darker shades so she did not feel conspicuous. After all, I'm pretty old myself, with my son in bed at home and twenty-four years to my credit, she reminded herself.

As soon as she entered the long ballroom, all golden polished floor, brilliant but shaded lighting and soft music, she was claimed, of course. She was popular with young men for her looks and gaiety and also for her courage in tackling the mouldering Tegydd ruins, as someone had put it, and bringing her illegitimate son home to live without so much as a blush.

First she waltzed with Stuart, then with Andrew, then with Dick. She had a stately turn around the floor with her host, and then she did an extremely lively polka with her father which left them both pink and breathless. After that she danced with Andrew, Dick and Stuart, and at suppertime they made up a very jolly table of young people, so that there was no difficulty about who was favouring whom.

As the evening wore on, Dot found herself with Dick, heading for the grounds.

'A breath of fresh air would do us both good, old girl,' he said, and his narrow, piratic face, with the lock of dark hair which hung over his brow and inspired so many young women with thoughts of Byron, made it seem an exciting and romantic thing to do.

Dot forgot that he did not like children; all of a sudden, after more than two years of celibacy, she found herself wanting a man. Dick simply happened to be nearby, but he would do! He caught her fingers and they escaped through some long french windows into the moonlit grounds.

It was a marvellous night. Behind them the castle loomed, as old as time, its round, battlemented turrets lit by the light streaming from the mullioned windows. Built by the English to subjugate the Welsh, it had brooded over the borderland for more than six hundred years; legend gave it no ghosts, but certainly now, in the moonlight, you would glance behind you as you went through the yew garden, almost expecting to see a headless lady in Tudor dress or a phantom hound lifting a leg against one of the statues.

Dot giggled at her own fancy, but kept very close to Dick, who was striding along with great determination and looking very like one of those Elizabethan adventurers whose portraits lined the beautiful, curving staircase. Presently they emerged from the formal garden and went down a path which threaded its way between trees – great oaks, tall elms, mighty chestnuts. One of the oaks was hollow but so huge that there was room for a man – and a small woman – to stand inside it. Dick was heading inexorably for that particular oak.

It was exciting in the wood in the moonlight; Dot kept catching her breath as first one scene and then another swam into view. The blackness inside the oak was a bit scary, but Dick pulled her into it, and into his arms, at the psychological moment, and it was no longer frightening; they were two kernels in a rather close-fitting nut, looking out on to the moonlight. Dick put his arms around her – he had to – and began to kiss her mouth. He was, she reflected dreamily, rather good at it. Presently she forgot she was squashed into a hollow oak tree and that, outside, the moonlight gleamed on the great pile of the castle and lit the revels of the guests in the courtyard and on the lawns. She only thought about what she was doing, and how long it had been!

However fond she may have been of lovemaking during her marriage, though, Dot found that a young woman used to the joys of a marital bed does not relish being seduced in an oak tree, no matter how hollow. The first time she heard her golden gauze catch on a roughness in the trunk she simply thought, *What the hell, let it rip!* and continued kissing Dick, which possibly gave him a wrong impression, for the second time it happened she stopped kissing Dick to unhook herself, and when his ardour became such that he began to try to get inside her beautiful evening gown, which meant that he pressed Dot's bare and tender back hard against the gnarled old trunk and also trod quite heavily on her satin-slippered feet, she was moved to tell him sharply to 'Get off!'

Apparently only remembering her initial response, Dick took no notice of this command and pressed on. Dot might be small but she was strong and she had never minded inflicting pain in a good cause, so she kicked Dick's shins as well as she could in the confined space, brought her knee into contact with parts of Dick which he would have preferred to remain unbattered, and punched him, eyewateringly, on the nose.

'Didn't you hear me? I said get off,' she said reproachfully, as Dick staggered back, endeavouring to clasp several portions of his person at the same time, an impossible task considering he still had one hand round Dot's waist. 'Really, men don't think! This dress is new, I don't want it ruined. And come to that I don't much fancy being raped in a wood. Though I suppose,' she went on thoughtfully, stepping out into the moonlight and examining her gown with anxious care, 'there are some who would think it very romantic.'

Dick muttered something catarrhally down his fast-swelling nose. He sounded sulky and Dot, glancing up at him, having ascertained that her gown was scarcely damaged at all, saw that he was looking quite cross and offended.

'What's the matter? I'm sorry about your nose, but better that than a black eye. People always seem to leap to the right conclusion about black eyes. What?' For Dick had muttered something else.

'I said you deedn't have hit be quite so hard,' Dick said. 'If you'd just said you didn't like it, that would have dode fide.'

'What? Oh, yes.' Dot brushed bits of oak tree out of her hair and off her shoulders and set off towards the castle. 'I said *get off* and you didn't, so I felt it was safer to prove I meant what I said.' She looked back to where Dick stood. 'Aren't you coming back with me? Oh, do come along and don't stand there sulking! I've got to go through the yew garden, and it's awfully creepy in there – I might get attacked.'

'Huh! I pity adywud who attacks you,' Dick said bitterly, but he followed her, nevertheless. 'What'll I tell beoble when they ask about by dose?'

'Oh, say you walked into a tree – I shan't split,' Dot said blithely. 'I'll have to hurry. I promised Andrew I'd have the next waltz with him and I'm sure that's a waltz they're playing.'

'You aren't going to marry any of them? Well, Dot, it's your decision, but I think you'll regret it. Being married is so lovely!' Jessica, sitting opposite her friend in Stevens whilst they both indulged in cream cakes and delicious coffee, had been regaled with the story of the midsummer ball at the time and had just been told about the final sad parting between Dot and Stuart, the only one to survive until now.

'Well, at the moment I'm quite happy as I am; happier than I would be if someone came along and started telling me what to do with the estate,' Dot said frankly. 'Perhaps marriage suits some and not others.'

'Dot, I've never asked, but . . . what about Tommy's father? Has he got anything to do with why you aren't keen on marriage?'

Dot giggled, then took another sip of her coffee.

'In a way. Let's forget it – I'm not going to marry. Not yet.'

'No, but have you written to Hywel? Mam writes to her sister Megan, but we only get little bits of information about Hywel. Have you written?'

'No. I might, one day, when I'm more settled. But I'm too busy now to want more complications.'

'I know how you feel in a way. I meant to write myself, just to show there was no ill-feeling, but . . . I don't know, it's a bit like opening old wounds, in a way. So I've not written yet, either.'

Dot took a third cream cake, examined it judicially and then bit into it; cream squirted.

'Heavens, aren't I messy? What I thought was, Hywel knows where we live and he hasn't written to us. Why not? I mean I shouldn't think your Mam would fail to mention that I was back home, would you? All that juicy scandal – came home with a little lad and not a blush did we see on that bold face – I was sure she'd pass that on.'

'Yes, I should think you're right there. And Megan would be bound to tell Hywel. When I was poking through Mam's letters searching for the address I had a look at some of them, and Megan says she reads the letters aloud to her family and they always enjoy them. And she gives Mam little messages from Hywel, too. Yes, I'm sure if Mam told about you being home Hywel would know.'

The cake was not very good after all. It was quite nasty; the

528

sponge was stale and the cream oily. Dot put it down on her plate and sipped at the coffee to get rid of the taste. The coffee was bitter.

'Yes, that's what I thought. So there's no need for me to write. If he . . . if he wanted to get in touch, he could.' She pushed back her chair. 'I'd better be getting back, Jess, or goodness knows what they'll be up to! We've got a field of barley ripening nicely, I want to take a look at that, and then we're trying a new way of mixing for cheese . . . I'd love to come to tea next week, though, and thank you kindly for the invitation.'

She left the low-ceilinged restaurant and hurried over to where she had arranged to meet Tom. They had come into town together in the car which her father had recently bought, and a hair-raising experience it had been, for Tom's secret conviction that a car was only a horse without legs did not make for good driving. Indeed, down the long hill from the village he had, she could have sworn, forgotten that he was in a mechanical vehicle; he had taken his hands from the wheel, gestured, turned to stare over his shoulder at someone else's good crops, and had it not been for Dot's warning cries she was sure they would have ended in the ditch.

I really must learn to drive myself, or he'll start risking Tommy's neck as well, she was telling herself as she made her way down York Street and through to Eagle's Meadow. That's why I feel so . . . well, so stale and unhappy, because I'm not looking forward to the drive home.

But she knew, in her heart, that it was not just the drive. It was the end of yet another small hope.

Twenty-Seven

'Dot, I don't say much, but that doesn't mean I don't notice much, either. You've been pale as a ghost for weeks and you've not got rid of that nasty cough, either. Here it is, halfway through August, and though I know we've had nothing but rain and then more rain you look peakier than you did last winter. You could do with a rest. And I mean a real rest, not just a day in Beeston for the horse fair.'

The three Tegydds were at breakfast; Tommy was tackling a man-sized meal with every sign of good appetite, Tom had finished bacon, egg, kidney and sausage, and Dot was pushing a fried tomato under an uneaten piece of bacon near her untouched fried egg. Neither she nor her son looked up as Tom spoke, but Dot heaved a sigh.

'I'm all right. I like work and I like Plas Tegydd. The cough's a nuisance but it'll go soon, I suppose.'

'You need a holiday, girl! You need to get right away, forget the place for a bit. You need sunshine, and nothing to do and lots to eat.'

'Well, we won't get sunshine anywhere in England and there's lots to eat here, only I'm not hungry.' Dot gave up the pretence of eating and put her knife and fork down on her plate with a cross little tinkle of silver on china. 'If I did go away for a week or two I'd probably die of boredom.'

'Hmm.' Tom returned to his paper, eating with a fork in one hand, then laid it down with a resigned sigh. He looked very much better after a couple of years of her rule, Dot decided. His figure was trimmer, his carriage more confident, and he looked happy.

'Look, Dot, how about Italy? You went there once and enjoyed it. Why not go back? The expense is no object. We're doing damned well with this place and the Wynd keeps the other two pits solvent. What do you say?'

'Oh, no, thanks, Father!' Dot was stunned at his remembering Italy and could not help visualising arriving in that country and walking slap bang into Carlo and his parents. 'I'll be fine now that the rain seems to have let up a bit. I'm sure the damp was bad for my cough . . . Oh, Tommy darling, do be careful . . . now look what you've done!'

Tommy had knocked his second boiled egg over. The yellow yolk puddled his plate, and Tommy, prodding at it with a bread-and-butter soldierboy, tipped the plate so that yolk ran on to the white starched tablecloth. Dot leaned over and slapped him, Tommy laughed, and Dot began to cry.

This absolutely unheard of reaction stunned both males present. Tommy stared, mouth agape, eyes rounding, and Tom got up and put his arms awkwardly round his weeping daughter's shoulders.

'There, you see? Once you'd have given Tommy a slap and then laughed as well. I'm not an observant man, and I know I'm not sensitive, but I'd have had to be a moron not to see you're unwell, and have been for many a week. Come on now, how about that holiday? If you think I could be spared I'd come as well. We could go to the seaside – Tommy would like that – or abroad. I don't mind going abroad for a couple of weeks. Or you could take the girl with you to give a hand and be away with no worries at all, because I'd take good care of the place.'

Dot stopped crying with some difficulty, for it had suddenly become essential that her unhappiness be given some rein, mopped her streaming eyes on her napkin, sniffed, and poured herself another cup of coffee. It would be fun, really, to get away; and Father was right, her cough was a niggling nuisance. It meant that she could rarely sleep a full night through and that in itself was tiring. But she would not dream of leaving him here. He meant to be so good, but he had ideas which did not fit in with hers and she had never completely trusted him not to do something quixotic, like buying some marvellous machinery which would cost thousands of pounds and would prove useless anyway. However, it would not do to tell him that, so she smiled instead.

'If you'll come with me, I'll go. To the coast, I think, because Tommy would enjoy that. Somewhere quiet, without a telephone, where we could lie on the beach or bathe or just take long walks.'

'Right – excellent. I'll book us into a decent hotel . . . we'll go somewhere with a bit of life, hey, so that we can get out of an evening. What about Rhyl?'

Dot was touched; she remembered Rhyl as a highlight of her childhood, but she had discovered since she had been at home that Rhyl had also been the place where Edie and her father had shared a little dreamhouse. It would not be easy for him to return there without her. However, she underestimated Tom Tegydd.

'No, it won't worry me, it'll give me great pleasure,' he told her when she said that going to Rhyl would only give him pain. 'I was happier there than I had any right to be, I daresay, but it was a different Tom Tegydd, living a different life. Now I can go back there, and remember how marvellous it all was, and enjoy looking back, but I shan't moon round sighing. It isn't in my nature to regret a pleasure passed.'

'Right, then Rhyl sounds fine to me. And Tommy will absolutely adore it.'

They went for a week and stayed for three and at the end of it they came home tanned, bright-eyed and rosy-cheeked, for they had been fortunate with their weather. Everything had been good: the walks along the prom in the evening, the trips to the theatre, watching the Punch and Judy shows, the long, sunny days on the beautiful beach. They all behaved like kids, wading through the warm low waters with shrimping nets and buckets and catching strange creatures – shrimps and prawns, tiny flatfish no bigger than a shilling – and they all enjoyed it tremendously.

'I'm happy to be back,' Dot said, as Tom steered the car quite neatly between the big stone gateposts and up the Plas Tegydd drive. 'Perhaps I'm happier because I've had such a wonderful time. My cough went, my suntan came, and I feel better than I've felt for years.

'That's just what I hoped,' Tom said heartily, drawing up in the stable-yard. He never stopped outside the front door. He seemed to feel that the car longed for its stable and should not be expected to wait to see that it had really arrived home. 'Well, here we are!'

'Home!' shouted Tommy, jumping out of the car and capering. 'Home home home!'

'That's right, love. And what's the first thing you'll do when we get indoors?'

'Wee wee,' Tommy said, making his grandfather roar with laughter. Dot giggled.

'Well yes, certainly, if that's your greatest need. But I was thinking about running up to the nursery to see Peggy. You'll do that after you've been to the toilet, won't you?'

'Yes,' Tommy said, jiggling. 'Mummy . . .'

'Oh!' Dot could not help laughing again as Tommy, desperation point obviously reached, fished briefly about through the leg of his shorts and began to water the mounting block. 'Now, love, seeing Peggy *will* be the first thing you do when you get indoors!'

'I can't thank you enough, Father, for that holiday,' Dot said that evening as they sat over cheese and biscuits and coffee, having disposed of Cook's welcome-home dinner in a remarkably short time. 'I didn't know how badly I needed it until we got there and I began to relax.'

'Good, I'm glad you enjoyed it.' Tom glanced craftily across at her. 'You're a good girl, Dot – did I ever mention it?'

'Once or twice.' She knew her father well enough to wonder just what was coming.

'Ah. You wouldn't like to do me a favour?'

'Aha, I knew it! What?'

'Love, I wish you'd come down the pits with me. Not all of them, if you'd rather not, but at least the Wynd, if you could bring yourself to do so. You see, I've always done my best to be fair to the men . . . I'm getting on a bit, though. Soon be seventy.'

Dot blinked. He could not be that old; he seemed so active and lively!

'And the men know you've never been below; there's whispers that when you inherit you'll sell the pits. Dot, I don't want you to do that! There are unscrupulous men about. They'd undo the good I've done, drive the colliers even harder than they're driven already, push men deep, past the point where it's relatively safe . . . they dread that. If you can't bring youself to do if for me, love, won't you do it for the colliers? When you've seen . . . you may still hate it, but you'll understand better why it's important that an owner doesn't just draw his money.'

'Of course I'll do it,' Dot said at once, ashamed of the way she had behaved in the past. 'I'm sorry, Father. I never thought of it like that. And I won't sell the pits – or, if I do, I'll make sure I sell them to someone reliable.'

'No one's reliable, not when big money's concerned,' Tom said sadly. 'Keep 'em, Dot, and do right by the men. The lad's fascinated by all things mechanical – you must have noticed that already. Not a bit of notice has he taken of that Shetland since he's been allowed to sit on the tractor. He'll take over from you and make a good job of it one day, and if you sell whilst he's too small to interfere you'll be doing him down. Will you promise me?'

'If you like,' Dot said uneasily. She had always intended to sell the pits the moment they came into her hands. She had not realised that she would be selling the men, too. Or perhaps she had realised; perhaps she was as singleminded, in her way, as her father had once been in his. Perhaps she had been prepared to see colliers suffer in order that her beloved home might benefit. 'Yes, I'll swear to it if it would make you feel better.'

'I'd like that,' Tom hesitated, then grinned at her. 'To tell you the truth, I've done my best to tie things up so you can't sell, but if you neglected 'em that would be as bad – perhaps worse. You must visit a colliery. If I'd visited the Wynd three or so years ago, I don't think there would be two or three hundred men buried under this house right now.'

'Under the *house*? My God, d'you mean Candle Deep is down there somewhere?' She indicated the floor beneath her feet.

'Well, approximately, yes. It gave me the shudders for a long time, but I've got used to the idea now and I reckon I've done enough penance for that neglect. Oh, regrets won't bring the

poor blighters back, but I've worked like . . . like a collier to
see that nothing like that happens again. I want to show you
how to make sure it doesn't happen again when I'm gone,
either. So you'll come. When?'

'I'll be pretty busy next week, settling in and checking up on
everything,' Dot said thoughtfully. 'The following week's the
same, and then there's the beast market . . . we've got stock for
sale. Shall we say in a month?'

'We'll say tomorrow,' Tom said firmly. 'No, don't look
doubtful; I might not be here in a month.'

'Don't be silly. I've never seen you look fitter. But tomorrow
it is.'

'Nervous, my dear? Don't worry, you'll soon get used to it.'

Dot tried to give a scornful laugh but it did not come out as
scornfully as she had intended; it was an altogether reedier
effort. She and her father were approaching the winding shed
where, presently, they would be issued with lamps before
descending in the cage to the bowels of the earth, just like the
real colliers.

It was not fear which Dot felt, however, or not fear in the
sense that her father imagined. She was about to come face to
face with an enemy who had stolen her father from her when
she had needed him most, had stolen her friend and caused him
to go far away, had very nearly stolen Plas Tegydd as well. Yet
she had triumphed; she had come back and weaned Tom away
from his total devotion to the mines, and now she could afford
to be generous. She must look her enemy in the face. She must
do it, but she did not expect to enjoy it.

Dot had already met all the staff who worked above ground.
They were friendly and curious to know her and when they
had met her they seemed to approve, which was pleasant. Now
they were alone save for a fireman and an overman, both of
whom would accompany them down to the pit bottom. At this
time of day the men were well into their shift; they had gone
down two hours earlier and would not be up for another four
or five. Dot, stepping into the cage and hanging grimly on to
the barred side, wondered whether she would be remembered
by any of the colliers; she did not often go into the village now,

though she visited the town regularly.

An order was given, a bell rang, and the cage plunged. Dot knew with her common sense that it was a controlled fall, but it was faster and more sickening than she had imagined and also more silent; there was a horrible hissing noise, a few clicks, and then they were just falling through the dark.

The cage stopped quite gently though and not with the spine-jarring crash Dot had been bracing herself for, and they were in a big space with narrow railway tracks leading off in all directions, tubs filled with coal standing by, and a couple of men hovering to see who was descending at this time of the day. The space was lit by lamps on the walls and there were wires and a couple of wooden huts, lit from within, which appeared to contain more workers.

'Come on, lass.' Tom opened the cage and they stepped out. Dot had been provided with a vast overall, a helmet and the aforementioned lamp. She and her father went over to one of the huts to greet the men inside, and then the overman who had come down with them, Willi Norman, said he would give them a tour of the pit.

'It's a good place to work, ask anyone,' he said, leading them into what Dot would have called a big tunnel but he referred to as a main. 'Best colliery in Wales, that's the Wynd. Different from years ago, mind, miss, but now it's a showplace, I tell you.'

'Oh, stop that Welsh sweet-talk, Willi,' Tom growled, though Dot could see he was pleased. 'Miss Tegydd won't believe a word if you go on like that. We'll go right down to the face where the actual coal-cutting is done, Dot, and you shall see everything. I wish you'd seen it years ago,' he added wistfully, 'when it was really bad. Then you'd know why we're pleased with what we've achieved here.'

So Dot toured the Black Wynd pit. She seemed to go along interminable passages, in some of which she could stand comfortably upright, in others through which she had to crawl. When you got near the face you nearly always had to bend double, though Mr Norman and her father kept insisting that no miner gave a thought to that. It was only water and gas that a miner disliked.

'There is water, mind,' Willi Norman said in his soft,

sing-song voice. 'Deep too, in parts. But we try to work round it when we can, and we don't go no deeper than the boss thinks is safe. Oh aye, a model pit it is!'

But model or not, Dot found it a weird and often frightening experience. The quiet settling sounds, the drippings and clickings and what sounded like long sighs, disturbed her and made the hair all over her body prickle with unease. Darkness had never much troubled her, but this was total blackness and she found that she was terrified that her lamp might go out. It was all very well in the main roads, which were lit, but what of the tiny side passages which seemed scarcely larger than rabbit burrows and were in utter darkness? Where the men worked they had light, but travelling to and fro they were dependent on their own lamps.

But the colliers were so friendly and cheerful! They talked to Tom and to her with complete freedom, having a moan about the showers that her father wanted to install, saying they would only lead to premature baldness and back pains, informing her succinctly that they were glad to be in work, but, though the four days was good, getting the social was not.

'Got to be a bloody prince, you 'ave, to get a penny piece out of 'em,' one man informed her. 'And if you *are* a bloody prince, they reckon you can manage!'

Yet they did not grumble about the four-day week. The work, they felt, was shared out so that everyone got some, and that was fairer than turning one man off and keeping three on. You had to admire them; they were cheerful, loyal to each other, and though she talked to perhaps a hundred of them she never heard a single man trying to outdo another. They shared the labour as they shared what little money there was, without claim or blame. Whether you pushed tubs up steep inclines or cut coal or shovelled it or led ponies, you were a collier and therefore you earned every penny the hard way. That was their attitude, and Dot admired them for it.

They had penetrated to the furthest point of the mine and were returning when Tom remembered the stables. Knowing how interested she had always been in horses he suggested that they should go along there and see if she had any suggestions for the welfare of the small inmates. Dot, who always kept sugar in her pockets, struggled to reach it through the flapping overall, and agreed that they really should not miss the stables; they had seen everything else, after all!

It was queer to enter a long room, lit by their lamps, for otherwise it was in darkness, and to smell a real stable smell. It was, Dot discovered, stronger and less pleasant than the Tegydd stable smell – it made your eyes water – but then it was not so easy to get rid of the urine-soaked straw down here. At the sound of their voices the five little fellows stabled here, though there were stalls and mangers for a couple of dozen, turned eagerly towards them. When Dot proffered the sugar they whinnied, eager for the treat, and she rubbed their ragged little ears and smoothed their necks, seeing that they were in as good condition as was possible in the circumstances but knowing that it was not good enough.

'Why are they stabled in darkness?' she demanded, as soft lips nuzzled the sugar from her palm. 'Would it be so costly to hang lamps up? It's quite a small thing, but an important one.'

'No, not costly, but . . .' The overman glanced at Tom, at the ponies, and then back to Dot. 'What do you think, Mr Tegydd?'

'I suppose we could put lights on the walls,' Tom said. 'Yes, we'll do that. Any more suggestions, ma'am?'

'Do they see a vet regularly? And I trust they are fed oats from time to time? They certainly work hard enough.'

She could not voice her disgust because it would only hurt her father, but she would better the lot of these poor little creatures if she possibly could.

'Vet comes in when he's called, about once a month; they get oats three or four times a week,' Willi Norman said. 'If you've seen enough, miss . . .'

They left the stable and began to make their way back to the pit's eye, where they would take the cage to the surface once more. Tom was exuberant, pleased with himself, and when they saw a light in the distance approaching from one of the side roads, he stopped, beckoning Dot to wait as well.

'You might like to see this, Dot. See the pony coming? This is a main road where the endless rope runs and presently the pony will bring his tubs up here, the lad will unhitch them, hitch them on to the endless rope, and they'll be drawn the rest of the way by that method. It's very cleverly done when you've a well-trained pony which knows what's expected of it; you watch.'

Dot was ferreting in her pocket for one last sugar-lump. As the pony, head low, leaning into his harness with the effort of getting himself and the tubs up the last stretch, arrived on the main road, she stepped forward to offer it and found herself pushed back quite roughly by the lad at the pony's head.

'Watch out, miss,' he said warningly. 'Most of 'em's all right but this one, Tuggem we call 'im, he's a real devil. Hates folk, he does, have your fingers . . .'

But he was interrupted; the pony suddenly gave a shrill whinny even as Dot ran forward to fling her arms around the pony's neck.

'My God, my God, my God! What have they done to you? Oh, my God, what have they done?'

'Dot, what is it? What's the matter?' Tom could only see her head pressed against the pony's filthy neck, her hand far too near its mouth. 'He's not hurt. You heard what the lad said – he's one of the vicious ones. He'll go for your face . . . get away from him!'

'Father, don't you *see*? It's Matchless, my Matchless, who I sold to Christian Markwell when I left home all those years ago. And all the time I searched and searched he's been slaving down here in the dark. That groom *lied*. I thought at the time . . . I'm sure, now! They *knew* he'd been sold for a pit pony and they never even told me!' She turned to the lad, who was watching her, open-mouthed. 'Did you notice? He *recognised* me! He knew me the moment he set eyes on me – that was why he whinnied like that!'

'Oh no, miss, he couldn't recognise you.' The boy's soft voice was matter-of-fact. 'Blind, he is, like most of 'em. Been blind since I worked here, and that's two full year.'

No lights in the stable. Why? Because lights would make no difference. The eager heads turned, but not to the light or the movement, just to the sound of people and perhaps to the smell of sugar. Tears were coursing down her cheeks, making white tracks through the coal dust. She kissed the pony's white star, almost hidden beneath the filth, and gazed into his big, velvet brown eyes.

Sightless, now. Milky with the blindness that comes of living in perpetual dark.

She would never forgive herself for what had happened to Matchless. The worst part was that if she had listened to her father and gone down the pit two years ago the pony's sight might have been saved. Useless to tell herself that she might have gone down at a different time of day or to a different part of the mine, so might never have seen the pony. Her fault was clear. She had known that local pits used small, sturdy ponies to draw their tubs and yet she, who prided herself on being a caring person, had not even bothered to go down the pit to see how the men and the small beasts were faring. It had been easier to stay on the surface and make self-righteous remarks whilst Matchless had suffered below.

She had the pony brought up at once, of course. It had not been easy to persuade her father's senior men that everything would have to be stopped whilst a pony – and a bad-tempered one at that – was winched up, hanging below the cage in a body-belt. Seeing how long it took and how ill-equipped they were to bring an animal to the surface, Dot asked what happened to ponies when there was a pit fire or some other disaster. There was an uncomfortable silence and then someone remembered that they had been brought up during the general strike; that was why they still had one or two body-belts.

'But when they're too old to work? Or when they're too ill?' Dot asked pitifully. The uncomfortable silence stretched.

So Matchless had hammered home what she had already known, in her heart. If you have a hand in something, no matter how small that hand is, then it is your business to see that what is done in your name is done properly and kindly. If you have any sort of a conscience, that is. It had been her duty to see how the pits functioned and she should have done it as soon as she got home, if only because the man she loved had nearly lost his life down here. Yet instead of Dot paying for her selfishness, Matchless, whom she loved, had paid.

When the pony reached the surface she would not hear of allowing him to be led home by any other hand. She waved Tom Tegydd off in his car and then set off along the quiet lanes. Her first impulse had been to take him to the Plas Tegydd stables and give him a feed of hot mash, a handful of oats and a good dollop of Jan's curative ointment for the galls and weals on his shoulders and body. But as soon as they got away from the pit she knew what he wanted, and it was not the stable or the oats. She could see it in the way he lifted his small head to snuff at the pure mountain air, at the way his ears flicked forwards and backwards to catch the sounds of the breeze stirring the leaves, birdsong, the tinkle of a stream as the day dawdled to its end. He wanted his old pasture, high up, with the thick hedges to doze against when night came and the scutter of rabbits as they shared the lush grass in the early mornings and late evenings. He wanted the owl's hoot and the nightjar's booming cry and grass beneath his hooves and fresh water to drink when he thirsted. He had had enough of stale air and darkness and imprisonment without trial.

They reached the gate leading into his pasture and he stopped; did he know they were there or was it just coincidence? Dot liked to believe he knew, as she took his halter off and led him by his mane through the gateway and into the meadow. He was condemned forever to darkness, of course, in the pit or out of it, but up here was the dark not friendly to him, with its night smells and the sounds he had heard without noticing for so many years? The ground sloped up, without holes or dips, and the stream had a piece of shallow bank down which he would scramble to get water. He might have a fall or two, but he was intelligent, and this was his natural element. In the depths of winter he might need to come down to the stables, but until the weather broke this was his place.

She left him and walked back to the gate, closing it softly. She did not leave immediately but stood for a moment, watching him. He did not turn his head towards her again but went forward carefully, feeling for each foothold in a way which broke her heart to watch . . . but with such courage! Only once did he stumble, and then he put his head down and checked on the grey nose of rock which had impeded him. He would remember it, perhaps, in relation to the gate. Then he went forward again until he reached the middle of the meadow. Here his head went down and he began to crop the grass. The tearing sound, the complete normality of the scene, brought tears to Dot's eyes once more. Matchless was back and she would take care of him as she should always have done, knowing that he bore her no grudge. He was said to be vicious, he had hated and feared the sling and the body-belt and the rocking upward journey swinging below the cage and all the miserable business of getting him on land without breaking his legs or sending him plunging to his death at the pit bottom, yet he had not once tried to bite or kick. She had been the only person to handle him, at her own insistence, and he had not so much as showed his teeth at her or laid back his ears. He was a gentleman and she loved him; he would never suffer again if she could possibly prevent it.

She stayed watching him until the dusk grew too thick to see him properly at all; he was just a sturdy little silhouette against the darkening meadow. Only then did she turn away, satisfied that he would come to no harm, that he could cope, and only then did he show that he was aware of a presence in the landscape other than his own. As she turned away she saw his head lift and heard the soft, breathy nicker of farewell which Matchless had always given when she left him.

'Goodnight, old boy. Goodnight, Matchless,' Dot called back, as she had always done, and then began to walk back the way she had come, between the high, rustling hedges.

She was terribly lucky to have been given a second chance with Matchless, for second chances are not often handed out in this life. What about Hywel, though? He, like the pony, had been lost. She had just about found him when Jessica had given her his address, and what had she done then? Nothing! Afraid of being hurt, afraid to lower her pride . . . it was the story of the colliery all over again.

What is wrong with me, she wondered, hurrying down the hill. Am I a coward, after all, when I thought myself brave and strong and sensible? I was afraid of the colliery and all the time it was hiding what I most wanted – Matchless. To be afraid to put something to the test was the worst kind of cowardice, because you were shutting your eyes, blocking out the bad with the good, the good with the bad. You might never get hurt that way, but you wouldn't know much joy, either!

I've done some bad things and some foolish things in my life, Dot thought, as she walked. Leaving Paoletta was so awful that she scarcely dared to think of it, and she supposed, doubtfully, that denying Carlo was pretty bad, too. And she had refused to go down the pits, when she had always known, really, that she ought. Yet still fate had been kinder than she deserved; she had found her pony.

She would not write to Hywel, she would go to him. It was odd how she made up her mind between one footfall and the next, and knew, with a tremendous inner exaltation, that she had done the right thing. Oh, he might be married with ten children, he might no longer even want to exchange the time of day with her, but at least she would know! She would not be blundering around like a child playing blind man's buff, she would have wrenched the stupid, self-inflicted bandage from her eyes and she would face whatever came.

She did just wonder about marriage; how could she marry anyone, when she was already married with two children? But she found it still did not worry her. She would marry, if she loved, and perhaps one day she might get her daughter back, but if not Carlo adored Paoletta and would look after her. One child each made it sound fairer.

One thing worried her; suppose her father did not approve of Hywel and disinherited her? Or her and Tommy, even? She stopped in the gateway where, in summer, the wild honeysuckle and the dog roses mingled. She looked down on her home, with its lights beginning to prick the dusk. She saw the fish-scale tiles on the onion domes built by some long-ago, ridiculous Tegydd who had wanted a faery-castle, and had built one with touches of the orient, touches of myth, combining all these things with the sturdy grey local stone. He had done a good job, Dot told herself, blissfully prejudiced. There could be no lovelier house than this, set like a gem in this fair land.

Could she risk losing it all a second time? For a man she had not set eyes on for a decade? Risk losing her father's affection, and the safe place she had made for her son?

She could. For Hywel, she could. Nothing venture, nothing win, she told herself grimly, continuing on down the hill. Her father, whatever his faults, was no snob. She did not think he would object at all if she sprang it on him that she was going to marry a very ordinary young man and not one of the landed gentry.

By the time she reached the stableyard it was full dark and

543

the stars shone brilliantly against a cobalt sky. She would tell her father that she had to go away for a week or so, and then if things did not go as she wished she could simply pretend she had been visiting a friend. As she entered the kitchen through the back door, Cook wagged an admonitory finger at her.

'Miss Dot, a terrible state your da's in. Better go straight to the drawing room. Where've you been at this time of night? He's been on the telephone, ringing everyone he knows, even the police in town to see if they know where you might be. Rang the station in town, then the station in Chester . . . in a terrible state he is. Sent back my good dinner untasted and would not so much as look at the wine.'

'I've been with the pony,' Dot said, scooting across the kitchen and snatching the door open. 'I'd better go and tell him I'm all right.'

Her father was pacing the floor and Tommy was grizzling on the window-seat. It was well past his bedtime. When Dot entered they both looked up, Tommy's face immediately breaking into a big smile and Tegydd's, despite an obvious effort for sternness, doing the same.

'Dot! Worried stiff I was! Where on earth have you been so late? You aren't a girl to miss a dinner but ours was served hours ago and no sign of you. I was worried . . . you went off with that pony they said was vicious . . . I looked for you in the stables because I knew you'd take him there, but there was no sign of either one of you. I didn't know what to think.'

'Well, Father, I stayed with the pony in the high pasture. I wanted to be sure he could manage the terrain, get down to the stream and so on, but it was all right. He's at home, you could see. And then I got to dreaming, leaning over the gate halfway down . . . you know how it is.'

'No, I don't. I'm not a dreamer, but I must say you've given me a bad hour or two. It was just like last time, you see. I felt you'd think it was my fault that I hadn't spotted the pony and blame me for the state he was in, and when you went off, just like last time, with Matchless, I couldn't help thinking . . . it was silly, but last time you'd gone and so had the pony. So you see, I worried.'

'Father!' Dot went over and kissed him on the chin. 'You

didn't think I'd go off and leave my child, did you? Really, shame on you!'

Even as she spoke the words a cold niggle of guilt bit at her. That was precisely what she had done when she had walked out without fetching Paoletta from school. Then she had not intended to deceive anyone. She had meant to return, to tell her father she was a married woman with a daughter as well as her small son.

'No, I knew you wouldn't leave Tommy. But I thought you might send for him later. Remember, when I first asked you to stay here you said it was impossible, you had commitments. I just thought . . . oh, Dot, I'm glad you're here!'

'I've got commitments here now,' Dot said. 'One of them is this young man – why on earth didn't you send him up to Peggy ages ago?'

'He wouldn't eat any tea so I said he might dine with us,' the doting grandfather admitted rather sheepishly. 'And then when dinner came I wasn't hungry so of course he didn't eat his meal either. Tommy, you must go up to bed now. Ask Peggy for some hot milk and biscuits.'

'And a piece of cake,' the miniature opportunist suggested.

'Good idea. A piece of cake as well.'

'And some pork pie?'

Dot hastily stepped in before Tommy asked for the moon.

'No, just cake, biscuits and hot milk, darling,' she said firmly. 'Bed!'

When Tommy had gone, too tired to object, Dot and her father re-ordered dinner and sat down to roast peasant. Whilst they were eating it, Tom suddenly put down his knife and fork, cleared his throat and spoke.

'Dot! There's something I have to say to you!'

'Fire ahead,' Dot invited.

'Well, you were a funny little thing as a child, and I was . . . very fond of you. But then I got it into my head that the only thing that mattered was to have a son to carry on the name. Up to this evening I thought I'd got my heir in young Tommy, and that was all that mattered. I was wrong; it isn't. I don't know why it is, but you – you've grown on me. I didn't want to rely on anyone – look what happened when I relied on Blanche –

545

but I found myself relying on you. And then this evening, when I thought you'd gone, run away to wherever you went all those years ago, I knew it wasn't Tommy at all, much though I love him. It's you, old girl.' Her father picked up his fork and stabbed the tablecloth with it. 'You care for the things I care for, and you've taught me to care for Plas Tegydd as I once did. I've even put the pits back to where they belong – they're very important, the men more than anything, but the coal takes second place now to the land. I realised this evening that if you went . . .' the tablecloth came in for another jabbing attack '. . . even if you never sent for the boy none of it would be worth fighting for; it would be sawdust, d'you see? No meaning, no reason for trying, no one to work for . . . with . . . whatever you will. I just want you to know.'

Dot smiled at him. 'What do you want me to know, Father? Go on, why can't you say it? I'm not just an ugly little gnome, am I!'

His embarrassment vanished; he grinned back at her, his eyes almost disappearing into slits behind his bunched-up rosy cheeks. He was immeasurably relieved that she had turned his confession of affection into a joke.

'Yes, you're an ugly little gnome, because you take after me – I'm an ugly old gnome! We're two of a kind and I've grown very fond of you, ugly little gnome though you are.'

'That's the nicest thing you've ever said to me,' Dot said. She got up from the table and went over to the window, twitching the curtains across as much to allow her father to regain his composure as to hide her own delight. Ridiculous to be so pleased because he had put into words what she had been reading in his eyes for months! 'And whilst we're on the subject of leaving people, you won't mind if I leave you and Tommy here for a few days? I find I've got to go and look up a friend of mine who lives some distance off. I can't tell you much because I don't know much, but I'll come clean as soon as I can.'

Over chocolate mousse, an excellent cheese board and coffee, Dot told her father a little of her quest. She was going to a friend, someone who had been close to her once; she tried to give the impression that she was going more to lay the ghost of a former love than to make contact with someone who might be a lover again, for she was suddenly sure that, having made her decision, she would find Hywel indifferent.

'I see. You won't be long, then? A few days? A week, maybe? Well, Tommy and I will do very well, you may be sure of that. We'll take care of each other beautifully. And I'll see your pony gets the best of everything.'

'I was forgetting Matchless! Perhaps I'd better not go tomorrow. I could leave it a week . . .' she was beginning, when she saw her father chuckle.

'Oh, Dot, Dot, if you're going, you go! You're too cautious, you should be more like me, impulsive! And by the same token, tell the chap you're going to see that your father realises he probably had a good reason for . . . for doing what he did, and tell him I won't hold it against him. Off with you now, up to your room and pack, and I'll take you down to the station after breakfast.'

Dot was in bed and about to settle down to sleep when it occurred to her that her father thought she was going in search of Tommy's father. No doubt he had always believed she had been deserted by some man, and had come home partly because of the disaster but also because she really had nothing else to go back to. But it did not matter what anyone thought. Since she would be going via Norwich, though, she might see if she could get news of Paoletta. If she knew her daughter was happy it would help her to feel less hideously guilty over leaving her.

Dot did not leave next day, after all, because she decided she would book her ticket, write to Mrs Blishen and ask if she could stay with her, and see Jessica. Jessica, she reasoned, might be willing to provide her with a good reason for visiting the Pettigrew family. There might be some message to pass on, some small gift . . .

Accordingly she explained to her father that she would not fly off without a thought, but would leave the following day, once she had booked her rail journey and arranged for somewhere to stay. He was agreeable, so later in the morning she went into town to book her journey and then came back via Jessica's cottage.

Unfortunately, Jessica was visiting her mother, or so Dot was informed by a small, grey-haired person with a head bristling with rag curlers who poked a thin, inquisitive nose over the dividing wall as soon as she heard Dot's knock.

'Oh? I'll go up there, then,' Dot decided. It was only a short walk and a couple of moments later she was knocking on Ella's door. Inside, there was a short scuffle, a murmur, and then the door was opened, very much to Dot's surprise, by a grey-haired, humorous-looking man she knew to be Glyn, Ella's husband. He recognised her at once, smiled and ushered her in.

'Morning, Miss Dot,' he said cheerfully. 'Would it be Ella or our Jessica you was wanting?'

'Oh! H-Hello, Mr Pritchard,' Dot said, her self-confidence deserting her. 'Er . . . well, let me see . . .'

'Dad's moved back in,' Jessica called from her seat by the fire. 'Told Mam when he left he'd do so when she stopped her grudgery and now she says she has, so he's moved back in. Nice, isn't it?'

'Oh! Yes, it's lovely.' Dot looked at Ella, who was beaming from ear to ear. 'I'm glad to see you looking so happy, Ella, I must say having Mr Pritchard back seems to suit you.'

'Only been back half an hour,' the elderly man remarked, but he looked pretty pleased with himself too, she noticed. 'Told her years back that if she wanted me to come home, then she'd have to ask, and stop putting on all them old airs, and this morning she came round, and back with her I came.'

'Just like that?'

'Ah, pretty well. Mind, I've been coming up once a week to see to the hens and give the garden a dig ever since I left, but not a word did we speak, eh, Ella? Not till this morning, that is.'

'It's a weight off my mind,' Jessica chimed in. 'Oh, come in, do, Dot, and stop hovering! Sit down and have a cup of tea. Da's just put the kettle on, haven't you, Da? You see, the thing was,' she went on chattily, 'I worried about Mam being here alone and Da being in town with that . . . that young woman. And then Peter got this job away and we're off in a week or so and when I told Mam . . . well, I think it made her wonder what the rest of her life would be like without me to pop in,

548

and with her and Da scarcely exchanging a word . . .'

'No, Jess, it did *not* make me think, you've got it all wrong,'
Ella said rather indignantly. 'Been meaning to tell Glyn how
sorry I was for what I'd said and done, been meaning to write
to Hywel to say the same, but I'd got into the habit, like, of
pretending to be right all the while and it isn't a habit that's
easy to break, so I just waited for someone else to do the
apologising. And then this morning my Tib came back.' She
indicated a fat and rather malevolent looking tabby cat which
was pressed as close to the fire as it could get short of actually
roasting. 'I wanted to tell someone – I'd been that worried
about her – but there wasn't nobody who'd care, not about
Tib. And then I remembered how Glyn had always cared and it
all seemed so foolish and so into town I went, and said I was
sorry. It didn't take much doing when it came down to it.'

'That's a lovely story, Ella,' Dot said sincerely, 'and I hope
you'll stay together and be happy for many years. But actually,
I came to ask you if I could help you in any way. I'm going
down to Norfolk to see a friend, and it happens she lives very
near the Pettigrews, and I wondered if there was any little thing
I could take them, from you. Or for Hywel, of course.'

'Well now, that *is* kind,' Ella murmured. 'There's that blue
gingham dress with the bows that wasn't big enough in the
bust for Jess; I've often thought how Megan could make good
use of it, if only she were nearer. You could take that, I
daresay.'

'Aye, and then there's the chicks,' Glyn added eagerly.
'There's a bit of luck you coming now, Miss Dot! Hywel, he
had hens in the back and each year we rear chicks. These
little'uns are from his flock and I've been searching my mind
how I could get 'em to him. Could you take 'em, if I give you
food and so on for 'em?'

'Yes, I'd be glad to,' Dot said. And presently, when she left
the cottage, she was carrying a white sash for Helen, two boxes
of turkish delight for the little girls and some chocolates in
case, as Ella put it, the blue gingham dress and a brown
cardboard box full of chicks and cottonwool for Hywel.

She had driven, shakily, into the village, and she drove even
more shakily going home, but she parked safely enough in the
stableyard and went in, laden. She said nothing to her father

549

about the gifts, though she did have to explain the chicks next morning, when he drove her down to the station.

'They're for the porter from his brother-in-law,' she said, crossing her fingers at this enormous lie. 'He asked me if I could bring them down when I booked my ticket yesterday.'

Tom grunted, narrowly avoided a dog which scooted out of his way, tail between surprised legs, and honked.

'Damned animals! Well, love, I'm glad you didn't plan to take the chicks all the way to wherever you're going. You won't tell your old father?'

'I will when I come back. Probably.' Dot, ever cautious, had only taken a ticket to the station sixty miles off, where she changed for the first time, so her father could not check up on her that way. She had never let the word Norwich pass her lips, for she felt uneasily that if her father knew about Norwich, or Norwich about her father, she would find herself with a husband she was far from wanting!

Tom came with her on to the platform, found her a carriage, and saw her aboard. Poor Dot, who had been forced to leave the box of chicks on the platform, suffered horrid fears that he would insist on remaining with her until the train pulled out, but fortunately he remembered that he hated wavings and kissings and all the paraphernalia of parting, so he bade her a gruff cheerio, told her that no matter what happened she was to remember she was a Tegydd and a hundred times better than any mere Englishman, and hurried out of sight.

As soon as he had gone Dot dived out of the train, grabbed the chicks to her palpitating bosom and hurtled back into her seat. Oh what a tangled web we weave, she told herself, even if we tell one very tiny lie over a simple little box of chicks! Those other enormous lies had already woven for themselves a ghastly muddle; better not to think about it, better to concentrate on the journey ahead.

It was strange to step out of the train at Thorpe Station and to feel herself two people and both of them scared to death of being recognised. She bundled straight into a cab and gave Mrs Blishen's address, and the moment she arrived she got into the house, closed the door, and then gave a great sigh of relief. Mrs

Blishen hugged her, Horry hugged her, Chappie, the little dog she had left with them, leapt up and down and barked and wagged his tail, and finally she sat down to a good old Norfolk high tea — ham, potatoes baked in their jackets, scones and butter, apple pie and hollow biscuits with best mild cheddar. After this princely repast she and her hostess settled before the fire.

'Well, dear?' Mrs Blishen's mild eyes beamed with affection. 'And just what hev you been up to? If you knew the fuss!'

'I don't; tell me about it.'

She heard how Carlo had advertised, asked every friend Dot had ever had, worried the life out of anyone who might know where she had gone, and had, at last, given up and moved back in with his parents.

'I'm sorry in one way and glad in another,' Dot said. 'Mamma Peruzzi is lovely — so's Pappa — and they'll take care of Paoletta and see that she's happy. I worried that Carlo might marry some woman who hated my little girl.'

'Why did you leave her, love?' Mrs Blishen enquired. 'When I heard I said, that she never did I said, not leave her little gal!'

'I didn't mean to, really I didn't. I left in an awful hurry, you see. I saw something in the paper and knew I had to go home. There had been a big accident and lots of people had been killed. I just had to make sure my family were all right. I was alone at home with Tommy so I left a message with the maid — she was at home, but sick in bed — saying I'd gone for a few days. I didn't *mean* to stay, but things were so bad between Carlo and me that once I got home I couldn't bear to come back.'

Mrs Blishen was nodding like a mandarin. 'That explains it. Is that why you're wearin' that rigout?'

Dot had arrived in all the splendour of a dark maroon coat with a matching hat. The hat had a half-veil and the coat a tall fur collar and a long, full skirt. Mrs Blishen had not recognised her guest until Dot had spoken.

'Yes. I didn't want to be recognised, and what with the veil and keeping the collar turned up — I nearly roasted — I felt it would put people off. You see, I'm so happy now, and everyone's accepted Tommy. My father adores him. He's made him his heir — he'll have all the estate and everything one

551

day. Our name's an old one, and Father would hate it to die out, but with Tommy he can have the name without the son-in-law and he wouldn't approve of an Italian one anyway. Father thinks all Italians are Mafia or ice cream salesmen.'

You could see Mrs Blishen shared Tom Tegydd's feelings, though she looked a bit puzzled.

'An old name? Oh aye, but aren't there a fair few Evans in Wales?'

'Well, yes,' Dot conceded, trying not to laugh. She had quite forgotten her alias! 'To tell the truth, our name isn't Evans, I didn't use it when I lived in Norwich because I was hiding from my father then.'

'Ah, I see.' Mrs Blishen nodded, looking wise. 'You was incogniscent, was you?'

'More or less. Mrs B., how come you know all about Carlo? I know you said he'd been round, but you sound as if you've been a fly on the wall in his homes these past two years.'

'I have, in a manner of speaking. My niece Rosie, she went along to the Royal Pavilion for a job in the kitchens, only your ma-in-law took a fancy to her. She did a lot of running around for the old lady, going shopping and so on, doing bits and pieces in that marvellous flat they've got, and then when trouble started with the boy . . . that's your hubby, my dear . . . the old lady asked her to go there for a few days. Which stretched. Oh, she come home with some tales!'

'Is Carlo planning to get married again?' Dot asked hopefully. He was a Roman Catholic and would not want a divorce, she supposed, unless he had another wife in mind.

'Well, no. There was a time when Rosie suspicioned it wasn't women he was after at all,' Mrs Blishen said guardedly. 'But then he took up with some female called Ida Gentian; the little gal didn't care for her at all nor her for your Polly. There was some sort of showdown and I gather Miss G. said your hubby was to choose between 'em. He come down quick on the side of Polly and Miss G. packed her bags and left the same night. My niece she say your Polly opened all the windows whilst she sang a song of glee and triumph – that was what she called it when your hubby asked. They had a good laugh about it, Mr Carlo and my Rosie.'

'And then?'

552

'Why, then he sold up the house and moved back in to the flat above the Royal. Rosie's with them and she's happy as a sandboy, your Polly. Spoilt by the staff, adored by her gran and grandad, and of course your hubby dotes on her. Rosie's partial, too; say she's ever so clever, ever so bright, and a good little soul as well.'

'Mrs B., you don't know how happy you've made me,' Dot said, hugging her knees. She was sitting on the floor, leaning against the chair into which she had sunk two hours earlier. She had reached the floor by comfortable degrees and now she smiled gratefully up at her hostess. 'I'm happy at home and I wasn't happy with poor Carlo. I can't tell you too much, but what Rosie said about his not being after women . . . well, he made me wonder, too. The only thing I regretted was leaving Paoletta, but I'm sure she'll be happy with the Peruzzis.'

'Very probably. Now, my woman, go you up to bed or you won't be up in time to catch your train tomorrow.'

Twenty-Eight

Nerves did not attack Dot until she was actually safely ensconced in a corner seat of the small, slow local train which would take her to the area in which Hywel lived, and then not even the long coat could stop her from trembling and feeling cold and edgy. Outside the window of the train the sun shone and the colours of early autumn glowed, but nothing could be sufficiently attractive to take her mind from her inner turmoil. She had been mad to come! He was bound to interpret it as another attempt to persuade him to marry her!

The journey seemed endless, yet she wanted it to go on for ever. Arriving was too horrible to contemplate, and since she had decided not to stop in Norwich on the way back she had all her luggage with her. Suppose — dreadful thought — he assumed she had actually wished herself on him and the family as an overnight guest?

The carriage was not empty, but her fellow passengers were all too dull to take her mind off her troubles. A couple of farmers, a couple of women going home after doing their weekly shop, an elderly farmworker so bent and crippled with rheumatism that he reminded her of a poor little mole. The women talked to each other, the farmers exchanged grunts over their newspapers and the farmworker ate. Stolidly he waded his way through the contents of paper bags, greasy little parcels and his pockets. Bread, strong-smelling cheese, a wedge of fruit cake, some apples, a piece of cold suet pudding, half a cold pork chop ... Dot watched, fascinated, as he produced object after object. Had he been raiding a pigbin, she wondered?

Presently she learned that she had not been so very far from the truth, for he saw her fascinated gaze on him as he produced yet more provender, and gave her a gap-toothed grin.

'Would you care for an apple, missie? Bin to moi sister's daughter's caff I have and she give me all the leftovers. Prime, they are.'

'Thanks very much, but I've only just had breakfast,' Dot said untruthfully. She had been too keen to reach the train to eat with Mrs Blishen and Horry. She had fought a sneaking urge to go into the city via Paoletta's school, just so that she could see her child and, hopefully, not be seen herself, but she had conquered it. She knew it was unfair to Paoletta and perhaps even unfair to herself. One day, she dreamed, she would go to Carlo and ask if she might have her daughter to stay for a week or two. Mrs Blishen had told her that when she had been away seven years Carlo could divorce her for desertion. It seemed unlikely that he would do any such thing, but she could dream, couldn't she?

The chicks were on the luggage rack. Poor little things, they had been leading adventurous lives for creatures so young! Horry had helped her to feed and clean them the previous evening, and he had so loved them! He had held them as gently as any one could, and carried them up to his face so that he could touch his cheek against their soft fluff, and he had watched them peck up their food and run about on their thin little wire legs with awe. He had not known anything so small and sweet existed, he seemed to imply, and their cheeps delighted him too, though the information that they would, one day, turn into hens had been greeted with some incredulity. Piglets became pigs, calves cows or bulls, puppies became dogs. But how, he seemed to want to say, could a ball of fluff become a large brown hen?

Because this was a little country train full of country people, the box of chicks had surprised no one, though on the express train, which she had joined for a brief period in its hurtling onward rush, astonished glances had gone to her cheeping box, which, now and then, tipped apparently of its own accord when all the small occupants had a fancy for the same side of their prison at the same moment.

'Be in in ten minutes,' remarked one of the women, and Dot, who had grown accustomed to the frequent stops and the shortness of most of her fellow passengers' journeys, glanced at her watch. Heavens, this train would finish its travels only one stop past her own, and that must mean either in five minutes or ten she would arrive at her destination. She was tempted to start titivating, to comb her hair and straighten her collar and start getting her luggage together, but she restrained herself. No point! At each of its frequent stops the train had hung about, sighing steam, until the last person, object or animal had made its leisurely way through the ticket barrier. Only then did the train, reluctantly it seemed, begin to mutter and make steam for the next stage of its journey.

The train drew in to another little country station and Dot saw that this was where she got off, though it was scarcely more than a halt; there were moon-shaped flowerbeds alongside the platform with masses of dahlias, sweet williams and salvias holding up their faces to the sun; two seats, painted green, and a sign with the station's name on it. Dot, burdened by the chicks, the turkish delight and a bag with the gingham dress and the white silk sash, was by no means the first passenger down on the platform, and by the time she had rescued her own small bag from the rack most of the other travellers had made their way into the road which she could see through a large barred gate to the side of the station building.

However a porter was weeding one of the beds so she approached him. He continued to weed; he was humming like a big bumblebee, tunelessly, but so natural and contented a sound was he making that she hesitated to interrupt. However, if she was to find out just where Hywel lived she had better bring herself to say something!

'Excuse me, I wonder if you could direct me to the Pettigrews' place, out on the marshes?'

The porter turned, revealing that he was white-haired beneath his cap and of portly build. He stood up, a hand flying to the small of his back and a grimace telling Dot better than words how painful the movement had been.

'Sorry, miss. I thought it was just the locals – didn't see you. Now you want the Pettigrew place. Well, it's five mile. You can't walk with that little lot and there in't no bus. Reckon you could run to a taxi, do you? Leastways, not a taxi exactly, but old Frid and his cart?'

'Reckon I . . . yes, I think I could manage that,' Dot said. But do I have to walk far to reach him? None of this stuff's heavy, but it's rather awkward to carry, particularly the chicks, because I have to keep the box flat.'

'Ar. Frid'll be outside. Here, give me a holt o' that.' He seized her case and the chicks and led the way out through the gate, ignoring the ticket barrier as if it did not exist. Plainly he stood upon little ceremony and looked upon the Great Eastern railway more as something which happened to run alongside his garden than a trust, for he had not so much as asked to see her ticket, let alone confiscated it so that she could not use it twice!

Old Fred was an ancient man in a battered bowler and long checked coat who sat on the driving seat of an equally elderly cart, to all appearances fast asleep. But as the two of them passed through the gate the porter shouted something and old Fred opened his eyes and cleared his throat, then spat into the dust.

'Lady want to get to the Pettigrew place,' the porter said laconically, heaving her case and the chicks into the cart. 'That's all right, Frid? Kin you tek her out there?'

'Ar,' Fred said. He slapped the reins against the neck of his large mottled horse which shivered its skin but otherwise continued to ignore the proceedings. 'Thass a good way. That'll tek more'n a moment.' He eyed her shrewdly, totting up her ability to pay the vast sum he was about to name. 'It'll cost, though.'

'How much?' Dot asked, more because she felt it was expected of her than from any particular interest. She would have paid pounds to avoid having to walk five miles with the chicks held out flat like a votive offering.

'Ooh, say one and tenpence?'

'Fine.'

'Oi orter've said two bob,' Fred confided as she climbed aboard. 'But that seemed a lot.'

'Two bob's all right as well,' Dot said with unimpaired cheerfulness. 'I may not be there long, though. How do I get back to the station again? I'm only visiting to take Mrs Pettigrew the chicks and a few things.'

'She's a hospitable woman,' Fred said, after thinking it over.

'You'll hev your tea there, no question. And there in't a train back to Norwich till six. Say I call for you at five, how would that be?'

'It sounds all right,' Dot said cautiously. 'Tell you what, if they're out or . . . or if they're busy, I'll walk back because I'll leave the chicks and the rest of the stuff with a note. How will that be? If I'm not back at the station by five, you'll fetch me.'

Whilst all this went on, the horse had remained motionless; plainly he did not move until his fare had been assured. But apparently old Fred was now satisfied, for he clicked, slapped the reins against Dapple's neck once more, and the equipage moved ponderously down as far as the station entrance, where it stopped again.

Dot was about to ask why when the porter reappeared. Before he had been in his shirtsleeves but now he had on a greenish-black jacket and he had straightened his cap.

'Arranged it, hev you?' he enquired sociably. 'Off are you, then?'

Dot was about to answer crisply when she saw the significance of their stop in the porter's right hand, which was held out ever so slightly.

'Oh, sorry, I nearly forgot. Thanks for bringing my things out.' She put a sixpenny piece on the edge of the cart and the porter came over, pocketed it, and thanked her before returning to his weeding.

Despite Dot's reservations, she thoroughly enjoyed the ride. Fred's cart was high and old-fashioned, but it meant that you could see over the hedges, where there were any, and the sheer beauty of the marshes, when they reached them, held Dot's attention. From the train they had merely seemed flat but now she could see the colours, the silver line on the horizon that was the sea, the pinks and purples of sea lavender and the gold of kingcups, the marvellous variety of greens and the beauty of the autumn foliage.

But out here the sky dominated everything. A great blue arc it was today, with tiny wisps of cloud an infinity above. The wind smelled of the sea, fresh and salt, and the marsh smelled good too. Someone had been cutting late hay and although Dot knew the quality was not equal to the spring grass it still smelled very sweet.

In the train she had been unable to concentrate on anything but her impending arrival at the Pettigrew place, yet now, with the open marshes around her and the sun on her shoulders, she did not even realise they were nearing the end of their journey until the horse began to slow down and, looking ahead, she saw a house at last.

It was quite a handsome house, reed-thatched, cob walls whitened, but as you got nearer you could see that it had not always been so. Once it had only been a small cottage, but someone had built on quite extensively and now it was a proper farmhouse. She said as much to old Fred.

'Ar. Used to be a dumpy little old cottage, but they built up and put more rooms on and made it into an E shape, without the middle bit, acourse – one bit of the E is stables, the rest is house – and now it's a real nice place. Why, they owns most of the land round here, them Pettigrews.'

'It's a lovely garden, too,' Dot said approvingly. When she had lived in Norwich she had always been impressed by the Norvicensions' love of flowers. At home the cottagers might have a clump or two of something bright and easy but most of the garden would be put to more practical uses. Middle-class people paid a gardener or an odd job man to work for them but were usually more interested in neatness – and good fruit and vegetables – than in flowers. But in Norfolk everyone pushed flowers into any available spare space. You would see a thick hedge of sweetpeas between orderly rows of cabbage, or lavender bushes, big and well cared for and purple with blooms, on either side of the turnip patch. And front gardens were marvellous when you thought that villagers, for the most part, toiled on the land all day. Yet they would come home and sow seeds and cultivate like mad until their gardens, no matter how tiny, were things of extraordinary beauty.

'Ah. Thass Miz Pettigrew; she do the garden. Thass always the farmer's wife wot do the garden.'

'She does it just how I like it best,' Dot said. From her perch she could see more dahlias, big clumps of clarkia and michaelmas daisies, but best of all the honesty, children's pennies, standing tall against the mellowing hedge.

'Ar.' The horse stopped and old Fred began to ease his creaking limbs out of what Dot had assumed to be a perma-

559

nent sitting position. She was wrong, however, for he climbed down, looking quite spry, and seized her case and the bag. 'Put it on the doorstep, shall Oi?'

'Please.' Dot fished around in her purse and found half-a-crown. She got down from the cart and followed her mentor up the little gravel path. He dumped her stuff down in the porch, took her money with a mumbled 'Thankee', and made for his cart once more. Dot waved to him, and then raised her hand to knock – and lowered it again. Oh, oh, how could she face whoever came to that door? But she knew she was being ridiculous and knocked hard, then stepped back with a thumping heart. Heavens, had she knocked too hard? Would it sound peremptory and demanding to whoever was within?

Her worries were in vain. No one came to the door and, on closer inspection, Dot wondered whether it had ever been opened. A spider had woven a web over the handle, and the whole structure looked so immovable that she hesitated to knock again. What a fool she would look on the wrong side of a door that was never used! She had better pick up her various bundles and go round the back.

She went to her right, and there was a narrow arch leading through into the back yard. It was more like a tunnel, really, since it penetrated the thickness of part of the house, and Dot trod warily along it, feeling rather impertinent to be actually on Pettigrew property and not merely at the door.

She felt worse when she reached the yard; it was a private sort of place, almost an extension of the farmhouse itself. It was, as the driver had said, hemmed in on three sides by house and outbuildings, but it was also hemmed in on the fourth side by a wide dyke. In order to go between their home and the marsh the inhabitants had built a sturdy bridge with a white painted gate on the yard side of it. It was a wide bridge, because, as she could tell, cows coming in to be milked, sheep being driven through for doctoring, horses returning after a day's work, all had to cross it, as did the carts, the tractors and the haywains.

You could not help staring at the view, though. So much space and lightness, so much sky, with the marshwater reflecting it and the sea not too far distant. She was still staring when someone spoke behind her.

'Good afternoon?'

Dot nearly dropped the chicks. She had not even thought of someone actually being out here in the yard. She had meant to go to the back door, knock, and speak to whoever was within and instead she had been caught staring at everything, more like a prospective buyer than an uninvited guest!

'I'm so sorry. Good afternoon to you!' Dot turned and saw that she had been addressed by a middle-aged woman with thick, grey-streaked hair and a worn, pointy-chinned face. She had once been very beautiful, Dot thought, and was lovely still, for her fine-boned features and large, well-spaced eyes had aged without losing their appeal. Dot knew it must be Megan because of a superficial resemblance between the two sisters, but because life had treated them differently their faces had grown apart. Ella's life had made her mouth tight, her eyes suspicious. Megan's face, on the other hand, was marked by life as well; you could see the faint traces of sorrow, pain, loss. Yet her lips still held a sweet and trusting line and her brow was placid.

'Have you come to see me, or one of my young people?' Megan crossed the yard and held open the back door invitingly. 'Do come in. We can't talk out here, and you must put your parcels down; your arms must ache!'

'No, not really. I came in Fred's cart from the station,' Dot explained, following her hostess into a big kitchen and taking off her coat and hat. 'Actually, some of these things . . . most of them . . . are for you and your young people. I come from your part of the world . . . North Wales, I mean. I suppose this is your part now . . . so I'm a messenger, really.'

'Oh? And your name?'

Dot felt her cheeks warm and hastily held out a hand.

'I'm terribly sorry. I'm completely unnerved by being caught staring in your yard! I'm Dot Tegydd and you, I can see, are Megan Pettigrew, Ella's sister.'

'The resemblance is still there, then?' Mrs Pettigrew chuckled. 'Now that I know who you are, I almost think I could have guessed; you are rather like your father – though very much prettier,' she added with a twinkle.

'Am I? He said I was the other day.' Dot put the box of chicks down on the kitchen table, untied the string and opened the lid. 'These are for Hywel, from his parents. They wanted him to have them because they're the descendants of his very own hens, the ones he reared from chicks. I've done my best to take care of them and I'm pleased to report that we haven't had any fatalities. I started out with fifteen and there are fifteen still cheeping.'

'That's very nice. He'll be so pleased.' Megan met Dot's eyes squarely. 'Did his mam send them specially? Was there a letter or a message?'

'It was Mr Pritchard who suggested it at first,' Dot admitted. 'But Ella wanted him to have them too. She said she was sorry for the way she'd behaved towards him. I think she'll write, given time. You see . . .'

Halfway through the story of Glyn and Ella's reconciliation the funny side of it struck Dot, and she and her hostess laughed until tears came to their eyes at the thought of Ella apologising in order to have someone to rejoice with her over her cat's return.

'It's not really funny,' Dot said at last, wiping her eyes. 'It's sad that anyone could be that lonely. Only you can't feel sorry for her because . . . well, I know she's your sister, but she did bring it on herself.'

'Yes; she always has. Now let's put the kettle on and have a cup of tea and you can tell me all the gossip which my sister never bothers to tell. And when they come in for their meal, you and Hywel can have a chat – it's him you've really come to see, isn't it?'

'No! Well, yes, in a way, but I had to come to Norwich on business and I thought . . .' Dot met Megan's gaze, hesitated, and was lost. 'Sorry. I was about to lie to save my face if . . .'

'If Hywel's not going to welcome you? My dear child, he'll be so delighted! He's friendly and easy-going but he's made no really close friends in the two years he's lived here – apart from family, that is. He misses his home . . . no, perhaps not his home, but he misses the village and the hills. And his friends, of course.' Megan went over to the sink and began pumping water for the kettle, raising her voice above the squeak of the handle and the rush of water. 'Coming from those parts, you'll likely know how Ella treated the boy; it doesn't do much for a man's self-confidence, that. Then there was that girl, Jessica.

Many a time I've wished I could get my hand to her.'

'I come from there, but I don't know much about what happened between Hywel and Jessica,' Dot admitted. 'Only that they decided they wouldn't suit.'

'Ha, so that's what she tells people! She jilted him, my dear, just went off after the disaster. Met someone more to her liking, no doubt. I don't believe for one moment that he loved her, but it hurt. That boy's been hurt too much. He's lived here two years . . . more . . . and he's only just beginning to shed the shell he'd built round himself to stop him being hurt again.' She looked shrewdly at Dot. 'Forgive me, but . . . you haven't come here to bring him news he'd rather not know?'

This was a facer; Dot knew she could not answer with a straight yes or no, because she still had very little idea how Hywel would greet her. Oh, she knew how she felt about him, but whether he would want her now merely as a friend or whether he would want a warmer relationship she could not tell until they met.

'Hywel's the only one that can tell you that, Mrs Pettigrew. You see, years ago I loved him and wanted to marry him. We had a sort of understanding, but it wasn't for there and then, it was for some time in the future. And then I – I needed to know how he felt so I went down and met him out of the pit and asked him straight out if he'd marry me. And he said no, and told me to go away, stay with one of my sisters and meet people of my own kind. I thought that was it, that it was all over. I thought I'd go away and forget him. Only I never have, not for one moment. It'd been seven years. I've . . . borne a child so I'm not w-without a certain amount of experience, but I still feel the same about Hywel.'

'You do?' Megan Pettigrew was putting the kettle on the hob but she straightened to give Dot a very sweet smile. 'That's wonderful! He desperately needs what you're offering . . . you are free to marry him, if he wants you to?'

'Yes,' Dot said bluntly. 'But I don't want him to marry me just because he's lonely and needs a wife. It wouldn't work. Everything needs balance. If you have a weight of love on one side and a feather of feeling on the other everything crashes. I wouldn't want that, not for Hywel or me. He isn't the only one who's been hurt.'

'Fair enough. I can't answer for him, because he almost never talks about home, not to me. Huw would know, only you seldom see one without the other. Incidentally, just to complicate things further Huw's been in love for two years and wanting to marry, but he hasn't been able to because of Hywel.'

'Why not? Doesn't Hywel like Huw's girl? But why would that matter? Surely it would make no difference?'

'That's what I say, but Huw says it's so easy already for Hywel to feel out of it, and his marrying would make it worse. But why I told you was because Huw's young lady, Helen, has done everything in her power for the past two years to find Hywel a girl. She's brought them back in droves, really she has. Blondes, brunettes, redheads; small, medium, large. And not once – not once, mind – has the lad shown anything but the most perfunctory interest in any of 'em. Except for one.'

'I know. Alice or Ellen,' Dot said gloomily. 'Jessica mentioned her.'

'Did she, now? But even Alice never got more than a few casual dates out of Hywel.' Mrs Pettigrew was pouring the tea but now she paused, with the big brown and cream patterned teapot poised above the cups. 'Helen chose Alice specially because she said Hywel had been in love with a girl once who was a bit like her. Small . . .' her eyes swept expressively from top to toe of Dot's five foot nothing '. . . dark-haired . . .' she jerked her chin at Dot's crisp curls '. . . and cheeky,' she finished, smiling. 'Do you know I'd imagined it was Jessica they were describing?'

'Oh no, Jessica's got beautiful red hair and she's tall,' Dot said. Her heart had begun to beat suffocatingly loudly and she knew her cheeks were going pink. 'Do – do you think Hywel meant *me*?'

'Well, was he ever involved with anyone beside you and Jessica?'

'N-n-no,' stammered Dot. 'I d-don't think so.'

'There you are then. Anyway, we'll soon find out.' She beckoned and Dot left her chair. Megan pointed through the window. 'See? That's Hywel and his brother, coming across the marshes. They'll be here in ten minutes.'

'Hywel . . . his *brother*?' Dot was staring with all her eyes.

Stan died, poor Stan. Would it be Luke? Or Dewi? But that chap's too tall. He's as tall as Hywel.'

'Good lord, didn't you know? Hywel and Huw are brothers.'

'Can I go and meet them? Please? If I go now, if I can surprise him, I'll be able to tell at once. He'll see me coming, he's bound to recognise me, and then I'll know, I'm sure.' She was at the back door, a hand on the latch, but good manners prevented her from leaving without her hostess's permission.

'Go on then,' Megan said. 'Tell them . . .'

Dot heard no more. She was pulling open the heavy back door and running across the yard. She flung the gate open and forgot to close it, she bounced briskly across the bridge not sparing a glance for the water beneath, and then she began to run in good earnest towards the two tiny figures in the distance. The marsh was good to run on, the ground firm yet yielding underfoot. Dot had always been a good runner and now she ran and ran until she had a stitch in her side and her breath was coming quick and short. Yet neither man seemed to notice her; they were deep in conversation and did not look up even as she drew nearer. Striding along, looking down at their boots as men will, they did not once glance up to where the small figure, panting along rather more slowly now with a hand to her side, was bearing down upon them.

Megan, watching her progress through the window, suddenly realised, as she saw Dot dart across the bridge, that, if the girl had not known Huw and Hywel were brothers, she certainly would not realise that they were identical twins. Worse, she had not seen Hywel for seven years. She had never seen him with a scarred face and, from the sound of it, did not have the faintest idea that he had been so tragically marked.

Megan dropped the teapot, which had been in her family for a century, shattering it on the quarry tiles, and ran out of the still open door. The girl was way ahead of her now, running like a deer, fleet and nimble, leaping from one tuft of grass to the next, now floundering into a pool but quickly up and out of it and on. Megan shouted her name, filled with an awful foreboding. It would all go wrong! The girl, poor little thing, was obviously deeply in love with Hywel, but it was the Hywel of seven years ago, not the Hywel of today, with the livid scar which bisected the right side of his face. She would see Huw, with the face that he and Hywel had once shared . . . oh, God!

Megan stopped shouting and concentrated on running. Over the bridge she hurried and on to the marsh, running like a girl again, determined to get to Dot before she reached the brothers so that she could prevent the dreadful wound which the child would unknowingly inflict on Hywel the moment she set eyes on Huw. Megan, less agile than Dot, plunged ankle deep into thick mud, lost half her apron on a wicked old briar which grabbed it and refused to let go, felt her neat bun of hair tumble about her neck, scattering hairpins to the wide winds. Still she kept on, but she was falling back; the girl had only a few yards to go, now . . . they were bound to look up . . . God, if you'll just let Huw speak at *once*, she prayed, let him give himself away with his good old Norfolk accent, then all might yet be well. Please, God, she prayed, running on, untidily, breathlessly, please, God, let Huw speak. Hywel's suffered enough. But her side was hurting, she could not see for the tears in her eyes, and if she did not stop for a rest she would surely kill herself.

She did not stop. She ran uselessly onwards, trying to call the girl's name, trying to attract Huw's attention. The boys continued to stare at their feet, Dot continued to run . . . It was like a nightmare! Megan stumbled on, praying in her mind for she was too breathless now to say a word aloud. God, let the girl fall, so that I may catch up! God, let Huw speak first! God, don't let my dear boy be hurt!

Dot was within three yards of them before either looked up. They both stopped, staring, incredulous. I must look a sight, Dot thought. By heaven, I must look a proper gypsy with mud all over my legs and one shoe gone, my hair all tangles from the wind and no breath left to say a word. But it didn't matter,

566

because Hywel was smiling at her, he was just as she remembered, the person she loved best in the whole world. She stumbled forward and fell into his arms.

Hywel held her, feeling the flutter and trip of her heartbeat against his breast as his own heart began to beat faster. She was here! Dot had come! She was in his arms, where she belonged. He wanted nothing more of life at that moment than to hold her, muttering ridiculous love-words into her tumbled curls, but as he stood there, totally absorbed in her, a picture flashed into his mind.

Huw, with a woman in his arms. A slim girl with golden-brown hair. A girl who, he realised with amazement, fitted with Huw as Dot fitted with him. Perfectly, as one half of a cockleshell matches the other.

It was Helen. For a moment surprise and delight were so strong that he forgot it had been a mind-picture only. He gave Dot a squeeze, found her face and kissed her lips quickly, and then turned to his brother.

'Huw, why didn't you tell me about you and Helen? I'd have understood, mun, and wished you joy!'

Huw grinned sheepishly; how he must have longed for me to come out of my self-absorption and realise, Hywel thought wonderingly. I've kept them apart without ever meaning to; yet they've never even hinted!

'Well, bor, I'm glad you know just at this moment! That was one thought I couldn't keep back! Now who's this young lady you're cuddling?'

Hywel laughed and put Dot back from him. Her eyes were shining and there was mud on her cheek. She was looking into his face as if he were an angel . . . he liked it!

'Sorry. This is Dot Tegydd; we were going to get married once, but things went wrong.' He put a hand under Dot's chin and tilted her face up to his. 'Shall we have another go, cariad?'

'Yes, please.' She turned to look at Huw, smiling. 'How do you do? You're Hywel's cousin . . . or did Mrs Pettigrew mean it when she said you were his brother?'

Megan, panting up beside them at this point, put her arm

round Huw and leaned on him for a moment before speaking.

'Yes, they're brothers, dear. In fact, they're identical twins. That's why I came after you, because I was afraid you might mistake them . . . I knew you hadn't seen Hywel for a number of years and I thought . . . well, others have mistaken them — their own mother did, so . . .'

Dot turned in Hywel's embrace and stared up at the ruined beauty of the face above her own. Then she looked across to Huw's handsome countenance.

'You'll have to explain what this is all about, because I'm lost, I'm afraid. I can see that they're alike, of course, but I couldn't mistake Hywel. I'd know him anywhere. We've been friends since we were small, you see, and he hasn't changed, not really.'

'Course I've changed, girl!' Hywel was trying to scold but his voice could not help its indulgent gentleness. 'All scarred I was in the accident. Quite hideous I look.'

'Oh, that.' Dot traced the outline of the great scar from the tip of his cleft chin to the spot where it disappeared into his thickly curling hair. 'I like it; it suits you.'

Hywel looked down at her and he thought of a thousand retorts and could say none of them because there was a great big lump in his throat. He could only smile, whilst tears glittered in his eyes.

But his brother was not so inhibited. He reached out a hand and squeezed Dot's fingers.

'You'll do, gal,' he said.